LAND OF THE FIRST
- SERVANT OF DARKNESS -

Simon J. Cambridge

Published in 2014 by First Thought Publishing.

ISBN 978-0-9927895-4-1

Copyright © 2013 by Simon J. Cambridge.

First Edition.

III

- SERVANT OF DARKNESS -

Kur-ur-ord Um-nalvaagei
Kur-pola Renod-doneis
Kur-logith Ao-aj-lareil
No-unka Iborn-ilmhz
No-unka Deran-od-torz
No-arka Bia-anodsii
Luj-husfam A-de-aozeis

Contents

1

THE DROWNED

Uhm-viufalz Pl-imzin-jir
Kor-ipab Jila-dr-pan
Len-z-ihd So-ith-kaoji
Karho-iks Odsa-pamjo
Armsoi-aih Sizaf-loaa
Rasai-jon Fenur-dahin
Dl-ith-pr zl-lir-eofjes

Its wings twisted by a persistent wind, the vessel struggled through a turbulent sea and slowly made its way back north. Above, the skies were dark, with clouds rolling in from the south, a rush of shadowed grey. Hills gradually emerged from the distances, grey like the clouds. Between them lay broken outlines, the ruins of a city.

Korfax turned away, his face sick with angry grief, but Gedonon did not. He remained where he was, rooted to the spot by numb horror.

Thilzin Jerris had been broken. Her great bridge was gone, as were her two great towers. Her high walls were high no more and not one of her fair spires remained. The monstrous wave had fallen upon her and shattered her stone.

Even the land to either side had not escaped the fury: cliffs, hills and valleys, all had been scoured of life. Everything was gone, everything that had clothed the land in colour and form, and only devastation remained, left where the uncaring waters had seen fit to cast it.

The destruction seemed endless, as did the stillness. Nothing moved except for the river, turbid and swollen as it flowed through the grim ruins, returning the last of its misery back to the sea.

Korfax could barely imagine how it must have been. They would not have had a chance. The great wave would have been over the horizon and on them in moments, before sweeping across the city almost in an instant, breaking everything in its path. The towers would have crumbled under its weight, walls pushed over and bridges torn from their moorings. Everything, but everything, would have drowned as the great wave swept on by.

Something hit the boat. Korfax looked down. They were passing through wreckage, and worse than wreckage. He looked away again. He did not want to see the drifting dead.

He glanced at Gedonon and felt the first stirrings of guilt. His own words, angry judgements, came back to haunt him. What use indeed the riches Gedonon had received from his hand? Though not by the Agdoain, Gedonon had still lost far more than he had gained. With one single sweep of its sword, fate had deprived him of his family and his home.

As if aware of his gaze, Gedonon turned slowly to look back at Korfax, his eyes dead things in his head, unfocused and dull.

"How?" he asked in a still voice.

"The wave," Korfax answered simply.

"Did you do this?" Gedonon asked.

Korfax took a step back. He held up his hands in the gesture of placation.

"No!" he said. "Neither did I know this would happen. If anyone is to blame, it would be Dialyas. He unleashed this power."

Gedonon took a step forward, and a light began to grow behind his eyes, a mad light.

"And who is Dialyas?" he asked.

Korfax stepped back again and kept his hands up. He did not want to confront Gedonon, not now, not amongst all this ruin.

"He is the one that I went to see," he said, "the one that unleashed the power that took away Lonsiatris. He is the one that created the great wave that broke Thilzin Jerris."

Gedonon clenched his fists and the madness inside him began to swell.

"No!" he answered. "I see more. If you had not gone to him, this would not have happened. You are the cause of this."

That was more than Korfax was willing to accept.

"And whose greed was it took me to Lonsiatris in the first place?" he asked.

Gedonon drew his sword and pointed it at Korfax, who in turn took another step back and dropped his hands. Gedonon was no longer listening, and nothing that Korfax could do or say would stop this now. All that would remain of this day would be regrets. Like Thilzin Jerris, Gedonon had also been broken.

Korfax did the only thing he could. With one hand he grasped Gedonon's blade, holding it tightly in an armoured fist, whilst he struck Gedonon on the brow with the other. Gedonon staggered and fell to his knees. Korfax snatched the sword away and threw it behind him, out of Gedonon's reach.

"I am sorry, Gedonon," he said, "but you are wrong. I spoke the truth when I said that I did not cause this. If you wish to blame anyone, then blame Dialyas." He looked down. "Not that it matters now. Dialyas has gone where neither you nor I can follow."

He looked at the city and then back at Gedonon, a mingling of pity and regret, then he cursed as he realised that if he wished to reach land again he would have to guide the ship to the dock himself, as Gedonon was in no fit state to do so.

When it was finally done, Korfax breathed a sigh of relief. It had been hard work, nudging the boat this way and that, so that it missed all the debris that lay beneath the waters of the harbour, whilst still staying on course for the one single pier that had miraculously remained intact.

He lowered the boarding plank and took a rope to tie fast the aft of the boat. After that, he tied the prow. Then he led Enastul on to the pier and looked back at Gedonon, who was still kneeling on the deck, staring with dull eyes at the ruin around him.

"I would wish you well," Korfax said to him, "but I have no words of comfort for you, not now. We are the bereft, you and I. All I can tell you is that you still live, and where there is life one can also find hope. May you rediscover it ere the end. I am not sure that I ever will."

Gedonon did not answer. He did not move. Korfax turned away and mounted Enastul. Then he rode off.

He rode through the broken city and tried not to see what lay across its stone, but he could not avoid it. He was compelled.

Weeds draped the walls, wreckage filled the roads and slime daubed the broken towers. It was silent, a heavy silence that weighed everything down.

Most ways were impassable, as stone, wood and flesh had been piled up in macabre drifts and mounds, great long drifts, great tottering mounds. Korfax tried to keep away from such things whenever he came upon them, daring to hope that he could avoid them entirely if he was careful. But then he found himself confronted by other sights instead, sights that were far worse. It was as though the city wanted him to see, wanted him to know what had been wrought by his deeds, whether he willed it or no.

On one road he came across the shattered hulk of a ship, lying like a fallen hill and blocking the way from end to end with its heaped up remains. Though its main mast had vanished and its deck was a mass of torn metal, a single pale arm rose up from its centre like a revenant, tilted at the cloud-strewn sky in grim salute.

In another place he found the dead piled up against a single door, a gruesome pile of bodies. Motionless, their eyes stared blindly, limbs entangled, bent this way or that. There were no other bodies on the street, just the detritus left by the flood. Korfax glanced at the door to which the dead clung and was perturbed to see the sigil of a healer upon the lintel. And where was she, he wondered. Was she gone or was she still within, drowning even now?

At one point his steed had to pick its way amongst the bodies of many children, each scattered carelessly across the entire length and breadth of a wide, open square. The wave had seemingly picked them up, all of them, from this place or from that, and swirled them around in its depths until it had drowned them all, and then, with unbelievable malice, put them all back down again, all in one place, like so many trophies.

At last he came to the great east gate, but even that had been thrown down, both of its towers leaning inwards like broken teeth. The guards were gone and the road beyond was empty.

And so Korfax rode out of the wreck of Thilzin Jerris and entered the wasteland beyond, a new land of broken rock and creeping muds. He spurred Enastul on and did not look back.

They watched him depart, two ragged forms in stained cloaks of darkest green.

"Why do we not act?" asked the first.

"We dare not," replied the second, "not against that one, at least not until we have both power and numbers at our back."

"I do not understand," said the first. "He is but one lone rider. Why do we not apprehend him?"

"Because of who he is! Though he is much changed since last I set eyes upon him, I cannot be mistaken. He rode out the wave. Few could have done that. He was ever the herald of dark marvels."

"Your answers make less sense by the moment."

"And that is because you never look beyond your bounds. You are of the Baltarith – and you will always be of the Baltarith. You do not aspire."

The first glanced angrily at the second.

"What do you mean by that?" he asked. "Explain yourself! Tell me why we do not act? If he is the cause of all this, then I for one would see him pay."

"But there is nothing to explain," said the second. "I am of the Noqvoanith. Accept it and be done. Leave your irksome questions in the place reserved for them. Do we act? Do we apprehend? Have you learnt nothing else in your time? In the Balt Kaalith one waits for knowledge. Only when our knowledge is as complete as we can make it do we act. Then our knowledge becomes our power."

"So enlighten me and gift me with power."

The Noqvoan looked at the Baltar and drew himself up.

"Change your tone! Change it or know my displeasure."

But even as the Noqvoan spoke, the Baltar drew out his sword and held it against the Noqvoan's neck.

"Change my tone?" he asked. "After all that has happened? My family are gone! My father! My mother! My wife! My daughter!"

The blade shook briefly and then became still again. The Baltar leaned closer, his eyes wide and staring.

"Change my tone? My life has been brought to ruin, and you dare to insult me with your arrogance? How shall I know your mind unless you tell me what is in it? All I have heard from you is 'do this', or 'do that', or 'do the other'! You have not yet given me one explanation, not one, since I rescued you from the flood. I have served the Balt Kaalith faithfully, all my life. I do not deserve this. So you will tell me what you know of this matter, or else you will die, Noqvoan, for since I saved you from the flood, your life belongs to me, and I will have satisfaction, one way or the other."

The Baltar stared hard at the Noqvoan, his sword steady in his hand. The Noqvoan did nothing and waited the Baltar out. The sword came closer yet, but still the Noqvoan did not answer, so the sword touched his neck and the eyes of the Baltar began to burn with a dangerous light. The Noqvoan glanced at the sword, then at the Baltar and finally relented.

"Very well," he said. "You are troubled, I see. Put up your sword and I shall apologise for my manner."

The Baltar did not move.

"Put up your sword, I say. Nothing will be served by this!"

The Baltar still did not move. The Noqvoan took a deep breath.

"So be it. I will tell you what I know. Will that suffice?"

The Baltar withdrew his sword a little, but he did not sheathe it.

"Say on," he hissed.

The Noqvoan looked to the east.

"I shall start with a name," he said, "and once you have heard it, perhaps you will consider it enough to assume your rightful place."

The Noqvoan paused a moment and looked significantly at the Baltar, who scowled in return.

"And what name might that be?" he asked. "I can think of none so dire that could explain…" the Baltar gestured vaguely about him, "… all of this."

The Noqvoan smiled.

"Then you have not thought enough," he replied. "What if I offered up the name of Korfax?"

The Baltar took a step back. He pointed at the east gate.

"That was him?" he asked incredulously.

The Baltar looked back at the road beyond the gate as if it were suddenly full of cavorting demons. Then he turned to the Noqvoan again.

"They said that he was mad at the end, mad with power and spite, and that the power inside him made of him both a traitor and a murderer. I heard that he fought with the Velukor himself and was cast from the Lee Leiulus. They said that he was dead."

The Baltar looked down but then held his sword up again.

"Do the dead come back to us now?" he asked quietly. "Do the vengeful dead return? That is one of the omens of the end!"

The Noqvoan closed his eyes as though at the limits of his restraint.

"Enough!" he said. "Cease your superstitious prattle!"

The Baltar held his sword against the neck of the Noqvoan once more, and this time he drew blood.

"You are in no position to mock!" he cried.

"I do not mock," the Noqvoan continued, "but you are being foolish! And put up your sword. Let me tell you what really happened."

The Baltar lowered his sword again and watched as the Noqvoan put his hand to his neck, feeling the cut. The Baltar waited with barely concealed rage.

"Say on," he said, "but do not think that I will ever forget your manner with me. Come the day and the hour, I will see you repent."

The Noqvoan looked heavenwards.

"May the Creator preserve me!" he sighed.

He looked back at the Baltar.

"Korfax survived the fall from Lee Leiulus," he said.

"And how do you know this?" questioned the Baltar. "Were you there? I had not heard if you were."

"I know for the simple reason that he appeared again in Emethgis Vaniad just before it was taken by the Agdoain."

"There were witnesses?"

"Geyadril Ponodol and Geyad Kurapan, to name but two. It was Kurapan who spoke of the encounter to the Velukor, and once the Velukor knew of it, so did we."

"But the Velukor said that he was dead."

"The Velukor was clearly mistaken. Besides, it became clear at the end that he suffered from a malady of the mind, like his father before him. Do not trust all that you hear where the Velukor is concerned."

The Baltar was outraged.

"Do not trust the Velukor?" he said. "Now what are you saying? Who do we serve if not the chosen of the Creator?"

The Noqvoan took a long, hard breath.

"Will you listen to what you are being told?! The Velukor was mistaken, and that is all that I am saying!"

The Baltar snarled for a moment, baring his teeth before looking away again. It had become a dance of violence between them. Passions long held in abeyance, grudging servitude, arrogant mastery, were finally seeing the light of day. The Baltar held up his sword and tickled the throat of the Noqvoan for the third time.

"So what now?" he asked.

The Noqvoan leaned back.

"Well, once you have removed your sword from my neck once more, I intend to go back and talk to the master of that boat."

He pointed towards the eastern docks. The Baltar bowed slightly.

"Then lead on," he said, "but allow me to ward you."

He gestured with his sword and they both headed back to the docks – the Noqvoan in front, the Baltar behind, his sword ever at the ready.

Gedonon looked up to find two others he did not know standing over him.

Though each looked dirty and dishevelled, their eyes were hard and keen and they both wore the cloaks of the Balt Kaalith. One held a sword. The other did not.

"You had a passenger," said the one without a sword. It was not a question.

Gedonon did not answer.

"We would know what you know."

Gedonon looked down. Why did they bother him? What did anything matter now? The one without a sword knelt beside him.

"Tell me what you know of him. It is important."

Gedonon did not look back up. Nothing was important any more. The other reached out to touch him. He drew back.

"Leave me alone," Gedonon said.

"I will," said the other, "but first tell me of your passenger."

"I will say nothing of him. I curse the day that he came to me. Ill-fortune followed in his wake."

"And many others would say the same. Ill-fortune follows him like a shadow."

Gedonon looked up.

"You speak as if you know him."

"Did he give you his name?"

"He only called himself Karin in my hearing."

"Did he?" came the answer.

"So you do know him!"

"Yes, I know him."

"Then tell me who he is."

"He is Korfax."

Gedonon bowed his head and shook. So that was it! No wonder the day was dark.

"They said that he was dead."

"I know that they did, but they were mistaken. Now, your story. Tell it to me, I must know it."

The tale emerged, long and slow and halting, but when Gedonon related how Lonsiatris had disappeared, the Baltar drew back and looked to the horizon.

"This one is mad. How can Lonsiatris be gone?"

The Noqvoan stood up and then glanced at the Baltar.

"Anything is possible where Korfax is concerned," he said. "I think this one is telling us the truth. It explains the wave. Come, we should discuss this elsewhere."

Leaving Gedonon alone with his grief, they moved away and found a convenient place to sit.

"What do you think really happened?" asked the Baltar.

"Korfax was on an errand, but he was betrayed somehow, if I read the situation aright."

"Yes, I see. According to Gedonon, Korfax cursed the heretics. He would not have done that if he still served them. I see what you mean."

"Good," said the Noqvoan. "You are thinking like one of the Balt Kaalith again. Recall his words."

'They have gone! They have fled this world, leaving the rest of us to fall before the foe. We that are left have become the price of their freedom. They have called down the arrow of time itself – from Kokazadah they have ensnared it. They have set themselves upon its shaft and even now ride its fire into the future. The heretics have escaped the world, though few will mourn their passing. More fool they! It is the rest of us that are the fools, for we are the ones that have been left behind, to fight on, and to die!'

"One of the Dar Kaadarith will need to explain this to us. However, we can be certain of one thing at least: the heretics have fled the world in some manner. Cowards! They would rather flee than fight."

The Baltar gestured about him.

"But where could they go? This world is all that there is. There is nowhere else." Then he lowered his voice. "Unless they went to the abyss?"

The Noqvoan scowled.

"Not to the abyss. They have not gone there."

"Then where?"

"The future! Think what Korfax said. 'They have called down the arrow of time itself.'"

"But how?"

"Korfax went to the Umadya Semeiel in Emethgis Vaniad and confronted Geyadril Ponodol in that tower's Hall of Memory. We learned afterwards that Korfax had taken the Kapimadar. It is clear to me now that he brought it back to Lonsiatris. And which heretic alone was of the Dar Kaadarith? That would be Dialyas, would it not?"

"And what is this Kapimadar?" asked the Baltar. "I have never heard of it."

"It was the reason for the downfall of Dialyas," answered the Noqvoan. "First he spoke out against the accepted wisdom of Karmaraa, and then he set out to prove that what he said was right. The Kapimadar was the result. All I know is that it was supposed to be able to change its nature according to the demands placed upon it. It was also deemed a failure."

"And how do you know this?"

"All of the Noqvoanith know it. It is required knowledge. Until his final exile, Dialyas remained unfinished business. It was necessary to know all that we could."

"But did not Korfax have a hand in his exile?"

"He was crucial. And that is the most interesting thing of all."

"I am not sure that I understand," said the Baltar.

"Nor I," agreed the Noqvoan. "We are missing something here, something of vital import."

"So what do we do now?"

"Have you still no mind of your own?"

The Baltar sneered.

"As you have continually reminded me, you are a Noqvoan."

"And what of your threat to make me repent?" asked the Noqvoan. "You held your sword at my throat. Will you subjugate yourself to the will of others only when it suits you? Or will you only submit when the decisions become too much and hard responsibility piles up about you? That is not service but selfishness."

"ENOUGH!" shouted the Baltar. "I know my place."

"Do you?" wondered the Noqvoan. "I wonder if you truly do."

The Baltar raised a fist and glared, but the Noqvoan held up his hand.

"You know nothing," he said. "You are merely the hand of the Balt Kaalith whilst I am its heart, its mind and its soul. I do not fear hard choices, I make them every day of my life."

"So make one now," hissed the Baltar. "Prove your worth to me!"

"Easy enough. We shall tell this tale to those that should be told. I will go to Othil Ekrin and alert our order there, whilst you will go to Othil Admaq and tell them what has been witnessed here this day. Othil Homtoh should also be told, but that will be inevitable, once you arrive at Othil Admaq."

"And why do you go east whilst I go north?"

"I go east precisely because that is the way that Korfax is going. It is not your place to inquire further. I am Noqvoan. You are Baltar. Do you equate your skills with mine?"

"Very well then," said the Baltar. "I will go to Othil Admaq. I would wish you success, but no doubt you would dismiss such benison as unworthy, coming as it does from a lowly Baltar!"

"Enough of your wounded pride," the Noqvoan said. "We have work to do."

"I will not forget you, Odoiar," said the Baltar. "Pray that we never meet again."

"And that is of little or no consequence to me."

The Baltar lifted his sword again, but Odoiar was quicker. His own blade blocked the Baltar's sword. A quick series of movements saw the Baltar's blade fly from his hand and Odoiar's blade at the Baltar's throat.

"The wheel turns, does it not?" said Odoiar.

"So kill me then," said the Baltar. "Or are you craven? Trust me, this will be the only chance you will ever have this side of the river!"

Odoiar turned away.

"Retrieve your sword and get you to Othil Admaq," he said. "And the sooner you are out of my sight, the better I will be pleased."

Out of the land of mud he came upon a tower set on the top of a high hill. The hill might have been green and fair once, but now it was grey. The tower looked whole, but its stone was begrimed and stained. Only the upper reaches of its walls and high spires remained untouched.

A row of bodies lay alongside the outer wall, bodies wrapped about in different fabrics and watched over by two figures. The first figure stood straight and stern, a staff in one hand, his other clutched at his breast. The second figure knelt before the covered dead and wept, all but lost to her grief. The standing figure was intoning something. Korfax could just make out the words.

"Behold the word of the Creator," came the voice, "the revealed promise, which is called amongst you extreme justice..."

The voice stopped and the standing figure turned towards Korfax.

"You!" he called out. "Stay! Declare yourself! Pay homage!"

Korfax did not stop but looked steadfastly ahead.

"Stay, I say!" the figure called again, leaving his place and striding forward, his staff held high like a commandment.

Korfax turned his head.

"If I had to stop at each place of death that I have passed this day, I would still be here a hundred years hence," he said.

The other stepped in front of Enastul and stood like a wall in the road. Enastul would have pushed him aside, but Korfax reigned in his steed and bade him stop. He looked down at the other.

This one was a Balzarg, cloaked and clothed in the traditional fashion, his house sigil gleaming proudly upon his brow. He looked the very image of dutiful service, but something behind his eyes betrayed him. They were cracked and fragile things, their inner light wavering and uncertain.

"There is nothing I can say or do," Korfax offered. "The dead remain dead."

"Callous!" accused the Balzarg. "Now you must make amends, I demand it. Pay homage to the passing of the house of Undir. My lord is dead. His daughter is dead. My mistress weeps. Have you no heart?"

Korfax looked away.

"It is for you to look to your mistress, as she at least still lives. And in the dark days to come all amongst the living will need comfort. But ask nothing of the accursed, lest you would add to your woes."

He spurred Enastul on and Enastul pushed past the Balzarg, knocking him out of the way. The Balzarg fell back, tumbling to the side of the road.

"Accursed you call yourself, so accursed you are, black heart!" he called, shaking his staff in the air. "May the Creator rot your unforgiving soul!"

Enastul cared not one whit, but Korfax glowered at the road ahead. Black heart? Rot your soul? What did the Balzarg of the Salman Undirith know? Korfax felt the gloom deepen about him. His fate must be written on his face.

Korfax stared at the long line of high cliffs before him. The view ahead was the same as the one behind. To his right, far below, lay the sullen sea; to his left lay a flat and featureless land that stretched as far as the eye could see.

Here was the Piral Zah, the land of solitude as it was marked on his map. Clearly the cliffs had preserved the land, but even if the wave had been high enough to wash over them, it would have made little difference.

He was alone at the edge of a wasteland, without and within, and he had begun to drown at last. His thoughts sank under an inner deluge that surged up from below, a flood that engulfed everything in its path. Where should he go now? What should he do? What was the point of anything any longer?

Korfax stared morosely ahead. Dialyas had fled the world and Lonsiatris, with all her people, was gone, gone from Uriel, gone who knew where. Dialyas had done exactly what he had said he would do – he had redeemed the Ell, just not all of them. The rejected and the scorned, the defeated and the lowly – they had all been saved, but no one else. The exaltation had come and gone, and those left behind had not even known it had passed. Soon though, soon they would understand, for those left behind would face the all but unstoppable Agdoain.

So here they were: the end of days, when the righteous were called to salvation and the guilty were left behind to face judgement and the consequences of their irredeemable sins. Who would have thought it?! Those that followed the chosen of the Creator were damned, and those that rejected such service were blessed. And here he was, the unwitting agent, left behind with all the rest. He would have laughed, if it were not so bitter.

Somewhere inside there was an inconsolable rage. He had been used and then tossed aside when his purpose was done, like a broken tool. Of all the betrayals he had endured, this was undoubtedly the worst. He found himself hating Dialyas.

So where had he gone? Where had he taken the land of the heretics? What wide and gentle sea in some far-off time and place now cradled its ancient stone? Who could tell? One thing was certain, though. Dialyas would rule. Who else would it be? Happy and sated and filled with contentment in an unstained world, surrounded by his many sycophants, Dialyas would be proclaimed the new Karmaraa by all he had deigned to save.

Korfax felt a sweeping sense of revulsion as he imagined how Dialyas, with false humility, would step backwards into his throne, forced there by his ever grateful followers. He would bow, his hands held up in mock denial, but inside he would smile as he prepared to pass down his self-deprecating benedictions from on high.

How far back did this go? How long had Dialyas planned for this moment? Certainly he had known Samor from the earliest days, when she was already of the Urendrilith and he was just an acolyte. No doubt they had liked each other, or at least admired each other, for that friendship had led to a privileged glimpse of the surviving prophecies of Nalvahgey.

Korfax wondered if that had been the spur. Perhaps Dialyas had seen something, glimpsed something, a possible meaning that had eluded all others. Perhaps it was this that had caused him to conceive the Kapimadar. But then, of course, in conceiving such stone he had stumbled upon his great heresy.

How deep went his play? How far back had Dialyas seen this coming, planning for it, keeping his guesses tight to his breast down the long years of waiting and saying nothing, even to those closest to him? Then, come the hour, he had pulled triumph out of failure and had fled damnation. Now all roads, every single one of them, led to the same destination: to suffering, to pain, to death and the world's ending.

Korfax went his weary way. He felt empty, used up and bleak. Was this how it was when all purposes were ended and all the goals of one's life were made void? He had not even known what it was that he had accomplished until it was too late. Had life become the plaything of the few, then? Did its mastery belong only to those that could gaze to the furthest horizon and beyond?

He bowed his head as Enastul took him on, carrying him over the great wasteland like so much baggage, for Korfax was too consumed by his own thought to care.

The perfidy, the cowardice and the sheer arrogance of what Dialyas had done all but stunned him. The Kapimadar had been created with but one purpose, and for a long while only Dialyas had truly known what that purpose was. The others that had helped him had not understood, not even at the end.

Virqol, Ponodol and even his father, his very own father, had been gulled by the liar. Earth, air, fire and water – all had been subsumed by the cunning of the deceiver, for only Dialyas had known the real truth.

Korfax clenched a fist and all but shook it at the empty air. His father, the potent fire behind the making of the Kapimadar, was dead, whilst Dialyas yet lived in some far-flung future. Dialyas was a thief. He had taken from others but had given nothing in return. He had taken from Sazaaim, from Ponodol, from Virqol, and what was the result? All of them were dead, but Dialyas still lived. He had clambered over the bodies of the drowning so that he might yet still breathe in the air for a little while longer.

Korfax glowered at the path before him. Even rage no longer sufficed. It was impotent. The last act was over before any had known it was even being played. For those left behind the oncoming night was to be their one and only fate.

So why was he still pursuing Doagnis? What advantage was there in her apprehension now?

Knowledge to follow Dialyas?

Unlikely!

Knowledge to defeat the Agdoain?

Possibly!

But Dialyas had not thought so. He had fled the world. Korfax kept his head down. Dialyas had fled the world.

Despair filled him, a despair unlike any he had ever known in his life before. It gnawed at him, robbing him of both his strength and his will. Emptiness beckoned, a single grey finger, bent like a withered hook. *Join with me*, it said, *join with me at last and end it all. It is the wisest choice, the only course left. There is no point any more, it told him. You have already guessed the truth. Your fight was over before it had ever really begun. But such is the way of the world. You live, you briefly struggle against the uncaring heavens, and then it all ends. What an absurdity! All your works come to dust! It is your only legacy. You are born, you live a brief moment and then you die and go to dust. To be forgotten is your only fate. Oblivion is the only answer, the only possible answer in this cruel and uncaring place. So stop the suffering and let it end. What else can you do?*

The siren song of the void had him. How different to his dream at Piamossin, which now sat inside him like an echo of himself. He had both risen and fallen in the brief space of just a few years, a life of ages compressed into moments. He had once believed that he knew what the heavens had in store for him, but then he had seen beneath the mask. Now he saw his fate, and the fate of the whole world, all outlined in the harsh light of reality. What hope remained?

He rode on without even the will to curse his lot. All was lost and everything seemed vain.

He headed east, for want of another direction. Ahead and to the north was a long line of low hills, the Leein Loh, or so they were named on his map, but as he looked at them now he wondered how it was that they had ever achieved that name. They seemed uninviting and drear – long, featureless slopes and wide empty summits.

So he came down from the Piral Zah at last, on to the low plains of the Piral Loh, and found yet more desolation. The great wave had come here and inundated everything. The coastline had been altered, new bays created and old ones removed. He could make out the ruins of bridges marking where the road had been, but of the road itself there was nothing. He saw no signs of habitation.

He stared out over great stretches of still water, sullen beneath the sky. The Piral Loh had become a swamp, a place of muds and stagnant waters, foetid and almost impassable. For a long time he stared at it. East, something inside him kept saying, go east. He did not want to listen, but eventually he succumbed. For want of anything better, he continued on his way.

He kept to firm ground where he could, but the going was not easy. The land would not rise again for many long days, and both he and Enastul had no choice but to endure the travails of the Piral Loh.

Fording each river he came to was not the hardest task, it was the land itself that delayed him, for the road had been swept away and its foundations had become a quagmire.

On the second day crossing the Piral Loh he came upon two ships anchored in a bay. There were smaller craft upon the shore and figures standing near to them. He saw armour, Branith no doubt, sent to assess the damage and look for survivors.

No sooner did he see them than they saw him. They waved. He did not wave back. Though he was in no mood for company, in this he had no choice. They were in his way. He could not avoid them.

He approached. Standing to the fore was a Brandril, clearly in charge and waiting for him. Korfax had no trouble assuming the role of the weary traveller.

"The Creator's light be upon you," said the Brandril.

"And upon you," Korfax answered.

"You have come far?"

"I have come down from the Leein Loh."

A look of surprise crossed the other's face.

"You survived the flooding?"

"When I saw how things were I kept to the higher ground," Korfax said.

"So you saw the floods?"

"I saw something of them, and I thanked the Creator that I had not taken the road. What caused it?"

"We do not know," said the Brandril. "A great wave swept the coast here. The further west we go, the worse it is. There are tales that have come to us, of flood and chaos. Many ports have been broken, or so rumour has it. I have not gone so far myself."

Korfax looked down.

"How many?" he asked.

"Again, we do not know. We were told to investigate. We have come from Thilzin Merenar. The land hereabouts is the worst that we have seen. I dread to think how it is further on."

"I cannot say," said Korfax. "I know even less than you."

The Brandril looked unsatisfied.

"Did you pass any other upon the road?"

"I have seen no other since I came down from the Leein Loh."

"And where do you go now?"

"Into the east."

"What is your business?"

Now there was the question. What could he say? That he had none? The Brandril might even go so far as to demand his aid.

"I am going to Othil Ekrin," he said.

"I asked for your business," said the Brandril, "not your destination."

"My business is my own," Korfax told him. Was there anger? Something had been stirred. He looked hard at the Brandril, and the Brandril looked hard back. They eyed each other for a moment.

"You look weary," the Brandril finally said.

"It has been a hard road," Korfax told him.

The Brandril pointed east.

"The going is easier beyond the headland," he said. Then he walked away, and that was that. Korfax watched him for a moment and then looked east. He could see no headlands.

14

He finally came to them after two more days. The land had slowly risen again, the way getting easier after the weariness of the Piral Loh. Then, over a long rise, they were before him, the headlands that divided the east from the west, a long line of hills ending in sheer cliffs.

Once he had achieved the highest point, he could see what the Brandril had meant. The land here was higher, and it had fared better. Had he reached the limit of the wave's influence at last? He hoped it was so. From here on the way might prove easier, and perhaps he would now find places where he could replenish his dwindling supplies.

To the north he could just make out the high plateau where Tylodir was said to be, across the flooded plains. He stared intently at the distant rise. Were there towers there, tall white spires safe behind high walls? He hoped it was so.

It was as he reached the end of the headlands that the land in front of him fell away once more, just as Rafarel pierced the clouds at last. Before him lay a wide bay, set with rocky spires and crouching stone. The land suddenly looked bright again, as though it smiled. He almost smiled himself to see it. He had forgotten he would pass this place. He had come to the Kordrilith Cho.

With Enastul following behind, Korfax walked the wide stretch of sea-washed sand and thought himself caught in a dream. To his left reared great stone pillars, their features lost to the elements. Some were squat and hunched, bent over upon themselves as though bowing, whilst others reared like great statues, unseen eyes gazing at the heavens. Though they seemed blunted, worn down by the tyranny of time, the spirit within them said otherwise. Deep inside, in each heart of stone, a light still danced.

He walked amongst them, the dancing giants, feet buried in sand, heads brushing the last of the morning mists. Here they had danced since the very beginning, dancing under heaven's gaze, dancing in joy. Behind them reared mighty cliffs, stern bastions that frowned down at the play below, but the cliffs were powerless against the dance.

The sea lay to his right, its green waves gentle on the pale sand that swirled across the beach. Further out, white-tipped waves flashed briefly whilst beyond the furthest movement the sea merged with the sky in a distant haze.

Korfax looked at sea, cliff and dancing stone. He smiled. He felt himself diminished as he walked his way, a child again, lost amidst the incomprehensible play of his elders.

He stopped. Where was his despair now? Suddenly there was only joy. He had been a fool! Oh, such a fool he had been.

This was the very thing that Dialyas had missed – the world. Dialyas had never seen the world. He had been so busy looking to the future that he had never seen the now.

All the wonders that Korfax had ever witnessed in his life came back to him, a brighter flood sweeping away the dark deluge. He saw again the sea rising up in fury as it burst over the walls of Tohus. He saw again the low clouds curling in upon themselves as they passed the airy tips of the Lee Izirakal. He saw again the Nazarthin Ozong from the railings of a sky ship, bathed in the glow of evening. He saw sunsets and dawns, red skies, black skies, blue skies. He saw the stars and the constellations and the mountains and the seas, and the beauty of creation came to him and filled him to his brim.

Tears fell from his eyes as he realised that he too had stopped seeing the world. Enastul nuzzled him, gently comforting the distress of his master, and Korfax stroked his steed in return and let the tears fall.

This was why he pursued Doagnis, this was why he lived. Whatever else Dialyas might think, the Creator was not done with this world yet. He, Korfax, had been chosen. He was here to preserve, and his charge was no less than the world itself. That was his purpose, to oppose its fall into the void; for all things have their opposite, and if Korfax understood anything, he understood that.

2

THE VOVIN'S SKIN

Pas-usfa Odur-farim
Oad-risin Fen-nht-orors
Chis-honli Isi-zafra
Edod-loag Odrox-odtor
Tel-dizihr Boaged-kaojon
Malin-zil Odna-innht
Unch-odix Od-ial-tharton

They watched carefully, quietly, three figures on steeds, hidden in the shadow of a shallow cave. Above them reared a great outcrop of stone. Below them stretched the eastern road.

Two bore great swords across their backs and sat both proud and straight, their pale faces open to the sky. The other, though, all but crouched in her saddle and hid herself away from the light under a deep hood and voluminous cloak.

"Might that be him?" whispered the one to her right.

"Quiet!" she hissed back, shifting slightly in her saddle. "I am looking."

The translucent stone in the palm of her hand did nothing. She frowned at it for a moment and then looked at the rider far below. Nothing. She would have put the stone away again but then she felt it change. She held it up once more and its pale light flickered, and then dimmed, before a rush of midnight flew out of its centre and eclipsed everything else. The transition was so rapid, so surprising, that she almost dropped the stone.

She turned to the others.

"Well now," she said, "it seems he is the one, after all. Now it begins in earnest."

"How hard do we follow?" asked the one to her left.

"Not too hard, not yet at least. We follow carefully for now. And neither of you will act without a word from me, is that clear?"

They both bowed to her.

"Come then," she said. "Let us begin. I have him now. He will be easy to follow. He has become the solitary tree upon the plain; he has become the lonely mountain."

The road, for the most part, was empty, but Korfax was glad to be upon it. Though there had been some flooding, this region seemed to have weathered the storm reasonably well. He saw little sign of damage to the road, and all the bridges he crossed were intact.

Occasionally he passed others. There were towers, small communities scattered about the road, but the people here kept to themselves, and those few that he passed did not greet him but merely glanced up before looking away again, intent upon their own business.

There was no judgement in their eyes, no suspicion, just a certain wariness. Korfax wondered if that was the tradition here, or whether it had arisen out of the troubles of the world. He knew little of this land or the ways of its people.

He found himself longing again for the north and the simpler courtesies of bygone days. Before the rising of the Agdoain the Ell had been more generous, more giving, less suspicious and not so preoccupied with their own affairs. He missed that now.

Come the night he either slept under the stars or, when he came to one of the few settlements that dotted the highway, in a hostelry. When in the company of others he kept himself to himself, his hood up, his face in shadow, and he always sat alone. It seemed to be what was expected of him.

He still garnered the odd glance, being taller and broader than most, with a pale skin and a strange accent. But most had eyes only for the great blade that lay across his back. Though sheathed and wrapped against the elements, it was a fearsomely large weapon, a kansehna of exceptional size. The unspoken threat hung in the air, and whenever Korfax met the glance of another, that glance was quickly turned away.

Only those that kept the hostels were friendly, if only to help lighten his purse. For, as each told him in their own way, these were dangerous times, what with the Agdoain and the floods and all. So Korfax continued his way eastwards and ignored the concerns of others. He had far more important things on his mind.

They followed their quarry discreetly, she ever to the fore, her escort always at her back. Every so often she stopped those that they passed, or those that they shared lodgings with, inquiring carefully of the tall dark rider and his great black steed. But all those that she spoke to told her the very same tale: 'He went that way,' they said, pointing to the east. Along the road, they gestured, always along the road and always to the east.

Korfax sat quietly in an alcove, a goblet of wine in his hand and an empty plate before him, his shadowed eyes peering into the distances.

The door to the hostelry opened and three entered. Two were armed, long swords slung across their backs and dark armour underneath travel-stained cloaks.

The other was smaller, hooded and hidden, but unusually purposeful. Korfax roused himself and watched them carefully, especially the hooded figure that led the way. There was a lady under that hood, he was certain of it, a lady of prominence and power. Only those of the Erm Roith, or widows, covered themselves so completely, but this one did not wear the orange of a Luahith, nor did she wear the habiliments of parting.

He watched and wondered. These three, for some reason, had caught his interest. Were they a threat, or were they just as they seemed – two escorts and their lady?

He looked away for a moment, ordering his thoughts in the ways he had been taught so that he could study them more carefully, but when he looked up again they had vanished. He glanced this way and that, but he saw no sign of them. No doubt they had gone deeper into the hostelry, seeking out its keeper, perhaps.

He readied himself and waited, trusting his instincts. Something was coming, but what it might be he could not tell.

She approached quietly and took the seat opposite, as if expected. She drew back her hood and smiled. Korfax passed a swift glance over her face. Her features were delicate and her skin was pale. She, like him, was not from these parts. He bowed his head to her but did not remove his hood.

"May the light of the Creator shine upon you," he said.

She raised an eyebrow as if the greeting was entirely unexpected.

"And upon you!" she answered after a little while. "But I think it would shine a little easier if you but drew back your hood. With all that shadow in the way you do not make it easy for the Creator to give you any kind of blessing at all."

"I prefer the shadow for now. Let the Creator's blessings fall where they may."

She raised the other eyebrow.

"So what are you hiding from?"

"And what business is that of yours? I did not invite you to sit with me. You invited yourself."

One of her companions leaned forward as if to offer an opinion, but she gestured him back.

"I saw you here, all alone, and I was curious, that is all," she said. "There are few like you upon the road hereabouts. I thought perhaps you might have an interesting tale to tell."

Korfax turned and gestured to the owner of the hostel. The owner came over carefully, eyes flicking from one to the other before settling at last upon Korfax, who finally drew back his hood.

"I would like some more wine, if that can be arranged," he asked. "Your best, if you please."

A single coin was held up, one single Sanizikal. The owner of the hostelry stared at it for a moment and then bowed in return. He smiled the most ingratiating smile that he could.

"The best? Of course. You shall have it by the flagon. As much as you can drink!"

Korfax smiled in return and handed the coin over. His guest watched him carefully as he did so, narrowing her eyes as she studied his face.

"That was most generous," she said, after the owner was gone. "The wine here must be moderate at best."

"Perhaps," said Korfax, "but I am expecting our host to suddenly discover something a little better in his cellars. Are you and your companions thirsty?"

She matched his smile.

"Most generous, indeed. I shall, of course, accept, but my servants have duties to perform."

She turned to one of her companions.

"See to my room, will you?"

He bowed and left. She turned to the other.

"See to our steeds."

He bowed and left as well.

Zizar waited for Boaza to join him. Boaza was not long in coming.

"Have you discovered which room is his?" Zizar asked.

"He has not yet taken one," Boaza replied.

"Then search his steed. It would be wise to discover his purposes, just in case."

"Are we not to kill him?"

"Leave that to our mistress. She is skilled in such matters. Our task is to watch and ward."

"I doubt he has left anything important in the stables."

"We have to be sure. Thoroughness, in all things, brings success."

Boaza bowed and left. Zizar went to his mistress's room and waited.

The wine came and it was, as Korfax had surmised, rather better than might be expected. Goblets were filled and Korfax held his up to his guest.

"Good fortune to you," he said.

"And to you," she answered. They drank and then the lady introduced herself.

"I am Tusrin Nar Tohtanef."

Korfax bowed his head slightly.

"An honour," he said. "I am Gallin Rom Hallai."

"You are a sword for hire?" she asked.

"Just a traveller for the moment," he told her. "I have been paid well for recent services."

"And have a taste for expensive pleasures, I see."

She looked at the goblet before her. Korfax took another sip from his.

"One acquires such things when one no longer serves another."

"You are from the north?" she asked.

"I am," he answered. "But what of you? I do not recognise your accent."

"I have been many places, so many, in fact, that I have given up belonging to any of them."

"But you must have been born. Where was that?"

She smiled.

"Now, Hallai, you know that I did not come here to tell you the story of my life, but rather to listen to whatever tale you chose to tell me."

"But simple courtesy demands you should at least satisfy my curiosity as well. Besides, how are you going to pay me for my time? A tale for a tale seems only fair."

Her eyes flashed slightly. It was brief, but telling. She was used to having her own way, and if Korfax was not mistaken, she had power. For some reason he suddenly thought of Doagnis, and with that he was instantly on his guard.

"And the wine," he asked, gesturing at her goblet, "is it not to your liking?"

She offered him a brittle smile in return and took a sip.

"The wine is very much to my liking," she returned, "but I like to take my time with such things."

Boaza entered the stables and walked past the many stalls. Where was the great black steed? There were no others here that looked even remotely like it. He looked from left to right as he passed from stall to stall, his frustration growing as he went. Was it stabled elsewhere? Then, right at the end, he found it. His quarry was right at the back, a huge and gleaming ormn contentedly nibbling at the grasses in its bier. He smiled. That was the very one indeed.

He walked confidently up to the gate of its stall and leant upon it, looking in. And what a magnificent beast it truly was. Black, all black, from head to foot, black, all black, from horn to tail. What a beast it was, with its laughing eyes and gleaming mane. He had never seen better. Here was a prize worthy of a lord, of a prince, even, not some wandering sword.

He looked it up and down and smiled. Would it not be fine to sit astride such a beast? Would the great black ormn not make a fine possession? And why not, he suddenly asked himself, why not? He was tired of the crumbs that fell from his mistress's table. Let him have something worthy for once. His smile widened. Consider it a spoil of war.

He opened the gate and came towards the black ormn carefully, his mind reaching out with calming thoughts, his hands held up in the gentling motion one used when confronting a strange steed, but Enastul was having none of it.

He looked down at this sudden interruption to his evening meal and snorted his displeasure. Who was this upstart? Enastul already knew who his master was, and he was a greater lord by far than this one could ever be.

Without any warning Enastul raised himself up on his hind legs and flailed his forelegs in the air, eyes wild as the stables shuddered with his sudden cry. The other steeds started at the sound and danced in their stalls in answer, whilst not a few even thrashed at their gates with their hind legs.

Boaza fell back from the lethal hooves. He was wrong. This one was a monster. He had misjudged the beast. It was untameable, and what a pity that was. But he still had to search the bags that hung behind it, so he drew his sword. Only one way to proceed now. He advanced again, sword before him, smiling darkly.

"Deny me, will you?" he said. "Not the best choice you could make!"

Enastul backed away, watching carefully. But the laughter did not leave his eyes. This one was a fool.

Enastul turned with a speed that belied his size. Faster than thought he struck, his hind legs a pair of coiled springs, his two hind feet battering rams. They caught the fool full upon his chest, and the fool flew. He flew through the air, broken and useless, before crashing against the far wall with bone-cracking force. Then he fell, all of a heap on the floor, where he remained, unmoving, his sword beside him still loosely held by a broken hand.

Enastul looked carefully at the unhappy wreckage for a moment, ears flicking this way and that, and then he turned back to his evening meal as if nothing had happened at all.

"So, your tale?" she asked.

"I passed through Thilzin Jerris and bore witness to its downfall," he told her.

She waited a moment.

"Whatever do you mean?"

"Did you not hear of the great wave?"

"Yes, there was flooding all along the coast. Further west it was worst, with some bridges being swept away, or so I heard. I have not been so far myself."

"Yet you are travelling from the west."

"I came down the road from Immil," she told him.

"And you have not heard what happened to Thilzin Jerris?" he asked. "It has been destroyed."

"You saw this?"

"I passed through its ruin."

Korfax took another draught of wine. It really was rather good. It was a pity he could not enjoy it as much as he would like. This lady was hard work. Every question, every word, was followed by a quick stab of thoughts, subtle barbs intended to sneak under his guard. She was adept, no doubt about it, but he was able to put her aside each time. From her expression, though, she was clearly finding his defences more than she was used to. There was only one certainty. She was not of the Balt Kaalith.

"Tell me what you saw," she said. Another stab of thoughts.

"The towers are gone, and the great bridge. The city is a ruin. The dead are everywhere," he answered, turning her thoughts aside.

"You did not stop to give aid?"

More stabs, this time from two different directions.

"To whom? The dead?"

He turned her aside again.

"No one was left?"

She tried to sneak in underneath.

"Perhaps a lucky few, but I did not see them."

He stamped downwards and felt her withdraw.

"Do you know what caused this calamity?" she asked.

"And how would I know that? It was a wave. Perhaps a great storm caused it. All I know is that Thilzin Jerris has been thrown down and her people drowned."

Tohtanef drew back. He could tell she was troubled. Both her failure to see him, and the topic of conversation, disturbed her greatly.

"The world has become a place of death," he told her. "One does not know what one will meet upon the road, or off it."

He watched her, but did not try for her mind, not yet. She, though, was clearly not happy with the way things were going. She dropped her hands into her lap. Korfax kept his eyes upon hers, and waited for her next move.

"So you seek death?" she asked.

"I did not say that," he answered. "But I have seen my share of it."

"Clearly, but you seem to be expecting it, nonetheless."

"That does not mean that I seek it."

"But you put yourself in its way willingly, I think."

"Hardly. Death is everywhere, like light. It is the intent of others that gives it focus."

He felt her stabbing at his thoughts again, but this time he stabbed back. She was hard pressed to still herself. Korfax smiled. He had barely exerted himself, and yet she was clearly struggling to keep him out. He withdrew and waited. Let her think herself inviolate.

"Who are you?" she asked.

"You have heard my name. Who are you?" he returned.

"My answer is the same."

"Undoubtedly. What do you want?"

"To know your purposes."

He took the plunge.

"Not for you, Arged."

She stood up and backed away. Korfax stayed where he was. They had an audience now. Others were looking up, sensing the tenseness in the air. Korfax waited easily, while Tohtanef gave him an unreadable look.

"We shall see," she said.

"We shall, indeed," he replied.

She left the room. Many eyes followed her, no doubt wondering what that had been about. Korfax took another cup of wine. He would not be the one to explain it.

Zizar waited. Boaza was taking his time. No doubt his mistress was still sitting with their quarry, if she had not yet disposed of him. He had seen her kill many times, mainly Balt Kaalith. She enjoyed such things, following the example of Doagnis herself. Zizar smiled. Now there was a daughter of the north. He had met her only once, but it had been memorable. She was beautiful, a soft beauty of curves and smiles, but there was hard stone beneath – the way she looked at you, eyes that drowned you and which pulled at your soul as though to rip it from your body. She had nearly slain the high council of the accursed west and had held at bay one of the most powerful in the land. He had no doubts that under her the north would rise again. Then let all others beware; vengeance would be swift and it would be terrible.

The door to the room opened and he felt Tohtanef enter. He stepped out from the shadows. Her face was troubled.

"What is it?" he asked.

"This one is not Balt Kaalith or Dar Kaadarith, but still he pursues our mistress. Also, he knows what I am and it clearly does not bother him."

Zizar frowned.

"Is he one of the Argedith, then?"

"That would be worrisome, if it were true," she said.

"But why? Surely he should ally himself with us?"

"And what if he believes in the old ways?" she warned.

Zizar drew back. That was unexpected.

"So what do we do?" he asked.

"We take no chances," she answered. "A silent death would be best. We will wait until later."

She looked about.

"Where is Boaza?"

"He hasn't returned. He has been gone some time."

"Find him," she ordered. "I need you both to be at the ready. Keep outside and watch the doors. Meanwhile, I shall prepare."

Zizar did as he was bade, going to the stables first. He did not expect Boaza to still be there, but he did wonder where he had gone. Boaza might be a little wayward, but he was not one for taking himself off without letting others know where he was going.

Zizar walked through the stables and soon found the body. He knelt beside it. Boaza was dead, broken and bleeding. From the look of it he had been hurled across the stables by some immense force. This had to be the work of their quarry. Sorcery! He had seen his mistress kill this way, calling up forces from the Mahorelah and then having them do her will.

He drew his sword and glanced about the stables. Was the force still here, waiting its moment to strike? He saw nothing, just the great black ormn quietly eating its supper. He turned back to his friend and bowed his head. Orders be damned. He wanted blood for this.

He made his way to the back of the hostelry and quietly climbed through a window into a storeroom. Then he crept along the wall to the door and peered out. There was his quarry, still drinking his wine. Zizar drew out his bow and readied himself. He must be quick but certain. He placed a poisoned arrow to the bowstring and pulled it back. Vengeance. It was his due.

Korfax moved just as the arrow was loosed. He had felt the threat, but he had not known from where it would come. Ever since Tohtanef had left him he had spread himself out, feeling his way through the surrounding air like the expanding roots of a tree, looking for the places of danger.

The arrow thudded into the wall opposite, just missing his head. He rolled, knocking the table and chairs aside. The others in the hostelry turned or stood. They had not seen the arrow. All they saw was Korfax drawing his blade, even as he rolled, before leaping out through the door.

Zizar cursed and went back out the way he had come. This one was good. He had felt the threat.

He climbed out of the window and felt ahead with his mind. His enemy was somewhere nearby, he was certain. He waited, with his back to the wall. There were sounds from within, voices raised in consternation. Someone had found the arrow. He reached further, but there was no sign of his enemy. Patience ruled this game, patience and timing.

Korfax waited across the road from the hostelry and watched. There was confusion inside. No doubt the owner and the other guests were in heated debate as to what was going on. He wondered what Tohtanef would have her minions do next, or would she act herself? He could only sense one mind against him at the moment. So where was the other?

He sighed to himself. He was not used to this contest of assassins. It was like a hidden game of Avalkar where you could not see the disposition of forces at your opponent's disposal. But it was worse than that, for there were no rules here. Anything could happen.

There was a sudden commotion of voices from the hostelry, and then silence. Korfax felt the touch of ice as a sense of sudden death filled the air. What had happened to everyone in the hostelry? Was it a summoning? What had Tohtanef done?

Zizar felt the summoning rather than saw it. His mistress had acted, slaughtering everyone inside the hostelry, probably with a cloud of poison. She liked such things, did Tohtanef.

He sucked in his breath. What if he had been in there? He wasn't expendable! No doubt she had intended to catch their quarry unprepared, but he wasn't in the hostelry either.

Zizar cursed again as he realised his mistake. He should have waited, not acted. This was his fault. He must make amends. He circled around the back of the hostelry, feeling with his mind. There was nothing ahead of him. He moved around to the other side. All he could sense was his mistress in one of the rooms above. There was no one else here. Where had their quarry gone?

Korfax stood up behind Zizar and released the silence in his mind. Zizar hissed in anger, even as he turned, striking out with his sword. But his sword struck the Qorihna and shattered. He fell back, a throwing knife leaving his other hand, but the Qorihna caught it upon a writhing blade and it broke into pieces. Not knowing what else to expect, Korfax extended his arm and his Qorihna all but speared Zizar to the ground. Black flame enveloped him and he was gone. Korfax drew back. There was only one mind left that he could feel now. Tohtanef. She was up there still, in her room at the hostelry, no doubt waiting with other sorceries at her beck and call. He wondered what to do. Should he confront her or should he leave?

No, he should confront her. He needed what she knew. If she had the way to Doagnis in her, then all the better.

He entered the hostelry carefully, his blade ahead of him. There were bodies here, the hostelry owner and the other guests, their eyes staring and mouths stretched wide. They were contorted as though they had died in pain. Korfax walked carefully past. He glanced up at the ceiling. Tohtanef would pay for this, if nothing else.

He went to her door and kicked it open. He entered. She was standing opposite, a pale stone in her hand. There was no sign of anything else in the room except for the furniture. It was empty.

"Was that utterly necessary?" he asked. "Did you have to kill all those others? You wanted me!"

"I wished to be sure," she told him.

"And yet still you missed," he said. "Not very good at this, are you?"

She stiffened at that.

"Better than you, I think."

"Why are you after me? What have I ever done to you?"

"That is for you to guess, and for me to know."

"Then have at it, and make your play. Show me what you can do."

The air seemed to thicken about them both. Korfax tensed briefly and then relaxed. He was ready. Tohtanef did not move for a moment, but then she tightened her grip upon the pale stone and a circle of green flame suddenly appeared about her. Korfax remained where he was, holding his sword up before him. Then he advanced, tilting his Qorihna towards her, even as Tohtanef began her summoning.

Tohtanef glanced at the sword and laughed.

"You may as well put up your sword!" she said. "That won't help you here."

There was an added radiance to her circle now, faint energies rippling to and fro. Korfax glanced at them. He had defeated such things before, but then he had been armed with a full stave. He looked at his sword. Could it breach such defences as it had with the Agdoain? The texts he had read said that the mightiest Qorihna were proof against any summoning, and his was the most powerful of all, but this was a new world for him. He did not know the Namad Mahorelah as one of the Argedith did, nor did he understand the limits. In the scheme of things this was a huge gamble on his part. He suddenly felt very uncertain.

It was as he was about to test Tohtanef's defences that three great forms dropped out of the air about him, things of muscle, claw and tooth. Korfax did not know what they were, not their form or their name, but he knew he had never seen their like before. Limbs they had in abundance, as well as eyes and mouths, and each glowed with a pale light. A dim burning smell filled the air about them, and Korfax saw, to his consternation, that they were dribbling corrosive fluids from their many mouths. Already the floor at their feet was fuming where they drooled. It took them only a brief moment to orient themselves, but once their many eyes had fastened upon him, they attacked.

They were fast, horribly fast, but his sword was faster yet. It writhed up before him and divided into three, one blade apiece penetrating the demons. The things screamed, a triple ululation, and the acid within them fumed upon the Qorihna's blade, hissing against its dark invulnerability before burning away and turning to vapour. Then the three creatures sank to the floor in flame and disintegrated to the last in a shower of the finest ash.

Korfax sighed and turned back to Tohtanef. He raised his sword up in front of him, one single blade again. The writings did not lie, and he suddenly felt like laughing. Not only were his weapons proof against the Agdoain, they were proof against other demons as well.

He advanced. Now he would test her defences. He let the tip of his Qorihna pass through her ring of flame. She stared on in horror as more flames boiled in the air about the blade, flames she could do nothing to abate.

Korfax let more of his blade enter the fire and it began to hum, almost as if it were singing to itself. The fires from Tohtanef's defences flickered along the blade and were consumed, one by one. The circle on the floor began to disintegrate, and Tohtanef sank to her knees, her hands at her mouth. As her defences flickered and died, she dropped her hands and stared up at Korfax. Her eyes were wide with fear.

"So you are one of us," she said in consternation. "They did not tell me."

"One of you?" he asked.

"One of the Argedith."

"And what difference does that make?"

"We must not fight amongst ourselves, we mustn't. That was how we were defeated before. That was how the hated west brought us down."

That was new. He stared down at her. In the past the Argedith had competed with one another, fighting amongst themselves to see who was strongest, who should rule. It was their way. The line of the princes had been the only force strong enough to keep them all together, and once the line was thought to be ended the fight for overall command had been fierce. Only with alliances had the north held together at all, those with less power allying themselves with those that were greater, but such accords had been fragile at best. So what of this?

"The Argedith have always vied with one another," he told her. "Only through conflict can the strongest be known."

"But that was how we lost," she answered. "We can no longer afford such luxury. We cannot weaken ourselves in such ways. We need all our strength."

She held out her hands in entreaty.

"Spare my life. I can be of service."

Korfax drew back a little.

"Why should I? You were ready enough to kill me before. And what of those others? You slaughtered them without a second thought."

"But you have proven yourself the more powerful. You are mighty, I can feel it."

She gave him a sidelong look.

"I could aid you. I know things you do not."

He stared at her. Was this another trap?

"Why should I trust you?" he wondered aloud. "You belong to your mistress, body and soul."

"Not body and soul," she told him. "I only serve. And I serve strength, as is our way, as you have said. We have always allied ourselves to the strongest."

"But why me?"

"Because I wish to live."

"Honest enough. Now tell me why I should trust you?"

"Because you have won. Because you hold my life in your hands."

"That is not enough."

"If you pursue my mistress, then there are only two reasons for doing so. One is power, the other is revenge. Is this a blood feud?"

She was trying to gain his sympathy. He could feel her in the air about him, a beguilement. You are alone. You are one. You need allies. He dismissed the temptation.

"That is not your concern," he told her.

"If it means life or death, then it is very much my concern," she said.

"Bondage in fear is the least trustworthy kind."

"And how do you think it is with Doagnis," she replied. "She told me to waylay you, told me to stop you by any means necessary. She does not value me except as the tool of her will. She spends the lives of others to preserve her own."

"Not unlike her father, then!" he said.

Tohtanef frowned.

"What do you mean?"

"That does not concern you either," Korfax answered. He stood over her now, eyes demanding.

"Prove that I can trust you – tell me where she is."

His blade extended and reached for her neck. She gasped as the black blade sang. Such a hungry sound. What was it, this great black blade? She had never seen the like, or had she? Something stirred inside.

"What is it you hold at my throat?" she asked.

"It is your life in the balance," he told her. "Now answer the question."

She stared at the blade, and an old memory came to her. There were stones in her family's keeping, stones that held remembrances. There were fields and forests, twilight towers and the far stars of evening. There were battles and sorrow, and the wielding of great black blades that coiled and burned. She gasped as she realised what she was seeing. This one was armed with a Qorihna! Gods below! A Qorihna! She all but shrivelled up inside. She did not want to die that way. Who knew what happened when Qorihna consumed their victims?

Korfax watched as Tohtanef shrank under the shadow of his sword. She seemed terrified now, terrified of his blade and terrified of him. How she squirmed.

"Please," she begged, "I do not know. She went east from here and then north. I do not know more than that. Have mercy, I beg you."

Mercy? He felt his mouth twist with nausea. He was not used to this, having another at his feet so abject in their fear that they would say anything, do anything, betray anything, just to stay alive. Perhaps it was an act, perhaps it was not, but either way he would not trust it, not yet. This one had already proven her ruthlessness by slaying everyone else in the hostelry. Let her submit, and then he would see what he would see. He knelt down and lifted her face. It was streaked with tears.

"Do not forget that you have just tried to kill me. Nor forget what you did in this hostelry. Innocents have died at your hands. Your tears come too easily, I think. Where is Doagnis? I will not ask again."

Tohtanef sobbed.

"I would tell you, if I could. I truly do not know. She left me here to seek you out."

"She knows that I follow her?"

"Yes!"

"Does she know who I am?"

"No! She knows only that you follow. She has seen it."

Korfax burrowed deep within her mind. She gasped and trembled, but nonetheless she did not dare even to offer token resistance. Korfax went everywhere that he could, but he found nothing that would tell him where Doagnis might be now. He stood back up and turned away.

"Nothing!" he said at last. He turned back again and looked down at Tohtanef.

"Mercy?" she whispered at his feet.

Seeing her now, Korfax felt all but ill. Her abject terror was not a lie. That life should be reduced to such beggary! And look at him; he was no better, flitting through her thoughts like a thief. But he had no choice. He had to see. He had to know.

He turned away. All he had seen were the memories of a life of dominance and fear, a life to which she clung all too greedily. Those above her visited fear upon her, and she doled out that very same fear to those below. And so it went on, the higher striking those beneath, whilst they struck those beneath them, all the way down to the bottom. He wanted nothing of it, nothing at all. He glanced back at her, and did not spare her his contempt.

"Very well, Tohtanef, you may have your life. But hear my words and act upon them, or you will know my blade at last. Go from here. Find another way to live. Turn aside from this path, or you will fall into the deeps and be swallowed by the mouths that ever wait there."

He walked out of the room without looking back. As he turned the corner there came a burst of light, followed by a short scream, sharp and piercing. Korfax quickly turned with his sword at the ready, but nothing else happened. He went back to the room and looked carefully inside.

A sense of heat met him. Ash and smoke floated upon the air, whilst the room itself was blackened and burnt. There was little to see of anything except smouldering remains. In the corner Korfax noticed a pile of blackened bones. He shuddered. Doagnis clearly did not take failure kindly.

In a place of shadow, veiled and alone, she leaned back and sighed. She looked at her shew-stone. It was still touched with darkness, which meant only one thing. Her servant had failed, in every possible way.

She rubbed her tired eyes and stood up. It had taken all of her skill to breach the fog of power that had encircled Tohtanef at the end, but the identity of her pursuer still eluded her. One thing, though, she had learned. Her shadow understood something of the Namad Mahorelah, and that was disturbing.

Sending burning energies through the shew-stone of Tohtanef had been her last gambit, but even that had failed. The only certainty she had was that Tohtanef had been broken in the encounter, and broken tools served no one.

She took a deep breath and hardened her eyes. Her tools must remain sharp. If they ever broke, then they were of no further use to her.

She turned to the prophecies of Nalvahgey, as she always did when she was troubled. She ran her finger over the many verses until she found the one that she wanted, and then she read it twice, just to be sure. Now, in the light of what had happened, it made better sense. She had simply misinterpreted it, that was all.

Despite their difficulty, the verses were like an addiction. They could tell you so much, but they could also badly mislead you. It was like a game her ancestor played, a lethal game. More than once the prophecies had led her to victory, but occasionally they had taken her in the opposite direction. Once they had almost got her killed. But she always came back to them, no matter the outcome. They were her great advantage.

Many of the verses still did not make sense despite years of familiarity, only falling into place as the events they described unfolded. Others were clear, but they were mainly those that referred to events far in the past. Some, though, gave her great hope for the future, especially when they talked of the rise of the Mikaolazith.

She flicked through the verses again, looking for guidance. One in particular stood out, and she smiled as she read it. She had read it before, of course, but now it assumed a far greater significance. She knew exactly what to do.

She turned to her shew-stone once more and parted the fires of time. She reached in with her thought and wrote one word upon the flames. Molpan. That would be more than enough. She withdrew and smiled to herself in satisfaction. Let her shadow follow the clue, and let it lead him to his death.

Korfax went to the stables to find Enastul. As he approached the stall he saw a prone body slumped against the far wall. It was one of the two that had come with Tohtanef, the one he had not yet accounted for. Korfax looked back at Enastul and pointed at the broken body.

"Did you do that?" he asked.

Enastul merely laughed with his eyes as he bowed his head. Korfax watched for a moment, incredulous, and then burst out laughing himself. He looked back at his steed fondly and then gently stroked Enastul's neck.

"What an ormn you are," he declared. "What a warrior!"

Enastul could only bow his head in agreement.

"Well then, my one and only companion," said Korfax, "I think it time we left. We have definitely outstayed our welcome here."

He mounted and off they went. Korfax did not look back, but he did say a silent prayer for those that had died.

Off the road, and much further on, Korfax sat under a tree and pondered long and hard. Enastul waited beside him, ears flicking this way and that as he dozed in the darkness.

Tohtanef truly had not known where Doagnis might be. She had received her orders and her guardians from her mistress and then been sent on her way. Doagnis herself had continued east, but the east was vast. He had his map, of course, given him by Dialyas, but he did not trust it. He would rather discover the whereabouts of Doagnis for himself than ever trust the word of Dialyas again. Besides, Dialyas had made his feelings quite clear in the matter. He did not want

Korfax to kill his daughter. The map could be deliberately misleading.

He drew out his logadar and searched through the prophecies. Perhaps help would be found here. One in particular caught his eye, and though he did not like it, it fitted well enough with the map. In the prophecy there was mention of a city without a wall, and on the map Dialyas had marked out the city of Thilzin Merenar as being of interest. He sighed. It was on his way, to the east and then the north, upon the banks of the mighty Patrim. It was his next port of call. He had often heard tell of far Thilzin Merenar. Famed throughout the world, it was, quite literally, a city without a wall – one of a kind.

But he still did not like it. Doagnis also possessed the prophecies, and she knew that he was after her, though how much she knew was another matter. What should he do?

He thought again of his confrontation with Tohtanef. There were too many unknowns, and it was clear that he did not know enough of her lore or the practices kept alive by the Iabeiorith. It was long past time that he found out.

If he were one of the Argedith, and he needed to find something in a hurry, the best way to do so would be to divine for it. He picked up his logadar again and looked for the texts that described the art of divination. Once he found them he read them carefully. At the end he felt nothing so much as surprise. If he had not known that he was reading the works of the Argedith, he would have said he was studying a tract upon the Namad Soygah itself. His mother had told him much concerning the discipline, and here it all was just as she had revealed it, in explicit detail.

Perhaps he should not have been so surprised. Much of the work here was based upon the writings of Nalvahgey, and she was the one that had created the Exentaser. But it was still strange to find such a meeting of minds in a work primarily concerned with the Namad Mahorelah.

He thought how it was now. Both sides treated the other with a contempt that made them all but blind. They were all so rooted in the certainty of their belief that each was now unsighted by the other's strategy. Each was as vulnerable as the other, by simple virtue of their unquestioning faith.

That was it, then. He would embrace both, and perhaps he would even put Doagnis out of reckoning!

Korfax decided that he would not divine for Doagnis directly, as there was a danger that she might notice his scrutiny. He would, instead, look for the places she had been and the people she had touched. It would be better to wring the truth of her whereabouts from her slaves than seek for her directly. And anyway, he needed to prepare himself well for that encounter.

He placed himself in the trance, shrank himself down to a mote and then parted the veil.

His thought reached up into the heavens and touched the weave. He moved himself forward, holding his desire clearly in his mind, and watched as the weavers turned upon their courses. There they went, the great spheres, circling the heavens, wheels within wheels. He watched them reach the moment when the angles of eternity spoke, then turned back again and looked down upon the world like a god.

It seemed altogether far too easy. Straight away he saw a city he did not recognise, a city without a wall upon the banks of a mighty river. He saw quick hands repairing a net and heard a name briefly whispered, that of Molpan. But then it all vanished away again and he was hurled out of the vision.

He was immediately on his guard. He remembered back to his mother's words, when she had tried to describe how one engaged the sight. Vision never came easily, she had told him; you had to fight it into being.

He thought of what he had seen. A city without a wall? That was easy. A hand repairing a net? The name of Molpan? It was almost as if he had been given them. It was a trap, it had to be.

His only advantage lay in seeing it, in knowing it was there. Other than that, if he wanted to find Doagnis, then this was the way of it. He would go to Thilzin Merenar and seek out this Molpan. It was his only choice.

3

DECEITS

Zim-hothil Pi-idtra-a
Iam-totchain Malzaf-pasorn
Log-luj-ed Pallar-unchihr
Doal-odvan Praholq-lehjo
Vah-telnis Farim-vors-zin
Zid-oddo Fenfel-uljo
Lan-ip-om Tonchis-vix-jir

The further he went, the more Korfax felt himself change. Each step, each footfall, seemed to increase the difference between what had been and what was. Ever since he had dipped his hands into its waters, the Namad Mahorelah beckoned to him as never before.

Every night that he could do so he awoke the logadar and studied its writings, the words floating in the air before him, serried ranks of bright strokes glimmering. He would read for a while, slowly working his way through the many works of his long-vanished ancestors, before shutting off the light at last and settling down to sleep.

But always the words seemed to stay with him, floating behind his eyelids as if still in his air, pulling at him, urging him to wake them again and read further.

Perhaps it was their disparate nature. At times they could be most frustrating. One text would say one thing and another would contradict it or present the same information in a completely different fashion. He was used to clarity, not obscurity. It was like a tangle of rope, an impossible knot. He would tug at the edges, pulling one way and then another, trying to simplify the labyrinth of intertwining meanings, only to find it made matters worse, not better.

Every night he fought with it, only to curse his failure yet again before lying down to sleep. Then, come the morning, he would set off once more into the east in pursuit of his foe. His nights and his days began to mirror each other, a long slow crawl that seemingly got him nowhere.

The temptation to give up began to grow on him, a counterpoint to the pull of the words. But he did not do so. When he had been in the seminary of the Dar

Kaadarith, he had been taught that persistence always brought a reward of some sort.

And so it proved, for on the twenty-eighth night from the start of his study, he discovered the hint of a hidden language, meanings hidden within meanings, a wordplay that he had not noticed before. His mistake had been to treat the Namad Mahorelah much like the Namad Dar – as facts to learn and processes to be applied – but it was not like that at all. It was an art, a passion, a language of the heart, not the mind.

As soon as he understood this, his dreams began to change. When had he ever found himself in such dark places full of rustling shadows and distant cries before? When had he ever crossed such interminable landscapes? His sleeping mind summoned skies that were a tumble of shadow, strange forests that were a struggle of paths, and he seemed ever to be groping his way through alien groves, over broken bridges or up towards dark heights crowned with blind towers and pale lights.

Wherever he went, strange creatures would accost him, snapping at his heels or barring his way, their mirrored eyes wide and liquid, their teeth long and dripping. At first they dismayed him and he found himself running from them, running back down again, back to the realms of light and looking ever for a way to escape. It was only by accident that he discovered the answer. Desperate at the last to fend them off, he drew out his sword, and when they saw it his pursuers fled, scurrying away to hiss nervously back at him from within their hidden places.

After that he found the dreams' power over him lessened. Indeed, he soon came to rely upon them, finding in them a strange counterpoint to that which he was learning. Symbols marched across his skies or were carved in stone and wood, and as he realised what he was seeing, so the Namad Mahorelah opened up before him, like a dark and shadowed flower.

There were still missteps, though. Occasionally, as he delved ever further into its mysteries, so the words of Asakom would come back to taunt him. To know the power of the abyss is to be seduced by it. Then Korfax would find himself back at some earlier point and the dreams would begin afresh, almost as if he was playing some gambling game and had just lost a throw. If this was indeed a seduction, then it was a far subtler affair than any that his teachers had ever hinted at.

So it went on. Understanding and the terrible danger that accompanied it. It was the thinnest of blades he walked upon now, the very real danger of the abyss set against equally real rewards. But he could not turn back, because if he was to confront one of the mightiest of the Argedith ever to be born into the world, he needed the knowledge.

When Korfax found himself in company, most of the talk he heard was of the flood. The south had paid a heavy price, it seemed. Many southern ports had been destroyed, Thilzin Jerris being but one of them. Sorcery was to blame.

Voices were lowered when such things were said, eyes wide and fearful. It was the work of demons, they said, the calling up of vile powers. Though no name was mentioned, there were always references to 'her'. 'She' had done this. This was 'her' doing. Korfax would always smile inside when he heard that. Little did they know.

Soon, though, another matter began to supplant the tales of the flood. There were rumours coming down from the north, hopeful tales that at last something would be done to put down the darkness. It was said that there was now a gathering of forces, the readying of armies. Levies were taking place, lords and masters calling to their subjects and asking them to honour their oaths. It seemed as if almost the entire east had risen up and was even now marching west.

Some of the rumours spoke of Noraud Noqmal, first-born son of Audroh Usdurna, and how he had stepped up to the mark, daring to grasp the standard that Onehson had let fall. Rallying behind him were some of the first council that had survived the loss of Emethgis Vaniad. There was Napeiel Valagar for one, Geyadril Chirizar for another, both to stand alongside Noqmal. Other names were mentioned – Vatamath, Orpahan, Tiarapax – names Korfax knew all too well.

Then he heard mention of the south, how the Tabaud of Badagar would lend his forces to the cause. Korfax thought again of his friend, Ralir, shaking as though possessed upon the floor of his chambers. Would he go north? Had he finally found strength enough to face his fear? Korfax heard no mention of his name, just that the armies of the south were being sent to meet with Noqmal.

Rumour piled upon rumour until it had the west rising up as well. Even Zafazaa was said to have declared himself for Noqmal, sending his first-born son to serve under the banners of the east. Korfax could not believe it. Proud Zafazaa humbling himself before the east? Was it a peace offering? Had the haughty west finally bowed its proud head so that it could serve something other than its own reflection?

It seemed that the fall of Emethgis Vaniad and the great flood that followed thereafter had finally spurred them all to action. No more, they had said, it was time to act. No more sorcery, no more terror. The forces of the abyss would pay!

Korfax sat alone and pondered. The west, the south and the east, all rising up. That would be an army to shake the very foundations of the world. Should he join it? His heart soared at the thought.

He would have to swear fealty to Noqmal, but surely Noqmal would forgive him in the name of his service, as Onehson had not. Then Korfax would prove his valour in battle. Imagine it! How he would drive the Agdoain back, back to the nothingness from which they had dared emerge. The world would be made safe again, the cowardice of Dialyas exposed for what it was and the name of Korfax spoken with honour once more.

But it was all a lie, a pretty fantasy. They would accept neither him nor his heritage. Besides, what of Doagnis? She would not remain idle whilst her enemies reasserted their primacy.

It was just another temptation, just another dream of power like everything else. It was enough to know that the Ell were no longer content to sit and cower in their cities, shutting themselves away from the storm without like children. It was not the time for him to reveal himself. Those he had told were either dead or gone, and none would speak of it again. The message was clear. He would keep his peace and follow his calling.

It rained. Into the east he went, riding the sodden road and crossing the swollen rivers, and it rained down upon him as though to beat him into the ground.

There were none upon the road now, at least none that he saw. The only time he found company was in the few settlements that scattered the long east road, and even then he kept himself to himself.

All the talk was of the gathering forces away to the north. Sky ships were now said to be ferrying the assembled might of the east to the edges of Ovaras, and the splendour of their banners was rumoured to cover the land from horizon to horizon. Such wonderful tales. It was hard to hear them and not be tempted.

He finally arrived at the Zinznah Patrim just as the rains failed. He came to a high cliff upon which stood a high tower, and he found himself looking out over the apparently limitless mouth of the river.

He watched as its waters poured themselves past the high walls of the headland. For a river this large the Patrim was fast, and there were many eddies and treacherous currents where it ploughed its way into the great ocean. Nor was it a river that twisted and turned in its long journey down from the distant mountains, it followed as straight a path as it could, carving its way across the land like a knife. Only at its end did it fail, unable to subdue the greater immensity beyond.

North and east lay the other bank, but Korfax could not see it. All he could see were brown and turbid waters washing themselves into the blue, a slow storm of sediment that boiled far out beyond the mouth of the river, before falling at last into the bottomless deeps.

There were two great towers that marked each bank, each set with a great piradar, but Korfax could only see the one that he stood beneath. Of the other, there was no trace, not even its light. It lay somewhere beyond the horizon, also set upon a high cliff but far beyond him now, far beyond the curve of the world itself.

It was said that only on the calmest of days could the tip of both towers be seen at the same time, and only then from a ship, and only if the sea master held his course to the very centre of the river.

Korfax watched the wide water for long moments, before turning aside. Now he must follow the riverbank to Thilzin Merenar, the largest port of all those that lined the Patrim and the only city of the Ell without an encircling wall.

It was just as he had seen in his vision. Thilzin Merenar sprawled, a chaos of towers and houses and roads that seemingly went wherever it would.

He was reminded of the roots of river trees, for ever appearing further and further away from the main trunk, ever erupting from the water clogged soil. That was Thilzin Merenar, a vast river tree made of stone.

So if the city was indeed a tree, then its trunk must be the mighty Umadya Zinznah, the river tower, with its huge piradar and its sonorous bell. There it was, somewhere near where the centre ought to be, strong and proud, a great tapering spar of stone.

It was said that even in the thickest fogs the light of the tower could still be seen, its incandescent beams piercing any possible gloom. Likewise the great bell. No storm, no matter how potent, could drown it out. The tower was both a warning to the unwary and a guide to the lost.

Korfax unconsciously straightened his shoulders as he looked up at the tower. It was a proud work and taller than he had expected. All in all, Thilzin Merenar, like Thilzin Jerris before it, was yet another wonder of the world. He found himself hoping that it would never suffer the fate of Thilzin Jerris or that of Emethgis Vaniad.

He made his way along the road closest to the river and marked where all the wharves were placed. Many piers and walkways stretched out into the river itself, clustered with the masts of ships both large and small. A few diarih circled them slowly, wings bent in the wind. That was where he needed to go. No doubt the street of the net makers would be near the wharves.

From the inside Thilzin Merenar took on another aspect entirely. It became a confusion of narrow streets, hidden squares and myriad canals, all crowded about by houses and towers. The houses were tall and narrow, and much of the time the world beneath their tall stone was in shadow. Seen like this, Thilzin Merenar appeared a furtive place. Even the main thoroughfare was not as wide as it perhaps could have been.

Korfax wondered if there had originally been a method behind its madness, for as he rode through its winding ways it seemed to him that any enemy trying to take it would have had to navigate its many narrow streets, streets that would only allow for single combat. As a strategy it had some merit, but Korfax doubted it had ever been tested in anger. No war had ever trampled the east underfoot, not even during the darkest days.

He finally found a waterside hostelry which suited his needs, out of the way and yet not so much as to be inconvenient. The hostelry looked settled with age and comfortable with its place in the world. Its keeper, though, was another matter. He was dour, with a sad face and a hard gaze, and just as he seemed to have lost all possession of his joy, so he had lost possession of his right arm. Korfax glanced briefly at the vacant sleeve for a moment but then gave the traditional greeting as if he had seen nothing at all.

"May the Creator's light shine upon you," he said.

The keeper held up the empty sleeve with his left hand. He had not missed the glance.

"The Creator's light has not shone upon me since I went to the wars in the north." He leaned forward. "So why aren't you up there? You look like a fighter to me."

Korfax raised an eyebrow.

"For the moment I am about other business," he said.

"And what might that be?" asked the keeper.

"That is my affair, I think," Korfax replied.

There was a long silence before the keeper eventually looked away, looking back out and over the fast-flowing river beyond.

"No doubt, no doubt," he said. "Well, I have many rooms available, some even with a view over the river."

"Then I will take one of those, if I may," said Korfax.

The keeper cast an eye at Korfax's sword.

"That is a strange blade that you carry," he said. "I do not recognise the design. And the pommel, from what I can see of it, looks new-forged. Have you used it much?"

Korfax looked back over his shoulder at his blade. The wrappings had slipped a little and he had not noticed. He turned back and looked hard at the keeper.

"It is older than it seems," he replied. "It has been very well kept."

"Even the best blades show some sign of wear," mused the keeper, "even if they have been infrequently used."

Korfax narrowed his eyes. Was the keeper deliberately trying to goad him?

"To see the true nature of something, one should look beneath its mask," he said.

The keeper drew back a little.

"I was merely making conversation. There is nothing wrong in that, or so they told me when I was young."

Korfax followed him with his gaze.

"They once told me that also," he said quietly. "So here is a sop for your curiosity. I have been fighting the Agdoain for many a year. I was at Othil Zilodar, on the northern frontier, and in Emethgis Vaniad when it fell. Having served the Velukor as best as I was able, I now find myself pursuing another calling."

The keeper scowled.

"I did not know that service to the Velukor could be stopped or started on a whim," he said. "I thought such service was for life. Or have you become craven? Are you one of those that argue we should leave the Agdoain alone so that they, in turn, will leave us alone? That is what they said after the death of the Meganza!"

Korfax waited a moment before answering. He did not like where this conversation was going. The keeper was trying to provoke him, he was certain of it. But was it simple bitterness or something else? Perhaps he should seek lodgings elsewhere.

"If that is your belief then I hope you take pleasure in it, for that is all you will get from me," he said. "Show me to my room or bid me begone. Either I stay here as your guest or I do not. Which is it to be?"

The keeper snorted as if satisfied at last.

"This way," he said.

Korfax looked out over the river and allowed himself a faint smile. Despite his host's demeanour the hostelry was peaceful and the room he was given was restful. In gentler times he could have been happy staying here.

As he looked out of the window he could see many vessels sailing up stream or down. Diarih followed a few of them, circling in their wake and waiting for a chance to swoop down upon the day's catch with eager and contentious cries. Around them the wider river flowed on regardless, glittering with the light of the day.

Korfax watched for a moment and then glanced up. Rafarel was travelling into the west once again and the day was getting old. It was long past time for him to seek out the street of the net makers, so he donned both his sword and his travelling cloak, placing one over his back and the other about his shoulders. He would walk, let Enastul rest in the stables below and eat of the sweet grasses in his bier. He at least had earned his supper, for he had not wearied in his stride ever since this journey had begun.

Korfax made his way to the docks, of which there were several. He asked the way of one of the merchants plying his wares in a small market situated on the eastern side and received excellent directions. So he came quicker than expected to the place that he sought, the place of the trap: the street of the net makers.

The street was broader than many he had yet seen in Thilzin Merenar, but it also seemed older, as though it was from here that the city had begun. Korfax found it a pleasure to walk along it without for ever stepping around someone or waiting while someone else came through a gap too narrow for two abreast.

Having studied the street and its denizens he found a convenient place to stand, in shadow and out of the way. Many walked by, intent about their business, but all the houses of the net makers remained quiet. Few were engaged about their craft this day. There was one that took his interest, though, an old Ell sitting beside his door, the tools of his trade on one side, a half-finished net on the other. But neither tools nor net were receiving his attention; instead, he seemed to be watching too, just as Korfax did now.

Korfax let the moments pass, his awareness spread out, gathering, sifting, until he was satisfied. This was the one he was after, he was certain of it. Done with watching, he walked over to one of the few net makers who was busy and asked, as innocently as he could, for directions.

"Excuse me," he said, "but I am searching for a certain Molpan, for I was told that I would find him here."

"Molpan?" came the reply. "Do you mean Lamadar Rom Molpan? If so, then that is him, over there. He sits outside the house of Viyal. Do you see him?"

Korfax gestured.

"That one, the one who does not work?"

"Yes, that is him," the other said. "But I warn you, he doesn't much like to talk." He leaned forward as if to offer up a secret. "Looks as though he has been there all his life, doesn't he?"

Korfax bowed his head, as he was expected to.

"But he hasn't," the other pronounced with a certain smugness. "He only took up residence last season."

Korfax smiled inside. Merchants and artisans were the same the world over. They did not miss an opportunity to pour scorn upon the others of their kind, trying to persuade all and sundry that their work, or their wares, were the best.

"Many here consider him immoderate in his craft," the other continued, "when he even deigns to attempt it. There are others in this street that are far better than he."

Meaning yourself, no doubt, Korfax thought.

"Thank you," he said instead, "but I have no nets I wish repaired this day. My business with Molpan is of an entirely other nature."

The other smiled indulgently.

"Well, that is your affair, of course, but I would warn you concerning him. He doesn't belong here. I think he has other purposes. I think he is here to hide."

Korfax frowned.

"Hide from what?"

"The war!"

"But surely that is no crime?"

The other looked less than pleased.

"Maybe not where you come from, but it seems somewhat dishonourable to me." He turned about and went back to his work.

Molpan sat outside the shadowed doorway and watched everything carefully. He wore the same clothing he had worn ever since he had come to this place, namely the ancient, the threadbare and the nondescript. A long cloak, a once fine robe, adorned his shoulders, and boots that had seen better days graced his feet. But it was all as it should be. His face seemed haggard, but even that was deliberate, the reworked parchment of his skin mapping a long nose, an unsmiling mouth and dark eyes that glinted as they flicked to and fro over the passers-by. He was as he was, waiting, ever waiting for words and commandments, for messages and orders. There was only one thing that occupied his thought at the moment, and he kept it in mind always. Watch for the fool that pursued his mistress. Watch for him, detain him and kill him.

It was as he looked to his right, just at the turn of the hour, that he first noticed the visitor. He caught the eruption from the shadows, purposeful, prideful even, a dark cloak and a shrouded mind, crossing the road and coming straight towards him.

He looked closer. Uncommonly tall, uncommonly broad and bearing a mighty sword across his back. Molpan stared. This one walked like a fighter, and though hooded against the failing light of day, there seemed to be a deeper shadow about him, something that actively defied the light. Was this him? Was this the one he had been waiting for?

He recited again the rhyme, his favourite, a strengthening rhyme that rode round and round inside, filling the gaps and plugging the holes with wonderful and resurgent energies. So he was well prepared when the stranger arrived before him and stopped. He looked up, frowning slightly, as the stranger bowed to him and spoke.

"Greetings to you. Am I addressing Lamadar Rom Molpan?"

The stranger's voice was quiet and deep and altogether friendly, but Molpan did not smile in return; instead, he kept his gaze on the stranger's shadowed features. After a long pause, he answered.

"And who is it wishes to know?" he asked.

His voice was as hard as he could make it. It must appear as if he did not want visitors this day. It must seem to all as if he was waiting for something important and had no time for distractions. But then the stranger inclined his head as though amused and spoke certain words that he could not ignore at all.

"I do, for I am one of those that follow the will of the Haelok."

Molpan started but quickly recovered. It was difficult not to be surprised by such a response, but that also was part of the plan. It was as his mistress had feared. One of their own had turned against her.

After a brief glance at the passers-by, to make sure they had not marked the greeting either, he cast a more searching look over the stranger. He must test this. He must be certain.

"You have an interesting turn of phrase," he said. "May I inquire where you learnt it?"

"From the Governor of the First Flame," came the response.

"And what else did you learn?"

"That the world has three levels, one above the other, the true order of creation."

Molpan waited a moment, marking the slight smile upon the stranger's shadowed lips.

"And?" Molpan prompted.

"That the order of creation was upended by usurpers so that the greatest was not the highest."

Now Molpan frowned. That was exactly the right answer. The phrases, the responses and the testing words varied with almost every encounter, and this stranger clearly knew the right things to say. It was hard not to be disconcerted.

"And what is the greatest?" he asked carefully.

"Sorcery," came the reply.

"And where would you find it?" Molpan probed.

"Within the dark heart," the stranger answered.

"And where might the dark heart be?" Molpan queried.

The stranger leaned forward and whispered the final answer.

"Veludrax Mikaolazith! Where else?"

Now Molpan leaned back. Exactly the right answer, except for the fact that everything had been changed. With the fall of Tohtanef all the words had been altered. He still had doubts, though. Perhaps not all knew of the change. It was difficult to talk to everybody when they were so widely scattered. Keeping his habitual mask he gestured to his door.

"You are most welcome in my humble abode," he said. Then he bowed and bade the stranger follow. They both went inside and the door closed behind them.

Korfax looked at the room to which he had been led. It was threadbare, like everything else.

"So, may I know your name?" asked Molpan.

"Uradin Rom Omatir," said Korfax.

"I do not know your house."

"I doubt that you do. Let us just say that the Uradinith were once called something else, a very long time ago."

"It is safe to say your real name here."

Korfax leaned back in his chair and stared full on at Molpan.

"So what of you?"

Molpan raised his eyebrows.

"You know it."

"Lamadar? No, I do not think so."

Molpan frowned.

"But why the suspicion? I have welcomed you."

"And we are also surrounded by the slaves of the west. Has their taint entered you, I wonder?"

A flash of anger crossed Molpan's face. That was an insult.

"Do you know to whom you speak?" he said.

Korfax sneered.

"Do you?" he retorted. "But speech is easy. Anything can be said with mere words."

Molpan stood up in outrage, ready to act, but Korfax was faster. He placed a hand against Molpan's throat and squeezed.

"Tohtanef is dead!" he said. "Someone pursues our mistress! I would know what you know!"

Righteous rage turned to astonishment in mere moments. Korfax watched carefully. It seemed genuine enough.

"You come from her?" Molpan asked, clearly disconcerted.

"I go to her," Korfax answered. "But I also track her pursuer. He is nearby."

"You are of the Haelok Aldaria?"

There was fear in the question. Korfax let all the contempt he could muster fill his voice.

"You are not that stupid!" he said.

"But she told me nothing of this," Molpan complained.

"And does she share everything with the likes of you? Besides, she does not know what I know."

Molpan scowled, despite his discomfort.

"But shouldn't you have gone to one of the chieftains?"

Korfax dropped Molpan to the floor as though in disgust.

"Fool!" he cried. "Who do you think it is now stands before you? I answer only to her."

Molpan bowed his head.

"I did not know," he said. "She did not tell me."

Korfax felt the ebb and flow of emotions around him and all but laughed. This had suddenly become all too easy.

"And when has that ever been an excuse?" he asked.

He sat back down and continued to glare at Molpan, but inside he smiled. All his guesses had been correct so far. Doagnis had resurrected many of the old ways. She was rebuilding the Argedith and she was rebuilding the Haelok Aldaria. Sorcery and the sword, two of the seven spears of the Iabeiorith. Everything he had taken from the mind of Tohtanef was being borne out.

"I am waiting," he prodded.

Molpan looked indecisive for a moment, but then his uncertainty was melded with another emotion, that of suspicion.

"But my orders also come directly from her," he said. "What should I do? I must have proof of what you offer, before I can say anything further."

Now he stared fully at Korfax.

"I have a shew-stone," he suggested.

Korfax felt a momentary flutter inside. He masked it as best as he could, but he was suddenly in turmoil. What had seemed ridiculously easy just a moment ago had become all but impossible now. If he revealed himself before a shew-stone, the game would be up. Doagnis knew his face, she had seen it. But how could he answer? To refuse would be illogical, but to accept would be suicide. He racked his mind for answers. Shew-stones were not unknown to him, but in the grimoires he had only given the accounts of them a cursory glance at best. He did not possess one, and the only time he had experienced that particular intimacy for himself he had been fighting Doagnis. There was only one way forward. Since his hand had been forced, he must take Molpan now.

He stood up and advanced upon his quarry, holding out his hand.

"Very well!" he said. "Since you do not trust me, you shall give me your stone. I will talk to her directly. Then perhaps you will be convinced."

But Molpan was not listening. He had already judged. His left hand made a brief movement in the air and four dark forms burst in through cunning trapdoors concealed in the ceiling.

Korfax fell back as they dropped around him, and only by ducking and rolling did he avoid the black darts they threw at him. He found himself thanking the long hours of training he had received at the hands of Ocholor and Ralir. Then he drew his Qorihna and let it speak in his stead.

It was odd, but he almost felt sorry for them. They had no defences that would stop his blade. In the merest moment it divided into four, knocking aside both dart and blade, before piercing each assassin almost at the same time.

Suddenly the room was empty again and only four piles of ash lay upon the floor. Korfax breathed deeply and looked about him sadly. That had not been his intent at all. But then he realised his greater mistake. Molpan was gone.

Molpan ran. Old he might have been, but he was still fleet enough of foot. Now, though, his life depended upon alacrity.

His mistress had tasked him with the death of her shadow, giving him a handful of assassins with which to accomplish the task. In the event of their failure, she had also given him a summoning, a curious invocation he had not come across before. He needed to be over water for it to work, which was why he was now running for the docks.

He thought again of what he had seen. Four assassins, some of the best of the Haelok Aldaria, had been thrown down with terrible speed. His mistress was right – they faced one of their own, and now her assassins were piles of ash back in his house. He thought of how it had been done, four bodies burned up by black and coiling blades of darkness. What was that? He did not know.

He felt back behind him with his mind. Was he being pursued? Yes, he was. Good! But he must not slacken his pace. Down alleyways he went, then over bridges, turning this way and that so as to confuse his trail, but he did not dim the light of his mind. He wanted to be followed.

Evening was darkening the world and the fogs were drifting in from the river as they always did at this time of year. Molpan ran into them, heading for that network of jetties that grew out of the eastern docks like a confusion of roots. He ran across the narrow gangways, the fog swallowing him up as he went. He came to the last jetty and slowed down, walking carefully to its end, as far out over the river as he could go. At the very end, where only a single piradar, set at the top of a long pole, cast its doleful light, he crouched down beside a collection of nets and pulled his cloak about him. To all intents and purposes he became just another shapeless bundle. Then he prepared himself for the silent summoning and waited.

He had been born under the auspices of water, and water had ever been kind to him, so he trusted himself to its caring hands and let its fogs surround him. He concentrated upon the summoning, ever alert for the sound of pursuit.

Deep in his tunic, in a hidden pocket, lay his shew-stone. He fingered it as he considered what he might say. His mistress would surely want to know all he could tell her concerning her pursuer, but he would only talk to her when he knew it was safe to do so.

After long moments he paused his preparations and allowed himself an instant of brief relaxation. He could no longer feel the stranger anywhere nearby. He had not followed after all. That was disappointing. Another way would have to be found. He drew out his shew-stone and prepared to talk to his mistress, but then a voice spoke his name from out of the darkness, a voice that was almost on top of him. His heart missed a beat. He looked up through a hole in the covering fabric and saw, standing over him, black sword in hand, the grim-faced stranger, poised and ready.

Korfax laughed to himself. Did this old fool think him a child? Few knew the arts of pursuit better than those trained by the Dar Kaadarith. Korfax had touched Molpan's mind at the moment of their first meeting, and he had latched on to it, pursuing its scent through the long maze that was Thilzin Merenar. Few outside the Dar Kaadarith, except for the Exentaser and the Balt Kaalith, even knew of the possibility. So here he was now, up a blind alley, if one considered the river to be impassable. Molpan could always jump in, of course, but Korfax was an excellent swimmer, and he had no doubt that he would easily catch his quarry in the river's turbulent waters.

"Molpan!" he said, gratified to see the indistinct bundle before him move, if ever so slightly.

"Get up! You have information that I want. You know what I am after, so tell me where she is and you will escape with your life. Disappoint me and I will feed you to my sword."

Molpan cast aside his cloak and stood up, shaking.

"I can tell you nothing," he said.

Korfax leaned forward and glared at Molpan. Shadows gathered under his eyes.

"That is not the answer that I want," he said.

Molpan swallowed in fear as Korfax took a step forward whilst his sword, seemingly sensible to his mood, twisted oddly in the fading light and moaned. Molpan stared at it, clearly disconcerted, his thoughts written all over his face. That was not a sword at all, he was thinking, that was a demon. Swords did not moan, nor did they bend as though they had a will of their own.

"What... what manner of blade is that?" he eventually asked.

Korfax let the shadow of a crueller smile drift across his face.

"What manner of blade? Can't you tell?" he asked.

"It is no ordinary sword," said Molpan, "I know that well enough."

"Of course it is no ordinary sword. But if you lack the wit or the lore to see what it truly is, then I will only appraise you of its mood. It is now impatient, much like its master. So tell us both what we want to know and spare yourself its wrath."

Molpan backed all the way to the edge of the jetty and rolled the silent conjuration through his mind. *Let this work,* he silently asked the darkness, *let me be safe.*

The sound of the river seemed all around them now, a rushing sound, almost as if the river itself was impatient. The fog thickened slightly and a vague stench of stagnant waters made the air heavy. Korfax frowned and sniffed.

"What is that?" he asked.

Molpan was a study in innocence and Korfax scowled back at him.

"I hope this is not some ruse, Molpan," he said. "I hope you are not summoning something, for I shall be most displeased if you are."

"No!" he answered, all the while continuing the summoning in his mind, rolling it on its way like an ever building wall about his thought.

"I am doing nothing. It is merely a passing chill, surely. What else can it be?"

He sank to his knees to beg. He needed time, time enough for the summoning to complete. Mercy had ever been the gift of the arrogant.

"I am not one of the Argedith, truly I am not," he sobbed into his hands. Then he grovelled to the floor at Korfax's feet. His mind was now split in two. In one part he rolled the summoning on its way, whilst in another he enacted abject misery.

"Please, please spare my life. I will tell you all that you wish to know."

Korfax stepped back as a vision of a grovelling Tohtanef came to him again. Nausea settled over him. He had seen this sickening sight before.

"Pleas for mercy fall too readily from the lips of those that serve your mistress," he muttered. "Tohtanef did the same as you do now, but it did her little good. She still died in the end, caught by the fires of Doagnis, fires that were intended to catch me."

Korfax looked back at the trembling Molpan. There was something in one of the pockets of his tunic, something that gleamed with a pale light. Korfax pointed at it.

"So here we have it again. Plays within plays! Not one of the Argedith? What do you say now, Molpan? What is that in your tunic? I sense the building of forces. What are you summoning?"

Molpan seemed to crumble as if undone, but inside he was furiously battling his way down into the depths. Only a few more locks to turn now, only a few more doors to open.

"But it is only my shew-stone," he wailed back. "They are the commonest currency. I was only going to talk to her. That was all."

Korfax tightened his grip on his sword and then loosened it again. That was certainly true. It was in the histories. It was how the empire of the north had been kept intact, even after the death of Sondehna. Was he judging too harshly? But there was still a sense of imminence in the air, a gathering of forces, so he drew his blade closer and looked this way and that. Something was happening. Something was coming.

He looked back behind him and shuddered. The land had been erased. He was fogbound, caught upon fragile stone with nowhere to go. Someone here knew his nightmares, or had guessed them. It was his dream from Piamossin all over again. Or was it?

The fog about him seemed to thicken as if fuelled by his doubts. The waters of the river began to invade the air and greedy vapours coiled about him, pulling at him, pulling him down. The river sucked at him, hungry and swift.

Korfax took another step back. This wasn't just his imagination. Something was coming. Something had been summoned and it had nothing to do with Molpan. Or did it? What was the trap here? He raised his Qorihna above his head and looked hard at Molpan.

"Come!" he said. "Follow me! I do not like this place. We shall go back to your house, you and I, and there you will tell me all that I want to know. And I promise you that you shall live, if you do."

Molpan remained where he was. He looked first at Korfax, and then he looked back at the river behind him. The summoning was here at last! He turned again to his pursuer and let his mouth widen in the slightest smile of victory. He had done it, as she had told him that he could.

"No!" he answered. "You cannot go back. Neither of us can."

The jetty about them both shuddered slightly, a faint vibration that did not subside. It was as though some immense heart now grappled with its foundations, winding its many arteries up the pillars of its supports.

Without warning limbs erupted from the water, great coiling limbs, faintly luminous and lightning fast. Korfax slashed at them with his Qorihna, and the sword severed them all in a dark and fiery blur, harvesting the pale flesh and burning it in black flame. A sound came from below, a liquid bellow.

Korfax looked at the coiling river that swirled about him. Whatever had attacked him was still down there, still under the water and below him. Korfax backed further away, retracing his steps carefully. He dare not fall into the water now.

More limbs came for him, and his Qorihna divided to meet them, slicing them all. Another bellow echoed up from the waters and they heaved. Korfax heard Molpan hiss, either in anger or in fear. He looked to where Molpan stood and saw that he was held in place, straining to hold the summoning together. Even as Korfax watched, there came a snapping sound, felt more than heard, and the summoning finally failed.

A vast limb shot out of the river and enclosed Molpan. Korfax caught the briefest glimpse of wildly staring eyes as the fleshy end of another limb entered his mouth and poured itself down his throat. Then Molpan was gone, pulled down with horrible speed into the river below.

For a moment there was silence, then the water at the end of the jetty boiled briefly as something was thrown back out onto the stone. Korfax caught a glimpse of gleaming bones, each separated from its neighbour as they tumbled down, vomited back into the air by the outraged water.

He tightened his grip upon his sword as a brief whiff of hot corruption drifted by. He shivered in revulsion and continued his slow way back to the land.

Back on the quayside Korfax breathed a sigh of relief. It was over. Whatever it was that had been summoned, it was gone. The air had cleared and the fog had lightened. He stared back for a moment at the mute pile of gleaming wreckage that had once been Molpan, before turning and running at last, all the way back to Molpan's house. He told himself that it was necessary, that Molpan's house was the only place he had left to look, but he dreaded it nonetheless. What other traps had been laid for him?

Back in the house Korfax found little of interest until he came upon a hidden compartment in a chest in one of the upstairs rooms. He would not have noticed it at all if there had not been a small piece of parchment sticking out. There was a crack like a closed door, and the parchment had been caught within its closing.

Once opened, the compartment revealed many scrolls, all smelling faintly of an unfamiliar scent. Korfax felt a momentary pang of guilt as he picked them up. This was prying, but greater needs drove him.

They were all letters from Molpan's daughter, one Tafamel by name. They were written in Hkomah script, easy enough to read, but Korfax thought them too stylised for his taste. Where was the flow, the rippling spontaneity? There was a certain artistry to such things, or so it had been drummed in to him by his tutor back at Losq.

It was not until he started with the third letter that he found what he was looking for. It seemed that allegiances ran deep in the family, for Tafamel mentioned 'the mistress' a number of times. Korfax smiled. Here was the prize that he sought: the name of a city, the name of a street and the name of a house. This Tafamel owned a hostelry in Thilzin Gallass, a port straddling the mouth of the Zinznah Fegenur. Thilzin Gallass was in the furthest east. Korfax replaced the letters as he had found them.

Thilzin Gallass was easy enough to get to. He could buy passage on one of the many merchant ships that regularly plied their trade up and down the coast. It would take perhaps fifteen days, if the sea master was in a hurry. And they usually were.

He hurried back to his room so that he could prepare himself for the morning.

She stared into her shew-stone and felt a dark anger. Molpan had failed. The assassins she had sent him were dead, and now so was he. The trap should have worked, but it didn't.

She turned back to the prophecies and read again the verse she had read before.

Now the words took on another meaning entirely. This was beginning to annoy her. It was almost as if someone had changed the prophecy when she wasn't looking.

So be it. If her shadow was as good as she had come to suspect, there was only one way he could go now, so she would set yet another trap, and this time she would make certain. Three was the way of it, after all.

Only overwhelming force would bring victory now, so that is what she would do. Her best servants would wait for him armed with the best summoning she could give them, and her shadow would fall to the very fires of destruction themselves.

4

FIRE AND WATER

Rox-anis Sal-depas-jon
Sal-drilin Alkar-ganihd
Im-leuged Roln-qu-idang
Agpiu-gros Aglan-jiouch
L-pilgem Oina-dr-pan
Ip-bigihb Bai-hon-mn-a
Brd-ipmap Od-unch-tolihr

The voyage seemed endless. Even with the zongadar in continuous use, the ship seemed hardly to be travelling at all. But with each dawning day the distant land slowly changed its nature as they headed ever into the east.

It was only when they passed the mouth of the Zinkao that Korfax finally understood how far he had yet to go. The Zinkao was so huge that one could easily believe oneself far out upon the great ocean itself, if it were not for the fact that the waters were fresh and fragrant and far gentler than any sea. Korfax stared out over the great expanse. The Zinkao made even the Patrim look small by comparison.

Though Korfax was the only passenger, none of the crew had much time for idle talk. They kept to their tasks and left Korfax to himself, a situation that seemed to suit both parties, for Korfax now found himself confronted by a deeply troubling puzzle.

If Doagnis was responsible for the Agdoain, then she must know something of the Namad Dar. But all the traps she had set for him were entirely sorcerous. Not in anything that she did, nor in any of the writings, could he uncover a single thing that remotely explained the Agdoain.

Up until the fall of Emethgis Vaniad her strategy had seemed entirely logical. Clear the north, keep the forces of the Velukor pinned upon the great wall and await the arrival of the Iabeiorith, who would then take up ownership of the land. But with the fall of Emethgis Vaniad things had become far less certain. If she was intent upon dominion, why not unleash the Agdoain in the other great cities? He knew that she had been to Othil Admaq, so why had she not loosed the Agdoain there? He did not understand it.

Certainly there were theurgies that did not rely upon any specialised knowledge of the summoner; instead, they took as their guide some proffered piece of the world and extrapolated a response therefrom. According to the writings, many of the Argedith, armed only with a handful of soil and a few seeds, had summoned forces from the Mahorelah that had then created entire gardens filled with strange and wonderful fancies.

The Namad Dar had taught him how the world was composed of self-repeating patterns, creation as an act of division and unfolding. But the Namad Mahorelah posited that the act itself was irrelevant, that it was only the result that mattered. Everything was seen as a reflection of everything else, the above mirroring the below, the below mirroring the above. For those that practised sorcery, that truth was so obvious that it was all but taken for granted. It was all they knew and all that they needed to know. Their lore, for them, was a thing of writ, while to Korfax the flaw was obvious. It was a trap with no way out!

The Argedith did not create, they merely manipulated. They had to make do with the materials that were to hand. He wondered if that was truly how it was with the Agdoain, not so much a new state of being, more an ancient malice given new flesh.

Grow like the Ell, the Agdoain were told, and so they did, mimicking that which they could never know. But Korfax felt uneasy with that answer as well. The Agdoain were not physically like the Ell at all. And what of his dream at Piamossin? What dark horror had pursued him that night? Perhaps this was not just the malice of Doagnis that now threatened the world but the echo of a mightier hatred, the hatred of the Ashar. Were they extending their powers at last, reaching up from their deeps to threaten the Ell as they never had before? But even that did not make sense. He thought again of Ash-Mir, hanging in the air outside his window. He remembered what it had said, but there was nothing in its words concerning the Agdoain at all.

Up until now he had thought it a great game of threes. He remembered playing it with his father as a child: sword beats shield, arrow beats sword, shield beats arrow. Only here the game was spread out over the ages, and it was far more deadly. The forces of the Velukor conquered the Argedith, the Agdoain conquered the forces of the Velukor and the Argedith rose up again to remove the Agdoain. Victory to the Argedith.

But was that the intent? Was there a deeper game of riddles and deceits? There was so much he did not know. At least his experience with Dialyas had opened his eyes a little wider, and from now on he fully intended to keep them as wide as possible. He was sailing on uncharted waters here.

So where did that leave him? Doagnis might know of the Namad Dar, but he knew that she did not employ it herself. She let her slaves do the work for her so she did not have to soil her hands with what she thought of as an unclean lore.

The Agdoain, in certain regards, were a mirror of the Ell. She may have made them, or set their creation in motion, but obviously, in filling them with the knowledge of the Namad Dar, she did not know what she had given them. Nor did she care. Her contempt for the lore was as blind as the Dar Kaadarith's contempt for the powers of conjuration.

So here he was, caught in the middle of a war of ideologies that granted no mercy, nor allowed any compromise. Neither side would bend, and that would only lead to an eventual breaking. It seemed to him at that moment that he stood upon the fulcrum of a balance. He could see what lay in each cup, but the occupants of each cup could not, or would not, look beyond their confining walls. He, alone, could see in the realms of the blind.

Korfax found himself wondering what Doagnis would say if she knew who it was that pursued her. No doubt his play with Molpan had set this off, but pretending to be one of the Haelok Aldaria had felt curiously apposite, as if that was where he really belonged. What would Doagnis do if she knew Sondehna's heir was on her trail with bloody vengeance in his heart? In his ever darkening world he found that singular conceit strangely comforting, like some black lullaby urging him down into dreaming.

But there was little comfort in his dreams either. As if fuelled by his awakening deeps, darker fantasies now rose up from below to disturb his sleeping mind.

Most common were those in which he proclaimed himself before the Haelok Aldaria and turned them from her service to his.

Less common were those in which he stood over her, a look of horror on her face, a sense of triumph on his, his Qorihna raised above his head and ready to strike.

And finally there came the rarest of all: singular visions where he held Doagnis against him in an unbreakable caress, one hand pinning her arms behind her, the other at her throat, cutting off her last breath even as he kissed her lips. His last sight was always of her staring and unfocused eyes as she slowly choked to death.

He always awoke at that moment, covered in sweat, his heart racing and his skin clammy. Sometimes there were words on his lips, words caught in the moment of saying or already said, but he could never remember what they were.

Every strong life was tainted with darkness, or so he reminded himself, but the dreams troubled him more than he cared for. He told himself that they came from the Urq, that unthinking other that lay within all Ell. It was the tempter, the liar, the dark self. He had long ago been warned to ignore such strange and destructive impulses, but he would never be able to make them go away. They would never leave. They could not. For better or worse, they were a part of him right up until the moment that he passed from the world.

After many days they came at last to the Minoaj Zinjil, the most easterly point of the mainland. As they rounded the headland Korfax caught a brief glimpse of a distant land, Lonekaniss, a dim rise above the horizon that marked the most westerly point of the eastern isles. Only the largest was populated, claimed by a hardy few who asserted their stubborn suzerainty by building great towers full of empty rooms on each of its many hills. Korfax could just about make out a few of them, dim spires appearing like upended swords.

The other isles were all said to be barren, whipped by even greater storms that rose up almost daily out from the eastern seas. Korfax wondered whether it was their proximity to the great gyre that caused them to be so chastised.

Though he did not want to appear too eager, Korfax still listened out for any news concerning the coming assault on Emethgis Vaniad by the forces commanded by Noraud Noqmal, but there was little to be told. The armies had already assembled and marched. The sky ships that had ferried the many thousands had not yet returned, so those that waited behind had only their fears and their hopes left to them. Maybe news awaited in Thilzin Gallass, but Korfax did not imagine that there would be any. Thilzin Gallass was almost as far as you could get from the centre whilst still on the mainland.

Her guest leaned back in his chair and surveyed the world beyond as if everything had been laid out before him in tribute. A thin, fluted vessel of fragrant wine waited on the table beside him. Its mate, a long goblet of pale crystal, he held in his hand.

It was evening and Rafarel was setting, and from the balcony where he sat, overlooking the river, the western side of Thilzin Gallass now reared blackly against its sombre light. Beyond the river, beyond the city, beyond the world even, Rafarel was going down in fire. On the opposite shore great towers rose up in stark silhouette, each black spire riding the roseate mists of evening. A few distant diarih flapped lazily across the sky, wings winking slow white flashes whilst below them a stately barge made its unhurried way in the opposite direction. To the west only the spires of the seventh bridge were visible. To the east the river vanished into opalescence, air and water merging at the limits of a dimming sky. The world was quiet.

Tafamel swayed gently out from her hiding place and came openly towards her guest.

"So, Gierozas, what do you think of my city?"

He turned his head slightly and glanced back at her.

"It is a rare jewel, Naray."

"Please," she said, holding up her right hand in denial, "do not call me that. I do not merit such an estate. Call me only by my given name."

He bowed his head to her and she hid her smile with her other hand. Though she might protest, the title flattered her vanity.

"You have the manners of a noble," she continued, dropping her hand again. "We are not used to such things on this side of the river. This is but a simple house, where the weary can rest amidst simple pleasures and so forget their troubles for a while."

She sat herself down in one of the long chairs next to him, a graceful movement, all of a piece. She inclined her head and peered sidelong at her guest. Though she tried to conceal it, her interest in him was obvious with every move that she made.

He was very tall and very broad, pale of skin but dark of cloth. His armour was strange, as was his weaponry, and he looked both young and old, as though he had strayed far beyond his time and place.

Many from distant lands stayed at her house these days, and she was used to far more outlandish costumes than this one sported, but he outmatched them in every way. Even a simple glance from his eyes was a delight to her. Something lay behind them, something deep beneath their waters, powerful and rare. Though she would not have admitted it to another, he drew her like a promise of wonderful danger. She had never met his like before. It was such a shame that he had to die.

"So tell me," she asked, "why have you come to Gallass?"

"I search," he said.

"And for what do you search?"

The faint smile in his eyes slowly faded away, eclipsed by a rising darkness.

"I seek someone," he told her.

"Oh?"

"I have heard it said you might be able to help me."

She frowned at that.

"I? Is it someone I know, then?"

"I believe that it is. I wish to know her whereabouts. I was hoping you could tell me."

"That depends."

"Depends?"

"On who it might be and what you intend to do with such knowledge."

"What I shall do is go to her."

"Just that?"

"Just that!"

"I am wondering what the consequences might be if I were able to give you such knowledge. Some might consider it a betrayal."

"I only wish to have words with her. What would follow after would depend entirely upon her answers."

"I remain unconvinced," said Tafamel.

"And what would convince you?" he asked. "Surety? How can I predict what she might say? Or do?"

"It is your intent that concerns me."

"I do not think that is your concern at all."

He lifted his goblet to his lips and drained it. She leaned forward and deftly refilled it. He bowed his head slightly in acknowledgement and lifted it again, taking another mouthful, whilst his eyes became distant as they gazed across the river once more. Rafarel had set at last and his fire was finally gone from the sky.

Only the stark outlines of the city towers remained, all silhouetted against the fading light, black against the dome of heaven.

They sat quietly for a moment, he watching the opposite bank, she watching him. Then he turned to her again and fixed her with his hardest stare yet.

"Let us to it, then," he said. "Where is Doagnis?"

Tafamel tensed and then relaxed. Here it came.

"Doagnis?" she asked. "What makes you think I would know anything of such a one?"

He laughed quietly and leaned back in his chair.

"Come now, I have already met with your father, so any further denial on your part would be an utter waste of time. Where is Doagnis? I will not ask again."

Tafamel was a moment composing herself.

"If my father would not tell you where she is, then neither shall I."

"He neither told me nor refused. There was not time."

"Not time?"

"He was too busy trying to kill me."

There was a long pause.

"What happened?" she asked carefully, clearly not wanting to ask the one question she dreaded. He did not spare her.

"I did not kill him," he said, "but your father is dead nonetheless. He attempted a summoning that was beyond him and paid the inevitable price."

"You lie!"

Tafamel stood up and backed away, one hand behind her back, catching at the handle of her hidden blade. He watched her and smiled sadly. The smile was almost regretful.

"Be thankful your mistress does not know that I am here. Otherwise I think your life would be forfeit also."

Tafamel backed away further. She made a swift gesture with her free hand and six others came out onto the balcony, five of them with swords already drawn whilst the sixth remained hooded and cloaked. Korfax looked at them all in turn and then back at Tafamel.

"But she does know," Tafamel spat at him. "These are my avengers. They will kill you for what happened to my father."

"Don't be absurd, child," scolded the hooded figure. "We are not here for vengeance. It is him that we want, this dark rebel that pursues our mistress. Yes, your father is dead, but we do not avenge failure. We curse it. Learn the lesson."

He gestured to the door.

"Now leave us. Your purposes here are done."

Korfax rose to his feet and, somewhat leisurely, placed his hand upon the hilt of his sword.

"Yes," he said, "Molpan failed, as did Tohtanef. And that should give you pause, I think. So I will make the same offer to you that I made to them. If you yield to me,

I will be merciful."

The other laughed and drew back his hood. He had a finely featured face, old and proud, but its lines were set with nothing but the deepest contempt.

"I do not know who you are, or into what long-forgotten house you were born, but this arrogant insurrection of yours, this imagined path to glory that you foolishly pursue, has run its course. We serve Doagnis, all of us, and you will not discover a single one of us that does not. You are out of step with the times, youth, for we do not ruin ourselves with such wasteful practices any more. Times have changed."

Korfax bowed his head slightly in acknowledgement.

"You did once," he offered. The other smiled mockingly in return.

"But as I said, not any more. We have learned the bitter lessons of the past and now understand all too well what we can afford, and what we cannot. Prideful rivalries brought about the long defeat and the victory of the thrice accursed west. That shall never be borne again."

"So how did you know that I would be coming here?" Korfax asked.

"It was obvious," said the other. "My mistress has seen you. She knew you would come here and she set us to wait for you. It was all foreseen."

"And your intentions?"

"We take you to her, of course. But under constraint."

"Then you can save yourselves a great deal of trouble," said Korfax. "Just tell me where she is and I will go to her myself, and of my own free will."

The other let his smile become a little crueller.

"Oh no! That is not how it shall be, not how it shall be at all. It will be our way, or no way."

They advanced but then stopped again, for a great black blade was before them.

It was fast, faster than any of them could have believed possible, for no sooner had Korfax extended his hand than his blade was in it. And no sooner was his blade in his hand than it had split into six parts and slaughtered the five guards, reducing them to showers of ash. Only a sudden circle of flame denied the sixth.

Korfax reigned in his sword.

"Tohtanef did what you are doing now, and she failed," he said.

The other looked back at Korfax for a moment, shock on his face. Then he increased his power and the circle of flame doubled. Two circles of flame, one inside the other, now surrounded the Arged.

"If that blade is what I think it to be," he said, "then you are to be commended. I did not know any had survived the wars. But even that will not avail you here. I am more than your match."

Korfax felt a certain abandonment fill him. He had heard it all before.

"So do your worst," he said. "You clearly have nothing to fear from me. But before you do, give me your name at least. Give me your name, and I will give you mine."

The Arged continued to smile.

"Names? You are no master of names."

"So where is the harm?"

The Arged snorted in contempt.

"Where the harm indeed! So be it. I am Kolors Enay Axayal, though what good that will do you, I cannot say."

Korfax gestured with his sword.

"The Kolorsith is it? Weren't they Gandao's people?"

Axayal narrowed his eyes.

"Yes, they were. So perhaps you understand a little better what it is that you face here. Gandao was mighty, as am I."

Korfax bowed and a mocking gleam filled his eyes.

"Mighty indeed, but you have not heard my name yet."

Axayal folded his arms and his twin circles of green flame all but boiled with his ire.

"Your name? Why should I care what you are called? All I care is that your death is on its way, even now."

Korfax raised an eyebrow.

"You think?"

"I know."

"Then let me disabuse you, for the name that I was given in the time of naming ..." and here he paused slightly whilst looking carefully back at Axayal, "... was Korfax."

Axayal gasped.

"You? But they said that you were dead!"

Korfax bowed his head.

"And how is it you are armed with a Qorihna?" Axayal asked. "How is it that you are versed in the Namad Mahorelah?"

"Needs must," Korfax answered lightly.

Axayal let out a long breath, almost a hiss.

"Well then, my mistress has prepared me well, even for this. I have been shown a conjuration that few of the Argedith have ever seen – and not one of the Dar Kaadarith at all. I see glories ahead for me, fool, but, alas, only torment for you."

Axayal raised his arms to the heavens.

"It comes," he cried, and even as he spoke a great gyre of flame suddenly burst out of nowhere, a roaring eruption of fire.

It was vast, a monstrous flaming vortex the size of a house. It lit up the night with a baleful glare, but in its depths a darker wheel turned, a place of insurmountable heat.

Korfax fell back, awakening his armour almost by instinct even as he shielded himself with his sword. The being above them both was impossibly powerful. Physically it was huge, but spiritually it was immense. It reeked of force. Despite himself, Korfax was appalled.

Axayal roared with laughter as he watched Korfax retreat. He had done it – him, him alone. He had done that which no other had achieved in all the collected ages of the world. Even his mistress had not accomplished this, or so she had told him.

"Do you know what that is?" he called out, his shrill voice piercing the incessant rumbling of the demon.

Korfax glanced quickly at Axayal but did not reply. Axayal grinned as if his triumph was all but complete.

"Above me waits a Givyalag, a demon of all but infinite might, almost like unto the Ashar themselves. But it is mine now, for I have brought it here and it will do as I desire. Curse in vain, slave of the west, and die in agony."

Axayal turned to the Givyalag and sent his will at it, telling it what it should do, but as the moments lengthened and the demon did not move, his face began to betray him. Consternation leaked across his features like an unwanted rebellion. He struggled with it for a little while, but then he began to realise the truth. There was nothing there to command, nothing at all. The thing had no mind. There was no way he could tell it what to do, for it would not hear him. He had summoned an idiot.

Korfax felt the shift in the air about him and glanced at Axayal. He saw the uncertainty, and then the fear. Korfax looked up at the demon. It remained where it was, seemingly content just to sit in the air above them both and roar like a furnace.

Korfax turned back to Axayal and offered the Arged an unkind smile.

"Well, here is a pretty tale," he said. "You may have summoned it, but can you control it?"

Axayal returned his gaze, anger and hatred filling his eyes.

"Do not mock me," he hissed.

Korfax gestured at the coiling fires above.

"Mock you? You mock yourself. I am not untutored, nor altogether lacking in lore. Like you, I can also feel something of what it is. You have overstepped your bounds. You have failed, just as the others did. The creature you have called up does not answer your will at all. It is altogether mindless."

He held his sword before him.

"Send it back, Axayal, send it back whence it came whilst you still can, before any real harm is done. And, in return, I promise to be merciful."

Axayal drew himself up in his circle and his eyes spat fire.

"You? Merciful? I think not!"

He looked up at the great fire in the sky.

"And send this back? Send back the greatest summoning ever achieved under the Bright Heavens? No!"

Korfax looked up at the mindless demon floating in the air above their heads.

"But Doagnis still surpasses you," he said. "She summoned one of the Ashar."

Axayal gaped.

"That is a lie!" he cried.

Korfax looked hard at Axayal.

"Then ask her when you next see her! She sent Ash-Mir after me."

"So how is it that you are still here?" Axayal sneered.

"Because she could not control her summoning, either." Korfax told him. "What strange symmetry you suddenly have, and what strange fantasies rule your lives! You have eschewed the old ways? What lie is that? You still try to outdo each other, try to outmatch each other with your power, but what do you gain instead? Nothing but bloody chaos."

Axayal roared and sent fires from his hands, but Korfax caught them upon his blade, which consumed them greedily. Axayal screamed in frustration.

"DAMN YOU TO DEATH AND DARKNESS!" he shouted.

Korfax would have answered, but a movement in the air above caught his attention. The Givyalag was moving at last. It was descending towards Axayal. Korfax retreated further and watched. What was it doing?

There was a sense about it now, a growing sense of hunger. Like great wheels beginning to turn, gathering pace and momentum, the Givyalag gradually awoke. It had felt the unleashing of powers, and that had been the spur. So now it descended and burned the air as it came.

Korfax fled the balcony, leaping down over the stone, but Axayal remained where he was. He could not move, not whilst he was constrained within his circles of flame.

Korfax heard the failing scream even as he fled the tower. He looked back. Not even a double circle could save Axayal from the Givyalag. It continued to descend, remorseless and imperturbable, and it consumed him even as it consumed the power with which he had vainly tried to defend himself. Korfax waited for the Givyalag to depart, but it did not; instead, it now fell upon the tower and began to consume that as well. Fire spread about it and the top of the tower began to slump in the heat. Molten stone flowed like water, running down the walls even as the tower came apart. Korfax ran out onto the street and looked back.

The Givyalag ate its way downwards, consuming everything as it went – the tower, its contents, every single thing that lay within its path. Axayal may have gone, but his demon still remained. Korfax would have laughed at the irony if the situation were not so dire. This writhing mass of flame did not even possess wit enough to return to the abyss at the death of its summoner.

He suddenly remembered that Enastul was stabled nearby. This accursed demon would take his steed as well as the tower if he did not act soon.

He raced to the stables and freed Enastul, quickly mounting as the fire began to fall. But it was only as he cleared the doors that the Givyalag finally arrived. Fire covered everything behind him, and then erased it all.

Ormn galloped up and many dismounted. There were Branith, their eyes alight with determination. There were four of the Geyadith with them, all hurling their summoned energies at the great, fiery demon even as they came within striking distance, but their actions came to nought. The drifting monstrosity did whatever it would, burning stone and air and water with equal facility, impervious to anything sent against it. Earth of air it swallowed, fire of water it drank, and nothing, nothing at all, seemed able to stop it.

The Givyalag moved away from the slumped remains of the tower and then moved on to the next, sensing perhaps a greater mass of stone, another piece of order that it could reduce to chaos.

Korfax found a vantage point and watched from there. Cries echoed up from below, the cries of the fearful, the cries of the dying. But what could he do? What *should* he do? This mindless oaf of destruction would go where it pleased, and no call, no threat, would persuade it from its course. It had become a curse upon the world, unthinking and elemental. It knew only destruction.

There were warnings in the texts – call always upon the lesser lest the greater command more than you – but that was no help here. He felt the beginnings of desperation. How in the name of all creation was he supposed to stop this demon? How was anyone supposed to stop it?

He took out his logadar and looked inside, but there was nothing in the resurrected words, nothing that spoke explicitly of such a monster. However, there were hints that began to quicken his heart. There were possible reversals, the putative undoing of summonings that had achieved the wrong purpose. The ancients, it seemed, had met with such situations before.

So, with his blade before him and his armour about him, Korfax went to the tallest tower that stood in the Givyalag's path and made his way, unseen, to the top. He stood a moment, preparing himself, emptying his mind, and then he called upon the abyss to open up above his head. He would send the demon back to the deeps with all the power that he could muster.

The demon came to him, hearing the siren song of home perhaps, but even as it approached the growing rupture it began to resist. Determination now stirred inside it. This place had not yet been destroyed. Was that not its purpose? Why leave when there was still work to be done? Inside it a dim consciousness had begun to form and Korfax could feel the slow rise, even now, like the resurrection of a memory, the reincarnation of an older self.

Korfax summoned more power to his cause, and more yet, making the hole above his head more potent with each passing moment, but still the Givyalag resisted. Though it had been plucked from its repose whilst still an idiot, it had begun to taste awareness again. It had been made to destroy and to take pleasure in it.

The demon became more certain, changing from moment to moment as it began to perceive its needs and its surroundings, recreating long-lost senses as it learned its molten body anew. Foetal eyes of incandescence suddenly blinked from within its inner darknesses, looking this way and that as they began to grasp something of the possibilities now laid out before them.

Korfax increased his summoning further and the Givyalag began to howl in denial as the deepening abyss pulled at its substance. Home beckoned, but home was sleep, and the demon did not want it. It wanted sensation again, it wanted pleasure and it wanted an endless feast of destruction.

The power increased. Korfax held a barely contained pit of darkness above his head and the fire before him touched its borders, but still it did not enter.

He needed a goad, something to persuade the demon to leave. There was only one thing in his possession that held such a possibility. His Qorihna. He paused. Dare he match it against this living gyre of annihilation? But conversely, dare he not?

He drew his Qorihna and pointed it at the great demon, but even his blade seemed to recoil from its heat. Korfax frowned. Was his sword reluctant? It pulled his hand back with it as it bunched itself up and thickened. Then he realised what it was doing. It was gathering up its strength for one almighty blow.

Black energies grew within it like the intake of a mighty breath. Then his blade roared one single, ear-shattering roar and flew upwards, striking at the Givyalag and impaling it upon a single tongue of metal. The Givyalag's incessant rumble trebled in pitch.

The choice before the demon was suddenly stark. Endure the black blade to extinction, or return home. It did not take it long to decide. It hurled itself into the darkness and the rupture closed behind it with a thunderclap. A hot wind briefly rippled the air and then there was silence.

Korfax looked at his Qorihna and pondered. It had seemed to know exactly what it should do. Had his blade met such creatures before? Or had it read its master's purpose instead? Korfax did not know, and once again his mighty sword worried him. What was it, really? Where had it come from, and what did it know?

He hid himself away and climbed back down. Only one thing remained to him now, Tafamel. She was his last link to Doagnis. If she had survived.

He found her amongst the wreckage, in a far corner of what remained of one of the gardens, the only survivor. But even so, she was dying still. He went quickly to her and cradled her burnt head in his arms.

"Tafamel, hear me. Tell me where Doagnis is. Look again for the blessings of the Creator, ere you go."

She gasped in pain but did not answer. He could feel her thoughts. She did not want to die.

"Tafamel," he implored. "Please, tell me what I need to know. You are dying. It cannot be prevented, but I can ease your way to the river if you tell me where Doagnis is."

She cried out. He reached inside her and blocked her pain, walling off the sensation. She sighed and opened her eyes, looking up at him.

"See how merciful the world can be?" he told her. "Now tell me what I need to know. I will ease your passing."

She looked away. She still did not believe she would die. She desired her life too much. He had no choice. He dived in, down into her depths and releasing the block on her pain so that he could see her thoughts. She screamed as the agony flooded back. But it was too much, all at once. She died even as he touched her memories.

He laid her back upon the cooling stone and stood up. She had died in pain, and for that he was sorry, but it could not be helped. He had to know.

There were scattered images and a name, the name of a place he had never been to before but would know anywhere. So that was it, was it? Doagnis was in Othil Ekrin? He would never have guessed. He turned about and made his way back to Enastul. Let others deal with the aftermath – he had business elsewhere.

She went to her window and stared out bleakly over the labyrinth of towers and bridges. With the coming of night the view was startling in its beauty, piradar lighting the towers, a million stars shining on stone and water, but she did not see it. Her eyes stared inward, and she felt a dark rage.

Axayal had failed. Though it hardly seemed possible, he had failed.

She had no idea what had happened next, for at the moment of his death all had gone dark. She would have to wait for the news to come to her by more conventional means. She turned and looked at the scrolls upon her table. One of them had a verse on it, a lying, malicious verse put there by her lying, malicious ancestor. No doubt Nalvahgey was laughing somewhere, far back in the distant past.

She walked over to the table and swept her arm across it. The scrolls scattered to the floor.

"Damn you!" she said, but there was only silence.

Korfax leant upon the rail of the ship and watched the endless world pass him by. It seemed as if he had been travelling upon water all his born days. Everywhere he went, every journey he undertook, water now dominated his every horizon.

Around the Minoaj Zinjil they went, before heading west, back along the coast, all the way to the mouth of the Zinkao and the great port on its eastern shore, Thilzin Pelemir.

Korfax alighted when they finally reached the port, and then he went in search of passage on a river ship, one that would take him all the way to Piralorm below Vasasan. It did not take him long.

Once settled on board he went to the rails and stared out over the river. The fragrant waters were slow and stately, utterly unlike those of the Patrim. Where the Patrim strode across the land by the fastest route possible, the Zinkao wandered where it would.

The Zinkao – so it had come to this! He was to travel the length of the Zinkao. It was said that everything life had to offer could be found upon its banks. It was a bold claim, but not one Korfax felt confident to doubt, for the Zinkao spanned almost a third of Lon-Elah itself.

The opposite shore was far beyond the horizon, and it would remain so for at least a day's travel. The ship would take the eastern side all the way through the Peisith Oadeas, the Woven Forest, across the lowlands and then on to Piralorm. From there, Korfax would have to walk the last few steps to Othil Ekrin. By ancient edict, only the steeds of those that served the great guilds were allowed within the city itself. Everyone else had to walk.

Night came on and the ship finally got under way. Thilzin Pelemir faded into the distance and the Woven Forest began to loom, a dark wall to the east. To the west the fading fires of Rafarel gradually dimmed and the stars came out to shine down from within the fires of their birthing. Korfax watched the world go by for a while, and then he went off to his cabin to sleep.

He awoke to find that little had changed. Only one bank was visible, a great green wall to the east. To the west there was nothing but water. They were deep within the outer boundaries of the Woven Forest now, but even here the Zinkao dominated all their horizons.

The sheer scale of the river silenced him. They had been sailing all night, but still the Zinkao was wider here than almost any other river he had ever heard of.

He stared down through clear waters at the distant riverbed below, watching the many and varied forms disporting in the depths. Argent shoals darted here and there, nervous glimmers of reflected light, whilst shadowed giants ever yawned at them with glinting teeth. Great and gleaming forms leapt and played before the ship's bows, whilst sinuous shapes of green swam along the banks or raised their flattened heads to gaze with unmoving eyes at the passing ship. Korfax watched it all in astonishment. So much life, so much he had never imagined.

Some of the beasts were named for him by a few of the crew, but their names did not do them justice. To Korfax they remained as he had first seen them, strange and mysterious, and he found himself preferring such conceits.

It took another three days to reach the heart of the Woven Forest. The Zinkao was much narrower here and the west bank was at last visible, a thin green line only just within sight. Many channels could be seen to the side, tributaries that came apart and joined again, branching this way and that, a veritable labyrinth of slow waters hemmed in by tall green walls. The main watercourse, though, remained their highway, a path of liquid crystal thrusting itself deep into the heart of Lon-Elah.

After the sixth day the trees on each side of the Zinkao began to thin, giving way to a wider land, a great wide wetland over which the river's many branches flowed. Now they travelled up the centre of the much narrowed waterway, and soon they would be able to see the edges of the uplands, the high cliffs that guarded the upper plains.

Come the seventh day and there they were, far walls of stone, just peeking over the horizon, a barely seen line of shadow below the cloud. The uplands were the food basket of Rasayah and a place of order. The lowlands had been left largely to themselves. They remained wild.

The main channel soon became the only way that they could go, for the rest of the land about them was a mixture of grassland, trees and long lakes. Ahead lay the small port of Piralorm, set upon the south side of the Zum Rolodir, the boiling sea that lay below the great falls of Vasasan.

Korfax could not see the falls, for they were still hidden by the distance, but he could hear their dim roar even now, even this far away.

They arrived at Piralorm amidst the omnipresent rumble of the falls, which still could not be seen, for one had to travel the length of the Zum Rolodir to do so, following its great curve around the cliffs of the uplands. Given the power of the falls the Zum Rolodir itself was never still, its waters continually lapping at the walls of Piralorm.

Korfax disembarked and looked along the quay. Until this moment, when he had not been on board a ship, he had ridden everywhere. But now he would have to part with Enastul whilst he went on to the city. An ancient decree, from the earliest days of its building, said that all should walk in the city. There were exceptions for the guilds, but he, a lone traveller, would only attract interest if he tried to claim a special case.

There was a hostelry beside the quay that he had been told was excellent in such matters, so he took Enastul there. The feeling, as he arranged matters with the owner, was strange, to say the least. He had not wanted to be parted from Enastul, but it had to be done nonetheless. Besides, Enastul would be in the hands of those that did this all the time. There were many hostelries on the outskirts of Piralorm whose sole purpose was to care for the steeds of those that travelled.

As Korfax released Enastul into the fields of keeping, the owner, Komanan, came over to stand beside him, watching Enastul with interest.

"A fine ormn indeed," he said. "I do not think I have ever seen better, not in all my days I have not."

Korfax was happy to agree.

"He comes of an ancient line born of the north. He is one of the few possessions that I would not be parted with."

Komanan looked at Korfax for a moment.

"I understand entirely," he said. "I will keep him for you, and I will keep him well. Besides, it would be an honour to have such a one in my fields of waiting."

Korfax smiled.

"Thank you again. I think the one thing that I have missed the most upon all the many roads that I have travelled are the simple courtesies that you offer now."

"You have travelled far, then?"

"From the uttermost north to the uttermost south. Now I travel the east."

"Far indeed."

Komanan bowed his head in calm respect and then turned his gaze back to the wide field, watching as Enastul raced across the green. Others raced with him, vying with each other to be at his side, but none could match him. His strength shook the ground. Komanan laughed quietly.

"Now look at that, will you?" he said. "The others bow to him already. That was quick. He has become the master of the herd merely by his presence. I was right in my assessment. Only the rule of the Ell will your steed allow."

Korfax thought back to a broken body in a stable far to the south.

"Not even that," he said quietly.

Korfax looked back at Komanan and felt a sudden lump catch in his throat. That was almost exactly the kind of thing that Chasaloh, keeper of the herd at Losq, might have said.

"If you do as you say," Korfax said, "if you keep him well, I will gift you with riches when I return."

Komanan made the gesture of completion.

"No need for that," he said. "I already have all the riches that I require."

He smiled.

"You have paid the requisite price. That is all anyone can ask."

They looked at each other.

"Thank you," Korfax said. "You are deserving of nothing but honour and praise."

Komanan smiled easily.

"And I thank you again. So let me say in return that I hope you find what you are seeking."

He gestured to the rocky heights above and the long road that wound its way upwards to the falls of Vasasan. Korfax looked up as well and let the smile fall from his face.

"I hope that also," he said. "I have been searching for far too long."

Korfax walked slowly up to the great falls of Vasasan, taking the northern side of the road. The road was steep and winding, scattered with those travelling to and from Othil Ekrin. There were a few of the travelling orders, Luahith mouthing orisons, Langith silent and sightful. There were even one or two swords, much like himself. The rest appeared to be about some business or other, up from Piralorm or down from the city. He walked in mixed company, which was all to the good, as it would make things easier when he eventually arrived at the city gates.

Eventually he achieved the wide expanse before the edge, where the road turned. He stopped for a moment and looked back behind him. The view was magnificent.

There it all was, stretched out below him: the river, Piralorm, the ends of the

Zum Rolodir and the great wetlands. He followed the Zinkao back into the distance where the wetlands merged with the sky in a distant haze.

He was high above the plain, and the port of Piralorm where he had disembarked was a mere toy to his eyes. Black dots, barely perceptible, moved to and fro upon the quay. He looked to the fields of waiting beyond the towers of Piralorm and watched the distant forms wander where they would. There were many shades – white, brown, yellow and black – drifting this way and that over the distant green. Korfax thought of Enastul. He was down there now, wandering with his own and drinking deep from the cup of mastery. Korfax smiled ruefully to himself for a moment before turning about. He did not look again.

He came to the edge and stopped at its walls. Now he could finally see the falls of Vasasan, revealed in all their glory. He had been told that the first sight of the Vasasan would be the one you took back with you into the river, and Korfax could only agree as he stared up in awe at the vast wall of water that fell endlessly downwards before him.

Stretching between immense pylons of obdurate rock was a huge expanse of tumbling cataract. Here the mighty Zinkao hurled itself from the many canyons it had carved from the uplands beyond, and its roar as it broke free from its enclosing walls seemed to shake the world.

The water fell into a veritable abyss, an immense hollow hidden under clouds of spray, deep and dark and ever moving. Down there, hiding the great cauldron, a seething whiteness moiled, over which curving bridges of light shimmered, the seven colours, pure and brilliant.

Korfax looked to the heights again and found his eyes drawn to the teeth of the Vasasan, an oddly regular spacing of curving spires projecting from the top of the falls. They were aptly named, for each great fang of stone seemed planted in some greater jaw, the jaw perhaps of an immeasurable beast that yet slumbered in death whilst the ever-rushing waters of the Zinkao tumbled over its eroded head. Korfax was minded of the legends of his childhood, of the giant that would awaken when the time was right. Once he had imagined that he had looked upon its limbs, cast carelessly across the soil of the north. Perhaps, here, he now gazed upon its teeth.

He moved on, continuing the long way up whilst the thunder the world's waters echoed around him.

The road gradually moved away from the falls, rising steeply to meet the upper gates of the city, far above the Vasasan, and like the Vasasan, Othil Ekrin remained hidden from view.

High walls and high gates awaited those that travelled the road, strung across what had once been an ancient waterway. The entrance was both wide and beautiful. Here the stone had been carved and shaped as if by water, a delicate swirl that rose up on either side to twin towers. Between the towers was set the gateway itself, a great wall fashioned like a waterfall itself. The gates, though, could not be seen, as they were drawn back into cunning recesses. To enter the city, one walked through a tunnel, much in the fashion of the gates upon the Komsel.

Above the gates and the guarding towers taller cliffs stretched to the north and to the south. There was no need for any wall. Korfax gazed up at the cliffs in satisfaction. The bones of the world were strong here – ancient, perhaps, but strong all the same.

He waited in line. The guards were questioning everyone; no doubt the events in Thilzin Gallass had heightened the need for vigilance. Korfax listened as each was dealt with in turn. The questions were careful but perfunctory. He smiled to himself. He had heard it all before. If this 'vigilance' was intended to catch such as him, it lacked a certain keenness.

The Branith that served the gates were clearly tired of their duty. They had been doing it for most of the day, and now they asked their questions as if by rote. Korfax checked himself just to make sure. All was in order. Even his mother would not have recognised the world-weary sword, dusty and travel-stained, that stood in line before the gates of the city.

"Name and business?"

Korfax looked sharply at the Branvath. That was curt. He had not been so with any of the others. Korfax felt a brief flash of annoyance.

"And may the light of the Creator shine upon you also," he said.

Korfax caught a glint of anger in the Branvath's eyes.

"I would greet you if I knew you, but I do not. So answer my challenge."

Korfax raised an eyebrow.

"I was never taught that familiarity and courtesy ever went hand in hand. However, if it please you, I am Naman Rom Evudal, formerly of Leemal, then of Othil Zilodar, then of Emethgis Vaniad. Having lost three homes in rapid succession I have decided to do without one for a while."

The Branvath looked uneasy for a moment.

"You have fought in the wars?"

Korfax let his voice adopt a wearier tone.

"Yes," he said.

The Branvath stared at Korfax, seemingly waiting for some elaboration on his part, but since none seemed to be forthcoming, he straightened up again. Korfax smiled to himself. If he guessed aright, this one had not yet seen anything of war at all.

"Then why are you not fighting now?" the Branvath asked.

Korfax became still. He decided he did not like the tone of the question or the manner in which it was delivered.

"I could ask the same of you," he said. "Suffice it say that I am about other business at the moment."

"And what business might that be?"

Korfax had had enough. Why the Branvath had chosen to pick on him, he did not know, but now it was time to put the Branvath firmly in his place.

"I seek work where I find it," he said. "But finding myself with a full purse I have become a traveller for a little while. I have heard it said that Othil Ekrin is beautiful, so I have decided to witness that truth for myself and perhaps gain employment here, before the Agdoain come at last to destroy it."

The Branvath blanched.

"That will not happen!" he said.

Korfax folded his arms.

"Will it not? And what do you know of it? I was on the wall during the siege of Othil Zilodar. I served in the watchtowers. I saw the fall of Emethgis Vaniad. What have you seen?"

Korfax glared while the Branvath worked his mouth as though tasting something sour. Korfax might have been tempted to say more, but then he became aware of a sudden stillness about him. He glanced to his left and to his right and saw that many others were now staring at him in horror. He cursed. He had drawn attention to himself, precisely the thing he had not wanted to do. He turned back to the Branvath.

"I am tired," he said, "and it has been a long journey. Let me pass, or forbid my entry. I find that I no longer care."

The Branvath stepped back and gestured to the gates.

"You may go on your way," he said. "I dare say we could use such battle-hardened veterans as yourself, even if you seem to have lost all faith that we may yet prevail."

Korfax looked back over his shoulder as he walked past.

"And you, good Branvath, should watch what you say. If I am any judge at all, I would say that you have not yet been tested. I would like to see how well you would fare against the enemy."

With that, he walked on through the gates. The Branvath watched him go and then turned about, only to find that everyone else was looking at him now. He could see the light of judgement in every eye. He turned away from them all and cursed the day.

In the shadow of the outer gates a figure clad wholly in darkest brown carefully watched the departing form of Naman Rom Evudal. Ears trained in the subtlest nuance of inflection and accent heard everything that had been said, and eyes trained to pick up the subtlest detail had watched every movement. So, having heard and having seen, the cloaked figure followed.

It was as he cleared the tunnel that Korfax finally came upon Othil Ekrin, and his black mood vanished as if ripped away by another hand. He all but came to a full stop in utter amazement.

Many of the places he had travelled to had been revelations – Thilzin Jerris, the great plain of towers on Lonsiatris, sprawling Thilzin Merenar and the Zinznah Zinkao – but the flower of the east humbled them all.

Once, long, long ago, there had dwelt here a garden of weathered stone, innumerable pillars of rock set in a great circular valley filled with many deep canyons. Around the pillars the waters of the Zinkao had flowed, this way and that as the whim took them, but then the Ell had come and they had built Othil Ekrin upon a wondrous foundation.

Everywhere he looked he saw spires and towers and great houses, all leaping up into the sky from their singular islands of stone. Bridges and causeways sprang between them in bewildering array, whilst below, far below, the waters of the Zinkao rushed through their depths, pristine and sparkling.

Korfax could only breathe. Such an astonishment it was, and so beautiful. Looking at it all now he could have wept with joy. Waters tumbled, spires reared and stone leapt bottomless gulfs. Who could contain it all with mere sight?

He had come to a labyrinth of almost perilous beauty, and nothing that he had ever encountered before could have prepared him for it. To see it was to drown in it, to fail even in its apprehension. Yet here he was now, within it, seeing it and knowing it. It spoke to him, to his depths, to that which lay below word, thought or naming. Here was the quiet passion that dwelt in the heart of the Ell, and seeing it all, all complete and in a single glance, he was spellbound.

He bowed his head. If Emethgis Vaniad had been the hand of the Creator upon the world, then here lay the heart. Here was the call of water, in all its beauty. Here stood the stone of making, in all its simplicity. Unbidden, he heard again words once spoken to him in the Umadya Semeiel.

'This world is larger than you know. There are sights you have never seen, lives you have not touched, people you have not known. Our world is so vast that you could travel it for an eternity and still not see all that it had to offer. Every moment, every feeling, they are here, somewhere, caught in crystal and stone, enough experience to drown us all until creation itself is ended.'

He sighed. Thilnor had said that to him on the day he had left the seminary of the Dar Kaadarith. How true it was. And that was why he was here. To preserve. Let the guards upon the gate be damned. They knew nothing. To each was given their due. And this was his.

He turned away. It was time to enter the labyrinth and seek out his enemy. If she were here, he would find her.

Korfax stood at the window of his room. He could not help it; it was as if he had been starved of sight all his life.

The hostelry he had chosen was in the northern quarter, but the room he had taken possessed the most wonderful view of the centre. As soon as he had been shown it he had claimed it as his own.

The hostelry sat upon one of the many great pillars of stone that dotted the forty-nine circles of peaks and chasms over which Othil Ekrin had been built. He had only to look down to see the dizzying depths and only to look up to see the airy heights. He was caught in the middle.

In the distance below lay the sharp flicker of many reflections, the wide waters of the Zinkao flowing on their way, for ever fed by the many tributaries that tumbled down from the encircling cliffs. From them, though, rising ever upwards, came spire after spire after spire. Over the many chasms many bridges leapt, some mere arches, others greater by far, pillared spans leaping the gulfs and sinking their great stone roots into the rock beneath. Permanence gave way to impermanence, solidity to fluidity, but all was in balance.

At the exact centre of the city Korfax could see the mightiest pillar of all, the Nazarth Nothoah. Its summit and sides were adorned with the Poamal Gevamah, the palace of the morning: a spiral of spires, a bewilderment of walls, steep roads and leaping bridges. It was the greatest tower of the city, the Poamal Gevamah, but it did not dominate; instead, it gently mastered. The many spires shone in the late light of the day, banners gently rippling in the breeze. In that place, in that ancient place, Audroh Usdurna, hereditary ruler of the Korith Zinu, had his being.

Korfax could not pull himself away from the sight; he was caught, like a prisoner, by the almost intolerable beauty. It was hard to think of anything else whilst in its presence.

He gazed at the Poamal Gevamah and thought again of Usdurna. No doubt he was there, even now. Korfax thought back to the last rites of Ermalei, when Usdurna had honoured him. Then he remembered his trial when Usdurna had spoken in his defence. Korfax looked away at last and his eyes swelled with a hot darkness as he thought of the betrayal and the loss that had followed.

For want of something else to think on he wondered whether Thilnor was still in the city. Thilnor had been sent back there after achieving his stave, to serve the second Geyadril of the city. Perhaps, though, Thilnor had gone west to fight in the battle to retake Emethgis Vaniad.

Battle! War! Othil Ekrin would not survive it, if it came. If Othil Homtoh was the hardest city for an enemy to take, then beautiful Othil Ekrin was surely the easiest. The high cliffs that surrounded it were also its one great weakness, because all the enemy would have to do would be to march across the uplands and climb down by the many ways to the city below. Korfax suddenly found himself wishing, with all his heart, that the Agdoain would never come here.

He stared about his room. It was long past time that he started his search. He had taken the image of a tower from the mind of Tafamel just before her death – one of many, set high upon the north face of a great pillar of rock not far from the centre on the northern side – but he did not know where it might actually be. The images were vague at best, and Tafamel had revealed neither the name of the tower nor even the district in which it was set. Her pain as she died had hidden almost everything from him.

He took up his armour and his sword, and then he covered himself in loose robes, as much to blend in as to hide himself. With a last look back he left his room.

If Othil Ekrin was a labyrinth to its citizens, then it was confusion incarnate to its visitors. Walking its many ways, Korfax began to appreciate what Thilnor had meant when he had said that you could traverse its streets for years and still see sights you had not seen before. Othil Ekrin surprised the eye with every turn of every corner. Here would be a new bridge, there a new courtyard or some as yet unexpected vista of plunging gulfs and soaring heights.

He took a wandering path, one that toured the many branches of the Zinkao as it came down from the north. At the start of his exploration it was hard not to take in the sights, daring even to think that he had both time and freedom to do so. The city was so full of life and yet so peaceful, and it was tempting to exult in the wonderful joining of stone with water that lay all about him. He could have easily forgotten why he had come here at all.

Each great island of rock that he came to he studied carefully, thinking all the while of the images he had taken from Tafamel, but none seemed quite right. Either the roads about them were wrongly aligned or there were not the requisite number of towers, or the towers themselves faced in entirely the wrong direction. But Othil Ekrin was a city on many levels and was cunning beyond his imagination. His task would take him many days at best.

The loose robe that he wore, of the kind preferred by the people of the city, blended him well into his surroundings. In a crowd he was hidden, but once out on his own it was a different tale. Then his size and his bearing gave him away. He stood out, no matter what he did. There were few like him upon the streets. All he could do was maintain the fiction that he was a simple sword of the north, easy enough as he did not have to change his accent over much. A strong Leemal brogue came easily to him, hiding as it did the softer tones of the furthest north.

Few appeared to notice him overmuch, but as the day grew older and his search became more directed, he began to feel the nagging sensation that he had missed something, that something was awry. It almost felt as if he was being followed, but every time he glanced over his shoulder or stopped on some pretext or other, looking surreptitiously this way or that, or yet even daring to feel behind him with his mind, he surprised no pursuit.

On his journey through the city, Korfax had come upon many sights, great towers rising above deep canyons or set about by still waters that gathered in this quiet lake or that or even balanced upon the edges of a waterfall. But when he came upon the great rift itself, Korfax could do nothing but stop where he was and stare at its fabulous beauty.

From the Poamal Gevamah to the falls of Vasasan it wound its intricate way eastwards, filled with the clearest water and adorned by delicate towers. Many shapely bridges spanned it and many hanging gardens softened the stone of its walls, but few boats dared the rushing torrent, for though the waters were deep, they were also swift and far too dangerous for any but the most skilled in such crafts.

Korfax leant against the finely carved parapet of the seventh bridge and took his ease. Here was a wonder of wonders, yet another jewel in the crown of the world, so he stood a while, lost in beauty and in thought, until a voice from behind disturbed him.

"So the great rift is to your liking, then?"

Korfax, surprised, turned about. There was an ancient standing there, or so he thought at first. She wore a fine dark cloak, much in the manner favoured by one of the bereaved, but she was also wrapped about like one of the Luahith and her face was almost completely hidden by shadow. Korfax smiled back at her.

"Of course, how can it not be?" he said.

"Am I right in thinking that you are from Leemal?" she asked.

"I am."

The other inclined her head just so and then turned her shadowed face to the river. Korfax watched her for a moment, wondering why she had struck up this conversation. She turned back to him, head still cocked on one side. He caught a brief glimpse of skin, very dark and smooth.

"And you are?" she asked him.

Korfax was taken aback for a moment, but he smiled and bowed to her all the same.

"Naman Rom Evudal," he announced. "May the light of the Creator be upon you."

Although he could not see her face, Korfax had the impression that she smiled as well.

"Thank you," she said. "Allow me to wish the same in return."

She bowed.

"So you are of the Namanith?" she said. "They were ever the most numerous! But, pardon me for being so inquisitive, it suddenly occurs to me that you don't quite have the look!"

Korfax raised an eyebrow.

"Really? And what would you know of it?" he asked.

The other laughed softly.

"I have been to Leemal," she told him, "but the Namanith that I met were much shorter than you."

Korfax raised himself up and straightened his shoulders.

"Shorter is it? Then may it surprise you to learn that I am one of the taller ones? Perhaps you do not know the Namanith as well as you believe."

Korfax gave his companion a studied glance. This one was not as old as he had at first thought. His senses were fully awake now.

"So," he said. "I have given you my name, but I am hearing no name in return."

The other clicked her tongue. In the south that was taken as a sign of annoyance.

"Ialdek Rom Kiafen," she said.

Korfax looked away again and smiled slightly. So she was of Badagar, was she?

"The Salman Ialdekith, is it?" he said. "And that is a strange thing also, for I do not recall any of you joining the Erm Roith. You are merchants, all of you."

He looked at her darkly but she waved her hand in dismissal.

"And who said anything about me being of the Erm Roith?"

Korfax gave her a sharp look.

"But you cover yourself up like one of the Luahith. Or perhaps it is simply that you have something to hide?"

Kiafen became very still.

"I have nothing to hide," she said. "Perhaps you are being overly suspicious?"

Korfax laughed now.

"Pardon me, but I am not the one with a head full of questions."

Kiafen remained where she was for a moment and then turned smartly about and marched off. Korfax watched her go. He had been right. She was much younger than he had at first assumed. But something about the encounter worried him, like an itch at the back of his mind. If she was following him, then why reveal herself? Was she testing him? If so, to what purpose? He watched as she disappeared into the distance, and then a darker thought occurred to him. Was she one of the Argedith? Did Doagnis know that he was here? He must remain on his guard from this moment on. This meeting had not happened by chance.

He walked on and found himself coming to the long market of the Piodo Vassass, the last before the great falls themselves. It was a long time since he had eaten, so he decided to investigate its wares.

There was little that he recognised. Though the smells were heavenly, he remained uncertain as to which of the many goods on offer would be best to try. He finally chose one of the more popular vendors and purchased two sticks of something they called gietey, spiced achir meat and roasted vegetables all pierced by a long thin stick of taanbar. He smiled gladly as they were passed over to him whilst he passed back two Sanhkdna in return. Payment given, he walked slowly on his way, consuming his purchase even as he went.

"So when did one of the Namanith develop a taste for gietey?" came a familiar voice.

Korfax turned to find Kiafen behind him, still cloaked, her face still in shadow. Korfax waved one of the sticks airily.

"Just now. And when did one of the Ialdekith make others' business their own?" he asked.

"Just now," she said.

Did she see him, he wondered. He raised up his defences, just in case.

"So we meet again. By chance, perhaps? Or perhaps not. Either way, what can I do for you now?" he asked.

"Conversation will suffice," she said.

"Really? You were in quite a hurry to leave the last time we met. Perhaps the conversation then was not to your liking?"

"Perhaps. Or could it be that I desired to give you a second chance."

"A second chance?"

"To explain yourself."

"And why should I do that?" he asked. "Who are you that you can demand such things of others?"

"You are not who you say you are," she replied.

"Neither are you," he accused, and that was that. Whoever this Kiafen was, he would find out her purposes. He reached out with his mind but met a barrier. If nothing else, she was very good at hiding herself. He pushed a little harder, and she took a step back.

"Stop it!" she hissed, even as she raised up more barriers to keep him out. He pushed on through regardless, but then he met with a wheel, a rolling wheel that ever threw him aside.

He withdrew, but now he was puzzled. She was not of the Argedith, he was certain. Neither was she of the Exentaser. He knew their touch well enough. She felt nothing like any of the others that he had met. So who was she?

He stepped closer and she took another step back. She looked poised for flight.

"What are you after?" he asked.

"And what are you after?" she replied.

He reached out with his mind again, full force, but this time she caught him off guard. She came forward, flicked out a hand and slapped him hard on his cheek. It was a distraction, for as her hand met his cheek, so her mind met his, a quick stab of seeking before he could react. Then she turned about and was gone, quickly vanishing back into the market before Korfax could follow. Even as he reached up to feel his cheek he reached out with his mind, seeking hers, but she was nowhere to be found. He frowned. Not many could hide from those trained by the Dar Kadaarith.

He was suddenly aware that others around him had been attracted by the altercation. Not a few were casting looks of disapproval in his direction. He had forgotten. Strong words and arguments in public were frowned upon in the east. He turned away and strode off, certain that eyes followed him all the way out of the market. Fate seemed to be conspiring against him. All his way into the east he had kept his head down, but now, here in Othil Ekrin, it seemed that the world had other ideas.

He wondered who this Kiafen might be. Given her mental skills she had clearly been very well trained. She was not of the Exentaser, nor of the Argedith, which left only one option, the worst of all. She was of the Balt Kaalith.

Or was she? If the Balt Kaalith knew that he was here, then they would have already moved to apprehend him.

He thought long and hard about it. Should he even return to his room? He decided he would not. Instead, he would hide himself elsewhere and watch. And if this Kiafen reappeared, he would show her another truth.

5

GIFTS OF PAIN

Mirith-iam Garur-imihd
Limihd-zas Ahzral-gemjer
Fe-in-od Dohim-lujaid
Krih-gembrin Chis-ouch-odvon
Oach-boa-ihs Om-l-vanzah
Voatrim-ihd Iolgem-ipoan
Ipur-jir Z-a-drpan

He stood upon a high wall, his armour about him and his arms folded across his chest. He stood in plain sight, but he was utterly invisible. Opposite was his room, and from here he could see everything – those that entered the hostelry, those that left, those that might enter his room and those that might wait outside, looking up.

After leaving the market he had found a small alley to hide in whilst he awoke his armour. Then, invisible, he had made his way back to the hostelry by the speediest route and found himself a decent vantage point. Now he waited and watched.

Since he had begun his watch, he had seen nothing untoward. Everything looked innocent enough, as far as he could tell, but he would not relax his guard, not even for a moment. If the day revealed nothing, then let him see what the night might provide.

He pondered the problem of Kiafen. Now that he had time to think he realised that she had been goading him. But why? For some reason he thought of Ralir and how he used to chide him when they duelled.

'You are too easy to anger!' Ralir had said. 'All I have to do is goad you and you rise up like fire. And that is why you lose.'

Yes, it was all too true. And that made him even more suspicious. Did someone here know him?

He looked skywards. There was a great golden wedge of cloud up there, rearing its lonely mass over Othil Ekrin. Look at it, staring down upon the world, watching him as he watched it in turn. Strung across the cerulean vault, the cloud leaned over the world, unconcerned and abstract. He smiled. You could not hurry clouds, or goad them, as they would do what they would do and the troubles of the world worried them not one whit.

The day turned to evening and then to night. Though the lights of the city were bright, the shadows were all but impenetrable. He flicked his gaze from hiding place to hiding place and was suddenly certain that someone was down there now, looking up and watching his window. He quartered the ground. In one place he found a shadow deeper than the rest. That was it.

Korfax fingered the pommel of his sword, and it moaned quietly back at him.

"Shall we?" he asked it, gesturing below.

It did not answer, but he felt the air about him thicken with expectation. That was enough for him. He stepped down from the wall and made his way back to the streets below.

A shadow stood within a shadow, and Korfax watched it as he approached. There was a figure there, utterly still, like some forgotten statue. He moved silently off at an angle. He would come up behind them and then he would see what he would see.

He crept closer, senses alert for the slightest change, but the watcher did not move. He came up behind them and raised his hand. The watcher suddenly ducked and rolled. Some sound, some tiny sound, the merest breath of air, had given him away. The watcher did not attack, though, and Korfax caught himself at the moment of moving, remaining exactly where he was.

From shadow to shadow they went, a blur of noiseless motion, before peering backwards and forwards, looking carefully all about, but Korfax already knew that he could not be seen; his armour could defeat even the sharpest eyes. So he waited whilst the watcher moved silently to another place of vigil before following as slowly and as quietly as he could. This time, though, he did not wait as before, but let his hand fall as soon as he was within reach.

The watcher moved at the last moment, falling away and lashing out with an armoured foot. Korfax dodged the foot and punched with his other hand, aiming for the head, only to find that the watcher had moved again and that he would miss. But his reach was long, and he caught the watcher's shoulder instead. That was enough. The watcher dropped and tumbled.

Korfax leapt over the tumbling body and turned, covering all avenues of escape. He undid the power of his armour and stepped out of the air.

The cloaked figure looked up to find him already standing over them. Korfax remained where he was and looked down, letting all the small details flow through his awareness. There was a sense of subterfuge in the air, as though everything – the clothing, the stance, the actions – was designed to mislead the senses. Korfax tensed and then relaxed. He had guessed aright.

"Well?" he said. "I have unmasked you, Noqvoan. Stand up slowly and carefully, and be aware that I know much concerning your abilities. Certain muscles you will not tense, certain movements you will not make, or I will put you down again. And I will not be so gentle a second time."

The cloaked figure stood up slowly.

"You do not fight fairly," came a voice. "I would like to know how you do that disappearing trick of yours."

The voice was light but husky. To a less practised ear it sounded nothing like the voice of one Ialdek Rom Kiafen, but Korfax was certain he could hear the faintest echoes all the same. He smiled.

"Say all the right things and I may tell you. Remove your hood, Kiafen."

The cloaked figure did so, letting the mantle part to reveal a lithe and slim body, feminine curves accentuated by the all-enclosing uniform of the Balt Kaalith. Her face was set hard and she looked angry, but even her anger was powerless to change the nature of her eyes, for they were large and delicate and Korfax found himself staring into them for long moments, struck by their strange innocence.

"I know you," he said, "and yet I do not. How strange is that?"

She raised an eyebrow.

"But I know you."

Korfax smiled slightly.

"And who does not? Well, say your piece; accuse me of treachery, call me a murderer, say all the things that you need to say. I care not."

"But nothing is ever that simple, Korfax of the Farenith. I have heard another tale concerning you."

"Oh?" he said.

She folded her arms in front of her.

"Yes. The tale that I heard has you as the victim of a conspiracy and a fugitive from subverted law. And that is a matter of the greatest concern to one of the Balt Kaalith."

"And who told you this tale?"

"No!" she replied brusquely. "It is my turn to ask a question. Why are you here?"

He hardened his gaze.

"I have no interest in answering your questions. You are here to answer mine. You have been bested, Noqvoan. To the victor the spoils."

She unfolded her arms and readied herself as though preparing to flee.

"I can be gone in moments," she told him, "and with you unable to follow. You dare not use your abilities in this place, as any of the Dar Kaadarith or the Exentaser would see you in an instant."

Korfax smiled again, but it was a colder smile this time.

"But I have picked up many another talent since my encounter with the Velukor's justice. I could follow you whichever way you chose to go, without anyone, including you, being the wiser. You have already experienced something of that, I think."

And then, to make the point, he vanished entirely, took a step sideways and then reappeared again.

She gasped briefly at the transition but quickly remembered herself. She looked askance at him and frowned.

"Well, it seems that, for the moment at least, I must submit. I cannot equal such deceits. But do not think that sight is the only sense I possess. We of the Balt Kaalith have abilities that you do not even suspect."

Korfax shrugged.

"I do not doubt it. So I grant you a boon. Let us play your game of question and answer. However, my only condition is that each of us must answer both fully and truthfully. No omissions and no obfuscations."

"I agree," she said. "Now answer my question."

"You already know the answer," he told her. "I hunt Doagnis."

She did not smile, but she did relax her expression somewhat.

"That is what I thought," she said.

Korfax stepped forward, menacing.

"And from whom did you hear it?" he demanded. "I told very few what I was about. Who have you interrogated?"

Instead of backing away, she held up her hands in the gesture of placation.

"It is not what you think," she said. "A friend told me."

"What friend?"

"Someone I know well. I gave them my word I would not speak of this to another. I now give it to you."

Korfax withdrew again.

"So that is it. Then you must be Adavor!"

There was no reaction, and Korfax felt a momentary sense of chagrin. When she cared to exert it, her control was excellent.

"No," she chided. "My turn now! What have you learned since you slipped the Velukor's justice?"

Korfax clenched his jaw.

"We do not have the luxury of boundless time," he said.

"The game no longer pleases you? But you set the rules!" she accused. "Come now, do as you said that you would and answer me."

Korfax walked over to a nearby wall and rested his hands upon the old stone.

"To tell you what I know will take most of the night," he said.

"I am patient," she returned. "The night is not yet old."

"But it will be by the time I have finished," he told her. "This tale touches on many things, some of which it will not be easy for you to hear."

"I am used to uncomfortable truths."

Korfax turned and stared at her, fully this time, and she backed away from the sudden fire in his eyes.

"You do not know what you are saying," he said. "How much terror can you bear?"

Then he advanced upon her, and though she turned to run he caught her arm, staring down at her, peering within as if gauging her capacity for revelation. She withstood his burning gaze as best as she could, but it was difficult. He was far too bright, far too dark and powerful. But she would not relent. She had always tested herself against such limits, so she tested herself once more and dared his gaze.

"Tell me, Korfax," she challenged. "Confess to me, reveal it all."

The light in his eyes burned even more fiercely for a moment, piercing even her shadows, but then he turned away again and dimmed his fire. He let go of her.

"Reveal it all?" he said. "I am not sure you know what that will cost you. I see the desire in you, to dare the fire, to dare the burning, but when it comes in the end know that you will still be unprepared. That is how it is with those of us who dare, though. None of us knows what it will cost."

He looked back at her.

"So be it, Noqvoan, I will tell you. Then you will wish that I had not."

He took a deep breath as though bracing himself for an ordeal. Then he began.

It became easier as he spoke, telling of the deaths of Asvoan and Abrilon, of his fight with Torzochil and the pursuit of Doagnis into the caverns beneath the Leein Komsel. He told her of the visit to his chambers by Ash-Mir. He spoke of his fall and his escape, but when he got to the death of Obelison, he stopped.

She was standing beside him now, looking up into his eyes. He could see the signs. His tale had begun to bind her to him. She could see the truth of it and she was greatly stirred. Her face had become altogether naked now, as though she had dropped all her masks.

"I think I begin to understand," she said. "But you must go on, Korfax. Such woe as I hear in your voice, such grief, it will only darken your soul if you keep it in the shadow. Tell it all and lighten your burden."

"So easy to say," he answered, "but so hard to do."

He looked down at her, the beginnings of tears in his eyes.

"Before I continue, at least admit to me that you are Adavor."

She smiled at last and her smile gentled her face even as it gentled him.

"I am," she admitted. "It is as you thought."

Then she hardened once more.

"Though I would like to know how you knew it."

Korfax smiled back at her.

"It is part of my tale," he said.

He spoke on, describing what happened upon the Lee Leiulus. He watched her darken as he spoke of Onehson's perfidy.

"Hard, you said!" she looked down. "Hard indeed."

"You think that the worst of it?" he asked.

"There is more?" she looked up again, clearly incredulous.

"Oh yes."

He told her of his flight to Othil Admaq, Ralir's aid and his description of

Adavor's mission to the land of the heretics. Adavor stopped him again.

"So Ralir told you? He gave me his word he would not speak of this. Who else has he told?"

"No one," Korfax answered. "I can assure you of that at least. He would not break his word lightly. I think he had a deeper intent. I think he wanted us to meet."

Adavor looked out over the city.

"Then I suppose I must be satisfied, but I will be having stern words with him when I see him next."

"But you found me all the same. Did he not get word to you that I might be coming?"

"It was pure chance," she told him. "I happened to be at the gate when you arrived."

"Why?"

She softened her gaze again.

"I will tell you after you finish your tale. So you followed my trail to Lonsiatris?"

"Yes," he replied, and then he went on to describe the journey and his encounter with Tahamoh, Samor and Dialyas. Adavor listened intently as Korfax told her of the mission placed upon him by Dialyas.

"This tale is winding its way to some momentous conclusion. Here is deep water."

Korfax laughed bitterly.

"Deep indeed. Did you know that the disappearance of Lonsiatris was my fault? I brought him back the Kapimadar, a stone created to ride the arrow of time. Dialyas used it to escape the world."

Adavor scowled.

"You of the Dar Kaadarith never did know when to stop!"

"Actually," he said, "there you are wrong. We did know. The Kapimadar was declared a failure despite the fact that it was not, and Dialyas was accused of blasphemy. It was why he was cast from the Dar Kaadarith. But the Kapimadar, even the disappearance of Lonsiatris, is incidental to this tale and I am ahead of myself. There are things you will hear now that I must ask you to keep secret until such time as I reveal them myself."

"Indeed?"

"I mean this, Adavor. This is life and death for me. You must swear it, on your word of honour, that the information I am about to divulge goes no further. You can tell others what you please about Doagnis, but not me. Yes?"

Adavor continued to scowl but she nevertheless acquiesced with a quick bow of her head.

"Then, in the name of the Creator," she told him, "you have my word."

Korfax bowed to her.

"I thank you for that small mercy at least."

She looked puzzled now, as though her answer did not merit such a response. But he did not give her time to interrupt further and went on with his tale, describing how he discovered the dark secret that his family had kept for seven thousand years. He watched Adavor's face as her emotions tumbled out from her, falling one by one across her face. She went from sympathy, to astonishment, to horror and then finally to fear. She even stepped back from him, staring all the while with wide eyes as though he had just prophesied her death. Korfax stayed still and let his story work its way inside her. Eventually she broke the silence.

"You are descended from Sondehna?" she whispered. "Your line is born of the Black Heart?"

He bowed his head.

"This is too much," she said, "too much. How can I contain such a revelation?"

He held up a finger.

"You gave me your word," he reminded her. "And you gave it before the Creator."

She looked down.

"But I cannot contain this."

She took a long breath before meeting his gaze again.

"Who else knows?" she asked.

"My mother, as does Baschim, the house Balzarg," he answered. "A few upon Lonsiatris heard me proclaim it, and Geyadril Ponodol knows it also. I confessed it to him first."

"And what did he say?"

"He was as shocked as you are now. And if it hadn't been for the attack upon Emethgis Vaniad, this knowledge might have become more widely known."

"Why?"

"There were many to whom my family owed an explanation. Why did we remain secluded in the north? Why did my father refuse to become Geyadril even though he merited such an estate a thousand times over?"

Adavor stared into the distance for a moment.

"But why do you burden me with this? What relevance has this to Doagnis?"

Korfax turned away and looked again at the city.

"I tell you this in order to prepare you for a greater revelation. You have yet to discover just how deep this goes."

With that, Korfax revealed the heritage of Doagnis.

"This time it really is too much," Adavor said. "If any other had told me this I would never have believed them. Doagnis is a descendant of Sondehna? Sondehna was descended from Nalvahgey? Deep water indeed. Our world is on the edge of an abyss, our enemies defeat us at every turn and suddenly the inheritors of the empire of the Iabeiorith appear again, the children of the darkest Ell ever to grace the Bright Heavens. We could drown in such waters, Korfax, we could sink without trace."

They stood side by side and stared out over the city. But Adavor ever and again turned her gaze back to Korfax, studying him as if his face had become a map she was compelled to comprehend. After several such glances he finally spoke.

"It does not work, does it?"

She blinked.

"What does not work?"

"Me, born of the Black Heart." He stared into the night, eyes abstracted. "From all the tales that I have ever heard about him, not once have I thought to myself that I would act as he did. I share nothing with him, nothing at all, except my blood."

"But how did you know what I was thinking?" she asked. "I did not feel you in my mind."

"It was obvious," he replied. "You kept looking from me to the city and back again. The question was written all over you."

He turned to her and gave her the most searching look she had ever experienced in her life. Not even in her harshest lessons had anyone punished her so. She tried to look away but he persisted, pinning her to herself. What was he looking for?

It ended as suddenly as it had begun. He released her. She stared up at him for many moments, trying to understand. Then she saw it. He had seen her fear, of him, of the darkness, and now he judged her in that light.

"You are right to fear," he told her. "The Farenith have ever been loyal, as steadfast as the northern stars. Few other noble families can claim as much. We were made by Azmeloh, made in gratitude for a life preserved. We were honoured by Anolei, for mighty deeds. Every single Velukor, from the earliest to the last, has taken comfort in the loyalty and the faith of the Farenith, but if such faith can be so misplaced, what else might have been missed down all the long years? What else might not now rise up to take its due?"

"But that is exactly why your tale is so terrifying," she said. "Your house has been the very word of service, and yet look at the secret it has kept. That such things can be hidden!"

She looked down for a moment and then caught his eye again.

"Is there much more to your tale?" she asked.

"Yes, there is, but nothing so dire or so dangerous as that which I have already revealed. I went back to Lonsiatris after the fall of Emethgis Vaniad. I did not linger, I could not, not even when horror covered her stones. I had to go back to Lonsiatris and give Dialyas the Kapimadar. I told both him and Samor what I had discovered, and they were not surprised by my heritage. It seems that the prophecies of Nalvahgey had already revealed my coming. But they did not know the history of Doagnis. I think that shocked Dialyas more than anything, though not enough to put him aside from his purpose. He collected himself enough to tell me where I might find her. So I told him to fulfil his part of the bargain and help preserve our people. After that I went off in pursuit of Doagnis and left him to do what he would."

Korfax suddenly grimaced.

"And that was when I learnt the true nature of his betrayal. As I left the isle, I saw it disappear right in front of my eyes. Dialyas was true to his word, after a fashion. He used the Kapimadar and saved our people, just not all of them. Where Lonsiatris is now, I do not know. Dialyas has fled the world. There is no curse dark enough that will assuage the fire that burns in me now."

He looked down.

"One more thing. The great wave that destroyed Thilzin Jerris was born of that leaving. To preserve Lonsiatris the southern shores were cleared of life. Dialyas should answer for that also. He knew what would happen once the Kapimadar was awakened."

He bowed his head once more.

"So there it is, the tale. Ever since then I have been following one lead after another. Doagnis knows she is being pursued, and she has set traps accordingly, but I have evaded them. She does not know that it is me."

"And so you seek her here," Adavor mused. "I know where she is."

"She is still in the city?"

"Yes, I have her. And that was why I was at the gate, watching for new arrivals to her cause. She has many of her people in the city now. I was about to alert my guild, but your presence and your tale change everything."

"How so?"

"I am thinking that one should fight fire with fire. She is powerful, certainly, and my order would be hard pressed to take her. Perhaps another way might be better. You have fought her before."

"You would ally yourself to me? Then lead me to her. Let me bring her down."

"But should I?"

"I am the only one that can match her."

"Are you? You missed her before."

"But I did not know then what I know now. I know her lore."

"Profane lore."

"Even so."

"But there is another reason."

"No!"

"I think there is."

"So what might it be?"

"Revenge!"

He sighed.

"I have scores to settle, but what of it? We all have scores to settle."

"As I thought," she said. "It is why I hesitate, amongst other things. I am not sure that I want the flame of vengeance at my back."

"I have full mastery of my passions," he told her.

"And what idle boast is that?" she returned. "Did you have such mastery when Onehson claimed your betrothed? Did you have such mastery when your father died in your stead?"

"ENOUGH!"

Black flame erupted about Korfax, running over his black armour and up into the air. It subsided slowly, but it left behind it a stain. Darkness now blackened the air where he stood like an echo, a shadow that moved as he did. Adavor crouched, ready to flee. Korfax looked alien to her now, a mask of flesh hanging from a stone-carved skull, bereft of spirit, or yet transcending it. What had she awoken with her rash words?

"How dare you!" he said to her. She watched as he pulled himself back from the brink.

"Who would remain unchanged by such events? Do you judge me so harshly?"

She dropped her gaze and stood up slowly.

"No, Of course I do not."

"But you do," he replied. "I have seen you. I have seen what you require. I have seen the heart of the Balt Kaalith. I must prove myself worthy."

He clenched himself, held himself still, eyes glittering.

"So be it!" he hissed reluctantly. "We will meet when you have decided how we should proceed. I will await your judgement."

He turned about and walked away. Adavor remained where she was, swallowed by doubt.

"Wait!" she cried out at last.

He waited, a shadow within shadows.

"Could we not meet upon the morrow?" she offered.

"Where?"

She struggled for an answer.

"Below the ninth tower?" she suggested. "Upon the Nazarth Ialdiss?"

"When?"

"At the turning of Safaref?"

"So be it!" he replied.

He stood a moment, looking at her, gauging her perhaps, but then he was gone, turning about, consumed at last by the darkness she had awoken.

Korfax stood at his window and gazed out over the city. There was a feeling of thunder in the air, as though a storm was brewing. Had he caused this?

He looked up at the early morning sky and frowned. There were no clouds at all. It was clear from east to west, filled only with the emerging blue of day and scattered sparingly with the last of the fading stars, dying flames of carmine and amber.

His armour and his sword lay where he had left them, in the furthest corner, lying carelessly amongst the periapts he had lifted from the ancient chest.

He stared at them all with distrust, but then he reached for his armour and partially awoke it. He bade it hide everything, all of it. The corner appeared empty now, as empty as it had been before his arrival. Nothing remained in the light. Keep it dark, he told himself, keep it secret.

He turned back to the window and thought of black fires. Where had they come from, those energies, rising unbidden at the testing words of Adavor? They felt too much like the fires he had unleashed upon the wall of Othil Zilodar. Visions of fiery holocausts swam in his head. This was not what he had expected at all. Where did such power dwell? Was he the master of himself, or were his powers the master of him? Dark questions sat upon him and burned him with their touch.

He must calm himself. He must control himself. What was the final test? Was it not power? He must not succumb to it! He must never submit to its siren call, otherwise he would become a beast, just as Samor had said.

Korfax turned his thoughts to the oncoming day. He must bathe and prepare, so he stripped off all his clothes and washed them in the adjoining room. Then he washed himself in turn, scrubbing hard at his flesh. He was tired of the dirt and the grime, but his need to cleanse himself went far deeper than that.

He had used the Namad Mahorelah, both with and without intent. It was as he had feared from the very beginning. The further he went on this journey, the more compromises he made. The old morality by which he had lived his life was being slowly eroded away, piece by subtle piece. What came next? The summoning of demons to do his will? Korfax shuddered. He hoped it would never come to that. Visions of vengeful Vovin clouded his mind.

After washing he donned the simple robe he had purchased and stood at the window again, pondering what to do next. Adavor was out there, somewhere. Was she gazing out over the waking world even as he did now, deciding what next to do also? Was she wondering whether she could trust him? Or was she thinking perhaps that it would be better if the Balt Kaalith alone tried to take down Doagnis? That would be a bad decision, the worst of them all. Doagnis would see the Balt Kaalith even as they learned of her whereabouts. No one was her equal in this, no one but himself.

He had seen her traps at first hand, and they were impressive. No other would have been able to escape them, but where Korfax was concerned Doagnis was out of her reckoning. He possessed powers of which she knew nothing – and that was where his advantage lay: her ignorance would be her downfall.

An old aphorism came to him, something Ralir had told him long ago, something whipped almost daily into the unforged of the Nazad Esiask. That which you cannot foresee will be the death of you. Korfax smiled, but then he dropped it just as quickly. There was another smile in the room; he could feel it, and the smile was behind him.

His first instinct was to turn, but he did not; instead, he probed gently with his mind to see who, if anyone, had entered his room. So it was only with mild surprise that he felt two minds behind him – not one – two minds possessed of a most familiar flavour. He readied himself, but before he could turn to the attack a dart slammed into his right arm, throwing him aside.

He staggered and the world staggered with him. The dart was poisoned and the venom was already doing its work. He stared back, tracing the flight of the dart to its origin. Balt Kaalith, as he had thought.

One held a sword, a light and long miamna. The other was similarly armed, but also held a small dart thrower, which was empty. Korfax wondered for a moment how potent the drug was and whether he had time to do anything about it, but then he remembered that this was the Balt Kaalith he was confronting, and they left very little to chance.

The shorter of the two smiled as though he saw what Korfax was thinking. Korfax recognised his face at least. It was Naaomir, the adversary from his trial.

"Good, you are ours once more."

Naaomir smiled a little wider.

"You seem somewhat changed since we last met. I would have had difficulty recognising you had I not been expecting you."

He gestured at himself.

"Just as you were clearly not expecting me."

Korfax did not move a muscle but continued to stare at Naaomir, who for his part paused for a moment, perhaps waiting for a rejoinder. As the silence lengthened though, his expression tightened. Finally he gestured at his companion.

"This is Noqvoan Okodon. Be assured she is most capable in all the ways of our order. You have no choice. You will surrender everything to us and place yourself in our care, or you will be compelled."

Korfax flicked his gaze at Okodon and then back to Naaomir. He briefly wondered whether Adavor had betrayed him after all, but he could not see it. That was not who she was, or he was no judge of character at all. His best option was to say nothing, so he contented himself with staring back at Naaomir with as much contempt as he could muster. But Naaomir did not care. He was far too full of himself. He clearly believed that he had already considered every conceivable contingency.

"If you are weighing up options for escape," he said, "I suggest that you discount them entirely. Many Balt Kaalith are here with me. There is no way out. Your abilities as a Geyadril of the Dar Kaadarith will not avail you. Besides, the poison in the dart is well on its way to robbing you of your senses, so what could you do?"

Korfax tested Naaomir's claim, by trying to control his failing muscles, but it was useless, as they were no longer his to control. He sagged against the wall and tried to focus his eyes. He stared at the bed, the floor and his hand, but his body was slowly betraying him. He cast a sour glance back at Naaomir. His tongue felt clumsy and slow.

"There are far more important things happening in this city at the moment, Naaomir."

Korfax could hear himself. He sounded stupid, or drunk. Naaomir walked carefully to the door that led to the other room and glanced inside, before turning back to Korfax and walking slowly towards him.

"If you are referring to Doagnis and the mission of Adavor," he said, "then do not concern yourself with it any further. We know all there is to know. Many loose strands have come together in this place. All we had to do was gather them up."

Korfax did not miss the boastful tone in Naaomir's voice.

"You were seen leaving Thilzin Jerris, and Adavor has been watched ever since she began to follow Doagnis; in fact, her interest in you is what led us here."

He stepped closer.

"We watch everything," he said. "So be assured that when Noqvoan Adavor comes before us again she will learn of our great displeasure. We take the dereliction of duty very seriously. That she pursues Doagnis is one thing, but that she does not inform us concerning you is another matter entirely. She is far too independent, a taker of risks. We do not approve of such things."

Korfax would have sneered, but his mouth had gone slack. Naaomir liked the sound of his own voice far too much.

"So that is how we have you," Naaomir continued. "You should have expected this. You, better than any other, should know us. We do not give up, and we leave little to chance. Like your capture, for example."

Naaomir now stood within a sword's length of Korfax and his blade was pointing straight at Korfax's stomach.

"And so to the house of justice!" he intoned, smiling all the while as Korfax began to lose his battle with the poison.

It closed in on him from all sides – dark walls ready to take away all that he was. He tried to fight it off, but to no avail. Naaomir's smile widened as he slid down the wall, and Korfax was unconscious before he hit the floor.

He awoke in a cell. There was a light in the ceiling and there was a door. The ceiling was high, higher than he could reach, and the door was almost invisible, with only the faintest of lines apparent where it joined with the wall. There was no furniture in the room, just a piradar set in the ceiling, lighting the stone with a faint yellow light. There was a small pot in one corner and a stone basin in the other. Korfax peered at the basin. There was some water in it and a stone faucet above it. The cell was much like those beneath the Umadya Levanel.

He stood up. He was naked and there was a faint mark on his arm where the dart had hit him. He walked to the door and ran his hands over the stone. It felt very solid and thick and he had the impression it would take a great deal of power to shatter it. He folded his arms. It was not completely hopeless; they still thought him just a Geyadril of the Dar Kaadarith, but he was far more than that now. He had studied the writings of Sondehna quite thoroughly and there were certain ways within them as to how he might effect an escape.

There were demons one could summon that could shatter stone, but he did not like that idea. What a blunt statement that would be. Then there were certain energies that could do the same, but he was unsure how much control he would have over them. Then there was the waiting place.

Waiting places existed as holes in the very fabric of the Mahorelah, small islands of calm to which the cornered could flee. Their only disadvantage lay in their impermanence. One could not stay within them for ever and one would always return to the place one had left. They were the last resort of the desperate.

Korfax shuddered as he realised the terrible temptation. He had once promised himself that he would not do this, not unless there was no choice. But then he asked himself: what choice did he have here?

It was as he was pondering his options that the door opened, sliding inwards on noiseless hinges. Naaomir stood there and behind him were two others – one was Okodon, tall and slim and silent, but the other he did not recognise. She was shorter, like Naaomir, and she looked strong, with bright eyes and a dark complexion. Korfax could not place her features and wondered from where it was she came.

Naaomir looked Korfax up and down and then smiled faintly.

"I would wager that you are still thinking of escape," he said. "Do not waste your time with such idleness. You cannot escape us as you did in Emethgis Vaniad."

Korfax moved back and leant against the far wall.

"Might I have some clothing?" he asked.

"No, you may not!" Naaomir said. "You will remain exactly as you are. I am not unmindful of your skills or your determination. We will not provide you with anything that could possibly be used to help you escape."

"So then, what now?"

Naaomir turned to the other two.

"Okodon is here to administer a preparation from various rare herbs that will help us learn the truth from you. And be certain that we will subdue you, should you become fractious. Turiam is here to interrogate you. You will tell her everything that you know, but if at any point she detects the slightest hint of evasion on your part, she has my permission to use a miradar."

As if to prove the point, Turiam held up a crystal with an angry red centre. Korfax unfolded his arms and came forward, staring at the crystal. He had heard of them, of course, but he had never seen one before. Nor had he ever expected to.

"A miradar?" he gasped. He did not hide his outrage. Turiam held a pain stone, a stone whose only purpose was the gift of agony.

"I did not know that any still remained in the world," he said. "Have the Balt Kaalith sunk so low? The Dar Kaadarith made only a few, and then only reluctantly. They are an outrage! Come the time of the repudiation, they were all collected and destroyed in our furnaces, or so it was said. Where did you get that one?"

The look on his face was such that Okodon immediately raised her dart thrower. Naaomir turned about to stop her, placing a hand over the thrower. He looked back over his shoulder at Korfax.

"An outrage?" he questioned. "You dare such accusations? You, a murderer and a renegade? You are the last one to accuse us of anything!"

He snarled with displeasure.

"Choose your next words carefully, traitor!"

Korfax all but ground his teeth together.

"Choose my words with care?" he hissed. "And when did we ever resort to torture and potions? The last people to engage in such activities were those who hunted out the last of Sondehna's forces. And their actions were universally proscribed, when it eventually became known what they had perpetrated in their zeal. Your order nearly fell that day, Naaomir. The repudiation could well have seen the end of the Balt Kaalith for ever. Choose my words with care? Miradar are an abomination. The Dar Kaadarith should never have made them!"

The light in Korfax's eyes was now piercing. Both Okodon and Turiam stepped backwards, disconcerted despite their advantage, but Naaomir stood his ground.

"You will not turn me aside," he said. "We employ the unprecedented because you are unprecedented. No Geyadril of the Dar Kaadarith has ever been declared renegade before. No seer could probe you, no mind overthrow you. We know that much at least."

"And there you are wrong!" Korfax told him. "Urendril Samor did exactly that and declared me innocent."

"Samor? What paltry lie is this?"

"No lie. I went to Lonsiatris. You know that I did. She was there, and she declared me innocent."

Naaomir smiled.

"I do so enjoy it when my charges betray themselves," he said. "That is precisely what I wanted to hear. Now I know which questions to ask."

"What do you mean?" asked Korfax.

"It was reported to us that you went there, and it was reported that you came back, riding out the flood born of the disappearance of Lonsiatris. You went to see Dialyas."

"You will get nothing further from me!"

Naaomir gestured easily.

"Be assured that I will, with or without your cooperation. Submit, Korfax, or you will be compelled."

Korfax drew himself up.

"So compel me," he said.

Without warning he sent the full weight of his mind at Naaomir, who staggered under the assault, falling to the floor with a scream on his lips. Turiam stared in disbelief, caught where she was by shock, but Okodon was made of sterner stuff. She fired her dart and Korfax felt the world about him dissolve into blackness.

He awoke to find himself upon a cold stone slab. There was a bitter taste in his mouth. He ran his tongue over his lips. They had forced him to drink something, perhaps that potion of rare herbs Naaomir had mentioned.

He could not move. His wrists and ankles, his neck and stomach, were all held by something hard and unyielding. He tested his bonds for a moment, but then Naaomir's face appeared above him, looking down.

"Yes, you have been given the potion," he said. "It takes some moments to work, but I am assured that it is most potent. The walls of your rebellion will succumb to it soon, I think."

Naaomir licked his lips, a look of satisfaction on his face.

"But before it takes you entirely, I thought I should tell you what is in my heart. The fires that are to consume you were brought upon you by yourself. You, Korfax, are ill. Though your body be whole, your mind and your spirit drown in sickness. Though you may curse us, we know what you really need. And you should be grateful for the burning, for only by the agony can you know redemption. For such as you, Korfax, the Balt Kaalith are salvation, not damnation."

Korfax lay upon the floor, his head still buzzing from the effects of the truth potion and the pain stone. He was back in his cell, a brief respite before they came for him again.

Though he hated to admit it, Turiam was good at what she did. If he had not been as strong as he was, she would have broken him by now. It was not easy to focus under the twin assaults of the poison and the pain, but somehow he had managed it, though it had cost him dear. The poison blurred the boundaries of the real with the unreal and made him all the more vulnerable to the pain. Just fighting it hurt.

Questions buzzed in his mind as the room about him swirled. It was almost as if he was back upon the cold slab, tied down, unable to move, whilst Turiam's disembodied face hovered above him, demanding, always demanding, the truth.

"The Velukor told us that he slew you. How did you escape?"

Even as the question echoed inside him he was back upon the Lee Leiulus, this time wrestling with the corpse of Doanazin over the body of Obelison, whilst Agdoain howled and swarmed below.

"You were seen stealing the Kapimadar. What did you do with it?"

Now he was in the Hall of Memory deep below the Umadya Semeiel and all the stones were filled with the mocking face of Dialyas, laughing at him with eyes of mad fire.

"You were seen riding out the great flood that destroyed Thilzin Jerris. What happened?"

Waters filled the room, waters in which the dead swirled. But all of them turned their sightless eyes upon Korfax as they swept on by, and they screamed at him through their dead mouths.

It is a lie, he kept telling himself, all a lie, whilst he hugged his secrets close to his chest and grappled with the fire that rippled over his body, up and down, up and down.

Come the end he was certain he heard Naaomir calling out from a distant place, calling for more potion and pain stones. He felt the beginnings of despair. They could pile on the pressure and the pain, day in, day out, and reduce his mind to a nub, if they so chose. Who would not fail under such an assault? He was doomed.

"My turn now, I'm thinking!"

Korfax pulled himself up and stared about his cell. That damnable poison they had made him drink still had a few illusions left to it.

"Who said that?" he called out.

"I did," came the voice again, just as the light in the piradar above him dimmed and went out.

Another light appeared in its place, less constant, a spread of flames licking over the stone of his cell. The light ran over the walls and the ceiling, the cold reflection of a paler fire. The fire intensified and something darker rose up from within, something burnt and blackened.

It moved towards him and Korfax drew himself back as far back as he could. He was appalled. Though it walked like an Ell and talked like an Ell, it had been broken almost beyond recognition. He felt his own pain pail into insignificance in comparison. This being should not even have had the power to rise at all, let alone walk with such purpose into his cell.

It was ripped and ragged, and it strode out of the pale flames as though from distances immeasurable. The flesh, where it still clung, was black and cracked, as if it had long cooked in a furnace, whilst the body was twisted and warped, as though great hands had wrenched it this way and that. Even its bones had been burnt, those that still remained, for there were gaping holes where entire portions had been torn out. But even now it still held itself proudly erect, and the pale flames in its empty sockets stared back at Korfax with utter contempt.

"Well, if this is not the final insult then I do not know what could be," it said. "So I am to give succour to the unholy get of the Black Heart, am I? Fate is not without a sense of irony, it seems! My sins return to punish me a thousand-fold. No wonder I have not achieved the river. Kokazadah binds me still."

Korfax knew that voice and wished that he did not. Mathulaa!

"First Doanazin, now you!" he said. "I must be losing my mind."

The burnt skull looked about his cell for a moment and then grinned back at him.

"You are in danger of losing much more than your mind, I'm thinking," it said.

Korfax tried to keep his composure, but it was hard. This was twice now that he had confronted one of his dead.

"And are you here to lecture me also?" he asked.

"No, child, I do not 'lecture'," came the answer. "I am here to remind you of that which you appear to have forgotten."

"And what have I forgotten?"

The burnt figure drew back.

"I was warned that you would be like this," it said.

"Like what?" Korfax asked.

"Disbelieving! Doubting even your own senses!"

"But you cannot be here."

"After all that has happened? You, of all people, dare to say that? You paltry thing!"

The blind sockets in the burned skull all but fumed and their inner flames brightened to near incandescence.

"But no one speaks to the dead!" cried Korfax. It was almost a wail.

The shade of Mathulaa hissed in consternation and curled in upon itself, like a tightening knot.

"Do you even deny your own fear?" it asked.

Korfax bowed his head but said nothing.

"Well, that is that then, isn't it?" said the shade of Mathulaa. "Even I can do nothing about that. If you deny the body, you deny the spirit, and if you deny the spirit..? Leastways, that is what they told me when I was young. But times have changed since my day."

There came a sigh, and the burnt figure almost turned away before looking back sharply at Korfax.

"But I cannot leave until I tell you what I have been called upon to say," it continued. "You have forgotten something, you slave. And whether you acknowledge me or not, truth is truth."

"And what is it I have forgotten?" Korfax asked.

"You have forgotten what you can do with stone."

Korfax stared up at the terrible apparition. It leaned over him now, and the stink of burnt flesh filled the air. He shrank from it as far as he could, into the stone beneath him, whilst the skull of Mathulaa stared back down at him with its rictus grin, blackened and broken teeth in a lipless mouth.

"Do I horrify you, young one?" it asked. "Do I remind you of all the abominations your accursed ancestor committed?"

"But I did not do those things," said Korfax.

It drew back again.

"No!" it admitted. "You did not!"

It held up a black finger and curled it like a hook.

"But you should never forget it either," it told him. "You are not Sondehna, merely the last of his progeny. Though his blood flows in your veins, you are not him. Never give in to the temptation as he did. Never become the victim of your own power. Remember your oaths."

"Is that why you are here?" asked Korfax. "To berate me?"

"I have already told you my purpose. I am here to remind you."

"Of what?"

"Your ability with stone, you deaf thing. What can you do with it? Can you not change its purpose? Or have you forgotten that also?"

"What?"

Now Korfax was confused.

"Didn't you change your father's stave?" asked the shade. "What did Dialyas tell you? What did the Kapimadar do? Who forged it? Whose blood is it runs in your veins? The clues are all there in front of you. The answer, once seen, is obvious, I'm thinking."

"Now what are you saying? Dialyas? He played me like a puppet and then fled the world! Many died because of him. Why should I want anything of him?"

The shade clicked its fingers, a rattle of bones.

"Fled the world, has he? So much for Dialyas! But does that give the lie to his wisdom?"

"The wisdom of a coward and a betrayer?"

"Truth is truth, fool, no matter its source! I always thought the Dar Kaadarith only saw what pleased their vanity, or their preconceptions, whilst blithely dismissing the rest as heresy. Now I see the truth of it. It was ever thus."

"So what am I to do, then? Ignore what I was taught?"

The shade pounced, its broken mouth all but spitting flames.

"Exactly! Ignore what you were taught!" it hissed. "Break free of your cage!"

Korfax clasped his head in his hands.

"So you are telling me that Dialyas was right all along? That every flaw in every crystal opens up onto the very same void?"

The shade drew back and bared its blackened teeth as if in triumph.

"No, I am telling you nothing. All I am saying is that you should remember."

"Then if that is so, what does it mean to me?"

The shade glanced up at the piradar in the ceiling for a moment.

"And are you really so stupid that you cannot see what is right in front of you? Or are you as afraid of the truth as you are of me?"

Korfax looked at the shade of Mathulaa carefully and then at the piradar. What was this dead thing saying? That he could consciously change the nature of stone? But the purpose of the piradar was set, wasn't it? Then how had he changed his father's stave? Passion? Was that it? Passion under will? But passion was the fire that fuelled the Namad Mahorelah. The Namad Dar was the devotion of reason. A marriage of the two?

As if he could see what Korfax was thinking, the shade of Mathulaa bowed in apparent satisfaction.

"And so my time is done," it said. "I have said what I came here to say. Now it is up to you."

The flames died and the broken body departed. The last thing Korfax saw was a burnt mask, a furious mask of blackened bone, glaring back at him out of the failing fire.

For a long time Korfax remained where he was. Had it all been a dream after all? But it had felt so real. Did the stink of burnt flesh still ride the air about him, or was it only in his mind?

Eventually he stood up and looked at the piradar above. Could he – should he – touch it? For some reason he thought of those black flames he had called up. There was something inside him, something that had opened up at the death of his father. Was it the fracture? Was that where the power lay, under the words, beneath reason, deeper than instinct and below everything that he was? Perhaps it was this that spoke to him. It was time to find out.

He picked up the small pot from the corner of his cell and placed it, upside down, below the piradar. Then he stood upon it. He overbalanced twice, the last gasp of the potion they had fed him, but on his third attempt he managed to hold his position, stretching up, one finger barely touching the cold surface of the piradar above. It was lucky he was as tall as he was, for the pot he stood upon was quite short. He concentrated. Long moments passed.

Suddenly, and with a brief shower of dust, the piradar fell from the ceiling, breaking its bonds with the stone in which it had been set. Korfax was so surprised he almost didn't catch it. Then, with it clasped safely in his hands, he stepped down from the pot as though from a throne.

At first it had just been like touching any piradar, any piradar at all – cold stone, cold heart, unyielding to both flesh and thought. But then, as he had concentrated, a strange thing had happened. The piradar had suddenly lost its uniqueness. It had floated in his awareness for a while, him uncertain, it uncertain, a swirl of possibilities. Then it had changed, even as he began to rediscover his purpose within his very own surprise.

The feeling had almost been like the forging of a stave, but not quite. Korfax smiled down at the piradar as it nestled in his hand. This simple light, this tiny crystal, had suddenly become his saviour.

Whether Dialyas and the others had been right or not, it was clear to him now that any of the lesser stones produced by the Namad Dar could be used like staves, their original purpose overridden, their singular communication with the void within irrevocably altered. But only if the adept was strong enough. And if Korfax knew anything, he knew that he was strong.

He spent the next few moments practising with the changed piradar, learning its strengths and its limitations. It certainly did not make him a match for a wielder of a full stave, but it would still allow him to express himself with more than adequate potency.

Satisfied at last, he moved to the door. He held the piradar in his left hand and made a fist. He concentrated, summoning up earth of earth.

The piradar grew brighter, shining now through flesh and bone, a hand held star of the deepest yellow. The door shuddered. The door shook. Korfax intensified his will and his grip, and the door cracked with a snapping sound. He pounded his left hand against the door, again and again, fury mounting on fury, until the door could no longer contain the forces being hammered into it and crumbled at last, great fragments tumbling out into the corridor beyond. Clouds of dust billowed and a sharp choking smell filled the air. Korfax took a deep breath and stepped through the thinning cloud. He was out. He looked up the corridor and immediately found himself confronting two of the Balt Kaalith, their faces frozen in identical expressions of shock.

Korfax concentrated again and raised the piradar up high in his clenched fist. A great wind tore past him, picking them both up and dashing them against the furthest wall. He lowered his hand and the wind subsided. He felt a mad laugh bubble its way up from deep inside.

This was too much. What rules could he not defy? He suddenly felt like a very lord of creation. He stood amongst the rubble of the door and laughed until his ribs ached, whilst all the while the fire of his will burned in his left hand.

When he finally sobered he went to the fallen. He bent over their unconscious forms and studied them both. One was near enough his size, so Korfax quickly removed that one's uniform and donned it himself. Then, still clutching the piradar, he made for the exit.

Naaomir was staring out over the city from his high window when Okodon came to his door. Naaomir waited a moment before turning.

"Enter," he said.

Okodon walked in smartly, as she always did, but her face betrayed her dismay. Naaomir did not miss it.

"What is it?" he asked. "What has happened?"

Okodon swallowed but did not answer immediately. Naaomir felt the beginnings of trepidation. It must be bad.

"Well?" he pressed.

Okodon bowed.

"Noqvoandril," she said. "Our prisoner has escaped."

Naaomir did not move. He could not. He suddenly found himself in the presence of impossibilities. He shook for a moment, a tremor of his entire being like a rebellion. Then he clenched his hands at his side, quelling the sudden uprising, before looking back at Okodon again.

"How?" he asked eventually.

"We are not sure," she answered. "All we know is that he shattered the door of his cell and overpowered the guards. Both are still insensible. One of them was partially naked when found."

"Is that all?"

"No. The only other thing of note is that the piradar in the ceiling of his cell is also gone. It was forcibly removed."

Naaomir hissed through his teeth.

"Well now!" he said. "Here is something the Dar Kaadarith have hidden from the rest of us. Such a possibility has never, ever been hinted at in all the reports that I have ever heard or read. I thought only staves could be used in such a manner."

Naaomir walked away from the window until he stood directly in front of Okodon. He stared up into the eyes of his subordinate.

"We have erred, all of us," he told her. "We have underestimated our charge. Yet again our knowledge has been revealed as inadequate. That is twice now. It must not happen again."

He took a deep breath.

"Has Korfax left the tower?" he asked.

"I do not believe so," she answered. "He may have taken clothing, but he does not know the passwords or the rhythms in this place. He should be easy enough to spot. But how will we subdue him? He is a Geyadril, one of the mightiest. He can pull power from stone."

"Forget that for the moment. We will deal with it when we have to. Has the tower been sealed?"

"It was the very first thing that I did."

"That is something at least. Method is the key. Method will recapture our charge. From now onwards I want all to use the higher passwords and be ready at all times to submit to scrutiny. I want weapons to be drawn. I want systematic searches and guards on all the exits. Those are our weakest points. Come, let us rally our forces, you and I."

Naaomir strode from the room whilst Okodon followed in his wake like his shadow.

Korfax crouched under a great table in a large, but empty, room. In one hand he held a star of yellow, whilst his other touched the bare stone of the floor.

This place was like the city – a labyrinth, a maze. It was difficult to see an easy way out. Stone barred his exit, and more than stone. He withdrew his hand and sat back against one of the sturdy legs of the table. He looked at the piradar in his hand and sighed. It was not enough.

On the walls around him were more piradar, illuminating the room with a harsh light. Korfax grimaced. They were far too bright. The Balt Kaalith did not understand gentleness.

He came out from under the table and looked up at them for a moment, even as another idea formed in his mind. If he could make a piradar perform like a stave, why could he not make one perform like something else, something like a qasadar perhaps? He smiled darkly at the thought. What would the Balt Kaalith make of that?!

He went over to the nearest piradar. He touched it with his fingers, and, after a small pause, it came away from the wall. This was getting easier. Belief fuelled his ability. He smiled to himself, enjoying the brief thrill of power and weighing possibilities in his mind like worlds. Then he travelled the room, taking all the piradar that remained and placing them in one of the many pouches that hung from his belt. The only light in the room came from the window now, that and the dim light from the piradar in his left hand, the one he had turned into a stave.

From out of the pouch he drew another. He held that one up for a moment and concentrated, trying to conjure in his mind the dangerous instability that made qasadar so destructive. After long moments he could feel the forces gathering within its heart, that special touch of chaos he had come to know so well. Then, as the forces mounted beyond his control, he tossed the fraying stone against the opposite wall and ran from the room.

Out in the corridor he sprinted for the stairs, racing time and calamity. But it was only as he arrived at the next landing below that the piradar he had left behind at last gave vent to its mounting fury.

A shuddering roar shook the tower and the stone under his feet trembled. A great wind whipped past him, carrying with it swirling rock dust and the stink of destruction. The force of the blast threw him against the wall and almost toppled him down the stairs. But Korfax gleefully picked himself up again and laughed long and loud. It had worked. It would all work. Now let the Balt Kaalith beware indeed. His egress from this place of torture had suddenly become far simpler. Closed gates would be opened, doors would be broken and nothing would be able to stand in his way. He continued on his way down to the main exit, holding his first piradar above his head so that it would light his way.

Genadol, second Geyadril of Othil Ekrin, sat by his window and read. Bright words floated in the air before him, languorous motes competing with the brightness of the day.

The treatise he had raised was a discussion on the use of the Namad Dar by the Agdoain. It was one of many such works now populating the archives of the Dar Kaadarith, and like all the others it was far from conclusive.

Genadol flicked the logadar with his mind and the words vanished. He looked out of the window and peered into the distance. Over there, far to the west, battle was engaged. Not for the first time he wished all possible success to the son of his prince. There was no news yet, nor would there be for a while, and like many in the tower he wished he had been one of those chosen to go.

A distant sound rumbled across the city. Genadol stood up. It was so alien, so unexpected, that he was a moment recognising it. Was that thunder? But the sky was clear! What was it?

Almost at the same time there came a knock on his door. He turned.

"Enter," he said.

Thilnor came in, breathing hard.

"Have you been running?" Genadol asked.

"Geyadril," said Thilnor, "there is something I must tell you."

Genadol gestured at the window.

"There was a sound I heard a moment ago," he said. "It sounded like thunder. Is that why you are here?"

Thilnor looked perplexed.

"No, Geyadril, that wasn't why I came to you," he said. "I came to ask you if you felt it just now."

"Felt what?"

"That stab of power."

Genadol frowned. Power? He stepped forward.

"No, I did not. What is this?"

"It happened a moment ago," Thilnor said. "Perhaps that is what you heard. I was down in the forges when I felt it. Udenar felt it, too, but he did not recognise it. It was a sudden stab of power, like a forging. But I have felt it before. There is only one person I know of that wields their power like that. Korfax is in the city."

Genadol stared.

"You are certain?"

"Very. It felt just like him."

"But Korfax? Here?"

Thilnor bowed his head.

Another Geyad approached. It was Udenar. He came to stand beside Thilnor.

"I have never run that fast in my life," he gasped.

Genadol waited for him to catch his breath.

"You felt it, then?" he asked.

"I did, Geyadril," Udenar answered. "But I have other news. On my way here I was told that a great hole has just been blown in the side of the Umadya Nudenor."

"A hole?"

"Yes, Geyadril."

"Qasadar?" Genadol did not hide his amazement. Udenar made the gesture of uncertainty and Genadol looked down, his thoughts racing.

"Gather up all that you can," he said eventually. "We will go there with all due haste. It seems that the Balt Kaalith have some explaining to do."

Naaomir picked himself up off the floor and stared in disbelief at the others about him.

"What was that?" he asked.

Okodon swallowed.

"I think it might have been a qasadar," she said. "I once saw the Dar Kaadarith wield them from the watchtowers during a visit. It certainly sounded much the same."

For the first time that Naaomir could ever remember, Okodon looked truly afraid. Naaomir could almost taste her thoughts as he looked at her. A destroying stone? Korfax had made a destroying stone? Of all the creations of the Dar Kaadarith, qasadar were the most deadly, indiscriminate slices of chaos that did not care what they destroyed. Naaomir cursed silently to himself. Korfax had outdone them again. If he had known that Korfax could now change the purpose of stone on a whim, then he would have had him slain on sight and paid for the consequences afterwards. How could he follow his calling if they didn't tell him everything that he needed to know?

"Is there any defence against such a weapon?" he asked.

"Only the Dar Kaadarith can say," she answered. "And that also is a problem."

"Why?"

"It is certain they will have felt the unleashing of powers. They are sensitive to such things. No doubt they are already on their way here. I imagine they will demand jurisdiction when they arrive."

Naaomir slammed his fist into the wall.

"This is our business, not theirs. They dare not intrude," he hissed.

"But they might," Okodon warned. "Audroh Usdurna favours them over us."

Naaomir looked back at Okodon with sudden fury. Without warning he cuffed her viciously across the mouth. She staggered backwards.

"You have failed me and our order," he told her. "You assured me, and on more than one occasion I might add, that all our preparations were more than enough to deal with this renegade. Now I find that Korfax could not only bring this entire tower crashing down about our heads, but that the Dar Kaadarith will become fully involved. Rectify this matter immediately and bring me the traitor's head. His knowledge, even his confession, is of secondary importance now. The integrity of the Balt Kaalith is paramount."

Okodon wiped the blood from her lip and looked at it. Then she stared darkly at Naaomir for a moment before marching off. As she went she gestured to others to follow in her wake, and by the time she had reached the main stairs she had at least twenty at her back.

Korfax stopped and looked down. There was much commotion below him. He had erred. He should have remained hidden and not tested his power. The Balt Kaalith now knew in what region he travelled and they were coming for him in force.

Competing ideas flitted through his mind like frightened things. He could drop more qasadar behind him, of course, and he could even blow out the walls of the tower, but he would also kill many by such an act – and that was not what he wanted. He would not kill, if he could help it. But how to escape? Then he remembered some old advice Ralir had once given him.

'When cornered, do the unexpected,' Ralir had told him. 'Put your opponent out of reckoning by taking the least likely course.'

Then he had grinned that well-remembered grin, a mock for fate itself.

'Trust me,' he had said, 'such strategies rarely fail. Fortune always favours those that dare.'

Korfax grinned like an echo. The unexpected indeed! A plan formed in his mind. His followers must be dissuaded from following too quickly. Using his changed piradar, he called up earth of earth again, undoing the stairs below him. With a crash and a roar the stairs collapsed. He ran back up, hoping that no one would be hurt as the stone tumbled down the tower.

The crash of the stone below echoed back up the stairway as he fled back upwards, whilst rock dust followed him in ever billowing clouds, ascending, even as he did, to the very top of the tower.

Okodon and the others were passing through the archives when the central stairway collapsed. Great blocks of stone tumbled down from above, blocking any access to the higher parts of the tower. Okodon ran to the blocked doorway and looked briefly at the rubble. She leaned as far out as she dared and peered upwards. Her eyes narrowed. Then she turned to one of the archivists that now stood at her side, staring at the wreckage in sheer disbelief.

"Korfax is heading for the top of the tower," Okodon told him. "Tell any others that follow us exactly that. Tell them that I have gone up the second stairway to the fifth level and that they must follow me there. The first stairway is destroyed to the fourth level and is now impassable."

Then she went on her way, along with her followers, leaving the archivist to stare in blank shock at the destruction.

With as many of the Geyadith as could be found at such short notice, Genadol took the quickest way possible to the Umadya Nudenor, the heart of the Balt Kaalith in Othil Ekrin.

As he marched through the tower gates, he looked up at the damage inflicted upon the tower itself. A great hole had been torn from its side and dust still floated lazily in the air about it. Only qasadar could do that to stone. His first thought was that of outrage. The wondrous symmetry of Othil Ekrin had been marred. Someone would pay for this, and they would pay dearly. He was tempted to lay the blame entirely at the feet of Korfax, but there was a more worrying concern. How could the Balt Kaalith possess such weaponry? And worse, was their vigilance so lacking that they could allow such a one as Korfax to gain and use them? He strode on, and by the time he had reached the tower itself, his outrage had reached its peak.

Naaomir was already waiting for him in the great courtyard. With him were several others Genadol did not recognise. He did not mix with the Balt Kaalith, no one did. They were dealers in secrets and watchers of heresy, keeping their own counsel in all such matters. But now their secrecy had become their undoing.

Genadol walked straight up to Naaomir, whilst those that followed him arranged themselves behind like an arrowhead.

Naaomir watched Genadol approach. Was that uncertainty that beat upon the wall of his chest, or at the wall of his will? Surely not! But to have this great mass of purple cloaks advancing upon him like a wave, whilst every eye in every head stared at him in judgement, was not something he was used to at all. The scrutiny of Genadol, particularly, was harder than he would have liked.

Genadol stopped just in front of Naaomir, but he did not bow or exchange pleasantries, as was the usual custom. Instead he stared directly into the Noqvoandril's eyes and held up his white stave like a commandment.

"I am given to believe that Korfax is here!" he said. "If that is so, then you will surrender him to us or step aside so that we may apprehend him!"

Naaomir drew himself up.

"You intrude where you should not," he told Genadol. "This is the business of the Balt Kaalith. The Velukor himself gave me personal jurisdiction."

Genadol remained utterly unconcerned. He merely tightened his grip about his stave and let faint energies flutter at its tip like a warning.

"Jurisdiction?" he snapped. "Is that the extent of your concern? If I were you, Naaomir, I would worry more about what you have let loose inside your walls than mere policy." He gestured at the hole in the tower. "It seems to me that you have far more serious questions to answer, to say the least."

Genadol waited, but his eyes flickered now with rising power. Each of the Geyadith about him became utterly still, awaiting the fall of the sword.

Naaomir felt dismay. Events were quickly spiralling out of his control. He missed neither the faint stir of power in the stave of Genadol nor the hard expression in the eyes of his followers. He found himself suddenly wanting to take a step backwards, and more than a step perhaps, but he kept his place and stood as tall as he could, holding up his stone scroll of office as if that was all the answer he needed.

"These are the courts of the Balt Kaalith," he announced. "We have final authority here. None enters or leaves without our blessing."

Genadol lowered his stave.

"You arrogant fool!" he said. "This is a Geyadril of the Dar Kaadarith you are holding at bay, not some petty heretic. He may have been cast from our order, but that does not mean that he has forsworn his power. Far from it! And how in the name of all the heavens did he get his hands upon qasadar? You should answer for that at the very least!"

Naaomir smiled coldly. Now he felt himself on safer ground. Here was one of the lies that he most wanted an answer to.

"He made it out of a piradar," Naaomir said. "I would like to know why you of the Dar Kaadarith did not tell the rest of us that you were capable of such feats. One must wonder why you have not employed such talents in our war with the Agdoain."

All the Geyad behind Genadol gasped. One of them came forward, his face dark with anger.

"What fantasy is this?" he said. "You describe the impossible. Once the crystal is set, it cannot be altered."

Another held up his hand.

"I see smoke and illusion – that is all! Ignore the lies, Demendal. Ask instead how the Balt Kaalith managed to get their hands upon qasadar in the first place. None leaves our vaults. It seems that the Balt Kaalith are guilty of theft, at the very least, and that is a great sin."

Genadol held up his stave again.

"Exactly!" he said, turning upon Naaomir.

"So what have you done that requires such dissembling?" he asked. "What iniquities have you committed?"

The forces behind Naaomir surged forward, cries of outrage from more than one of them. Lies and theft? They were the Balt Kaalith! Naaomir held up his hand. He stared back at Genadol.

"Iniquities? I am not the liar here!" he said. "So explain this, Geyadril! Korfax was held in a place of keeping. We had taken all the precautions we deemed necessary, but somehow he used the piradar set in the ceiling to break open the door and incapacitate his guards. Then he collected up every piradar he could lay his hands on, taking them from walls and ceilings as though picking fruit. It was only afterwards that he did that!"

Naaomir pointed at the gaping hole in the tower.

"He turned the piradar into qasadar. You will explain this to me."

Another Geyad stepped forward.

"Geyadril, there is something."

"What, Udenar?"

"The power Thilnor and I felt in the forges was not unlike that of a forging itself. Also, Korfax changed his stave at the battle of Othil Zilodar."

Genadol paused and then turned.

"That is certainly true," he said.

Udenar paused and looked even more uncomfortable.

"Do you remember the debates when we were at the seminary, before Dialyas was dismissed from our order?" he asked.

Thilnor summoned up the courage to speak.

"Korfax knew Dialyas," he said.

Genadol offered Thilnor a stern smile.

"And you knew Korfax. I understand entirely."

He turned back to Naaomir.

"Are you absolutely certain of this?" he asked.

Naaomir smiled in self-righteous triumph.

"You see how your accusations come to naught, how you are caught by your own lies? Dialyas? Korfax? Yours are the very courts of heresy!" he accused. "Go from here and do not return. When this matter is concluded it is you who shall be called to account, not I."

Genadol stared back at Naaomir as if he could not quite believe what he was hearing.

"And what strange world is it that you suddenly live in?" he asked. "Have you not heard what has been said here? Korfax changed his stave. It is a matter of record. Now you tell us that Korfax can turn piradar into qasadar? This must be understood clearly, before we even begin to consider how Korfax may be detained."

"There is no time for this," Naaomir insisted. "We have jurisdiction."

"Korfax destroyed an entire army of Agdoain," said Genadol, shaking his finger as if lecturing a recalcitrant child. "Do you honestly think you can stand against such might? This peril must be met with understanding."

Naaomir would not be moved.

"I understand it all too well," he said. "We have a traitor and a renegade to put down. This is our calling, not yours."

He held up his stone scroll of office once more, like a barrier.

"You will leave these courts, Genadol, you will leave them and let the Balt Kaalith be about their business. I have every right to deny you, and be assured that I will pursue this matter to the highest level. Usdurna is not the regent, Zafazaa is, and he has no love of either heretics or traitors. Begone!"

Genadol took a step back. All the other Geyad braced themselves for the inevitable. Genadol brandished his stave.

"I have no time for this," he said, and as he spoke the last word, he slammed his stave into the ground.

Every one of the Balt Kaalith present was thrown into the air, like so many limp bundles, as a shock wave of force took both the court and the tower in its unforgiving grip. Naaomir was thrown backwards, tumbling head over heels until he fetched up against the far wall. Genadol lifted his stave again and the tremors stopped. He turned about. All the Geyad of the Dar Kaadarith stood waiting, unmoved by the power Genadol had unleashed.

"Udenar?" he said.

"Geyadril?"

"You have recorded all of this?"

"Indeed, Geyadril."

Udenar held up a kamliadar in evidence.

"It is all here, Geyadril," he said, "every single word."

"Good," said Genadol. "Go now to Audroh Usdurna. Do not deviate or allow yourself to be put aside. I want the Audroh to know exactly what it is that has transpired here today."

Udenar bowed and turned swiftly about. He soon left the courtyard and in moments was riding back across the bridge to the tower. Genadol turned and, ignoring the dazed and the fallen that still lay upon the ground, strode into the tower, his followers at his heels.

Korfax was on his way to the last balcony when the feeling came to him that he was being pursued. He looked below and saw movement, many dark shadows quietly circling the great spiral stairs in his wake. He looked up. He was near the top and there was only one exit above him. He could run, of course, but perhaps he could delay the pursuit somewhat and so give himself a little more time to prepare. He took out a piradar from his pouch and placed it on the stairs at his feet. Then he climbed up a few more steps and sat down in the shadows and waited, calming his mind and building up his energies.

Soon enough, Okodon came into view, as silent as she was fast. Korfax silently applauded her stamina. She wasn't troubled by the long climb at all. If nothing else, the Balt Kaalith trained their acolytes well. Korfax doubted the Nazad Esiask could show any better.

He stood up and held the piradar in his hand high. It blazed through his flesh, lighting up like an earthbound star. A wind out of nowhere blew around the walls and was gone.

Okodon came to an immediate halt, as did those who followed with her. Many shielded their eyes. Korfax lowered his hand and let the light fail.

"Come no further and make no move to apprehend me," he said. "Instead, study the stairs between us. You will see a thing."

Okodon said nothing but did as Korfax suggested. She saw it immediately, a piradar, sitting in the middle of the stairway and glowing faintly with an uncertain light. Korfax watched as Okodon frowned but still did not speak. Korfax smiled.

"That, my good Noqvoan, is no longer a piradar," he told her. "You must have realised what I can do by now, so I will say it as plainly as I can. What you see before you is a qasadar. I have changed it from its original purpose and I have but to let go of it with my mind for it to shatter the top of the tower. Come any closer and I will unleash it."

Okodon scowled.

"What do you want?"

"I want you all to go back the way that you came."

"And if we do not?"

"I will release the qasadar."

Okodon grimaced.

"You will kill yourself if you do so."

Korfax laughed quietly. He held up his piradar and let it shine.

"No, I would not. Instead I would ride the air away from the destruction. This is now a stave of air. You should go back, Okodon. I do not desire your death or that of your followers."

Korfax backed away to the top of the stairs, keeping his eyes on Okodon, who for her part did not move. Then the tower shook and Korfax involuntarily glanced over his shoulder. Power had been unleashed somewhere below. The Dar Kaadarith had arrived, and they had arrived in force.

His distraction was precisely the chance that Okodon had been waiting for. She flicked out a small object from her hand, a throwing disc of Laidrom, sending it straight at the crystal upon the stairs. Her aim would have been astonishing to any that had never been trained by the great guilds, but Korfax only had time enough to note its accuracy with sad approval.

With a precision borne of a lifetime of practise, the spinning disc struck the glowing crystal and bounced it against the wall. From there it bounced back again, over the edge of the stairs and out into space. They all watched as it tumbled down into the gulfs below, before the distant echo of its landing came back to them again, a musical tinkle as it fell into the ruin below. There was no explosion. Okodon narrowed her eyes as she saw the ruse, and then she raced up the stairs again.

But Korfax had already moved. He hurled himself out through the last door and onto the highest balcony of the tower. His ploy had both failed and succeeded. There would be no other chance for any such a stratagem again. Instead he must follow the only plan he had come up with. He must leap from the tower and guide himself into the river below, using only his power to control his descent through the air. To say it was risky was an understatement. Even with a stave it was well-nigh impossible to do, but with these changed piradar? Korfax truly did not know.

He jumped up onto the edge and turned, a piradar in each hand. Behind him Okodon raced into view, aiming her dart thrower. Without a second thought, Korfax leapt backwards into the air, and the world tumbled about him as he fell.

Genadol had only achieved the second level when he felt it. Someone was wielding great power nearby. He turned to the others and saw with satisfaction that they had felt it as well. Good! There were no dullards in the service of the Dar Kaadarith here. He was about to speak when Thilnor stopped him, pointing out of the nearest window.

"Geyadril, look! It is him. There he is."

Genadol looked to where Thilnor pointed and saw a falling figure, its cloak flying up behind it. Someone had hurled themselves from the top of the tower. But even as Genadol watched, he noticed that the figure fell strangely.

First it would plummet like a stone, but then it would slow and stop, hovering as though balancing upon a knife edge. Then it would tip over and fall again, plunging downwards until brought to a halt once more, as if tumbling down some vast but invisible flight of stairs. And on each inconstant platform it would hang, before falling again, tumbling through space, end over end. And so it continued: plunge, stop, tumble, halt.

With each tumble, the figure moved further away from the tower, and from what Genadol could judge, it was heading for the river far below. Genadol watched in disbelief for a moment and then looked at Thilnor.

"Explain this to me. What is he doing?"

Thilnor felt stunned. How could he answer? This was all beyond him. Korfax had occasionally been rash, but this?

"I am not sure, Geyadril," he answered at last, "but I think Korfax intends to fall into the river below by using the air to gentle his descent."

Genadol looked around him, eyes full of questions.

"Has anybody ever done such a thing before? I have not heard tell of it if they had."

None answered. Thilnor turned back to watch the dark shape fall into the chasm below.

"Geyadril, there are stories I have read, stories from the wars of those that found themselves caught in high places with little chance of escape."

"And?"

"Of the few that chose this course, even fewer survived, and then only with good fortune. Maybe Korfax thinks that the river will break his fall if his power cannot."

Genadol squeezed his stave in sudden frustration.

"However this ends, we must witness the conclusion. Come," he beckoned, "we go to the river."

Korfax was in trouble. This was like dancing upon the tip of a sword. No sooner did he achieve a steady updraft of wind, enough to gently lower him to the ground, than the air about him would rebel and he would find himself tipping over and hurtling downwards again. He could not surround himself with enough of a shield, as the stones in his hands were too imprecise. Oh for a stave! The only thing he could achieve with any consistency was his aim for the river. He was right on target for the deepest part, but it would do him little good if he could not slow himself down. The river was still far too shallow.

It was only as he dropped past the edge of the upper ravine that another idea came to him. He had been using the two piradar in his hands to control the air about him, but what if instead he reached down and raised the river up so that it would cushion his fall?

He concentrated again and summoned water of water, sending his force downwards, down into the flowing torrent beneath. But he had little time left now. The water and the rocks below it came rushing up to greet him. Deep though the river was, the rocks over which it flowed would kill him if he continued at this speed. He pulled with all his might and the water below him rose up, pulled from its courses. First there was a mound, then a hill and finally a veritable tower to catch his mortal remains.

He struck the water. It was cold, cold enough to make him gasp. He fell through it, down with a dangerous speed. But its depth was enough. Just!

Encased in green light he rose to the surface again and let his power diminish. The waters duly subsided and Korfax laughed, breathing deeply as he broke through into air. He swam to the shore, easy strokes against the current. Luck was still with him. He had escaped his prison and foiled his pursuers. No matter how many followed him now, no matter their power, they would take a long time to come down this far. He was right at the bottom of the city and on the wrong side of the river.

As he hauled himself up onto the bank he suddenly had the sense that he was being watched. He looked up quickly, eyes moving this way and that, ready to bring his power to bear, but all he found was a child staring back at him in amazement from the river's edge. Korfax breathed a sigh of relief and smiled gladly as he stood up, casting his wet hair behind him. The child stared back at him, her eyes watching carefully as he came to her. Korfax stopped before her and knelt.

"Please," he asked her, "which is the best way back up to the streets?"

The child said nothing but raised her hand to point behind her. Korfax followed her finger and saw a distant stairway cut deep into the rock. It was steep and narrow, but it would take him all the way back up to the second quarter. He laughed when he saw it.

"Thank you," he said, taking her hand and kissing it in gratitude. She remained amazed. "Thank you," he repeated, releasing her hand.

She did not answer, watching him but not moving otherwise. He looked at her for a moment and then smiled as he took out one of his piradar. It was one of the twain that he had changed into a stave of air. He handed it to her, bowing.

"No act of kindness should ever go unrewarded," he told her.

The child took the piradar carefully, peering at it as though it was a mystery. She smiled at last. Korfax bowed his head in acknowledgement and then went on his way. But the child followed him with her smiling eyes whilst at her breast she held the rarest of gifts, a crystal imbued with a heart of air.

Genadol looked about him as they left the courtyard of the Umadya Nudenor. He glanced at one of his followers.

"Peikan!" he said. "The Balt Kaalith must know where Korfax has lodgings within the city. Find out. Force the issue, if you have to, but go there with Demendal, just in case. If they insist on going with you then that is fine, but remind them that we have jurisdiction. I will follow Korfax with the others. If all goes well I shall send messages or come myself. Beware, though. If Korfax escapes me and comes to you, remember at all times how powerful he is."

Peikan bowed.

"He shall not get by us," he said.

He turned to Demendal.

"Come!" he said. Then they both ran off as though the very fire of the Creator was at their backs.

Genadol and the rest fanned out in pairs as they descended, covering as many of the ways down that they could, but when they arrived at the riverside it was clear that Korfax had already made good his escape. Once they were all assembled again Genadol gestured back the way they had come.

"We shall retrace our steps," he said. "Though I doubt he will return there, Korfax's lodgings are our only recourse now."

But then Thilnor pointed further up the river.

"Look, Geyadril. Look at that child, over there."

Genadol looked to where Thilnor pointed and so saw her, standing upon one of the large boulders at the side of the river, a blue light caught in her hands, hands held to her breast. They all hurried forward and soon surrounded her. Genadol leaned forward.

"May I see what it is that you have?" he asked.

He held out his hand. The child looked at her treasure and then took a step back. Genadol withdrew his hand.

"I will not take it from you," he promised. "I can see that it is a gift. Such covenants have always been respected within the Dar Kaadarith. But may I not even have a glimpse, the merest touch?"

The child pondered this for a moment as Genadol held out his hand again. She looked solemnly into his eyes for a long time and then finally gave him the stone.

Genadol clasped it tightly and probed it with his mind. Deep within it, far down inside, he found the echo of Korfax. But the power that Korfax had passed through the stone was altogether staggering. It was as though the crystal had been remade in a forge. Genadol shuddered and handed the crystal back to the child.

"Thank you," he said. "I think that you have gained the rarest of treasures this day."

The child offered him a shy smile in response but dropped it when another stepped forward, breaking the moment with his demands.

"Geyadril! That is no toy you have left in her hands. It should be taken. It should be studied."

Genadol remained unmoved.

"I gave her my word," he said.

The other would have argued but it was Thilnor that interrupted them both.

"But, Geyadril, what did you feel?" he asked. "Can we not know that much, at least?"

Genadol turned to Thilnor and smiled sadly.

"What did I feel? I felt Korfax, his achievement, his triumph. But we cannot follow him. We cannot go where he has gone. We lack the power. I think we should seek out Peikan and Demendal as soon as we can. I am suddenly certain that they are not up to the task that I set them in my ignorance. And now I find myself wondering whether any of us are at all."

6

VIOLATIONS

Bama-as Chis-iol-pirjon
Ix-lognei Van-krus-driljir
Gi-nadar Vonzil-laraih
Nuj-uhmje Odran-doal-je
Ur-tonihs Gahasp-vanihd
Gem-sanith Othpa-qasje
A-dr-pan Landril-ujir

Korfax paused outside the hostelry where he had been staying. Would the Balt Kaalith be waiting for him inside? And what of the Dar Kaadarith? His choices had become difficult again, but he was already defined by them. He had to recover his belongings, for then, and only then, would he truly be safe.

He took the narrow lane that would take him to the rear of the house, staying ever in the shadows. No one was about that he could see or feel, but that didn't mean that the Balt Kaalith were not there at all. They were past masters at hiding themselves, and if he actively sought for their thoughts it would only alert them to his presence.

That was it, then. He must use his changed piradar. He had given four of them the attributes of each element: there was one of earth, one of air, one of fire and one of water. But he was tired now. Even he had his limits.

He brought out the one of air and wove a spiral wind about himself, in order to deflect any of those poisoned darts the Balt Kaalith were so fond of. In his other hand he held the piradar of fire, his chosen element. That had been the easiest to prepare and would prove the best offensive weapon. He entered the house and quickly went to his room.

As he reached his door he paused. This was far too easy. Were there others nearby, watching and waiting? He did not know but he could no longer risk the time to look. He opened the door slowly and peered inside. Again he sensed no disturbance, so he entered as quietly as he was able.

The room was empty. He walked over to the corner where he had left his belongings and studied its emptiness. It was as he had left it, invisible and inviolate. He thanked the fates. Though the Balt Kaalith had taken everything else, they had not found this. He smiled and looked deeper. His sword was revealed, as was his armour and his bag of periapts, lying on his great black cloak.

He breathed deeply and stepped back, readying himself to release the illusion, and it was at that precise moment that he glimpsed a sudden movement out of the corner of his eye.

Two of the Balt Kaalith had appeared behind him almost as if they had stepped through the walls. One, a Noqvoan, had been hiding in the shadow of the other room and the other, a Baltar, had stepped through the outer door. Korfax was impressed. He had neither seen them nor felt their presence in any way.

"Drop your power and surrender," said the Noqvoan.

"I think not," Korfax replied.

A third figure moved into the light from the other room. It was shadowed by a fourth. Korfax closed his eyes in sudden chagrin and cursed. It was all but over. The third figure was a Geyadril, his white stave, both the badge of his office and the measure of his power, held before him in both hands. He was slight of build but full of confidence. Behind him followed a Geyad, taller and broader but already of far less consequence. The Geyadril overshadowed all others in the room merely by his presence. Korfax glanced at each face in turn, but he did not recognise any of them.

The Geyadril spoke.

"I think you will," he said. He gestured with his stave and Korfax reluctantly dropped his shield and lowered both of the piradar. His converted stones were no match for the full stave of a Geyadril.

"How is it that you work with the Balt Kaalith?" he asked.

The Geyadril smiled lightly.

"As soon as Geyadril Genadol learned of your presence, the Dar Kaadarith took jurisdiction. A report is being laid at the feet of Audroh Usdurna even now. Noqvoandril Naaomir will have much explaining to do. But, in the meantime, you are to be apprehended."

The Geyadril looked at the two Balt Kaalith. They came forward, ready to act, but then Korfax held up one of his changed piradar and it flickered with a dangerous light. They stopped where they were and glanced at the Geyadril.

"Forgive me," said Korfax, "but I would rather not remain in the company of the Balt Kaalith. I have suffered too long at their hands."

He turned to the Geyadril.

"Naaomir had me tortured. I will not place myself in their care again."

The Geyadril held up his stave and energies flickered along its length.

"Did you not hear what I said?" he said. "The Dar Kaadarith have authority here. The Balt Kaalith will do exactly as I tell them. Once you submit to my authority, then we can turn our attentions to other matters. But that is how it will be."

But Korfax did not submit. As quick as thought, he changed the stone in his hand. For a moment it blazed brightly, but then it altered, filling up with a strange and uneven radiance. The Geyadril gasped in horror and gestured quickly to the two Noqvoan to stand back. They both frowned but did not move. The Geyadril turned to them.

"Get back, both of you! That is a qasadar that he holds."

They both did as they were told, each now with a wary expression. The Geyadril turned back to Korfax.

"By the powers," he exclaimed, "I would not have believed it if I had not seen it for myself."

Korfax smiled easily enough, but his weariness was fast becoming a thing of torment, and the strain of holding the qasadar stable made it worse with every passing moment.

"I suggest that you and your friends leave this place while you still can," he said. "I am holding it stable for a little while yet, but how much longer I can continue to do so is a moot point. I am already rather tired."

One of the Balt Kaalith stepped forward. It was the Noqvoan.

"Though we do not seek it needlessly," he said, "we of the Balt Kaalith do not fear death."

Korfax looked over his shoulder at him.

"Then you are even greater fools than I originally thought you to be. A qasadar does not just destroy matter, it also destroys spirit. It is the very essence of negation."

The Noqvoan and the Baltar moved back again and both of them suddenly looked afraid for the first time. But the Geyadril snorted and a smile played upon his lips.

"What utter rubbish!" he said. "Whatever else you have, Korfax, you have a nasty imagination."

The unnamed Geyadril turned to the Noqvoan.

"Pay no heed, Omloa, he is playing with you. Ignore his words."

Korfax turned back to the Geyadril and smiled as gently as he could.

"We are all running out of time here," he said. "If I let go of this," he shook the qasadar back and forth in his hand, "then a goodly portion of this house gets blown all the way to the Mahorelah."

The Geyadril narrowed his eyes.

"I have been thinking," he mused. "I am not so certain you would do this. This is some ploy on your part."

The Geyad behind him stirred.

"But look at it!" he hissed. "You have just seen him do it. How can you doubt your own eyes?"

"Because I do not believe that Korfax will kill himself, that is why," said the Geyadril.

Korfax looked at the Geyad and then back at the Geyadril. The Geyad was clearly convinced, but the Geyadril was not. What could he do?

"Well," he said, "perhaps you are right. Perhaps that is not my intent."

He held the stone up.

"But then again, perhaps it is."

Korfax changed the stone once more. Red light erupted from its core and the Geyadril, caught off his guard by the transition, gaped in astonishment.

Korfax thrust the transformed piradar straight at him, and a summoned wind struck the Geyadril full in the face. He was flung against the far wall as though he suddenly weighed nothing, and there he slumped, falling to the floor in a heap. A dribble of blood dropped from his lips.

The Geyad behind him raised his stave, preparing a reprisal, perhaps, but his shock made him slow. Korfax was already moving and his summoned air fell upon the Geyad. He was hurled back, just like the Geyadril, back against the wall, where he dropped his stave and then fell across the limp body of the other. He did not move again.

Korfax turned about to find that both of the Balt Kaalith were almost upon him, their faces a strange mingling of astonishment and determination. They moved almost without thought, each drawing a sword and a knife as they advanced. Korfax had time for one thing only, so he slammed the transformed piradar into the floor. The stone of the floor broke as if it had been struck by a great hammer.

The room, the entire building, bucked with force. Cracks tore across the floor and the ceiling and both the Noqvoan and the Baltar were hurled backwards, dim energies flickering up from the floor and over their bodies. Their knives were twisted into useless shapes and their swords were shivered into pieces.

Korfax remained where he was, kneeling on the floor. He had exhausted himself. He could perform no more acts of power. He was drained to the dregs.

He coughed and felt blood upon his tongue. He tasted it with resignation. Maybe he had gone too far. He blinked furiously for a moment, clearing his vision, and then turned to retrieve his belongings. He released the illusion and watched as his belongings emerged from behind it. But then something slammed into his side and he tumbled against the far wall. Someone had survived his assault after all. It was the Noqvoan, Omloa.

Korfax rolled away, breathing heavily. That had hurt. He felt around for his piradar but it had been knocked from his hand. He looked up and saw his assailant. Omloa still held the hilt of his shattered sword in his left hand, but his right hand was broken, a twisted clutch of fingers held tight to his breast. Blood was running from several cuts on his face and he swayed even as he stood, but Korfax did not mistake the determination in his eyes – if it was the last thing Omloa did, he would take Korfax down.

Even as Korfax tried to stand, Omloa was on him again, turning his body, dancing on the ball of his left foot and letting the heel of his right lash out with blinding speed. It struck Korfax solidly in the chest and he was flung backwards again. The next thing he knew he was lying on the floor, staring at the ceiling and sucking in air. Omloa stayed where he was, half crouching and limbs at the ready.

"I don't know whether to knock you into submission or kill you," he said. "The only thing that would really settle this argument would be a blade. I need a weapon in my hands to make sure of you."

Korfax tried to get up, but another blow to his ribs convinced him otherwise.

"Do not move!" ordered Omloa. "More of the Dar Kaadarith will arrive soon, so if you wish to surrender whilst still in one piece, I suggest that you do not give me reason to subdue you further."

Korfax lay back and clutched at himself. He was really hurting now. His extravagant use of power and the blows of Omloa were taking their toll at last. Then he heard Omloa move away. He looked up and saw that he was staring at something by the bed.

"A sword!" he declared. "A big one, too! A kansehna! Now that I can use. But how is it here? I thought we took all your belongings."

He turned to Korfax.

"Another of your tricks?" he asked.

Korfax sat up and stared. Omloa had seen his Qorihna. Korfax felt a thrill of fear course through him. Omloa did not have the faintest idea what it was he was about to lay his hands upon. Words heard long ago tumbled into his mind, words his father had once spoken in warning.

'Only those of the blood can touch it. The black sword will answer to no other. To touch it would mean their death.'

Korfax reached out, imploring with his hands.

"Omloa, I beg you, do not touch that blade. It is not what you think it to be."

But Omloa did not listen.

"Again? You may fool me once, Korfax, but never twice."

He lifted the Qorihna up by its hilt and smiled.

"This is a mighty blade indeed. I have never seen the like. And it is so black. What metal is it made of?"

But even as he spoke, the sword squirmed in his grasp. He stared at it in consternation as it writhed in his hands, but he did not drop it, not even when it began to scream.

Korfax could do nothing but place his hands over his ears. The sound was an utter agony. It tore through the air like outrage. It was as if violation had discovered a voice. Hard flesh, beaten out upon a cruel anvil, screamed for restitution.

Omloa stared in horror as the blade and the hilt transformed. Like a skin, all its surfaces peeled back, layer upon layer upon layer, only to reveal yet more blades beneath, and yet more beneath them, until a veritable forest of black fronds waved in the air above him. The hilt enveloped his hands in a coil of roots, holding them in place. Then the blades lengthened and grew, dividing and subdividing as they reached up to the ceiling until it looked as though some great black tree had sprouted from the ends of Omloa's arms. The black roots swarmed up and over Omloa's shoulders and about his body, holding him immobile in a strangling darkness. For a moment the Qorihna swayed in the air, filling the room with boiling shadows, each blade wailing with its singular voice, a dissonant choir. Then the branching blades turned back upon themselves, falling silent as each bitter tip bent over to hover in front of Omloa's horrified face. It was almost as if they regarded him in some strange fashion, looking inside him, judging him perhaps. Then, having judged, they acted, each tip tearing inwards, burying itself in his naked flesh. In the moments that followed, Omloa was both swallowed and sliced and burned in equal measure. The blades covered him in a squirming blackness and he disappeared utterly from view. Korfax turned away, sickened and terrified. A single scream filled the air, a scream of terrible fear, of utter agony. Then it fell gradually away into infinite distances, falling beyond the borders of the world before vanishing at last.

It was only when silence returned that Korfax dared look back again. There was no sign of Omloa, not even the ash of his demise, and the great black sword, his Qorihna, lay alone upon the floor as if nothing had happened at all. Korfax stared at it. It might have been his imagination, but he thought he sensed an air of righteousness about it now, as though it had assumed the shade of a great beast, some feral immensity which had just seen off a rival and now lay back down to sleep. Korfax almost turned away, leaving the room and his belongings behind him. But he did not. He could not. He needed them far too much.

He walked back to the Qorihna and looked down at it. His heart hammered in his chest. He reached down with his left hand to take it up but withdrew it again before his outstretched fingers could touch the hilt. He stared at his left hand. It was shaking. Korfax clamped his right hand over it and closed his eyes.

"Would you do that to me?" he asked the sword.

It did not answer.

"WOULD YOU DO THAT TO ME?" he roared.

The sword still did not answer. Korfax clutched at himself to hold back the fear. Indecision racked him. He had made a pact with unholy powers. Was he about to pay the price?

He reached forward for a second time. He needed the sword. However fearsome its attributes, it was his only weapon against the Agdoain and he needed it. Only now did he truly understand just how appalling the risk was. This was what his father had really feared, all those years ago. Korfax bowed his head and wept. He was cursed. Doomed. He had dared to play with powers he barely understood and now he was paying the price for his folly. Only here, on the other side of the divide, were the consequences revealed at last, when it was already too late.

No one understood Qorihna – none of the Argedith, not Sondehna, not even Nalvahgey, though she had been the one to drag the thing out of the Mahorelah and somehow bind it to her bloodline. But such powers had a history of turning upon their masters, finally rebelling against the long ages of their servitude.

Korfax shuddered. In his mind's eye he saw the Qorihna scream again, coming apart and coalescing like a swarm of writhing limbs, a tree of a thousand blades and a thousand voices, each branch hungry for his flesh. It took him long moments to hurl the foul image from his mind.

He had chosen this road. Him. No one else had chosen it for him. He had done this, him alone. His father had denied it, but he had accepted it. Now he must pay the price.

So Korfax forced himself to touch the sword.

A faint sighing sound came to his ears, or his mind, perhaps, a sigh of contentment, a brief song of happiness. And as he picked it up, the hilt seemed to nestle against his hand, a brief shiver of satisfaction. Korfax closed his eyes in relief. His sword knew its rightful owner and loved the hand that held it.

He breathed deeply and looked again at his black sword. His Qorihna was back in the place it longed to be and all was right with its world again. He stood back up and looked about. Neither the Baltar, the Geyadril nor even the Geyad had moved. Korfax said a silent prayer for them all and left the room at last, taking his belongings with him. But it would be a long time before he could remember the hapless Omloa without a cold shiver running up and down his spine.

Genadol stood in front of his prince and told as much of the tale as he knew, whilst Urendril Nimagrah stood on one side and Noqvoandril Naaomir stood on the other. Every so often Usdurna looked at Naaomir as though he could not believe what he had just been told. When it had all been said at last, he stood up and looked down at the Noqvoanadril. Then he spoke.

"This tale astounds me," he said. "How did you possibly think that you could contain Korfax? Have you learnt anything at all in this affair? Clearly you have not. You persist in repeating the mistakes of the past! Having failed with Korfax once, you try again. And then you fail again. We are defined as much by our limitations as by our capabilities, and being able to recognise such boundaries is a sign of true self-knowledge. It seems to me now that you are utterly incapable of such a feat. You did not seek help, you kept everything to yourself, and as a consequence there has been both death and destruction in my city. How do you justify yourself in the light of that?"

Naaomir clenched his jaw.

"Justice has always been the province of the Balt Kaalith," he said.

Usdurna glanced at Nimagrah, who did not say anything, though her expression was most eloquent.

"You forget, Noqvoandril," he said, turning back again, "I was there at the trial of Korfax. I saw then exactly what it was that your justice meant. You bowed too much to the whims of the Velukor and too little to the law."

"That is heresy!" Naaomir spluttered. "The Velukor's word is the law!"

Usdurna leaned forward.

"Heresy, is it? That word falls too readily from your lips. To disagree with the Velukor is not to commit heresy. The Velukor's word is not the law. That is why there is a council, to moderate and to dispose. That is the writ of Karmaraa, or would you disagree even with that?"

There was no answer.

"Consequences!" continued Usdurna. "Because your order bowed to the Velukor on that day, we lost the one weapon we needed in our war with the Agdoain. My son fights even now against the evil. How much more hope would he have had with Korfax at his side? You deliberately hobbled us so that your order could ascend. Blind, stupid greed and arrogance! The Balt Kaalith is not the world, Noqvoandril, nor the word."

Usdurna closed his eyes.

"Shall I remind you who Korfax is and what he did? He is the son of Sazaaim and Tazocho, of the Salman Farenith, most loyal and most steadfast. He turned the battle for Othil Zilodar! He changed his stave! The signs were written upon the stone even then, and still you refused to see them for what they were. You, the Balt Kaalith, brought him down for your own selfish purposes. You were the ones that sowed the seeds of doubt in the Velukor's mind. You were the ones that pushed him so that he would break. Now look where we are. Because of you we have a renegade adept of the Namad Dar loose in our city, a renegade who can perform acts of unprecedented power. We needed Korfax with us, not against us."

"But he is a traitor," Naaomir insisted.

Usdurna turned away.

"You will not give, will you? You are blinded by yourself, Noqvoandril. You believe you are right and the rest of the world is wrong. So be it. All further discussion has become irrelevant and you leave me no choice."

Usdurna turned once more and filled himself with his authority, standing as if carven from the stone of the tower. His gaze fell down with all the weight his long life could give it and Naaomir looked back up in sullen hatred. He knew where this would go now, it was obvious. Usdurna would rule against him and banish him from the city. His only regret was that he had failed.

"I cannot dismiss you from the Balt Kaalith," Usdurna said, "nor can I strip you of your authority and rank, but I can banish you from my city. You are no longer welcome here. You are to leave Othil Ekrin immediately. You will present yourself to the regent and the high council in Othil Homtoh. No doubt you will seek to overturn my judgement, but know that I will not bow in this, not even to Zafazaa. Begone from my sight."

Usdurna turned to Nimagrah.

"I wish you to represent me in this. You are to go with Naaomir. You have my full authority. I will send an entire parloh with you. When you speak, it will be with my voice, and when you act, it will be with my will. Zafazaa may feel he can ignore me, but he cannot ignore you."

Nimagrah bowed and turned to Naaomir.

"Shall we, Noqvoandril?"

Naaomir gave her a dark look for a moment and then turned about and strode from the chamber. Nimagrah merely smiled and followed him. When they were gone Usdurna turned to Genadol.

"So how do we proceed?" he asked.

Genadol breathed deeply.

"I am not sure." he answered. "Korfax can do unprecedented things. This whole matter has moved to realms that are completely outside my experience."

He paused.

"There is one thing, though," he continued, after a moment's thought. "I have a Geyad in my service that once knew Korfax quite well. He told me that Korfax used to confide with Ralir of Badagar, and, according to the Balt Kaalith, there is a connection between Ralir and a certain Noqvoan currently in the city. Also, Korfax and this Noqvoan have met before this hour. I think we should seek her out."

"And who is this Noqvoan?" Usdurna asked.

"Her name is Adavor," said Genadol. "She is currently on a mission to learn all she can of Doagnis."

"Doagnis!" Usdurna exclaimed. "Our problems multiply with each hour that passes. A renegade Geyadril of the Dar Kaadarith, and the mightiest Arged since the wars – is it certain that Korfax pursues her?"

"Yes, Audroh. Of that, at least, we are certain. Noqvoan Okodon assured us it was so. She may have been Naaomir's second, but at the end she discovered that she had little love for her master. Okodon can be trusted in this, I am sure of it. She certainly gave us all the aid that we required once it was clear that Naaomir had overstepped his bounds."

Usdurna walked to the window and looked out over his city. Somewhere out there two beings walked, one a servant of the dark abyss, the other driven beyond himself by fate, but both dangerously powerful. And his son, heir to the throne of Othil Ekrin, was leading an army, the largest army that had ever been assembled, against the all but infinite Agdoain. He suddenly felt impotent.

He feared for the future as never before. A vision came to his mind, a vision of Othil Ekrin toppling down, her towers tipping over, her stone cracking as the earth opened up under her like a mouth and swallowed her whole.

Genadol watched Usdurna. For a moment he saw darkness in the old prince's eyes, a round darkness that peered out briefly and then was gone again. Genadol looked to the window, wondering, not for the first time, where this would all end.

She was caught, though how it had happened was a mystery. When Korfax did not meet her at the appointed hour, she had gone on alone. She had returned to the place that she had found, a high tower where many of the Haelok Aldaria were wont to gather. Some she knew, having seen them on Lonsiatris, whilst others she did not.

She had watched the comings and goings for a little while, awaiting her moment, but then something had come upon her, a dark vapour that seized her by her throat, or her mind, and the next she knew of it she was naked and bound upon a frame of stone, stretched to her limits by four cruel metal bands at her wrists and ankles.

She looked about her. The place of her confinement was both dank and dark and there was an unclean smell to the air as though mounds of ancient filth lay piled up nearby. She tested her bonds, but they were more than enough for her, as was the stone to which they were fixed.

"Good, you are awake at last."

Adavor looked around. Doagnis walked out from behind the stone frame to stand before her, her face calm and her eyes glinting.

"I wondered how long you would be unconscious," she said. "Such summonings are rarely precise, unfortunately. But here you are at last, awake and at our pleasure."

Adavor cast her eyes over her captor. It was the first time she had seen Doagnis close to. She was not as tall as Adavor had imagined she would be, and her face seemed almost innocent in its childlike beauty, but Adavor was not fooled. Though Doagnis might sway like a gentle beguilement under her sumptuous robes of black, her large eyes had a fire behind them – a deep, dark fire. Adavor reminded herself that this one had outplayed the high council itself, and even Korfax had been bested by her, coming too late to prevent her escape. Adavor smiled. At least Korfax would not allow such a thing to happen again. Doagnis saw the smile and frowned.

"You are amused?" she asked. "Not the response I would have expected from one in your current predicament. So tell me, slave, what has caught your fancy?"

Adavor smiled a little wider.

"Nothing of consequence," she answered.

Doagnis came a little closer and Adavor gasped at the cold thrust that suddenly pierced her. The weight of Doagnis's mind was terrifying, a deadly weight that filled her up to the very brim with pain. Doagnis took another step and even increased the pressure, if such a thing were possible.

"That is not the answer I desire," she said. "So, please, tell me your thoughts. Tell me what amuses you; I would so much like to know."

Adavor did not answer. Instead she began to recite a rhyme to herself, a circle of words like a wheel. Round and round it went, gathering momentum as it turned upon itself, hurling all other thoughts aside.

Doagnis touched the wheel and grappled with it, but for all her strength, and it was considerable, Adavor had the better of her for a moment. It was a simple enough trick, the wheel, but it was effective nonetheless.

Doagnis withdrew. If she had been pressed for time she would have forced the issue, but now she intended to take a more leisurely path. Here was a rare opportunity to teach the hated Balt Kaalith a lesson they would not forget.

She watched as Adavor relaxed ever so slightly. She smiled and then turned away, beckoning to the shadows. Another walked out from behind the stone frame. Adavor recognised him immediately. This was Mirzinad, one of the Haelok Aldaria favoured by Doagnis.

"This one remains stubborn," said Doagnis. "She has decided not to acquiesce to our demands. It would please me if you would convince her otherwise."

"Mistress!"

Mirzinad bowed. He did not smile, but Adavor caught the sudden anticipation that sharpened his eyes, and something inside her shuddered at what such anticipation might mean.

"How far do you wish me to go?"

His voice was mild, almost as if he was discussing some matter of little or no consequence.

"I think a small taste of what is to come would be appropriate. Let her understand the consequences of defiance."

Mirzinad glanced at his intended victim, running his eyes slowly over her, pausing here and there until stopping between her legs.

"That will be hard in some respects," he said. "Her tail is firmly in place."

Doagnis moved closer to him and took him by the arm. She led him away and smiled sweetly back at Adavor as she did so. Then she leaned closer and drew out the smaller of Mirzinad's two knives from his belt. She tapped him lightly on his chest with its tip.

"You could always cut it off!" she said.

He came to the meeting place and searched it thoroughly. There was nothing, no sign from Adavor and no indication where she might have gone. He looked up at the surrounding towers. None of them matched the image in his head, so Adavor must have gone on from here when he did not show up. But where, though? His options were diminishing by the second.

Ever since his escape from the Balt Kaalith one struggle after another had consumed him. He had changed the nature of stone, he had fought his own, he had witnessed something of the true nature of his Qorihna and now he intended to confront Doagnis. The last few hours had compressed into moments, and he felt himself rushing headlong towards who knew what. He only hoped that whatever lay in wait for him would not prove to be evil.

If he was seeking someone, or something, and he did not know where to find them, he would have once asked the Exentaser for help. But he was alone now and there was no one to whom he could turn. Rigid adherence to tradition had become a cage. No one was self-sufficient any more.

There was another way, if he would but take the chance. An act of summoning would find Adavor, but that was the one thing he had vowed never to do. Need sat on him like a goad. He knew there were powers he could summon that would aid him.

This was it. He stood at the very last boundary, beyond which there was no turning back. Yet again came the temptation, the solving of problems with power and yet more power, and then more power after that. It was the eternal stream. Once its waters were tasted, the memory would sit for ever in the mind, and the only way to satisfy the desire would be to come back to drink from it again. The thirst, though, was eternal. The water – the cool, the wonderful and necessary water – dragged one back to it time after time, as each taste became more potent than the last. Driven by need, he was heading down towards the well-head, drinking its upwelling waters even as he went, immersing himself ever deeper in its substance. Eventually he would reach the source and, after that, there would be no hope left for him at all.

Wanton abandon welled up inside. What foolishness was this, he asked himself? Did it truly matter now? Today had been a day of miracles, both of the bright and the dark. All he had left to him was his fate. Let him trust in that or in nothing at all.

He opened up his logadar and studied the words. He read the requisite passage and grimaced. It was easy. It was also wrong. But he had no choice; he needed to find Doagnis, and the only one who knew where she was, the only one he could trust, was Adavor. He looked at the words again as they floated before him, projected in the air above the logadar, and there, drawn in a dark script of dim fire, was the way to open the inner doors of his vision and the outer doors of the upper deeps, the very antechamber of the Mahorelah itself.

Fascination had him. This was his birthright. This, once ritual and tradition had been cast aside, was who he was. So he read the text once more and memorised the details.

When he had first begun to read the lore of sorcery it had dismayed him how many periapts he must procure and how he must prepare them. He had almost given up in frustration at how arcane it all was. But he did not. The Dar Kaadarith had already taught him that persistence brought its own rewards.

'At the last,' he had read towards the end, 'an adept need not bring anything to the ritual other than the ability to visualise such periapts as are described herein – the ritual shield, the ritual sword, the ritual brazier and the ritual cup. The adept must be able to smell the burning herbs, be able to draw the ritual circle, be able to hold up the many periapts, but only in the mind. If all are held clearly by the inner vision, then the rite will be just as successful as if the ritual items were themselves employed. But even better it is to behold the very essence of the ritual itself as a distillation, as a single burning thought, without all the encumbrances of pedantic realism. Here lies the heart of true mastery, and here lies the lightning stroke of power. But one must be pure in this, and very certain, for take one misstep in any direction and the forces that wait at the portals of the Mahorelah will consume your immortal soul.'

Comforting words! But Korfax needed the warning, as it would hold him to the path. That was his purpose and it was how he had been trained as a Geyad. Visualisation was also the key that unlocked the door of the Namad Dar. As he had already discovered, the two disciplines were not so different after all. In each, any change in the nature of reality was produced by the will, and the will alone. Trinkets, amulets, swords and potions all served the same purpose; they helped the untrained mind to focus. But the trained mind was another matter. It had already achieved the requisite state.

He closed his eyes and prepared himself, but all the while another thought sat at the back of his mind like a black stone. He was about to do the very worst thing of all, to summon another being into servitude.

Adavor hung limply from her restraints. She was bleeding from many cuts and she was bruised in many places, but she had not submitted. Though Mirzinad had violated her, many times many, she had not given him any satisfaction at all. Even when he had cut off her tail, an utter agony in itself, she had kept her silence. He had hurled himself against her mind as he had thrust himself against her body, striking her with his fists, raking her flesh with his claws, even biting her with his teeth at the end, but she had not given in.

There was one light in her mind. Here was the final test. Here she would prove herself against all the pain and the suffering her enemies could provide. She must forget her body, the pain, the outrage and the humiliation, and concentrate only upon the light.

Mirzinad stood before her, a sour expression on his face. He had wanted to be the one to break her, but she had beaten him. She even allowed herself a mocking smile at his expense.

In rage he drew back his hand to strike her, to strike her head from its impudent neck, but the blow never fell. An imperious voice stopped him, a voice he could not ignore.

"Enough, Mirzinad! Control yourself!"

It was Doagnis.

"I did not expect you to succeed," she said. "You are here to do my will, not deny it. Break her beyond recall and you will earn nothing but my approbation!"

Mirzinad dropped his hand and withdrew with a bow. Doagnis came forward, treading daintily, careful not to step in one of the many patches of blood that now spattered the floor. She looked up at Adavor, false pity on her face.

"Now tell me what I want to know and the suffering ends. It is so utterly simple."

Adavor dredged up all the rebellion that she could muster and spat it at Doagnis. Doagnis fell back in shock before frantically pulling out a piece of cloth from one of her sleeves and wiping her face with it. Mirzinad surged forward, but Doagnis stopped him with a gesture. She finished making sure that every single stain was gone, before looking at Adavor again, but when she did so her eyes were poison bright.

"That was very ill-advised, slave," she hissed. "Now matters will be the worse for you. I wonder what worth you will find your intransigence in the face of a Baramak."

Doagnis gestured impatiently to one side and two others of the Haelok Aldaria struggled reluctantly forward bearing a strange-looking cage supported between two very long poles. It was from this that the stench came. A large, dark entity thrashed about slowly inside. Adavor tried to ascertain something of its nature, but all she caught were glimpses.

There were eyes, wet eyes, a great many of them, large and small, dotted across a body of indeterminate shape and size. Everything shifted from one moment to the next, texture, form and colour. She saw limbs, a great many of them, but she could not count them. Sometimes hooked claws poked through the bars of the cage, and sometimes something softer oozed slowly through the holes, almost as if the entity caressed its prison, both loving and loathing at the same time. Doagnis smiled sweetly at Adavor.

"Believe me when I tell you that not all things can be endured," she said. "Do not mistake me in this, slave, for this is your last chance. If you do not satisfy me now, then I will leave you to the tender mercies of the Baramak for as long as it wishes to play with you. And at the end, when it has finished doing what it does best, you will beg me for oblivion."

Adavor stared at the cage. The histories had told her of such things, and her training had not spared her the possibility. She knew that she might one day come to it, to die in terror and pain, far from succour, far from hope. She had known of such things in her mind, but her heart now told her another story entirely. The reality of it all was so much worse. Oh, the desire to give in, the desire to tell her captors everything they wanted to know, swelled within her now. But that was the test, and she would not submit.

Korfax followed the being he had summoned. It flitted across the fabric of the city like some darting plague, infecting each stone it passed over with a brief mottling pattern, a shifting stain that paused before moving on again. It was a finding mist, a barely sentient force, something born of the shadows that lay in the depths of the Mahorelah.

Korfax cursed it even as he followed it. He tried to comfort himself with the thought that the finding mist was simple, a force with no thought, a thing of no sentience, but he knew that he was fooling himself. Its outer simplicity had already displayed a certain inner subtlety. It now sought Adavor as if it knew exactly who she was. It understood the concept of seeking and it understood the concept of finding. How could it not be sentient?

Korfax doubted that any knew it was even there except for himself. And no one, of course, could see him. He wondered if Doagnis would feel the mist. She was certainly sensitive to power. But perhaps, or so he hoped, the mist was too far down the scale of her ambition. Would she even suspect such a play? And in her pride, would she even look?

Korfax smiled to himself. What a surprise that would be! He had a sudden desire to see that surprise written all over her face.

Doagnis smiled back at Adavor as she hung upon the stone frame, walking slowly away all the while, her wide hips swinging this way and that like an enticement. The Baramak sulked within its cage, its many eyes dividing their attention between its summoner and the proffered prey. Doagnis reached the door and turned slowly about, lingering upon the threshold whilst the others dutifully left before her. She looked back meaningfully at Adavor.

"You stand upon a threshold, slave," she said, "just as I do. I have but to leave this room and you will experience such an abyss of suffering as you cannot possibly imagine. But I am nothing if not merciful. Since you have no idea as to what truly awaits you, I will allow you a brief moment with the Baramak. And, I assure you, you will understand then. By the time that I return, I think you will be more than willing to tell me everything that I wish to know. But if you are still not convinced, even after that..."

Doagnis offered up another smile and left the room. The Baramak made a gurgling sound. Adavor stared at it in puzzlement. Doagnis had not released the thing from its cage. Or so she thought.

The cage split open. It broke in several places, like a shell, like an awakening seed. Then Adavor realised how wrong she had been, for the cage was not a cage at all, but a part of the creature itself. The demon, the Baramak, had deliberately shut itself inside its own body. But now, as it unfurled its anatomy, she could appreciate its true nature. She bit back a scream.

The Baramak gradually raised itself up from the floor, the remnants of its cage-like integument becoming flush with its many dripping surfaces. All of its eyes were now upon her, and its many and varied limbs uncoiled and twitched in anticipation. Then it danced, caressing itself as it went – a sick and revolting prelude before it was to come to her at last and enfold her in its vile embrace.

Doagnis stood upon a balcony and looked out over the city. She was ill at ease. Ever since the capture of Adavor a feeling had been growing on her that something, somewhere, was wrong. And she had felt like this before. Every time one of her servants had failed to kill the one following her she had felt this very same feeling. It was like a great weight about her neck.

The sound of footsteps came from behind. She turned. It was Ronoar, and his face was pale.

"What is it?" she asked.

"Dire news, mistress," he answered. "Korfax is here, in this city. I have just had report of it. It seems that the Balt Kaalith and the Dar Kaadarith search for him even now."

"Korfax?" she gasped, astounded. "But he was supposed to be dead!"

"Indeed, mistress."

"Come with me!" she commanded.

She went to her apartments. He waited outside as she entered. She went straight to her shew-stone and saw that it was dark. Its pale light had been almost completely eclipsed and featureless night now spilled from its depths. But even as she looked, the last of its light began to die.

It meant only one thing. Her shadow, her accursed shadow, was on her heels again and this time he was very, very near. It took a moment for her to still the rise of panic, but now she understood. Korfax was her hunter.

She felt dismay. She had been outplayed in some way. If Korfax was indeed the shadow that had been pursuing her for all this time, then how in the name of all the dark heavens had he managed to escape her snares? Not even a Geyadril of the Dar Kaadarith could have evaded her traps, not now – they no longer possessed such insight. Think of it! Tohtanef had called up three Zibra, Molpan had summoned a Rapalen and Korfax had survived both encounters. She had even passed on her knowledge of the Givyalag to Axayal and Korfax had seemingly ridden out that storm as well. Three entities, all of ever-increasing power, not known in any of the writings or the bestiaries, had been defeated in battle. The rumours from the furthest east, especially, were the most worrying. Apparently the Givyalag had caused much damage, even slaying Axayal ere it departed. Many had died, but her shadow had not. He had seen all her traps and evaded them. And the proof of it was before her, for the centre of her shew-stone was midnight.

"Ronoar!" she called.

"Mistress?" he answered, coming to stand at the door to her apartments.

"We are leaving!" she said. "We are leaving now! Leave behind as few as can be spared. Tell Mirzinad that he is in command."

Ronoar peered back at her uncertainly.

"We are leaving?"

She pointed at her shew-stone.

"Now! Korfax is here. He is coming for me."

"Korfax is your hunter?"

"Yes, I am certain of it, and the wrath of the great guilds will surely be following in his unsubtle wake. We should not be here. Mirzinad will stay. Tell him that if Korfax does come here, and he manages to slay him, I will elevate him to the position of first. That will be incentive enough, I think. He will buy us the time that we require."

Ronoar swallowed and bowed, his mind seething with questions, but they could wait. He understood one thing above all others. Duty first.

The tower seemed empty, but Korfax knew that it was not. He could sense others here, other minds lurking behind its quiet walls. This place had all the makings of a trap, with Adavor as the bait.

He entered through the door and followed the finding mist down many flights of stairs. He saw no one until he reached the bottom. He heard the sounds of movement above, and looking up he caught sight of two scurrying figures in dark robes. They looked like servants, the way they were dressed, the way that they moved, clutching at their burdens and their heads bowed. He would have turned about, but then he remembered the finding mist. He had to follow it. As it was bound to him, so he was bound to it.

The finding mist took him to a door behind which something snarled and gurgled. Korfax shuddered. What had been left here to greet him? And what had it done to Adavor? He drew his Qorihna and opened the door.

The Baramak was only the merest moments away from her when it let out the most appalling howl. Adavor opened her eyes and saw that it was impaled upon black fire. Flames erupted along its length as the substance of its flesh bled away into nothing. In no time at all it was reduced to floating flakes of ash.

Adavor looked about her, trying to see what had destroyed the creature, but there was nothing there. Then, right in front of her, the air rippled and Korfax stepped into view. She uttered an involuntary gasp at the shock. She had been saved at last.

He said nothing to her, but his eyes were as hot as they were eloquent as they marked her torment. He released her quickly from her bonds and caught her carefully in his arms, before lowering her gently to the floor. It took all her self-control to put down her hysteria as she wrestled her terrible fear back into the shuttered darkness from which it had emerged. Korfax, meanwhile, undid his great black cloak and placed it about her, covering her nakedness like a comfort. Then he knelt down beside her and held her whilst tears fell down her cheeks.

"We should leave," he said quietly. "The trap that has been set in this place has not yet been sprung."

She looked up at him.

"What trap?"

"Can you not feel it in the air?" he asked.

"I am in no fit state to feel anything," she told him. "They... raped me... amongst other things."

Korfax stared down at her and his eyes lit up with astonishment and rage.

"They *raped* you?"

She bowed her head. More tears fell. He held her closer and she sobbed against him.

"They will regret that," he promised her. "They will regret that utterly."

"And what, pray tell, will we regret?"

Korfax looked up. Others were at the door, crossing its threshold one after the other, each dressed in the habiliments of the Haelok Aldaria, swords drawn and eyes glaring. Their leader stepped forward. Adavor started with sudden fear and then caught herself. Her eyes filled with hatred.

"Mirzinad!"

She spat the name like a curse. Korfax raised himself up to his fullest height and stood over her.

"Mirzinad, is it?" he asked.

"The very same," Mirzinad answered, bowing slightly. "Well now! Our mistress was correct. Here you are, just as she said you would be."

Mirzinad hefted his sword. Faint fires ran up and down its length. Korfax watched the blade carefully. It was not a Qorihna, but it was not an ordinary blade either. It had been invested with power in some way, potent energies wrenched from the Mahorelah, no doubt. The same seemed to be true of Mirzinad's armour, for it, too, gleamed with a dim and orbiting fire.

Korfax waited, not yet drawing his own sword or awakening his armour. If they did not know of the powers at his disposal, maybe they would be overconfident. So he played to the gallery and kept his hands at his sides.

"And where is your mistress?" he asked. "I would have words with her."

Mirzinad smiled grimly.

"Oh, you will have words with her. You will have many words with her, more than you would be willing to part with, I think."

Mirzinad fingered his blade.

"We know about you, Korfax. Our mistress has told us all about you."

He gestured with his sword.

"Surrender, if you please. You are over-matched. There are seven of us."

Korfax tilted his head.

"Only seven?" he questioned. "I am insulted!"

Adavor laughed quietly at the jest, but Mirzinad only widened his smile.

"Your mockery is badly out of place," he sneered.

Korfax smiled in return.

"Then we have symmetry, you and I," he answered. "For I think the same of your confidence."

He gestured at the walls.

"Have you not been paying attention to the world outside? Who do you think

129

put that hole in the side of the Umadya Nudenor? And why are the Dar Kaadarith and the Balt Kaalith running this way and that across the city? They hunt me, even now, but they cannot find me."

He dropped his smile.

"I am not unskilled, nor untutored," he continued, "and I have already slain many of your followers. Now, if you surrender to me and tell me what I want to know, I might be merciful."

Korfax felt Adavor tense under his hand, but he gently squeezed her shoulder. She relaxed again. Mirzinad, meanwhile, took another step into the room. His companions spread out to either side, seeking to surround both Korfax and Adavor.

"As I said before," Mirzinad replied, "we know all about you. And I think you have been altogether too busy this day. You must be so very tired after so much activity."

He held up his hand, and in his grasp he revealed a small and oddly shaped stone that gleamed with a dull light.

"This is a ralaxdo," he announced. "It shows me things. And what it shows me now is that you have quite exhausted yourself. You have a blade, I see, but no stave. I think that you will find us more than adequate to the task of bringing you down, so do not trouble us with tales of your skill and your power. I am the only one here able to grant mercy, so surrender to me and you might earn it. Refuse and the consequences will be dire."

Korfax waited, his face neutral.

"But where is Doagnis? I thought she at least would come to gloat."

Mirzinad took another step forward, but his eyes never left those of Korfax.

"There is plenty of time for that. Do you surrender?"

"Sadly for you, I do not," said Korfax.

Mirzinad smiled gladly.

"Then, happily for me, your end is come."

Korfax reached over his right shoulder with his left hand and grasped the hilt of his sword, and it flowed eagerly from its sheath. Then, with his right hand, he held Adavor at his feet whilst he gave full rein to his blade. It reared up above him and then echoed his will with a howl of rage.

With its strange cry still hanging in the air it split into seven parts. Then, even as they raised their blades, it slashed down at all of the Haelok Aldaria that dared threaten its master. Six of them vanished in fire, brief sparks of mortality caught upon a flame too potent for flesh, but Mirzinad somehow managed to parry the seventh blade with his own. The Qorihna reared up once more and snarled, seven blades coming together again as one. Now it writhed with a darker anger. It was not used to being denied. Korfax frowned as he felt his blade's rage in his mind. Sometimes it seemed to be the very mirror of his own, but at other times it seemed altogether far too independent. He thought of the hapless Omloa again.

With all the others gone, Korfax stepped from the side of Adavor and took the fight to Mirzinad, only to find his Qorihna blocked again and yet again by the sorcerous blade of his foe. But Mirzinad's blade was weakening, for every time the Qorihna struck it, it sucked the informing energies out from it, drinking them down, piece by stolen piece. Mirzinad fell backwards, step by faltering step, and now his eyes were full of fear.

"What manner of sword is that?" he gasped as the black blade smashed against his defences for the sixth time. Korfax offered up his most regretful, and his most mocking, smile yet.

"You do not recognise it?" he said. "How paltry you latter-day Haelok Aldaria have become. I am so very disappointed!"

Mirzinad spat.

"No, I do not recognise it. What should I know of the foul lore of the Dar Kaadarith?"

Korfax laughed at last and his Qorihna echoed his laughter with a gruesome chuckle of its own.

"But this is no product of the Namad Dar," he said. "For the blade I hold in my hand is a Qorihna."

Mirzinad widened his eyes in astonishment. Shocked beyond any possible answer, he was speechless at last. Then Korfax bared his teeth and swept his Qorihna down for the seventh time.

Mirzinad's sword came apart in a shower of molten shards and the Qorihna passed through Mirzinad's armour before biting deep into his flesh. Then, even as Mirzinad screamed in agony, the Qorihna reduced him to a pile of ashes and its flames greedily consumed him.

It was done. Korfax stared at the ashes upon the floor for a moment and then went quickly to the door. He peered outside, but there was no one else about. He even risked sending his thought abroad, seeking, hunting and looking, but the tower felt truly empty at last.

He turned back to Adavor. She wasn't moving. He leapt to her side, fearing the worst, but found that she had only passed out through pain. He stroked her hair for a brief moment and then prepared himself once more. There were healing theurgies he could summon, energies that could be pulled from the Mahorelah and used to feed the energies of life. He quickly looked them up in his logadar, read how they were to be employed and then called them into being.

Adavor was bleeding from a number of wounds, so he healed those first. Then he saw the worst of it. Her tail had been cut off. He closed his eyes and shuddered. Fury filled him and he was a moment gathering himself. Then he ground himself back down and set to the task again.

When it was done he laid her back in his cloak and stroked her hair again. He looked upwards. They had seen him coming and no doubt had left in a rush of fear. Good! Perhaps they had been careless, leaving something behind that he could follow.

He stood up and made to leave the room. He looked back at Adavor. Would she be all right? It was a chance he would have to take. He strode from the room with his Qorihna held before him, keeping it in his hand so that its hungry song would fill the tower around him like a warning, just in case.

He went through every room and corridor, dark shadow and singing sword, beast and master, the perfect match it seemed. But more than once Korfax wondered to himself which was which.

When Adavor awoke again she found Korfax's cloak still about her, but Korfax himself was nowhere to be seen. She was no longer in pain. She looked for cuts and bruises, but there were none. Even where her tail had been she felt healed skin. Korfax must have done it. But how? And where was he? She slowly got to her feet. Though her wounds had been healed, her mind had not. She felt ill-used, and the memory of what had been done to her made her crouch back down on the floor and hold herself tight. Alas for her tail.

As she clutched at herself, she noticed the ash piles, seven of them, scattered here and there. She remembered that much at least – Korfax striking at them with his black sword of fire. Then she must have fainted.

About the furthest pile lay a few fragments of still smoking metal, shrinking even as they fumed. She looked at the brittle remnants, curling in upon themselves like so many pieces of smouldering fabric. They would be gone soon. Adavor looked hard at them.

"I hope there was pain," she muttered.

The door opened behind her and she turned about in fear, but Korfax stepped in to the room and she breathed a sigh of relief. He looked down at her.

"How do you feel?" he asked.

"I am less than I should be," she said, "but I can still travel."

She gestured at the ash heap in front of her with her toes.

"Did he die in pain?"

Korfax suddenly looked troubled as though stirred by a guilty memory.

"I do not think that anyone caught upon my blade dies well," he said.

Adavor looked down.

"I am sorry that I missed it," she said.

Korfax did not answer for a moment. He sheathed his sword and came to her. He stood before her and then reached out, holding her shoulders.

"I would much rather slay the Agdoain than our own people," he said.

Adavor looked back up at him, her gaze sharpening.

"Be satisfied, then. I consider any servant of Doagnis to be as low, perhaps even lower. At least the Agdoain do not betray their own kind."

Korfax grimaced.

"You think so? Then you do not know the Agdoain as well as you believe. In their extremity they will even consume their own."

He turned away. She did not deserve his admonishments, but he was on fire inside. He looked at her again.

"I saw what was done to you. I healed it as best as I could. Forgive the intimacy."

She looked at him intently.

"Forgive you? You saved my life," she said. "I am already deep in your debt."

She reached up and touched him.

"You are such a strange mixture," she told him. "Gentleness and rage."

There was a long silence, and then Korfax drew back and held up some clothes.

"I found these as well."

Adavor sighed in gratitude.

"My badges of office," she said.

"It is all there," Korfax told her. "It has been carefully kept. I imagine they intended some subterfuge with it."

Adavor smiled at him as she reclaimed her uniform.

"And now you lessen my dishonour," she told him. "You erase it, even. Thank you."

Korfax frowned.

"What dishonour?"

"No Noqvoan must ever relinquish their badges of office."

"One who does not let their riches fall from their hands at need has already set one foot within the river."

Adavor took the rest of her clothes from him.

"We all have our different ways," she returned.

Once dressed, she gave him back his cloak.

"What now?" she asked.

"I have searched this place," he said. "They left in a hurry, leaving much behind. Some of what they left is..." He paused. "...troublesome."

Adavor looked up in surprise.

"Troublesome?"

"I doubt it," he said.

"Doubt? What do you doubt?"

"Doagnis – her intent!"

"Her intent?"

"I don't understand it. You should see it and tell me what you think. You may know more than I."

"Where is it?"

"Follow."

He led her from the room.

The tower was large and labyrinthine, filled with many rooms and many winding stairs, thereby making its geography difficult to remember, but Korfax

133

was certain of the way to go. He took her along a corridor hung with a few old and threadbare tapestries and then up a single flight of stairs, which were cut into the very rock on which the tower itself had been built. Along another corridor they went until they came upon two sets of stairs. Korfax took the left, taking her up three flights and past two small landings, both empty of ornamentation but not of the detritus of panic. Adavor could see how it had been. The place had been stripped in a hurry. On one of the landings there were shards of pottery where something had been dropped. On another there were stains upon the rock, dark drips that trailed all the way back down to the lower doors. She found herself hoping that their fear had choked them.

At the top of the stairs Korfax led her into a huge room, its great windows giving a wide view of the western quarter of the city. But Adavor had no time to stop and stare, for Korfax led her out of that room and into another, a darker, smaller room, almost an annex. There was a table there, its top scattered with burnt parchment. Three fragments had been laid out as if for inspection. Korfax passed his hand over them all.

"Read those," he said. "I rescued them from a still smouldering pyre."

Adavor leaned forward and passed her eyes over the neat script imprinted upon the surface of each piece. It was easy to read. Whoever had written it had used Nanhtah script, square and solid. Adavor read all of it, before turning back to Korfax.

"I see what you mean," she said.

Korfax passed his hand over his face whilst looking askance at the pieces of parchment.

"It could be a ruse, of course," he murmured. "Doagnis has planted some subtle snares for me before now."

Adavor did not answer for a while. She read the parchments again and then looked back at Korfax.

"But this tells me that the Haelok Aldaria are actively engaged against the Agdoain."

She held up the pieces in turn.

"These are the remains of reports on the disposition of forces. I see victories here, reports of victories, and Korfax, I can verify two of them at least."

He looked at her as if she suddenly appalled him.

"You can verify them?" he hissed.

"Yes," she said. "The Balt Kaalith have known of at least two of the events documented here. There was the sudden and mysterious diminishment of Agdoain forces at the pass of Madimer. Then there was the complete cessation of hostilities around Gozer. These are matters of record. Many of my order wondered what this portended at the time, but now you have found the answer. Doagnis was responsible."

Korfax seemed to shudder and his eyes became dark and bloodless.

"I cannot accept it," he said. "That Doagnis is fighting the very creatures she has called into this place? She is of the Argedith! What you call up you can put down again! It is writ!"

She held up one of the pieces, a fragment of a letter.

"But look at this one," she said. "Someone called Axayal is telling Doagnis that he still cannot divine the origin of the Agdoain. That also is suggestive."

Korfax looked darkly at the fragment.

"What of the tale of Orpahan? What of that?"

Adavor took a deep breath.

"It was unclear who that was."

"Not to me, it wasn't," he told her. "She was there, at the statue. Asvoan herself confirmed it. This is some game she is playing, pointing us in one direction and then going in another. She is responsible for the Agdoain, she has to be."

"Korfax, I know that you hate her, but think for a moment. What if she is not the one responsible? I think..."

Suddenly he swept his hand across the table, scattering the fragments. Adavor watched the rage rear up in his eyes.

"AND I DO NOT CARE WHAT YOU THINK!"

Within an instant his face was a hand's breadth from hers and his eyes were two molten pools of fire in his head. She shrank back. The fury had taken him again. He stood over her now, dwarfing her, and as she stared up into his burning eyes she felt herself suspended over a chasm, a deep, dark place where rage, grief and self-loathing battled with each other, sculpting and re-sculpting their firmament as they fought for control. She dragged her sight away from the blackness and looked down, suddenly terrified of the passion that boiled in front of her.

"There is a saying in the Balt Kaalith," she ventured. "Reason saves, passion damns!"

"THEN IT IS A SHAME THAT THOSE OF YOUR ORDER DO NOT FOLLOW SUCH SAGE ADVICE!" he roared back. Then he turned and left the room. It was as though a sword had suddenly sliced the air between them.

His voice came back to her from the other room, far and distant, but crystal clear. Adavor found herself more afraid of the stillness than she had ever been of anything else in her life.

"Once upon a time," came the voice, "I stood upon a wall, filled to the brim with a rage and a grief I could not contain. I destroyed my enemies by the hundred, by the thousand, but it did not suffice. My father lay dead at my feet." There was a pause. "I changed stone. I saved the city." Another pause. "But only for a little while. The city fell, and I fell with it. I lost my honour, was betrayed and scorned. But the darkest hour was yet to come."

She knew what was coming next.

"I lost my love."

She closed her eyes. Such pain there was, such dreadful pain. She went out to join him, fearful of what she might find, but he was not how she thought he would be. He was staring out of the great window, staring through the world beyond and reaching out to other places, the dark places that lay on the other side of his heart. He turned to her even as she approached, and she saw the fracture behind his eyes.

"It must be Doagnis," he told her. "She was the one at the statue. She was the one who threatened the council and killed Abrilon and Asvoan. She is the one behind all of this! It must be her! It has to be her! I need it to be her!"

7

RUIN

Kia-zilef Thila-rasjon
Ix-qisged Mirk-ralinji
Turso-eoi Talul-a-arn
Ton-dr-pan Zintorz-uje
Dl-ith-pr Bai-ks-vimihs
Tolbig-qo Krg-us-a-ul
Map-ipnis Vorzum-jijiz

A single sky ship appeared over the city. It span down to the great landing field and almost crashed into the ground, so fast was it moving. All its doors were flung wide and many stumbled out, but all made way for the single rider who emerged at last, a rider bearing a single burden. All bowed their heads as he passed by, whether sick or broken or even dying, and few raised them again for long moments afterwards. The rider went all the way to the Poamal Gevamah, where he dismounted and entered, carrying his burden before him.

Genadol watched as Napeidril Undariss walked steadily into the throne room. None barred his way. In his arms was a body, limp and unmoving, wrapped about in a blood-stained cloak of purple. Undariss stopped before his master but did not bow. Instead, with a face of stone, he set the body down upon the floor at the feet of his Audroh. Then, and only then, did the stone begin to crack. Grief racked him and Genadol dreaded the words that he knew would follow.

"Audroh of the Zinu, most venerable and most wise, behold your son," Undariss cried out. "Great deeds are his, most worthy of song. I bring the body back to you, but alas for the spirit, it has already fled."

Another stepped forward, Falra, wife to Noqmal. She did not say a word but sank to her knees before the body and bowed her head. She remained utterly silent and shook with grief. Others came to comfort her. Usdurna did not move. He sat like a statue, one with his throne. Genadol looked up at his prince, saw the stillness and stepped forward himself.

"But what of the battle? What of the Agdoain?" he asked.

Undariss turned his brittle eyes to the heavens.

"We slew them by the hundreds of thousands," he said. "Rivers of fire we raised, storms of crystal air and the Agdoain that came against us were burned and crushed beneath our feet. Though the foe flowed from Emethgis Vaniad like unending corruption, we slaughtered them all, even to the very last. But it availed us not. From the north another army came, greater by far than any we had heard rumour of, and they fell upon our rear and slaughtered us in our turn."

"It is a defeat?"

Undariss closed his eyes.

"Of the mighty host we sent west, only a few rode out the storm. I came back with but two hundred at the most. Few of the Dar Kaadarith or the Balt Kaalith survived, and few of the Nazad Esiask either. The sword of doom has fallen and we are no more."

He looked down and sank to his knees.

"We have failed, even in this. I also come with a warning. The Agdoain pursue us even now. They are coming here."

"At least we have time to prepare, then," said Genadol, but Undariss made the gesture of denial.

"They will be here within the hour," he said.

All stared at Undariss.

"But how is that possible?" asked Genadol. "Even if the road was straight, Othil Ekrin is at least a hundred days' hard march from Emethgis Vaniad."

Undariss wiped his hands over his eyes.

"In our retreat we took a single sky ship," he said. "The others we left behind and the Agdoain took them. As our ship turned about and headed east, I saw the grey horde swarming below, filling up the ships we had left and making them fly. They follow us, but they are not so skilled in the art of flight. Make no mistake, though. We saw many of the ships we had abandoned rise up, covered with Agdoain. We saw them turn and follow us, and though they travel slowly, they come with great speed nonetheless."

It was as they left the tower that they saw the sky ship. Korfax pointed at it.

"There is something wrong there," he said. "Look at it."

Adavor looked up to where he pointed. There was a sky ship, indeed, but it did not gleam in the light. Instead its hull was dark as though it had been smeared with shadow. Its flight was erratic also, strange and wandering. Even as it cleared the cliffs of the upper lands it began to come down to the landing field, barely missing the stone as it staggered through the air. They both watched it sink lower and lower, and Korfax felt the touch of ice. He knew, even before he saw them, that there were Agdoain on that ship. He could feel them, their emptiness and their hunger.

The sky ship came closer and they could see that its skin crawled. Agdoain heaved upon the gleaming metal, movements like waves, rising and falling as the journey's ending roused them from their sleep.

Diseased and failing, the sky ship dropped onto the landing field at last and broke apart, cracking like some immense and rotten egg. Countless Agdoain poured outwards, spilling like grey yolk, a vile tide, fully grown and ravenous.

Korfax drew his sword and stared in horror. How was this possible? What had happened? Adavor pointed upwards.

"Look!" she said.

Another sky ship was descending, and it too swarmed with the grey, whilst another appeared beyond that and another beyond that. They formed a disorderly queue of vengeance, dropping out of the sky and down into the heart of the city. The grey hordes had come to Othil Ekrin at last, falling from the sky in their tens of thousands.

Korfax ran with Adavor along the great east road. Most of the sky ships they had seen had now come down across the city. Some had crashed into towers, others had fallen into nearby ravines, but all of them had spilled their cargo of grey. Everywhere they looked they saw the signs of growing battle, the smoke of conflict darkening the pristine air like an outrage. Distant shapes scurried across bridges, while frantic movements filled the streets and the squares. The great tapestry that was Othil Ekrin was beginning to unravel in a tangle of panic and fear.

Korfax rubbed at his armour and then touched his sword. Then he looked about him as though suddenly lost. Adavor watched for a moment.

"Korfax?"

"I cannot leave!" he said.

"We must pursue Doagnis," she told him.

He looked at her, but his eyes were dim. He gestured vaguely upwards.

"But what of the city?"

How strange he seemed to her now, shrunken and diminished. His fires were all but gone, doused by his doubts.

"We must pursue Doagnis," she insisted. "It is the only purpose left to us. She must be stopped. If we remove her, then we have one less enemy to worry about."

Korfax looked about him again.

"But she has fled this place," he said. "The Agdoain are here. Othil Ekrin needs me." He gestured vaguely at the city. "I have already witnessed the fall of Emethgis Vaniad. I do not wish to see Othil Ekrin suffer the same fate."

"But what can you do?"

"I can fight."

"Then you would die," she told him. "You cannot fight all the Agdoain that were ever spawned. They would overwhelm you by sheer weight of numbers."

Korfax turned to plead with her.

"But I cannot just run," he said.

"You must. We have to..."

A hissing roar interrupted them. As if summoned by their name, many Agdoain dropped down onto the road from the wall above and landed before them both. They crouched and hissed for a moment, but all too soon they rose up again and advanced, mouths grinning and weapons raised.

Without a thought Korfax drew his Qorihna. With an enemy before him he seemed to gain stature again, his fires building and his rage rising. Adavor breathed a little easier and then drew her own sword as well, mirroring it with her knife. But then Korfax turned to her and pushed her roughly back.

"Get behind me," he ordered.

Adavor turned on him. Now it was her fires that rose up.

"Why?"

"You have not seen these weapons in action. I would shield you."

She looked even more offended.

"You will not! I will fight, as is my due. I am not untutored in the ways of battle."

And with that she leapt forward. Korfax spat a curse and then followed after her. Adavor clashed with the first Agdoain, adroitly turning its blade with her own so that she could stab upwards with her knife. It blocked her with its shield and stepped back. But then something came between her and it, and the Agdoain disintegrated, dark fires erupting from a sudden wound that reached from its groin all the way to its gullet. It crumbled to the ground in smoking ruin and all too soon there was nothing left except a pile of ash.

Adavor stared about her, but she could not see Korfax at all. The Agdoain advance fell apart as something tore its way through them all with a terrible speed, leaving only ashes in its wake. Adavor was still staring about her in disbelief even as the last grey shower fell to the floor. Then Korfax reappeared in front of her, his sword moaning in his hand as though in the throes of some hideous ecstasy.

"What was that?" she asked. "What did you do?"

Korfax looked back at her carefully as he sheathed his sword.

"That," he replied, "was my Qorihna. Now do you see why I warned you? The weapons I wield are far beyond your experience. I can walk straight up to the enemy and strike them down without them even knowing what it is that slays them. My intention wasn't to shame you, Adavor, but to preserve you. Can you truly say that you can match me when I wield such might?"

Adavor stepped back.

"Perhaps not, but I can still aid you, can I not?" She gestured at the sword. "I can see now why you think you can kill Doagnis. Before this day your weapons were but words on a scroll. Having seen what they can do, though, I find myself wondering how Karmaraa ever managed to be victorious at all!"

"It is a long story," said Korfax. "Suffice it to say that Sondehna was not using this Qorihna nor wearing this Qahmor when he went into battle. He was betrayed, as many have been that dared trust another with their life and their love."

Usdurna stood by the window and watched as his city began to fall to the enemy. Beside him stood Genadol.

"We have failed," said Usdurna. "There are no words that I can say, no powers at my command that will change the inevitable. My city dies with me. My son is dead and my line has ended."

"But there is still an heir to the throne," said Genadol. "What of your son's child? What of him, Audroh?"

"An heir to a broken throne and a broken city? I would not have that; rather, I would have nothing at all."

Genadol gestured to the door.

"We should leave, Audroh. We should leave now."

Usdurna turned and stared at Genadol. The singular look Genadol had glimpsed earlier now sat fully in Usdurna's eyes. They had become unfathomable again, eclipsed by the light of a strange and ailing moon.

"Leave?" Usdurna said. "I shall not leave my city, my beauty, my jewel." He looked out of the window again. "Who has your beginning in glory..." he cried. Tears began to fall. "Long she was in the building," he said, turning back. "Great she was in her youth, but now death takes her at last. She is sinking, sinking fast into the chaos that awaits us all. She should not suffer."

Usdurna put out his hand and placed it gently on the shoulder of Genadol, but Genadol could feel a tremor there, a dim quiver like the rise of fever. He stared back into Usdurna's eyes and the moon-driven depths stared back out at him, luminous and still.

"She should not suffer!" Usdurna insisted. "If your favourite steed is struck with a malady which cannot be cured, what do you do? If there is no power in the world or the heavens that you cannot summon to your aid, then you ease it on its way, do you not? Allow no suffering; that is our creed. But now my city suffers and there is no way to redeem her. We should help her on her way, Genadol, we should help her on her way."

Genadol swallowed. He tried to see what Usdurna was thinking, but something held him at the borders. He could feel nothing but a whirling confusion beyond, as though some great gyre turned within the mind of his prince, hurling anything aside that came too close. Usdurna stared back at Genadol for a moment, and then his grip strengthened. Usdurna had suddenly become strong, horribly strong. Genadol tried to twist out of his prince's grasp, but Usdurna followed him, tightening his hold. Bones bent under the force of his hands and Genadol winced at the pain.

"Do not deny my will in this," Usdurna told him. "You will obey me! You must obey me! You have no choice!"

Usdurna struck Genadol across the throat. Genadol fell backwards to the floor, fighting for breath and shocked into inaction by the speed of the attack. He rolled over, clutching at his throat as Usdurna snatched his stave from his hands and slammed it into the floor. The room shuddered and Genadol was thrown backwards, all the way to the wall.

"Do not try to deny me," Usdurna said. "Though you have served me well, like your father before you, I will not forgive you if you disobey me now. Leave this place. And may this be the very last mercy that I ever grant you."

Usdurna ran off. Genadol staggered to his feet. That someone so old could be so fast! Still rubbing his throat, he ran after his prince.

Usdurna was heading down, taking one of the many stairs down to the gates. Genadol followed, trying to persuade others to stop the Audroh by shouting ahead, but either they did not understand, or they would not. Stop the Audroh? The very thought! The mad pursuit continued.

Genadol expected Usdurna to go through the gates and out into the city, but he did not. Instead he kept going down, down to the lower levels. Genadol followed. What was Usdurna doing?

Down they went, ever down, to the lowest levels of all. Here began the foundations, below even the river, sunk in ages past deep into the bones of the world. Usdurna ran to the centre and stopped there, holding up the stave. Genadol arrived just in time to feel Usdurna reach into his stave and take hold of its power with his mind. Then Usdurna sent that power spiralling downward into the rock beneath them both, driving it deeper and deeper, as far down as he could. Genadol stared in horror. He was too late.

Usdurna had been a master of earth many, many years ago, but he had never used his power again after he had ascended to the throne of Othil Ekrin. He had once been strong, by all accounts, but the power he wielded now was nothing short of terrifying. Genadol was held immobile by his shock. Were all the rules he had lived by all his life about to be overturned? First there was Korfax, able to do things with the Namad Dar that no one had thought possible. Now a mad old prince was giving a lesson in power to a Geyadril at his peak. The world had suddenly turned upside down.

Genadol could feel what Usdurna was doing, could feel him grasp the bedrock deep beneath the city. Then he felt Usdurna shake it, as though two great hands burrowed down into the deep rock and pulled the roots of the world apart.

The ground shook. Korfax turned and placed his hand upon the stone at his side. He stared at Adavor in shock but did not speak. She looked back at him in consternation.

"What is it? What is happening now?" she asked.

"Someone has awoken the stone beneath our feet," he told her. "I can feel it. A master of earth has reached down into the foundations beneath the city and is overturning them. By the Creator! Such power!"

"How is that possible?"

"I do not know, but we must find shelter. This will destroy everything."

"Is it some device of the Agdoain?"

Korfax concentrated, even as the ground began to shake with ever increasing fury.

"No," he said, "not the Agdoain. This act is by Ell hand alone. I can feel it, but the touch! It is like chaos. Whoever has done this, whoever has touched the stone, they intend to bring Othil Ekrin crashing down about us all! Everyone will die! The Agdoain, the Ell, everyone!"

Adavor looked about desperately.

"Where is safest?" she asked. "Above or below?"

"Neither," he answered, standing up. "We are too late. There is no time. It has already begun."

The stone, the towers, the roads and the bridges, everything about them shook. Cracks appeared up walls, across roads and down into the bedrock. The ground began to dance under their feet and they found themselves unable even to stand. Korfax caught hold of a naming post and reached out for Adavor, but she had already fallen too far from him. The road beside them now bucked as though some great subterranean beast flexed itself below the surface, and Adavor was hurled even further away, rolling back down the shallow incline. Korfax made to follow her, but before he could take even a single step, the ground before him lifted up with a tormented groan. He clutched back at the post and watched as a chasm appeared, a great tear in the ground belching dust. In moments it had widened further than he could jump, pulling the road apart even as it grew. Then it lengthened, splitting the wall on the other side, before making its way up the great pillar of rock beyond that. He stared upwards as the towers and houses above him began to come apart slowly and fall. In moments he would be engulfed.

As he stared upwards, so it happened again, even as it had when he had lifted his father's stave, or duelled with the Agdoain or changed a piradar into something else. The moment came, but this time it fell upon him like the lazy fall of sunlit motes. Mere moments seemed to last for ever whilst his mind flew this way and that like a thing possessed.

In the grimoires of Sondehna there were many things one could do to escape danger, but the one that came to him now was the same one he had considered in his cell in the Umadya Nudenor. He must summon himself out of the world to a waiting place. There, he had had a choice. Here, he did not.

His mind became a point, un-dimensioned, dark brilliance and intolerable fire flashing downwards like an all-piercing sword. Stars, the heavens, illimitable night, all flew up and away from him, whilst the black abyss opened at his feet and he found what he was looking for. It lay below him, down in the darkness, and seeing it he went to it, just as a mountain of rock toppled slowly down from above to crush him.

One moment he stood upon the crumbling road, the next he stood somewhere else.

He peered at the surrounding gloom with eyes suddenly able to accept anything. It had worked. He had hurled himself away from danger, out of the world, out of the Bright Heavens themselves. He had summoned himself all the way back to the Mahorelah, and of all the acts of sorcery, this surely had to be one of the strangest.

He stood now within a pocket of air, a bubble, suspended in a matrix that was neither stone, nor metal, nor flesh. He stifled a shiver of loathing. Safe he might be, but this place was not one in which he would choose to linger.

He shied away from the confining walls that contained him, for they gleamed unpleasantly as though coated with slime. But neither did they move, though it seemed that they should, being ribbed and folded and set with many blind and drooping orifices. There was a hint of transparency as well, as though something waited outside, lurking deep within the walls or beyond them, but try as he might, Korfax could not see anything except a vague suggestion of dim unmoving forms.

The light, such as it was, was drear, and it seemed to come either from his presence or from the air itself, which felt both damp and stale. Korfax breathed with reluctance, suddenly fearful that some taint or sickness might enter him and make a new home for itself inside. Visions of demons swam in his head, but he saw and felt nothing untoward. Unpleasant as it was, there appeared to be no real harm here. He was safe enough, for the moment.

He looked down and noticed a small scattering of detritus near his feet. Amongst the less recognisable items he discerned the remains of a scroll, its edges crumbling and discoloured. There were also what appeared to be a few coins, each covered by a dark mould as they spilled from a folded piece of dirty cloth. He bent to examine them.

He reached for the cloth, but it was too fragile and came apart as soon as he touched it. A faint scent came to him as it disintegrated, the faintest hint of a perfume he could not place. He thought of flowers long faded, years past, innocent moments taken under a younger sky, but then it all vanished beyond recall and he found that he held nothing between his fingers but so much dust. He rubbed the dust away and carefully picked up a few of the coins.

The coins were blackened and corroded and details were difficult to descry, but even by their touch, Korfax knew that they had long outstayed their day. They felt ancient. He studied them carefully and found that the best of them still showed a few remaining characters from their initial casting, so he rubbed away the all-consuming mould and managed to reveal a name. The name was old, far older than Korfax would have liked. The coin he held in his hand had been cast during the reign of Aolon, and Aolon had been the father of Sondehna. That made the coin well over seven thousand years old. Korfax shivered and dropped the decaying sliver as though it had burned him. The clash of the present with the past was too disturbing.

He turned to the scroll next. Should he touch it? Dare he? What would it reveal?

It appeared more robust than the cloth, but even so, both ends had wholly succumbed to the ravages of time. Nor could the writing upon it be easily read, but Korfax persisted all the same, despite the dim light.

The script was fine but uneven, an older variation on Nanhtah, for the words were different, strange in unprecedented ways and oddly formed, so it was a long moment before he could extract their meaning. When he did so he soon realised that he held a letter in his hand, a letter from a lady to her lover, from one Jernis to one Ramenur. Korfax did not recognise either of the names. Time had swallowed them both.

'Ramenur, my love, if you discover these few paltry words then I hope that you will forgive me for leaving. I stayed as long as I could at the threshold, but I fear it will not prove long enough. The hunters have been at my heels ever since the fall of Melluhdril, and I am become weary with flight. It was only as a last resort that I came here. No one saw me, or so I thought, but I cannot be entirely certain. No doubt I will find out when I return, for return I must.

'I fear I will find them waiting for me. They know all our ways, it seems. They are both cunning and ruthless and have made of the river a great and hungry mouth.

'I am in an agony of fear, knowing that I must eventually leave, whilst dreading it as well. They are everywhere.

'The one hope I have is that they have not yet discovered the place from which I came, or how I achieved it. I know that none would talk openly of it, of your house or of mine, but they torture those that they capture and not all possess the strength to endure.

'So I have nothing left to me but hope, hope that you will follow in my wake, hope that our hiding places are still a secret known only to us.

'If you follow me, and I pray to the Creator that you do, know that there are no safe ways to the south except for one. With luck I hope to make it to the Pisea Gonos, and from there I shall cross the southern plains to Thilzin Jerris.

'Though I long to be with you, though every moment apart is an agony, I have a fear that this is merely the beginning of a far greater suffering that is to come and that we shall not meet again this side of the river. I live in hope that I shall see your sweet face once more.

'May the Creator's light shine upon you during this unending darkness, my life and my love.

'Jernis.'

Korfax bowed his head. The writer of this letter was as much an Ell as he was, whatever the Balt Kaalith might say otherwise. He could imagine himself writing such words to Obelison in his extremity. He wondered what tale lay behind the little he had encountered here. Had Ramenur ever followed his love? Had they been reunited again across the far seas? Given that the scroll still lay here, forgotten and decaying, he doubted it. Ramenur had never come to this place at the very least.

Korfax put the scroll down next to the coins and stared about him. How many other such places lay scattered throughout the Mahorelah, tiny caches of frozen life sealed off from the rest of creation, and what might still lie within them, forgotten by all? He did not know, but he could offer a guess. He looked at his armour and his black sword. There were secret places yet, secret places waiting to be discovered. Who knew what memories or what calamities filled them?

A strange temptation to leap from one to the other, to see what he could find, came to him, but he turned away from it. He knew the temptation, and he denied it. It was not his fate to become some dark and shadowy voyeur for ever sating himself with the memories of other lives.

It was said that the waiting places had been made – all of them – carved from the substance of the Mahorelah for times yet to come. It explained some of the more curious tales from the histories, how sometimes one of the Argedith would vanish when cornered, going into a room or a cave from which there was apparently no escape. But when a search was conducted, they could not be found. Korfax, though, understood the danger. All one had to do was to wait for them to re-emerge again. For waiting places were just that – places to wait, not to linger. The safety was an illusion. One could not wait for an eternity.

From the letter Korfax guessed Jernis had been fleeing from the fledgling Balt Kaalith, 'The hunters' as she had called them. No doubt they had tracked her to Othil Ekrin, and there they had lost her. Given the tone of the letter, she had possessed little hope she would escape. She had written to her lover in the throes of despair, and clearly she expected to be apprehended when she left this place. They could not follow her here, but they might linger nearby and catch her when she re-emerged from her impermanent sanctuary.

Even as he pondered, Korfax became aware of a growing sensation. It was as though he was being pushed from the inside out. Now he understood the last part of the letter and the warning in the grimoires. Any waiting place would ultimately reject those who waited, returning them whence they had come, whether they willed it or no. If he unclenched that part of his mind that had brought him here, he would return to the place he had left.

It was just as he remembered this fact that an unpleasant thought occurred to him. What if the place he returned to was now solid rock? When he had left Othil Ekrin he had been under a falling mountain. What would he find when he returned?

Like Jernis before him, he now knew that terrible feeling. He dreaded to go, but he also knew that he could not stay.

So he took the chance. Holding his breath he plunged back to the world from which he had fled.

Bright light fell upon him as he dropped down out of the air, only to land upon a large and uneven slab of rock. He fell to his knees and coughed as a storm of dust swirled around him.

His view was limited. He stood upon a portion of prostrate wall, surrounded on either side by dim and jagged shadows. He had been lucky, or so it seemed. Fate was not finished with him just yet!

He stood straight and called out.

"Adavor!"

There was no answer. He scrambled higher and called again.

"Adavor!"

There was still no sound. His voice fell flat in the dusty air. He looked this way and that, but swirling clouds obscured everything. If Adavor was alive the only way to find her was with sorcery again.

As before, he called up a finding mist, letting it coil about him as it awaited his will. He collected his thoughts and feelings and let the mist take the scent of Adavor from his mind, as he had previously. If she was still alive the finding mist would gain her; otherwise, it would leave, revealing that she was already dead. So his heart quickened with hope when the finding mist darted forward. He followed it eagerly, but as before it was quicker than he. Every so often it stopped, swirling upon itself and waiting for him to catch it up.

Korfax found himself wondering if this was the very same mist he had conjured before or whether it was another one. He watched it carefully for some sign of recognition, but he saw nothing that would identify it. The mist had no distinguishing features that he could see, and it remained as it ever had been – a mottled pattern informing the substance over which it passed: stone, air, fire or water.

The mist led him through the dust-laden air to a huge tower, overturned and broken like the shattered spine of a giant, and then swirled before it. As Korfax came closer, though, the mist vanished as if swallowed up by the stone beneath. He fairly leapt to the place the mist had once occupied and found that there was a window there, a window that now lay at his feet. He looked below and saw the dim glimmer of the mist waiting for him just at the limit of his sight. He clambered reluctantly over the threshold.

This was a risk. What if the finding mist sank below water? Or went through a gap too small for him to follow? How far should he go? The summoned mist had become a mechanism, his mechanism, the very slave of his thought, following the commandments of its calling and blind to everything else but the task it had been given. He felt the guilt rise up inside, but he thrust it back down again. Once more, he had no choice. If he was to find Adavor then this was the only way left to him.

It was like some lethal game: step this way and die, take this choice and live. It would be like that until the end, he guessed. But what of the mist? Once summoned, it had no choice at all.

Inside the tower everything that was not reduced to splinters or rubble was either upside down or lying on its side. Korfax could see chairs, tables, pottery and crystal, all strewn, all wrecked, and underneath it all, at the very bottom, lay what remained of the occupants. None had been spared.

He turned away from the upturned ruin and concentrated instead upon the mist. But the mist did not care and went ever downward, descending through the many cracks in the overturned world, dropping further into deep night.

There were occasional lights here and there, piradar that had been spilled from their fixings or yet clung precariously to this wall or that. Korfax took a few, just in case, and as the darkness grew deeper, he held one up before him, lighting his way.

Eventually he came to another window where the finding mist waited for him. Beyond the broken window lay an impenetrable curtain of black.

The mist darted down into the darkness, but Korfax held out his light, peering downwards before joining it. The ever-present dust made it difficult to see, but he thought he could make out the tilted wall of another tower just below the one he now occupied. There seemed to be a reasonable gap between the two. He dropped down and looked about. The two towers crossed each other between immense walls of shattered rock. He looked at the chaos and the ruin that lay about him. His reason told him that Adavor could not have survived such a cataclysm, but his heart, and the mist, said otherwise. Either way, with his summoned guide leading him, he would soon find out.

He followed the mist along the sloping wall of the second tower, all the way to another window. For the second time he dropped into an overturned world. Through this tower the mist led him, down inverted stairs and across walls instead of floors until he emerged at its shattered top. Great leaning rocks made a temporary roof above him, but below him lay water, a gathering pool here, the merest trickle of a stream there. He must be nearing the level of the Zinkao at last.

The mist led him to a pile of rock beyond one of the pools. There lay the cracked remains of a huge carven archway, still sturdy enough to keep the massed rock above it at bay. Below it was a tiny space. The mist stopped and, having completed its task, vanished back to the realms from which it had been summoned.

Korfax called out.

"Adavor?"

He waited long moments, holding his breath. He called again, his heart quickening. Then a quiet and answering cry came to him from deep under the arch and he breathed a grateful sigh of relief. He went to the gap.

There was a large stone in the way, almost as large as he was. It would take all his strength to move it. He set to the task.

He moved the stone aside. There was a hole behind it, a small gap. A hand flickered there for a moment, seeking purchase. Then it vanished again. Korfax removed more stone, careful not to disturb anything, because although the arch looked solid enough, he knew it could crumble at any time.

He reached inside and took hold of an arm. He pulled firmly and brought Adavor out. She gasped in pain all the way.

Her right arm was broken, as were several of her ribs, and she had deep cuts and lacerations across her legs, back and head. But the fallen arch had miraculously preserved her life.

Korfax summoned his healing theurgies, setting her bones, mending her skin and stemming the flow of blood. Being conscious, she cried out in pain every time he applied the summoned energies. The process was not gentle, and he winced every time he felt, or heard, her bones snapping back into place. Finally she fainted, a mercy perhaps. Korfax continued until he could do no more. Then he waited for her to awaken again, watching all the while the level of the water about him.

She awoke at last, her face peaceful. She breathed gently for a moment, her eyes unfocused, but then she saw him and looked long at him.

"So you save me again!" she said at last.

"I did what any other would do," he answered.

"But only you could do it," she returned with a smile. She reached out to touch him.

"No other has saved me as you have. Twice have you done it now. Perhaps it has become my destiny to be the one that you for ever save."

Korfax felt the stirrings of unease as he divined something of her emotions. She was giving herself to him, and she was giving herself willingly.

"I would do this for anyone," he told her, but the look on her face said she clearly did not believe him.

"No," she said. "You would not. I have already seen your power and the dreadful spirit that informs it. Only those touched by the Creator have such fires within them. Only those that can tip the balance of fate can do what you have done. And only those that serve the Creator can preserve the Creator's chosen. Am I to be one of them? I tremble at the consequences."

Korfax looked at her as if she horrified him.

"I am not what you think I am," he said.

"But that is not so," she told him. "I know who you are now, even if you still deny it. You are the one who pulls miracles out of destruction and chaos."

Korfax looked away.

"You have not lived my life," he said. "You have not seen what I have seen. I am followed by an ill wind that seeks ever to destroy what I would preserve."

"No!" she said, pulling his face back to hers. "Our world is beset by a foe, a terrible foe that will stop at nothing to destroy and despoil. You are the Creator's answer to that foe. You have turned the evil of the past to a force for good. You have become our banner."

They climbed through a ruined world. Korfax took the same route that he had taken down and Adavor clung to him, letting his strength lift her. What else could she do? She was weak and broken despite the healing he had given her. But there was another, deeper reason. Korfax was her saviour and she had silently vowed to herself that she would not let go of him, ever again.

They emerged into the light at last and Korfax stared out over the ruins as he helped Adavor to stand beside him. Then they both turned about to regard the ruin that enclosed them.

Vapours still coiled upwards, drifting this way and that on the southerly breeze, but the view was much clearer now than it had been when he had returned from the waiting place.

Scattered across the jumbled expanse surrounding them a few sad towers still leaned brokenly at the sky. But between them lay a chaos of rock and water, and there was a silence the like of which Korfax had never experienced before. Occasionally the distant fall of broken stone would disturb it like an echo of what had gone before, but that made the omnipresent silence all the more oppressive, not less.

The entire foundation of the city had sunk and the collapse had created a great circular depression, a vast steep-sided bowl across which lay scattered the sad remnants of its former glory. The canyons had all gone, along with the cliffs and all the towers of rock. The labyrinth had been levelled. But even now, even through this titanic wreckage, the Zinkao continued its irresistible way, following new courses, filling new chasms, ever eager to make its way back to the great ocean beyond.

Korfax watched the water pooling distantly below. A lake was already beginning to take shape around the shattered stump of the Nazarth Nothoah, now the lowest part of what remained of the city. And given the potency of the waters that flowed in from the uplands, the lake would grow quickly.

Strangely enough, the walls of the Vasasan still remained intact. Like a great ridge they stretched to the east, and though the Vasasan was silent now, it would not be so for too long. The falls would soon thunder again when the Zinkao reached them. But that would not happen until the incoming waters had all but drowned what remained of Othil Ekrin.

Adavor stood at his side, still holding on to him for support.

"Where do we go now?" she asked.

He gestured at the ruins around them.

"Walking across this will be perilous," he said, "but the level of the water is rising so I see no choice in the matter. We should head for the south-eastern gate, as it is the closest. We take the highest road that we can."

They scrambled up a hill of detritus and broken boulders, teetering precariously on its sharp and volatile slope. The incline was steep and the footing was treacherous, ever threatening to tip them back down onto the ruin below. More than once an injudicious step would dislodge a rock or start a small landslide. Then there would be a brief rushing sound as the shattered remnants of Othil Ekrin settled further downwards, before silence returned again.

Above them lay the walls of a broken tower, below them – far below – the ever rising waters of the Zinkao slowly pursued them like a promise of drowning.

Korfax, when he was not helping Adavor, peered at the edges of the ruins. He would occasionally catch the odd glimpse of movement here and there as the fortunate few that had survived scrambled out of the sunken wreckage as best they could. To his relief many he saw were Ell, but then he began to spot a few Agdoain as well, scattered groups of gleaming grey that had also weathered the cataclysm, clawing their ugly way up out of the rubble.

It came to the point when Korfax and Adavor could go up no more. They had to go back down again. They had no choice. The way was blocked by immense boulders and unscalable heights. Their path took them back to the water's edge.

Now their world was circumscribed by narrow ways and swirling waters, occasional flotsam drifting past, bobbing in the swell. There were bodies also, part or whole, drowned or broken, turning this way and that. Korfax watched it all with burning eyes. So much lost! So many dead!

It was as they came to a long curving bay of broken walls that they saw a huge tree, drifting into the fragile slopes beyond them. It went this way and that and then it waited, caught between two broken walls that stretched out like jaws. On its great trunk lay a body, clinging for dear life. Korfax stared down. Were they alive?

He removed his armour and much of his clothing, and then he dived into the water and swam to the uprooted tree. He pulled the body away from its place on the great trunk, and then, supporting it with one arm, swam slowly back again. Adavor was waiting to help him back up, bracing herself against the stone and using both her arms and her legs as best as she could.

Back on dry land Korfax placed the body on a flat slab. For a moment he breathed hard. The water had been cold. Then he looked down at who it was that he had saved, and he felt the world tilt about him even more. He knew who this was. He recognised the face and could not be mistaken. It was Thilnor, his friend from his days in the seminary of the Dar Kaadarith, who now lay dying at his feet.

Though he was bruised and cut, none of his wounds appeared mortal. But whilst he was still alive, for some reason he was not breathing. Both Korfax and Adavor tried to revive him, Adavor breathing for him whilst Korfax massaged his chest. Long moments seemed to pass with no reaction at all. And just when Korfax felt it was all to no avail, Thilnor drew breath at last and started coughing. Korfax sagged with relief and then shook him gently.

"Wake up, Thilnor. The river does not have you yet," he said.

Thilnor coughed and spluttered. He opened his eyes.

"I know that voice."

He looked up.

"Korfax!" he breathed. Then he lay back again and closed his eyes. "It had to be you. It could not be any other. You were ever the master of miracles."

Korfax frowned and was suddenly all too conscious of Adavor at his shoulder. He did not have to look at her to feel her sudden approval, for it filled the air about her like a flame. Of all the things Thilnor could have said, that was the worst. Korfax suppressed a sudden rise of rage. They were so wrong. He was no saviour; he was anything but.

"How do you feel?" he asked Thilnor at last, careful to keep his voice as neutral as possible.

"As weak as a child," Thilnor said. "But how did you find me? I thought myself surely dead. There was a dream of tumbling, then the cold of deep waters, then darkness."

"You were clinging to the trunk of a tree," Korfax told him. "Where were you when the city began to fall?"

"The Poamal Gevamah."

Korfax stared back at Thilnor.

"You were at the heart of it? Then you are a master of miracles yourself! You have come a long way indeed. We are approaching the south-eastern gate. You must have fallen into one of the canyons before the swelling current brought you here. But the chances of that happening must have been small indeed."

Thilnor bowed his head. They sat and rested a while, but no one said another word. Thilnor stared at the sky, drinking in the light, Korfax stared at Thilnor, wondering at the chances of the world, whilst Adavor stared at Korfax and dreamed.

Though weak, Thilnor could walk. He leant upon Adavor while Korfax warded them both. Together the threesome made their uncertain way on towards the ruin of the south-eastern gate, the rising water ever at their heels.

"Korfax?"

It was Thilnor.

"Yes?" answered Korfax.

"What manner of sword is it that you carry?" Thilnor asked.

"It is a sword, that is all," Korfax told him.

"No," said Thilnor, "it is much more than that, I think. It is strange, unlike any kansehna I have ever seen. It is so very black."

Korfax glanced back.

"I do not think that you would like the answer to your question," he said.

"What do you mean?"

"Just that – you would not like to know."

Thilnor frowned.

"Korfax, just tell me why, will you? I cannot conceive of anything so dire that I would rather not know it. Knowledge brings its own rewards, or so they taught us at the seminary."

"They did not know this, my friend."

"Come, Korfax, please, tell me what your sword is. I sense power."

Korfax stopped and sighed.

"Do not mistake me in this, Thilnor. Some things are better left in the dark."

"And I think I deserve an answer," said Thilnor.

They looked at each other.

"So be it," said Korfax. "But don't say that I did not warn you. It is a Qorihna."

Thilnor staggered and Adavor steadied him.

"A Qorihna?" he said. "In the name of the Creator, that cannot be. They were all said to have been destroyed."

Korfax did not answer but turned away instead. Thilnor took a moment to think.

"Very well then," he said, "let me ask you a different question. What are you doing with a Qorihna?"

"Wielding it," said Korfax. "What else would I be doing with it?"

"Korfax! Please! Help me in this! A Qorihna? That is a weapon of sorcery. No one should use such a thing. Help me to understand this."

Korfax turned for a second time and looked back carefully at Thilnor.

"You wish to understand? Really? I beg to differ. You already do not like what you are hearing, so imagine how well you will like the rest."

Thilnor frowned and turned to Adavor.

"Do you know what this is about?" he asked her.

"I have heard this tale," she said.

"Then will you tell it to me? Will you tell me why my old friend is armed with such a weapon?"

"I will not," she said. "I am sworn to silence. Besides, your questions are irrelevant. It does not matter. If the hand that wields the power is the hand of a saviour, what more can be said? Accept it for what it is and consider yourself blessed. Did he not save you?"

Thilnor did not miss the sour look Korfax gave Adavor.

"Very well, keep your secrets, the pair of you, but I know more than you think. There were few stories of hope from the fall of Emethgis Vaniad, but one of them comes back to me now, a strange tale told by a certain Branvath, Nudenil Rom Chursaq by name. He believed he saw a black rider on a black ormn who swept the Agdoain aside as if they were chaff. The Balt Kaalith dismissed it as nothing more than a fantasy, but the Exentaser looked deeper and saw the truth. They shared what they saw with a few others. Have you anything to say to that, Korfax?"

Korfax stopped and held himself upright. His eyes had that faraway look again, remote and emotionless, as though he had dipped his hand in some deep pool of power and now drank deep of it. Thilnor felt daunted, despite himself. He suddenly wondered into what strange realm Korfax had now passed. It seemed a very long time before Korfax finally answered.

"I rode Enastul," he said finally, "the finest steed ever sired of the north. Born of Norimeh and Hellus, Enastul was the child of a match that even the Creator could not have bettered. I rode him into battle, and with his help I slaughtered the foe. I slaughtered them by the hundred, by the thousand, even, but that was not enough. Though I wielded the mightiest Qorihna, though I wore the most potent Qahmor, even I, astride Enastul, the prince of all ormn, could not turn the tide alone. And so Emethgis Vaniad fell."

Korfax turned about and looked at Thilnor, who in turn shuddered at the dark light that now fell from his eyes.

"But there will come a time, I promise you," said Korfax, "when nothing shall stand in my way. There will come a time when even the grey void shall fill itself with regret that it ever dared face me in battle."

Korfax withdrew and moved on. They followed him. After a long while he spoke again, but he did not turn his head.

"I have told you a thing, now you must tell me a thing in return. Who destroyed Othil Ekrin?"

"I am uncertain," said Thilnor. "Just before the cataclysm I was told that my master, Geyadril Genadol, had been seen pursuing the Audroh to the foundations of the tower. He ever cried out to those that he passed that Usdurna had gone mad and must be stopped. No one heeded him, but then the tower came apart and it was too late. That is all that I know."

"Usdurna?"

Korfax stopped in his tracks. He was clearly shocked.

"But he was merely a master of earth, nothing more. Where did he gain the power to summon such devastation?"

Thilnor shrugged.

"All saw how he was when Undariss returned with the body of his son."

Korfax held up his hands and stared at them as though they suddenly appalled him.

"Is that it?" he asked. "Is it grief that has caused all of this?"

He looked at Thilnor again. Thilnor bowed his head.

"I believe it," he answered quietly.

Korfax wrung his hands at the heavens.

"Why?" he cried at the sky. "Why must it always be grief? Why can we never find power in joy? Why must we be tormented so? Why must we suffer like this?"

But the sky did not answer him, and neither did Adavor nor Thilnor. Instead they both looked where Korfax stared, seeing only the clear blue vault and the lonely brilliance of Rafarel. If the Creator was listening, there was no sign to say so.

They moved around another broken tower, passing from rock to rock at its shattered base. Beyond the tower lay another, and beyond that stretched a huge mass of tumbled stone like a long ridge.

Korfax was silent now, silent and alone. Neither Thilnor nor Adavor spoke to him – she out of respect, he out of fear.

They were making for what appeared to be a road. From what they could see it seemed likely that it would take them much of the way towards their destination, but first they had to scale a long slope of loose stone and earth.

They reached the top at last. It was no road. Great slabs of stone lay there, the remnants of the ancient walls that had once encased the entire valley of Othil Ekrin. Beyond them reared the scarred rock from which the slabs had fallen, new stone, new cliffs, cracked and raw like open wounds.

Korfax led whilst Adavor and Thilnor followed. Below and behind them, in the far distance, the remnants of the Poamal Gevamah had almost vanished beneath the quickly rising waters. A lone spire like a twisted limb still madly defied the oncoming flood.

The day lengthened. They began to hear far sounds, some behind, some ahead, echoing back and forth across the ruins. No doubt the survivors were gathering as they all headed for the gates. The sounds ahead grew louder, and there were now clear cries of alarm and the clash of arms. Korfax gestured that Adavor and Thilnor wait. He crept forward to the next rise and peered over. Below him he saw the last thing that he had wanted to see at all. A fight.

Several Agdoain were attacking a small group. Though badly outnumbered, the survivors were holding their own yet, but their lives could only be measured in moments. They were ultimately doomed if no help came to them, for even if they fought off their present attackers, more Agdoain were scrambling up towards the affray, no doubt called on by their siblings. Only three of the Ell were armed.

There was a Bransag with a lance, another with a sword and what appeared to be a Noqvoan with a knife. Behind them crouched four others.

Without a second thought Korfax drew his sword and leapt into the fray, vanishing from sight as he did so.

Thilnor went to the edge with Adavor and watched the onslaught. If he had ever doubted the efficacy of Qorihna and Qahmor, he had no doubts now. Where there had been perhaps forty Agdoain, only the ashes of their demise drifted on the breeze. Korfax had burned his way through them all like a harvest fire.

Those he had saved stood and stared at the miracle, but then they fell back when Korfax stepped out of the air. One of them, the Noqvoan, held up her knife.

"You?" she said.

Korfax turned and looked back. Here was another surprise, but not an entirely welcome one.

"And greetings to you, Okodon," he said. "One of the fortunate few, I see."

Okodon looked Korfax up and down, clearly trying to marshal her wits.

"I suppose I should thank you for our lives."

Korfax raised an eyebrow.

"You suppose?"

Okodon straightened her shoulders.

"And what would you prefer? Honesty or insincerity? We both know each other. You are a traitor and a murderer both."

Korfax drew himself up and his eyes glittered.

"So be it, then! But I have no interest in what you think. I am far more interested in how you managed to survive..." He gestured about him. "... all this. The Umadya Nudenor is far from here."

"I was pursuing you," Okodon replied. "After your escape from the hostelry I remembered a report that Adavor had been seen frequenting the Piodo Voadiz. And since I knew that both you and she were pursuing Doagnis, I thought that perhaps you would not be too far behind her."

Korfax looked long and hard at Okodon, until Okodon finally bowed her head and looked away. He gestured back the way he had come. Adavor and Thilnor revealed themselves from above. Okodon looked up at them both for a moment and then scowled.

"So I was right," she murmured to the broken stone at her feet.

"Yes, you were," answered Korfax, "and your guesses have preserved your life. How fortunate for you! The Creator has some purpose for you yet, it seems."

Okodon looked back at Korfax briefly, but his expression was unreadable. She then turned to watch as Adavor and Thilnor scrambled down the slope, ending up beside Korfax. Okodon looked at Adavor especially. Adavor met her gaze and smiled coldly. Okodon scowled in return.

"You may have his protection for now," she said, "but do not think that you will escape our judgement. Eventually you will have to answer for your actions before the Noqvoanel himself. Though you may have forgotten it, you are still of the Balt Kaalith. The rules apply even to you."

Korfax laid a hard hand against Okodon and pushed her backwards.

"Do not flaunt the name of your order in front of me," he said. "I know exactly who and what you are. Adavor has far more honour in my eyes than you could ever achieve in seven lifetimes."

Okodon staggered away but managed to retain her footing.

"And what is that to me?" she said after a moment. "You are a renegade. You are a traitor. I did what was required by the law."

Korfax advanced.

"The law?" he laughed. "Miradar? Truth potions? You are a torturer! You are a slave to torturers! I have no doubt that you have done many questionable things in your time, but believe me, I know the worst of them now. I remember what was done to me."

Thilnor reached out and carefully touched Korfax.

"Miradar?" he asked.

Korfax looked back at him.

"They used them on me in the Umadya Nudenor. They were the last of the few that were given to them by Efaeis, I believe." He turned to the others standing nearby, staring at this exchange with varying degrees of astonishment.

"Do you understand, all of you?" he asked. "That is your precious Balt Kaalith for you. When the law no longer suffices, when it no longer serves their purpose, they would willingly break it. Just like the Velukor did when he broke my betrothal!" Korfax now turned back to Okodon and the contempt in his voice was like a whip. "You are all carved from the very same stone, the very same! My father said it truly. You change with the wind."

Okodon glowered but could not meet the gaze of Korfax for long.

"I was only doing my duty," she offered in return.

Korfax glanced about him. Many looked darkly at Okodon now. Yes, they understood what was being said here. He turned back to Okodon and took a step forward, staring down at her.

"Your duty?" he hissed. "And how many others have said the exact same thing when confronted with their crimes? See yourself for what you are, Okodon." He looked for a little longer and then turned to the others. "Come," he said, "let us go to the gates. We should leave here."

One of the Branith came forward.

"You are Korfax?" he asked.

"I am."

"They say you are a traitor and a murderer."

"I am neither."

"You saved us, and for that I thank you."

Others echoed him. Korfax gentled his expression and gestured at the ruins about them.

"But I could not prevent this," he said. "Come, we should go ere more of the Agdoain arrive."

They followed the high ground all the way to the gate. Other survivors joined them, a ragged few in small groups or singly. All of them stared at Korfax, at his strange black armour, his long black cloak and the huge black sword that nestled snugly across his back, whispering his name when they heard it and bowing their heads when he looked in their direction. Korfax did not like what it told him. He had become an object of fear.

They achieved the gates just as Rafarel dipped below the western heights. The Zinkao had risen rapidly behind them and there was now a vast lake of brown waters lapping at the walls of the Vasasan itself. Soon the waters would tumble over the top and Vasasan would speak again, but the wreckage of Othil Ekrin would be covered by turbid waters for many years to come. Only if the Zinkao ran clear again would those in future times be able to see the ruins below. Then weeds would grow to soften the hard and broken stone, and tornzl would play amidst the ruins, darting this way and that, their gleaming bodies catching the light in memory of what had gone before.

Korfax looked for the enemy, but no Agdoain were to be seen. He did not trust it. They had not seen the last of the foe. Many had survived the fall of Othil Ekrin.

They crossed the ruin of the gate. Others were here – Branith, more survivors, a few that had travelled up from Piralorm.

When Korfax led his small band out, many stopped and looked. Who was this tall stranger in black? When they were told, many came just to stare. That was Korfax?

They stopped at the brow of the slope. Below them the world looked utterly at peace. The only thing missing was the sound of the Vasasan. Korfax turned to Thilnor.

"I have a gift for you," he said. "No Geyad should be without his stave."

He drew out the child stave of fire that Ralir had given him.

"You will be needing this, I think."

Thilnor stared at the stave.

"Where did you get it?"

"It was a gift from a friend. Your need is greater than mine. I doubt there are any others of the Dar Kadaarith that survived."

"What do you intend to do now?" Thilnor asked.

"Adavor and I will pursue Doagnis."

Adavor smiled at that.

"It is only right," she said. She turned to Okodon.

"Do you contest this?"

"No," said Okodon. "Others might, perhaps, but not me. I know when I am over-matched. Besides, I owe Korfax my life. That should count for something." She glanced at Korfax. "You will bring Doagnis down?"

"That is the task I have set myself," he told her, "and it is also the task given to Adavor. You should honour it."

Okodon would have answered, but a Brandril pushed his way roughly through the crowd and confronted Korfax. He was not ragged, like many of the survivors, so Korfax guessed he had come up from Piralorm.

"They say you are Korfax," he said.

Korfax looked him up and down for a moment and then he folded his arms.

"And may the Creator's light shine upon you also."

There was a ripple of whispers from the onlookers as others drew up to watch this new confrontation. The Brandril drew his sword and pointed it at Korfax.

"I am not daunted by your reputation," he said. "My duty is clear. You shall be put under constraint."

He was about to signal to the others with him when Adavor stepped forward, raising her hands in the gesture of intercession.

"Brandril!" she declared. "Do you know what I am?"

He glanced at her.

"You are a Noqvoan," he said.

"So you recognise my authority?"

"Yes."

"Then put up your sword. Korfax is under my care, and I declare him innocent of all the crimes he has been charged with. I, Adavor of the Balt Kaalith, say this!"

Korfax would have said something as well, but then Thilnor stepped forward. He looked at the Brandril and then gestured with the child stave Korfax had given him.

"And I am Geyad Thilnor of the Dar Kaadarith," he said. "Without Korfax, I would be dead, as would many that are here."

There were bows of assent from some of the others, but the Brandril was still not persuaded.

"I accept your authority also," he said, "but in this I cannot allow Korfax to go free. He has been declared a traitor and a murderer, and by the Velukor no less. I believe his authority is greater than yours."

Korfax laughed darkly at that.

"I have no time for this," he said. "Stay here and play your silly games of precedence, if you wish, but I have better things to do than debate whose authority is the greater."

He turned to walk away and the Brandril made to follow him.

"Hold!" he ordered, raising his sword. Korfax stopped and turned back.

"Do you know the name Doagnis?" Korfax asked him.

"Of course," said the Brandril.

"I hunt her," Korfax told him. "You would do well not to stop me."

The Brandril would have spoken again when a cry went up.

"BEWARE! AGDOAIN! AGDOAIN!"

Everyone turned. Agdoain were there, scrambling over the ruin of the gates, a great many of them. Korfax cursed and drew his sword.

"Adavor! Thilnor!" he cried as he ran back. "Protect them!" he commanded as he vanished from sight.

Those that watched stared in utter disbelief as an invisible force carved its way through the centre of the Agdoain. Only Adavor moved.

"Quick!" she cried. "Form a defence! Korfax will not be able to kill them all."

Okodon joined her and then Thilnor. Finally the Branith joined them, whilst all the others, the survivors and the onlookers, ran back down the long slope to Piralorm.

The Agdoain spread out, scattering as they came. Some ran at the Branith and some at Adavor and Okodon, while others ran on past and pursued those that were making for Piralorm.

Thilnor summoned fire from the child stave and tried desperately to burn as many as he could, whilst around him the Branith formed a shield wall, cutting down any of the foe that came too close. With them were Adavor and Okodon, fighting side by side, their blades a flicker of light. But there were just too many of the foe. The shield wall broke and soon Thilnor found himself flanked only by Adavor and Okodon.

Korfax stopped. There were no more of the enemy before him. He had sliced his way through their ranks and had come out the other side. He looked back and saw the lights of summoning. Thilnor was hurling fire of air to keep the Agdoain at bay, whilst Adavor and Okodon protected him. The rest of the Agdoain were running on towards Piralorm. Dim cries echoed up from below. No doubt some of them had caught up with the survivors.

He ran back towards the others, but even as he tried to reach them he saw the last of the Branith fall. Then the Agdoain were upon Thilnor, who was already sorely tested.

Korfax watched as Okodon was knocked down, watched as she rolled over the ground to avoid the thrust of grey blades. He ran towards her and slaughtered all the Agdoain that harried her. Then he turned just in time to see Thilnor catch a blade on his arm. Thilnor gasped and dropped his stave as he clutched at the wound. More Agdoain closed in and Korfax leapt upon them, burning them all up with his blade. He looked about. Where was Adavor?

He found her at the edge of the cliff, three against her, forcing her back. He ran to aid her.

She killed two with her blade even as he closed upon her, but the third grappled with her and then they both tumbled over the edge.

Korfax cried out, a single 'NO', and dived after them.

They fell through the air, down to the Zum Rolodir. He saw Adavor and the Agdoain grappling with each other, and then the water hit them.

It was cold. He was a moment getting his bearings, but then he caught sight of her. Adavor was hardly moving and the water was stained red. The Agdoain had its blade through her. Korfax screamed his denial and was on the demon in moments. He thrust his blade through it, and the demon came apart.

He reached for Adavor. She was not moving at all now, so he opened the abyss in his head and dragged her from the world.

He laid her upon the substance of the waiting place and tried to staunch the blood. She stirred even as he held her.

"Where are we? What is this dim cave?" she asked.

"It is a waiting place," he told her.

She coughed and blood dribbled from her lips.

"I do not want to die," she told him. "I have to stay with you."

She gasped in pain as she tried to reach up to touch him.

"I claim you as my own," she said. "No other will stand in my way. You are the Ell of my dreams. I will not be denied in this." She sobbed as he stroked her hair. "Save me?" she asked. "Three times pays for all."

He looked down at the gaping wound in her stomach. There was nothing he

8

DUET

Gi-ippei Niho-ors-jon
Fen-iamtil Far-nimin-jes
Om-vanord Odsong-antel
Ip-saban Ds-soi-ranaid
Ip-ouch-nil Mn-a-od-e
Pol-lardril Obin-olsag
Luh-torzu Odsob-achar

He rode south and west, heading away from the Adroqin Chiraxoh. Somewhere ahead of him, under the eaves of a distant forest, hidden by encircling hills, secreted in caves, his quarry lurked.

He kept a watch for the Agdoain as he went. Though they had suffered great losses during the battle for Emethgis Vaniad and the fall of Othil Ekrin, they still remained a threat. One could never tell where they might appear next.

Korfax could not imagine the strange seasons that ruled them, waxing and waning across their grey and empty heavens. Was there even a rhythm to it? Mathulaa had once thought so, but Korfax had never found any clue to it in all the days since. They rose and they fell, like everything else in the world, but each rise was mightier than the last, and they kept what they conquered.

Three great cities had fallen, two by the power of the Agdoain and one by the hand of a mad old Ell, a last desperate bid to destroy the foe. The task ahead of him seemed all but insurmountable now. It had taken the rest of the world a thousand years to clear the north of sorcery. How long would it take to remove the Agdoain?

Korfax grimaced. It would take as long as it needed to. They would never stop, not unless the power that ruled them could also be stopped. And that was his only purpose now, to seek it out and end it.

He reigned in his steed and stroked its side.

"I promise you that we shall not be parted again, you and I. Not until all our battles are won or lost at last."

Enastul raised his proud head and snorted his agreement. His great horn flashed brightly as it caught the light.

Forty-nine crouched like stones, each peering carefully down into the valley, intent upon the enemy below. In the valley, right at the bottom, Agdoain prowled, a great many of them.

One of the watchers briefly raised a piece of polished stone and flashed a message to the ridge on the opposite side. A brief flash came back. The stone was put back in its pouch and the owner looked down again. For a moment all was still, then, without a word, all the Ell on that side of the valley drew out small black rods, dark crystal vials filled with a slow and viscous fluid. They shook the vials and placed them in slings. Then they whirled the slings about their heads, suddenly standing, almost as one. The vials flew out from their sheaths.

Down they went, down from both sides of the valley, a brief and unexpected rain. They landed amongst the Agdoain and shattered. The Agdoain started and snarled upwards at the hills, but even as they turned green vapours erupted, quick and silent and all-encompassing, filling the valley from end to end with a lurid sea of cloud. As quickly as it had blossomed the cloud dissipated again, fading away like sunburnt mist.

The Agdoain were gone, but so were the trees, the bushes and the grass. Nothing remained except for the thickest bones, here a limb, there a shield, oblique upon the barren earth, all slowly decaying back to the nothingness from which they had emerged.

Korfax, invisible upon the ridge, felt the world shift about him. New shapes and possibilities coalesced out of the air. He felt unsteady, as though even the ground under his feet had begun to shift. It was true, all of it, everything he and Adavor had uncovered in Othil Ekrin. Doagnis was fighting the Agdoain.

But what was her purpose? If she had raised them up, why set her forces upon them? It did not make sense. He felt cold inside.

At least the green vapour was not a mystery. It was spoken of in the histories. Many of the Argedith had used acid clouds in the Wars of Unification, slaying friend and foe alike in their mad desire for victory. It was a vile weapon, indiscriminate and ugly.

Korfax caught himself. Could not the same be said of qasadar? Were they not just as indiscriminate? Did they not destroy the land as they destroyed everything else? Think of the desolation they had wrought beyond the watchtowers to the north. In war there was no high ground. To win was all.

He shook. He was being dismantled, piece by bloody piece. Everything he had believed in, everything he had taken stock by, seemed fragile and broken now. There were no more certainties left. Nothing was true and everything seemed permissible.

So what should he do? The words circled in his mind. Doagnis fought the Agdoain! Doagnis fought the Agdoain! It was true. But what else was true? He had to know it all. He had to be certain.

Korfax watched as her forces left the hills on either side of the valley, quietly dropping down the slopes and taking no risks upon the pale scree. They knew how to use the land to their advantage and were well-armed, not only with bow, shield and sword, but also with other weaponry. Knives, darts, glaives, slicing wire; Korfax had never seen such a fearsome array. No member of the Nazad Esiask would ever use such things, for them it had to be the shield, the lance, the sword and the bow. Those were the weapons of honour, or so it was said. But the forces of Doagnis followed another way, and they had beliefs other than those of the Nazad Esiask.

He followed them down, keeping a discreet distance and staying on firmer ground when he could. Down in the valley a thorough search was in progress, a search for survivors. Korfax, for his part, was certain there were none, but he understood the need to make sure.

As the search came to its end a rider appeared, garbed all in black. Korfax moved closer so that he could listen to what might be said.

The rider had an air about him, both proud and dismissive, as though nothing would please him. Korfax noticed the rider's sword. It looked somewhat like a kansehna in form, but it was far more like the weapon Mirzinad had wielded. One of the searchers came forward and made the salute of the Haelok Aldaria, left hand to the right breast and then to the brow, sweeping away again with a bow. It was as if the Wars of Unification had not happened at all. The Iabeiorith walked the world once more.

The rider saluted in turn and then dismounted.

"Well?" he said.

"It is the same as all the others, Enay," came the reply. "Once more we have a complete victory. These Agdoain have no answer to our weaponry, it seems. None appears to have survived the attack."

The Enay looked about him as though sniffing the air.

"Good! Very good! I will report back, of course, but you are to carry on. A small force of Agdoain was seen crossing the Leein Noratoh to the north of here. Your orders are to seek them out and deal with them also. You have enough vials, I presume?"

The other bowed again.

"Indeed, Enay. We have more than enough."

The Enay mounted his ormn.

"Then I will not keep you from your duty. I expect you to have completely eradicated the Agdoain from this region by the end of the third day from now."

Without a backward glance, he rode off. Korfax turned away and headed quickly back to where he had left Enastul. This one would lead him to the commanders of the Haelok Aldaria, and from them he would find out where Doagnis was at last.

Across the wide sky great lines of cloud stretched, gently sailing the upper heavens, the last light of Rafarel caught upon their edges. Korfax looked up at them, following them from the distant east all the way to the uttermost west. Watching their stately procession, he began to question himself. Why was he here? What was his purpose now? He travelled another wasteland. The more he discovered, the further he went, the more he lost. Even his pursuit of Doagnis was no longer what he had thought it to be, and beyond it, on the other side, what would follow? He could not see. He was naked in the dark.

Part of him shouted find her, find Doagnis and bring her down. Make her answer for all the things that she has done. She has killed mercilessly. She has slain, she has tortured. She should answer for those crimes at least. There should be justice!

Another part laughed. Justice? It was already dead. The Velukor had murdered it. Many still clung to the corpse, hoping for some small sign of life, but they were deluding themselves. Justice? There was no justice left in the world.

So what was it, then? Duty? Honour? Redemption? His honour had been stripped from him, and given the blood that flowed in his veins he would never get it back. Nor would he be forgiven, no matter how many Agdoain he slew. Though he might save the world a thousand times over, the west would never forgive him his crime of being born of the north.

That left only vengeance. The Ell, of all persuasions, had ever taken the spilling of blood as the sign to take up arms. Abrilon was gone, as was Asvoan, both dead in the belly of a demon called up by Doagnis. Adavor and Obelison were gone, casualties of war. But it was no longer as simple as that. Even the fires of vengeance did not suffice, for he had moved on again. Too many deaths had followed him from Lonsiatris to Othil Ekrin. He needed a better answer.

It had taken him a long while to realise it, but he was closer to Doagnis now, closer than he had ever been before, in both senses of the word. She was over there, under those hills, gathering her scattered forces and building an army. And yet she was here within him also, the last daughter of Sondehna, trying to raise up again the dark empire of old. He frowned. But that was his temptation, not hers.

He felt her shadow in his mind like a stain, tainting and enticing him. What was the old warning? Study the devices of the enemy too closely and you will become the very thing that you hate? Korfax could not deny the wisdom, for there was a darkness in him now that had not been there before, a great and guilty darkness that tasted of forbidden things, of sorcery, of heresy, of the long-forgotten past he had once desired more than anything else, dreaming the impossible dreams of innocent youth. But the never-ending furnace of his life had re-forged him yet again, making him over, burning away all the old hopes, all the old dreams, all the fears and desires and leaving them as ashes in his wake.

So here it was at last, the only possibility left to him. He was of the house of the Mikaolazith. He was its last prince and there was no other. Alone, he had become absolute.

But a prince was not a prince unless he ruled. Ruins listened not. What if he should proclaim himself and retake the north? Then, perhaps, something new might be born. He thought of the north, thrice crushed, once by the Agedobor, once under the heel of the west and now by the vile claws of the Agdoain. He clenched his fists together. Yes, there was purpose in him yet, a purpose all but forgotten in his pursuit of Doagnis. He would fight the Agdoain until either he died or they were exterminated. And then, perhaps, after the dust had settled, if he still lived, he would reclaim his birthright. But first he needed allies.

He had to be strong. The Iabeiorith were ruled by certainty. If he revealed himself to them they would know his heart and they would follow him.

He must be ruthless. The Iabeiorith had always understood necessity. He would know the truth of Doagnis, and then he would slay her for her crimes, just as he had promised, back when his anger was green.

He would be terrible. There was only one thing the Iabeiorith claimed fully as their own – the power of the darkness. So he would let his own darkness fill him to the uttermost brim. It was his right, his heritage: his and his alone. This tragedy, this hope, was his! So let the followers of Doagnis become his followers instead, for he knew the final altar at which they abased themselves. For it had a name, that altar, and its name was Mikaolaz.

So saying, he faded away, he and his steed, until not even the vaguest shadow remained behind to betray their presence. Then he rode slowly and purposefully into the hills and went to meet his doom.

He rode quietly through the encampment and allowed himself the slightest of smiles. They were well-hidden, all of them. Sorcerous mists were everywhere, shielding everything from sight, from the ear and even the mind's eye. The tents and the pavilions were all cunningly concealed within the wider woods, blending with the foliage and the land about so that only the hardest search would reveal them. But then the searchers would have already had to penetrate the confusing labyrinth of mists that swirled around it all like a great wall.

Only one of the Urendrilith would have been able to sniff them out, perhaps, or maybe not even one of them. Perhaps Samor or Asvoan, but very few others. Asvoan was dead though, and Samor had fled, dwelling now within the bosom of Dialyas.

Korfax was tempted to laugh at the thought. In his time he had mastered them both. Asvoan he had dismissed and Samor he had flattened with his power, nailing her to the very floor at his feet. They and their order no longer mattered.

He rode on, catching glimpses of training duels, the making of arrows and darts, even the forging of swords, where energies were pulled from the outer darkness itself and imprisoned in metal.

The scent of cooking drifted past him from this place or that, shapes in the mist moving to and fro, dimly lit by conjured flames.

Beyond the woods reared a long line of hills, the Leein Affa, or so the map said. This was the place, the final place, he was certain of it. Here he would find her, deep within the hollow hills, deep within their caves. If he knew anything of Doagnis, he knew this. She always felt safest when hidden within stone.

He tethered Enastul in one of the many stables, hiding him carefully amongst the others that waited there also, bidding him patience with a single thought. Then he went a-hunting, the scent of Doagnis guiding him on his way.

She entered her inner sanctum, home and safe, happy in her purposes. She moved comfortably, her shields and walls falling away from her even as she advanced, but when she reached the very centre, she faltered.

There was a sudden sense of wrongness in the air. She looked about her, eyes darting over the trappings, the appurtenances, the periapts, the tools and the stones, but nothing had been touched since she was last here. Everything looked much as it had before.

The scent-stones she had set to burn only this morning were a little smaller perhaps, but their vapours still freshened the air. The were-fires she had set in the ceiling still glowed with their accustomed light, undiminished. Her sanctuary, to all appearances, was as it had always been, namely a place of comfort and retreat. But something was wrong, and she could feel it.

She looked inwards, concentrating, and quickly realised that she had felt such a sensation before. It was almost as if she was back in Othil Ekrin again, that sense of danger and mounting panic. She turned about, breathing hard, and looked straight at her shew-stone.

It was black, utterly black, filled to the very brim with featureless night. There was no light within it at all. When had it ever been so dark?

She stared at it, mesmerised. How it burned, like a hole in the world. The sense of peril in the air was now so intense that it all but made her giddy. What had she missed? Who or what had invaded her sanctuary? It could not be Korfax, could it? He was dead, wasn't he? She took a careful step backwards and felt something touch her neck, something hard and sharp, like the tip of a blade. She stopped where she was and froze.

Something waited behind her, rearing up in the brief moment between sensing and seeing, almost as if it had stepped through some hidden doorway. She thought of defences and conjurations, of energies and summonings, but nothing seemed even remotely adequate to the power that now stood at her back. She was utterly undone.

Terrifying possibilities loomed in her mind. Not since one of the Ashar had climbed up through her conjuration in Emethgis Vaniad had she felt such power. She shuddered inside. Was that it? Had that monstrous being returned to ask questions she could not possibly answer?

She took a deep breath and steadied herself, remaining where she was, letting the power at her back bend over her like a storm, letting it see her so that she could see it as well.

There was something else now, a sense of abeyance, as though what stood at her back was not yet ready to act. Did it want something? Was there a chance – the slimmest of chances – that she could grasp at? If so, she would take it, with both hands. Who knew what might result?

"Neither move nor speak, Doagnis!" said a voice, deep and quiet and horribly cold.

Another involuntary shudder took her. Whatever this was, it knew her, and she understood the threat all too well. She held herself in a vice-like grip and stilled both her panic and her fear whilst her mind raced like a thing possessed.

There were two powers behind her now, not one as she had originally surmised. The power at her neck was both hot and dark, a hungry force that swayed back and forth in her mind like an undulating frond. A hint of melody came to her, as though it sang to itself. She closed her eyes, a long slow blink. What in all the world, or below it, could it be? She thought of all the terrors that dwelt in the Mahorelah, but none of them was remotely similar.

The other, the one that had spoken, was further back. She tried to see it, but she could only catch glimpses. This one was obscured in some way, hidden from her by a wall she could not breach. But she could not doubt its potency, for it beat against her like a dark furnace.

So they waited: the silent singer on its leash, its darker master, and Doagnis, their prey.

"Good," the voice announced at last. "You have sense enough to know when you are over-matched. Turn around slowly, Doagnis, so that I can see you. But be warned! Your death will be swifter than you can possibly imagine, if you do or say the wrong thing!"

She did as she was told, hating the commandment even as she feared it. She was not used to this. Others were here to do her will, not the other way around. She turned as slowly as she could, and so came face to face with the threat.

At first she felt nothing so much as a sense of disappointment. How could she have been so easily fooled? Before her was merely a very tall Ell, clad from head to foot in strange black armour and wielding a very large sword. A brief sense of chagrin took her. Had she been duped? But as she looked, she saw deeper and realised that her first assessment had been so much closer to the truth.

To begin with there was something very strange about the sword. It was uncommonly large for one thing, larger than the largest kansehna, perhaps, and it was black, black in all its ways, from its pommel to its tip. It looked almost as though it had been carved rather than forged, and she could think of nothing like it that she had ever seen before. The air about it misbehaved somehow as though the sword rippled with a hidden heat, and within, under its skin of metal, there were subtle movements, its many curved surfaces shifting rhythmically as though the sword breathed. She found herself wondering whether the sword was a sword at all, whether it was a mask for something else entirely, and she decided that she did not like that idea at all.

She turned away from the great black blade and studied its master next, but the great armoured shape did not move. Its black armour seemed akin to the sword, for it also shifted under her gaze, just as the sword had, made of the very same substance no doubt, black, all black and playing with the meagre light that fell upon it. But there was also a gleam to its surfaces, as though it seeped fluids, and briefly, now and again, the ghosts of pale energies ran across it like fleeting clouds.

Doagnis swallowed in a throat gone dry. What did she face? What power was this? Had she awoken too much, summoned too much and so strayed out of her depth at last? She had no answers, none whatsoever. All she could do was ask.

"What are you?"

The other did not move, but she felt the echoes of a smile somewhere, a mocking smile at her expense.

"What am I?" the cold voice questioned. "You will know soon enough. First, though, I have questions for you. Answer them well, and you may yet live."

There was an answer that would supplicate this apparition? A flood of relief threatened to undo her even as she clung to the chance. There remained something she might yet be able to exploit. But even as she wondered what advantage might be hers she felt another in her mind, watching her thoughts even as she tried to hide them away again, snatching them back, each and every one of them, out from her head with a chill hand.

The sword came to within a hair's breadth of her throat. She widened her eyes and held her breath, awaiting the worst, but the sword came no further. She still lived. Then she realised what had just happened and she stared back in fear. The sword had moved all by itself, elongating so that it could come closer. The blade's master spoke again.

"Do not seek advantage in this, Doagnis, nor consider such a possibility at all. You have not yet satisfied me. Perhaps you believe there is some stratagem that will avail you, some power at your beck and call that will save you from me." The apparition laughed, brief and mocking. "Disabuse yourself of such fantasies, they will mislead you. There is nothing that you can say or do that will turn me aside. I desire your fear at the very least, for you have visited it upon so many others, after all."

Then, like some counterpoint to its master's voice, the sword began to sing, a quiet moaning sound that sent an icy shiver down her back.

"Know fear, Doagnis!" came the cold voice again, and she did, despite herself. Fear filled her, all-encompassing, deeper and more potent than any she had ever felt before. It was all that she could do to keep it in check.

"What manner of blade is that?" she asked, trying a distraction, any distraction, to keep her fear at bay.

The other laughed again, but now the laugh was almost regretful.

"You do not know? You truly do not know? Even now? You disappoint me. I thought that you, at the very least, would recognise it as soon as you laid eyes upon it. You have already witnessed what it can do. Do you truly not see it for what it is? My sword, like its long-vanished brethren, has a history, a very long, a very bloody and a very famous history."

Doagnis went still. A famous history? Memories nagged at her – tales of battles, of terrible weapons, black blades that could change their shape and which sang with the will of their masters. She shuddered. It could not be, could it? Despite her fear she suddenly felt incredulous. She studied the sword before her, the great black blade that sang, that changed its shape and echoed the will of its master. Could she doubt it?

"Is it a Qorihna?" she dared, hoping against hope that it was not.

The other bowed its head slightly. Doagnis went still inside. By the Ashar! A Qorihna? But there were no more Qorihna left, or so she had been told. Even those miserable shells that had once been proudly displayed on the walls of the tower of the Nazad Esiask were not Qorihna. They were only the remnants of certain sad imitations left over from the last few days of the Wars of Unification.

But now, here before her, was something else entirely. She looked at it again and found herself marvelling at its dark and awful symmetry despite her fear. She closed her eyes. Think of it. One of the mightiest weapons ever forged of sorcery was at her throat even now, a monstrous weapon plucked from the Mahorelah itself. For even the greatest feared Qorihna. And how right it was that they should; Qorihna were fatal.

She decided not to believe it. By all accounts this fantasy could not be, should not be. Qorihna were said to be extinct. This was an imitation, a fraud. She was being deceived.

"There are no more Qorihna left in the world!" she announced. "They were all destroyed."

"So you do not trust your eyes or your ears?" came the counter.

"It is an imitation," she responded.

"No, Doagnis, it is not. Nor is my armour," followed the rejoinder.

Doagnis's eyes opened wider. Yes! If the blade was indeed a Qorihna, then the armour surely must be Qahmor. Qahmor? What dark resurrection was this?

"Who are you?" she whispered.

"Can you not guess?" it replied.

That was it. Now she knew. Her first guess had been right and she almost cried out with the revelation. There was danger in the air, her shew-stone had turned black and an Ell stood before her, threatening her life. Who other than Korfax had ever done such a thing before? But Korfax? He was supposed to be dead, wasn't he?

She almost laughed at the thought. And how many reports of his demise had she heard? She should have learned by now. But something was still very wrong. Korfax? Korfax of the Farenith, son of the most loyal house to the Velukor, standing before her with a Qorihna in his hand and wearing Qahmor? The world seemed to tilt about her, falling away into impossible deeps until it all rose back again and a new world took its place.

Think on it! It answered so many riddles. Now she could see how he had escaped all her traps. She had set snares fit for a Geyadril of the Dar Kaadarith, but Korfax had no longer been such a creature. And, as if to confirm her thoughts, he let his armour uncover his face so that she could see him.

She watched the black roll back, undoing itself like pliant flesh. If ever she had needed confirmation, here was the final proof. Only Qahmor was ever said to act in such a way, as supple as a second skin but as impenetrable as a wall. She stared at it for a moment, marvelling at its astonishing properties. But then she looked again at the face that had been revealed and all her doubts fled her. She knew that face, for it had flitted darkly through her dreams and her nightmares for many a season. She knew that face, for the face was the name. Here was Korfax indeed, Korfax in the flesh.

He looked paler than the last time they had crossed paths, and grimmer, but she could see that the change in him went far deeper than that. When she had last laid eyes upon him he had been the Meganza of the Velukor, filled with the inconsiderate fires of unthinking loyalty, potent and proud. But he had become a far subtler affair since then, for he was both renegade and traitor now, and he had travelled an altogether darker road.

She thought of how he had once bested a Babemor, broken her circles and then put down three Azadra, all in succession. She thought of how he had nearly killed her in the labyrinth of stone under Emethgis Vaniad. She thought of how he must have evaded all her traps as she made her way to Othil Ekrin. He had even put down the Givyalag in Thilzin Gallass. He had always been mighty, she reminded herself, but now something else had been added to the mix, an underlying darkness she could almost taste. It was strange, but with the onset of revelation, her fear took on another quality entirely, almost as if it had become a helpless ecstasy instead, a feeling she had only ever entertained in her darkest fantasies. It was as though she suddenly found herself drowning, her death already upon her and enfolding her in its flames, and yet all of a sudden and surpassing sadness, exquisite and beautiful.

"Korfax!" she finally breathed. "You have found me. Yet you come in a most unexpected fashion."

She took another breath.

"Are you still the Velukor's executioner?" she dared, glancing at the sword. "Would not your former master question your choice of weaponry?"

"I have no masters now," he told her. "What I do, I do alone."

"So what must I say that will stay the executioner's hand?"

"You must satisfy me."

"And how will I do that?"

"You will tell me about the Agdoain. How you called them up and how you intend to put them down."

She started.

"How I called them up? But I did not."

"I think that you did. You were seen at the statue of Efaeis on the day, the very hour, when the womb of the Agdoain grew up from below and tore out the heart of Othil Zilodar."

"I was not there," she said.

The black blade snarled and she swallowed, breathing hard.

"Lie to me again," said Korfax, "and that will be that. You were seen by Enay Orpahan. He called out to you and you ran away. Orpahan showed Urenel Asvoan what he saw and she confirmed your presence. Now tell me the truth and do not lie to me again."

It took her a long moment to calm herself.

"I wanted to see what it was," she said eventually, her eyes fixed upon the blade. "It was already there when I found it. I do not know how it came to be."

The black blade shifted slightly.

"I am telling the truth," she hissed.

"Prove it," he said.

"My forces are already engaged with the Agdoain. We kill them even now," she offered.

"I know," he said. "I have seen. That is how I found you. But it proves nothing. You could have raised the Agdoain up as bale for your enemies and fodder for your troops. Now that the north is cleared, all you need do is march in and take it, setting the Iabeiorith on the road to empire and glory once more."

"I did not raise them up," she insisted.

Korfax paused a moment.

"Your mother then!"

"No! Why do you think I have anything to do with them?"

"You are of the Argedith."

"But they do not come from the Mahorelah."

Korfax paused again.

"Not from the Mahorelah? Perhaps that is true after a fashion. Perhaps they only grow here. But someone is responsible. I find the timing of your insurrection more than a little interesting."

"I simply took advantage of their arrival, once I discovered their flaw."

"What flaw?"

"They have no answer to the Namad Mahorelah. They do not employ sorcery."

"Which is why you raised them up in the first place. They clear the north for you and then you take it back. The logic is irrefutable."

"But I did not call them up! I did not!"

Korfax leaned in.

"Prove it to me. Show me your mind."

Doagnis drew back.

"No! You shall not know my thoughts."

Korfax clenched himself in preparation.

"Then," he said, "for the death of my father, for the deaths of Abrilon and Asvoan, for the death of my beloved, the torture of Adavor and all the unspeakable horrors you have unleashed upon the world, I sentence you to death."

"WAIT!" she screamed, even as the black blade touched her throat. She lifted her head – she had to, she could not avoid it. She could feel it there, pulsing metal eager for her blood. A song came briefly out of the darkness once more, thrumming against her neck, before silence returned. The black blade waited and pressed itself against her in an eyeless stare.

"Please!" she implored. "Wait, you are wrong. I admit to the deaths of the Geyadel and the Urenel, of course I do. But why would I not seek their deaths? They were my enemies, as was everyone else upon the high council. I am of the Argedith, born to it. I had no choice. What mercy would they have shown me in their turn? But I had nothing to do with the Agdoain."

"SO SHOW ME YOUR THOUGHTS!" he roared. And then he stormed her fortress.

She could not stop him: he was in, through and out the other side in moments, through doors she had not even known were there. He touched nothing but her knowledge of the Agdoain. She was horrified and amazed, all at the same time. The power of him was frightening. He had not uprooted her secrets, nor gone down the dark lanes of her life, but he could easily have done so.

She watched as he withdrew, tears of rage following in his wake. The only satisfaction she had was that he had his answer, and he did not like it.

"Thief!" she hissed back at him, clenching her fists. "Ravisher!" She paused a moment, breathing hard. "Are you done violating me?" she asked.

The blade was back at her throat in a moment.

"And what of Adavor?" he asked in return. "Should I spare you her fate? You would have had everything that she was, given enough time. I was far gentler with you than you were with her. And don't worry about your precious secrets. They are safe. I took the answer to my question, and that is all that I took."

She breathed hard, thinking fast. What could she do? His powers were unprecedented.

"How did you do that?" she hissed again. "How did you enter my mind? That should not have been possible."

"A trick learnt from the Exentaser," he told her. "Samor once did it to me."

She held herself still, gradually willing herself to calmness again. She was being outplayed here. She must seek for an advantage – any advantage – and pursue it.

"Do not think to shame me with Adavor," she said. "She was of the Balt Kaalith. Do you know what they did? If it is crimes you seek, then look to their history." He did not answer. "You have nothing to say?" she pressed.

"I have as little love for the Balt Kaalith as you," he answered, "but Adavor at least was honourable. She did not deserve what you did to her."

"And if you knew what I know, you would not think so."

"I know more than you can possibly imagine."

They stared at each other for a few more moments, she considering her options, him waiting her out.

"So what now?" she eventually asked.

Satisfied, he relaxed a little.

"Now we talk," he said. "That you have nothing to do with the Agdoain is one thing, but that you are the only force that can stop them is another."

Doagnis felt herself caught by that. She was the only force that could stop the Agdoain? What was going through his mind? An alliance? He was mad! The others would rather die than accept him. Perhaps she could garner some advantage from this situation after all.

"They are a great threat. They should be removed," she offered.

He lifted his head a little.

"Something we can both agree on."

She did not smile, but something inside her leapt at his answer. She was right. He wanted an alliance. He saw her, or the forces under her command, as a way to stop the enemy. Here was her way out. Time for a few questions of her own.

"And now that we have settled that, I would like to know how it is that you have such weaponry."

She flicked her eyes at his blade.

"I am sure that you would," he returned. "But you are here to answer my questions, not me to answer yours. Do not make the mistake of thinking this a meeting of equals, Doagnis, for it is not. You are under my hand. Do or say the wrong thing and you will die. I have seen enough of you, your taunts and your traps, to know what it is that I am dealing with. Remain as you are, and know that your life still hangs in my balance."

She sneered at that.

"If you are seeking an alliance against the Agdoain, the last thing you should do is kill me."

He smiled.

"And what of the old ways? Only the strongest shall rule?"

That was not the answer she had expected. She must not forget that he was, in certain ways, steeped in her lore.

"That no longer applies," she told him.

"Does it not?" he asked. "Axayal vied with you, whether you deny it or not. He laughed when he called up the Givyalag, claiming that the mightiest summoning was now his. But he was not so pleased when I told him you had already surpassed him by calling up Ash-Mir."

She felt a return of fear and fought hard to push it back down again. She had forgotten that, too. Korfax had survived both encounters. He clearly knew something she did not. Could she get him to reveal it?

"Axayal was one of my best precisely because he was ambitious," she said. "Only the hungriest vines reach the light. But he knew his place well enough, or I would not have trusted him. How did you best him?"

Korfax laughed quietly, albeit without humour.

"You honestly believe you have changed, don't you? But still you all try to outdo each other, powers vying with powers, until you reach your limits and attempt to go beyond them. You deceive yourself. Axayal could not control the Givyalag, just as you could not control Ash-Mir. What a fine symmetry you both have."

"Ash-Mir was an accident," she snapped back, and then she bit her tongue. She had not meant to say that. Calm, she told herself, remain calm.

He looked curiously at her for a moment.

"What an interesting admission. It came here of its own free will? I did not think that was possible."

She held herself as still as she could. Only self-control would avail her here.

"It climbed up the path of my summoning," she continued. "I was going to summon a Givyalag, but Ash-Mir came instead."

"Then you are more fortunate than you know. If you had called up the Givyalag, you would now be dead, like Axayal."

"Why?"

"Givyalag are uncontrollable. The one Axayal called up was a mere idiot. He could not control it because there was nothing there to control. It killed him and then started to destroy Thilzin Gallass. I had to persuade it to leave."

Her eyes widened.

"How did you do that?"

Korfax gestured at his sword.

"That is why I have you at my mercy, and why you can do nothing about it."

She looked at the sword for a moment, weighing possibilities. Qorihna were outside her experience. She stood now in the realm of unknowing.

"Why should I believe you?" she said.

"What choice do you have?"

"What do you want, then?"

"To see if I am wasting my time."

"Wasting your time?"

"Talking to you. I want to know if you can truly change. I want to know if you can be better than you are."

"In other words you want me to be more like you," she sneered, "like those taught by the inglorious west? That will never happen. I know what they are. I

176

know what manner of creatures made you."

"And I know that your hatred will be the death of you," he countered. As if in answer his sword sang, a long, low moan. She looked at it and then back at him.

"Hatred?" she spat. "What do you know of hatred? I was born into a world the like of which you could never understand. From the moment I arrived all hands were turned against me for no better reason than I was the daughter of my mother. I grew up alone, watching everything that I said, everything that I did, so that I would not betray who and what I was. Fear is my heritage, and that is the way it has been ever since, for me, for my mother and her mother before her, all the way back to the times of unification. Do you know what it is like to live under such fear all your life? The only time I ever stopped hating the world I had been born into was when I could bring a piece of it crashing down. I tried to have the council killed? What of it? They would have condemned me to death at the very moment of my apprehension."

She drew a deep breath and her eyes returned his cold fire.

"You come from the places of peace," she continued. "I do not. For those of my line, the Wars of Unification never ended. For us, Karmaraa and his spawn are the true evil in this world. Do you know what they did? Do you know what really happened? The Iabeiorith were slaughtered, all of them. Only those poor few that fled to Lonsiatris were spared. The fiction you have believed all your life is a foul lie. They did not retreat and despoil the land; it was the forces of the west that erased what they found even as they advanced. Only a few managed to flee at the end, fleeing to Lonsiatris, but Creator forfend if any were caught. No trial, no justice, no carefully considered sentence of servitude, no chance for mercy. No matter who you were, your fate was sealed as soon as they laid hands upon you, even children. Death by burning! It is said to be an utter agony. But what do you care? Suffer not the Argedith to live? Is that not the creed of the Dar Kaadarith? You do not know what such words cost! Only the west in its self-righteous hatred could conceive such works of pious cruelty. Only they were arrogant enough to believe they were doing the work of the Creator. I tried to kill the high council? Who of my people would not have leapt at the chance? So whilst the rest of you were distracted by the Agdoain, I made my attempt. I saw the greater chance and I took it! And I nearly succeeded. I will not plead for my life, nor can you make me, but I will tell you this. You are the one born of lies and deceit, not I."

He drew back a little, watching her. There was a look in his eyes, measuring, seeking. Did he see how the words cost her? Did he even believe her?

"A pretty speech," he said at last. "You play the victim well. Lies and deceits, though? That is your province, not mine. False passion has ever been a tool of the Argedith."

"I AM NOT FALSE!" she screamed back at him. She could not help it. Damn him for pushing her. He seemed to sense this somewhat, because he pulled back a little more and took his blade with him. But it was still pointed at her throat.

"The first victim of war is always the truth," he told her. "But do not try to tell me that the Iabeiorith were innocent either. I know what happened at Peis-homa. I know what really happened."

They stared at each other for another long moment. She was the first to break the silence again.

"So you want me to be like you?"

He deepened his gaze.

"No, I did not say that! What I want to know is, can you be better than the west?"

She almost laughed at that, despite his intensity.

"So that is it, is it?" she said. "That is the measure of your desire! Vengeance!"

Again she sneered.

"Why should I do anything for your comfort? You were declared traitor by the very powers you revered, yet still you abase yourself before their blood-stained altars like some slave."

Korfax narrowed his eyes, even as their fire sharpened.

"I learned how things should be from my father and my mother," he told her, "and not from any other. They venerated truth and honour, but love was their currency – love and trust. The west only desires power at any price, just like you."

Now she did laugh, but it was bitter and harsh.

"And who taught your mother and father?" she asked. "Whose hand raised them up? You are born of the lies of the west. I know who made your house!"

She matched his coldness.

"It is so easy to accept such things when your world is safe and you are cosseted," she continued, "when the majority thinks the same way that you do, when you follow the herd and believe that you know what is right and what is wrong. But the real world is not like that. I dwell in another place, in the shadows, feeling my way through the darkness out of harsh necessity. I have to weigh my judgements on less forgiving scales than you, and frequently I have no choice but to keep my own counsel. There are many things you do not know, Korfax, and memories are much longer than you suspect. My one guiding light, the one thing I hope for above all others, is for restitution, the restitution of my people."

Korfax peered at her as though she had surprised him.

"Who would have thought it?" he mused. "Your father said almost exactly the same thing to me when I spoke to him last. I did not expect to hear such sentiments from you."

Doagnis felt a momentary stab of resentment.

"My father? What did you ever know of him? Are you going to teach me, his very own daughter, who he was?"

Korfax did not answer. Doagnis took another deep breath before continuing. It helped, bolstering her inner defences, keeping her calm and keeping the fear and the rage at bay.

"All you ever saw was the beguiling mask," she said, "and that, no doubt, is what attracted you to him in the first place. And do you really think that you were the only one ever to be so dazzled? Why do you think my mother married him? She wanted her child to be of the best, so she chose of the best. But she did not own him. Nor did he own her. They deceived themselves and each other just long enough to see me into the world. Then they all but parted. My mother got me and the continuation of our line, whilst my father..."

She paused, looking away. She had never imagined how much such words could hurt. She looked back at him. Why was she even telling him this? He did not care.

"I think I can guess what your father gained," he said.

"What?" she asked, looking up surprised, despite herself, and finding his expression curiously regretful.

"The complete prophecies of Nalvahgey," he said.

"You saw that in my mind, you thief!" she hissed.

"I did not," he said. "My mother was of the Exentaser. She taught me something of her art. I know how to find what I need."

She looked incredulous.

"Then how did you know?"

"I guessed."

She stared at him for a long time.

"You guessed?"

"There were many clues, and it took me a long time to put it all together: your father's alliance with Samor, his interest in time, the things that he said and did. When I confronted him at the end, he eventually admitted it."

She continued to stare.

"Yes!" she said finally. "The entire prophecies of Nalvahgey. So here I am! A scrap of life for a scrap of parchment! My life has ever been sculpted from such stone." Her eyes glittered with old memories. "When I learned that, the mask was gone. I saw him for who he truly was – selfish, grasping, wrapped up in his own affairs. He manipulated others to suit himself."

Korfax became almost insouciant.

"Not unlike your mother, then," he returned.

Doagnis flared like a new-lit beacon.

"How dare you! They were not even remotely the same. My mother understood her duty and the harsh necessity of her heritage. She saw what she had to do, saw what was written in the prophecies, and she bravely took her chance. She had a line to continue. That was her purpose, a purpose she understood all too well. When she told him what she was and what she could offer, all it would have taken was a single word from him, one single word in the right ear and my mother would have been taken and killed. She took such a chance with Dialyas, such a chance! A former Geyad of the Dar Kaadarith? Who would have thought it? But she did take the chance, and here I am, desired, foretold and necessary. My mother served the greater need; my father served no one but himself."

"Yet you went to Lonsiatris to say goodbye to him."

Doagnis all but screamed her answer back.

"Are you really that stupid?! I went to him because I wanted to kill him. I hated him!"

"Yet, when you confronted him you found that you could not," Korfax returned gently.

The tears came again – she could not stop them. She berated herself for her weakness but could do nothing about it. For some reason Korfax elicited a response from her: fire and water, pain and regret. It was as though, no matter what she did, she was vulnerable to him.

"I said goodbye and that was all," she told him. "He was my father. He was the last of my blood. There are no others now. My mother is dead. All I have are servants and slaves."

Doagnis became still again and Korfax dropped his gaze as though troubled. Then he looked back at her. She waited for what he would say next.

"You have never known love, have you? Not really. I think I begin to understand you a little better."

His eyes were gentler now than she had ever seen them before. What was this? Was that compassion? She did not trust it. She would never trust it. She looked back at him with all the contempt she could muster.

"You understand? What could you possibly understand in any of this?"

Coldness filled him again, even as he smiled, but even his coldness was not untouched by this strange new gentleness.

"So we come to it at last," he said. "You think you know who I am, but you do not." His smile became almost rueful. "Your father changed my life, though I did not realise how profound the change was until it was almost too late. He showed me how wrong my understanding was, how wrong the Dar Kaadarith were, and he led me to a revelation that I neither desired nor wanted. But I have had to accept it nonetheless, for it has since become my salvation. As for him? He is as you have said. A mask, selfish, proud, using others for his own ends. Come the time he fitted me to his bow and loosed me. Unwittingly I did his bidding, because I thought it would serve my purposes, but never was an arrow so cheaply bought. When I learned how I had been cursed I went back to him with rage in my heart but, like you, I could not do the deed. I still did not understand. At the end, having done his bidding, he dropped me like a hot stone and fled the troubles of this world like a coward."

Doagnis waited. There was more to learn here, much more than she had expected, she could hear it in his voice. Where was this confrontation going now?

She knew that Lonsiatris was gone, and she knew that her father had been involved in some way. The tales she had heard, the great light, the great wave, had been all but unbelievable, but they were true nonetheless. Lonsiatris was gone, and nothing could she discover of its fate. Even the rarest theurgies she possessed told her nothing of the matter. Now, though, she heard hints that her father was entirely responsible and that Korfax had been at the heart of it.

"What happened?" she asked carefully, her voice as neutral as she could make it.

Korfax clenched his jaw before answering as though he caged a deep anger.

"Your father had me steal something from the Umadya Semeiel. It was the Kapimadar, a crystal with power enough to breach the ramparts of Kokazadah. He told me that it could be used as a weapon to help defeat the Agdoain. My price for this treachery was your whereabouts. He sold you to gain me."

Doagnis stared at Korfax again.

"He sold me to you?"

"Yes! Thus the greater thief set his snare for the lesser. What a fool I was. Dialyas took the Kapimadar and, when I was safely on my way, invoked its power to send Lonsiatris into the future. He has fled the troubles of this world and taken all the heretics with him. Dialyas told me once that he sought the restitution of the Ell. I thought that he meant he wanted to change the world, to make it better. I even thought he might find a way to stop the Agdoain or send them back from wherever they came. But he did not. All he wanted was to flee. Now those of us who are left behind must face the Agdoain. Dialyas has betrayed us all."

She closed her eyes and blinked away more tears. Her father had sold her to Korfax? That was hard. Cruel hard. She looked back at him.

"I knew I should have killed him," she said. She held up a hand. "Will you not at least put up your sword? I am not your enemy now, clearly I am not. Enemies have ever been known to forget the past and embrace the future. We have both been betrayed – you by the Velukor and both of us by my father. I knew nothing of your story."

Korfax did not drop his sword; instead, he held her gaze and his eyes became hard again.

"Betrayed indeed!" he said. "But what, I wonder, are you thinking of now? Are you seeking advantage still? Are you still looking for a way to escape me? How far can I trust the daughter of Dialyas?"

"I am not him."

"But you are his daughter yet. Ovuor sought him out because of prophecy. She knew that the child of his loins would bring about the rise of the Iabeiorith. She tried to beguile him, but when that failed she offered him something she knew he could not resist. And that was how you came to be. One of my masters, Ponodol, called it a perversity. Should I agree with that? It is said that each life is for ever marked by its conception. So how much of their spirit remains in you, I wonder?"

"I cut my teeth on such superstitions," she hissed back at him. "You have been reduced to hunting for excuses. You do not believe anything that you are saying at all. You still do not want to believe that I can tell the truth. Is that Korfax the traitor I am hearing, or have you not yet thrown off the shackles of the west?"

Korfax did not move.

"Neither," he said. "But should I trust you at last, you who has sought my death on so many occasions?"

"No more than you!"

"But you used your servants in much the same manner as Dialyas used me. What would happen to me if I turned my back upon you now?"

"Tohtanef, Molpan and Axayal all knew the price of failure. It is our way, a way that has existed since before the Wars of Unification, a way that we of the Iabeiorith are all born to. If we do not fear, then we do not fight. If we are captured, then we will betray. Flesh has always failed, so when we fail, we die. The dead tell no tales."

Korfax let a look of knowledge slide across his face. He smiled darkly back at her.

"The dead tell no tales? Are you sure of that?"

"What do you mean?"

"What did I say to you before? You do not possess all knowledge, Doagnis. The dead can indeed tell tales. They can berate. They can accuse. They can reveal."

She did not see his meaning at all.

"And how many have you slain?" she asked.

"But that was not what I meant. So let me ask you this in return. Is there no room for honour and loyalty in your creed?"

"Honour and loyalty are easy enough when you have a full belly," she told him, "but the famished have ever had to fight for their scraps. They know a different honour and a different loyalty."

She paused a moment before speaking again.

"It may surprise you to learn that many are indeed loyal and honourable as you understand the estate. But we live in perilous times, and many need a goad. Harsh necessity, I said."

"And I heard that also. But I also think that you took a certain dark pleasure in the humiliation of Adavor, as did Mirzinad, before he learned the error of his ways."

Doagnis almost spat her answer back.

"But what did you expect? A spy from the hated Balt Kaalith was suddenly under my hand? Given such an eventuality, why should I not use her as I saw fit? I had no love for her or for what she represented. If I had told her that I had nothing to do with the Agdoain, she would not have believed me. Besides, I was responsible for an attack upon the high council itself. She and her masters would not have wasted their breath on me if I had been in their power. I intended Adavor to be a reminder to those that followed in her wake that I could be just as ruthless as they."

"Perpetuating the old cycle of pain?" he said.

"They started this," she returned.

Now Korfax really laughed. Doagnis drew back. Naked scorn filled the room and she waited in silent rage for him to stop.

"That does not become you, Doagnis," he finally announced, catching his breath. "In truth, it does not."

He leaned towards her again and raised up his sword. He bared his teeth.

"They did not 'start' this at all. No one can be said to have 'started' this. The beginnings of this hatred are lost in the long-vanished past. The Iabeiorith and the Korith Zadakal have been at each other's throats ever since the world began. But if you really wish to place the blame on someone, then look no further than Sondehna himself, for it is certain that neither of us would be here now if it were not for his infatuation with Soivar."

Doagnis bared her teeth back at him. How dare he say such things? She had a sudden desire to rake him with her claws.

"And what do you know of such matters?" she asked. "Sondehna desired her but was denied. I would wager that the tale you have been told is nothing like the truth! History has ever been written by the victors." Cold filled her. "And did you not desire?" she asked. "And were you not denied also?"

Korfax smiled coldly in return.

"True enough. But I still know more than you."

"You know only what they taught you."

Korfax snorted with barely concealed disdain.

"And by that token, so do you."

"But I know more about Sondehna than you ever could," she said.

A barely concealed look of satisfaction crossed his face now, almost as if she had just walked into a trap.

"So present your proof!" he said.

"Not for your eyes, scion of the Farenith! You will merely have to take my word for it. You know nothing!"

Korfax let his lips curl up in a dark smile, a crueller smile by far than any he had offered her up until now.

"No, Doagnis," he said, "you are wrong. I already know your heritage, but do you know mine?"

She stared at him. What was this? Where was this going now?

"My heritage?" she asked carefully. "What could you possibly know of my heritage?"

He returned her stare for a moment, teeth and eyes in savage agreement, and then glanced beyond her.

"So you desire revelation, after all," he murmured. "Let it be, then. Consider that casket of yours. What of that?"

Doagnis felt a chill run down her back.

"What casket?"

He pointed past her.

"The one you keep over there." He gestured at the back of the cave. "The one no one else can open."

"I do not know what you are talking about," she said.

"Really?" he replied. "The very first scroll I picked up stated it plainly enough, I thought."

Doagnis almost staggered.

"You've seen it?" she hissed.

They stared at each other for what seemed an age. Then she threw up her hands in panic, summoning fire, summoning rage, but before she could complete the conjuration, Korfax was upon her, wrapping his free arm about her and pinning her arms at her side. She gasped in astonishment as his mind calmed the burgeoning energies, casting them aside even as he called up the waters of banishing with his unspoken thought.

They stared into each other's eyes, hers wide with rage and fear and his suddenly filled with a strange sorrow.

"So there it is," he said.

She struggled, but Korfax only tightened his grip further. He was far stronger than her, and he still held his Qorihna in his other hand.

"No one must know!" she said, weeping with rage.

"Why?"

"No one must see me! No one!"

Korfax raised his head, though he still held her with his gaze. There was something careful in his eyes now, as though what she said puzzled him.

"But why? Why must no one know that you are of the line of the Mikaolazith, that you are descended, in direct line, from Soivar?"

She closed her eyes and sagged in his arms. Here it came at last, her own, her very own nightmare. She had known what he was to say, but actually hearing the words spoken all but broke her. Her darkest fears filled her. Failure! She would fail. Let this be known anywhere and her followers would rebel against her. All her plans would fail.

Soivar was the betrayer. She was the one that had brought down Sondehna. That was the dark secret, the unforgivable crime. The taint of betrayal could not be removed, no matter how long the line survived. Sons became fathers and daughters became mothers.

In her mind's eye she saw them, the assembled might of the Iabeiorith. They would stand over her and curse her for the betrayal. She would plead with them, ask them for forgiveness and show them that she had made them mighty again, but they would still deny her. Soivar had betrayed their prince, and she was born of Soivar.

There would be a room where they would incarcerate her, or worse torture her, for that would be what she deserved in their eyes. And at the last, when all the requisite words had been said, when all the necessary rites had been enacted and all the obligatory humiliations performed, there would be that wheel, that horrid and brutal wheel to which they would chain her naked body, stretched to its limit and pierced by the seven spears, over and over again until all life was extinguished. Then her remains would be buried, deep and dark with no remembrance over them. Her line would be ended and she would be no more.

She shuddered and looked back at Korfax. There was concern upon his face now, a sudden empathy that shocked her almost as much as his invasion of her mind. From threatening her life and violating her sanctity he had come to this? There was a pain in him, she could see it, and she did not understand it, not any of it. It caught her, even in her fear. He had called this a trial, offering her death if she did not satisfy him, but now, having revealed his knowledge of her ancestry, he clearly wanted her to live. If this was a trial, then whose was it really?

Korfax spoke to her, gently musing.

"So that is it," he said. "That is what you fear: the truth, the taint of betrayal!" He smiled sadly down at her. "How terrible must be your loneliness. And how terrible your fear. But you, at least, are innocent of that. You were not the one to betray Sondehna. Instead, you honour the memory."

"Honour?"

"By your choices. By bringing back the Iabeiorith despite your fears. We are alike in so many ways, it seems."

"How are we alike? I am nothing like you!"

"But you are, and more than you know. Haven't you asked yourself where my weaponry comes from?"

"Some long-forgotten hoard? Something stolen from the Balt Kaalith?"

"And you should know better than that."

Korfax released her at last and stood back. She breathed deeply even as she rubbed her numb shoulders. He had all but crushed her as he had held her to him. She would have fled then, but instead she found herself compelled to stay. She had to know the final answer, the answer she knew was coming.

Korfax held up his sword and she felt the sudden clench of power. The cave walls vanished into great distances and darkness rolled in from each quarter. He became a black and shadowy cloud. Potent energies flickered here and there and all the other powers in the cave were suddenly subdued. Doagnis felt deep cold swell about her. Then, just as quickly as it had come, it vanished again and Korfax stood before her as before.

"This is not just any Qorihna, Doagnis," he told her. "This is *the* Qorihna: the first, the only, the one Nalvahgey originally took from the Mahorelah, the one she gave to her son. This is that very same Qorihna, the one that Aolkar used to quell the Agedobor, the very first of them all."

Doagnis sank to her knees in shock. What was Korfax saying? Few, precious few, knew that the son of Nalvahgey was indeed Aolkar, or so she had thought. She stared back in horrified wonder.

"But how can you know this?" she asked. "There is no record of that anywhere else in the world. Abhimed never spoke of it, and only Aolkar knew the truth. It is a secret that has been kept by the Mikaolazith for generations. The only other, in the whole world, who knows anything of this at all is Ronoar, and he is my servant. He has never spoken of it to anyone, and I would swear my life upon it. So how do you know this? I demand that you tell me. How do you know this?"

He held her with his gaze.

"Because, like you, I am descended from father to son, in line unbroken, from Haelok Mikaolaz Audroh Sondehna."

He let the words hang in the air whilst Doagnis stared back up at him.

"You lie!" she said, but there was no strength in her voice.

Korfax gestured to the back of the cave.

"Then tell me how it is that I can open that casket of yours?"

She did not answer.

"I once possessed its twin," he told her.

Doagnis clutched at herself as if to keep her still within the world.

"Adraman vanished!" she said. "The male line vanished!" she accused. "Only the female line survived," she whispered.

He knelt down and looked long at her.

"However you may deny it, it is the truth," he told her. "How else can I open that casket of yours, a casket which will only open in the presence of the pure bloodline of the Salman Mikaolazith? But there were things in my casket that you do not have in yours, because they cannot be duplicated. After all, the son of Sondehna was to have everything that belonged to his father."

Korfax lifted up a small, nondescript bag from its hiding place upon his belt.

"Here are the heirlooms," he said, "passed from father to son since time immemorial. A gift from our long-dead mother, from Nalvahgey herself!"

He held it towards her and she stared at it, unmoving. The sense of stored power within the bag was so strong that it made her fingers itch, even now. She was horrified. There were no periapts in her possession that came even close.

"What is in there?" she dared at last.

He looked at the bag for a moment as if measuring it, but then he looked back at her again. His eyes glittered darkly.

"Look! Know! It is the very proof that you seek."

She tried to see what Korfax was thinking, but she failed utterly. His revelation still had not sunk in. It was as though her life had entered a waiting place all of its own. She felt herself suddenly cushioned from the world, remote and no longer in control. There was a wind somewhere, a great wind, and if she listened carefully enough she could hear it bearing down upon her even now, ready to lift her up and deliver her into the courts of chaos. She shuddered. Events had taken the least expected turn of all. She looked at the bag. Dare she touch? Dare she look? But Korfax leaned closer and offered up the last temptation.

"So, are you going to take it? Don't you want to know the truth?"

Doagnis closed her eyes. She dared not, for this was not only temptation but also admission. But she was on fire inside and her fingers were already burning with the power she could feel before her. So she took the proffered bag carefully and gingerly opened it up. She found four objects inside.

First of all she took out a heavy disc of black stone that was filled with shifting lights, glittering like a horde of gems. She turned it over and over, staring at it as if she could not quite believe what it was that she was seeing. It took her long moments to put it back down again.

She took out the next object, a short rod of a hard and dark blue wood, hollowed with a core of airy luminescence. But even as she held it up its core all but ignited and bright blue energies spread out over all its surfaces, both inside and out, daring even to swarm over her hand as well. She dropped it and the energies faded away again. She stared down at it for a moment and then looked at her hand as if the energies had burned her, but her hand was as it had ever been.

She took out the third object, a small red dagger forged of a substance that seemed to burn continuously with phantom fires. She held it as far from her as she could, tentatively grasping it by the hilt, even as she marvelled at its impossible radiance. Then she put it down carefully, down beside the blue wooden rod, but its fires did not dim.

Finally, at the last, she took a shallow cup out of the bag, a cup of the smoothest green in which slow-moving waters lay. But no matter which way the cup was tilted, the waters remained where they were, at the bottom of the cup, rippling gently all the while.

The whole of creation seemed to open up inside her head. She had, before her, the fabled elements of Nalvahgey. They could be nothing else. Nothing, not anything, could remotely feel like this. It was almost as if legend sprang to life at the touch of her hand. She placed the cup down again and closed her eyes. Here they all were: earth, air, fire and water. Here they were before her, at her feet. She had completion within her grasp.

It was all too much. The most potent tools ever made for the practise of the Namad Mahorelah were now in her possession. She suddenly had such power in her grasp as only the giants of the past had ever dared to wield, and then only sparingly. With these periapts Nalvahgey had subdued the Agedobor. With these periapts the north had become the strongest power in all the world. Silent tears coursed down her cheeks as the truth finally filled her.

Korfax looked down at her. See her there, kneeling before him, caught in revelation. How vulnerable she was now. He had thought her callous and cruel, possessed of a heart of the coldest stone. But now he found himself seeing the world through her eyes.

How strange it was. There were so many echoes of his own life in what she had said. Were not all hands raised against him now? And like her, did he not hate the west also? He thought of Zafazaa and his plots against the Farenith. He thought of the Balt Kaalith and their self-serving duplicity.

His life was replete with turning points – the attack upon Losq, his mercy towards Mathulaa, the death of his father, his fall from grace, the death of Obelison, the origins of his family and the death of Adavor. Now here he was, seeing it in another. What would it do to her?

He watched as Doagnis carefully put the periapts back inside the bag before clutching it all to her breast in sudden ecstasy. He watched the tears even as they formed, watched as they swelled in her eyes before falling down her cheeks in uncounted numbers, and he found himself moved as had never expected to be. He suddenly understood, so keenly that it hurt, what it must be like to lose something as if for all eternity, only to have it given back again, pristine and pure. For so much had indeed been lost to the past, so much had been burned and trampled, or slain. But here, at last, was something of great worth that had survived the long and careless years unstained.

He watched as Doagnis closed her eyes and covered her face with her hands.

"They are yours," he told her. "I give them to you as proof of my sincerity."

She opened her eyes and dropped her hands. She stared at him as though he had suddenly become miraculous.

"You give them to me? You give them to me freely?"

Korfax heard the intensity in her voice, and he suddenly felt a deep well of emotion rise up inside. It was all that he could do to answer calmly.

"I do. You know how to use them better than I. But if you do not trust what I say, then look inside. As I looked inside you, look inside me. See the truth for yourself."

Doagnis stared at him. Look inside? Dare she? She paused, afraid. But then he reached out and touched her, and before she could do anything to stop him he was there, within her, showing her who he was. She could see him, all of him, with an intimacy she had never experienced before. Nor could she turn away from him, for he was everywhere. Everywhere that she turned, he was there before her.

She was not used to such a gift. In her world she took, neither asking nor waiting for permission. She took what she desired and threw it away once she no longer wanted it. But this sharing, this wonderful sharing, made everything she had ever experienced before seem crude and unlovely. How much better was this gentle merging of thought. He finally withdrew and she found herself alone again. She tried to look at him but was unable to meet his eyes.

There was a part of her that sneered at what had just happened. You must not be touched by this, it said, you are alone because none can match you. You are the ruthless pinnacle, ruthless by necessity, ruthless by right. But she could not listen to that voice, because she had seen another truth. She had seen Umadya Losq, the far north, a place she had never been but which nevertheless filled her dreams. And in that place had been love, family, sharing and belonging. Seeing this hurt her in ways for which she was totally unprepared.

She felt as if she were a child once more, unsure, uncertain. Seeing him now in this strange new light, she felt something tighten in her breast, something she had never felt before in all her life. It was a sense of coming home, the one place she had never truly known. And it was Korfax that had done this – him, her avowed enemy. He had come to her with death in his left hand and mighty gifts in his right. They had fought each other with words and thoughts, revelation piling upon revelation, until the words and the thoughts had all fallen into a great furnace and the final truth, the only truth that mattered, had emerged from the ashes.

Korfax was of her blood. He was of the line of Sondehna, he knew who she was and yet he forgave her. That Soivar had betrayed Sondehna meant nothing to him. Her nightmare was no more.

The revelation circled and circled until she realised the deeper truth. Her nightmare was no more. The fear was no more. That he was here, now, preserving her life, changed everything.

It was the prophecy, the great prophecy that the Mikaolazith would rise again. She could see it before her. With Korfax at her side none would stand in her way.

It ached inside, tumultuous yet still. This was why she had not been able to slay him. How could she? He was her other half. He was a part of her, the fulfilment of her destiny. A place long dark and crushed down now saw the light again. Love! She had never thought to know it. She looked up at him and saw him as if for the very first time. Something inside began to sing.

Without thought or hesitation, she came to him all in a rush and flung herself into his arms.

"Thank you," she cried, her longing filling the air about her like a conjuration of fulfilment.

"Now I understand," she sobbed as she held herself to him.

She looked at him and her eyes were empty of everything but tearful joy and fearful adoration.

"We are kin," she murmured, "brother and sister, you and I!"

"You are my completion," she whispered as she tightened her hold upon him and bowed her head to his breast.

Korfax heard the words as though they tumbled down around him from the heavens.

We are kin!

What mighty words!

He had not considered that.

He lifted his hands away from her, even as she clung to him, and looked at each in turn as if he no longer understood their purpose. Then he placed one about her carefully, slowly following it with the other, gently, hesitantly, as if not fully understanding what it was that he did at all. But as the moments passed he held her closer to him, and closer still, tighter and tighter until he finally let the moment engulf him completely.

How strange was this? He swallowed hard. Of all the answers to this confrontation, this was the least expected. Or was it?

She was right, of course. Out of their shared lives came the one inescapable truth. Fate had spoken yet again. This was why he had come here. His fate knew that which he did not. They were together, as it was ever meant to be. They were kin, brother and sister, two halves of the same sundered stone, the last saplings of a once mighty tree. He held her tighter still and felt a dark happiness fill him from the inside out, a sense of finality he knew he could never put into words. A dark fire unfurled within and began to roar. Here was where the world finally turned. Here was the mighty apex of his life. Here, finally, the false light was eclipsed and the true darkness was revealed at last.

9

HIDDEN

Totch-agzar Chimim-namouch
Lan-a-ged Odix-sibji
Ip-komail Tolah-ajon
Om-eonaih Fensa-zomain
Chis-pei-i Kursih-vanzaf
Pa-ors-a Ikrus-doalne
Od-iparm Sb-tal-lijiz

He sat upon the high seat and she knelt at his feet. He drank of the dark wine and she ever replenished his cup.

He studied the cup. It was fat and richly carved, and he found its lavish absurdity pleasing in a way that nothing else had ever pleased him before. It was deep and sensuous, much like the wine that it cupped and so different from the memories of his youth. Then it had all been light and subtle, but now he found the richness in his hand more apposite to him than anything that had gone before, so he partook of the wine again and looked down at Doagnis as she waited upon him, staring up as if he were some god to be so gladly appeased.

That, at least, he understood. She wanted to do this. She wanted to please him. After all that they had been through – the hatreds, the rages, the pursuits, the lethal games – it all came down to this. He had become her fulfilment.

It was strange and yet not so. He also felt a sense of completion, as if he had finally achieved the meaning of his life. It was as Doagnis had said. Brother and sister. The words fitted exactly!

He savoured the wine, tasting it on his tongue, or in his memory. It had come from Badagar, or so Doagnis had said, but he had never encountered its like before. She had named it Oucheis, but he did not recognise the name. He wondered if Ralir had ever tasted it. He frowned. What would Ralir say if he could see his old friend now?

He looked at Doagnis and saw that she was looking at the elements again. She kept on going back to them, almost as though she feared they might suddenly disappear. As he watched she held up the short rod of blue wood and it ignited with energies even as she touched it. Then it sat in her hands like a gently burning scroll.

"You know what this is, of course?" she said to him.

He lowered his cup.

"Do I not?" he returned. "You hold the Taankab. With it are the Ksral, the Vepna and the Hktal. I know each and every piece and have read the contents of each and every scroll. During the long seasons that I pursued you I steeped myself in the lore. But you are the one with the skill to realise their true potential, I think. Unlike me, you have pursued this knowledge all your life. You are a true daughter of Nalvahgey." He paused and stared into the deep distances. His eyes darkened. "Just as I, no doubt, am a true son of Sondehna."

But she did not notice. Instead she was consumed by the sight of the Taankab, holding it up before her like an offering, gloating even as she worshipped its miraculous existence. He watched her as she gloated and found even that expression a thing of strange beauty. It had all changed, all of it. The way he thought, the way he saw, the colour of the world.

"The Taankab," she sighed. "With this I can summon the mightiest demons and not worry for the consequences."

Korfax smiled coldly at the thought.

"You seemed to do well enough without it, as I remember. You possessed Torzochil, you summoned a Babemor and then you sent three Azadra against me. You even managed to escape the attentions of Ash-Mir."

Her smile faded and her eyes filled with a more troubled light.

"I was lucky," she said. "The Hung God had other business than my soul, it seems. So how did you escape?"

Korfax smiled back at her in reassurance, but inside he still shuddered at the memory.

"It knew who I was," he told her. "It even said so, though I did not hear it at the time. Then it left of its own accord."

He looked down.

"I think it wanted to ally itself with me."

She turned away and he watched her carefully. He had the feeling she did not like what that told her. No doubt, like him, her old life battled with the new. Up until this moment she had been singular, strong and defined by the loneliness of power, right at the centre. There was a part of her that did not like it when others displaced her. She had a jealous streak, something all the Argedith seemed to share. He understood. It would take time for them both to adjust to their new accord.

She glanced at the Taankab again as if in reassurance.

"Before this moment I thought I had power enough to avenge the long defeat, the deaths, the dishonours, the terrible crusades. But now? It is almost as if Karmaraa achieved nothing. The last seven thousand years have come to nought and the Iabeiorith return to take back what is theirs."

"But you forget the Agdoain," he reminded her. "They must be dealt with, before we can even consider the west."

He leaned back in his chair and took another draught of wine. "But once they are gone," he continued, "there is one in particular that deserves my attention."

"Who?"

"Zafazaa! I owe him for many things."

She held up the bag and placed the Taankab carefully back inside. The expression on her face suddenly reminded him of Dialyas, a carefulness of calculation.

"Revenge, is it?" she mused. "You were always such a one, I think."

"Such a one?"

"Fuelled by vengeance."

"Not always, but there are many that I would like to thank for the parts they have played in my life. Alas, some are no longer within reach."

He drank the last of the wine. She watched him for a moment.

"You still love her, don't you?"

"Who?"

"Obelison."

He felt a brief surge of rage. Was it the memory of loss? Was it guilt that he had so quickly forgotten her? Or was it rather a sudden sense of chagrin that he was so easily read?

"Foolish question!" he snarled back at her.

She moved away from him. There was fear in her still. Korfax lowered his gaze as he rolled his cup betwixt finger and thumb.

"I am sorry," he said. "Some wounds can never be healed."

After a moment Doagnis returned to him again.

"I am sorry, too."

She laid a timid hand upon his knee.

"I did not mean to cause you pain."

Korfax reached out and touched her hand for a moment, stroking it.

"I know you did not," he said.

He took a deep breath.

"Yes, I still love her. But only the memory. She is gone. She entered the river during our flight from the Velukor, and one should not long for that which can no longer be."

He looked down at his cup.

"So yes, you are right, there is vengeance in my heart, but I reserve the greatest portion for whoever is responsible for the Agdoain."

Doagnis smiled, gentle now, consoling.

"Well, without them you would not have come to me," she said.

Korfax gave her a searching look. She did that so easily, shift from one state to another. He wondered briefly if she had hidden herself from him in some way. One moment she was like Dialyas, all slyness and manipulation, and the next she was as cold as her mother, before becoming warm and sensuous again, like now. Who knew what tricks Doagnis had within her?

He decided to test it. He leaned over her and his hand played upon the hilt of his sword. She glanced at it and Korfax did not miss the sudden flicker of fear in her eyes.

"You kneel at my feet," he said, "and you pour wine for me, but do you do this merely to assuage my wrath? I have wanted vengeance on you for such a long time."

She drew back a little.

"But what of it?" she answered. "I was just as eager to kill you."

True enough, he thought.

"I knew who you were," he continued, "and still I wanted your death."

She turned him aside almost as easily, whilst lifting up the bottle and pouring more wine into his cup.

"But now you have discovered another truth," she returned. "We learn by our mistakes. They forge us. Now you have found other targets for your unanswered rage."

Another good answer.

"And what then, sister mine?" The words were out even before he could consider them. He stared back into the depths of his goblet. The word hung there. Sister! He stared at it, savoured it. He looked back at her.

"What would you like to happen once the Agdoain are cleansed from our world?" he asked.

She smiled up at him, the look on her face suddenly the most loving he had ever seen. His ill-considered words had ignited something in her, some deep feeling long-buried that now rose up to take its place in the light.

"Why," she said, delicately moistening her lips with her tongue, "then the works of Karmaraa will finally be overthrown. I have no love for him or his heirs..." she paused for a moment, "... and now, I think, neither do you."

She came even closer and he felt the nearness of her. Her eyes had become deep, dark pools and her lips were parted almost in invitation. She sat upon his lap and took his head in her gentle hands and laid it against her breast. But even as she curled herself about him a sound from behind them both broke the moment. Someone else had entered the room.

Ronoar stood in the doorway. Doagnis stood up quickly, suddenly startled.

"Ronoar!" she said, a nervous smile flitting across her face. "What are you doing here?"

He bowed.

"But surely, mistress, you have not forgotten? It is the turning of the hour of Iasznna."

Korfax leaned forward, revealing himself from within the shadow of the high seat. Ronoar started, looking from Doagnis to Korfax and then back again. Doagnis laughed lightly.

"Yes! The fifth hour!" she said. "Of course! But let ritual become our servant for a little while. It is rarely ever so. I think we deserve its service once in a while. So come to me, Ronoar, come to me now and meet our newest ally."

Korfax stood up. Ronoar took three steps into the room and stopped, his eyes never leaving those of Korfax.

"Mistress! I know who this is," he said "Though he is much changed I still recognise him and you will not persuade me otherwise. This is Korfax. How can he be our ally? He has promised us death ever since our paths first crossed."

"Not quite true, Ronoar," Doagnis said. "I once met Korfax in my father's house, a long time ago. He did not promise me death then. As for the rest? Consider it an honest mistake. Korfax has discovered new truths since he last crossed our path. He has decided to embrace his heritage and join with us."

She said it lightly, her tongue tripping over the words as though they were nothing, a mere song, but Ronoar clearly did not trust anything where Korfax was concerned. He scowled in response.

"Has he mastered you so easily, then?" he asked. Then he drew his sword and held it before him in the attitude of defence.

"The Dar Kaadarith know many ways to get inside another's mind!" he continued, but Doagnis merely looked back with fond regret, even as she clasped her hands to her cheeks in mock dismay.

"Come now, Ronoar. Do you really think this a glamour?"

She smiled and then walked around the chair and over to her shew-stone. No darkness crossed its depths now. It was altogether pale and clean. She stroked it as if to thank it for its honesty and then held it up.

"Look! No darkness here," she proclaimed. Then she gestured back at Korfax. "Korfax has come to me bearing gifts I cannot ignore. And he has brought himself, a greater gift by far, for he has shown me who he is. It seems that the Salman Farenith have kept a wonderful secret from the rest of us for a very long time."

Ronoar still did not move.

Korfax looked at Doagnis for a moment before turning his attention to her servant again. He studied Ronoar carefully. Though they looked nothing like each other, there was something of Baschim in Ronoar, and how that likeness burned. He wondered at it. How deep did Ronoar's history go? How long had his house served the line of Sondehna?

"And what secret would that be, my mistress?" Ronoar asked at last.

"That the Farenith are not the Farenith at all, but the Mikaolazith. Korfax is a direct descendant of the male line."

She spoke the words with such nonchalance that Korfax found himself staring back at her in sudden amazement. That such truths could be uttered so lightly? It was another challenge, surely.

Ronoar, meanwhile, seemed to stagger. He turned back to Korfax just as Korfax turned away from Doagnis again. Their eyes met. Ronoar could not imagine it. What was this? He took a small step forward.

"You are..."

He stopped and almost choked as he gazed back at his mistress again.

"Mistress, please, tell me this is no jest. Do not play with me so!"

Korfax stepped forward. Ronoar stepped further back in sudden fear.

"This is no jest, Ronoar," said Korfax. He reached over his shoulder and fingered the hilt of his black sword.

"How long have you served the house of Mikaolaz?"

"A long time," said Ronoar. "Since the earliest days."

"Since the time of finding?"

Ronoar frowned as if not expecting such a question. "Yes!" he declared.

"A long time, indeed," said Korfax. "There are few that have served so faithfully for so long."

Ronoar, at the mention of his own heritage, drew himself up. There was a certain pride in him now.

"You will not persuade me with sweetened words," he said. "I serve only certainty."

"I know. So what of the word of your mistress? But if that is not certain enough for you, then I will also tell you also that the greater casket of Sondehna has been in my family's possession for over six thousand years. And if that is not sufficient either, then I will tell you that I have upon my finger Sondehna's ring, that I wear the Qahmor of Sondehna, that I bear the Qorihna of Sondehna and that I can open the casket of your mistress, a feat only a child of direct descent can accomplish. And finally, if you want even more proof, Ash-Mir proclaimed me a son of the house of the Mikaolazith to my face, if somewhat obliquely."

Ronoar blanched and muttered, almost to himself.

"My mistress ever wondered how you survived that encounter."

Korfax smiled.

"I might tell you the story some day, if you still possess a willing ear, that is." Korfax dropped his smile. "And one other thing," he said. "I have given your mistress four gifts lost since the time of Sondehna. They have been in my family's possession since the earliest days of our house."

Ronoar was a moment answering.

"What gifts?" he asked.

"The elements of Nalvahgey," came the answer.

Ronoar gasped. He looked at Doagnis and she held up the bag. The weight of revelation finally became too much for him and he fell to his knees, staring at the stone below. Korfax could see it written in him. It was too much. He served and he had believed that he knew what it was that he served. But now something greater had returned out of the lost years, something that made his service greater also, made it mightier. Once again a child of the line of the stewards could serve the house of the Mikaolazith as they were meant to.

"Then you are my Haelok!" he said. He raised his hands in supplication. "Forgive your humble servant his doubts, great prince. I have kept faith with the house of Mikaolaz all my life, but it was always believed that the male line had passed into dust. It was only with the greatest difficulty that the female line survived at all."

Korfax smiled. Haelok! Great prince! Yes, those were his titles now, and how good they sounded.

"There is nothing to forgive," he told Ronoar. "You are as you are."

Ronoar let out a long and shuddering breath as if he had just attained his heart's desire.

They sat together and thought, or rather Korfax sat with Doagnis whilst Ronoar stood at hand, ready to serve as always. The question before them was simple. How to have the others accept that Korfax was now their ally?

"We should tell them who we are," said Korfax. "They would take it as a sign that the Iabeiorith will rise again."

"No," she counselled. "They should judge you by what you do, not by your blood. That is how I come to occupy my position. I am the best of the Argedith. None can gainsay it."

He looked at her for a moment.

"Very well. So what am I to do, then?"

"Convince them with your power. Show them what Qorihna and Qahmor can do. Let their imaginations work for you. Once they realise that you have embraced the way of the Iabeiorith, they will not doubt you then."

He looked long at her for a moment.

"What is it that you really fear? Is it the taint of Soivar? But what if I stand beside you and say that I absolve you of all guilt in this. Surely that would do?"

She smiled sadly.

"No! Not even you can order such a thing. The daughter becomes the mother. Even you cannot gainsay that, no matter how mightily you proclaim it."

Korfax turned to Ronoar.

"And what say you?"

"This secret has been kept down the long years," Ronoar said. "It should never be revealed. The Iabeiorith have filled themselves with tales of times past all throughout the long years of exile. Their glories and their defeats fill them. There are many stones of memory taken from those days, days of happiness when the Iabeiorith ruled and days of woe when they were defeated and cast out. It is their truth, and the darkest of all their tales is that of Soivar and her betrayal. She is named traitor and, as it is written, any of the female line must carry that taint also. It is of the blood, and the blood must always have its way. This is the heart of the

Iabeiorith."

"That is hard," Korfax said. He reached over to Doagnis and took her hand. "I understand traitor all too well. But you did not do this. It was Soivar's choice – and her choice alone."

Doagnis smiled.

"No," she told him. "This cannot be. You must accept this. I do. As it was with my mother and her mother before her, I also will not live under the shadow of another. I will prove myself alone. It is how it has always been."

She stood up.

"I think that all we should say in this matter is that your house was once called something else, a name lost to the dark years, and that your heritage remains unknown. Let them judge you by what you do, not by who you say you are."

Korfax paused a moment, thinking. He had found himself enjoying the moment when Ronoar had called him prince. How right it had felt. But Doagnis was correct in what she said also. He needed to prove himself to the others. He needed to earn their trust. Finally he bowed his head.

"So be it," he said.

Ronoar bowed to them both.

"Then I will gather the chieftains," he said.

Korfax walked into the main cave and stopped. Ronoar stood before him like a herald and Doagnis stood at his side, her arm in his, like a mistress. All the chieftains of the Haelok Aldaria that were assembled stood up, some with curiosity on their faces, others with confusion.

Korfax had been told their names, their real names, and had smiled even as he heard them. More secrets from the past. Here were representatives of the Vordekassith, the Noldurissith, the Rameldurith and the Korzuldurith. So many forgotten names, so much that history had declared as dead.

Their chief and captain, Teodunad, Teodunad of the Korzuldurith, looked up and stepped forward, his interest obvious. But Doagnis ignored him and smiled sweetly at all in turn.

"I come to you now with great news," she announced. "It seems that we have a new ally this day – one that has been our greatest foe has become our greatest friend instead, bringing with him mighty gifts. Rejoice, I pray you, for his change of heart."

No one spoke. They all looked at Korfax. Teodunad stepped further forward.

"This is him, mistress?" he asked.

"It is," she said.

"But how can that be? You once told us that our greatest foe was Korfax. It was also said that he died in the wreck of Othil Ekrin. So who is this that stands beside you?"

"It is Korfax, of course."

She inclined her head just so, and he scowled. He placed his hand upon the hilt of his sword, as did many others. All now looked darkly at Korfax and the air thickened.

"Mistress, surely not!" exclaimed Teodunad. "You cannot mean it."

He gestured at Korfax.

"This is the Enay of the Salman Farenith? This is the Meganza to the thrice-cursed Velukor?" Teodunad now turned to the others. "This must be some ruse, some ploy by the slaves of the west. First they make us believe that Korfax is a traitor and a heretic, then they set him on our trail and finally he infiltrates us. Then, come the requisite hour, he will betray us."

Korfax folded his arms. A look of amusement tilted his lips. Doagnis merely looked hard at Teodunad.

"And do you honestly believe such a plan would fool me, Teodunad?" she asked. "Conspiracies and subterfuge? I think I know them better than most. Korfax has shown me his heart. I know who he is. He has given me undeniable proof of his commitment and has come to me bearing mighty gifts."

Teodunad looked down for a moment in expected humility, but then he shot a venomous glance at Korfax.

"Then why does he not speak on his own behalf, instead of standing there, smiling in cryptic silence. Many of us have died at his hand, and do not think that the rest of us shall easily forget it!"

Korfax laughed quietly.

"Come now, Teodunad," he said. "Do you really regret Mirzinad's passing? Would he not have taken your place had he slain me? Do you honestly regret that?"

Teodunad scowled and there was a faint rustle from behind. Some were smiling at that. Korfax glanced about, catching where the smiles lingered longest, but Teodunad was not done.

"We know who you are, puppet of the Velukor."

Korfax let his own smile fall away.

"Puppet, is it? You and I shall come to blows, Teodunad, if you do not curb that rash tongue of yours. What has your mistress just said?"

Korfax let his hands fall to his side. Ronoar glanced at Doagnis and they both withdrew to the side, leaving Korfax alone. The hall became quiet. They could all feel it, that sense of imminence, but they did not know what it might portend. Teodunad glanced to either side, wondering belatedly, perhaps, if he had dared too much and too soon.

Korfax drew his sword. What Teodunad had taken for a very large kansehna suddenly writhed in Korfax's hand like no sword he had ever seen before. Disconcerted, Teodunad took a step backwards, but then the blade elongated, following him even as he retreated, tracking him like a predator and only stopping at last when it was within a hand's width of his face. Then it sang quietly to him.

Teodunad heard the song, almost within his head, rising and falling like a long, drawn out moan. The tip of the sword swayed slightly, and Teodunad was suddenly certain that it was looking at him. He felt his skin crawl. He looked back up reluctantly at Korfax and saw the darkness that sat behind his eyes.

"Teodunad," said Korfax, "you might be surprised to learn that not everything is a lie, or a plot, or counterfeit, that sometimes you do indeed hear the truth. I have a heritage that has been hidden since the times of the wars. My ancestors, like yours, once fought for the north."

Teodunad was still not convinced. He pointed an angry finger back.

"Your ancestors fought for the north? Where is the proof? You stand there, threatening me with a sorcerous blade, and then you ask me to accept your word? I accept nothing of you. Thousands of years of blood are upon your hands, and I, for one, shall not forget it."

Korfax laughed.

"Teodunad, do you not hear the words coming out of your mouth? I am threatening you with a sorcerous blade? Think what you are saying! I, a former Geyadril of the Dar Kaadarith, hold a sorcerous blade? Do you not see what that means?"

Teodunad looked perplexed.

"I once believed other than I do now, I admit it," Korfax told him. "I once swore an oath in the name of Karmaraa that I would not suffer the Argedith to live. I have since come to greatly regret it. But how many here have been betrayed by the very powers they were raised up to believe in? Few know what that costs. But that betrayal sent me down a path I would not otherwise have followed, and it brought me here, back to the place I truly belong, back to the Iabeiorith."

He gestured at the sword with his other hand. "But it is a sad reflection on what the Haelok Aldaria have become that you do not recognise what kind of sword it is that I wield."

Teodunad looked again at the sword. Korfax withdrew it from Teodunad and let it coil in the air above him. All watched it in stunned amazement. What dancing thing was this? What demon, wrenched from the darkest deeps, could make mere metal live like that?

Korfax looked back at them all.

"My armour should also give you pause for thought."

His armour seemed to pulse now, and the dark shadows of phantom flames flickered up into the air.

"That is impossible!" said Teodunad. "You cannot be wielding a Qorihna. Nor can that be Qahmor..."

Without any warning at all, Korfax vanished, and he vanished entirely. Not a trace of him was left. With the exception of Doagnis, all those assembled either gasped or turned away, poised as if to flee. Then Korfax reappeared again.

"But how can you have weaponry such as that?" Teodunad asked in clear amazement. "It was all said to have been destroyed."

Korfax sheathed his sword again and it moaned back at him as if he had just denied it its due. He took a deep breath; sometimes it was hard to cage his sword unbloodied. Then he gathered himself and looked hard upon Teodunad.

"There is much more to this story than you know, Teodunad, much, much more. But Doagnis has asked that all of you judge me by my actions, not my words. So, for the moment, ponder this. How is it that I possess such weaponry, how is it that I have mastered them and how is it that I can do this."

He gestured in the air, a brief beckoning of the fingers as if he called to something just out of sight. Then he stretched out his right hand as if to grab it and an oily mist quickly occluded the hand, a sick yellow mist that boiled even as it coiled upon itself, over and around his outstretched and grasping fingers.

Teodunad gaped, as did all the others. Korfax was performing sorcery. A Geyadril of the Dar Kaadarith was performing sorcery? They all understood exactly what it meant, for such an act carried with it an immediate sentence of death. What was happening? The world suddenly seemed to have turned itself upside down.

All of them gazed, mesmerised, as out of the slow mist a great shape fell, slithering down and onto the floor. Long sinuous coils writhed and twisted, mounting up into a great and boneless hill of muscle. A head reared and a mouth gaped as the creature turned and bowed to its summoner.

Korfax directed it with his mind and it obeyed him utterly. He directed it to the assembled chieftains of the Haelok Aldaria and made it bow to each in turn. Then he had it pause, willing it to stillness, before speaking through it.

"Teodunad!" announced the great worm, its voice crude and brutal. "I know the Namad Mahorelah. Once I was sworn to fight such lore, but that oath means nothing to me now. Now I embrace the way of the Argedith as the one and only salvation of the Ell. With such lore the Agdoain shall be driven from our world. With such lore the wrongs of this world shall be put to right again. So ask yourself this. Is this truly the action of a lackey of the west, or rather that of an ally?"

The great worm paused a moment and cocked its all but featureless head on one side. Then, having used the creature to its fullest, having given it speech and purpose far beyond its dim understanding, Korfax allowed it to depart at last. The great sinuous form turned about and slowly vanished, diminishing in size as though swallowing itself up in its all too cavernous mouth. The dark mist about it dissipated before vanishing away entirely, and only then did Korfax drop his right hand back to his side.

"I am not your enemy," he told Teodunad. "My eyes have been opened. Have yours? Judge me by my actions, not by your prejudices. You might be surprised by what you come to see."

Korfax sat in her apartments and partook of the Oucheis again. But this time Doagnis sat opposite him, her hands in front of her and her back straight. She had taken up another aspect of herself, something harder and colder. She puzzled him now. What was she thinking?

Though he did not show it he felt physically ill from the summoning. He had not thought it would be like that. The creature he had called was relatively harmless, a carrion eater from the abyss of Utih. He had thought it would cost him nothing to pull the beast from its repose and make it dance to his will, but touching the beast's thoughts, commanding it and feeling its dim bewilderment like an uneasy dream, had been like bathing in slime. He felt soiled, dirtied and abused. The experience had been nothing like calling up a finding mist, which had been clean and quick, like the slash of a knife. He hoped he would never be called upon to do such a thing again. Better to rely upon his sword and his armour and the calling up of blind energies.

"That was a most impressive conjuration. I have never seen better," she announced.

Korfax glanced at her. There was a look in her eyes, a troubled look. Had he unsettled her? His summoning had been, after all, quite unexpected. Perhaps she was unused to others taking the initiative. He bowed his head, hiding the brief and sickening memory of the summoning deep down inside. He must be sanguine at all times now, especially with Doagnis. She would take his distaste as a sign of weakness.

"Thank you," he offered. "I find the Namad Mahorelah apt enough to my will." He looked up at her. "Now I have a question for you. How did you possess Torzochil? Demons are easy enough, as I have just demonstrated, but the texts say that only the weak or the willing can be possessed. Torzochil was neither."

Doagnis looked uneasy.

"She had a weakness," she said.

"A weakness?" Korfax was surprised. "She was first of the healers. What weakness could she possibly possess in that regard?"

Her discomfort increased.

"As you were able to enter my mind through doors I did not know I possessed," she said, "so I was able to do the same to her. She was susceptible."

"How?"

"Healers, by the very nature of their art, open themselves up to others. Though they have barriers and walls about them much as the Exentaser, there is one path inside them they cannot seal. It is the conduit through which the healing energies travel."

Now it was the turn of Korfax to be surprised.

"And how do you know this?" he asked. "I have never heard of that before."

"You will not find it written down, and no text speaks of it," Doagnis continued, "but there was a time when only those that practised sorcery could heal. When Nalvahgey first created the Exentaser they practised both the art of prophecy and the art of healing. Gradually the disciplines grew apart and there was a split. The

Faxith were born."

"The Faxith employed the Namad Mahorelah?"

Korfax was incredulous.

"Yes," Doagnis answered. "Not so surprising, if you think about it. Nalvahgey did the same before she eschewed it. Healing involves the replenishment of energies, and those energies must come from somewhere."

"But they use apiladar! They no longer use the Namad Mahorelah."

"Indeed, but the pathway remains. Once such a door is opened it can never be closed again. I exploited it. Reread the texts and you will see what I mean. So much has been forgotten since the time of Karmaraa, so much that was once wise to know."

There was a long silence. Korfax sat and thought. Here was yet another tale from out of the lost years, another stone falling from the crumbling edifice upon which Karmaraa's victory was built. He found himself wondering how much more there was. He would have asked Doagnis but she had stood up, making as though to leave.

"What is it?" he asked.

"There are things I must attend to."

She walked away.

"Is there anything I can do?" he asked, standing as well.

"No," she answered. "Stay here. We will talk again when I return."

"But what shall I do?"

"Do nothing," she said. "Learn patience. Give yourself time."

Then she was gone.

He sat alone and pondered. Suddenly, or so it seemed, his life had come to a stop. What should he do? What was there to do? There was nothing.

It was strange, but he no longer knew himself. His encounter with Doagnis had gone to places for which he was not prepared. He could never have foreseen such a conclusion. Now here he was, alone in her cave and missing her company, even though she had only been gone a few moments.

'Give yourself time,' she had said. Yes, time! Time to learn how to stop moving, time to adapt to new rhythms and new people. Yes, the Iabeiorith! That was it. These were supposed to be his people, but he did not know them. Perhaps he should find out.

He left the cave. The others watched him, those that were about, but no one spoke to him. He went to one of the guards and asked where Ronoar might be, but he was told he had left with Doagnis.

It seemed that Doagnis was want to go off occasionally on her own. When Korfax inquired after an escort, the others looked hard at him.

"Ronoar is with her," said one. "It is her will. She does not tell us her intent and we do not ask. Those of us that serve find themselves well content with that."

Korfax saw the expression on each face as they looked back at him. He took the hint.

He found himself wandering aimlessly. He felt ill at ease. The others in the encampment kept away from him. Most kept their eyes downcast when he approached, but a few seemed barely able to hide their hostility. If he asked a question, he got an answer, but it was usually terse. No one wanted to know him. He was distrusted, so he stopped asking questions.

He went to the stables and sought out Enastul. There were others there before him, three of them, all looking at his steed from a distance. They were talking quietly to each other, admiration and appreciation for such a fine ormn.

They turned as he approached, but they did not speak. He bowed his head to them, but they did not bow theirs back. His expression darkened, and something of his fire entered his eyes. They quickly left. He watched after them for a moment and then went to Enastul.

Enastul greeted him happily enough. Korfax looked about him. Whoever managed the stables had tended to Enastul well. His bier was full, there was plenty of water and someone had even brushed him down, coat, mane and tail.

"So you let someone else touch you, did you?" he asked. Enastul bowed his head for a moment and then went back to his bier. Korfax smiled and stroked him for a moment, then he turned about to leave, only to find another looking in at him. She was hard of face, with a weary expression. She was staring at him as if not quite sure what she was looking at.

"He would let no other come close," she said.

"You have looked after him?"

"Yes. Many wanted the privilege, but he would only allow me to come near. Even then I had to bow my head to him before I could approach. He is proud."

"He is. Thank you for seeing to him."

She gestured at Enastul.

"He serves you," she said. "Few would do that."

Korfax started.

"I am not your enemy," he told her, "not now."

She looked as if she did not care one way or the other.

"Words are easy. Words cost little."

Korfax gestured towards his steed.

"Can I at least know who to thank for this."

She did not smile. Instead her expression tightened, if such a thing was possible. She pointed at Enastul.

"I am here to be his friend, not yours."

She turned away and left.

When he eventually made his way back to the cave, he found Doagnis and Ronoar only recently returned.

"Where have you been?" he asked.

Doagnis smiled.

"Elsewhere."

She caught the look on his face.

"Don't be so suspicious," she said as she walked back with him to her apartments. "I like to practise things on my own, summonings never before attempted, new possibilities. I like to be alone when I do such things."

"Of course," he answered, and he left it at that. But inside he wondered what the real answer was. The hostility he had encountered had put him on edge.

"What is it?" she asked.

"When you were gone I tried to talk to some of the others, but all I received back was enmity."

"As I said before, you must give yourself time."

"Perhaps I should tell them who I am, after all. Then they will trust me."

She grabbed him by his arm, her face suddenly stern.

"I thought we had already discussed this!" she said. "Do you have any idea what the consequences would be? Have you any idea what it would be like for those who do not follow our cause to learn that an heir to the throne of the Mikaolazith has survived, to learn that one of the most honoured houses in all the land has been but a mask for the most reviled? You blamed me for the Agdoain! What would they not blame you for?"

Korfax looked at the rock at his feet.

"But the Farenith are honoured no more. Onehson saw to that."

There was a pause. He felt Doagnis let go of him, and he looked up once more. She had a troubled look on her face now.

"What is it?" she asked. "Is that doubt I see? Are you regretting your choices now? Do you regret our new alliance?"

"I suppose I am tired of being doubted and reviled," he said.

"But they have good reason."

"Do they? I have given them my word."

"And they have learnt, through bitter experience, that not all words can be trusted."

She looked at him for a moment as if measuring something.

"Come!" she finally said, leading him back to her apartments. Once there she set him in a chair and then went off to the back of her cave. It was not long before she returned with a dark and glittering stone.

"Here is something I think you should see."

Korfax looked at the stone. It was much like the one Mathulaa had used to show him the fate of Peis-homa.

"That is a stone of memories," he said.

"It is," she replied. "This is the Apnoralax Angelus."

"What is on it?"

She did not smile.

"Revelation."

She looked utterly serious now.

"This stone will show you the truth."

Then she came closer and placed her hand upon his breast. She looked long into his eyes.

"I want you to know our anger," she finally said. "I want you to know our rage. This will help you to understand why we are the way that we are."

Korfax sat in the chair and stared into space. He felt numb, without sensation, a dull sack of flesh without passion or fire. The world had gone flat around him, all its colours fading to grey.

He knew, as if it had been burned into his very soul, that what he had just witnessed was the absolute truth. It reminded him too much of the vision Mathulaa had shown him of Peis-homa. But this was of another order entirely.

The stone Doagnis had set before him had taken him back in time, over six and a half thousand years, to Lontibir, a land of ill omen set in the turbulent seas of the north-east. Now it was barren and sad, a dark land few were inclined to visit. Some even said that it was a gathering place for lost souls, those who did not, for whatever reason, make it back to the river. Korfax, though, now knew the real truth.

Once upon a time there had been a great tower built upon its highest hill, around which had been set a great many halls. An ancient lord had reared it as the seat of his house, raising it up in the long-vanished past, and his heirs had owned it for a little while, until the time of Sondehna. But then Sondehna had passed into the river and the armies of the west discovered it in turn and took it for themselves. They made of it a holding place, for it was vast and lonely and it suited their purposes perfectly. All the folk of the Iabeiorith – all the captured, all the surrendered – were to be taken there to linger briefly under its shadow, but from its shadow they would never emerge again.

Now Korfax understood the tale of Jernis and Ramenur. He could feel the terrible partings, the many crossings of the Adroqin Perisax and the Adroqin Chiraxoh as the defeated and the fearful fled, trying to elude the forces of the west. He thought of the suffering, the hardships and the sacrifices. And all because of that one stark tower upon Lontibir.

For the lucky few, the very few, Lonsiatris became their final refuge. But for the thousands left behind, for the luckless and the condemned, the tower on Lontibir was to be their only fate.

Korfax saw again the dark horror of it. It could not be true, could it? That the peace of the last six and a half thousand years had been born of this dark evil? To think of it was bad enough, but then to enact it? This was a horror beyond all horrors.

Did anyone else remember this tale? Perhaps there had once been a record of the atrocity kept in the Umadya Levanel, but the Umadya Levanel had now been eaten by the Agdoain, and who knew what had happened to all the records there. Perhaps another record lay still in Othil Homtoh. The highest in the west would surely have known what had come to pass during the day, but what of them now? Would they have been shown the secret, passing it on like a dark guilt from father to son, down the long years, never to be mentioned, never to be spoken of, only to be kept? Korfax thought of his own heritage and wondered what other secrets had survived the long years.

The stain of this crime, though, fell ultimately upon the throne. The long peace had been bought with blood, innocent blood, so much blood that Lontibir could never again be washed clean of the stain. Now, once more, its dark past reached down from the north like a shadow, to poison the entire world.

The wars were finally turning against them and the Iabeiorith were retreating, holing up in their many enclaves and fighting with desperate defiance against the unstoppable vengeance of the west. But they knew that it was the only thing that they could do, for the Balt Kaalith and their servants were rounding up every known family of the Iabeiorith, everyone from the conquered territories, and sending them all to Lontibir. Unbelievable tales crossed the land, passing from tower to stronghold, terrible stories that the Balt Kaalith, in the name of the Velukor, had ordered the unthinkable.

Sorcery was a disease, they had decided, a disease that must be cut out, root and branch, flesh and bone, and never again be allowed to grow. The towers were to be torn down, the cities were to be unmade and the Balt Kaalith were to fall upon the children of the Iabeiorith like a great flock of okanam and sweep them all away in their claws.

Few made it to Lonsiatris, only a few thousands from all the wide lands of Lukalah. Other families came to the empty spaces, other families uprooted by the war, and they set up home there, new families devoted to the rule of the saviour, the Velukor, chosen of the Creator. But on Lonsiatris the ragged few that came to hide under the shadow of the Gohedith knew the terrible truth.

Korfax saw it all again in his mind's eye. He saw the captured stripped naked and chained together in long lines, before being herded from land to ship and packed into the holds as tightly as was possible, so that none could sit or lie. Some still glanced about them with the light of rebellion in their eyes, whilst others just bowed their heads in utter submission at last. Fathers stood angry and fearful, mothers wept and children stared this way and that, wide-eyed and confused as they looked out upon a world gone mad.

There were hard faces on those ships, faces that stood over their captives and were set in stone: features unmoving, shuttered eyes, each as blind as a mirror, reflecting the suffering about them but not seeing it, not seeing it at all.

So the ships left the land, one after the other, each set of wings spreading their blood-soaked limbs and staining the pale light of morning with ruddy shadows.

To Lontibir they came, each creeping into the one shadowed harbour and furtively unloading its cargo onto the darkened wharves.

There they were held in long lines, before being driven up the long road to the tower, to the Umadya Ialith as it had come to be known, where the smoke of burning rose ever upwards into the sky, night and day, day and night.

Each unhappy band struggled its weary way to the tower, a trail of tears trodden many times many. They entered through its stark walls, walking up the unforgiving steps to the mighty gates beyond. Some dared ask for mercy from their captors, some implored of the heavens, whilst others merely cursed under their breath or yet spat their broken contempt upon the stones at their feet. But none tried to escape. None could. Defeat had already taken them, writing its grey lines in all their faces. They had already failed. They had become the dead in waiting.

Through the great gates they went, through the gaping stone jaws, entering the darkness beyond in one single, unending line. And so the tower ate them, and they never came out again, but all the while dark smoke coiled from the blackened crown, one long exhalation of atrocity, the never-ending consummation of flesh and fire.

For many long years afterwards the Umadya Ialith remained upon that lonely peak, pointing its cold stone throat at the passing clouds. Then, finally, after the present had buried the clay of the past, they came back again to tear down the tower. The single stark finger of its accusation was undone, stone by blackened stone, and each piece was taken back to the ships that waited at the shore, a strange reversal of the trail of tears that had once led in the opposite direction. Then each ship took its allotted cargo out into the great ocean beyond and dropped each sullied block into the deepest, darkest depths. Dismembered and drowned, the tower ceased to be.

On certain nights, though, or so it was rumoured amongst those who occasionally passed that way, the tower sometimes reappeared. For many a year afterwards its smoky spirit was said to rear up again from its broken foundations, its cold stone gullet belching redness at the sky, vomiting up the sickly glow of its terrible heart into the night above. With the passing years the rumours became legend, and the legend passed into forgetfulness, and the memories faded away until all that was left was Lontibir and its brooding grief. No one ever went there again – no one wanted to. But few could say why.

Korfax dropped the stone from his hand and stared emptily at the floor. His family had known nothing of this, and he found himself wondering how many actually did. Those that had perpetrated the deed had fled the north and kept the hideous secret to themselves. That there were records somewhere Korfax did not doubt. He wondered if even Zafazaa, Audroh of the Korith Zadakal, knew of this.

Of the guilds, he could only be sure of the Balt Kaalith. They had known, certainly. They kept everything. He even suspected that Naaomir had uncovered this singular fact, so proudly had he displayed the vault where the unrepentant had been buried alive.

But the memory, like an unquiet spirit, would refuse to die. It cried out for restitution. Some in the Balt Kaalith would hold on to the necessity, as would those few of the noble houses in the west that had been involved, but they would never speak of it openly. They knew, in their blackened hearts, that if this thing were revealed they would be reviled for ever more.

Doagnis approached him quietly from behind. She looked at him with fear and trepidation. This had been a risk on her part, for she knew all too well what fire filled his soul. She saw his blank and empty face and her own eyes glittered with remembered pain. Then she dropped her gaze and came to sit before him, holding his hands in hers.

"There was no easy way to tell you this tale," she said, "but perhaps you understand me a little better now. All of the Iabeiorith know what you have just seen, if only because it is told to each child that is born to us. But this stone, the Apnoralax Angelus, that is a trial reserved for only a very few. Only the strongest are able to withstand such brutal truths. This memory was brought to us by one who escaped the flames, the only one to do so. Malatar Pasen Angelus saw the horror herself, saw it all. Though she entered the furnace, her power saved her. She conjured herself back into the Mahorelah and out from it again, and so she was able to bring her terrible vision back to the rest of us. Her escape, her salvation, became the beginning of the hope for restitution that we now enact in her name, and in the name of the Creator. But the Iabeiorith have grown numerous again only by being as ruthless as those that persecuted them. And as we do not forget, so we do not forgive. But the end is fast approaching now and the day of judgement comes headlong towards us. It is nearly here, but with the chaos caused by the invasion of the Agdoain, we can take the main chance at last and pay our persecutors back for their crimes, even as we preserve our world from the foe. And for each life that they took we shall take one of theirs in turn. A hand for a hand, a soul for a soul, until justice be finally done, in the name of the Creator."

Korfax lay back and stared at the ceiling. Tears fell. "In the name of the Creator..." he murmured. He closed his eyes. "The wrongs of this world have become like an ever mounting hill of shackles about our feet. Soon we will be unable to walk under the weight of them. I think that there will come a time when even the Creator will have had enough of us, and we shall all be thrown back into the black pit from whence we came. Maybe that is why the Agdoain are here."

"No!" she chided. "I will not believe it!"

"But the exaltation has been and gone!" he told her. "Your father has fled the world and we, the poor damned fools that are left, the sons and the daughters of insurmountable sin, remain to face the wrath of the Creator."

Doagnis clutched at Korfax.

"You cannot believe that," she insisted. "You must not believe that. I did not show you this truth so that you could despair so."

Korfax looked up at her.

"What I believe? Everything has been thrown down! Where now is the honour? Where now is the mercy? Where now is my belief in love, in justice, in mercy and the goodness of the pure heart? Where are they now? There is nothing left to us but the harsh void. Chaos has us all in its ineluctable grasp and we have become its playthings."

Doagnis looked now as though she regretted showing him the stone at all.

"No, Korfax, no! You are wrong. Let me show you new things to believe in. Let me show you destiny, the righting of wrongs, the possibility of justice again and a people finally at peace with themselves. That is the message I wish to bring – the end of the tyranny of the lords of the west, a glorious future ruled by a glorious empire."

She leaned over him, her hand on his cheek.

"Let me restore your faith in all things. Let me fill you with the righteousness of our cause, with revenge, with justice."

Her face came closer to his.

"And let me restore you to love, brother mine, my one, my only."

She leaned in and kissed him upon his lips, lingering. She drew back and held him to her, and he let her soothe away his pain.

Days passed and the camp prepared to pack itself up and move on. The muster was coming, when all the scattered forces were due to come back together again. There was a place set for this very purpose, deep in the grasslands to the south. Come the eve for departure and all made ready to leave; all except for Teodunad, who sat alone and pondered.

All his plans and dreams lay in disarray. It used to be that Doagnis would smile at him with affection, especially when he carried out her will. But now she had eyes only for another, and she hardly seemed to know that he was there at all.

Korfax and Doagnis! What was it between the two of them? There was something going on, something deep and dark and hidden. One only had to watch her eyes. She followed him everywhere with her gaze. And not only Doagnis but Ronoar also – and that was even more puzzling. Ronoar was fiercely loyal, suspicious of anything and everything, even Teodunad, whom he had known for many a year.

Teodunad had to admit, though, that Korfax was impressive. He was tall, broad and strong, and long years of battle had hardened him. You could tell, just by the way that he moved, that he was not a warrior to be trifled with. Teodunad had no doubt that Korfax had slain far more than his due.

But that was not the problem. Teodunad also understood the way of war. He was a warrior himself, one of the best, born to command. Warriors were easy enough to deal with, if one knew the right things to say. But Korfax was not just a warrior. He was also a power.

He had been a Geyadril of the Dar Kaadarith, learned in all the ways of the Namad Dar. After he had turned the battle for Othil Zilodar they even made him Meganza to the Velukor, though it was clear now that the position had been a cage rather than an honour, for the rumour was that even the Velukor had been scared of the power Korfax had wielded on that day.

Teodunad thought the stories from the siege of Othil Zilodar somewhat exaggerated. Korfax had slaughtered a million of the foe? Surely not! But that was not all. There was another strange rumour that Korfax had found a way to turn the stones of the Dar Kaadarith from their original purposes.

He did not understand the lore himself, merely what it did. But those that did understand such things were perturbed by the tales. It spoke of unprecedented power, power no other could match.

Now here he was, amongst them, and one of the Argedith no less, powerful in the ways of the Namad Mahorelah. He had defeated Tohtanef, Molpan and Axayal in battle, and that was no small feat. He was even armed with Qorihna and Qahmor, weaponry not wielded since the end of the Wars of Unification themselves.

Teodunad thought about that. Korfax was armed with Qorihna and Qahmor, the ancient weaponry of the Haelok Aldaria elite. How he had come to possess such things Teodunad did not know, but it was certain that Korfax knew all there was to know concerning the requisite rituals and passwords. It was as though he had been born to the Haelok Aldaria, born to its very heart. And for Teodunad, that was the strangest mystery of all.

There was a secret here, a secret to be uncovered, and he was not the only one to think so either, for others watched Korfax just as carefully as he did. But Korfax did not put a foot wrong. He kept to the path and said and did all the right things.

So here was the task. How could he, Teodunad, resume his rightful position at the side of his mistress? How could he supplant Korfax, remove him and bring him down, without weakening the cause or hurting his mistress? He did not know. It was time, perhaps, to learn a little patience.

10

BEGUILEMENTS

Cho-ged-a Sihil-pa-aih
Doal-odvan Amao-raqlar
Om-unch-ord Krih-askith-saq
Boror-hon De-opors-stl
Tran-quting Ged-hominas
Fas-kapihd Z-pao-nimin
Bog-tilorp Ixnis-anorn

Over the low hills they went, a long line of dark figures astride dark steeds. At their head rode Korfax, like a lord, with Doagnis beside him, like a bride, he on Enastul, she on Orsael, newly named and newly taken. Ronoar rode behind and warded them both like a careful and caring escort.

Teodunad led the main force, leading them like the dutiful servant he was, seven paces back. But his eyes ever bored holes in the back of Korfax's head.

They had come to the wide grasslands on the south-eastern side of the Adroqin Perisax. About them the land rose and fell in long ripples of green, wide and all but featureless, a sea of leafy blades seemingly without limit. Great clouds marched across the blue vault above, and a cool wind rippled the grass at their feet. Korfax breathed deeply and smiled.

"Such air!" he said. "It is good to be out again, crossing the wider world. I have not been to this place before, but this country we travel through now is much more to my liking than any cave."

Doagnis offered him a smile, but there was more than a hint of indulgence about it.

"Having spent most of my life in hiding," she said, "I am not so averse to the darkness. The shadow has ever been my ally."

Korfax looked back at her and then glanced behind at Ronoar. Even Ronoar had a happy air about him now, for all that he looked straight ahead with his habitual expression of stone.

"And what do you say, Ronoar? Inside or out?" Korfax asked him.

Ronoar bowed his head.

"I am just happy to be where I am," he said.

Korfax turned back to Doagnis and flicked his eyes at Ronoar. She looked behind her briefly and smiled. She leaned closer and her voice was soft.

"I think that Ronoar has discovered the contentment of his soul at last. What was thought to have been lost for ever has been found again. He serves a completed house and all is well with his world."

"A blessed condition indeed," said Korfax, "to find again what was thought to be lost."

"And you," she asked, "have you never found anything that was lost?"

He turned away, the light in his eyes fading a little.

"What is lost remains lost," he said, before turning back to her again.

"But one can always find new things to replace the old."

She bowed her head as if satisfied and looked to the front again. Korfax watched her, following her profile. How unlike she remained, so unlike any other that he had ever met before. She was not as tall as Obelison had been, nor as athletic as Adavor, but she had her qualities, did Doagnis.

For a start she was more voluptuous than most, curvaceous and sensual, with fuller lips and a fuller figure. She belonged to an older world, perhaps, like Mathulaa, a darker world. Korfax found himself running his gaze over her, dwelling on her curves. Doagnis glanced sideways back at him.

"And have you finished your inspection?" she asked. "Do I meet with your approval?"

Korfax looked away, suddenly embarrassed.

"That was unforgivable. Please excuse the familiarity. I do not know what I was thinking."

Doagnis laughed knowingly.

"Oh yes you do. But I forgive you, nonetheless, because I also understand."

"And what do you understand?" he asked.

"That you thought you knew what the world was, only to have it torn away from you. You believed that you served honour and truth, only to discover that there was no honour and no truth. You have been both slave and warrior, puppet and master, thief and fugitive. You have seen loved ones die, seen enemies grow legion, seen miracles, seen despair, discovered that your friends were your enemies and your enemies were your friends, found hate where you only expected to find love and love where you only expected to find hate. Is it any wonder that I fascinate you? I am your completion, as you are mine. As for your attentions? I love you for them as I love no other. They make me feel real, they make me feel whole."

Her eyes flashed even as Korfax looked at her.

"Love?" he asked.

Doagnis smiled her deepest smile yet.

"Yes, brother mine, yes! Though you were my enemy, and I was yours, that is all behind us now. How easily hatred slips into love. Each extreme of the circle falls into the other as though finding consummation, and only those who have never known such a condition can believe that it does not exist. They do not understand because they are singular. But you and I have seen it for ourselves. So I look upon you with new eyes, for by your side I will realise the long dream of our house. And for that, and for many other things, I love you."

Far out upon the undulating plain they made their camp, in between three lines of long, low hills. And in the wide valley called Vuriless they camped within the sea of grass. It was a forgotten country now, marked only on maps. Like the Piral Jiroks that lay far to the west, few ever came here at all.

Sentries were placed just below the brow of each of the surrounding hills, their eyes turned ever outwards, but nothing crossed the horizon. The Iabeiorith lay anchored in the green sea and had only the stars for company.

In the great tent at the very centre of the encampment Korfax sat at the table and slowly drank his portion of wine. Doagnis had retired and a few of the chieftains of the Haelok Aldaria sat at the table with Korfax. None spoke to him, but they all eyed Ronoar with ill-concealed curiosity, for he stood at Korfax's shoulder with proud and shining eyes. Korfax glanced at them occasionally and then turned to Ronoar.

"Ronoar? Sit with me, will you?"

Ronoar looked surprised and leaned over to speak softly.

"I should not. My place is at your shoulder, to serve you as I may."

Korfax dropped his smile.

"Then serve me by sitting with me."

He gestured at the place beside him. Ronoar did not move. Korfax pointed emphatically at the seat.

"I desire speech," he hissed, "that is all."

Ronoar bowed at last and sat on the chair beside Korfax, waiting expectantly. Korfax was a moment gathering his thoughts.

"Have you seen the way the others look at me?" he asked.

Ronoar bowed his head sadly.

"Yes, I have."

"I do not like it. I would do something about it."

"I know. I wish the situation were otherwise, but my mistress feels that this is for the best. Trust will only come with time."

Korfax looked into his goblet.

"She is cautious, and her caution has served her well up until now, but we are fast approaching that time when such caution will become a hindrance. Battle is coming. The gathering of the Iabeiorith is coming. We will soon reveal ourselves to the world. And if they knew who I was, they would all feel differently, I know it – I feel it."

Ronoar bowed his head again.

"They do not know her ancestry, either. She rules, as is fitting, as the mightiest of the Argedith. But, be assured, when the time is ripe, this story will be told again." Ronoar leaned closer and his voice whispered gently in Korfax's ear. "But there is another consideration. When you forge Qorihna for them, when you give them Qahmor, when you lead them into battle, they will not doubt you then."

Korfax lay back in his chair and drained his goblet. He looked hard at Ronoar.

"And are the Haelok Aldaria so easily bought with gifts and sorceries? Does no one look at another's heart and know the truth of what he or she beholds there?"

Ronoar looked down, a sad smile still upon his face.

"Hearts have always been complicated creatures," he said. "Their whims and wants blow with the wind." Then he looked up as if filled with a joyous light. "But show them your might in battle, show them your power, and they will bow before you as I do, and they shall name you master until their dying day."

Korfax looked away and did not answer.

The night found him on his bed, staring up at the rippling fabric, unable to sleep.

A wind whistled through the camp outside, a cold wind from the west, fluttering the pennants of red and black and shaking everything with its unquiet fury. Its many rhythms should have cradled him, but they did not. Instead he turned this way and that, trying to quieten his mind, but his thoughts ever turned to Doagnis.

Ever since they had ridden across the sea of grass strange fantasies had risen up to disturb the landscape of his mind. Now, with nothing else to occupy it, his mind resurrected those fantasies and hurled them back at him as though to taunt him.

She seemed always to be before him, a flickering form in many guises. She became a lady of the court, wrapped about in a gown of the finest illis, before becoming an assassin darting through a window, enclosed about by dark fabrics, and then she turned into a rider galloping across a plain with her cloak and her hair streaming behind her, and in every guise she assumed, she drew him like a guilty pleasure. Her eyes beckoned and her figure ever caught his gaze, either in stark silhouette or in the light of day, her soft curves drawing him in, inviting his touch.

Korfax rolled this way and that and cursed fulsomely. He had never known the like. He desired sleep, not fantasy, but his unruly mind would not relent. Like an elusive scent or a song at the edge of hearing, the thought of Doagnis tantalised him.

It had not been like this with Obelison. He had known her in the instant he had met her and he had given himself to her without question, as she had to him. Their thoughts had become entangled and the heavens and the deeps had opened up about them both. But with Doagnis? He no longer understood himself at all.

Eventually he hurled himself from his bed and went out into the other chamber to get some more wine. Wine would help him sleep. But, instead of wine, he found Doagnis instead, already waiting for him in one of the chairs, straight of back, her hands resting lightly upon its arms.

Korfax stared at her as though he could not quite believe she was there, but she looked back up at him with a smile that was almost luminous.

"So here you are at last!" she said. "I was right after all. Neither of us can find comfort this night."

He watched her as she stood up slowly. Such a simple movement, but her rising was like the swelling of a slow fire to him.

"You should not be here at this hour," he said.

Doagnis took a step towards him, shadow and light from the flickering were-fires rippling across her, the light revealing, the dark concealing.

"Should not? And why is that?" she asked. "I will be wherever I please. And where I please to be at this moment is here."

Korfax stared down at her. She was clad only in a simple gown, its fabric shimmering as she moved, touching her curves and releasing them again. Korfax dropped his gaze.

"Are you not cold?" he said. "The wind is not gentle this night."

Doagnis came forward and placed a hand upon his chest. And, as if to answer his question, he could feel the warmth of it, the heat of it, as though her fingers burned at his touch.

"Then warm me, Korfax, I pray you, and protect me from the unkind air."

Korfax shuddered. He both desired it and feared it, all in equal measure. She wove a siren song in his mind and in his heart. An old memory came to him and he saw Asakom again, long dead in the ashes of Emethgis Vaniad, standing tall before a class of eager acolytes, finger upraised as he told them of the many powers of sorcery.

'And there is one power that is the most deadly. It is that of beguilement, of enchantment. An Arged can enchant the mind of her victim, singing a song he will find irresistible. Many, some even of the Dar Kaadarith, have fallen prey to this insidious power. Though they are all gone, we yet maintain a record of this most perfidious form of attack, for its ultimate goal is possession, the Arged possessing her victim, owning him body and soul. He becomes enslaved and she can summon him like a demon for ever more.'

Korfax stepped back. Was this what Doagnis was doing? It seemed to fit the description, and yet, strangely, it did not. He turned away.

"This is too soon," he said.

"You resist me?" There was dismay in her voice.

"I resist myself!" he told her.

Doagnis was silent for a moment. Then she walked around him and looked up at him, breathing deeply.

"Korfax, you know what I want. I desire the love of a peer. I want it. I demand it.

I deserve it. I want to sit beside you, to eat with you, to ride with you, to sleep with you. I want to be with you always, our powers to entwine, our bodies the same. I am hungry for you, Korfax, as I have never hungered for any other. Do not reject me now, I beg you."

She sank to her knees, suddenly trembling. Korfax clenched his fists and closed his eyes. She begged him. No Ell should beg of another, ever. A vision of Tohtanef danced briefly in his mind. Horrified, he reached down and pulled her up again, staring deeply into her eyes.

"You should not beg!" he said. "You must not! I do not reject you, by the Creator I do not, but my feelings confuse me. I am on fire inside, and if I surrender to it, I do not know what will happen."

Doagnis laid her head against him.

"Then surrender to your fire, just as I have surrendered to mine. None of us knows the next moment, because the now is all that we will ever have. There are dreams, there are prophecies, minds drifting upon the sea of time, but they are all thrown down by the now. The now is all we can ever claim. So be with me now in this waiting time. Be with me now in this waiting place and forget the unformed future for a little while yet."

Korfax held her against him, before taking her back to his bed. They lay together upon the softness, he looking at her, she looking at him. Then his world dissolved in burning, and he suddenly found himself revelling in the fire.

He awoke alone and was glad that he did. He stared upwards at the rippling fabric of the tent, still worried by the wind. He looked up at the ripples and wondered what it was he had done.

But it had been so good. So what did this mean? Or did it mean anything at all? He lay back and pondered.

At last he raised himself from his bed, and donning a heavy robe he went out into the main area of the tent. Doagnis was already there, at the table, being waited upon by Ronoar as usual. Both looked up at his entrance, Ronoar bowing, Doagnis smiling.

"Will you join me?" she offered.

Korfax paused.

"Please?" she asked.

He acquiesced and sat opposite. Ronoar offered fruit, bread and meat. He took some of each and tried to appear as relaxed as he could.

"So then," he asked, "what is the news of the day?"

Doagnis smiled fondly.

"The camp is astir and the muster has begun," she said. "Several companies rode in late last night, or so I am told, and many more rode in earlier this morning. But they are only a handful. The greater number is still to arrive."

"And what are the houses of those that have come?"

"We have the Nourissith, the Olangerith and the Kolorsith."

Then Doagnis paused and looked sideways at Korfax.

"Once they learned of it, they questioned your presence. The Kolorsith, especially, are proud. They will need to be convinced. They have not forgotten that Axayal failed because of you."

Korfax sighed. Here it came again. He glanced at Ronoar, but Ronoar said nothing. He looked back at Doagnis.

"Have you spoken with them?" he asked her. "Have you told them how it was?"

"No, not yet, my love."

She stroked his cheek, the briefest of touches. But all too soon she drew back again.

"I thought rather that you would prefer to deal with the matter yourself."

She smiled and Korfax raised an eyebrow.

"Is this to be another test, then?"

Doagnis became still and her smile disappeared. Was that dismay he saw? Had he hurt her with his doubts? He held himself in a vice-like grip. He must be strong now. Sondehna had been strong and he must be the same.

Doagnis leaned closer, her eyes wide.

"No, Korfax, not a test. Never that!" She leaned closer still. "Not after last night," she whispered. Korfax stared down at her and felt a shiver of pleasure. Last night! He would have leaned closer also, but Doagnis had already receded. She looked back at him carefully now.

"I think it would be wise if you were to show them all exactly where your loyalties lie. Show them what it is that fires your heart. Otherwise, I think, they will never bow to you. And we cannot have that. They fear me, but even that is not enough, not now. They should fear you, for it will not do for you to hide behind me."

Korfax looked away.

"Would it not be simpler just to tell them who I am?"

Doagnis laid a careful hand on his.

"Why do you persist in this?" she asked. "That dream is too powerful to dream yet. Keep the secret for now, as I do. Let them only see your power and teach them to fear it. Then they will serve you willingly – as they serve me."

Too soon she withdrew her gentle touch, the most fleeting of caresses. Korfax stared at the goblet set before him and looked at its contents. It smelt familiar. So rather than brood upon Doagnis, he turned to Ronoar instead.

"What is this that you have set before me?"

"Hudo juice, my lord. It both cleans the palette and awakens the mind."

Korfax smiled slightly.

"I once knew someone in the seminary of the Dar Kaadarith who swore by the Hudo. The last I heard of him, he had returned to Othil Homtoh. I wonder if he still partakes..."

The curtain covering the front of the tent suddenly swept aside and seven entered. Korfax did not recognise any of them, but they all had the air of command about them. The insignia of forgotten houses lay across their shoulders, and each stared back at Korfax with undisguised hostility. Two of them even kept their hands upon the hilts of their swords. The leader stepped forward and bowed to Doagnis.

"Mistress, we come to do your bidding. But first we must question the presence of this one."

He pointed at Korfax.

"We do not understand why you have him here. We do not question you, only him. We would know why he is to be high amongst us. We would know why he is to command. We doubt him."

He stood tall again and looked with undisguised contempt at Korfax.

"All know his tale. None trust him."

Doagnis smiled and leaned back.

"So, let me understand you," she said. "You do not question my word, and yet you question it? I think you had better explain yourself further!"

The chieftain was about to speak again, but Korfax interrupted him.

"I have had just about enough of this!" he said.

All the chieftains stared back at him.

"I was speaking to my mistress," said their leader. "Not to you."

Doagnis seemed about to do something, but Korfax was already on his feet. He drained his cup, never taking his eyes off the chieftain as he did so, and then he placed it most carefully back down upon the table. Releasing the cup with a gentle stroke of his hand he walked around the table and stood with his arms folded. They all stepped back slightly, except for their leader. His gaze now burned just as hotly as that of Korfax.

"I understand that you do not trust me," Korfax told him. "It is regrettable, but at least it is honest! But that you question the will of Doagnis? Who has brought you here? Who has shown you how to reclaim what is rightfully yours?"

Korfax unfolded his arms.

"Doagnis has shown me the truth. I have seen the Apnoralax Angelus. After seeing it, when I finally came back to myself, I cursed those that could conceive such acts and then carry them out. Their names should be cast into the lingering place, and never should they have rest. Their deeds should be carved upon stone so that they are never forgotten and their shame naked for all to see. That I once served the west I now regret, utterly. But that I should choose, of my own free will, to ally myself to Doagnis and to her cause should give you pause, at the very least."

Another of the chieftains laid his hand upon the hilt of his sword and snarled back.

"Your words are nothing – easily said and easily forgotten. You have killed many of us, and I for one would see you answer for that."

Korfax clicked his tongue in gentle derision.

"And you have clearly not listened to a single word I just said!"

He gestured with his right hand and then extended it. A red blur flew from out of his palm and hovered before him. There were wings and there was a body, but the wings fluttered faster than the eye could catch, and the body flexed like a dance of knives. The thing squalled as it hung there, held in place only by the power of his mind. Everyone stepped back, and even Doagnis looked shocked, though she did not move or speak. Korfax smiled at the assembled chieftains as they retreated from him in a huddle of fear.

"This," he told them in his most conversational voice, "is an Azadra."

All eyes were now upon the red blur. Korfax widened his smile slightly. They already knew exactly what it was, but he decided that he would remind them of its propensities nevertheless.

"Azadra are fast and deadly and enjoy fresh meat. At the moment, this one is held where it is entirely by the force of my will. Were I to release it," and here he paused meaningfully, "you would die before you could even raise up your swords. When the time comes you will all be given ample cause to trust me. But, until then, you will hold your peace, and you will trust the words of your mistress instead. How greater than you is she? If she trusts me, then so shall you!"

Korfax narrowed his eyes into cold slits.

"Is that clear?"

He gestured with his right hand, his middle finger curling into that of a hook. The Azadra screamed with pain. Everyone flinched at the sound, even Doagnis, but Korfax ignored it all, even the distress of the demon, and took a step forward. The demon advanced with him, dancing above his outstretched hand like some impaled flame. Now it came close to the first chieftain, and all he could do was to stare at the flickering redness that hovered directly in front of his face.

"Now you will leave," Korfax said quietly, "as Doagnis and I are enjoying a quiet meal together. Go! You are dismissed."

Stunned silence greeted his words. Then, with hurried bows, they all left, one after the other.

Korfax gestured again and the Azadra disappeared as though sucked out of the world through a sudden hole. He sucked in his breath also and walked back to his place at the table, before sitting back down carefully again. That had been hard. Azadra were not the easiest of creatures to command. As they flickered in the air so they flickered in the mind. Doagnis looked back at him with wonder in her eyes.

"Now there was a surprise," she said. "When ever did you learn to do that?"

Korfax looked at his unfinished meal. It suddenly revolted him, especially the strips of cured meat. What had he promised himself? No more summonings? Yet here he was, doing exactly that. It was his anger, it had to be. It did not care. He glanced at Doagnis for a moment. How should he answer?

"It is in the writings," he finally said. "It is all in the writings. In the Dar

Kaadarith, visualisation is the key to unlocking the power within the crystal. With the Namad Mahorelah the same applies. It merely becomes a matter of will."

Doagnis took a deep breath, her eyes still wide.

"But to summon one of the Azadra!" she exclaimed. "That was dangerous, almost foolhardy, I think. They are notoriously fickle. What if it had eluded your grasp?"

Korfax became still. Good question. His anger had made him reckless, but he could not tell her that.

"Did you not tell me that a demonstration of power would suffice to keep the chieftains in line?" he asked. "So what have I done here? Pardon me if I decided to make it an impressive one."

Doagnis laughed nervously.

"That it was, my love, that it was. But please do not do any such thing again. Azadra have a nasty habit of slipping the leash."

Korfax dropped his gaze. He frowned at his right hand and thought of Torzochil, a bloody pile of flesh slumping down to die upon a cold floor.

"Like Torzochil, you mean?"

The words were out before he could consider the cost. The sudden condemnation in his voice curdled the air, and there was a long silence. Korfax could hear Doagnis breathing deeply as though she fought to contain herself. Finally she let out her breath in a long, drawn out sigh.

"I thought we had agreed to leave the past in the past. What is done is done, and it cannot be undone. Or are you going to rebuke me further? What of all those that you have slain? Shall we count numbers, you and I, a tally of the dead like debts owed and payment received?"

Korfax looked up and met her angry stare with one of his own. His eyes burned darkly now, with hurt and pain.

"I was neither rebuking you nor raking up the past," he snapped. "I was merely stating facts, the truth of what I beheld. The last Azadra could not close with me, so it attacked her instead. That was all that I was saying."

Doagnis seemed to shrink in upon herself for a moment and Korfax had the sudden feeling that he had shamed her in some way. Now he felt guilty in turn. He leaned forward and placed his hand upon hers.

"I meant what I said. I will not bring up the past, nor accuse, nor blame. I am the last one to do so. My heritage is the blackest of all. I saw what Sondehna did to Peis-homa. I know what my ancestor was capable of. And too often have I felt that self-same darkness within me."

Her eyes widened as they looked back into his.

"You said that before, as though you had been there. What have you seen?"

Korfax took a deep breath.

"You trusted me enough to show me the Apnoralax Angelus," he said, "so now it is my turn. There is a story that you do not know. It is well known that I once went north to find the source of the Agdoain, but what is not so well known was that I, and those that were with me, had help. We were saved by the last of the Korith Peis, an Arged by the name of Mathulaa. He it was that showed me what happened to Peis-homa. His ancestors had been there, and he had an apnoralax that retained the memory of it. To say that Sondehna was cruel that day would not describe the full horror of it. They denied his will and he was not merciful."

Doagnis did not look at him for long moments. Instead she exchanged a glance with Ronoar, before standing up and walking around the table. She turned to Korfax with a complex look in her eyes now, as if she was not at all certain what it was she was seeing.

"How does that make you feel?" she asked. "How does that make you feel knowing that you are of his blood?"

Korfax spread his hands upon the table and glowered at its surface.

"We are all forged by our fate – he by his, me by mine. All of us are caught in the places that were forged for us. Sondehna destroyed Peis-homa and Efaeis destroyed Veludrax Mikaolazith. Hate begets hate. Destruction begets destruction."

Korfax kept himself still, slowly fighting his anger back down again.

"Sondehna trapped himself by his choices, taking Soivar and so calling up the wrath of Karmaraa. But Karmaraa trapped himself also, starting a war it took a thousand years to complete. What terrible symmetry they had. Their clash at the Rolnir was all but inevitable. Soivar's betrayal tilted the balance and led to the downfall of the north. Sondehna was once taught a dream, the dream of empire, but the beauty of Soivar seduced him from his reason, and in taking her he brought about his own downfall. His love for her destroyed him, and I think he knew it at the end. I understand that. I too have been betrayed by those that I once loved. I too have stood upon the battlefield and felt that terrible hatred. I too have felt the horrid power of it, felt its seduction, the cry of anguish that will not stop, the burning fire that will not be quenched. I know what was in his heart when Peis-homa fell, and I mourn for both that city and for him."

Doagnis came to him then and sat in his lap, cradling his head. Now her eyes were gentle again.

"Ah, my love, now I see you. You fear your destiny and desire it also, thinking it will end your pain."

She raised his head and gently kissed his lips.

"But you should not fear any longer, for there is hope now, hope for all. Our people are a power once more, a power ruled again by their rightful masters. Now it is our turn to 'Stretch-forth-and-Conquer', for we, and only we, hold salvation in our hands. Karmaraa passed from this world over seven thousand years ago, yet still the others follow his words in their blind adherence to the dogma of dust. The Ell have been frozen in time ever since, and what a terrible price they have paid for the folly of a few. But we are here again, bringing our people out of the dark days and back again to the light, that fierce light that was always our gift to the Bright

Heavens."

Korfax put his arms about her as she lay against him and held her tight. She returned his embrace and they remained together for long moments. But then he suddenly realised that Ronoar was no longer with them, and for some obscure reason it bothered him. When had Ronoar left? Why had he not sensed it? He had, in the past, taken pride in his ability to notice all that happened about him. It was how he had been taught, But something inside him had changed, something fundamental: he was no longer who he had been at all.

Tales of Korfax's talent for summoning spread throughout the camp, and he found himself being watched ever more carefully when he went abroad. The hostility was still there, but now it was mixed with curiosity as well. There were no other warriors that were also of the Argedith.

One, in particular, seemed to make it her business to follow him. She was Opakas, most powerful of the Argedith after Doagnis now that Axayal was gone. But she did not come close. It was only when he was alone, taking one of the many paths up into the surrounding hills, that she finally approached, climbing up from behind.

She was old, by the look of her, but vigorous, and she was simply dressed for one so high in the Argedith. She came to stand before him at last, but all the while her eyes searched his face.

"You are Opakas," he said.

"And you are Korfax," she replied, smiling.

"What is it that you want?" he asked.

"Speech will suffice," she returned. There was a long pause. Her smile widened. "So much for speech," she laughed.

Korfax took a long breath.

"I do not know what you want me to say. No one trusts me. No one believes that I should be here. All I get from anyone are unfriendly words and glances."

Opakas gestured easily.

"Not as true as you might believe. I am here. Have I been unfriendly?"

"No, you have not. But the day is still young."

She laughed again.

"Is it any wonder that you believe all are against you? Look at how you are yourself."

Finally he smiled.

"True enough," he agreed.

He studied her. He could see the light in her now, the strength. He had no doubt that she knew her craft well. But as he studied her, so she studied him. Finally she spoke.

"I do not see her death in you."

"Whose death?" he said.

"Tohtanef," she answered.

He looked away. It was inevitable, he supposed. He had killed more than a few of the Iabeiorith in his time. But at least, in this, he was innocent.

"That is because I did not kill her," he told her. "At the end I had her at my mercy and I spared her. It was more than she deserved, though, after what she did."

"What she did?"

"Doagnis sent her to kill me. She confronted me in a hostelry upon the far southern road. She killed everybody in it with a poison cloud. The cloud was intended for me. Obviously, it missed."

"That sounds very much like her," Opakas said, looking back at Korfax. "But you did not kill her at the end?"

"I did not."

"Then how did she die?"

"There was a fire."

Opakas frowned.

"Was it a summoning?"

"Yes," said Korfax. "It was intended to catch me, much like the poison cloud, but it missed also."

Opakas pursed her lips.

"Why are you asking me this?" Korfax wondered.

"I have my reasons," she returned. "So you are saying that she killed herself?"

"No!"

Opakas smiled.

"And you will not say who it was!"

"Perhaps it would be best if the past was left in the past."

"Perhaps, but I have another question for you. How is it that you know the art of summoning so well?"

Korfax tapped the hilt of his Qorihna.

"My house kept a secret. Part of that secret lay in writings. I taught myself from them."

She stared at him for a long moment.

"I was told that, but I find the tale curious at best. Your house was one of the most faithful to the Velukor, yet here you are, bearing mighty weapons born of sorcery and keeping forbidden works. Is that not a curious thing? Who would have thought that the Farenith had two such different faces?"

Korfax did not know how to answer that.

"Silence? Again?" she said.

"There was a prophecy," he replied.

"A prophecy?"

"Yes."

"And you will say nothing further?"

"No!"

"And you do not know where your house originally came from?"

"No!"

She drew back a little.

"That is a lie," she accused. "You have a secret."

She watched him for a long moment, but he waited her out.

"So be it," she said at last. She glanced at his Qorihna. "I have also been told that you will be forging Qorihna and Qahmor for the Haelok Aldaria. May I see it? I have never before seen one outside of a vision."

Korfax drew it out. It moaned slightly as it came forth. She reached out to touch it but he drew back in alarm.

"Do not!" he told her sharply. "You may look, but you must not touch. No one may touch this blade but me."

She looked at him archly.

"No need for that!" she said. "I have no intent other than curiosity."

"But you do not understand," he warned. "If you touch this blade you will die. It is tied to my bloodline. I once saw another try to take it up, and my blade awoke in his hands and tore him to pieces."

There was another long silence. Opakas stared up at him and then at the Qorihna. She frowned and then looked back at him again.

"It is tied to your bloodline?" she asked carefully.

"Yes."

"That is rare, almost unprecedented. Very few tales speak of such things."

Korfax felt uneasy now. He could see the look on her face. Opakas clearly knew something.

"Very little is known of Qorihna," he said. "They are a mystery."

"That they are," she agreed.

She looked him fully in the eye.

"There is something about you, Korfax, something I find myself wishing to know. You are not born to our ways, yet you have taken to them as if you were. The Namad Mahorelah takes years to master, yet you have done so in a very short time. You are a power, apt to the ways of the Iabeiorith and a dark flame in our midst. I find that most intriguing."

She gestured at his blade.

"Thank you for letting me see your sword."

She turned about and went back the way she had come. She glanced over her shoulder at him.

"Be assured, though, that I shall be keeping my eye upon you," she said. "Like your blade, you also are worthy of study."

He watched her departing back and wondered what this meeting would lead to.

Korfax said nothing of the encounter to Doagnis; instead, he kept his own counsel. Besides, Doagnis was fully occupied with her own affairs. Come the end of the day he went to his bed alone and dreamt.

In his dream he found himself in the dark, but he was not afraid. Though great folds of swirling cloud and vapour curled about him, he did not fear them. They were here at his behest, or so it seemed to him. He was waiting for something, waiting upon a high place, for soon the veils would be lifted and glories would be revealed.

He raised his right hand, gesturing that the dark clouds depart. They obeyed him, slowly at first, but then with gathering speed. The air about him cleared and he found himself upon the topmost pinnacle of a mighty tower, black from base to apex, rivalling even the Umadya Pir with its dark majesty.

Below him stretched a mighty city, almost as large as Othil Zilodar had been, its many spaces filled with mighty towers, all hewn of the same black rock. And everywhere that he looked under the louring clouds he saw sorcerous lights at play. They danced over the streets and the gardens, they danced over the towers and the houses and they danced over the city and the walls, filling it all with a potent and mystical radiance.

He watched them play for a while, sensing within himself a feeling of completeness he knew he could never describe. Then he looked up at the sky again. It was time.

He did not know how he knew it; he only knew that it was. He raised his left hand and Vovin roared down from the north to disport for his pleasure. Proud and mighty though they were, ill-enduring any dominion, they came gladly at his command, eager and joyful, delighting to honour their summoner. They swooped and they soared, they circled and they roared, and their eldest flew before him, hovering as though caught upon a tower of air, bowing its great horned head in grateful servitude. So he bowed in turn and felt himself smile, cold and hard. This was his due.

He looked down. Below him, in each of the mighty squares, upon each great field of dark flagstones, a vast army waited. Black armour, black helms, they roared their allegiance to their master above. He drew out his own sword in response and held it up above his head.

The sword sang. It flexed and rippled as its weird and mouthless voice encompassed the city. All fell silent to hear it, even the Vovin, for it was a song of limitless power.

Korfax all but leapt out of his bed even as he awoke. Though he had never witnessed such a sight before in all his life, he knew instantly what it was that he had just seen. He had seen Veludrax Mikaolazith itself, the black city, the greatest ever built by sorcery alone. Though no image of that place now remained in the world, his thought had pierced both time and space and he had seen the throne of the mighty in all its dark splendour. The vision both exhilarated and terrified him. It took him long moments before he could calm himself again.

As he sat upon his bed a thought came to him. Karmaraa's successors had destroyed that city stone by stone, leaving nothing behind. For all its might and power Veludrax Mikaolazith had fallen and passed into the night. It was a warning he dared not ignore. Nothing endures for ever. All things end.

He found himself wondering what might have happened if Karmaraa had failed. What if Soivar had not deceived her lord and master, what would have happened then? Korfax shuddered. He knew the answer to that question all too well – Lon-Elah would have fallen into darkness and Sondehna would have eaten the world in his mad desire for dominion.

The next day saw the muster of the Iabeiorith continue, whilst the camp within the encircling hills grew and grew again until it filled the valley from end to end.

Korfax occasionally watched as the warriors rode in, each now proud and fearless in the light of his reinvented vision. Their families followed behind in great wains, wives haughty, sons and daughters dutiful but also carefully curious, peering now and again out at the world beyond from behind their coverings. A great city of tents awaited them, a vast and impermanent city, riding upon a sea of grass hidden only by a greater immensity without.

Occasionally he caught sight of Opakas, and every time he saw her her eyes were upon him, but she never came close. Korfax wondered what was going through her mind.

When he was not watching, or being watched, he studied and studied again the process for making a new Qorihna. Not much was said in the grimoires as to what effect this had upon the original; instead, all that was offered was that the parent appeared unaffected by the process and that the children were always lesser in power. Korfax read it all again and again, but each time he prepared himself to attempt the task, he found himself loathe to begin. The memory of the hapless Omloa always returned to trouble him.

So it was a long while before Korfax actually summoned up the courage at last to make a new Qorihna. But dare it he did, laying out his great black blade and placing his hands just so upon its surface. He thought of beginnings and felt the substance divide under his touch. Then he reached out with his mind, thinking the requisite thoughts, feeling the requisite sensations, and throughout it all his sword remained calm and unmoving, bleeding its darkness back into the air, a boundless night like an infinite stream of lifeblood. Come the moment, Korfax reached forward into the breach and felt his hand catch hold of a sliver, the merest quivering sliver wriggling slowly under his fingers. He grasped it with his hands and knew that he had achieved his aim.

He felt an odd sense of familiarity take him as he pulled the struggling darkness back out from the heart of his sword. He laid it to one side and watched it carefully as it grew in size, shaping itself accordingly. It was like a birth, and yet unlike any birth he had ever heard tell of. His Qorihna seemed entirely unconcerned. It lay there, quiescent and apparently unmoved by what had just happened. Korfax reached out for it and picked it up, but it felt exactly as it always had. The birth of the new Qorihna appeared not to have affected it in any way, shape or form that he could perceive. It was as though the birth had never happened at all.

Korfax thought back to his youth, when he had once helped Chasaloh with the foaling of a new ormn. Then the foal had struggled its way into the world, staggering up on its new feet as it had tried to go every which way at once. The mother had not the strength to help it, being weakened by the birth, lying yet upon the gentle straw. Instead she had groaned at the pain. How fragile that scene seemed now. Qurihna were not so frail, and with the birth mere moments in the past, the parent remained as strong as ever whilst the child became fully grown with a speed to defy belief.

Korfax put his own sword down and stared at the new Qorihna, before reaching out to touch it. Then he hefted it in his hands. It was slightly smaller and seemed duller in comparison to its parent, but when Korfax wielded it he could feel the power of it. There was one subtle difference, though. This new-born sword did not respond of its own volition. Rather, it echoed his thoughts as though it had no life other than that of its wielder, taking up the will of its master like an echo. Korfax frowned. Maybe here lay its one weakness. It had entered the world without the experience of its parent. It, like everything else that lived, had to grow, learn and experience. Then, perhaps, it would know what it was, and it would speak at last with its own voice.

But as Korfax stood there, feeling the new Qorihna and wielding it, sweeping it this way and that, he noticed a gradual change in the air about him. There was a watchfulness circling him, as though the world had suddenly filled with eyes. He looked about him in puzzlement. What was this? What had flavoured the air? Then he caught it. It was his very own sword that was looking back at him. Though it possessed no feature, no face, though it had not moved from its place at all, Korfax immediately knew that it was looking at him. The feeling was odd, worrying, as if his sword had suddenly become a thing of judgements and jealousies.

Korfax shuddered and felt cold fingers stroke his spine. He saw again that unfortunate of the Balt Kaalith, Omloa, and he heard again in his mind that terrible scream of outrage as his sword had wound itself about its violator before consuming him in a lethal nest of blades.

Korfax put down the new sword and gingerly picked up his own. But even as he reached for it, it came into his hand, squirming against his flesh and gently moaning its resurgent joy at the touch of its master once more. Korfax took a deep breath. He understood at last, and what a relief it was.

"And did you really think that I had forgotten you? You should not have. You are mine."

Korfax smiled for a moment and then became very still. An odd feeling of duality filled him.

"Nor should you forget it. I am your master until the very end."

The words were spoken before he could stop them. They seemed to come from somewhere else. He awoke as if from a dream. What had he just said? What had he just meant? But his sword had heard the words all the same, and now it moaned its pleasure in response, squirming fondly in his grasp.

A sound came from behind him and he turned. Doagnis stood there, staring at the new sword. He quickly dissembled, putting his own Qorihna down and gesturing at the new one.

"You have made one!" she cried, her voice all but breathless with excitement.

Korfax suddenly felt excited himself. He came to her and stood beside her. She looked up at him, eyes wide, and he smiled back gently.

"It was not so difficult," he said. "The process, whilst daunting, is actually quite easy. And it is just as the grimoires say. There are no ill effects suffered by the parent. This one is as potent as it ever was."

Korfax gestured at his own sword and Doagnis looked at it with a curious expression. She looked back at him again and her eyes were uncertain.

"As I entered, I heard you speak to it. I have never heard that they understood speech, or that they even had a mind of their own."

Korfax reached for his blade and held it up before him. He stroked it and it sighed gently with each touch. Doagnis watched him carefully and shuddered inside. Korfax almost touched it like a lover. She tried to distract him with her thought, but Korfax had eyes only for his sword.

"This one is so old and has known so many masters," he told her. "It is altogether wiser than its children." He turned to her and held up a warning finger. "But I must warn you of this at least."

She stepped back from the sudden harshness in his voice, but Korfax did not spare her, not now. This was dire.

"No other can touch my sword except for me. For another to touch this blade would mean their instant death. It knows only me and will allow no other to come near."

Then Korfax dropped his gaze and gestured at the new sword.

"The child, though, is another matter entirely. Anyone can use it – anyone. It is new-born, an innocent, a mind yet to be awakened."

Doagnis stepped forward again, reluctant but resolute. Korfax watched her. She was vying with him now, he was certain of it. He watched as she carefully reached out to touch the new blade. Then, when it did not react, she ran her fingers up and down it, watching the play of energies across its dark surface.

"Marvellous," she said at last. Then she frowned and looked back at Korfax.

"Tell me," she said, "tell me in all truth, what exactly are Qorihna? Do you know? Do you really know?"

Korfax held up his own sword. He caressed its blade and it sang faintly for a moment and then fell silent again.

"I do not," he said. "Nalvahgey pulled this one out from the abyss and tied it to her bloodline in some way. There are no records that might reveal to us what was done that day, but something happened, something vital. No other Qorihna has ever been found in all the ages that lie between that time and this. All others that have ever been have been born of this one. It is the eldest of its kind."

He smiled at his blade.

"I have often entertained an odd fancy that there are indeed no other Qorihna to be found anywhere, not in the whole of creation. This one is the first of its kind. And, in some strange way, it has tied itself to me, as though it is grateful for my touch. But it will accept the touch of no other." He looked back at her, still smiling. But his smile was no longer gentle. "And it is quite adamant about it. I handled its child for only a moment and suffered the distinct impression that this one became jealous."

Doagnis, already unsettled, started in surprise.

"Jealous?" she asked, backing away.

She gave his sword a black look and muttered something quietly under her breath. Korfax tried to catch what she said, but he missed it entirely.

"What was that?" he asked.

"Nothing of consequence," she answered. "It is only that I feel uneasy employing powers I do not fully understand."

"But that wasn't what you said at all. So what was it, really?"

Doagnis gave him a sharp glance.

"Only that there is an old saying I rule my life by. Call always upon the lesser, and not upon the greater, lest they command more than you."

"I have heard that also," he said. "But the male line of the Mikaolazith, all the way back to Aolkar, has ever owned this Qorihna, and it has never failed them."

Korfax held up his sword and flourished it.

"This is an affair of the blood, Doagnis, and such things speak to the deepest parts of us. I may not understand exactly what my Qorihna is, but I know what it will and will not do. It will never harm me, ever. Nor will it harm my heirs."

The Qorihna moaned again as if in agreement. Doagnis watched it for a moment, her expression all but unreadable. Then she looked away again.

"So be it," she said. "If you are happy, then I am happy also. But heed this warning at least. Do not ever step outside the bounds you know with powers that exceed you. For once such rules are broken, the world changes and things are never quite the same again."

Korfax sighed and lowered his sword.

"And I know that, too, to my cost."

He took a deep breath and squared his shoulders. Then he turned to her and pointed at the new sword.

"So, let us go and present this to Teodunad. That, at the very least, should assuage his distrust somewhat."

Doagnis smiled in agreement, but her smile was brittle, and Korfax knew that she remained troubled by it all.

They found Teodunad greeting the latest arrivals. With him were his aides and many of the highest chieftains as well. All were arrayed in their finest, each assuming their most powerful pose, but when Doagnis came amongst them they all dropped their stances and bowed to her in turn. Korfax, though, was another matter. When he followed after her, stopping at her side, many reared back up again, passing hard glances over him. One or two even laid their hands upon their swords, though they did not draw them. They had heard the stories, but Korfax no longer cared. Here was a moment he had long looked forward to.

He stepped up to Teodunad and held up a long bundle in his hands, a long black bundle bound about by many layers of black cloth, like an offering.

"What is this?" asked Teodunad.

"It is a gift," answered Korfax.

Teodunad frowned and did not take the bundle. Korfax merely smiled in return before turning back to look at Doagnis.

"Such a surly welcome!" he said. "I am not sure that Teodunad deserves my gift after all."

Teodunad sneered.

"Nor am I sure that I want anything from your hands. I still do not trust you. An allegiance once changed can change again."

Korfax laughed openly and Teodunad could only scowl. Korfax held out the long black bundle again.

"I understand your suspicions, Teodunad, but I doubt that any of the Haelok Aldaria have ever received such a gift before, not since Sondehna's day at the very least. Take it, and I assure you you will like what you find within."

Teodunad took the bundle reluctantly and slowly unwound the cloth, his frown deepening with each turn. But when the new-born Qorihna was revealed, his eyes widened and he all but gasped. Korfax smiled in satisfaction.

"No true Chieftain of the Haelok Aldaria should ever be without his Qorihna," he said.

Teodunad almost dropped the revealed sword in shock.

"You are giving me a Qorihna?" he asked.

Korfax widened his smile.

"Freshly forged from my own," came the answer.

A strange battle of feelings flickered across Teodunad's face. There was horror and there was delight; there was pride and there was remorse. Korfax watched it all with understanding. The others, the chieftains, looked on in utter confusion. Korfax studied them all for a moment and then turned the knife in the wound.

"And after I have furnished you all with Qorihna, I will show you how to make Qahmor as well. Then you will truly be a fighting force to be reckoned with. Then you will truly be the Haelok Aldaria."

He turned about and walked away while the chieftains stared after him, not daring to believe their ears. Doagnis watched him go and frowned. She felt the stirrings of trouble deep inside. That had not gone the way she had expected it to. Korfax had not waited for her. He left now as if he was the master, and she found herself not liking what it told her.

After the gift of the Qorihna to Teodunad, Korfax noticed a not so subtle change about him. The hostility was lessened, and many even dared bow to him in greeting, if somewhat carefully.

That was something at least. But they were still wary of him, for did he not have a foot in two camps – the Namad Dar and the Namad Mahorelah?

So Korfax began his second play and made more Qorihna, and he gave them in turn to the many chieftains that followed. Now the tide began to turn in truth, for many bowed openly, calling him lord, for did he not give gifts, powerful gifts, sorcerous gifts that made the Haelok Aldaria mighty again?

Finally Korfax showed them all how to pull Qahmor from their own swords, a far simpler process to that of the birthing of Qorihna. Soon, across the length and breadth of the great encampment, dark energies flickered here and there as the newly born weaponry was exercised and learnt.

Shadows danced through the air as warrior after warrior discovered how to use each new Qorihna and each new Qahmor. And chieftain after chieftain came back to the great tent to offer tribute in return.

Doagnis looked upon it all with gentle acknowledgement, as if everything that happened was already her due, but Ronoar watched each unfolding moment with glowing eyes, as if each new day was an unexpected gift.

Later, after a particularly long day, Korfax sat with Ronoar in the late evening. No others were near. Doagnis had left earlier to commune with her inner circle, the best of the Argedith, discussing matters of lore.

The failing light lengthened the shadows, darkening the world as it fled. But it was a glad darkness, a starlit darkness, jewels cast across the sky above whilst the minds below played with fantasies and dreams.

Korfax turned to Ronoar.

"Tell me, Ronoar, is this more to your liking?"

"What do you mean, Enay?" Ronoar asked.

"The muster, the distribution of weaponry, the rise of the Iabeiorith?"

"Yes, Enay, it is much more to my liking. But to be by your side? That is the best of all. I feel like Adraman of old."

Korfax leaned back.

"Ah now, and there lies a mystery. What did happen to Adraman at last? I know that he vanished without a trace, but I find myself wondering if you might know something more of it."

Ronoar suddenly looked less than happy.

"And so you touch upon the heart of the matter, Enay. Here is the one attainment of his service that I do not wish to emulate. I believe that he sought too much and failed in the seeking."

Korfax waited a moment.

"I am not sure that I follow you," he said. Ronoar took a deep breath.

"He tried to follow in the footsteps of his master. He studied all the arts of sorcery, though it was forbidden for servants to do so at the time. The tale is that he overreached his aim and a force from the Mahorelah took him."

Korfax looked carefully at Ronoar.

"Do you know more than you are saying?"

Ronoar swallowed as if fighting some inner compulsion. Korfax laid a gentle hand on his shoulder.

"If you would rather not speak of it, I will understand."

Ronoar bowed his head.

"But you are here, Enay. I feel safe by your side."

He looked up.

"There was a tale I heard that he summoned something dire, for what purpose I do not know, and that the summoning went very wrong."

"As it can ever do so, if you are not careful. Have I not seen it myself?"

Ronoar lowered his voice.

"Yes, but the tale is that he desired to make a pact."

Korfax was intrigued.

"A pact? There are few forces in the Mahorelah with whom such a thing is possible." He now leaned forward. "Who has told you this tale?"

"It is known by the female line."

"How?"

"The daughter witnessed what occurred. Though she forgot nearly everything, that particular detail was found within her mind."

"But what did she witness?"

"A great shape in torment and Adraman bowing before it."

Korfax leaned back and stared into his goblet of dark wine. He saw again that chill and horrific form outside his window in the Umadya Kallus, inverted, tortured, pleasured, stretching and suffering on some invisible frame. He saw again its bald head, no other features on its face but a wide and gaping mouth with a furious eye within.

"Ash-Mir!" he whispered.

Ronoar sighed.

"Yes, Enay, that is the tale. Adraman summoned Ash-Mir. To what purpose I do not know, but he failed where you conquered."

Korfax looked back at Ronoar.

"Ash-Mir spoke to me. I did not understand much it said at the time, but now I begin to see further. A little more of the puzzle falls into place, but not all of it. So why would Adraman summon Ash-Mir? What was the nature of the pact? He must have been desperate."

"Or mad, Enay," suggested Ronoar.

Korfax smiled grimly.

"Perhaps that also," he mused. Then he turned back to Ronoar.

"Doagnis knows this tale?"

"Yes, Enay, but do not speak of it to her, for it has troubled her greatly since she left Emethgis Vaniad."

Each fell back into their thoughts as the last rays of Rafarel vanished from the sky. Korfax thought of many things – of the fall of Sondehna, of the murder of Soivar and the vanishing of the children, of Adraman and of the female line – but for some reason the face of Opakas kept appearing to him as though there was something about her it was needful for him to know. Finally he turned to Ronoar once more.

"Tell me about Opakas," he said.

Ronoar looked up in surprise.

"Opakas? She is of the Noje-ethith," he answered.

Korfax waited for more, but none was forthcoming.

"Just that?" he prodded.

"There is little to tell, Enay, but why do you ask?"

"We have spoken, she and I. She watches me. Apparently I 'interest' her."

"She watches everyone. She is second only to the mistress."

"Is there anything else you can tell me?" Korfax asked.

"She had rivalry with Axayal, Enay. Beyond that I cannot say."

Korfax leaned forward.

"Rivalry?"

"Yes, Enay. I think they would have killed each other if the mistress had not forbidden it."

"Then I suppose she is not unhappy that he has entered the river."

"I think, Enay, that she would have much preferred to have done the deed herself."

Korfax leaned back again and glowered at his wine.

"I will never understand such thinking."

Ronoar bowed his head.

"But that, Enay, is how it was after the death of Sondehna. Without its dark heart, the centre could not hold. Memories are kept alive in the Iabeiorith. It is all that they have had for so many years."

Teodunad held his Qorihna in his hand and stared into its dark depths. Korfax had gifted the Haelok Aldaria with great power, power not seen since the days of the old wars. He wondered at the possibilities.

Now he could truly believe that the dream was possible, that the Iabeiorith would rise again and that a new empire would overturn the old order. Even the great might of the Agdoain no longer appeared quite so insurmountable.

Teodunad had seen the look in his mistress's eyes. She, like many another, loved power, and Korfax was mighty with it. But he had known her longer than Korfax, and he had seen how quickly she could tire of her toys. One had to keep her amused to stay by her side, and woe betide you if you ever competed with her or failed to do as she asked.

Korfax was beginning to win the hearts and the minds of others and Teodunad could see the day coming when Doagnis realised that Korfax was no longer hers to command. When his influence became too much, she would feel threatened, and Doagnis was always at her best when she felt threatened. No doubt she was already wary of her new ally, wary of his influence and of his power. He did unexpected things such as summonings and the giving of gifts. He already competed with her just by his presence. Eventually he would surpass her, and that would be something she would never allow.

How would she repay the one that removed him? She would thank them. Until the coming of Korfax she had been the power, but now she had a rival. Leave it too long and Korfax would be unstoppable.

Teodunad ran his hand across the black blade. Here was real power. His dark sword and his dark armour were the mightiest gifts he had ever been given. Korfax had made a serious error. It did not even occur to him that he had brought about his own doom. He could not conceive that his gifts might be turned against him. In the Iabeiorith one kept the greatest power for oneself, one did not go spreading it abroad. Teodunad smiled. All that would be needed was an excuse.

11

ASCENSION

Nisra-jon Norith-luhjo
Zafjil-jir Pi-in-pimjon
Aldon-dril Gedlon-bamjes
Gi-mn-a Nt-qor-kanji
Kam-zienaich Mir-stl-homin
Zad-elan Odais-de-arp
Ka-henor Fen-pl-danihd

That next morning found the muster all but complete. And though it had taken nearly all the days of Alohan, Korfax considered the time well spent.

He was always there when the gifts were given, but with the last of the Haelok Aldaria entering the great encampment, that particular purpose suddenly came to an end.

As Korfax had given his gifts and explained them, so he had come to know a number of the chieftains. Many had changed their opinion of him, it seemed. Now they were in awe of him, of this giver of mighty gifts. Conversation was still not always easy, but some at least were more forthcoming than others. The youngest of them, Dosevax by name, of the house of Gondohar, seemed especially friendly, as did Aodagaa of the Vordekassith, second only in command to Teodunad himself. Teodunad, though, remained aloof and would allow only a certain grudging acknowledgement whenever their paths crossed.

Korfax decided to take a tour of the encampment. With him went Dosevax, along with a number of his followers. They were all young, much as Korfax was, and he detected a certain eagerness in them, an eagerness to be seen alongside a power. He suddenly wondered if this was what concerned Teodunad. Did Teodunad see Korfax as a rival? There was a rumour from some quarters in the camp that Teodunad had once aspired to the position of consort, desiring to stand at the left hand of Doagnis herself, but Korfax thought that those who spoke of such things considered him beneath her, though they did not say as much openly. Teodunad also inspired fear.

After the tour Korfax took his steed up to the summit of one of the enclosing hills, and many went with him. At the summit, they all stopped. Most looked out over the great sea of grass, gazing towards the horizon. Korfax, though, turned away to look back instead at the vast encampment below.

"I understand that we have nearly thirty thousand warriors gathered here now," he said.

"Yes, we do," Dosevax said eagerly. "But it will be difficult to equip them all in time, I fear."

Korfax smiled at that.

"I am sure that each of the forgers I trained will be able to do the job in hand. From the many Qorihna I have made, more can be made in unlimited number, as can Qahmor. They will all be equipped in time for our first test in battle."

Dosevax smiled in return.

"I await it eagerly," he said.

Korfax looked carefully at Dosevax.

"I know you have fought the Agdoain before," he said, "but that was warfare by stealth. This will be different. You will ride openly into battle and there you will meet the foe blade to blade. It is not an easy thing to describe."

Korfax suddenly found all their eyes on him. How the world repeated itself. He had done this before, standing with those innocent of battle and carnage whilst trying to describe the chaos and the eternal now that occupied such places.

"For more than a year I faced the Agdoain from within the great watchtowers," he said. "We would pummel them with qasadar, ride into their ranks with sword and shield, rain fire down upon them. The land to the north of the great wall became pitted and scarred and stained, a smoking ruin, a nowhere, a wasteland of crawling muds and shattered stone. It will remain as we will not, a lasting testament to the horror of war. When forces are equally matched, stalemate is the only outcome. When we thought we had the advantage, the enemy would surprise us. And fighting with the Agdoain has ever been thus. It is like fighting with a reflection."

He paused a moment and then held up a hand.

"But the one advantage," he continued, "the one advantage we have left to us is that the Agdoain do not employ the Namad Mahorelah, in any form whatsoever. I have fought them with Qorihna and Qahmor, riding unseen along the streets of Emethgis Vaniad, and they could do nothing to stop me. But I was alone, and they took the city by sheer weight of numbers."

He lowered his hand. Talking of the fall of Emethgis Vaniad brought it all back again. A terrible day, one amongst so many. He bowed his head, as much to hold back the loss as the anger. When he raised it again, his gaze was fiery.

"But the Haelok Aldaria shall be victorious. All who yet dwell on Lon-Elah are counting upon our success, whether they know it or not."

Dosevax looked hungrily at the vast camp below.

"I wonder what the assassins of the west would think of that."

Korfax twisted his face into a snarl, surprising them all.

"Assassins? That is not what I would call them. They are honourless, all of them. They are cowards, still subsisting upon the pickings of the victories of the past as if such victories were their own."

He turned to Dosevax.

"No matter what we do, they will not accept it. They will not accept it even if we brought their crimes out of the shadows of the past and into the light of day. But they will acknowledge one truth at least, though it stick in their throats till they die. History has always belonged to the victor, and I do not doubt that victory will be ours once more."

Dosevax looked sideways at him.

"I have heard it said that there are a few among them on whom you would have vengeance."

Korfax raised an eyebrow. Vengeance? Oh yes, there was a desire for that, certainly.

"Yes," he said, "it is true. But now I find myself wondering if any of them are worth the effort. What would I do if I had Zafazaa before me and at my mercy? I do not know. Three times he tried to bring my house down, to dishonour it, all because my mother once spurned him."

Dosevax bowed his head slightly.

"I have such tales belonging to my house – feuds, slights, vows of the blood."

"And was satisfaction had?"

"Not always."

"It was ever thus."

"You have seen the Apnoralax Angelus?"

"I have."

"Would you have satisfaction for that?"

"From the perpetrators I would. But they are long gone now."

"And what of their inheritors?"

Korfax looked into the distance for a moment.

"Whose wings are thorns to stir up vexation..," he murmured to himself. Then he turned back to Dosevax, who was waiting with a puzzled look on his face. Korfax smiled. "They are the sons of sons of sons," he said. "Seven times seven have been the generations. I doubt many have kept the memory alive. Some of them, perhaps, the Balt Kaalith, hiding it in secret shame. But none of them did the deed. For me it would be enough to see their swords broken and their heads hung in shame. They are cowards, all of them, hiding behind words and shirking deeds. They have no honour in my eyes. Perhaps it would be best if we rose above them and proved that we are better than they. Let it be their shame, not ours. Too long has our history been written by cowards! What we need now is truth and honour, and the healing of the world."

Dosevax looked at his companions and then back at Korfax.

"Teodunad does not say that. He says that we should purge the guilty."

Korfax laughed a short, sharp laugh.

"And who are the guilty? Answer me that! We need to learn from our mistakes, Dosevax, not repeat them."

"You would be merciful?"

"I would take their power away from them. And that, believe me, would be a punishment far greater than death."

"So you would let them live?"

"Yes, I would let them live. But in shame, shunned by the world without. Let them rot behind their walls. Let them rot!"

Dosevax frowned.

"Does Teodunad know that you say this?"

"Teodunad," Korfax whispered. He turned to Dosevax. "What do you think? What is your opinion?"

Dosevax did not answer for a moment. Then he pulled himself up in his saddle.

"I follow the code of the Haelok Aldaria. I am not here to think," he replied.

Korfax gave Dosevax his hardest look yet.

"Then you have learnt the wrong lesson. What is the fault of the west? They did not listen to others or to the better natures of their hearts. You make the same mistake they have ever made. Their unbending adherence to ritual and tradition has already doomed them. Ignore the mistakes of the past, Dosevax, and they will return to your ruin!"

Dosevax wheeled his ormn about, before galloping back down the hill to the camp below. His followers glanced worriedly at Korfax for a moment, before following in his wake.

Korfax sat in the great tent and sipped his wine. The doors were tied back and he could see everything that passed in the camp to the north. It was, he had come to decide, his favourite direction. Everything happened in the north.

He had found himself coming more and more to appreciate the gentle orderliness of the life that now gathered itself around him. The camp made him think of older days, when a more wandering life was to be had, people travelling from place to place as the seasons took them, planting, hunting and harvesting, before moving on again.

He drank his wine and smiled as two young children scampered in the distance, each flourishing a play sword as though it were deadly. They fought for a while, mock blows, mock deaths and mock victories, until their play was interrupted by the mother of one. She stood there, pointing at her child in admonishment whilst the fading light of day outlined her in fire. Downcast at the sudden interruption, her child walked back to her slowly, waving goodbye to his friend even as his mother's arms claimed him. But the other, still fired by his imagination and his remaining freedom, turned about and ran in the opposite direction, sword aloft and eyes still fierce.

Korfax stared after the running child and suddenly felt a strange longing. He had never played like that at Losq. There had been no other children to play with. His time had always been spent with his elders. It was only when he had stayed at Leemal that he had joined in the games of others. But that had been an infrequent joy, only once a season or so. He felt the loss of his youth with a poignancy that seemed almost physical, a brief stab to the heart followed by a long ache. He turned to his flagon of wine and poured himself another cup.

The wine was Girril, fine, dark and old, another surprise from the seemingly inexhaustible supply of Doagnis. Korfax remembered that Ralir had liked Girril as well. One thought led to another and he found himself wondering what Ralir was doing. Was he preparing to weather the oncoming storm, or was he fighting even now?

The rumours had the Agdoain biding their time. Having consolidated their capture of Emethgis Vaniad, and then having suffered both defeat and victory in the ill-fated attempt to retake that city, followed by the cataclysm of Othil Ekrin, they had retreated and waited, and waited again, much like they had done after the taking of Othil Zilodar. No doubt they were building up their numbers, their growth, like their desire for conquest, in tune with some alien season only they could sense. And no doubt the time would come soon when they would march once more. Mists would swarm towards the southern cities, over the Piral Jiroks, over the dry lands, grey mists, mighty mists, wet with the foe. The Agdoain would go south and conquer.

Korfax felt sure that once they had taken Othil Admaq, Othil Homtoh would be their next target. Then their victory would be all but complete. None of the other towers and cities was mighty enough to stop them. He pondered the mystery of their genesis. Who had called them? Or had they been sent? No one knew the answer, not even now, though many had gone looking.

Korfax considered the first city of the west, Othil Homtoh. He had never been there. It was, by all accounts, the smallest of all the great cities, but it was also a fortress the size of many mountains. And it was the most holy. The long, slow rule of the Korith Zadakal, and the uninterrupted line of the princes of the Zadakalith, had seen to that. It was said that little had changed in the city since before the time of Karmaraa. Korfax smiled to himself. Now that he could believe. The west kept itself frozen in time and, with the victory of Karmaraa, sought ever to freeze the rest of the world.

As he toyed with his thoughts, mirroring the play in his mind with the cup in his hand by running it through his fingers from one side to the other, the faint echoes of a commotion came to his ears.

He looked up. The sound came closer. A crowd was approaching, growing in numbers as it came marching through the camp. There were several figures at its head. Korfax sat up straighter. Two of the leaders pulled a third, a single Ell bound about with many ropes.

Korfax stood up and put his cup to one side. Pausing only to take up his cloak, he strode towards the crowd. They were making for the tent of Teodunad.

As Korfax approached, he noticed that the prisoner was dressed much as one of the newly arrived, in dark leather armour and a heavy cloak. With his face all bloodied and bruised, he looked weary, but he still struggled against his bindings as though he had not yet abandoned the possibility of escape.

Korfax looked with distaste at his wounds and secretly applauded his rebellion. Memories of his incarceration by the Balt Kaalith came back to him. Then he looked harder at the face. It suddenly seemed familiar. Did he know this one? He went closer.

As the crowd reached their destination, so Teodunad emerged from his tent with two of his aides, Herenir and Orimal. Teodunad glanced at Korfax, bowed his head curtly in acknowledgement, and then walked towards the prisoner. Silence fell. Teodunad looked directly at the one who walked beside, the one not actually holding the ropes.

"Speak!" he ordered.

This one stood to attention.

"It appears that we have a spy in our midst. He was seen in Aodagaa's tent, going through manifests, the communications, all the private scrolls."

"Your proof?" Teodunad demanded.

"This one is of the Mazzurith," came the answer, a hand holding up an emblem on a torn piece of cloth. "He is not of the Vordekassith. What business did he have there?"

Teodunad offered an anticipatory smile.

"And where is Aodagaa now?" he asked with barely concealed scorn.

None missed the implication. Korfax glanced around him for a moment, marking the looks on every face, before turning his attention back to the prisoner.

"He was inspecting the boundaries," came the answer. "Word has been sent."

Korfax took another step forward and stared more closely at the captive. There was definitely something familiar about him. He began to taste things, a sense of aloofness, a touch of self-righteousness. The captive glanced his way, a look in his eyes. Recognition? That was it! Korfax had met this one before. He let his feelings wash over him, digging through memories, names, faces and voices. Finally he spoke.

"For one whose origin is in doubt," he said, "your captive seems to have been rather harshly treated. Surely it would have been enough just to restrain him."

All eyes turned to Korfax. Teodunad frowned, but one of those that held the rope smiled.

"He did not like it when we questioned him. Indeed, he became most impolite with us, until we taught him better manners."

There was a rustle of laughter from the crowd, a hungry sound that made Korfax shiver. They had become a mob. He waited for the laughter to die down. There were many ways to deal with a mob. An appeal to self-interest was one, but Korfax decided that this was perhaps the time to exercise some more authority. And perhaps this prisoner would help.

"And how many of you did it take to subdue him?" he asked.

The other looked displeased.

"I do not see why that matters?"

Korfax smiled darkly in return.

"Indulge me."

The other looked sour and glanced at Teodunad.

Korfax folded his arms.

"And why do you look to Teodunad? He does not know the answer. Or is the number larger than you would like?"

The other looked down.

"He took five of us before we could hold him at last."

"Five?" Korfax asked. "Are any of them here?"

"They were all sent to the healers," said the other.

"Then he possesses a more than common fighting skill," Korfax replied. "So tell me, did he fight like one of the Haelok Aldaria?"

The other would have answered but Teodunad strode forwards and held up a hand.

"Korfax, why do you interfere?" he asked. "This is no business of yours."

Korfax looked back at Teodunad for a moment and then gestured at the crowd.

"If we have a spy amongst us, it is very much my business. I have questions I would like answering, that is all. And do you not have questions also?"

"I do, but that is no concern of yours, either!"

That was entirely the wrong thing to say, and the few that stood beside Teodunad knew it. Korfax drew himself up and turned the full force of his gaze upon the first of the Haelok Aldaria. There was a sudden swelling of darkness in the air, a hint of rising powers. Many in the crowd stepped back.

"Have a care, Teodunad," Korfax said quietly. "You have reached my limits at last. I will no longer tolerate your scorn. Do you think that you know me? Do you think that you know what I am and what I can do? You do not! You are as ignorant of me as you are of this spy. No doubt you will question him and learn nothing. Then you will torture him and learn nothing. Following that you will have him put to death, just in case. Crude, stupid and wasteful! There are better ways to find the truth of the matter, better and quicker."

Teodunad chose not to see the threat and laughed instead.

"Who are you to tell me what to do? I am the first of the Haelok Aldaria! My word is law!"

So that was the way of it, was it? Korfax clenched his fists and then unclenched them again. Now he would see the heart of the matter. He reached out with his mind and went through the unseen doors. Into Teodunad he went, and there he looked. Teodunad's desires were written large, written in fire: his desire for Doagnis, his desire to kill Korfax. There it was, as clear as day. Plots, stratagems, opportunities given and opportunities wasted. Korfax withdrew again and prepared himself.

"And who furnished you with Qorihna?" he asked. "With Qahmor? Who has made the Haelok Aldaria as mighty as they were when they rode at the side of Sondehna? Who has done this? Yet still you scorn me. I am done with you!"

Teodunad reached up to touch his blade as though to draw it, but Korfax had already read his intent. He leapt high and kicked Teodunad full in the face with a booted heel. Teodunad flew back and lay still, hand still clasped to the hilt of his Qorihna. Korfax landed lightly and then went to stand over him.

"YOU DARE THREATEN ME WITH THE VERY SWORD THAT I GAVE YOU?" he shouted at the prone body. He turned to the others.

"Does any other here wish to challenge me also?"

No one spoke. They could all feel the threat in the air, the gathering of forces. He waited a moment until every gaze was cowed, and then he turned to the prisoner.

"You are a Noqvoan of the Balt Kaalith," he accused.

"No!" said the prisoner. "You are wrong. I am Mazzur Rom Lindar. These others are... mistaken."

Korfax leant in closer.

"No, that is not your name, nor your house. You knew who I was, even before you heard my name. We have met before, I am certain of it. Open yourself to me."

The other would have answered but then gasped in pain as Korfax stormed his mind. He did not bother with subtlety this time; instead, he strode through the hard-held walls and battered them down with sheer force. No doubt the Noqvoan would have held out against Teodunad, but Korfax was another matter entirely. The old oaths of his past were finally broken. He was in a hard place full of hatred and fear, and if that was all that these fools respected, then so be it! He would be as they, taking what he wanted and begrudging the least little thing. Then they might sing another song.

The prisoner grimaced and then slumped halfway to the ground, groaning with the pain. Korfax held him for a moment longer, clenching his power ever tighter. Visions of Naaomir swam in his mind, before he found a name at last. Odoiar!

He would have laughed at the surprise were the matter not so serious. Odoiar the estimator? Odoiar the herald of woe? How the wheel turned. Here was the very same Odoiar he had struck in the face and challenged to a duel as they flew over the wreck of Leemal. How small the world had become.

But Odoiar had changed. His face had been altered. He had been disguised, well enough for others, perhaps, but not well enough for Korfax, who now drew back. He released the prisoner, and Odoiar fell to the floor, insensible at last.

Korfax stood straighter and looked at the guards.

"His real name is Noqvoan Kalan Nar Odoiar. He is of the Balt Kaalith. He and I have had dealings in the past. But fear not, he is alone. He is the only one to follow us and infiltrate our camp. Noqvoandril Naaomir set him on our tail. He has no idea what it is that he seeks, and unhappily for him he has just found it." He gestured that they follow him. "Bring him to the great tent and bring a healer with you. I dislike treating with damaged goods."

None of them moved. One glanced at where Teodunad still lay. Korfax held out a hand and fires suddenly enveloped it, bright fires that made a pillar in the air. No one could mistake the threat now.

"Did you not hear what I said?"

"But what of Teodunad?"

"Leave him where he lies," Korfax spat. "Let him wake in his own good time. And if the fool still wishes to face me in combat, let him come and find me." He turned to the rest of the crowd and let the flame boil higher. "Do you hear what I say? Teodunad stays where he is. The one that touches him before he awakens again will answer to me. Now depart in good order. This evening's entertainment is at an end."

He turned about and walked off. The crowd dispersed behind him, and many glanced at his retreating back in fear.

Korfax sat back down at the table and poured himself another cup of wine. He looked at the food and sighed. He picked up a single kwanis and sucked at it. Suddenly he was no longer hungry.

Every time something like this happened he lost his appetite. It was almost as if the very expression of his power provided him with all the sustenance he needed.

It was not long after he had sat down that the guards brought Odoiar to him. Their manner was much changed. They bowed humbly before him and did all that he asked with dispatch, untying Odoiar before mounting a careful watch outside.

Odoiar, though, looked back suspiciously at Korfax. His wounds had been tended to and he seemed to have recovered his senses somewhat.

Korfax poured him a goblet of wine and filled a plate with food for him. Then he gestured at the table.

"Sit! Eat! Drink, even! Recover your senses. I would talk with you."

Odoiar looked at it all with suspicion. Korfax sighed. He took a careful sip from Odoiar's goblet and then took a slice of meat from Odoiar's plate and made great play of putting it in his mouth, before chewing and swallowing it.

"The wine is not drugged," he told his reluctant guest, "nor is the food poisoned. I meant what I said. Eat and drink. I already know everything that I need to know concerning your mission."

Odoiar took the wine and gulped it down. Korfax laughed quietly.

"Were Ralir here, he would teach you how better to handle such excellent fare."

Odoiar put down the goblet.

"Ralir of Badagar?" he asked.

"The same," Korfax said. "I imagine you remember him also. He was there, on that sky ship, the one that took us to Leemal."

Odoiar sat back and looked speculatively at Korfax.

"Do you still desire a duel?"

"Of course not! Besides, you would not survive it, not now. I am not the youth you once knew."

Odoiar looked down.

"Clearly," he said. He glanced at Korfax. "So, shall I thank you for saving my life?"

Korfax smiled indulgently.

"Yes, I think that you should. And have no fear for the future. None of the others will interfere now. Not whilst you are in my custody, at least. Nor do I apologise for invading your mind. You would have done the same, were our positions reversed."

Odoiar sat back.

"You are aiding these people?"

"I am."

"Why?"

"The answer might surprise you."

"I never thought to find you allied with Doagnis."

"Nor did I, once. But times have changed. These people now represent the one hope for victory."

"I cannot accept that, or you in their company. You were the Meganza. You changed stone."

"And the Velukor decided to take what was not his to take."

"But... sorcery?"

"The Agdoain are vulnerable to it."

"You swore an oath."

"So I am to abide by my oaths whilst the Balt Kaalith and the Velukor can do just as they please, is that it?"

"That is not so."

"But it is!" Korfax snarled, leaning in. "Believe me it is! I know what you are, I know exactly what you are!"

Odoiar kept as much distance as he could. It was hard to match that gaze, those eyes of dark fire.

"I have learned much while I have been here," he said. "You have armed these people, Korfax. You have armed them with terrible weapons, weapons that you somehow brought with you. So now I have a question for you."

"I think I can guess what it is."

"Where did you get the weapons from?"

Korfax leaned back again.

"I am not going to tell you a single thing. Leave it be, Odoiar. Know when enough is enough."

"Very well, then," Odoiar said. "But you hide a secret, Korfax, a terrible secret. I see it in you."

"Then you have a good imagination, Noqvoan of the Balt Kaalith."

Korfax smiled and then fixed Odoiar with his hardest stare. Odoiar twisted uncomfortably in his seat.

"They did a good job," Korfax told him. "I would not have recognised you at a glance. But I was also taught to look deeper. Your order errs seriously in that regard."

"And look at you also," answered Odoiar, "consorting with heresy. They were right to incarcerate you."

"Lies built upon lies," Korfax said. "I was incarcerated because the Velukor feared me. It is as simple as that. Which of us broke the law first?"

"He was the Velukor."

"And does that excuse him?"

Odoiar tried to match the gaze of Korfax, but he could not. Every time he looked he had to look away again. That he persisted at all said something for his determination.

"They told me that you were pursuing Doagnis," he said. "But when I heard of the fall of Othil Ekrin, when they said that you had died, I wondered to myself whether it was true. So to find you alive again does not altogether surprise me, though I confess I had not thought to see you allied to the slime of the abyss."

Korfax slammed a hand into the table. Odoiar jumped despite himself.

"Be careful with your insults, Odoiar. Remember that you do not know everything. This camp and this army are our people's last hope of victory over the Agdoain."

Odoiar still did not retreat.

"You are powerful, Korfax, and though it goes against my better nature, I think you are also still somewhat honourable. But I know where my loyalties lie, and you will not intimidate me."

Korfax laughed at that.

"Won't I? You are already intimidated. I stormed your mind as if you were a child. You cannot meet my gaze. You know the kind of power I wield. Your determination is all that you have. As to loyalty? I used to be like you. I thought I knew where my loyalties lay as well. However, when matters came to a head, it became clear that I did not. You must have been told all that has happened since my victory at Othil Zilodar, so you know somewhat of the truth, but I'll wager they didn't tell you everything. Did you speak to anyone else other than Naaomir?"

"No."

"Pity, you might have learned something better."

"So what do you intend now?"

Korfax leaned back in his seat.

"You will be my messenger. You will give the high council my words. When I come to Othil Homtoh at last, I will expect them to know my will."

Odoiar looked surprised.

"You will come to Othil Homtoh?"

"It is inevitable," Korfax said. "First we will destroy the Agdoain and then we will come knocking on the gates of Zafazaa. There are crimes for which he and his followers must answer."

"What crimes?"

Korfax became still and his eyes grew cold, dark pools of ice.

"Ask them about Lontibir. Tell them that I know its history, all of it, and that I hold them accountable."

"I do not understand," Odoiar said.

Korfax looked unkindly at Odoiar.

"I have heard it said, on more than one occasion, that the Balt Kaalith wait for knowledge before acting. So let me gift you with knowledge. Then you will understand and be able to act. But this knowledge comes with a warning. Once you see it, I think that you will wish that you had never looked in the first place."

"I still do not understand."

"Oh, but you will, Odoiar, you will."

Korfax was still at the table when Doagnis rode up. Odoiar was deep into the trance of the apnoralax and Korfax was watching the shifting patterns on his face as the full horror of the tale of Lontibir was revealed to him, piece by horrid piece.

Doagnis walked smartly over to Korfax. She was angry.

"I have heard a number of things concerning you, things I think we should discuss."

Korfax looked back at her and folded his arms.

"Say what it is you wish to say."

She pointed at Odoiar.

"This needs privacy."

Korfax flicked a hand in dismissal.

"He cannot hear you."

She looked at Odoiar again and frowned.

"What have you done to him?"

"Shown him what happened on Lontibir."

Her anger deepened to outrage.

"Why? Why do you show an outsider our pain?"

Korfax met her stare.

"He is to be my messenger. I wish them to know that justice comes for them, that the crimes of their houses are known to me and that they will not escape my wrath. As they have dishonoured me, so I will pay them back in kind."

Doagnis almost hissed her answer.

"And do you think that you are the only one here with scores to settle? So what of my plans? What of my desires? I am not sure that I want a Noqvoan of the Balt Kaalith taking knowledge of us back to the west."

Korfax glanced at Odoiar and saw deep pain etched into his face now. He wondered what Odoiar was seeing. Apnoralax did not show the same vision to everyone, not like oanadar. For some the trance passed quickly, but for others it was long, drawn out and slow. Apnoralax gave up their secrets according to the disposition and the power of the person involved, making the transaction an oddly personal experience. Korfax turned back to Doagnis.

"So," he grated, "what is your will in this matter?"

"Do not you take that tone with me!" she snapped, and Korfax surged to his feet.

"OR WHAT?" he roared back. He threw the table aside and came straight at her. Doagnis retreated, but he was too fast. He grabbed her by her shoulders and crushed them in his hands.

"What will you do?" he snarled down into her face. "Attempt a summoning? Call up another Babemor? I have power enough at my beck and call to lay low any demon you could call upon! I am sick and tired of being treated as if my opinions do not matter. I have armed the Haelok Aldaria. I have made them mightier than they have ever been since the fall of Sondehna and still I have to endure the scorn of fools like Teodunad!"

Doagnis struggled in his grip, staring back at him angrily.

"Let go of me!" she said, quietly, slowly. He did not; instead, he tightened his grip.

"You do not include me in your plans," he accused, "so why should I include you in mine?"

She blinked.

"You are hurting me," she said. Now she was frightened as well.

He lessened his grip somewhat, holding her gaze. Then he released her at last and turned away. He went over to the table and picked it up, placing it back where it had been. He sat back in his chair and looked hard at her. She had not moved, except to raise her hands to her shoulders and rub at them.

"Was that absolutely necessary?" she asked.

"It got your attention, did it not?" he said.

"Is that how it was with Teodunad? Did you want to get his attention as well?"

Korfax stood up and came at her again. She stepped back, fearful again, still rubbing her shoulders where he had grabbed her.

"You know what I can do!" he told her. "I looked inside him. I saw his intent. If he had fully drawn his Qorihna and slain me with it, would you have thanked him?"

She looked up in shock at that.

"No!" she cried. "You know I would not."

He waited, measuring, seeking.

"I did not know what was in his heart," she said.

Still he did not answer.

"I did not know what was in his heart," she repeated. It was almost a plea. Korfax bowed his head at last and turned away.

"I grow weary of this," he said. "I give but only receive scorn in return."

"After what you did today," she offered, "I doubt that any here will scorn you again."

She looked at Odoiar. He was still deep in the trance.

"At least you might have waited until I returned to do this."

Korfax sat back down and folded his arms across his chest.

"You have been gone many days, without anyone being the wiser. I had no idea when you might be returning. So, sister mine, unless you tell me your thoughts, how can I know what they are?"

Her eyes flickered.

"Not so loud," she said. "That must not be revealed."

Korfax did not move. Doagnis watched him, and as the moments lengthened she realised he was clearly prepared to wait her out. She took a deep breath and gathered herself up.

"Very well, then. It appears that there is fault upon both sides. I am used to having everything my own way, just as you are. We should reach an accommodation, you and I. We must not argue, Korfax, not us."

Korfax subsided and the fire in his eyes dimmed. But again they did not go out entirely.

"What do you propose?"

"A division of labour."

"Say on."

"In military matters I will give you complete control. You have fought the Agdoain for many years and are hardened by battle and war. All will acknowledge your experience in this matter. But as to policy, you will give me complete control."

"But policy always dictates military objectives."

Doagnis sucked in her breath sharply.

"I have been planning the ascendancy of the Iabeiorith all my life. You have not. I think deference is due!"

Korfax thought about that. Though he did not like to admit it, she was right. He would not give in, though, not yet, not until he was certain that this was more than mere words.

"I tire of serving others," he told her. "I tire of having that service taken for granted or thrown back in my face as if it was of little or no consequence. I once honoured the throne, giving all that I could in its service, but I was thrown down by those that thought more of their own selfish needs than the needs of all. I am beginning to wonder if the same is not happening here. I have shown you all where my heart is. I have armed the Haelok Aldaria and made them mighty. I have given everything, cast aside all that I was so that I could be one with the Iabeiorith. I have accepted your truths, embraced them and made myself over in your image, but still you account it of little worth."

There were tears in her eyes now.

"But that is not so," she said. "I know your heart in this, none better. We are two sides of the very same stone."

She stepped forward and sat beside him, placing her hand upon his chest. He could feel the heat of her.

"It has never been my intent to treat you like that," she said, "never. I know how you have been hurt. I know how you have been betrayed and lied to. But I now give you the Haelok Aldaria. They are yours, so long as you accept that I know the best way to achieve our aims."

Korfax was silent for a moment. He so wanted to say yes. He could feel her against him, the closeness of her, that siren song in his head. He watched her tears, watched them fall. How vulnerable she was under all that hardness. How soft.

"Very well," he said at last. "I accept."

She smiled gently and slowly wiped away her tears. He watched the easy gesture and narrowed his eyes. Was this a play on her part, even now?

"But there is a condition," he said.

She looked up at him, and he wondered whether she did it a little too quickly. Had her tears been replaced by her fears?

"What condition?" she asked carefully.

"Teodunad – I want him gone!"

"He has served me faithfully and well."

"Faithfully and well? You believe that? Still? After what I saw in his head? He is a crude fool, full of pride and ambition. He wants me dead. If I had not stopped him, he would have drawn his Qorihna against me!"

She looked down.

"I do not know how the others will take it."

"They will do what you tell them. Besides, who is it that has made the Haelok Aldaria mighty again? It was not Teodunad! And I know of at least two chieftains who would not be sorry to see the back of him. Need I remind you how willing you were to let Mirzinad become the first, if he could slay me?"

She glanced up at that.

"I thought we agreed to leave the past in the past!"

"We did. So leave Teodunad in the past also. Or does he mean more to you than you are saying?"

She took a sharp intake of breath and he saw it in her eyes. She had known of Teodunad's desire and had played upon it.

"So you are not as innocent as you would like others to believe, I see," goaded Korfax. "Guess what else I saw in his head?"

She drew back in shock.

"No! You cannot believe that. I have never been with him. You must know this."

He leaned in closer and looked at her.

"Prove it!" he challenged.

"You are jealous?"

"That is Teodunad's sin, not mine!"

She did not answer.

"Either you get rid of him, or I will," he pressed. "If I am to be first, as you have proposed, I will not have him beside me. It is him, or me."

She sighed.

"So be it. It will be as you ask."

She waited a moment.

"And what do I get in all of this?"

"What?" he asked. "You made this proposal! You know what you are getting. Two sides of the same stone, as you said. Is this not what you desire?"

"You do not trust me?"

"I do not trust Teodunad."

"But do you trust me?"

"I am here, am I not?"

"That is not an answer."

"Judge me by my actions."

She took another long breath.

"I find this hurtful."

"As do I."

She came closer.

"I will only be with you," she said.

He looked at her. Was that true? The look in her eyes, their softness, was compelling, and he found himself drowning in them once more. Would he trust her again? He would. He reached out and took her hand.

"Then I apologise for my anger. When I saw what was in him, I was enraged. Once betrayed, you ever look for it in others."

She smiled.

"I would never betray you. You must know that."

He stroked her hand.

"Then I accept your will in this matter and in all such matters. And you shall see the fruit of it soon enough. By the time we go to battle, the Haelok Aldaria will truly be a force to be reckoned with."

Doagnis turned away and looked at Odoiar, her smile dropping from her face.

"So what of him?"

"I had thought to make him my messenger," said Korfax. "I want them to know fear. I want them to know that I am coming for them!"

He turned to her.

"I had no intention of letting him take any useful intelligence back with him," he continued. "Besides, he knows little enough as it is."

Doagnis all but breathed a sigh of relief. She smiled at him and laid her head against him. He caught her scent. How wonderful it was. He realised how much he had missed not having her by his side.

"Then that is the way it shall be," she said to him. "But first let me make sure, just in case. There are potions, along with certain sorceries, that can seek out and remove unwanted memories. Once I am satisfied, then he can return as a warning to the proud lords of the west that their last days are upon them. Yes, that will serve my purposes after all. We will set them another riddle to solve. I suddenly find that I like that. I like that very much."

Korfax looked down at her.

"And Teodunad?"

Her smile dropped away.

"I will deal with that also."

They held a council. The seven chieftains were there, Vordekass Enay Aodagaa, Gondohar Enay Dosevax, Nolduriss Enay Ambriol, Olanger Enay Ralendu, Rameldur Enay Ortal, Nouriss Enay Vandalim and Daniss Enay Dorlamu. Many of the Argedith were there also, led by Noje-ethith Enay Opakas. There was silence when Korfax entered beside Doagnis.

She turned to them all.

"Do any here doubt that the Haelok Aldaria has been made mighty by the gifts of Korfax?"

No one spoke.

"Do any here doubt that Korfax has shown himself to be one of us?"

A few stirred uneasily, but still no one spoke.

"Do any doubt his prowess in battle or his experience against the foe?"

More silence.

"Do any doubt his power as one of the Argedith?"

It was clear that many had guessed where this was going now. That Teodunad had threatened to draw his sword against Korfax was well known. That he was not amongst them now made what was coming next all too obvious. It was Ambriol who stood.

"I wish to speak."

"Say on."

"All these things are true," he said. "Korfax has greatly aided us. But many still doubt that he is one of us."

Korfax glanced at Doagnis. She bowed her head. He stood up to face Ambriol.

"There are many here that I have come to admire. You are one of them, as are Aodagaa and Dosevax. When I gave you Qorihna and Qahmor, you accepted them graciously. You have never judged me by what you have heard – you have only judged me by what I have done. That is fair and just and I honour you for it. I understand your doubts, given who I am, and I understand that you find it difficult to accept me. So let me tell you something you do not know."

He paused for a moment, catching the eye of Opakas. She was watching him carefully, a faint smile on her lips. He looked away again.

"A long time ago the Farenith had another name," he continued. "I cannot tell you that name, only that my house came to forget itself, and for a long time it dwelt in ignorance. Eventually, though, the past returned to us and we became its regretful guardians. That is why I have a Qorihna. It came to me out of times long gone. What I can tell you is that my house once fought for the north. My house was once of the Iabeiorith."

Ambriol was not moved.

"That is not a surprise to many here," he said. "But even that knowledge does not clear the air. You once swore oaths to the hated west. What of those?"

"Those oaths were sworn in ignorance, and those to whom they were sworn have revealed themselves as liars and thieves and murderers. I have renounced my former life. It is no more. I will only add this. Before you all, I will swear a new oath of allegiance, to the memory of the Salman Mikaolazith, the house of princes. I will honour that memory with my dying breath, and if I fall in battle, I will do so gladly in that name."

There was silence again. Ambriol looked long at Korfax.

"Do you swear before the Creator that you are of the Iabeiorith?"

"I do!"

"Do you swear by the Creator that you have renounced your old allegiances and you have embraced the ways of the Haelok Aldaria with all your heart?"

"I do!"

Ambriol bowed his head.

"From what I have seen of you, you have never deceived, and your actions have followed your words in complete agreement. I, for one, am satisfied. I accept you as first."

Korfax smiled and bowed.

"It will be an honour to fight beside you."

He sat back down, as did Ambriol. Doagnis stood again.

"Then I declare it done. Korfax is named first of the Haelok Aldaria. Do any object?"

There was no dissent.

Afterwards, as the gathering began to break up, Aodagaa came to Korfax. He saluted but then looked hard at him.

"I have never seen Doagnis be with another as she is with you. Many have noticed it. There is something between you, a bond, a secret, something mighty."

"I cannot tell you what you want to know," said Korfax.

"The Farenith were made by Azmeloh," Aodagaa said.

"An act of gratitude for an act of selfless bravery, given in ignorance."

"I have no love of Teodunad," Aodagaa told him, "nor do any of the others. He was first only by right of succession, but he was ever proud in his dealings with others and would accept no counsel unless it flattered him. However it is, though, many still see him as our first, no matter what Doagnis might say."

"Judge me by what I do," said Korfax, "and let all others do the same."

"But what is to become of him?"

"That is for Doagnis to say."

Korfax would have turned away, but now Opakas came forward. Aodagaa inclined his head to her and moved away. She watched him leave and then looked back at Korfax.

"And so you advance," she said.

"Do you object?" he asked.

"Not at all. I think all are beginning to see where your heart lies."

"Are you still watching me?"

"It is difficult to take my eyes away from you, you burn so brightly."

"But I still serve Doagnis."

"I know. And that also is a puzzle."

He caught the gleam in her eye. Did she know the truth?

"It should not be. Doagnis rules, as is her right," said Korfax.

"So we are told every day of our lives. But many are beginning to ask the same question that I have been asking for a while now. What name did the Farenith once have that the last son of its house can step so mightily into the ranks of the Haelok Aldaria?" She now leaned in closer. "Consider how the echoes of the past come back to haunt us. Consider how the world loves to repeat itself. You asked me if I was still watching you, but I am not the one that should be watching at all. You are the one that should be watching now. Keep watching and you may see a thing."

She turned and walked away, leaving Korfax to ponder.

For many days afterwards Korfax spent all his time with the chieftains and their followers, teaching, listening and discussing. He described the Agdoain, their way of fighting, the power of the Ageyad and their habit of fighting in threes.

It soon became clear to the others how much their tactics and strategies would have to change. Korfax, though, made it abundantly clear. Though all had practised with Qorihna and Qahmor, learning their ways as best they could, it was only in the presence of the enemy that they would truly understand what their weaponry could do.

He spoke to them of lines of force, invisible to the foe, its components spread widely to allow free rein to their dark blades. They would be like scythes upon a harvest day. Many liked the idea, and not a few began to discuss variations, adaptations, fighting on foot, fighting on steed. When this happened, Korfax stepped back and let the others take the floor. The Haelok Aldaria understood well the classic tactics of warfare, but adapting them to the new weaponry fired their imaginations and their blood.

Eventually Korfax turned to the Agdoain siege towers and how they might be brought down. When he suggested the conjuration of fires, though, many looked dismayed. None knew the art. He was surprised by this, but then he offered to teach them, there and then. Many were amazed at how easy it was, and soon the encampment was full of inconstant flames as the skills were passed on. Korfax watched it all with growing pride. Wherever he went now, the others smiled at his approach, bowing gladly.

Eventually Ambriol came to him alone after another long day of discussion and planning and sat beside him as he took a cup of wine.

"I did not think that I would ever say this, but I am glad now that you are the one to lead us. Teodunad would have failed in this task. He did not plan, he did not discuss and he did not teach or pass on skills and gifts. He cared for nothing but his own counsel – and rarely did he offer it. Always it seemed that nothing would please him."

Korfax looked down.

"So why was he chosen?"

"Right of blood. Loyalty to Doagnis."

Korfax frowned at that.

"Mirzinad might have replaced him."

Ambriol drew back and looked hard at Korfax.

"An even worse choice. They are both carved from the very same stone: proud, unforgiving and arrogant."

Korfax bowed his head slightly.

"Both you and Aodagaa were born to lead. I have learned a lot from you."

At that Ambriol smiled, something it seemed he did rarely.

"Now you are being overly kind. Of the two of us, you are the one that has fought in many battles, not I."

"But battle is the stuff of chaos. I have been lucky."

Ambriol laughed at last and leaned forward.

"Humility, generosity, honesty and truth – that is what I have come to see in you. You were born to us, whatever Teodunad might think. I do not know your history, but I thank the Creator that you have found us at last. With you beside us, we will be victorious."

He got up, bowed and left. Korfax watched him go and pondered the words of Opakas.

When not engaged in deep discussion with his chieftains, he watched the practise sessions, skills with the bow, skills with the glaive, archery and, of course, swordplay.

Dosevax was one of the best with a sword, and Korfax would frequently come to watch as he duelled, admiring his skill as he threw down each and every opponent he came up against. It was not long before Dosevax noticed and offered Korfax a blade. Korfax accepted, and soon the two of them were duelling with ever-increasing ferocity. Come the end, when Dosevax somehow managed to disarm him, Korfax was laughing with the joy of it.

"You are the best I have ever seen," he said as he went to retrieve his blade. "I am not even sure that Ralir of Badagar could match you."

Dosevax bowed and smiled.

"And you are the first opponent that I have had who could truly match me. There were several moves there that I have never encountered before."

Korfax hefted his sword.

"I would be glad to teach them to you. But even so, you still managed to counter them."

He turned to Dosevax.

"We must do this again."

"It would be my honour."

And so it went on. Doagnis would occasionally come to watch, or listen, as the Haelok Aldaria grew stronger and stronger. She would watch Korfax with glowing eyes. She was also true to her word. Teodunad was nowhere to be seen, and for that Korfax was immensely grateful.

Every evening, as they dined together, she would sit beside him and they would talk softly of the day's affairs, she telling him that she was happy that all was going so well and that the Haelok Aldaria were now indeed a force to be reckoned with, while he would thank her for her love. Then they would retire and lie together, her scent and her warmth filling him as he held her close. He could not remember when he had ever been happier than he was now.

But it could not last. There came a day when Dosevax came to Korfax, a look of puzzlement on his face.

"I have just heard a thing," he said. "Did you know that Doagnis has created a personal guard?"

Korfax started in surprise.

"A personal guard? No! Why does she need such a thing? She has us!"

"Many are concerned by this," Dosevax said. "Doagnis always said that we should eschew the old ways, that we must not compete with each other, but some have come to believe that Doagnis has not fully done this. They think she vies with you. No one likes it when those who make the rules break them on a whim."

Korfax sighed.

"I will talk with her. I will find out what this is about."

"One more thing – Teodunad is to lead it."

Korfax had difficulty controlling his anger. Dosevax watched as Korfax clenched his fist and then unclenched it.

"Do you wish for an escort?" Dosevax asked.

Korfax looked up, surprised.

"Do you think I need one?"

"It is long past time you had an honour guard. You are the first, after all. But for now I will come with you, as will Aodagaa."

Korfax bowed his head.

"I am honoured."

"You deserve all honour. You lead us well. Teodunad never did."

They marched through the camp, Korfax flanked by Dosevax and Aodagaa. They found Doagnis talking with Teodunad outside the great tent. To Korfax, the conversation appeared more than a little intimate.

He stopped and bowed. Dosevax and Aodagaa bowed as well. Teodunad looked up with his habitual scorn but hid it quickly again, as Korfax was there, and not in good humour.

"My lady," he said, addressing Doagnis. "Please explain your will to me."

Here he gestured at Teodunad.

"He has served me faithfully," Doagnis said. "We are going to war. I thought a personal guard would be prudent."

"And I would have given you one, gladly, joyfully, if you had asked."

She smiled. Korfax thought it a little forced.

"I thought this better," she said. "You know that I like to do things my way."

"But him?" Korfax gestured.

Teodunad did not move, but his eyes burned.

"You know what I think of him," said Korfax, "and I know what he thinks of me."

"Even so," she said. "He has served me well in the past. I cannot forget that."

"But he is a thing of divisions. He divides to no good purpose. Ask of the others and they will tell you how he treats those he considers beneath him. Divide and rule? A divided army is a weakened army. Who would follow such a one? What victories would be gained?"

Now Teodunad moved.

"I might surprise you there! There are still some who are loyal to me."

He glanced pointedly at Dosevax and Aodagaa. Both of them stood straighter.

"Korfax is a better leader than you could ever be," said Aodagaa. "He shows us how to fight. He makes us mighty. What did you ever do except hand out orders and curse those that did not do your will as you saw it?"

Dosevax did not speak; instead, he held out his hands. Fires grew there, pulled from the abyss. Teodunad scowled.

"Korfax has taught us true power," Dosevax said, extinguishing the flames with a flourish. "We are now where we should be," he continued.

Teodunad would have answered but Doagnis held up her hand.

"Enough of this!" she ordered. "I will not have it."

She turned to Korfax.

"You and I will speak together."

He bowed to her, and then he turned to Aodagaa and Dosevax and bowed to them, before following Doagnis inside.

"Why do you do this?" she said, whirling about. "Why do you set them against me?"

"I have not set them against you!" he said. "They are concerned, as am I. A personal guard? They do not understand. I do not understand. They think you no longer trust them. The Haelok Aldaria were always the elite, but now you appear to be saying that they are not!"

"Of course I am not saying that."

"Then why have you created a personal guard?"

"I felt the need. Teodunad has served me well, as I said before."

"What did you say to me? Did you not say that he would be out of my sight?" She looked back at him sadly.

"I thought enough time had passed for the healing of wounds. Clearly it has not. I know there is contention between you, but Teodunad fully understands my will in this matter. He knows how much I care for you. All he desires is to serve me."

"All he desires is you!"

"That is not so."

"I saw it in him."

"And perhaps all you saw were your fears. I know you. When you first came to me you were full of doubt. You hated the hostility others gave you. But look at you now. You lead the Haelok Aldaria. All see your worth. Your pride has returned to you, as it should, but do not let it turn to jealousy. Allow others to love me. Do not deny me this. I would be served and loved by all."

"That is not what I meant."

She came to him and placed her hand upon his chest, the one gesture she favoured above all others.

"Nor is it what you think it to be," she told him. "I hear tell that you are to have an honour guard. I would have the same. It is time, I think."

She looked up at him, her eyes soft.

"Would you begrudge me this?"

"No! You know that I would not."

"And is Teodunad not of the Haelok Aldaria?"

"He is. But..."

"Then my personal guard is of the Haelok Aldaria, is it not? See how your doubts vanish at the slightest touch."

He stopped where he was and looked down at her. All his questions and concerns suddenly lay at his feet in a confused pile.

"But Teodunad..."

"Forgive and forget, my love," she said as she reached up and kissed him with gentle passion.

"Who do I sleep with every night?" She kissed him again. "Only you," she whispered.

The kisses became passionate and she became as fire in his hands.

12

REVEALED

Ur-doalji T-van-zida
Do-krusors Drol-ne-uras
Rannil-sj Ton-lujh-eijon
Alkar-fis Vim-a-dr-pan
Moz-od-klei Rox-ad-e-arp
Krih-mn-a Pl-im-pamin
Odzen-do Pilaih-risorn

It was morning the next day when a scout rode into the camp. He had come from the north-west, from the watch that was kept upon Emethgis Vaniad. He went straight to Doagnis and bowed to her. His message was simple. The Agdoain were marching south in vast numbers. She went to Korfax.

"You know what this means?" she asked.

"Yes," he said. "It is what I expected. They intend to take Othil Admaq. This is exactly what they did in the north. They built up their numbers and then came south."

"What do you think we should do?"

"We fight. It is time. If we break camp now, we will, in all likelihood, beat them to Othil Admaq by at least a day. Then we let the siege begin. The Agdoain will soak up all the punishment that they can, and once they have depleted the defences they will attack in force. That is when we make our move, when the Agdoain commit everything to taking the city. That way we will be certain to get them all."

He watched her. There was uncertainty, and something more.

"What is it?" he asked.

"I had intended to go north. I was intending to retake Lukalah."

He smiled.

"That is what I thought. But here is the thing. If the Agdoain take Othil Admaq, our task will be all the harder. We cannot allow them to increase their hold upon our world."

She smiled also, seemingly agreeing with his assessment, but she looked distracted. He watched her face.

"Are you afraid?" he asked.

She looked up at him.

"Aren't you?"

"I have fought in many battles," he said. "You have not seen even a single one, or witnessed anything like it."

He came forward and placed his hands about her.

"You are a power," he said. "Do not doubt yourself. I serve you with my life. All my skill, all my experience, I lay at your feet. But I promise you this. Come the end you will have a victory the like of which this world will have never seen before."

She took a deep breath and smiled.

"Your certainty reassures me, but this is the great test we face here. In this we will be forged. In this we will declare ourselves. There is no turning back once we start down this road."

"Do you doubt me?" he asked. "I have fought with these weapons and I know what they can do. And once the fury fills the Haelok Aldaria, they will know it, too."

They rode for the Pisea Gonos. They passed through the green lands of the lower plains, crossed the young Patrim by one of its wide fords and came by quiet ways to the east side of the Adroqin Perisax. The land about them was empty, no doubt cleared by the rumour that the Agdoain were coming south. They saw no one. All had fled to the cities.

Korfax rode at the head, his honour guard behind him. Beside him rode Aodagaa, shadowed eyes scouring the land.

"They have all fled," he said as they passed yet another empty tower.

"It was what happened in the north," Korfax returned. "My father had everyone moved to the cities, where they could be defended. The Agdoain were too numerous, and it was difficult to know where they would strike next."

There was a long pause.

"What was your father like?" Aodagaa asked.

Korfax smiled.

"He was strong. Once his mind was set, you could not change it. But he also served, and if he was given a duty, he did it, come what may. He was the best of the north."

"You miss him?"

"Greatly, though I am not sure what he would think if he saw me now. He died preserving what he wished could be true. At least his service to the throne did not fall into mockery."

"Is that what turned you?"

"Somewhat. When those that rule do not abide by their own laws, tyranny is at hand. Our people have never been well-served by such things."

Aodagaa frowned.

"So what of Sondehna?"

Korfax glanced back.

"He made one wrong choice, and from that everything else followed. I grieve for what could have been."

"Your house kept no memory of it?"

"Not as you would think of it. We remained guardians, bound by prophecy. The lore and the weapons were kept hidden and each generation was sworn to secrecy."

"At least you were born in the north," said Aodagaa. "That is something I do not have."

Korfax smiled.

"You are born of the north," he said. "I listen to you now and I hear the accents I grew up with. You are born of the north."

"Until now," Aodagaa said, "memories were all that I had."

"Soon you will have more," Korfax reassured him. "Once the Agdoain have been swept aside we will remake the land in our own image, as it was in the beginning."

They rode on for a while in silence.

"So you believe that Sondehna should not have taken Soivar as his bride?" Aodagaa asked.

Korfax thought for a moment. How could he answer such a question? He would not be here now if it were not for Soivar.

"That was the act that started him on the road to ruin," he said.

"But surely it was his defeat at the hands of Karmaraa that sealed the fate of the north?"

Korfax's smile became dark. If only they knew.

"And history has ever been written by the victors," he answered. "Who knows what really happened."

Aodagaa frowned again. He watched Korfax carefully for a while.

"You know something," he said at last. "Opakas was right. You know something you are not telling the rest of us."

Korfax turned at that and looked sternly at Aodagaa.

"What else has Opakas said?"

Aodagaa met his gaze and did not flinch.

"That you can be trusted. That we should – all of us – put our faith in you. She did not say why that was, only that she believes you are not yet ready to relinquish the role of guardian."

Korfax looked away.

"I cannot answer you in this," he said. "I wish that I could, but I cannot."

Aodagaa bowed his head as if entirely satisfied.

"She also said that would be your answer and that I should not let it concern me."

He gestured ahead.

"I have always preferred actions to words anyway, and you have already shown your worth to the rest of us."

They made their way over the pass and then followed the mountains to the south. Soon they came upon the tributary of the Hoknodoss, much as Korfax had when he was first on his way to Lonsiatris. It was not far now.

They camped on the eastern side of the hills above Othil Admaq, just as the Agdoain crossed the horizon on the western side. Guards were set, sorceries conjured and the vast sprawling encampment was hidden from view.

Korfax went with the chieftains to the head of the pass. With them went the vanguard. They stared out over the plain as evening fell and the lights of Othil Admaq lit up the sky. On the horizon to the north a mist boiled. The Agdoain.

"How many are there likely to be?" asked Ambriol.

"More than you can count," Korfax replied. "They will cover the land. Though Othil Admaq be twice the size that it is, they could still surround it."

There was a long silence. Korfax glanced about him. They were afraid. Greatly afraid. He understood.

"Hear me well, all of you," he said. "Anyone who is not afraid before a battle is either a fool or already dead. You need your fear. Do not despise it – but do not let it conquer you, either. You will understand once the sword is in your hand and you ride out to face the foe. Remember what you have learned and think upon the words from the Namad Alkar:

"'Without constant practise, a warrior will be nervous and undecided when facing battle; without constant practise, those in command will be wavering and irresolute when the crisis is at hand.'

"This is what you have done," he told them. "You are ready. Believe it."

They rode back into camp. Korfax went to find Doagnis and found her but lately gone, along with Ronoar. He would have made nothing of it, but then one of the guards told him that another had gone with them.

"If you are concerned, Enay, Teodunad went with her, to ward her."

Korfax looked up.

"Just Teodunad?"

"Yes, Enay. She asked him. She wanted to be careful, what with the enemy being so close."

Korfax thought about that. It seemed a fair precaution.

"Which way did they go?" he asked.

The guard gestured to the hills.

"Into the hills, Enay."

Korfax glanced up into the darkness.

"Thank you," he said.

The guard bowed. Korfax strode off.

Suspicions clouded his thoughts. Though he tried to put them aside, he could not. He simply did not trust Teodunad. What was Doagnis doing? Was she with him? Had she bound him to her with more than simple loyalty? Jealousy grew like a fire, feeding his suspicions until he could no longer stand it. He must know what was occurring.

Sorcery was his only means. He took out his logadar and trawled through the texts. There were many ways of divining the here and the now, but the best of them involved the use of a shew-stone. The way it was described made it sound like a directed vision, albeit far more immediate, more like a projection of consciousness.

The thing was, he did not possess a shew-stone and they were remarkably personal objects. He then thought of Doagnis. What of hers?

He threw the logadar aside. Damn it, he should be more trusting. But he had seen inside Teodunad. He knew what Teodunad desired. He paced up and down, trying to calm his thoughts, but he could not. He had to know, or he would burst.

He awoke his armour and slipped out of his chambers. Invisible, he stole inside hers. He went to her shew-stone and took it back with him. Once back in his chambers again he closed the drapes and sat down with the stone in his hands. He hurled his mind inside it and the stone went dark at his touch.

Doagnis, he thought, Doagnis, and his mind flew over a twisted landscape of rocks and trees. He could see everything, hear everything, but it was all warped and bent out of shape, as though his thought was some great hole into which the world could pour itself.

He came upon Teodunad, standing guard at the entrance to a cave. Beside him stood Ronoar, a burning rod in his hand. There was no colour, though – everything seemed to be shades of grey. Korfax felt trepidation.

Into the cave he went, a mote, a heavy mote swimming through the spaces that lay in between. He found her ahead, walking carefully through the darkness, another burning rod in her hand. Where was she going? What was her purpose?

He followed her ever deeper. The rock they passed through became filled with dark holes of all sizes, as though nameless things had gnawed their way through the stone, taking this course or that.

At one point she stopped, peering back into the darkness, almost as if she believed she was being followed, but she turned around soon enough and made her way on.

Up ahead another light grew, a pale and dead light that waxed and waned. Doagnis stepped forward into the light. She had come to a vast cavern, tall and wide. Great stone roots coiled downward from the ceiling or collected together in sheets. Occasionally one would drip, watering the rock beneath, and there stone shoots grew slowly upwards, each blindly seeking the roof. Korfax followed at her shoulder, watching with disquiet the dead light that grew about them both. Then he heard a vague rustling sound and something slithered through the air towards them both.

Korfax stared. What was this thing? The size of a head, or maybe larger, it boiled and fumed as it hung in the air. There was a covering of sorts, a cloak of leathered slime, pitted and scarred, shifting from moment to moment as though whatever lay underneath writhed and pulsed. Shapes rose up or fell back down, unpleasant approximations of form and purpose, but the cloak covered everything. The more Korfax saw of it, the less he wanted to know.

Doagnis bowed to it and it bobbed up and down.

"All proceeds as it should," she said, her voice echoing in his mind, a curious doubling.

The thing seemed to roll inside its cloak of slime, a rhythmic wave of movement that orbited its body. Korfax stared in horrified fascination. Vapours coiled about it for a moment and then its voice gurgled out – an oily sound as though thick fluids had learned to speak.

"You do not sound as certain as your words."

She paused.

"It is Korfax," she said eventually. "Sometimes he is hard to contain. Always he pushes."

"You have beguiled him?"

"He loves me."

"Love does not suffice. You know what we told you," came the thick voice. "We remember Sondehna. We told you how it was with him."

"I know, but Korfax is precious to me. Besides, he is the only one of us that truly knows battle. He is strong, mighty, most worthy to command my armies, and I would be a fool to cast him aside. I have summoned him. He is mine and he does my bidding."

"Always?"

The question squirmed its slow way through the air. She did not answer.

"There is a saying amongst us," continued the other, "one you know very well. Call always upon the lesser, lest the greater command more than you. You have called upon Korfax and bound him to you. But what if he should command more than you?"

"That will not happen. He loves me."

"And do you love him?"

Doagnis was a moment answering. Her face was clenched now, as though she fought with herself.

"Yes!" she said eventually, almost as if it were an admission of weakness.

There was another long silence as the humped thing rolled upon itself. Korfax had the distinct impression that it was greatly disturbed.

"We do not trust love," it said at last.

Doagnis narrowed her eyes.

"Who I choose to love is not your concern."

"All things are our concern."

She made a cutting gesture with her hand.

"I did not come here to discuss this but to impart some news. The enemy have laid siege to Othil Admaq. Now is our great chance to prove our worth."

"We know, but the people of the south are nothing to us. Why should they be anything to you?"

"The Agdoain must be stopped."

"Yes, the Agdoain must be stopped, but why not let others do your work for you?"

"That is not what Korfax counsels. He says that we should not allow the Agdoain free rein. We should crush them wherever we find them. I agree with that."

"So he does your bidding, does he? Do you rule, or do you not?"

"I rule, but should I not listen to the counsel of others also?"

"It is weak! We despise it. Only the strongest shall rule, all others must follow."

Her face twisted in anger.

"Be careful what you say to me, Arzulg," she hissed. "My toleration has limits. Do not ever call me weak again!"

The humped thing drew back a way and its motions slowed.

"We have advised you well in the past," it said. "Does that count for nothing now?"

"And I have given you much in return. Do not forget that either."

"We do not."

"Good!"

"But this matter of Korfax – he bothers us. He is mighty. He is wilful. He knows who he is. What if he should declare himself? Your traditions demand that only a prince may rule. He is a prince. You would be weakened."

"I have convinced him otherwise. Besides, I have an agreement with him. I rule, but he commands the Haelok Aldaria."

"That will satisfy him for only a little while. He will change his mind. He is of the line of Sondehna. He will not be contained. We have an agreement with you. We do not have an agreement with him. You should rectify this."

"What do you mean?"

"Get yourself with child. Then you will no longer need him."

The anger returned and Doagnis drew herself up as if preparing to strike, one hand low, the other high.

"How dare you!" she hissed. "I think that is up to me, not you!"

"But we see your desire," came the thick voice. "You may hide from yourself, but not from us. That is why we stay with you. You are much like us in many ways. Fulfilment is transitory. Desire is continual. You desire. Do as we do. Take what you want and discard it when it no longer pleases you. It is the only way."

"But I want him beside me."

"No! You do not! You mislead yourself. You have desire, but that is all that you have. The longer he is beside you, the less you would want him there. We know this. We see it in you. Satisfaction and contentment are the heralds of death. They are surrender. They are the end. Only desire is continual."

"But who could replace him?"

"Your child."

Doagnis paused for a moment, peering sidelong at the other.

"I see you," she said. "You would have me hobbled by a child, wouldn't you? Is that your real intent, to gain more than you already have by weakening me with burdens?"

"No, that is not what we desire at all. We desire your strength. A child would strengthen you. Consider, your child would have everything. The dark sword would belong to your child and your child would have an agreement with us. That would mean that we would be safe from the threat of the dark sword. That is our only desire. We must be safe. There are so few of us left."

"Are you certain that is all that it is? I know you. You are never satisfied, or so you have said on many occasions in the past. Perhaps you now feel that your influence over me is on the wane? Perhaps you feel that my child might prove more tractable? Is that not what you desire? More power? More influence? All things ordered according to your will?"

"No, it is Korfax that we fear. Think! Once you have a child you will no longer need him. We agree with you that he should win this war for you, but once you are victorious, then you can dispose of him. All tools outlive their usefulness. Is this not what you believe?"

There was another pause.

"I will not be hobbled by a child," Doagnis said finally. "I will rule for as long as I see fit and I will endure no rival, be they of my own flesh or no! No other will stand above me. As for Korfax, once the Iabeiorith are victorious, once the world bows down before me, then we shall see what we shall see."

"But what of us?"

"You desire your safety, I understand that. You fear Korfax and the dark sword, but how can the dark sword harm you if the hand that wields it remains in ignorance? Has my line not kept you safe through all the dark times? Have I not kept you secret all these years? You have guided me well in the past, and I am not unmindful, but take care how you step beyond my bounds. Leave Korfax to me."

"So be it, but do not forget our warning either! Call always upon the lesser, lest the greater command more than you."

The humped thing moved off. Korfax watched it go. There were small tunnels in one of the rock faces. The humped thing glided up to one of them and then vanished inside. Its light went with it.

Korfax withdrew from the shew-stone and sat for a moment, filled to the brim with deepest cold. Then he shook himself and stood up, before making his invisible way back to the chambers of Doagnis. There he replaced the shew-stone, putting it back exactly where he had found it, before retracing his steps, all the while holding himself still and not daring to think what it was he had just witnessed.

Back once more in his own chambers he sat quietly and let what he had seen tumble through his mind. He thought of the name he had heard. Arzulg. He knew it, knew it well, for he had read of it in the histories. It was a name from the past, a terrible name from the time of Nalvahgey and the Black War. Arzulg had been the ruler of the Agedobor.

The Agedobor! They still lived? He felt dark. How many had survived? A conversation came back to him from long ago and on the other side of the world, when he had sat with his former master, Ponodol, and discussed a troubling tale from the ancient wars.

'The Agedobor appeared like a sudden plague whilst Nalvahgey was still young. Some say they were a curse from The Creator, planted as a torment to the wicked. They killed, they despoiled, they conquered and they ruled. They were a terrible breed. Every single one of them had the power of summoning within it as if born to it, and only the best of the Argedith could ever match them. They possessed an undying hatred for all that went on two legs, and woe betide any that they conquered, for all that fell under their dominion received only torment and death in return. They were beaten back, of course, beaten back to the dark places, to caves and pits that knew no light. For long years they ruled the darkness into which they had been driven, a terror to all that chanced upon them, until the Wars of Unification finally swept such wreckage from the land. So the forces of Karmaraa vanquished them at last and they passed from the world, falling back into the darkness from whence they came. Nalvahgey gave them their name, the Agedobor, for that is how she saw them, but what they called themselves was never discovered. Only one name has come to us out of the dark years, that of Arzulg, their ruler, but nothing more than that.'

The Agedobor! He shuddered. How old they must be, how so very old. Thousands of years in the darkness, full of hatred and desire. He could not imagine it, the long slow fall of ages. And here they were again, as vile as the tales made them, shapeless horrors under cloaks of slime.

He thought of Doagnis and shook, not with fear, but with rage. Was this a betrayal? That is what it felt like. Words tumbled through his awareness:

'I have summoned him. He is mine and he does my bidding.'

'I will rule for as long as I see fit and I will endure no rival, be they of my own flesh or no! No other will stand above me.'

Images from a dream returned to him, a dark dream where he caressed her and strangled her, both at the same time, killing her even as he loved her.

He felt his hands grip his chair. He felt the chair break. He stood up, dropping the pieces to the floor. He wanted to scream, to roar, to tear everything apart in fury, but he did not. There was more – other words, things said that gave him pause.

'And do you love him?'

'Yes!'

Was that true? Something inside told him that it was. Something else denied it. He stood upon the blade once more, the bitter apex, but he dare not surrender to it. Instead there was still much to consider, much to weigh in the balance. It was not as simple as betrayal. This alliance of hers, handed down through the years, had not been started by her. It was something she had inherited, something she had grown up with, an alliance of likenesses, hatred matched with hatred. She hated the west and the Agedobor hated everything.

No doubt one of her line had begun it long ago, an alliance of convenience, knowledge for protection. No doubt the Agedobor were grateful, thankful for their survival, but what now?

'Get yourself with child. Then you will no longer need him.'

It was clear the Agedobor wanted rid of him, but he had the answer to that at least. He knew what they feared – his sword. Should he seek them out and assuage his wrath? Another voice intruded.

'I will not be hobbled by a child. I will rule for as long as I see fit and I will endure no rival, be they of my own flesh or no! No other will stand above me. As for Korfax, once the Iabeiorith are victorious, once the world bows down before me, then we shall see what we shall see.'

Where was her love for him now? She had declared herself for him, hadn't she? Or was she simply telling the Agedobor what they wanted to hear?

In the darkness, in his black places, he suddenly saw how it was. He was Sondehna, whose god was wrath and anger; she was Soivar, whose goddess was betrayal! But she feared that part of her, didn't she?

It was at that moment that he felt her return. She went straight to her chambers. She was alone. No doubt she had much to think about. He suddenly had the urge to go to her and pull everything that he could from her mind – her thoughts, her memories, her secrets. He almost made to leave, but then he stopped as another thought came to him. He went cold.

Like a blinding light it dominated him. She was the daughter of Dialyas. Of course! Now he understood what he should do. She played the same game as her father, pulling all the strings to make the puppets dance. So be it. He would match her, but this time he would not let her go as he had Dialyas. This time he would take the game to its bitter end. Then let true purposes be revealed.

The morning found him in the hills, his honour guard beside him. He had risen early so that he could watch the unfolding siege.

He stared downwards, watching with barely concealed fury as the innumerable enemy surged across the plain. His eyes burned and his hands itched. He so longed to unleash his weaponry. No doubt the others thought he was preparing himself for the battle yet to come, but they did not see the fury inside. He no longer saw the Agdoain below him; instead, he saw her, her face, her terror as he fell upon her with his sword.

He held himself still and let his fury build, stirring the crucible slowly, carefully building it up to boiling point. Battle would come soon, and it would be good to let his rage speak at last.

Aodagaa came to stand beside him. No word was spoken and both watched the unfolding siege in utter silence.

The Agdoain broke against the walls of Othil Admaq like waves, falling and rising, grey lightning erupting from their crests to wreak havoc upon the walls above. Flames and storms thundered back against the grey, and their collective might was almost always enough to hold back much of each attack, but occasionally the grey was victorious, and so the defences weakened a little more.

There were the wrecks of sky ships out on the plain, lying together or singly. Some had even crashed into the city, for there were broken towers and the rising of smoke.

Agdoain siege towers lay against walls, clasped to the stone as though to leech away its very substance. The Agdoain ever swarmed up their sides, only to be beaten back by a host of swords, but it could not last. Othil Admaq was doomed.

Aodagaa stared down at the seething hordes, clearly unsettled by the sheer number of them.

"We are to fight that?" he asked, almost a whisper.

Korfax smiled coldly but did not turn around. His gaze was consumed entirely by the battle below.

"Do not be swayed by the size of the task," he said. "I assure you, they will fall before us like the hollow things that they are. They will neither see us nor comprehend us. Though they outnumber us a hundred to one, a thousand even, we will sweep through them like a fire."

Korfax paused before turning around at last.

"So have no fear. You will understand soon enough."

He reached out and clasped Aodagaa by the shoulder.

"Ready our forces and wait. The time is almost upon us. I go to consult one last time with Doagnis. When I return, I will have one more thing to say to you. You, all of you, are about to learn a mighty secret."

Then he turned and strode off, without waiting for a reply, and Aodagaa watched him go, wondering what was coming next.

Doagnis watched the approach of Korfax and felt a shiver of fear quite unlike any she had ever felt before. She stilled it as best as she could, hiding it away deep inside where no other would see it, but now she felt the words of Arzulg rise up instead to echo in her mind:

'There is a saying amongst us, one you know very well. Call always upon the lesser, lest the greater command more than you. You have called upon Korfax and bound him to you. But what if he should command more than you?'

The others bowed before him as he approached, for they could do nothing else. He had become the very image of imperial wrath, cold and furious and unstoppable. Spectral vapours filled the air about him, coiling vapours that drifted at the edges of sight or at the edges of the mind. He had summoned up his full power at last, and both his armour and his great sword danced to the rhythm of his thought. She could feel the rage and the anger burning in the air about him, the desire to spill blood, to slaughter the foe. She felt utterly daunted by the sight.

But when he finally stood before her, he bowed to her. And though he did not smile, his voice was gentle enough.

"We are ready," he said. "All you need do is watch. You will not need to aid us with a summoning. We will fall upon them as the very wrath of the Creator. You will see."

Doagnis was a moment answering. She looked up at Korfax and saw how he simmered, the boiling fire caged behind his eyes. But it was a cold fire. Woe betide any that dared cross him in this hour. Seeing him like this, standing in his presence, she could truly believe at last that he was of the line of Sondehna.

After a long moment she eventually found her voice and took pride at how steady it sounded.

"It is good to see you so confident," she said, "but I will stand watch, even so. I have lived by my caution all these long years past, and I see no reason not to continue to do so, even now."

"As it was then," he said, "so it is once more."

He bowed again and then left her presence with a decisive swirl of his great black cloak. She wondered what he had meant.

She felt fear. She had never seen him like this, so absolute, so elemental, so cold. It was as though he had crushed himself down to a single point and a single purpose – to defeat his enemies, to utterly destroy them, to spill their blood upon his altar and to remove them utterly from the world. But would that assuage the fire in his heart? Would that ever be enough now, for power fed upon power, and in the end it fed only upon itself.

Korfax went to the guards that kept Odoiar. He bent over the prisoner and reached inside his head, looking long and hard. Doagnis had been true to her word. Only vague impressions remained, and all useful intelligence regarding the Haelok Aldaria was gone. The tale of tears still remained, of course, but now Korfax added a message to it, a message for one person only. Odoiar looked blearily upwards as Korfax withdrew.

"I have been ill used," he said.

"Then you know how I felt when I was under your hand," Korfax replied.

He turned to the guards and handed a kamliadar to one of them.

"You have your orders," he said. They bowed.

He went to the stables, to Enastul, his great black steed, and Enastul, sensing his master's mood, neighed until the stables shook with the sound.

"Enough!" Korfax commanded. "Now is not the time. Save yourself for the battle ahead."

But Enastul tossed back his head and his great black horn caught the light, brilliant gleams flickering upon the darkness. Korfax held up his hand.

"It will be time soon enough. We will ride out, you and I," he promised.

Enastul neighed again, rearing up, hooves striking the air.

Korfax relented at last.

"And you were ever wilful," he said. "So be it, then. Let the time be now. Let battle commence."

And Enastul, having got his way, subsided. Korfax mounted, a shadow upon a shadow. Then the horned darkness erupted from the stables, a darkness armed with a great black sword.

Korfax rode up and his honour guard rode with him, their eyes now filled with astonished wonder and fearful joy. Who was this mighty lord they followed now? Was this truly Korfax, or was this some greater shadow from out of the past? Their fear and awe held them all enthralled.

Korfax drew up before the Haelok Aldaria and cast an imperious glance along the lines. It was time.

"Before you lies the uncounted foe," he said, voice and mind reaching out to touch them all. "I know your uncertainty, I feel the doubt within you. You have never been tested in a battle such as this. But do not fear, not now, for I, too, have seen such a day. This, for you, will be as a great forging. Your power, your skill, will be yours to finally know. And when you see what is in you, and what you can do, your fear will vanish."

He paused, judging them, listening to them as they listened to him.

"There is only one thing more to tell you, for now is the moment of revealing, when you finally understand all that has been wrought in your name and in the name of our people. I wish you to know this. I wish you to understand who it is that leads you out into battle at last."

He paused again. They were waiting upon his words now. They knew he was about to reveal something, something of might and power that would lift them high. He let the expectation rise and took them upon the crest, showing them his thought even as his voice rang out.

"Many have wondered where my Qorihna came from. Many have wondered who I am to hold such power, to know the things that I know and do the things that I do. Now I will reveal to you the answer, for the armour that I wear once belonged to Sondehna himself, and the sword that I wield was once his sword, the first and the only. And who could I be to wield such power but the heir of Sondehna himself. I am that one. From father to son, in line unbroken, I am that one. For a great secret has been kept all these long ages past, a great secret that I reveal to you only now. For I am your Haelok. I am no longer of the Farenith, for that house was born of chance and ignorance. I declare myself at last. I am Sondehna's heir of the house of the Mikaolazith, and I am your prince."

They all felt it then, all of them, for Korfax opened his mind to each and every one of them and they felt the utter truth of it even as his thought unfurled within like a dark and swelling blossom, revealing all that had lain hidden.

The chieftains stared at him in wonder. All stared at him in wonder. Then his guard slowly turned their steeds about and bade them bow as they bowed themselves, and it rippled outwards, a great falling, steed and rider both, all bowing as the truth sank in. Korfax was the heir to Sondehna? Korfax was of the Mikaolazith? It was the darkest of revelations, and yet it was the mightiest. Who now could doubt victory? Who now would doubt him?

Aodagaa stood again and came before him, his eyes filled with tears.

"Now I understand," he said. "You are come back to us. Our victory is complete. The west has lost. Karmaraa failed."

Korfax bowed his head in return.

"Karmaraa failed," he repeated.

The other chieftains did the same, tears of wonder, eyes alight. There were roars and cheers from the assembled army. Korfax looked at them all.

"It is done," he said.

Then he drew his great black sword and held it above him. Black fire erupted from its tip.

"To battle!" he cried. "Let the foe know the fire of our hearts!"

And they took up his cry, that ancient cry, the battle cry of the Haelok Aldaria, and they raised up their blades and hurled fire into the sky.

"Let the foe know the fire of our hearts!" they cried with a single voice. Then they poured forth, Korfax at their head, black flames, dark flames, burning the air about them, before they faded away into shadow and rumour and so passed into battle.

Ralir rode the walls of Othil Admaq and watched as the powers about him ebbed and flowed like an uncertain tide. It was Othil Zilodar all over again, but with a terrible difference. This was his home that was under threat.

It was decided that they should use the remaining sky ships to drop qasadar upon the advancing horde, but then the Agdoain had answered with sky ships of their own, no doubt a remnant of the great fleet lost at Emethgis Vaniad. So they had crashed their sky ships into those of the city's, and brought them all down. It was an obvious play and one that should have been thought of, but now it was too late and there were no more sky ships left.

So they had launched qasadar from the walls, many times many, destroying the foe in uncounted numbers, but still the Agdoain came, as innumerable as the sands they had crossed.

When at last there were no more qasadar, then the battle began in earnest, siege towers advancing, vines climbing, fires burning and arrows flying. Chaos!

It was in a brief lull as a new wave of enemy advanced that one of his aides came up to him and bowed.

"What is it?" he asked.

"It is Geyadril Vatamath, Nor-Tabaud," offered the other.

Ralir glanced over the aide's shoulder and saw many riders approaching. Vatamath was leading them and, even from this distance, Ralir could tell that Vatamath was in a darker mood than usual. Ralir waited with ill-concealed distaste. He had never liked Vatamath, not since he had first met him. Humourless and demanding, prideful and arrogant, he was all the things Ralir despised. But Ralir kept his dislike to himself, as he kept a great many other things, hiding behind his humour and his rank and laughing as though nothing mattered at all.

Vatamath drew up before him and Ralir smiled his best smile back.

"So, Geyadril, and here you are. What wonderful news do you have to give me now? Has someone discovered a hitherto unnoticed horde of qasadar? Does our foe flee in confusion? Are we victorious at last?"

Vatamath scowled. Though he had only known Ralir since the fall of Emethgis Vaniad, he still did not know how to take him. It was as though Ralir took a positive delight in infuriating others at the expense of himself. Vatamath had been told there was a reason for this, and that he should forbear, but he could not stop himself from grinding his teeth together whenever he and Ralir crossed paths.

"I have nothing so good to tell you, Nor-Tabaud," he said. "Our forces are too evenly matched. We are caught as Othil Zilodar was. The enemy have far greater numbers than we do, and for every two of them that we kill, they in turn kill one of us. As ever, we find ourselves duelling with a mirror. Though we take a tower down, another grows in its place. The Geyadith are exhausted, the Branith are exhausted and soon the inexhaustible enemy will breach our defences and swarm over our walls. Then the city will be lost."

Ralir smiled without humour.

"Well then, I am glad that I drank the last of the Ertil Pelarr last night. At least if I die now I will not have time enough left to mourn its passing. Not unless some saviour comes to our aid, that is."

Vatamath kept his peace only by the greatest of efforts. How Ralir loved to goad. And how barbed were his comments. This one, though, was at least understandable. Ralir had fought during the first defence of Othil Zilodar. It was hard not to draw comparisons. Vatamath sighed and let his anger lessen a little.

"I am pleased to find you in such high spirits, Nor-Tabaud," he said. "I am sure you are a comfort to all that follow in your wake."

Ralir let his smile fade away completely.

"No, Vatamath," he replied, "I do not think you are pleased at all. I think you are anything but."

Vatamath did not change his expression one whit.

"And do not think that I misunderstand either."

Ralir laughed grimly.

"Of course you understand. That was my intent. Like all war masters I wish for advantage. So I wish that my old friend was beside me again. At least, by his side, I never suffered defeat."

"Then you will wish in vain. He is dead, drowned in the boiling sea, lost in the wreckage of Othil Ekrin."

Ralir smiled in mock sadness.

"You know, I have been hearing so many tales of his death lately that I have come to disbelieve them all. Onehson said that he slew him, but then Korfax is seen in Emethgis Vaniad. Two of the Balt Kaalith see him ride out the flood that destroyed Thilzin Jerris, then he turns up in Othil Ekrin. So what are we to believe now? That he is supposed to have drowned in the boiling sea at the foot of the Vasasan? The only thing I know for certain is that my old friend has led the world a merry dance these last few years. If we survive this siege, I hope to live long enough to be there when he stands up behind you all and laughs."

Vatamath scowled. As Nor-Tabaud of Othil Admaq, and as a Napei of the Nazad Esiask, Ralir was responsible for the entire defence. He did not shirk his duty, but deep inside the seed of cowardice had been sown, and who knew when it might rise up again to claim him.

All knew it, many professed to understand it, but Vatamath hated it. Nor could he change what was. He had to accept it as he accepted everything else. One could not change what was.

Ralir watched Vatamath out of the corner of his eyes. In the past few seasons he had come to understand his world and its occupants all too well. He could see Vatamath's thoughts as though they were written upon his face. And it was the same with all the others, even his father.

Though they treated him fairly, though they waited upon his word, they did not fully trust him. He did not blame them. He was the one that had run. He was the one that had been unable to face his fear.

He felt a momentary despair, a shadow of his old nightmare rising up to haunt him again. He thrust it all back down inside. He had no use for despair and visions of horror, not now, not ever again. He had a task to perform, and perform it he would.

Another was riding towards him along the wall road, a Branvath from one of the eastern watchtowers by the look of his insignia.

"Nor-Tabaud," he bowed after dismounting.

"What is it?" Ralir waved his hand impatiently.

"Nor-Tabaud, you should come and see."

"See what?" Ralir demanded. He suddenly felt irritable and intolerant. He was tired of second-guessing others. Let them speak plainly for a change. But the Branvath was not paying attention. There was a look on his face, a look of disbelief and wonder.

"Nor-Tabaud," he gasped, "it is easier if you just come and see it for yourself. I cannot – I will not – describe it."

Ralir bit back a rebuke even as he caught sight of the Branvath's suppressed excitement, bubbling up inside him and dancing in his eyes like a sudden and unsung spring. Ralir looked at the surging waters and chose to see hope in them. Something had happened, something marvellous, so he dared to dream of miracles again.

He looked about him. No one else had observed the transition. He smiled to himself for a moment before gesturing roughly to the Branvath, who turned his steed smartly about and all but galloped back the way he had come. Then Vatamath leaned over, pitching his voice so that only Ralir could hear his words.

"You do not fool me," he said.

Ralir merely laughed in response.

"And why would I even try to?" he asked, before spurring his mount to follow that of the Branvath.

Vatamath followed afterwards, his eyes full of warnings, and the honour guard fell in behind them both and thundered along the wall road in their wake.

Further along the east wall the Branvath reigned in his ormn and pointed beyond the city. Ralir and Vatamath stopped beside him and looked out over the smoke of battle.

For a moment Ralir saw nothing. Why had he been summoned here? He looked this way and that, quartering the seething chaos, and he was about to question the Branvath when he saw it at last. The Branvath had been correct. Words were inadequate. The unbelievable was happening. The Agdoain were retreating.

They were being destroyed. All along the eastern wall it was happening, like a wave of surrender. The Agdoain were falling back, falling away from the walls of the city itself, whilst the defenders put up their weapons in turn and stared down in disbelief. The Agdoain had turned their backs upon Othil Admaq in a vain attempt to counter the bizarre threat that had suddenly taken them from behind. Something was eating its way through their eastern flanks.

A great shadow boiled to the east, a wall like a vague and uncertain storm that rippled at the very edges of sight. Inside the storm there was nothing except, perhaps, a vague confusion of dimly perceived forms. Like a phantom fire it flickered, yet where it went it licked the land clean of the foe. Behind it, far out beyond the heaving shadow, the distances stretched, ominously empty of anything that lived.

As the shadow came closer it became clear that something else preceded it. To the fore it strode, a great hole of air, flexing and shifting, its borders ever changing. At its edges the Agdoain burned, their bodies briefly writhing as dark flames undid them, but nothing crossed its empty boundaries, and its unsighted centre remained inviolate.

The invisible power moved on, the greater shadow behind it, cutting a great swath through the massed ranks of the Agdoain. Ageyad reared up and spat their grey energies into the shadow, but they too were swallowed whole. A siege tower was caught upon its edges, writhing as dark fire undid it, collapsing down in pieces that burned up even before they touched the ground. Nothing stood in its way, and slowly, inexorably, the infinite sea of the foe was reduced to ash.

Ralir turned to Vatamath and pointed at the flickering shadow.

"What is that?" he said. "What comes to our aid?"

"I have never seen the like before, ever," said Vatamath.

No one spoke again; instead, they all waited and watched, spellbound, as the siege of Othil Admaq was lifted. The Agdoain retreated and retreated again, a squalling mass of baying flesh, grey mouths, grey bodies, grey blades, a tumult of screams. But all were unequal to the fearsome and silent shadow.

Two rode along the wall, flanked by an escort. Ralir recognised them both – Urendril Nimagrah and Uren Payoan. Nimagrah was much like Vatamath, proud, humourless and demanding, but Payoan was quiet and thoughtful. She was the real power here. She was the one that had visions. Vatamath turned to Nimagrah.

"What is it? Why are you here?"

Nimagrah ignored him. She had eyes only for Ralir.

"Nor-Tabaud, you must hear this. Payoan has been granted a glimpse of what aids us. She knows what that shadow is!"

Ralir turned to Payoan and she bowed her head. Then she pointed at the empty spaces and heaving shadows that continued to swallow the Agdoain hordes beyond the wall.

"I saw," she said. "It was only a glimpse, but there are Ell down there, an army of Ell, and a power is with them that I have never seen before. They are surrounded by forces that I cannot penetrate. Instead all I see are glimpses, of skins like shadows, hiding and shielding, of great black limbs that ripple with strange energies, for ever changing shape as they cut the enemy down and consume them in dark fires. The Agdoain fall to ash before them."

Ralir stared at her. That was not what he had been expecting at all.

"I don't understand!" he said. "Powers that cannot be seen? Coiling limbs that cut down the foe?"

Vatamath, though, understood all too well, and he felt his world crumble about him. An army of Ell hidden by shadows? Weapons that changed their shape? Powers that could not be named? By the Creator! He saw, in his mind's eye, a terror from the blackest histories he had never imagined he would ever hear of again, not even in his worst nightmares.

The look of dawning horror on Vatamath's face alerted all the others. Ralir turned upon him and took him by the shoulders.

"Do you understand this?" he asked. "Do you know what this is?"

Vatamath looked at Ralir as though appalled.

"I did not know what it was before, but I do so now," he said. "That description lies in the archives of the Dar Kaadarith."

He gestured at the dim shadow.

"It seems that your miracle has come at last."

"And what do you mean by that?" Ralir said.

"Have you never studied the histories?"

Vatamath turned to Nimagrah.

"Urendril, have you seen this also?"

"No!" she said. "This vision belongs to Payoan alone."

"But you have guessed?"

"I have a fear," she said.

Vatamath looked away, beyond the wall. His voice was chillingly remote when he answered.

"Payoan describes Qahmor and Qorihna. She speaks of the profane, of monstrous weapons not seen since the ending of the Wars of Unification. You are, all of you, witness to the rebirth of the Haelok Aldaria. This is the work of Doagnis. That we should live to see such days!"

No one answered. Instead they turned to watch the shadow in uneasy silence as the siege of Othil Admaq ended and the Agdoain were forced to retreat ever further before the relentless assault of the oncoming darkness. Behind the retreating masses, the bodies of the Agdoain, whether warrior, beast or Ageyad, had all but vanished. Even the last of the towers had crumbled, mighty as they were. Finally the shadows were gone, leaving behind nothing at all of the foe except a great sea of ash, countless swirling piles of ash that smoked gently in the fitful breeze.

For a long while all was still. Then something shivered in the midst of the ash heaps and disjointed shapes emerged as if pulling their substance out of the very air itself. Many stared, not quite believing their eyes, as three steeds appeared with three riders. Two were utterly black – black steeds and black armour – while the third was dressed simply and looked to be bound about by ropes.

For a moment they remained, all three, and then the black riders turned their steeds about and rode away, disappearing, vanishing away like so much mist. Now there was only one.

The single rider came slowly towards the wall. Ralir signalled that he should be met and taken inside. With all due dispatch, this was done. Ralir went to meet the rider and find out what this was all about. The others, Vatamath and Nimagrah, followed.

Down by the great gates he found the rider being tended to by a healer. She turned when he arrived.

"Nor-Tabaud," she said, bowing her head. "He has been drugged, but otherwise he seems in good health."

"What drug?" Ralir asked.

"I do not know," she said. "His thoughts are in disarray. I think certain of his memories have been removed."

Ralir looked up.

"Is that possible?"

The healer made the gesture of uncertainty.

"I know of at least one herbal preparation that can induce forgetfulness. Perhaps that is what has happened here."

"Who is he?" Ralir asked.

The rider looked up. He was clearly having trouble focusing his eyes.

"I need to speak to Ralir," he said.

"I am Ralir. Who are you?"

"Odoiar," came the reply. Ralir frowned.

"I remember you," he said. "You are of the Balt Kaalith."

"I have a message for you," Odoiar said, "and for you alone. No one else must know it."

He drew out a kamliadar and gave it to Ralir.

"I was told to tell you to listen to it alone. Then you will understand."

He sank back and closed his eyes.

"So tired," he whispered. "So tired."

Ralir stood up and looked at the kamliadar. He did not need to ask whose voice was within the stone, he was already certain.

Doagnis stood before her shew-stone and waited. Victory was theirs, swift and all-encompassing. How wonderful it was. She felt the fire inside, that wonderful fire of success. What an ecstasy it was. She looked in her stone and watched as the riders arrived at the camp, and she saw how their eyes glowed. Yes, she told herself, that was exactly how she felt. Exultant. It would all work, all of it. Bless Korfax, bless him. He had given her the greatest gift of all – assured dominion. With this power they would encompass the world. She prepared to go out, to see Korfax, to thank him for this marvel.

She touched her stone and closed it. She stood up and went to the door of the tent, only to find Teodunad waiting for her, his face a picture of dismay.

"Mistress, you did not tell me," he accused.

"Tell you what?"

"About Korfax. He is the Haelok! He is born of the line of Sondehna! Did you know this?"

Doagnis went dead inside. Teodunad took her silence as his answer.

"You knew this and you did not tell me?" Teodunad said again. She saw fear on his face, utter dread.

She sent him away with a flick of her hand and waited for the approach of Korfax. All the chieftains were there, as was a huge crowd, all following and cheering. Others were arriving, their faces enraptured. The news had gone everywhere. Soon she was an island of dismay in a sea of jubilation.

Korfax arrived before her, smiling down. Then he dismounted and everyone around her, all of them, dropped to their knees and bowed their heads. She stared at them all and then back at Korfax. There was no victory for her after all. She had lost everything. Her people were no longer hers, they were his. With one simple stroke he had stripped her bare.

"Shall I bow also?" she asked, barely able to contain herself. He came to her side and took her by her hands, looking deep into her eyes.

"I think now is the time for you and I to talk," he said.

The coldness she had seen before was still there. Battle had not assuaged it. It was almost as if he was confronting her for the very first time. Something had changed between them, something fundamental. It was not simply that he had declared himself; it was something else, something far more dire.

She would have removed her hands from his, but she could not. He held her fast and she could not compete with his strength. He kept his smile, but his grip tightened, a warning perhaps, before he turned to the others.

"We have a victory," he said. "Let there be celebrations. All of you rejoice. The Iabeiorith have come into their own once more."

The crowd rose to their feet cheering. Korfax turned to Aodagaa.

"See to it," he ordered. "See that all feast well this night. Doagnis and I will celebrate in private. I know that Doagnis and I should be there with you, but let this night be yours instead. To you the victory. To you the joy."

Aodagaa bowed, as did all the others.

He led her inside and she could not resist him. Once inside he released her and folded his arms. She turned away, doing her best to maintain at least some illusion of control.

"I told you that I did not want this," she said.

"And I heard you," he replied. "But I have said nothing about you, I have only revealed myself."

"And taken everything away from me," she hissed.

"No, I haven't done that, either," he said. "Besides, authority is given, not taken."

She looked at him over her shoulder. He remained where he was, arms folded, eyes cold.

"When were you going to tell me about the Agedobor?" he asked.

A fit of trembling coursed through her and it took all of her self-control to suppress it. He knew! So that was it. But how?

"You followed me," she accused.

"No!" he replied.

"You had me followed, then."

"No!"

She turned about. She was frightened now. That meant he had used sorcery in some fashion, and she had not seen or felt it. She looked at him. He still had not moved, but the air about him was haunted and uneasy. His power was there within him, unforgiving, judgemental and ready to act. She read the signs. He believed that she had betrayed him. Of all the crimes she might commit, he considered betrayal the worst.

"Then how?" she asked. "How did you know?"

"You really should have listened to me when I told you to get rid of Teodunad. If it had not been for his continued presence, I would not have been suspicious."

"What has Teodunad to do with this?"

"Do you know why I spied on you?" he asked. "I was told that you had gone off with Ronoar and that Teodunad had accompanied you. You have gone off with Ronoar before, but never with Teodunad. So why, I wondered, would you take Teodunad with you now?"

He paused.

"Do you know what I thought? I thought that you wanted to be with him despite what you told me. Imagine my surprise when I discovered the truth."

"You still have not told me how," she said.

He gestured to the side, pointing at her shew-stone. She understood the implication well enough. If he could do that, then nothing could be hidden from him.

"Then you know that I was not with him," she said.

"Of course, but he is no longer the problem."

She held herself still. Where was Korfax going now?

"I heard everything that was said," he told her. "I heard what Arzulg said to you, and I heard your replies." His voice was quiet, distant and abstracted. "It seems you truly are a daughter of Soivar!" he said.

Doagnis began to back away. It was her nightmare, her dark nightmare come back to her. She felt the threat. Soivar was the betrayer of Sondehna. One word from Korfax and she would be revealed. It would be the undoing of her. She stared at him, watched as he became still and sharp, as though he had narrowed himself down to the point upon which his anger balanced. Something was coming, some terrible retribution, and she was powerless to prevent it.

He came at her without warning. He grabbed her by her shoulders, as he had before, but this time he lifted her bodily from the floor. She gasped at the pain as his fingers crushed her flesh, his claws digging deep. He stared down at her and she looked back up at him. She was utterly at his mercy. She shuddered. He looked cold now, cold and still, like the quiet air that heralds a storm. They looked at each other for long moments, him deadly still, magisterial almost, she remaining as submissive as she could. She hoped it would be enough, but then the storm broke about her.

Korfax all but tore her clothes from her body. She would have fallen, but now he grasped her by her hair, holding her up by one hand as he stripped her with the other.

"Korfax!" she cried, trying to fend him off. "Please!" she pleaded, her hands trying to hold him at bay, but he would not stop.

"But isn't this how it was meant to be?" he hissed at her.

She suddenly realised that she was naked. She felt more vulnerable now than she had ever felt before. Where would this go? What had she caused?

Korfax had become a thing of elements. As he tore away the last of her garments he lifted her up again like a great wind and threw her upon the bed. She had never felt such rage and strength before. She had, in the past, considered herself strong, but now Korfax taught her how mistaken she was. She was a piece of storm-tossed wreckage before him, and like a storm he would do with her what he willed.

"So you would not be hobbled with a child, would you?" he snarled into her face as he landed hard upon her, flattening her under his weight, even as the question flattened her like the fall of mountains. Now she understood. Here was where all her choices had led her at last.

Korfax had revealed his heritage precisely because the Agedobor had told her that he must not. Now he would give her a child precisely because she had not wanted one. He would punish her, and it was her fault. She had asked for this.

"Open to me!" he demanded, pressing himself against her.

She could not.

"Open to me!" he demanded again. "Remember Adavor?"

The coldness of the threat undid her. In her mind she saw a sharp knife tapping wantonly upon a breast plate.

"Open to me!"

Reluctant, sobbing, she uncurled her tail and he took her.

He took her with fire and with rage, and the rage of battle became the rage of betrayal. She would receive everything she was due, many times many, and he would give it to her. He took her again and again, on and on and on until she thought she would surely die indeed. He held her down, with his body and with his thought, and she was helpless before him. Pain and pleasure tore through her, and she was hurled between their competing peaks like a broken child. But come the moment when he entered her mind and forced her to conceive, forced her to call down the energies from above, there was such an explosion of ecstasy that she thought the river had her at last.

It was done. He rolled away from her and she lay quietly under the bruised air. He came close one more time, his mouth against her ear.

"Now you may kill me, daughter of Dialyas," he whispered, and her eyes went wide with terror. He turned away again and she glanced over. He was lying with his back to her, utterly vulnerable. She stared at his back, tears rolling down her cheeks, and then she turned away herself and curled up into a ball.

13

DESCENT

Fas-alkar Gil-thar-poljo
Luj-vanin Oded-log-pir
Mo-zod-kon Pra-hal-renjiz
Nis-nujith Z-devan-doal
Tel-risji Od-daz-oach-falz
Yo-odser Fen-a-dr-pan
Eof-odvon Dan-mn-a-ain

The dim light that presaged the rise of Rafarel cast its gentleness against the fabric of the tent but was powerless to pass inside. Doagnis dared a silent sob. Korfax had hurt her in ways she had never imagined he would.

There had once been a Korfax that would never have acted so, but she had changed that.

There had once been a Korfax that would have fallen upon his own blade rather than commit such violence, but she had changed that as well.

There had once been a Korfax that had been gentle and loving, but she had changed that also.

She had done this, ensnaring him in her purposes, beguiling him, leading him on and setting him on the road that she required, with no thought for his needs at all. For a while it had been a gentle and passionate dance between them, but then he had begun to rise, his power, his presence, making itself known, and the Agedobor had seen this. Then the betrayal began in earnest.

Yes she had hurt him, but he had hurt her also, and everything else in between. She thought again of that ecstasy, pain and pleasure indivisible, a single thing, the two suddenly made one.

Was this how it was meant to be? Surely it was not supposed to be like this, was it? Once, long ago, she had read what she could of the poets, of the joining, of love, but she had never found such pain, not in any of their words. Instead they had spoken of light, of a wonderful and never to be forgotten sight, of the coming together of souls, of a merging, of eternity itself. She grimaced. That was not what she had experienced at all. She clenched her teeth as she remembered the many verses. The dreamers who wrote such words were liars and deceivers, all of them. What did they know? What did they truly know? They knew nothing.

She looked over her shoulder and studied him. He was still asleep, his eyes closed, his breathing slow. He no longer had his back to her and she could see his face, still fierce even now. And looking at that face she found in herself a sense of pity at last. He had fallen because of her. He had once been one of the high, one of the mightiest, but she had never occupied such an estate. What must that have been like?

He had shown her something – a brief vision of purity, pure service and love, like a dream of the poetries of Kommah, but it was all an illusion, all of it, a fabrication raised up in contradiction of what really was. It defied the truth. The Bright Heavens were blind to such things. Only the Ell gave names to their perceptions, each different from the other, the separation of mortality. Gods were born otherwise, already knowing.

She lay back down again and sensation stirred within her. She felt again the deep pain of their union and that strange desire that wanted it to happen again, and again, and again.

She rolled away from him, closing her eyes and squeezing out the tears to ease the burning. Why did life have to be so cruel? Where was the comfort she deserved? Was it gone beyond recall? Things might have been very different had his needs not clashed with hers.

And that had become the dividing line. They had crossed each other and were now reaping the harvest. Only she had received the worst of it. She hated the revealed equation. The feminine had always been subjugated by the masculine. They were supposed to be equal, two principles coeval, but one had always been more equal than the other. Only princes ruled. The world was as it ever had been, a thing unbalanced.

Korfax pondered as he lay still. He could feel her wakefulness, her thoughts turning this way and that, a tumble that rolled through the air above them both. He remained where he was, watching and waiting, feigning slumber.

It had all happened exactly as he had imagined it, except that he had not killed her at the last, but had, instead, invited her to kill him. The game was played out, the betrayal seen and the shade of his dark ancestor appeased. But what of her? Where would it go from here?

He waited until the requisite moment and then sat up, stretching himself in apparent contempt, before staring over his shoulder at her curled back in studied disdain.

"Well!" he said at last, "I see that you have spared me. You are not a true daughter of Soivar after all, it seems."

Doagnis seemed to start, huddling further into herself, but then she turned her head to look back at him. He stared at her and could not mistake the pain in her eyes or the stain of tears upon her cheeks. Part of him was revolted by what he saw, not her as she was, but as the consequences of his actions. He did not look away, though. It was too late for contrition. What was done was done indeed.

Doagnis swallowed at last and looked down. Under his hot gaze she felt curiously submissive. What had been awakened here? What was this? Why did she suddenly want it all to happen again?

"You did not warn me that you could be so fierce," she said.

He snarled, a brief bearing of teeth.

"Nor did you tell me that you took the role of Soivar quite so seriously."

"I did not want to kill you. I never did."

"Not true. You only stopped trying to kill me when you found out who I was. Then you became something else."

She sat up but remained curled into a ball, hiding herself from him.

"Soivar the betrayer," she whispered.

"Except that the story is untrue. We both know what really happened. Soivar's children did not burn with her upon her pyre. Her betrayal was of an entirely different kind."

"It was still a betrayal. Now others will ask what really happened, and the truth will come out. I still cannot reveal myself."

"Trapped by your own desires!" he mused. "Fearing her legacy, you were doomed to repeat it. You should have faced it from the very beginning, and then none of this would have happened."

"But what do we say to the others? I am with child."

"That is simple. We tell them that the succession is secured. They will be happy. You will be happy. Even the Agedobor will be happy, if they are capable of such a thing."

"And what of me?" she asked.

"Consider yourself mine!" he told her. "You shall be my 'mighty light and burning flame of comfort'. You are a power for always and always, as you ever wanted to be. As you have given, so you have received."

Korfax raised himself and strode out of the tent. The camp was astir. Ronoar came forward. There was fear.

"Haelok," he bowed carefully.

"Ronoar," Korfax announced with forced joviality. "Good news. Your mistress and I have joined. She is with child. The line of the Mikaolazith continues."

Ronoar could not help it. He stared in utter astonishment. Then Korfax leaned closer and set his words so that only Ronoar would hear them.

"I know about the Agedobor," he said. "I know all about her betrayal. See that your deeds reflect your words from this moment on, or you will know my wrath. Remember the fate of Adraman!"

Korfax walked off, and Ronoar stared after him in terror.

Those that met him bowed low, smiling and happy that their Haelok was come again. He talked with some, small things, the doings of the day, the pride of victory, desires for a better world.

He came upon one of the chieftains, Ambriol, who bowed to him and offered undying fealty once more.

"There is no need for that," Korfax said, "you have already proven yourself a true son of the Iabeiorith. You were mighty in battle."

Ambriol smiled.

"It is the joy, my Haelok. We are where we should be once more, and we have you to thank for it."

Korfax gestured behind him.

"Doagnis also had much to do with it."

"But you are the Haelok," he answered. "To you the glory. You are our dark centre. We are whole once more."

Korfax looked down for a moment, gathering his thoughts.

"I would like there to be a meeting, a gathering," he said. "I have some things to tell you and a duty to perform. I want Teodunad there also."

Ambriol bowed.

"I will see to it, my Haelok. When shall it be?"

"Within the hour."

Korfax moved on and finally found the one that he was looking for. Opakas. She was with the others of the Argedith. They all turned and bowed, their eyes glowing.

"Haelok!" they cried in unison.

He smiled and turned to Opakas.

"May I have a word?"

"Of course, my Haelok," she said.

She turned to the others, and they bowed again before leaving.

"So now you know," he said to her, and she came forward and knelt before him. She reached out and took his hand, revealing the ring he now wore. She kissed it tenderly and then looked up at him with adoration.

"We searched for so long," she said.

He smiled.

"So that is the answer," he said. "Your house was one of those that sought the male line."

He reached down and lifted her up.

"What happened?"

"We dwindled until only my house remained. They continued to look, hoping against hope that the line had survived. There were hints, suggestions, but then the Balt Kaalith came and the search was ended. A child was sent south, carrying memories, and that was the last of it."

Opakas held up a dark stone, faintly iridescent. Korfax looked at it. He could imagine what it contained.

"You already knew, didn't you?" he said.

She bowed her head.

"I guessed, my Haelok. You said things, things that only a child of the line would know."

"My Qorihna."

"Yes," she answered.

Now she looked fully at him.

"Why did you not say who you were at the very beginning?" she asked.

"There is a certain wisdom in gaining the trust of others first," he answered. "Let them see who you are, then tell them at the last."

"It is a good reason and wise, but it is not the truth."

He looked at her for a moment.

"It is the only truth that I desire now," he said.

Opakas reached out again and touched him gently.

"Beware, my Haelok, take care where you place your trust. I would not have it that I lose you again."

He smiled.

"I know. But believe me in this. That lesson has been well-learned."

At the turn of the hour they all came together, the seven chieftains along with many of the houses of the Iabeiorith. Doagnis stood beside Korfax, doing exactly as he had instructed her, smiling at all, acting with grace and reserve, keeping herself as she had always been. But inside she dwelt in a sea of fear, for she could feel him watching her, still looking for the slightest sign of betrayal.

Korfax came forward and drew her with him. She looked at the faces around her. How radiant they were. She could feel their love for him, and she now bathed in that reflection. Old regrets stirred. How much better it would have been if that love had been aimed at her alone.

Korfax spoke.

"We have a victory, as I knew that we would. For we are the Iabeiorith, the true inheritors of the north, mightiest ever to take up arms under the gaze of the Creator. Now begins the long road to take back what is ours."

He looked at them all, encompassing them with his gaze.

"I am truly blessed in your service. My life is yours. I am your will, a will of equal hearts made whole again and blessed."

He gestured to Doagnis.

"With victory comes the promise of the future. Doagnis and I are now made one, which is as it should be. Let her love of our cause be your fire, as her love is the cause of mine. Let her be repaid a thousand-fold, for in her I have placed all my hope."

They all turned to her and gave her their adoration. It felt wonderful, that surge of devotion, but neither had she missed what Korfax had said. In her he had placed his hope. Another warning. She would know fear all her life.

Korfax turned to Ambriol next.

"Bring him forth."

Ambriol bowed and gestured. Teodunad was led to the centre. There was silence. He would have spoken but Korfax held up his hand.

"You know who I am?"

"Yes, my Haelok."

"How will you serve?"

"With all my heart, my Haelok."

"See that you do."

Korfax walked towards Teodunad.

"I grant you this mercy so that all may know it. You can continue to serve the lady Doagnis, even though I know what you desire. But know this also. If you step where you should not, if you reach for that which is not yours to take, I will fall upon you with all the wrath of the abyss at my back, and I will bury you in eternal darkness. Be warned."

Korfax stood over him, staring into his eyes for a long moment, and then he gestured with his head.

"Leave my presence now, and remember your oaths."

Back inside the great tent Korfax gestured that she sit.

"Now you and I are joined in their eyes. They will come to love you rather than fear you. Do you see now how things could be?"

She sat quietly, utterly submissive now she was alone with him.

"What do you intend next?" she asked.

"I will meet with Ralir, alone," he said.

"You will go to him?"

"There is a secret place we both know. I have told him where and when."

"Where is it?"

"It will no longer be a secret if I tell everyone where it is!"

"You do not trust me?"

He looked at her. She took a deep breath and plunged on.

"You trust him, then?" she asked.

"With my life," he said.

"Why would you do this?"

"I would have an alliance."

"An alliance?"

"Yes, an alliance. He is my friend. Besides, if the Agdoain are to be swept from the world, then all possible force must be bent upon them. We still do not know their origin. We should remain cautious."

"But we are hated! Why would they ally with us?"

"Because we have just saved their city. Because they know who it is that commands. And because of that, and other things, they will think very hard about everything that we have to say to them. Remember, I have revealed the truth of Lontibir to them."

"I do not like it. No one else will like it, either."

"What did we just do?" he asked. "Did we not just save Othil Admaq? Why did we do it if not to prove to them our worth? I think you do not understand our people. But perhaps I should have done what you would have done. Perhaps I should have let the Agdoain destroy them, as the Agedobor suggested? That, after all, would have been so much easier!"

She shrank back from him.

"Is that the whip you will use upon me for the rest of my life?" she asked.

"You had the agreement with them, not I!" he said. "I but remind you of how we got here."

"They have helped me in the past. They have helped all my line."

"Only because it suited their purpose to do so. You know what they are, none better. The histories do not speak well of them, and for once I believe the histories speak truly. But now things are changed. They still need you, but you no longer need them."

"They are mighty. It would be wise not to anger them. They know things others do not."

"That could be said of many. Besides, there are only a few of them left..."

He paused and the air about him sharpened.

"... and I have a black sword."

She sat still, looking down.

"This is not what I wanted."

"So you have said. It is not what I wanted either, but this is how it is. There was one thing you said to Arzulg, one thing alone that preserved you. Arzulg asked you if you loved me. You answered yes. Remember that, as you remember everything else. Your choices have brought us here. This is your doing. So for the sake of that answer I now give you one chance to redeem yourself. Do not waste it."

By the old tower he waited. No others were there. Few knew of this meeting – only his father and his mother. No one else.

He leant against the stone and thought long and hard. He had no idea what he was going to say except to offer his gratitude. Korfax had saved his city.

But he was also worried. Korfax had embraced dark powers to do it. His friend had become the very thing he had once sworn to destroy.

Korfax appeared right in front of him astride a great black ormn. It was almost as if he had just stepped out of the air. Ralir stood up and stared in amazement.

"That was impressive," he said.

Korfax dismounted and smiled.

"One of the simpler skills I have learned," he said.

They looked at each other.

"You have changed," said Ralir.

"As have you," answered Korfax.

"I imagine there is a story that explains all of this?" Ralir said, gesturing at the dark armour.

"There is," said Korfax, "but we have no time for the particulars. I think the important thing here is that I now command a force that can destroy the Agdoain, and I am willing to ally myself with any that would see the Agdoain threat ended for once and for all."

"You know my answer to that," said Ralir, "but there are others here that will deny you. You have embraced sorcery."

Korfax took a long and deep breath.

"No doubt," he said. "And no doubt these are the very same fools who would cling to the blind dogmas of the past even as the sword of battle comes down upon their necks. Three great cities are lost. What will it take for them to realise that we are on the edge."

"Better to die untainted than live in damnation," Ralir quoted.

"And do you think that of me?" asked Korfax.

"You know I do not."

Korfax stepped forward and held out his arms. Ralir came to him and they embraced.

"Thank you for saving my city," Ralir said.

"I am just glad I was able to get here in time," Korfax returned.

They drew back from each other.

"I am not sure I like the darkness," Ralir said.

"It takes some getting used to," Korfax told him, "but it is necessary. It is Qahmor, and over my back, a Qorihna."

"Where did you get them?"

"My family kept them."

"Your family?"

"A secret long held."

Ralir looked long and hard at Korfax.

"Why?" he asked.

"Prophecy," Korfax said simply.

Ralir grimaced and Korfax smiled.

"Some things never change," Korfax said. "You never were one to trust in prophecy, or vision. But I have had a harder road, and I have had to trust in it. I would be a fool to deny its power now."

"So what is this secret? Can you tell me?"

"I fully intended to. You should know this. You should know who you are dealing with, after all. But I warn you. You will not like it."

"You are my friend. I trust you with my life."

"Thank you. You are a good friend."

Korfax looked meaningfully at Ralir.

"I am born of the line of Sondehna," he said.

Ralir stared. For a long moment he tried to understand what he had just been told.

"You cannot mean it!" he said at last.

"But I do," assured Korfax, "and it explains so much, if you think about it. Why have the Farenith been so strong for so long? Why did we bury ourselves away in the north, remaining humble? Why did my father refuse to become Geyadril? Why is it that I possess the Qorihna once wielded by Sondehna?"

Ralir looked appalled but said nothing.

"You react exactly as I imagined you would," Korfax told him. "But there is more. The line of the princes of the Iabeiorith has another surprise buried within it – Nalvahgey! She is the power behind the throne. Aolkar, son of Abhimed, was her child, though the histories do not say so."

Ralir turned away.

"This is too much. Too much!"

"Perhaps," said Korfax, "but that does not stop it from being true. I have proof undeniable. You can tell the Exentaser that I have the entire prophecies. I will give them a great gift."

Ralir looked back at him, clearly uncertain.

"They will say that you are trying to buy their allegiance," he said.

"Well, we are in the south, after all," Korfax answered, leaning back against the stone. "So who is first of the Exentaser now?" he asked.

"Kukenur is still there," said Ralir, "but she is in Othil Homtoh. Nimagrah is here."

"So they escaped Emethgis Vaniad, did they?"

"Yes, but few others managed it. Geyadril Chirizar is in Othil Homtoh and Geyadril Vatamath is in Othil Admaq. He came to the city after the attempt to regain Emethgis Vaniad. The Agdoain followed those that fled east."

"So they could gain the sky ships!"

"Yes. That was unexpected."

"Perhaps not," said Korfax. "The Agdoain were ever our mirror."

He paused for a moment, before glancing sidelong at Ralir.

"So what was the battle to take Emethgis Vaniad like?"

Ralir looked down.

"I cannot say. I was not there."

Korfax bowed his head.

"I am sorry," he said. "I should not have asked."

Ralir did not answer. Regret filled him and he did not speak for a while. Eventually, though, he stirred again.

"Korfax," he said, "do you know what the Agdoain are? Do you know how they come to be here?"

"No," Korfax said, "and no. All I can say is that they do not come from the Mahorelah. I do not know their origins or what it is that commands them. The grey void still remains a mystery to me."

He stared into the forest about the tower.

"Do you remember what Mathulaa said?" he asked.

"The heavings of Zonaa," Ralir answered. "I did not like the sound of it then and I like it even less now."

"But it is all that we have," Korfax said. "That and my visions of the void. I know no more. I ponder it often and yet still find nothing."

There was another pause.

"It has been a long road," said Ralir.

"And a hard one," Korfax answered.

"How did this happen?"

Korfax looked up, surprised.

"What do you mean?"

"How did we come to be here?" Ralir asked. "How did this all come to pass?"

Korfax sighed.

"Do you remember me telling you how my father saved my mother and I at Losq?"

"Yes."

"That was a lie," he said. "I did it. I picked up the black sword and slew the last of the Agdoain with it. That was where it all began for me. My father told me afterwards that the Farenith were its guardians. What he did not tell me was that we were not the Farenith at all, but the Mikaolazith. When I eventually discovered the truth my life became dark for many days. But that truth has since become our salvation. Only the Namad Mahorelah suffices. Only sorcery can defeat the Agdoain."

"I do not know what to say," Ralir said.

"There is nothing you can say," Korfax answered. "It has happened the way that it was meant to happen. Those damned prophecies of Nalvahgey. Doagnis resurrected the Iabeiorith so that I could rule them."

"The way it was meant to be?"

"Yes, I have declared myself to them. They see me as their prince. They call me Haelok and bow before me. I am where I was meant to be. We do now what we were meant to do, to rid the world of the Agdoain. It is the only hope that I have."

"And what of Doagnis?" Ralir asked.

"She knows her place," Korfax told him.

"I do not like the sound of that."

"Neither do I, but that is how it is. I have bound her to me. I have tamed her."

"Tamed her?"

"Let us just say that she understands the alternatives."

"It will be hard for the others to accept anything to do with her."

"Leave that to me," Korfax said. He then paused a moment. "One last thing," he said. "Did you speak to Odoiar?"

"Yes," said Ralir.

"Did he tell you about Lontibir?"

"Yes, he told that tale to many. Few would entertain it."

"Believe it," Korfax said. "It is true. The Wars of Unification became an excuse for slaughter. The west became as bad as the north. Sondehna committed the horror of Peis-homa and the west replied with the horror of Lontibir. Hate begets hate."

He turned to look at Ralir.

"We need a better answer than that," he said.

Ralir stood up.

"So, when shall our embassies meet?"

"You set the time. Let us meet at the head of the pass. It is wide there, and open."

"Halfway."

Korfax smiled.

"Halfway is good. I await your message. I will have someone waiting at the pass."

Korfax reappeared before the sentries and they came down and bowed to him. He gestured back towards Othil Admaq.

"I will be expecting a message from the city. I need a presence at the top of the pass to receive it. As soon as it arrives, bring it to me."

They bowed and went to carry out the order.

Aodagaa came to Korfax as he rode back into the camp.

"My Haelok," he said. "May I speak with you?"

"Always."

A careful expression came over the face of Aodagaa.

"My Haelok, what of Doagnis?" he asked.

Korfax smiled.

"Do not be afraid to ask hard questions, my friend. I have seen your heart, as you have seen mine. Never speak anything but your mind with me."

Aodagaa bowed his head again.

"My Haelok, many have not forgotten how she ruled us. She ruled with fear. She played one against the other. We followed her because there was little alternative. But now we see a different truth."

"I see. And which do you prefer?"

"Honour! True service! To know once more that I serve the dark heart of the north."

Korfax understood. The dark heart of the north. Here was the true darkness beloved of the Iabeiorith. It was not evil or wrong, it was the night reclaimed, the beauty of darkness set in harmony with the light. All things made known by their opposite.

"Then here is what I will say of her," Korfax said. "She thought it best that I prove myself to you."

"She would deny us your truth?"

"Say only that she desired a more cautious strategy. Before I declared myself, I let myself be known by the rest of you. Did you not like what you saw?"

Aodagaa smiled.

"I understand. It was well played. You showed us who you were. Then you showed us who you were again."

"It did not happen quite the way I thought it would. It was my suspicions of Teodunad that forced my hand."

Aodagaa let out a long breath.

"He has always desired to rule. What shall be done with him?" he asked.

"Leave him now," Korfax answered. "He has sworn himself to me. You were there. Let that suffice. He has, at least, been faithful to her, so let him remain as her servant. Let all find the place best suited to them. Let there be no rancour. I want no division amongst us. I want us whole. Let us be the people we should be, not what others have made us. We are the Iabeiorith. Let it be our time once more."

He came to her and found her sitting alone, almost as if she had not moved since the last he saw her.

"Have you thought upon your choices?" he asked.

She looked up at him.

"You have taken everything from me," she accused.

"No less than you would have done with me. But you would never have given it back again."

"I find it a bitter gift, and broken."

"Only because you made it so. If you had been honest with me from the very beginning none of this would have happened."

"I know it."

"I could have cast you out. I could have gone to the others and told them you were the very image of Soivar, but I did not. Instead I have kept my word to you and said that you shall remain by my side. You will rule, as will I, and the north will be ours."

"Made over in your image?"

"No! Made over in the image of old. Before the wars it was the best place to be. It shall be so again."

"A gentle place?" she asked. "A quiet place of forests and hills that knows only peace?"

"And why not?" he returned. "I once showed you Losq. You loved that. I saw you at play in the images. You wanted it."

"That was before. Now I find myself remembering a life that was, the life of the hidden where everything was certain and I was safe in the shadows."

"Now you deceive yourself. That was also a time of hatred and fear. I showed you gentleness. You once shared my bed with gladness."

She flinched.

"Will I ever know your touch again?"

He stared at her.

"That depends."

"On what?"

"On what you desire."

The message came quickly. They would meet on the morrow at the head of the pass between the hills. And so it proved.

The embassies met halfway. On one side there was Korfax and his honour guard, Aodagaa and Dosevax to either side. Opposite them stood Ralir with his honour guard. Beside him was Urendril Nimagrah and Geyadril Vatamath. There was no one from the Balt Kaalith or any other guild.

Korfax dismounted, along with Aodagaa and Dosevax. Ralir did the same, along with Vatamath and Nimagrah. They met halfway. Korfax gestured to Dosevax.

He bowed to Ralir, to Vatamath and then to Nimagrah.

"Nor-Tabaud Ralir, Geyadril Vatamath, Urendril Nimagrah, may I present Haelok Mikaolaz Audroh Korfax, hereditary ruler of the lands of Lukalah and Audroh of the Iabeiorith."

He withdrew, eyes gleaming. Korfax stepped forward and held up a logadar. He turned to Nimagrah.

"A gift for you," he said. "No doubt Ralir has told you what this is."

She stared at the stone and then back at him.

"It is true, then?" she said. "The Nor-Tabaud told us who you really are, and from whom you are descended. The blood of Sondehna runs within you?"

"Yes."

"It is hard to believe."

Korfax gestured at the logadar. She took it carefully.

"Why do you give me this?" she asked.

"So that you may understand. I am not just the heir of Sondehna, I am also of the blood of Nalvahgey, of Aolkar, of Akiol, of Aolon, of Haldos, of Noqor and all who lie between. But I am also the son of my father and mother, of Sazaaim and Tazocho. Do not be blinded by a single name. Think to yourself who I am and how I came to be here. I was once Nor-Enay, Geyad, Geyadril and Meganza. I was also Enay of the Farenith. Who would you speak with?"

Nimagrah took a deep breath.

"With Korfax," she said.

"Good!" he answered. "And what of you, Vatamath?"

"You raise up the names of your house like a wall," Vatamath said. "I do not know who you are."

"Yes you do," Korfax told him. "You once sat in judgement over me. You were there when the council made me Geyadril. You were there when I became Meganza. You know much of what happened in those days."

"You also said that you loved Abrilon, yet here you are, allied to his murderer," Vatamath accused.

"And here you are, still loyal to a tyrant," Korfax countered.

"What are you talking about?" Vatamath retorted. Korfax pointed to the city.

"The banner of the Velukor still flies above Othil Admaq, I see. Did they not tell you what he did? Did they not tell you how Lanarin died?"

"The Velukor said that you did it!" Vatamath answered.

"Did he?" Korfax said. No one missed the derision in his voice. "Onehson lied," he continued. "He did it. He killed his entire guard to get to me. He was a tyrant and murderer both. I did not kill Obelison, she died during the fight with the Agdoain. I did not kill Lanarin, or any of the Imperial Branith. Onehson did the deed."

Korfax turned back to Nimagrah.

"Another gift!" he said. "The truth!" And he showed her.

She staggered at the speed of it. Korfax was in her mind and out again before she could stop him. He left images behind, a tale, a hideous tale, and she was a long while regaining her composure.

"Samor showed me how to do that," he told her. "She did the same to me, after a fashion."

Nimagrah stared at him for a long while and then looked at Ralir and Vatamath.

"I will need to think on this!" she said. Then she glanced at Vatamath.

"Believe what he says," she told him.

"This is incredible!" said Vatamath.

He turned to Korfax.

"These accusations will not stand," he said. "All saw how you were with the Velukor."

"He broke Kommah!" Korfax answered. "How would you have dealt with that?" He took a deep breath. "What is this to be?" he asked. "Another trial? I already know the duplicity of the Balt Kaalith, better than you. Naaomir had me tortured with a miradar."

"I know that tale also," Vatamath said.

"Good, then you know what followed."

"Much of it is hard to believe."

Korfax drew out a piradar. He handed it to Vatamath.

"What is this?"

Vatamath frowned.

"A piradar," he said.

Korfax took it back, held it up and changed it into a stave of fire. He handed it to

Vatamath again.

"What is it now?"

Vatamath stared at the stone for a long while.

"So it is true," he said at last. "You can change the purpose of stone."

Korfax smiled without humour.

"The gift of Karmaraa."

"But you are of the line of Sondehna."

"Yes, I am. But, thanks to my mother, the holy blood also runs in my veins. So what does that tell you?"

Vatamath did not answer. He was confused now, disturbed by everything that had been revealed. Korfax waited a moment, watching him, before speaking again.

"Very well, then! I have another question. Have the Balt Kaalith opened up their archives to you?"

"No, of course not," Vatamath said. "They deny the tale of Odoiar. They say that it is a fiction created by sorcery."

"Yet the council of the Dar Kaadarith was willing enough to accept my testimony concerning the fate of Peis-homa. That came from a similar source."

"But Peis-homa is historical fact!"

Korfax would have laughed at that.

"Now you are not thinking at all, Vatamath," he said. "Who gets to write the histories? Who would be willing to admit that they allowed the extermination of an entire people? The Iabeiorith did not burn their land, destroy their towers or poison their wells as they retreated! The forces of the west did it, removing the stain, just as they removed the stones of Veludrax Mikaolazith. It was an abomination! No wonder the war took a thousand years! The Iabeiorith were given no choice. How many innocents ended their lives upon the pyres of the Balt Kaalith?"

Korfax held up his hand.

"One more thing. Lonsiatris! I also know what happened there. Dialyas did it. I brought him the Kapimadar because he told me he could use it to thwart the Agdoain. He did not tell me that he would use it to escape this world."

"Escape the world?"

"He has taken Lonsiatris, and everyone on it, somewhere else. He did not tell me his plans."

"The great wave?"

"Was his doing."

"But you gave him the Kapimadar?"

"Neither I nor Ponodol knew what he intended. The deed was done in hope. Dialyas betrayed us all."

Vatamath looked down.

"We need a long time to consider this," he said. "You have told us so much, so much that is dark, that is miraculous. As it was when I stood in judgement of you when you were to be Geyadril, so it is now. I look at you and do not know what I see."

Korfax smiled.

"To know a thing you must ask yourself what is it, what is its nature? What have I done, Vatamath? What acts have I committed? What is the truth of me?"

Vatamath looked away. It was too much.

Korfax turned to Ralir.

"So! Will we have an alliance? I am not Sondehna – you know this. I do not want the world, but I can help to preserve it."

Ralir smiled.

"For my part I accept."

He turned to Aodagaa and Dosevax.

"You have fought beside him. He is your prince. Is he not honourable?"

Aodagaa bowed his head.

"Greatly! He has shown us the true heart of the north. I would gladly die in his name."

"As would I," said Dosevax. All the others of the guard were smiling.

Ralir looked at them all.

"You saved my city," he said. "To you I would open my doors and shower you with gifts. But the greatest gift you already have: the love of my friend."

He turned back to Korfax and they embraced.

There were sounds of riders. Others were coming, green cloaks, the cloaks of the Balt Kaalith. Ralir turned in fury.

"I told them not to come!" he grated.

Two dismounted and came forward. They were masked. The first removed his mask. It was Odoiar, back to his usual self.

"I am here at the behest of another," he said. "And he is here to speak on behalf of the Balt Kaalith."

Korfax hissed through his teeth but said nothing.

Odoiar turned to the one at his side. This one revealed himself. It was Naaomir.

Korfax drew his blade and it howled.

"WHAT IS THAT PIECE OF FILTH DOING HERE?" he roared.

Ralir leapt before Korfax.

"Hold, Korfax, hold! We are an embassy, as are you."

Korfax slowly put up his sword, but it moaned as he caged it again. Many cast worried glances at it. They had seen something of what it could do.

"You see?" said Naaomir to Odoiar. "That is the kind of creature he is – sorcery incarnate!"

Korfax turned to Ralir.

"You did not tell me that he was here!"

Ralir took a deep breath.

"He came here after Othil Ekrin."

Korfax drew back.

"Why did you not tell me?"

"I thought it best not to say, given what happened between you. I wanted this alliance to go ahead. I know how you feel about the Balt Kaalith. I wanted this meeting to be between us. I wanted them to have nothing to do with it."

Naaomir stepped forward.

"Which is precisely why I should be here," he said.

Korfax turned upon him.

"Then you had better state your will! The sooner you are out of my sight, the better I shall like it."

"You do not daunt me," Naaomir said.

"Then you are a fool!" Korfax spat back. "I just lifted the sword of the Agdoain from your unworthy neck! They would have been over your wall and at your throats if I had not intervened."

Ralir stepped forward again.

"Korfax, please, this serves no purpose."

"On that, at least, we can agree," Korfax sneered. "The Balt Kaalith do indeed serve no purpose."

Naaomir made the gesture of dismissal.

"We shall have no alliance with the likes of you," he said. "We shall deal with the Agdoain ourselves, and by the word of Karmaraa, we shall prevail."

Korfax laughed. He laughed long and loud. He turned to his followers, to Aodagaa and Dosevax.

"Do you hear this?" he said. "Do you hear these proud fools? Three great cities lost and still they believe they will prevail in the end!"

Naaomir turned to Ralir.

"Tell him how it is!" he said. "Tell him you do not have authority in this, neither do the Dar Kaadarith or the Exentaser!" Here he looked at Vatamath and Nimagrah.

"Tell him where the power lies. Tell him who has the final say."

Korfax started.

"Who has the final say?" He turned to Ralir. "Have you lied to me?"

Ralir drew back.

"No, of course not."

"But if you told them not to come, why are they here? Why can they so blithely disobey you? You are Nor-Tabaud."

Ralir took a long breath to calm himself. He stared at Naaomir.

"It seems they have a hold over Zafazaa. I do not know what it is. He issued an edict to say that only the Balt Kaalith can speak with his will. He will not listen to any other guild."

"And when were you going to tell me about that?" Korfax asked. "You, best of all, know how he was, how he tried to bring down my house."

"Which only validates his actions," said Naaomir.

Korfax turned to him and pointed his finger.

"I was not speaking to you," he hissed. "You will keep your silence or I will no longer recognise your embassy."

He turned back to Ralir.

"Well?"

"Perhaps I should have told you," Ralir said. "But I thought we should take it one step at a time."

Korfax half turned, running a hand over his face.

"I grow weary of this," he said. "It seems ever to be my fate to put my trust in others and then have that trust abused. First Doagnis, now you! This was a mistake."

He turned to Vatamath and Nimagrah.

"It seems you now fight a war on two fronts, the Agdoain and the Balt Kaalith. I have shown you the truth. Do with it what you will. There is nothing more to say."

Korfax turned away to leave, but then Naaomir stepped forward.

"Indeed!" he said. "There is nothing more to say but this. You are the spawn of evil and it is my solemn duty to rid the world of such as you."

A dart flicked out from hidden folds in his robe, straight at the neck of Korfax. It flew, a blur of motion, straight at the naked skin. But then it bounced, striking armour, for the Qahmor had blossomed to catch it, leaves of metal rising up in the instant the threat was perceived.

Korfax bared his teeth, and his eyes were black. He stared down at the dart. They all did, caught by the shock of it. Korfax reached down and picked it up. He peered at it. The tip was wet, poison no doubt.

The Haelok Aldaria surged forward and suddenly every throat was marked with a black blade. Korfax held up his hand.

"Hold!" he commanded. They waited upon the word of their prince.

Korfax turned to look at Naaomir. He said nothing but held up the dart. It burst into flames in his hand and was reduced to ash in moments. Then he reached out with his thought, and Naaomir screamed. His scream pierced the air, echoing from the hills, and he fell to the ground, writhing, jerking, until he finally stopped and lay very still.

Korfax stared down at the body of Naaomir for a long time. Then he turned and looked at Odoiar.

"This was an embassy," he said, his voice still and dreadful. "You have defiled it. You are without honour. You are no better than the Agdoain."

He glanced at Ralir.

"We are done here," he told his friend. "I trusted you, and you have betrayed that trust. Go back to your city and await whatever end the Creator sees fit to bestow upon you. I want no more of you." He looked at the others. "ANY OF YOU!" he roared.

He gestured and the Haelok Aldaria withdrew. He mounted and rode off. His guard went with him, and as they went, they vanished away until they were utterly gone from sight.

Ralir stared down at the twisted body of Naaomir. There were tears in his eyes, but not for the dead. Korfax, his friend, his oldest friend, who he had loved like a brother, had rejected him.

Odoiar came to stand beside him.

"Now do you understand?" he said. "Now do you see what you would have allied us with?"

Ralir turned and stared at Odoiar. Then he drew his sword and, in one easy motion, took off his head.

He ran to his steed and mounted it before anyone could stop him, and then he galloped madly towards the south. No one moved. They stared after him and wondered what they would do now.

When the embassy returned all could tell that something dark had occurred. The face of the Haelok was terrible, a black mask of rage. They all watched in fear as Korfax passed by, going to the great tent alone. He spoke only once, telling the guards that no one, but no one, was to disturb him. Then he went inside.

Aodagaa and Dosevax turned back with bowed heads and went to find the others so that they could tell them what had happened.

With Teodunad at her back Doagnis went to the guards. She saw the fear in their eyes, even as she asked to enter, but they refused her. The Haelok had spoken.

She would have remonstrated, but she knew that her authority was no longer as high as it had been. She felt anger, then rage and then fear. She turned about and went to find Aodagaa and Dosevax. At least they would tell her what had transpired.

She found them with all the other chieftains. Aodagaa was telling the tale. Doagnis waited at the edge, and listened.

"So it failed, then!" said Ambriol, after Aodagaa had finished.

"If it had not been for the Balt Kaalith," Aodagaa said, "we might have had an alliance, but there is little hope of that now. The Balt Kaalith are as they have ever been – defilers and murderers both."

"That has long been known. It was a fool's hope."

Doagnis turned at that. It was Teodunad, muttering under his breath, but his voice carried and all turned to look at him. Some even put their hands on the hilts of their Qorihna. Aodagaa stepped forward, eyes dark with anger.

"It would be well if you said nothing else," he warned. "It is not your place to speak at all. Remember who you are!"

Teodunad glanced to either side and saw nothing but angry faces, ready to leap to the side of Aodagaa, who now turned to Doagnis.

"The Haelok grieves," he told her. "He will see no one now, not even you. His friend betrayed him. He has become tired of betrayals!"

She started at that.

"What do you mean?"

"Perhaps you can tell me, my lady," Aodagaa said. "We all heard it. When he berated his friend the Haelok said that he had grown tired of others abusing his trust. He named you. We all saw his friendship for Ralir and what that meant to him. We all saw how he was when that friendship crumbled to dust. My lady, in the brief time I have known him, Korfax has only ever shown me honour. He has opened himself to me as no other ever has before. It is a trust I would never betray. He is my prince and I find that I would lay down my life for him. What say you to that?"

She went still inside. Damn them all. They would never have dared speak to her in such a fashion before Korfax declared himself.

"But why would I betray his trust in me?" she said.

"Because you desire to rule alone," Aodagaa told her.

"No!" she said. She looked at all the others about her. None of them was looking at her with any favour.

"We have not forgotten your way with the rest of us," continued Aodagaa. "You ruled with fear, but he does not do this. He treats us honourably."

There it was again. Honour! She could come to hate that word. She could come to hate it greatly.

"And have you forgotten what I did?" she said. "Have you forgotten all that I have done?"

"No," said Aodagaa. "When you came to us you found a people of regret, living on old memories, hoarding them in the hope of better days. Then you told us that those days were at hand. You raised us up, gave us hope and promised us the north. But soon we discovered that it would only be on your terms. You threatened death to any that denied your will. We have not forgotten either the good or the bad."

"And have you forgotten my power?" she said.

Aodagaa did not withdraw.

"No," he said, "even that is clearly in our thoughts. But I have been shown another truth. As I said, the Haelok showed me everything. He showed me how he put down the Zibra of Tohtanef. He showed me how he dealt with the Rapalen of Molpan. And finally he showed me how he put down the Givyalag called up by Axayal. He has opened himself to all of us. He told us that he wanted us to be the best that we could be, and we saw that in his heart. He told us that we were not slaves but lords. That is a promise of service and honour I can only repay with my loyalty and my life. How do you answer that, my lady?"

She looked down.

"My life and his have been very different," she said. It was all that she would allow.

"That is true," Aodagaa said. "But he has rejected much that he used to revere so that he could embrace us. Will you not do the same? Will you not show yourself to us now? We have seen a different way, a better way. We would embrace that and be stronger than we were."

"And if he did not trust me," she said, "would I be carrying his child?"

Another voice intruded.

"But Soivar carried the children of Sondehna, and we all know what happened there."

There was stunned silence. Opakas stepped forward.

"It seems we have come to a time of revelation," she said, holding up a dark stone in her hand.

"This has been in the care of my house since the dark days. My house is the only one remaining of those that searched for the male heir. Here is a memory of that search. Until Korfax came amongst us that was all this stone was, just another memory lifted from the long defeat."

She turned to Doagnis and their eyes met.

"Then Korfax arrived, and I saw things in him that awoke a faint hope in me. I saw Qorihna and Qahmor. I looked back in this stone and I wondered." She put the stone away again. "Now my hope has been answered, as have many questions. There is one, though, that concerns me. Of what line are you, my lady?"

There were many sharp intakes of breath. The implication was obvious. Doagnis felt fear once more, fear great enough to overturn her anger.

"Be careful what you suggest," she replied, but Opakas did not retreat.

"I suggest nothing," Opakas said. "I only ask the question."

Aodagaa looked from Doagnis to Opakas and back again. He bowed his head.

"The Haelok told me the tale of how his Qorihna and Qahmor survived the battle of the Rolnir."

"Yes," said Opakas, "that tale also has gone far and wide. There was a betrayal, just not the betrayal everyone believed it to be. Both children survived. Soivar did not end the line of the Mikaolazith."

She looked carefully at Aodagaa.

"Did you know that the Farenith always had sons, never daughters?"

She turned back to Doagnis.

"Your line has always had daughters, I believe. Were there ever any sons?"

Doagnis felt the fear mount. Opakas knew! She knew!

"What has that to do with anything?" Doagnis said.

"I see a tradition, a ritual reaching far back in time. I see the cage of prophecy. Korfax told me of it."

"What else has Korfax told you?"

"Nothing," Opakas said. "Nor would I ask. It is for him to say – or you."

"What is it that you want of me?" Doagnis asked quietly.

"Honesty!" Opakas answered. "You understand our concerns, my lady. Betrayal can come in many forms, even to the most loving soul."

Doagnis held herself in a vice-like grip. Now she saw it. Now she saw what Korfax had done to her. She was trapped in the very nightmare she had sought to escape. She was with child and she had betrayed him. She could see it in all their eyes. Accusations swirled about her.

"What do you intend?" she asked.

"You do not see it, do you?" Opakas said. "He loves you. If he did not love you, he would not be trying to protect you. But memories are longer than either of you know. None of us are fools. I know your fear. The daughter becomes the mother."

Doagnis thought long and hard. What was she to do? There was one hope. Mercy. It also was Korfax's gift to her. Opakas was right. If Korfax did not care for her she would not be here now. This was her one chance to take things back. She had ruled by fear? They did not know what fear was, nor did they know her. She was always at her best when threatened.

"I understand," she said at last. "So let me prove my worth to you once more. Let me prove my worth to him."

They all looked at each other. Silently, it was agreed. Aodagaa bowed his head.

"Very well, my lady. If you can gain him what he desires, none will ever doubt you again. We will honour you all the days of your life, and we will do so gladly, if for no other reason than you have repaid his love for you."

She went back to her chambers in the great tent, with Teodunad trailing in her wake. She was who she was, she told herself, she should never have forgotten it. She should never have let Korfax distract her from herself. Her way was the way of fear. It was the only way that she knew, so let her take them all again in fear, as she had before. And to do it she needed a summoning of such power, such dreadful majesty, that they would all bow down before her and never rise again. It was her one chance to take back what was hers.

Ronoar waited at the threshold. She turned to him even as she arrived.

"They know who I am," she told him. Ronoar bowed his head in sorrow.

"Korfax told them?" he asked.

"No, Opakas discovered it for herself. I shall be avenged on her for that. I shall be avenged on all of them."

Teodunad gestured carefully.

"My lady, I am not sure this is wise. She has the favour of Korfax, and Korfax is the Haelok."

"But I carry his heir!" Doagnis told him. "Korfax will be your task. He grieves, and when he grieves he is vulnerable. He desires death. And I shall give it to him."

Ronoar and Teodunad exchanged glances. She could almost taste their reluctance.

"My lady, what do you intend?" asked Teodunad.

"Are you loyal to me?" she asked in return.

"You know that I am," he said.

"Then prepare yourself. When I am ready, you will go to Othil Admaq and demand their surrender. If they refuse, you will remind them of Peis-homa. Is that clear? Then you will come back here and await my will."

Korfax drank. He sat on his long couch, in the great tent, and drank. If it could pour he swallowed it, and no one stopped him or berated him, because no one dared. His face had become a blank mask and only his eyes remained alive, dimly burning with a dark and sullen fire. Dark shadows flitted carelessly in the air about him as he ran his hands across his blade while it lay in turn across his knee like some monstrous instrument of music. And as he caressed it, so it sang to him, a gentle song of blood, a lullaby of slaughter.

She watched him from her shew-stone. He had gone beyond her, beyond them all, stepping ahead to dwell in the places denied all others. He grieved for lost things, and the Haelok Aldaria grieved with him. It was betrayal, the darkest of crimes.

She shuddered at the song of the sword. It had a hungry sound to it, a thing of lust that drifted across the encampment like a curse. No one who heard it remained unmoved by it.

The story had travelled the camp. Agreement had been close, an alliance had been possible, but then the Balt Kaalith had showed up to spoil the feast. One of them, Naaomir by name, had even broken the ritual protection of embassy by firing a poisoned dart at Korfax. She had smiled at that. Stupid Balt Kaalith! They had forgotten what Qahmor could do. They were living shields, aware of everything. Only greater power could unlock them.

Then Korfax had slain this Naaomir with only his thought. It was terrifying and astonishing and it filled her with both dread and wonder. Few had ever managed that. It was said to be a sign of the greatest power, the greatest strength – to kill with a word!

She had heard it said by others in the camp that Korfax had become the word of the Creator amongst them. That filled her with dread as well. He surpassed her in so many ways. Now she must surpass him. She thought she knew how.

Teodunad rode invisibly up to the walls of Othil Admaq, his followers beside him. He undid his power right before the gates. Those high up on the wall scurried this way and that. Teodunad could taste their fear. They had rejected the Haelok Aldaria. They had every reason to be fearful.

He called out.

"Bring forth the Tabaud of Badagar! Send forth the betrayer of our Haelok! I have words to say to him."

The walls remained silent for a while, and then a voice came down from above.

"And who is it that comes so rudely before our gates."

"I am Teodunad. I speak for the Haelok."

"Then I am Bodurass and I speak for the Tabaud. What does your Haelok want?"

"He wants your surrender. He wants you to submit to his authority."

"Is that all? I will see what we can do!"

"Do not mock!" Teodunad warned. "This is your last chance for redemption. You betrayed his embassy. Do not think you can do such a thing and not pay for it."

"And you can go back to the abyss," said Bodurass. "Return when you have something sensible to say."

Teodunad looked up, glaring at the blank stone.

"Do not tempt me," he said. "I would rather be anywhere else but here, slave of the west. Instead, I do my duty as befits my station. My Haelok offers you two choices, mouth of the Tabaud."

"And what are they?"

Teodunad ground his teeth together in a snarl, but then he remembered what Doagnis had told him. He smiled up at the wall.

"That you can either surrender or you can be crushed underfoot. Have you never heard the tale of Peis-homa?"

There was a long silence. Teodunad felt something in the air about him, the gathering of forces. He looked to his guard. They felt it too.

"Draw your swords!" he told them.

Fire rained down from above.

They were caught within a storm of flame. It licked all about them, but their blades and their armour held it all at bay. Teodunad laughed. He turned back to the wall, and his voice, made great by summoned power, echoed from tower to tower as it crossed the city like a mighty wind.

"So be it, children of Badagar, you have given my Haelok his answer. What comes next will not be of his doing. This choice is yours. Revel in the time left to you, it will not be long."

They galloped from the walls, lightning and flames falling about them. But their unleashed swords caught the flames and consumed them, and their flickering armour cast a shield about them, a shield of such might that all the gathered powers of the Dar Kaadarith upon the wall were not able to shatter it.

Teodunad arrived back in camp and went straight to Doagnis. He told her what had happened and she smiled. Then she told him to keep watch in the camp. If a chance came he was to act, otherwise it would be up to her.

She went to the cave where she had met with Arzulg, and she set to her work.

She placed the shield of Nalvahgey, the Ksral, before her, a dull glitter of black gems, and lifted up the Taankab, its blue flame covering her hand. Then she opened the gates all the way to the thirteenth abyss and appeased each guardian in turn. Then she paused. Now she had to speak the words. It was a thing peculiar to the being she was about to summon. It wanted to hear her voice. It wanted to taste her life.

She looked up into the empty air and down into the deeps. She spoke the words.

"Oh you that dwell in Utih, most mighty in the places of the abyss. To you it is said: behold the commandments of the Creator, whose eyes are the brightness of the heavens."

Above her, over her head, something began to swirl. A vague green motion tumbled slowly, growing and thickening, pulsing ever larger until it blotted out the roof of the cavern. Doagnis spoke again.

"Oh you that govern, that order all things in the name of the most holy. Arise! Serve the heavens. Govern those that govern; cast down those that fall; come forth with those that increase and destroy the accursed. Let no place remain the same; add and diminish until the all is ended."

The tumbling green immensity took on a sickly hue. A stench as of decay fell out of it. Clouds grew and pale fires rippled across them, splitting and burning them, and they fell inwards to create a hole, a cavern, a rolling confusion of ever-revolving forms. A great wind filled the air and Doagnis had to shout her words over its roar, straight into the cavern itself.

"Arise, move and appear to our comfort, which the Creator has sworn unto us in all justice."

Something now fell down out of the tumbling maelstrom, a pale form that grew and grew until it had eclipsed everything else. Doagnis cried the last words, almost screaming them into the maelstrom.

"Open the mysteries of your creation, and make us partakers of your knowledge."

It emerged even on the very last word. Like a nest of bloated worms it unfolded its immensity above her and then gazed downwards.

There was a vast face, a furious mask of bleached bone. There were many eyes of unequal size, white pools unmarked by iris or pupil. There was a great mane of limbs, fat ropes of flesh that coiled and uncoiled as they gulped for air.

Doagnis stared upwards. Here it began.

"Great Ash-Tel, hear me. I am in need."

The vast face above her did not move.

"I COME AND I GO AS I PLEASE! WHY SHOULD I DO WHAT YOU ASK?"

Doagnis froze. Her mind raced. How could she answer such a question? In the scrolls she possessed it mentioned briefly that Nalvahgey had spoken with this being, but not what she had said nor how it had answered. Neither had the Agedobor told her anything of use. She had been told to follow her instincts, and that was all they had said. Doagnis steeled herself and held up the Taankab like an offering.

"I called you with this, great Ash-Tel. I called you so that your worship would not die from this world. The blood of Nalvahgey runs in my veins, and I would honour you as she did, but I am in great need."

The great face came a little closer and a few of its eyes closed as if in pain. From the others a pale light fell.

"I REMEMBER HER."

Doagnis waited.

"SHE WAS FULL OF GRIEF."

Doagnis frowned. What did that mean? She thought furiously, ever aware of the great face looking down at her. She swallowed and spoke again.

"We all grieve, great Ash-Tel, at the time of grieving. But now we live in the time of strife. I need your succour, great Ash-Tel. Will you give it to me?"

The face dimmed for a moment and all the eyes closed. Then they opened again, all of them, and they bled pale liquids, rivulets running this way and that across the bone.

"SHE ONLY SPOKE TO ME! SHE DID NOT SUMMON ME! WHO ARE YOU TO DO SUCH A THING?"

Doagnis wanted to flee. She could feel the regard of the dead god almost as a physical thing. It came closer and closer, before stopping just the other side of the shield. It regarded the shield for a moment and then looked back at her. She suddenly had the feeling that she was utterly defenceless before it, that if it wanted to it could cross any boundary at all. What was she to do?

Now she was a supplicant at last, but was she too late? The face bent over her, descending slowly as if already relishing her end.

"But I thought you would welcome this!" she cried in desperation. "Others of the Ashar have come here! Ash-Mir came to me when I called!"

The great face drew back again and there was a sudden hint of speculation in the heavy air.

"SO YOU WERE THE ONE THAT AWOKE US? YOU WERE THE ONE THAT TOUCHED US WITH YOUR DREAMS?"

Its eyes brightened as it drew back further.

"TELL ME YOUR DESIRES!"

If Doagnis considered the question a glimmer of hope, it was soon dashed by the expression on the dead god's face. She was being judged here. She had to answer Ash-Tel now, or her soul was forfeit.

"I have enemies. They need removing. They are an obstacle in my way. I intend to resurrect the old ways. That is why I have called you to this place. But I need your help."

"I SEE MORE THAN YOU!" said the face. *"I KNOW WHO YOU ARE! I KNOW WHO YOU ALLY YOURSELF WITH!"*

Then the face dimmed slightly, veiling itself in shadow as if pondering its choices. Doagnis stilled a fit of trembling. She had never been in such peril before. The face brightened again and looked at her, and its mane of worms writhed and squirmed.

"VERY WELL! I WILL AID YOU. BUT SOULS ARE THE BARGAIN. WHAT CAN YOU PROMISE?"

Doagnis almost wept with relief, but she dared not. She dared not show the slightest sign of weakness, even now, so she turned smartly about, pointing to the entrance of the cave.

"Follow me, Great Ash-Tel, and let me show you your prize."

She picked up the shield and held it before her, then, with the Taankab held high in her other hand, she walked out of the cavern. The great form followed in her wake.

Like some monstrous shadow it anchored itself to her shoulders, and she could feel its breath upon her neck like the exhalation of a corpse. She tried to ignore the stench, but it surrounded her on all sides. It was everywhere and it was all she could do to stop herself from gagging.

It seemed an age before they reached the cave mouth, an ecstatic journey of fear and horror for her, but at the entrance she stopped nonetheless. Ash-Tel, though, did not. Instead it swept over and around her and buried her alive.

For a moment she felt herself bound about by great coils, coils that squeezed her until she almost could not breathe at all. Heavy darkness covered her, pregnant with stifling wrappings and cloying earths. Her mouth was filled with sudden clay and her limbs were trapped in tight and binding fabrics. She was buried below, pulled into the ground, down into the failing places, the places beyond all hope. But even as a scream of insurmountable fear rose up from inside, the sensation passed on by and she found herself back again in the light, whilst Ash-Tel rose up above her. It unfolded itself again and stared back down with its blind eyes and she swallowed in a mouth that was altogether dry. She pointed at the city beyond. The city remained her one great distraction. Every other purpose within her failed in the face of such might.

"They dwell there, great Ash-Tel, in that place. There is the prize. There are your souls. There dwell the ones that would refuse your truth."

Ash-Tel looked where she pointed.

"ARE THEY YOURS TO GIVE?"

"They are! They were offered an alliance in all good faith, but they betrayed our embassy with violence! They are betrayers. They are accursed."

"SO BE IT, THEN!"

For a moment it hung unmoving whilst a vast and unknowable sorrow spread outwards into the air. Then it shrank in upon itself and she stared in fascinated repulsion as the dead god swallowed its own face, sucking its illusory flesh inwards, features spiralling, substance bleeding, all of it falling away into the dark distances as though down an ever-widening maw. Limbs coiled and span about the vanishing face, spinning ever faster as they fell inwards. The whole contracted down to nothing and then exploded upwards into the sky.

Now a hideous cloud spread itself across the heavens. It pulsed and it roared and its chaotic heart beat with dim green fire. It rolled towards the proffered sacrifice and passed its blind regard over tower and wall, then down onto Othil Admaq it fell, passing through air, through stone and through flesh. Ash-Tel sat upon the city and compressed it with its terrible weight.

Those of the Iabeiorith that saw this fell back in silence and all but fled as screams filled the air. Some covered their ears with their hands, some cast themselves into the dirt at their feet, whilst others merely stared back over their shoulders, transfixed in terror as vast, translucent limbs began to writhe across the jewel of Badagar. And as those limbs went about their work, the dead face of Ash-Tel rose up beyond the highest tower like some insane dawn.

Vast Ash-Tel became, a shape beyond size, a form beyond all limitations, eclipsing the city, eclipsing the world. The sky darkened and even Rafarel dimmed, hiding himself away from the atrocity that now boiled and writhed across the greatest city of the south.

Othil Admaq slumped. Domes cracked, towers leaned, walls sagged and the stones of the city decayed, bowing at last under the intolerable weight of death. The city fell, all of it, rotting down into the earth as its substance was leached away.

On the walls, in the streets, wherever they stood, whatever they were doing, the citizens of Othil Admaq were caught in innumerable green coils, impaled, every one of them, by the dead god. They were silent now, beyond terror and fear, caught in the last agonising instant as their lives were taken from them, ripped out and sucked into the pulsing limbs.

Ash-Tel moaned and sighed, and a great wind passed over the land, singing sadly of the glories of death. Then came a silence more dreadful, more profound than anything that had yet preceded it. Like a presage of the end it fell. Nothing moved; nothing could. A dead weight held the fragile world in its imponderable fist and squeezed.

It ended at last. The silence lifted and Ash-Tel gathered itself up, a sad green mist that rose up into the sky, before floating slowly back to the place where Doagnis still stood. And there it stopped, right in front of her, regarding her for a moment with its sad dead eyes before quietly vanishing away.

Doagnis remained where she was. What had she done? It took her long moments to realise that she had not moved at all between the sending and the returning. She must be in shock. What had she done? None of her ancestors had ever dared such an act, but now here she was, standing alone on the other side, and the madness she had dreamed of in her arrogance was already history.

She stirred, thinking of all the rituals of necessity. Was there something she should have done? Was there something she had forgotten? But all she could think of was the spectacle that had just been laid out before her. What would be its consequences? What would be its conclusions? No one had ever done such a thing before. She had stepped beyond all boundaries at last.

Ronoar came to her, coming to her as he had ever done in the past, coming to her when her work was complete. But this time something had changed. Before he had approached her as if it was his proud duty; now, though, he bowed before her like a slave.

"Mistress!" he said, reluctance in his every line.

She swallowed and smiled, but no matter how she stiffened the mask of her face, it suddenly felt inordinately fragile.

"It is done, Ronoar," she announced like a triumph.

"Yes, mistress, the city is very quiet. The walls have collapsed, the gates have fallen."

Doagnis turned away from him. How fearful he was. But that was not what she wanted from him. Her pride all but conquered her at last and she felt a sudden surge of almost limitless rage. She turned about again. Did this fool not appreciate, even now, what she had accomplished here?

"Of course it is quiet!" she all but spat back at him. "Nothing has been left alive in there. They are all dead! Who will not now bow down before me? I can call up death! They dare not disobey!"

Ronoar became even paler, almost ghostlike, as he bowed his head. Doagnis turned away again, hiding her thoughts. It was true. She had indeed stepped beyond all boundaries. Ronoar did not understand. And if he did not understand, who else would? Who else could appreciate the depth, the breadth or the height of what she had achieved this day. She composed herself and turned about for a second time.

"Do you not understand?" she asked him. "Do you not? Do you truly not see what I have done?"

Now she let her full wrath fall upon her servant, her pride boiling in her breast.

"So even you fail me at the last," she said. "Have you no sense at all beyond your petty boundaries? I have just become the greatest of all the Argedith. Not even Nalvahgey dared such a thing. I have finally called up one of the Ashar to this world and I had it do my bidding. Do you hear me, Ronoar? IT... DID... MY... BIDDING!"

A small part of her mind itched with the lie, but she ignored it. She had already wilfully forgotten how close she had come to her own extinction.

Ronoar fell to his knees at last.

"But, mistress, such power, so many consequences – did you not say only to call upon the lesser...?"

"FOOL!" she cried, raising her fists above her head. "Fool I said and fool I mean! Get out of my sight, if you have not the wit to see what this means. Send Teodunad to me. He, at least, will acknowledge my achievement. He understands faithfulness. I would have him come to me and pay homage. Only he will do now."

Ronoar remained where he was. Doagnis stared at him for a moment and then all but lost her self-control.

"GO!" she screamed.

Ronoar turned and ran, and for the first time in his life he wondered whether it was because he was eager to be about his mistress's business, or because he simply wished to get as far away from her as he possibly could.

14

GRIEF

Entel-nis Fen-arp-bada
Rel-ajiz Ged-nilus-orh
Othil-ix Od-von-torzu
Unchim-dril Tol-a-dr-pan
Luj-gelje Pam-d-ton-i
Kurvan-tios Mikaol-azmed
Od-orsor Nisan-farain

Korfax stirred. Someone had touched him. He looked up. It was Dosevax.

"What is it?" he asked like a curse.

Dosevax swallowed.

"My Haelok..."

"What is it?"

"My Haelok, I know that you did not want to be disturbed, but something has happened."

Korfax stood up.

"Something has happened?" He stretched and looked out across the camp. "So, what is it?" he asked.

"Othil Admaq has fallen, my Haelok."

Korfax started and then became very still.

"What did you say?"

"Othil Admaq has fallen."

"WHAT?" Korfax lifted Dosevax high into the air. "FALLEN?" he roared.

Dosevax, terrified, could only bow his head.

"HOW?"

"My Haelok, after we came back, all could see how you were grieved. But we heard you talk of betrayal, and we wondered at it. Aodagaa confronted Doagnis. He doubted her. We all doubted her. But when Opakas questioned Doagnis about her heritage, that is when she told us what she would do."

Korfax dropped Dosevax to the ground and stared down at him.

"What she would do?" he asked.

"She said that she would prove herself to us. She told us that she would gain you what you desired."

"What I desired?"

"That is what she said. But then she called up a being, one of the Ashar. She bade it destroy the city. We did not know that she would go so far. We did not know she had such power. All are terrified, my Haelok. It is as though the end of the world has come."

Korfax continued to stare down at Dosevax for a moment, and then he turned away and buried his head in his hands.

He walked the streets of Othil Admaq alone. The silence weighed him down, as did the stillness in the air, and he felt as though he wandered in some long-forgotten ruin, a wasteland of the failed and the broken.

Not even pausing to don his armour or take up his sword, he had leapt upon Enastul and then ridden like fury to Othil Admaq, hoping against hope that what Dosevax had said was not so. But then he had seen it for himself, and his world had fallen.

Everywhere he looked he saw empty buildings, some tilting perilously, others wholly collapsed. The air he breathed tasted stale as if some vital element had been taken from it, and even the stones underfoot looked fragile as though wormy with ancient rot. Othil Admaq had crumbled, and in the towers that still stood windows and doors gaped like mouths echoing silent screams. The jewel of Badagar was a jewel no more.

In front of him, up and down each street that he passed, he saw the scattered clothing. It lay in piles, little piles of empty garments, stretched out or tumbled in disarray, bereft and abandoned. The people of Othil Admaq were gone, their bodies stolen away, and all that remained was the rotted cloth that had once covered them.

Here lay the armour of a Bransag, tarnished with rust; there lay a child's gown, a mute tumble of discoloured fabric.

Korfax knelt beside the gown and held out a tentative hand, reaching gently for a fragile sleeve. But the fabric came apart at his touch and the gown fell to dust in his hand. A single sob escaped him. Tears blurred his vision.

For how long he stayed there he did not know, but when the clatter of approaching feet disturbed the sad silence about him, he came back to himself once more.

He felt the feet stop behind him. Silence fell again until a mocking voice broke it for once and for all.

"So here you are! How apposite to find you in this monument to failure."

Korfax did not turn. He knew the voice, but it was a long while before he could remember clearly to whom it actually belonged. Teodunad – the one-time first of the Haelok Aldaria.

Korfax looked back at the remains of the dress. Teodunad, his impatience and his gloating mockery obvious in his voice, spoke again.

"Look at you!" he declared. "So I am to follow you, am I? I think not."

Korfax still did not move, but now his stillness solidified, as though he slowly turned to stone. His tears stopped their falling and vanished instead in puffs of vapour whilst something harder stepped up to occupy his flesh. More pitiless than stone it seemed to be, deeper and darker and far more absolute. And as he filled with adamantine darkness, so he finally stood. But he did not turn, not yet. Instead he spoke, and his voice echoed as though it fell upwards from immeasurable depths.

"Who sent you?" he asked. "Was it her? What does she want? More death? Does she want me dead now, like this city? Is that what you have become, Teodunad, her executioner?"

Teodunad did not hear the threat in Korfax's voice. Instead he snorted, hands upon hips, jaunty with his own derision and his rediscovered pride.

"A poor scion of Sondehna you prove yourself to be!" he said. "I always thought you soft and pampered, but now I see the truth of it. This was necessary, you drunken fool! They refused us! If they are not for us then they are against us. Have you not learnt anything from the past? What did Sondehna do to Peis-homa? Do you now regret your inheritance? Or your history? Should I remind you who it was that declared himself before the battle? It is as I thought from the very beginning. You are soft, born of softness, born of ease and luxury. Our mistress assures our victory with such actions. The lesson of Othil Admaq will subdue the world. None will dare rise up against us now. Here is where your choices have brought us, but you have not the stomach for it! I am right to remove such as you from the world. You are not fit to rule the Iabeiorith."

Korfax turned around slowly and looked at Teodunad, not just with his eyes but with his entire being. Teodunad had drawn his Qorihna and awoken his armour. His followers drew back. Teodunad turned and looked at them.

"Cowards!" he spat.

"But he is our Haelok!" said one of them.

"He is unfit to rule," Teodunad said.

"But he is unarmed," said another.

"And when has that ever been an excuse?" Teodunad sneered. "I do now that which has been done so many times before. Only the strongest shall rule, and that will be her."

Teodunad turned back and raised his sword. It howled. He ran at Korfax and slashed downwards, but the blade did not fall. It remained where it was, as though it had pinned itself to the air. It would not move. Teodunad stared up at it in utter disbelief.

Korfax also looked up at the blade. For a moment he seemed caught by the spectacle of Teodunad trying to drag his reluctant blade through the air, but then he reached up for the blade himself and he took it from Teodunad.

Teodunad fell back, horrified. What had just happened? His blade had refused to kill Korfax! He could not think, he could not act. Korfax stood over him and raised the Qorihna above his head. He brought it down upon Teodunad, and Teodunad came apart in a fountain of flame. Korfax let go of the sword even as it pierced its former master, and both sword and armour shattered, each destroying the other. In moments, the merest of moments, all that was left of Teodunad was a mute pile of ashes, one more death amongst the uncounted millions that had filled the city.

The followers of Teodunad fled, running back to their steeds, terrified by what had just happened. They raced from the city and back to the camp, and soon the rumour of what had occurred spread like wildfire.

Korfax rode back slowly to the great tent and all fled the rumour of his approach, even those that had sworn their lives to him. His face was almost white and his eyes were almost black. To those that saw him it suddenly seemed that something else had taken possession of their prince, some terrible demon filled with all the vengeance and the wrath culled from out of the lost years. So they turned away and ran, glad at last that it did not seek for them.

Korfax paused only to take up his sword and don his armour. Then he looked up into the hills. That was where she was, he was certain of it. He walked up the long path, and as he walked, his armour changed about him, curling and twisting its shape. Shadow swallowed him like a cloud, flexing like two great wings, and his eyes became lights in his head, each gleaming in the darkness of his rage.

Only Ronoar stood his ground. He knelt before the oncoming storm like an old and twisted stump and wrung his hands at the shadow, even as it loomed over him. A voice, hideously bleak, rolled down around him like distant thunder. He grovelled in the dust.

"Is she up there?" asked the voice.

Ronoar kept his head down. What was he to do? Behind him was his mistress of many years, besotted with her sudden power, drunk to the very brim with summonings and drowning in a mad dream of divinity, whilst before him came vengeance incarnate, a storm of such power that it seemed to have no limits at all.

Ronoar was caught between the hammer and the anvil, caught at last upon the hard blade of his service. All his life he had served the house of Mikaolaz, but here he was now, trapped in the very middle while the last two children of Sondehna sought each other's death.

"Haelok, please!" he begged. "I know what is in your heart, but I beg you, please do not do this."

The darkness paused.

"She is up there, isn't she? She is up there in the caves, in her favourite retreat, her favoured place of refuge, where she can hide herself away from the world and dream. It was ever her delight."

Ronoar waited, hoping that the storm had abated. But then it turned upon him with redoubled fury.

"MOVE ASIDE, RONOAR," it roared, "MOVE ASIDE! I WILL HAVE HER LIFE FOR THIS!"

Ronoar stayed where he was, still wringing his hands at the darkness even as it boiled over and around him. For a moment he was alone in a black coldness that stole the very heat from his bones, but then it passed on by like a mercy. Looking back over his shoulder he saw the winged darkness follow the path that stretched up behind him, all the way into the hills beyond.

Doagnis felt the approach of Korfax even before she saw him. The ground seemed to tremble at his touch and the air became chill. She had seen what had happened, before her shew-stone went utterly dark. She did not mistake the import. All her choices had come to this and here would be the final play. Terror clutched at her breast, but she reminded herself once more that she had always been at her best when danger threatened. So she clasped the four elements to her and ran to her place of summoning. Soon the cave echoed again to the sound of her voice as she called up the only help that she could.

Korfax entered the cave and stopped. Doagnis was here, as he knew that she would be, but so was another. Behind her reared again a vast shape, the very same that had destroyed Othil Admaq.

He looked up at it and then back at her. The shadow fell away from him and his Qorihna was quiescent in his hand, but his face was skull-like now, oddly mirroring that of Ash-Tel, and no emotion stirred at all in his fiery eyes.

"Doagnis!"

He spoke her name, but his voice was altogether dreadful. Something had been added to it, or taken away. Doagnis shuddered. To her it seemed then that Korfax was no longer an Ell but something else entirely. As she had crossed a boundary in her extremity, she found herself wondering what boundary he had crossed in turn and from what well of nightmare he now raised this terrible aspect of himself.

He raised his hand and pointed a finger at her.

"You killed Othil Admaq, you and that pale thing at your shoulder. Both of you shall pay. I desire nothing but your ending."

"But I carry your child," she warned.

"THEN YOU CARRY A CORPSE!" he roared back.

Doagnis felt her heart stagger in her chest. Who was this? What was this? No Ell, certainly. Had he lost himself to the darkness at last? Was this Sondehna before her now, the darkest monster ever to trouble the dreams of the Ell?

"DO I KNOW YOU?"

The voice of Ash-Tel soughed like a great wind. Doagnis turned and stared at it. What did it mean? How could Ash-Tel know Korfax?

Korfax looked up and returned the gaze of the dead god. Though he was far smaller than Ash-Tel, to Doagnis he suddenly seemed equal. Size became the illusion now, and the bones of the world seemed to shift to accommodate this new truth.

"I know you," Korfax replied.

"IS IT YOU?" came the great voice. "I WAS TOLD THAT YOU WERE HERE, BUT I DID NOT BELIEVE IT. I THOUGHT YOU LONG GONE."

Ash-Tel advanced slightly and stared down at Korfax with its many blind eyes.

"BUT I SEE IT NOW IN TRUTH. I WAS WRONG. IT IS YOU. YOU ARE COME BACK AGAIN."

Ash-Tel drew back and its face was dismissive.

"YOU SHOULD LEAVE THIS PLACE," it said. "YOU CANNOT BREAK THE COVENANT, NOW OR EVER. THIS GRACE WAS GIVEN YOU BY THE UNITY. REMEMBER YOUR OATHS."

Korfax raised his Qorihna.

"You butcher an entire city, you murder the innocent by the thousand, by the million even, and still you have the audacity to bid me remember my oaths?" The darkness erupted around him again. The mad rage in his eyes reignited and he drew himself up. "I will burn you and your mistress upon the very same pyre."

His voice swelled as he repeated his threat.

"DO YOU HEAR ME, ASH-TEL? THE VERY SAME PYRE!"

Ash-Tel shuddered.

"YOU THREATEN ME? YOU DARE? YOU SHOULD KNOW BETTER THAN THAT! RAISE MATASTOS AGAINST ME AND YOU WILL KNOW THE UNDYING RETRIBUTION OF THE ASHAR FOR ALL ETERNITY!"

But Korfax was no longer listening. He unleashed his sword and uttered such a cry that his voice cracked the stone of the cavern itself.

"AND WHAT DO I CARE FOR THAT? YOUR TIME IS DONE!"

He raised the sword above his head and gathered up his power. Around him night blossomed, a blackness writhing with the darker limbs of his sword. So Korfax came at Ash-Tel, and they met at the very centre of the cavern. There they clashed, whilst the rock about them trembled and broke apart.

Doagnis cowered, her hands over her ears. She had not understood all that had been said, but one thing had struck her like a bolt of light. Ash-Tel had named the Qorihna. It had called the blade Matastos.

She shook with fear. Apocalypse! That was its meaning. A black window opened in her mind. In what dim and distant past had such a weapon been forged? When had it been given such a name? Apocalypse? What terrible struggle had caused it? She suddenly felt as if she had unwittingly stumbled upon the last pages of some great and awful story.

She turned to look at the battle that raged behind her; she could not help it, she had to look. Someone should see it, she told herself, someone should witness it, even though it turn them mad.

For Korfax, it was like fighting immense serpents within an inky sea. Vast green mouths would come at him from each and every side. And as they came at him so he would cast his Qorihna back at them, its many blades writhing in their deeper darkness, eager to burn and consume. And somewhere, hovering nearby, was the bulk of his foe, a dead face with dead eyes that circled ever around him, just out of reach.

Energies flickered from limb to armour and back again. Then the armour in that place would smoke and fail. Korfax would slice the limb, severing it, his Qorihna consuming it in flame and song, and Ash-Tel would moan with pain and withdraw, but the dead god seemed to have an inexhaustible supply, and for every limb it lost, two more would appear.

Soon his armour was gone, corroded away to nothingness, and Korfax found himself naked, with only his sword to protect him. And now, from every direction, limbs came at him, their tips opening on vast and toothless maws.

He began to fail. Even his rage was not enough. He was doomed. A brief glimmer of doubt took him and blossomed. Fight one of the Ashar? What had he been thinking?

It was as despair threatened that he heard the song of blood in his head again, the real song, the potent song from his childhood that he had all but dismissed since that day, the one true song from when he had first taken the great black blade in his hand. And with his recognition, his Qorihna truly awoke in his grasp. His childish imagination had not made it more than it was, not at all; instead, he was the one that had forgotten.

The great song spoke to him again, untrammelled at last by any other power, and he understood its message at last. Using other forces, other potencies, even those that were coeval with the blade, dimmed the might of the one true Qorihna. When it was alone, when there was no other power with which it could compete, when its wielder was unfettered and could submit to it entirely, then, and only then, could its real power speak.

But there was a price to pay. There was no controlling such power, it was chaos incarnate. No will could master it, for all became subservient under its rule, whether they chose to do so or not. That was the purpose of Qahmor. It allowed the wielder to remain in control. It was a shackle, but a most necessary one.

Now he understood. That which submits, rules. He remembered back to that time when he had been but a child, when he had slaughtered three Agdoain as though they were nothing. He let the full song of the Qorihna fill him at last and he laughed with terrible abandon as he bathed himself in its power, even while he submitted to its desires.

Doagnis felt the shifting battle within her mind as Ash-Tel drove Korfax ever back, stripping away his armour before preparing to consume his soul. She felt a curious sense of duality. Part of her marvelled at the power she had drawn down into the world, but another felt nothing but regret that Korfax would die.

She caught the fires of his mighty defence, but she already understood that Ash-Tel would inevitably win. She was safe from her brother's mad ire. She allowed herself a little sadness. Though Korfax was the equal of any Ell that she had ever met or read about in all the histories, in the end he was just as flawed. All of them were flawed. None of them could see the truth. She turned away, finding herself suddenly unwilling to watch his death. But then she heard his mounting laughter, in the air and in her mind, and she turned back again despite herself. She stared upwards in utter astonishment.

Korfax had grown and his Qorihna had grown with him. He seemed to have fused with it, for his skin was now black and metallic, suffused with a darkness that yet gleamed with a terrible light. But his sword? That was now a light itself, a black light that burned the eyes and blinded them.

Korfax had vanished, his features were gone, and instead there were just two eyes, two great eyes like burning holes where his head should be, and from them lightning fell.

A giant laughed as it hewed at Ash-Tel, who now moaned and thrashed in despair. Limbs shattered stone, limbs crushed the air, but it was all to no avail. Blow after blow rained down upon the hapless god, the many blades of the Qorihna parting its unliving substance, harvesting its dead limbs like a scythe through corn. Then, finally, the Qorihna was hefted high and all its blades were made one. Down went the killing stroke, deep inside Ash-Tel, all the way to the hilt.

There was a scream that staggered the air, a storm of darkness that tore the rock of the hill apart and a stench the like of which Doagnis hoped never to know again.

Ash-Tel ended.

The cavern vanished as a wave of sick green fire expanded outwards. The air filled with golden sparkles in their wake, golden stars that swirled and danced. The ground shook, the air ignited and she was tossed carelessly aside like a limp bundle. She landed heavily and knew no more.

When she came back from the darkness, she found herself in the light. The cave, the entire top of the hill, had vanished, blasted from the world by the ending of the dead god. She lay under the gentle light of day.

Korfax stood in the same place, the exact same place, from where he had delivered the killing blow, a pale statue, his sword quiescent in his hand. The fire in his eyes had dimmed and a golden light filled the air about him. It swirled, that light, rising and falling, rolling in the air as it circled, orbiting his unmoving body.

Doagnis looked about her. Everything was gone. Her periapts were nowhere to be seen. She stood up and staggered away from Korfax, searching the ground. Her head throbbed and there was a pain in her ribs and her stomach. It was difficult to see and her vision blurred from moment to moment, but as she stumbled across the shattered stump of the hill, she became vaguely aware of distant cries from the valley below. No doubt the destruction of the hilltop had hurled debris everywhere.

Something gleamed in front of her and she knelt to pick it up. In her hand she found pieces of charred wood, smoking fragments that seemed to dim even as she studied them. There was a blue vapour, the remnant of their failing substance. She almost sobbed as she realised what they were. She held, in her hands, the last fragments of the Taankab.

She stayed where she was for a moment, before casting one hateful glance back at the still unmoving Korfax. Then she staggered away, making her way to the opposite side of the hill. All she wanted now was to escape, to leave this place and its mad destroyer, and she could think of only one other that would help her.

Korfax stood in a timeless place. Visions flew past him – great abysses, vast depths, immense vaults, pits filled with squirming things, limitless halls where the dead floated endlessly upon the sullen breeze. He was filled with such sorrow that he would have fallen to his knees and wept, but he did not.

He stood upon the borders, the blood-drenched mists of a thousand battles curling before him. Here was the miraculous place he had once seen from afar – the eternal twilight, the peace after the slaughter.

Golden shapes wandered here and there within the mists, phantom figures slowly dancing in circles but never coming closer or moving further away. He heard voices, some crying, others calling out, but they were distant things. Who were they? Was he truly caught between worlds, hearing the echoes of those on the other side of sight, those that walked unseen?

The mists parted and a golden shape came towards him. Then it was joined by another, then another. They spiralled inwards, and as they came closer, so their shapes became more certain. Limbs they had, and torsos, but they were yet cloudy things, ill-defined, as though their boundaries were still imprecise in their memories. Only their heads took definite form, assuming faces both familiar and strange.

The first that came forward seemed like Tabaud Zamferas, but its character was entirely subsumed by another. Here was serenity, certainty, clarity and peace. It was as though the life of Zamferas had been a piece of parchment, wrinkled and creased by ill use, only now to be smoothed out and straightened, its stains erased and its imperfections healed.

"Zamferas?"

Korfax stared at the apparition as it looked back at him calmly. It had the eyes of Zamferas, certainly, but there was more here than just the Tabaud of Othil Admaq. There was an echo of something else, of knowledge, awful knowledge.

The apparition did not speak, but instead it held his gaze for a moment. Korfax found its scrutiny uncomfortable. He felt naked before it. But then it bowed to him and moved on, its features fading, its form losing coherence again. Finally it was gone.

Another came forward. This one looked like Vatamath, but a Vatamath with all the pride and the arrogance washed out of him. There was stillness instead, an unmoving compassion that understood everything that it saw. Again, like the previous apparition, this one held his uneasy gaze for long moments, before it too bowed and vanished.

And so it went on, and on again, face after face, form after form. Some he thought he knew, the names of the departed, Tharah, Payoan, Nimagrah, but others filled him with greater disquiet. There were children here, some so young they could not be more than a season old. But all looked at him with that same intelligence, as if they knew everything there was to know.

He began to feel that he could not endure this procession, as though each gaze was a judgement for actions he had not yet taken, but he could not stop it. He was powerless in this place. Each looked at him and then fled, and he could do nothing but stand and accept their strange regard.

It seemed endless.

But then the faces changed.

Now he saw feral masks, faces painted in black and white swirls, one eye black, one eye white. Black eyes, white eyes, a strange dichotomy he found the hardest to understand. Who were these? Some looked like Ell, but others did not. Many had the heads of beasts, muzzled, beaked and horned. They rose up before him like an army, proud and mighty, but also strangely humble. And they bowed before him as the others had.

In their wake came the night, the world darkening in its sorrow, and Korfax fell at last into its grieving depths.

"So you weep? How apposite!"

Korfax looked up. He saw a pale form standing over him. There was a face, coalescing from his grief. It looked down at him and spoke again.

"I should thank you, perhaps, for freeing all the dead from bondage, but that is all that I will ever do for your comfort."

Korfax found himself staring up at Adavor. She hung in the air and dripped with water, and there was a gaping wound in her belly, the same jagged wound where one of the Agdoain had caught her. She looked down at him, her eyes watery-pale in her bloodless face, but for all their seeming blindness, they burned inside with pale fires.

"Adavor?" he said.

"Yes," she answered, "it is me. And I am surprised that you even remember my name. Or perhaps it is that you would rather not. Is that guilt I see?"

"What do you mean?"

"You lay with her!" she accused. "You lay with my torturer and got her with child! What a creature you are. Have you no shame?"

He took a long and shuddering breath.

"You know the truth of it."

"Do I?"

"If you truly are one of my dead, then you know what happened!"

"Ah, yes. As Mirzinad took me, so you took her. I suppose I should take some measure of comfort from how it all ended, but I do not. Before her betrayal you lay with her gladly enough. You allowed her to beguile you with her softness."

"Yes!" he said. "Beguilement! Betrayal! None of this was my fault."

"No doubt those lies satisfy you," she returned, "but they do not satisfy me. I see you – all of you. I had hoped you would prove worthy of me, that you would be the one who bowed less to his lust than to his honour."

"Are the dead always so unforgiving?" he asked.

"And what do you care?" she hissed. "You will dismiss this as a dream, just as you dismissed all the others that came before. Life is wasted on the living."

"So why are you here, then?"

Her eyes intensified.

"Against my better judgement I come to you with counsel, the last you shall receive before the end. Three is the limit and there will be no more from this time onwards. I am the last of your dead. I cannot tell you why it should be so, but that is the way that it is."

"So what are you here to tell me?" he asked.

"You have one last choice to make," she told him. "Make the wrong one, and you will fail. You will understand, come the time."

"More riddles? Is that all the dead have to offer? Riddles?"

"But riddles can be so instructive."

"So Doanazin said."

"And you still have not understood what she told you!"

"I understood at the end, when Lonsiatris vanished behind a wall of lightning. I understood well enough then."

"Now comes the blame," she said, "the blame for others; always the blame for any but yourself."

"Then you do not know me as well as you think," he said. "I know where the blame lies, none better. It is my fate that I curse."

"Well now, here is another revelation. If you understand that, then you do not have so far to go as I thought."

"That we make our own fate? I once cut my teeth upon such considerations."

"But only the teeth grew."

"Where are you leading me? Doanazin led me to my heritage. Mathulaa led me to my power. What is your purpose?"

"I come to you with the noblest gift of all," she said. "I but point you towards your destiny."

"My destiny? But I have long known what that was: to slay the Agdoain."

"No! That is incidental. Your destiny is other."

"More riddles. What pain do I have to endure now? Doanazin cost me my trust. Mathulaa overthrew my teachings. What must I lose now?"

"Everything! Whoever loses everything wins."

Korfax bowed his head.

"Everything?"

"Everything! You must hazard it all. It is, after all, why you are here in the first place. To win is to lose, and to lose is to win."

And with that Adavor vanished. Another took her place, climbing over the shattered lip of the hill. It was Opakas. She was alone.

"Haelok?" she called.

"I am here," he said.

"Are you hurt?"

"I am whole."

She came closer and peered at him.

"I saw what you did."

He looked at her, saw the fear in her and the hope.

"What I did?"

"You slew one of the Ashar. You destroyed Ash-Tel. If someone had told me the tale, rather than seeing it for myself, I would not have believed it. You are mightier than any other that has ever walked the world."

"And darker. And more foolish," he told her.

"No!" she said. "Doagnis is the fool, not you. Fear of her heritage trapped her in the very cage she sought to escape. She became the betrayer because she sought to deny the very thing that made her what she was. You only gave her the chance to do otherwise."

"I had more than a hand in her betrayal."

"But it remained her choice. I knew what kind of creature she was, long before you ever came amongst us. You have seen something of it. Did she not slay Tohtanef at the end? She spent her servants lavishly, playing them against each other. She was cruel."

"She also raised you up."

"Yes, that too. It was what blinded many of us. She was a thing of opposites. She would have given us the north, and then taken it away again."

She looked him over.

"Are you certain you are without hurt?"

"I was preserved. My sword preserved me."

She held up her cloak.

"I am not cold," he told her. He pointed back to the camp.

"We should return."

"When I understood what had happened, I bade the others wait," she said. "What of Doagnis?"

"She is gone. I do not know whether she lives or is dead."

"Perhaps she still lives. Ronoar is gone also. He fled."

Korfax looked down.

"Let her go," he said. "Her teeth have been pulled."

"But she carries your child."

He grimaced.

"It is her child, not mine. I disown it."

Opakas bowed her head.

They walked off the shattered hillside in silence. Though he was naked, he did not care. Let his flesh be caressed by the elements, he told himself, let them touch him and know him. It was how it should have been from the very beginning, naked before the world, nothing hidden. Only that which was hidden was guilty.

He looked at the ruins of Othil Admaq.

"Too much has been lost," he said.

"But at least it can be replaced," she answered. "We are still here."

She smiled.

"Let that be 'a window of comfort' on this dark day," she quoted.

"You have hope?"

"I do. You have returned to us. You are of the mighty. We will prevail."

Further down the hill others rode up to them both, his honour guard and the chieftains. One of them was leading his steed. They stopped before him and all bowed their heads. Aodagaa dismounted and led Enastul to his Haelok.

"My Haelok, we saw the destruction of the hill. Opakas bade us wait as she climbed up to find you. She told us what you did."

Korfax looked at them all.

"What I did!" he said. "I am to blame for this. If you desire another way, I will renounce my titles, my heritage, and put my life in another's hands."

Ambriol stepped forward.

"Do not despair, great prince," he said. "We know much of what has passed. You trusted. You hoped. What else could you do? That is who you are. This was unforeseen. She betrayed you. She desired to rule. She would never have been satisfied with anything less, no matter what you did. As for us? We are yours till the life leaves our bodies. We will follow only you. You are our heart and our whole."

They rode back to the camp. Korfax was now wrapped about by a cloak. All came out to gaze upon him, their eyes full of fear, even terror, but also wonder and hope. Once more tales had gone far and wide. Their great prince had put down one of the Ashar. The shades of Othil Admaq had been appeased. It was a tale of astonishment and dread.

Korfax came to the great tent and entered. Opakas came with him, as did the chieftains. They waited whilst he found a simple robe and donned it. Wine and food were brought. Korfax sat and ate.

"What is your will, my Haelok?" asked Aodagaa.

Korfax looked up.

"What is yours? What will you have?"

Aodagaa smiled.

"That we retake the north. That we end the threat of the Agdoain. That we go home."

Korfax looked at the others.

"You all wish this?" he asked.

They all bowed in agreement.

"And also that you lead us," said Ambriol. "That is our will as well. We desire no other."

Korfax smiled at him.

"Thank you. You deserve all honour, all of you. From this moment on I shall try to be the prince that you deserve."

He turned to Opakas.

"And I name Opakas first of the Argedith and first counsellor. I need her wisdom, now more than ever."

Opakas bowed to him.

"And I shall not leave your service, my Haelok, not whilst there is a breath in my body. I have found you. You are the conclusion of my purpose, the long purpose of my house. Now all things are in their proper place."

There was a meeting, the last before they broke camp. All that were high were assembled and Korfax stood before them.

"I have little to say," he said. "We all know the task before us, we all know how the rest of the world sees us, but we are their one hope, whether they know it or not. Without us, the Agdoain will eat the world. Therefore, my plan is simple. We ride north and we take Emethgis Vaniad. There is a womb there that must be destroyed. That is our first task."

"And beyond that, my Haelok?" Ambriol asked.

"We find the source. We find who or what is behind the Agdoain, and we destroy it."

"Do you know what it is?" asked Opakas.

"Beyond what I have already told you? No, I do not," Korfax answered. "An old Arged, last of the Korith Peis, once described the Agdoain as the heavings of Zonaa."

He paused a moment, remembering the grey.

"I have, before this day, encountered a force, a grey force of dissolution. I have felt it many times since, especially when fighting the Agdoain. It dwells within them and orders them, but what it might be I cannot say. It is monstrous and powerful, a bringer of terror and nightmare, but it does have a weakness."

Many looked up at that.

"A weakness, my Haelok?" asked Aodagaa.

"The Namad Mahorelah. Would its slaves be vulnerable to that lore if it was not?"

Korfax held up a logadar.

"Here are the complete grimoires of Sondehna, taken from the works of Nalvahgey. They have belonged to my house since the earliest days. I now give them to you, all of you. By the time we face the foe, they will face an army of Argedith. We will be again what we once were – the mightiest ever to walk this world."

When he was alone with Opakas again, he waited whilst she perused the contents of the logadar. Eventually she looked up and smiled.

"There is so much here," she said. "Such a gift, and you give it freely."

"It does come with a price," he told her. "I intend it to be used."

She looked long and hard at him.

"You are a marvel to me. You give and you give, but I have never seen you take."

"I have taken."

She did not drop her gaze.

"Rarely, I think."

"I have taken," he said. "I have demanded, been proud, been forceful and vengeful. I have bowed when it suited me and rebelled when it did not."

He gestured at the logadar.

"There is one thing that you should know. I have not told the others this, and it is not written down, but you should know it. Doagnis had a pact with the Agedobor."

Opakas looked suitably shocked.

"And I thought that they were no more."

"As did I, but I saw her meet with Arzulg and I heard its words."

Opakas grimaced.

"I understand that they are not a pleasant sight."

"No, they are not, so whatever it is that lies beneath their coverings, it must be hideous indeed."

"Then that explains why she would take herself off at times. Ronoar knew?"

"And Teodunad at the end. It was an old pact, reaffirmed by every daughter of the line. Arzulg wanted Doagnis to kill me. It wanted her to take my child and then kill me."

"And you confronted her with this?"

"After the battle for Othil Admaq. I was not gentle."

"So that is why you declared yourself and why she was so subdued. I wondered what had caused it. But if you knew that, why did you spare her?"

"Because it asked her if she loved me, and she said yes."

"Will you tell me the tale?"

So Korfax told her everything: the whys, the wherefores, the history, what he did, what the result was. At the end Opakas sat very still for a long while.

"I did not know you could be so cold, or so brutal," she finally said.

"There is a rage in me," he answered. "Sometimes it speaks."

"So I see."

"You think less of me now?"

"Sometimes, when I look at you, I do not know what it is that I see. When you rise, you rise to the very heights. But when you fall, you fall all the way. I cannot condone what you did to Doagnis, but I find I cannot judge you, either. Betrayal, especially a betrayal such as this, would be a sore trial for any of us. It squeezes the life out of us and consumes us with hatred. But you may come to rue this in the years ahead, especially when the child decides it is time to seek you out and ask you why."

"Then I will tell it the tale that I have told you."

"And what good will come of that, I cannot say. I am no seer."

He looked long at her in silence. Finally he spoke.

"Will you still be my counsellor?"

She smiled.

"Of course, and your friend. You need me more than ever, I think. It is my task now to keep you upon the path. But have no fear, my Haelok, I shall not let you stray."

"Thank you for that mercy at least. I am not sure that I deserve you."

"Oh, you deserve me, make no mistake about it."

Korfax drew out another Qahmor from his blade, from Matastos, another collar of unfolding armour, as mighty as the one he had lost to Ash-Tel. Only Opakas stood beside him now, waiting upon her Haelok and watching.

It did not take long for the new armour to be ready. Korfax hefted the Qorihna again, probing it with his mind. Again it seemed unaffected by the whole procedure, as though the birthing of new Qorihna and new Qahmor were nothing to it, a natural function of its being.

"You are a wonder to me, Matastos," he said, "a terrible wonder."

At the mention of its name, the sword stirred. It sang quietly for a moment, its surface shimmering. Opakas looked darkly at it.

"None of the others has names, nor do they accept them when given. They are only echoes, it seems, echoes of thoughts and of will. But yours is different. It has a will all of its own."

Korfax stroked the blade.

"It loves me," he said.

"Loves you?" she looked up, astonished.

She looked back at the blade.

"It is a beast?"

"Perhaps."

"You do not know?"

"No."

"But it has a name."

"A terrible one. But then it is a terrible weapon. It can slay gods."

She waited a moment and then gestured outside.

"It is time to go," she told him.

"Yes," he agreed. "Tell the others to assemble. I will speak to all before we depart."

She bowed and left.

He went out from the tent and rode to a high rock set above the plain. All were waiting for him, everyone. They covered the wide plain, a sea of expectant faces waiting with trepidation for whatever their Haelok would say. He stood upon the high rock alone, covered in his dark armour, his fearsome blade across his back. He sent out his thought and touched all their minds.

"We have passed through fire," he said. "We have been forged. But that forging did not come without a price."

He paused a moment, bowing his head.

"Doagnis has gone. No doubt you all know the tale of this by now, so I shall not tell it again. Rather, I shall ask you for your forgiveness for the part I played in it."

A rustle of whispers coursed through the crowd.

"Doagnis desired to rule, and that is no sin, for many have desired it before now. But her life was born of hatred and fear, so she meted out that hatred and fear upon others. That is who she is, a choice she found that she could not deny at the end, for we are all the sum of our lives."

He held up a hand in the gesture of warning.

"She raised you up and brought you back to Lon-Elah. For a time I fought her in ignorance. I did not know who I was. Rash oaths I swore, oaths that I have since come to regret. But when I found out who I was, everything changed. Then I came to her, and together, for a while, we knew the comfort of shared covenant. But she was already tainted by her fear of her past, and she continued the fight. She knew that she was of the line of Soivar, and her fear of discovery drove her to do terrible things. She has paid for her choices, as we all have. When the mighty fall, they do not care what lies beneath. They crush it in their despair."

Now he made the gesture of appeal.

"And so I stand before you, repentant to the last. I ask for your forgiveness and would know your will. What say you? Will you follow me once more? Will you accept me as Haelok?"

It was spontaneous, hands held up in the gesture of acceptance, a single cry from every mind, every voice as one.

"You are our prince," they all said.

Korfax dropped to his knees and bowed to them. There was utter silence. He stood again.

"Then from this day forward let there be no division amongst us. Let us be whole. Let us march to the north and reclaim our land, and let nothing stand in our way."

All now dropped to their knees in turn and bowed to him, to their prince, their Haelok, last child of the Mikaolazith.

They broke camp and crossed the hills, riding down to the ruins of Othil Admaq. Few spoke. As they followed the road, passing under the walls, many looked up at the crumbling stone. Soon they came to the road north, the great road bestriding the desert. Along its wide way they went, a great dark line rising up above the sands. To the north they went, leaving death, betrayal and the darkest of miracles behind them. Their great prince had slain a god. All they could do was follow.

He watched from the wall, as still as the stone about him, as the dark line wound its way by, riders, wains and walkers, an entire people on the move. At the head, no doubt, was Korfax, leading them all to war. To the north they would go, leaving nothing but grief in their wake.

He turned back to his city. Moments ago, or so it seemed, this place had lived. Now it was dead, as was everything in it.

Death had come and he had seen the storm of its passing, even as he had sat alone upon the heights, brooding, ever brooding, upon his choices. He should have told Korfax the truth, he should have trusted his friend and he should not have slain Odoiar.

After the death of Odoiar he had fled to the hills, there to hide. He was a coward. He could not face any of them, not now. He had slain Odoiar in his despair and he would have to pay for that crime.

He had wondered what his mother and father would say. Would they understand? They knew his heart, knew that he desired only what was right. But what would they say of the murder of Odoiar? He should not have done that, no matter the provocation.

It was as he had sat there, high in the hills, that he had seen the day darken around him. Then had come a coldness and a sense of rising powers. He had looked up, stood up even, as the storm flew across his sky, dark and writhing. But then it came – death and worse than death.

The storm had descended upon the city and his world had ended. It fell upon his city and pleasured itself upon the stone. He saw the pale face rise up, he saw the city sucked dry and he knew then that far more had been lost this day than his honour.

Eventually the storm had departed, leaving the city broken behind it. Everything was in ruins! Everything? His family? The realisation felled him and he had fallen to the ground, curling in upon himself. He felt emptiness. He had not been there. He had not been with them when death had come. But he had not thought, had not believed that such a thing would happen. He had dropped his head to the dirt at his feet and wept. He had drawn his sword and struck the ground with it, again and again, until he could do it no more. But still the tears had rolled down and still the despair filled him.

Eventually he got up again and walked the grief-stricken road down into the ruins. All he had ever cared for was gone. All that he had ever loved had died. Even Korfax. There was no Korfax any more, just a dark shell, a dead thing that walked the world in his place, a thing of rage and vengeance.

Though he had no tears left to shed, Ralir felt their departed ghosts still falling from his eyes. Where had it all gone so terribly wrong? Why did the Creator allow such things to be?

Now here he was, upon the wall, watching as the Iabeiorith left, that dark line of vengeance that had eaten his city. It took a long time for them to pass, but eventually they were done, moving on, a diminishing darkness heading north.

He watched in stillness, and the stillness consumed him until he could no longer move. He became a point, dimensionless and frozen. Even breath seemed to cease.

Darkness came, the fall of night, and still he stood upon the wall. He thought of vengeance, but had not the fire. He could not face Korfax. He could not face his fear. He thought of hurling himself from the heights, or falling upon his sword, but he could not do it. He clung to life yet, still upon that dreadful ledge, unable to face what waited below.

A voice came to him out of the night.

"Well now, it seems you no longer desire your life but do not have the will to end it. Perhaps I can be of service?"

Shocked to mobility, he turned. She stood not seven paces away, sensuous curves and dark robes coiling. But her eyes held him. They pulled at him. Drown in me, they said, burn in me. He could not look away.

"I know your pain," she told him. "I can ease it."

He was a moment answering.

"Who are you?"

"You know who I am, Ralir of Badagar. You have heard my name many times before."

Ralir shook his head but did not look away. Her beauty held him, innocent like a child's, but so knowing, so dark.

"We have met? I do not think so. I think I would have remembered you," he said. She laughed fondly.

"No," she said. "We have not met before. But you do know me. I am Doagnis."

He would have leapt back, run perhaps, but suddenly he was surrounded by small, self-luminous globes that hung in the air. Forces held him. He could not have fled now, even if he had wanted to.

"Do you see them?" she asked. "My allies? Do you know what they are? Do you recognise them?"

Ralir stared about him. There were eight of them, eight pulsing, dripping forms. They moved and shifted under their coverings, unpleasant suggestions of form, and they laughed at him with thick, liquid voices. Ralir could not help but look at them, and he knew, with utter certainty, that he did not want to see whatever it was that lay beneath their slimy robes.

Doagnis came closer and pulled his head back to her with her hand.

"They are the last of the Agedobor," she whispered.

Only his eyes moved at that, widening with shock. He knew the stories, tales told out of the long years, tales of the Black War. When he had studied in the Umadya Madimel he had read of them. The Agedobor. They were a horror, and to be at their mercy was said to be the worst fate of all, for they loved the suffering of others and lusted after it as if it was the greatest prize in all of Creation.

Doagnis stepped back, holding his eyes with hers.

"Here is my desire," she said. "I will leave this place and follow Korfax, my loving brother and the father of my child."

For a moment she caressed herself, hands moving down, over her breasts to her belly, where they played for a moment.

"I will follow him," she continued, "but I will not strike. I will wait until he has defeated the enemy, until he has crushed the Agdoain."

She smiled.

"That was the mistake the others made, those fools of the west. They hobbled him before he could win this war. They did not understand his purpose. But I do now. Tools should be used until they can be used no more, not thrown away before their time. Korfax is the mightiest ever to stride out across the world. I know. I have seen. He can slay gods!"

Now she looked away, eyes filling with remembered terror as she stared down into herself, down into memory.

"He can slay gods," she whispered. She looked up again. "So I will not touch him until his task is done," she said.

She reached down into her robes and drew out a knife, long and sharp, a brilliant blade and the blackest of hilts.

"But once victory is complete, once it is certain that the Agdoain are defeated, then I will act."

She held the knife up.

"I will end his life. I will walk up behind him and stab him through his mighty heart."

She moved to within a hand's breadth of Ralir's face.

"But I cannot do this alone," she told him. "My brother knows me all too well, the touch of my mind, the sound of my voice. I will need your assistance. I will need you."

Ralir understood. He tried to speak, to scream his denial, but he could not. He was held in place and could not move.

"Arzulg!" she said, looking to the side.

One of the Agedobor came forward.

"Let us empty the vessel," Doagnis told it. "Let us empty it so that we can fill it up again with our desire."

She walked away, turning her back and casting her hood over her head. Clearly she did not want to watch what was about to happen. Ralir quailed at the prospect. The Agedobor called Arzulg rose up to hover immediately in front of his face. He could see every detail now and he did not want to. Its coverings were shapeless drapes of leathered slime. Something writhed underneath and a stench came with it, a stench as of excrement.

"Feast upon my glory," it said, and it parted its coverings.

When it was done, when what lay beneath was hidden again, Doagnis turned about and came back to Ralir. He now hung limply in the air and stared emptily into the distance. She came close, cupping his slack face in her hands and staring intently into his eyes. They were all but empty.

"He is gone?" she asked.

"Almost!" said the one she had called Arzulg. "I withheld at the last, though it was difficult. There is nothing so satisfying as watching the spark depart, but a corpse is of no use in this endeavour."

"Good," she said. "Only one more thing to do." Then she leaned in and kissed Ralir full upon his all but lifeless lips.

15

THE AWAKENING

Bor-pirjo Krih-dial-orje
Unchod-lam Yoi-kom-eaih
Manipal Ahz-zar-meqis
Bl-chis-iam Gem-gah-atil
Krg-qohil Ar-is-odtel
Kah-tabix Odson-dr-pan
Od-urq-pl Var-a-kao-jo

She awoke to a dim grey dawn. For a long time her thoughts wandered, sick, fragile things, ever struggling to shape themselves, only to fall apart again before they could fully form.

She remembered conflict, a vague memory of violence and horror, but it seemed another age and another life ago. She tried to see, but her thoughts hid from her, fading even as they fled.

There was fear somewhere, a dim apprehension that sat within her like an itch too deep to scratch. Something below all thought, something deeper than her bones, had marked the passage of time. Whole seasons have come and gone, it told her, and things are no longer what they once were.

She tried to see where she was, struggling against a heavy reluctance, but it was to no avail. She could not move, and she could not see beyond the grey veil that shrouded her.

Why was she so weak, she wondered? No intelligence came to her, though. She fought against herself for a while, but it all came to nought. In the end she fell back again, down into the depths, drifting downwards, down through the ever shifting landscape of her mind like some heavy cloud, drowsy with sleep.

A light grew about her, brightening the featureless grey. She turned to face it, but there was nothing there. For a long while the light was all she could see, but then, finally, a vague outline began to form. She watched as it coalesced, growing ever more certain, ever more sharp. Eventually she could make out the silhouette of a tall figure, tall against the brightness, but there were no features to speak of, none at all.

She waited as she watched, waiting for the figure to speak, but it did not. Was this another phantom, she wondered, something from her unruly mind?

Then, as if in answer, a voice spoke to her, a voice out of the all-encompassing grey.

"So you are with us once more? Long have we struggled to bring you back from the brink, and it was uncertain if you would ever return at all. You were so reluctant it was all but certain that we had failed. But here you are again, back from your deeps."

Was it the figure that spoke? She tried to raise herself up to see better, but she could not. Her weakness held her down, and more than weakness, for she seemed to be held in place by bindings, bindings that were soft but not overly yielding.

"Where am I?" she asked. Her tongue crawled in her mouth.

"Safe," came the answer.

"Safe?"

"From the troubles of the world."

"Who are you?"

"Your saviour."

"Why am I bound?"

"For your protection."

"From what?"

"The troubles of the world."

She closed her eyes and followed the circle of words, a never-ending spiral that rolled on and on and on. The voice filled her head, so gentle, so calm. She could feel herself wanting to succumb, but something inside her rebelled. She was awake now, it told her, and she needed to remain so. To return to oblivion would be wrong. She willed herself to look again. The silhouette was still there.

"Good!" it said. "You no longer desire sleep! Perhaps you are ready to go further."

There was a pause.

"Your timing is almost prescient."

She struggled with the words, with her thoughts, trying to marshal them.

"What has happened?" she asked. "How long have I been lying here? Where is Korfax?"

"So many questions," came the answer, "so many irrelevancies. As for Korfax? No doubt he is the reason you are back. Your spirit has heard his thunder, felt his mighty footfall upon the land and so it has returned to your flesh. You have purpose once more."

"Who are you?"

"Who am I? Have you not guessed?"

There was a pause.

"Truly?"

There was another pause.

"You seek a name, but what is a name, really? All names are veils. They hide what really is. Just as this face does. It also is a veil, hiding what lies beneath. We are vessels, mere shells. You see the shell, but only within is the truth. The other showed me this. For a long while I did not understand, but then it became clear at last, when Emethgis Vaniad was taken."

She heard a hint in the voice, a chilling hint.

"Where am I?" she asked.

"You are in Emethgis Vaniad," she was told.

She thought about that, and felt a slow coil of fear.

"But you said Emethgis Vaniad had been taken."

"Yes I did. But don't you understand? You and the city share the same fate. Emethgis Vaniad has been taken by the other, just as you have been taken by me."

"I cannot see you."

"Can you not? Then let me show you. Here I am."

She saw.

"You?" she gasped.

"Me!" he whispered.

"Release me at once!" she cried.

"That would not be wise!" he said. "You are still weak. You might damage yourself."

She tried to move but could hardly raise even her hands. It was useless. She glared at him, hurling all the rage and loathing that she could.

"You are vile!" she told him. "You are loathsome! Is this really what you desire? Do you truly believe that what you cannot achieve openly, you will achieve by subversion. I hate you!"

He looked back at her sadly.

"You do not know what you are saying," he said. "You do not understand. I will return when you have come to your senses."

He turned and left.

She lay alone for a long while, wondering, occasionally trying her bonds, but it was no use. She was weak, like a child.

There had been a struggle amongst stones and dust, the Agdoain coming for her, ever coming for her, Korfax fighting them off, ever fighting them. But then it had all gone grey, like the sudden tide of death, and everything had faded down to nothingness. Beyond that she could not go.

Eventually he came back to stand beside her, looking down.

"Have you come to your senses?" he asked.

"That depends," she answered.

"Upon what?"

"Upon what you choose to tell me."

He tilted his head.

"Ask your questions!" he said.

"Where is Korfax?" she asked.

"Korfax?"

"Where is he?"

"You would ask that, still, after what he did? I am astonished, truly I am."

He looked away, fingering his chin.

"Unless, of course, you desire revenge," he mused. He turned back to her once more. "Is that it? Do you desire revenge?"

"Revenge?" she questioned. "Revenge for what?"

Now he looked utterly perplexed.

"How do you think it was that you ended up here?" he said. "He killed you!"

Her mind went blank. Korfax had killed her? But she was alive! It was a long moment before she could speak again.

"I don't understand!" she said.

"You were fighting the Agdoain," he told her. "He used his power and he killed them. But you were caught in the fire. And that is how you were found. He deserted you, believing you dead by his hand. He does not care. But I do. I have healed you."

"You said that he killed me?"

"You were on the edge. You were nearly gone. But I brought you back. He was the one that abandoned you, not I."

"He thought I was dead?" she whispered.

He paused for a moment.

"You do not remember?"

He turned away.

"Well, perhaps you do not. But it was his power that broke you. As he broke his enemies so he broke you. He was never the subtlest of souls."

She could not think. What had happened? She remembered the Chanorus, riding by the Lee Leiulus, finding the pool and fighting the Agdoain. She remembered the last stand, when they were surrounded. She remembered Korfax wrestling with one of the Ageyad. Beyond that, nothing.

"It must have been an accident," she murmured.

"Believe what you will," he said, "but his was the hand that nearly cost you your life. He confessed as much to me before he escaped. He thought you dead. I thought him dead. Such are the symmetries that rule our imperfect lives."

She waited a moment.

"He escaped? Where is he now?"

"Why do you care?"

"You know why."

He looked at her with distaste.

"You love him? Still? After what he did to you?"

"It was an accident. He was trying to preserve me."

He sighed.

"Believe what you will until the world teaches you otherwise."

There was silence for a long while.

"Why am I here?" she asked.

"I have been healing you," he answered.

"Why?"

"I would have thought that obvious."

"Where is Korfax?"

"That again? I suppose nothing will satisfy you until I give you an answer. So let us just say that he is where he has always been, deep in the arms of rebellion."

Now it was her turn to sigh.

"You will not tell me, then!"

"I will answer you in any way that I see fit," he said.

"Why won't you tell me the truth?"

Now he looked incredulous.

"The truth?" he said. "You are clearly not ready for the truth. I tell you Korfax killed you, you say that he did not. I tell you that I healed you, you tell me you do not understand why. It is clear to me now that you will accept nothing that I say."

He drew back for a moment, waiting for her to say something, but she did not.

"So be it!" he said, his face in shadow.

"Korfax is trying to unite that which cannot be united," he told her. "He is trying to join opposites. He will fail. Then, once he realises this, he will come here and try to destroy what cannot be destroyed. As always, he aims far too high. He will miss and fall, as he has ever done so. All things die in his ungentle hands."

He leaned in closer.

"He is an oath-breaker and a betrayer. He has willingly embraced the forbidden lore. He does not care how he achieves his ends, just so long as he achieves them!"

She stared up at him

"The forbidden lore? What forbidden lore? He is a Geyadril of the Dar Kaadarith, the mightiest there has ever been, save one. He turned his father's stave white!"

"Yes," he said, "and I have not forgotten it. But that is not what I am speaking of. Forbidden lore, I said. Korfax would embrace profanity, in all its ways."

"You speak in riddles."

He smiled at that, drawing away from her.

"Do I? Or perhaps it is merely that you are simply unwilling to hear what I am saying. Do you remember Doagnis?"

She felt herself go very still. Something in his voice warned her. Something was coming, something she would rather not know.

"She was the one that tried to kill the high council," she said. "She killed my father."

"Indeed," he replied. "Your father was murdered by Doagnis, and Korfax was sent to apprehend her. But he failed in the task and now Doagnis is the very one that your so-called beloved is in league with! Forbidden lore, I said. How much will it take for you to be convinced? He throws you down, leaves you for dead and then allies himself with the murderer of your father?"

She struggled feebly against her bonds.

"It isn't true," she cried. "It isn't true. You are a liar."

"It is true. Believe it. I do not lie," he returned.

He leaned in closer once more, a gleam of teeth in the darkness.

"I am here. He is not. I healed you. He did not. You lie here alone. He takes one of the Argedith to his bed. Draw your own conclusions."

She heard the words but could not believe them. It was spite, all of it, malice and spite. She watched him leave, and then she let the tears stream down her face.

It was some time before he returned again.

"Are you now ready to resume your life?" he asked.

She did not answer.

"Do you hear me?"

"Release me from these bonds and then you will hear me," she hissed.

He laughed quietly at that.

"Your powers are no match for mine, or the other. The tricks and the wiles you have learnt in your brief life will not avail you here. The other is as far beyond you as you are beyond the things that sleep in the muck of the abyss."

She looked at him.

"What is this other that you keep babbling about? Have you become mad at last?"

"Will there never be an end to your questions?" he sighed. "I suppose not. You know so little, after all. You struggle into this world, an empty mind waiting to be filled, but then, after all too brief a moment, you leave again, still just as ignorant as when you first slipped in through the door."

He paused and looked at her, as if measuring something.

"I said that I should not leave you in ignorance, but I am at a loss as to how to explain the other to you. You see, the other is like nothing that you can imagine!" He smiled to himself. "Now there is comedy!"

She frowned.

"I never thought you a babbler," she said, "but you have become one now, Explain yourself!"

He looked down at her and his sudden humour vanished as quickly as it had arisen.

"Explain myself?" he said. "I do not have to justify a single thing to you! I have not forgotten what you did. You denied me!"

He turned away for a moment, a hand raised, closing on empty air. Then he turned back.

"But I must not leave you in darkness. I will show you my purpose, whether you truly wish to see it or not, for I believe you to have a singular destiny. When I am done, you – and you alone – will be the one to understand. You will know the great truth."

"Which is?"

"That nothing lasts for ever!" He paused a moment. "It is time," he said. He moved to her side. "Come with me."

"Where?" she asked.

"Where I am going, of course."

"But I cannot move."

"Yes you can!"

Her bonds vanished as though suddenly sucked out of existence. She tried to rise, but it was as though the bonds were still there. She could barely move at all. She looked down at herself. She wore only a simple gown. Beneath it she could see her body. She had become thin, a famished shadow.

"What have you done to me?" she cried.

"I?" he said. "I have done nothing to you. It was Korfax did this, not I. You have slept longer than you should and your body has become weak. That is all."

"Then how can I come with you if I cannot even get up?"

He raised an eyebrow and tilted his head slightly.

"Here," he said, "a gift for you, one of many I shall give."

Energy suffused her limbs. She gasped in astonishment. It was like being flooded with gentle fires, fuelling fires that returned her to herself. She could move. He smiled at her.

"Am I not generous? Am I not considerate?"

He leaned forward and all but lifted her off the bed with one hand.

"Come," he told her. "We must not be late."

"Late for what?" she asked.

"Late for what we need to be in time for!" he answered.

She pulled away in exasperation.

"Which is?"

"You will see."

He held her by her left arm and all but dragged her with him. She tried to resist, but she might as well have struggled against a mountain. He was stronger than stone.

He marched her through corridors, through halls, through doorways, down stairs, down, ever down, but she did not recognise where she was. There was little light and everything was in shadow.

They finally achieved two great doors, which opened silently even as they approached them, and beyond them waited rank upon rank of Agdoain, warriors and Ageyad both, thousands upon thousands of them, drooling even as they bowed down before him, cowering in abject fear.

She instinctively drew back, but he marched her on, straight towards them, even as they tumbled to the ground and kissed the stone. For a moment it seemed that she rode out on the crest of some irresistible tide, a grey flood, a deluge that would sweep everything else before it.

She shrank from them, even as they prostrated themselves, and she would have run but he held her up, his fingers digging into her arm as he forced her on. She looked back at him with dull incomprehension. What was this?

The Agdoain were terrified of him, and she began to feel the beginnings of terror herself. What was this thing that walked beside her? It looked like an Ell, it talked like an Ell, but the Agdoain feared it unto death. That which had never feared, that which had willingly, gleefully, spent its flesh by the hundred, by the thousand, was afraid at last. She could see it written on them and in them, in every grey and quivering line of their foul bodies. Even their beasts were terrified, bowing their mighty shoulders to the ground and mewling in fearful supplication, but her escort looked neither to the left nor to the right as he dragged her on. He ignored them as though they were not even there.

Finally she understood. The Agdoain were his, his slaves, to do with as he pleased, to use as he would, in any way, shape or form that he desired. He was their master. He was the one that had called them to the world. He was the enemy. It was the worst of all betrayals – and the most hideous.

She looked about her for want of something else to think upon, and suddenly she realised that she was not sure where exactly it was in the city that they were. The skyline of Emethgis Vaniad had changed since last she had seen it.

She turned to look behind her and saw the Umadya Pir rearing darkly against the sky. That had been the place of her confinement, the place where she had lain like a dead thing for all this time. But how different it was now. Its light was gone and vine-like growths now fattened themselves upon its stone. Sickened, she looked away again.

It took her a few moments, a tower here, a wall there, but she began to piece it together. Before her should have been the Umadya Zedekel, the Umadya Semeiel and the Umadya Nogarel, but they were gone. Empty sky yawned where they had once reared their mighty forms, and all she could see was broken stone and rubble. That was where they were going, though, to where the great tower of the Dar Kaadarith had once stood.

After passing through the wreckage they arrived at the edge of a pit, an immense hole that had been ripped from the city's heart. Some distance below lay what was left of the foundations. She looked down. Stone glistened unevenly back at her as if it had once melted and flowed, only to solidify again in strange frozen whirls. Many colours were stirred into its surface, chaotic and random, and long cracks ran this way and that.

What had happened here, she asked herself, what calamity had so burned the city?

She turned to her escort and he smiled back at her with such emptiness that even she felt like tumbling to the ground before him in terror. It was vile, dead, a mockery, the yawning of an abyss wider than the great pit before her and far deeper. She wanted to run from that smile, to run and to run and to never turn around again. But she could not. He held her fast. He gestured at the pit.

"The one that achieved this still lives," he told her. Even his voice was changed now, echoing as if rising up from great distances.

She stared into the pit. Now she understood. When Othil Zilodar had fallen, someone had destroyed the furnaces of the Dar Kaadarith rather than let the Agdoain gain them. The same had happened here. Now, as if ignited by her thought, she felt a sense in the air about her, a rumour in the ground at her feet, the ghost of an intense heat.

"I have only one regret," he announced.

She looked back at him, but he was not looking at her. His eyes stared into the distance instead, lightless and dull.

"When I saw the Umadya Semeiel erupt in flame, when I saw it destroyed, I was angry. How dare they break my city? How dare they?!"

He clenched his jaws and the muscles rippled, fat worms pulsing. An image came to her then of being eaten alive, consumed from within. She felt sick at the thought and tried to pull away once more, but he held her tight. He looked down into the pit.

"But I was not thinking," he said. "I was suddenly back in the cage that holds the rest of you, acting without thought, obeying the dictates of the flesh. That is my regret."

He clenched his jaws again.

"I punished him," he spat. For a moment there was malice and the hint of fire, but all too quickly it was gone again.

"Even in the worst of choices, though," he continued, "there lies a lesson, if one has wit enough to see it."

He gestured at himself and then at her.

"We live in the land of flesh, and flesh has its own ideas. The will proposes but the flesh disposes! Denial! That was the lesson, and I have learnt it well. I will never make such a mistake again. I should have preserved him for just such a moment as this, not punished him. It would have been far better if he had been the one to bear witness to his folly, not you. But all such desires are vain in this imperfect place. The arrow moves in one direction only. You only ever get one chance."

He paused for a moment, looking out at her through the mask of his face.

"And so it falls to you," he said. "Two purposes served, not one. I brought you here so that you could understand. Then you can explain it to him. Let his imagination see it, rather than his sight. Let him know the full extent of his folly. Let him know the full error of his ways."

"And what am I to understand?" she asked. "Defiance?"

He laughed quietly to himself, almost a hiss.

"No! You already understand that. You are here to understand the truth."

"What truth?"

"My truth."

"Which is?"

"That we are nothing!" he announced. "That we are prisoners! That you and I and all of us are nothing more than the slaves of time, to be spat out and swallowed up by a blind, uncaring creation, that both flesh and will are illusory, that all our works are dust."

He bowed his head slightly.

"Better that it all end," he said.

She stared at him. She did not know what to say. He smiled his empty smile again.

"Watch and you shall see," he told her. Then he turned to the pit.

There must have been a signal, but she did not catch it. Crude doors she had not noticed before opened below her, and out into the light staggered the last ragged remnants of the city's once mighty populace.

Here were the last few, the very last, those unfortunate few that had not managed to escape when the city fell. She could not imagine what it must have been like, the panic, the horror, as the Agdoain erupted over the walls.

She thought herself thin now, but the prisoners below were emaciated, starved and naked, bones and skin with barely the strength to stand. A lifetime of torment had fallen upon them, or so it seemed, but still they possessed enough of themselves to walk out into the light unbowed. For a moment she watched them with desperate pride – their rebellion, their defiance, lifting her even as she tried to reach out to them. But he would not let her.

She understood what was to follow, and her heart went dead inside her. These ragged few walked into an arena. She turned to her escort and raised her free hand in supplication.

"Please, do not do this," she asked. "You do not need to. Please let them live. I understand now. I understand!"

His smiled widened, its abyss stirred by an even deeper rupture.

"You understand?" he laughed. "I do not think so. If you understood you would not ask for their lives. No, you do not understand at all. You must see this with your own eyes, you must experience this with your own flesh. You must feel it, know it, have it written in bloody words across your sight! Only then can you truly appreciate my truth, for only then will you understand its poetry. Why do you think I preserved you in the first place? You are here to stand at my side and bear witness!"

She would have knelt, begged even, but again he would not let her.

"Please," she cried. "Do not harm them!"

The rupture deepened, and his eyes gleamed down at her like stagnant pools.

"Harm them? You still do not see! Harm them? I will not harm them. It is creation that harms them! It is creation that has brought them to this place and this time. If creation was so benign they would not be here and the possibility of suffering would not exist. As for me? I await their release. I await the moment their burdens are lifted! I await the end of their pain! That is what I wish for. They are blessed in this, as you will be when you understand what it is that you really see. Are not all things made known by their opposite?"

She had no answer. What could she say? She stared up at him in horror, even as he turned her about with his brutal strength.

She looked below again, trying to mark each ragged face, trying to preserve them all in her memory. But for some reason her eyes kept straying to two that waited in the midst of the crowd. She did not recognise them, did not know them, but they drew her like a fire in the night.

The elder held the younger against her breast, her eyes closed, her face beatific. This one had already accepted her fate. The younger had closed her eyes also, but clung to the elder as though to a narrow ledge. This one did not accept what was to happen at all. There it all was – one single glimpse, the old waiting for the sword to fall, the young believing it could not.

She tried to reach out. She wanted to go to them, to save them, but she was denied. The brutality of it had her weeping.

There must have been another signal, but again she did not see it. The Agdoain around them picked themselves up and now streamed past them both in ever-increasing numbers, a torrent of limbs and bodies. They encircled the pit, spreading out on either side, each stopping at its appointed place before leering down at those that waited below.

Eventually the pit was surrounded. Rank upon rank waited above, thousands of them leaning eagerly over the shattered edge, a single sightless stare of lust. Those that stood below merely looked up, eyes wide and mouths closed. For what seemed an age each regarded the other, predator and prey. The grinning horrors gloated while the ragged prisoners waited silently with fear and resignation in their eyes.

Her companion raised his arm and the Agdoain turned to him, almost as one, as if he had suddenly become the only voice in the whole of creation. Like a god he held them, his upraised hand their only purpose, their only doom. He kept his hand raised for a long time, a very long time, and she thought she caught a glimpse in his eyes of a dark joy, the veriest glimmer of rapture. So this was what lay under his truth! Mere dominion!

He lowered his hand again and released them, all of them, and they poured over the rim, a grinning flood of grey. Those in the pit made no sound at all as they contracted to the centre whilst the grey flood advanced upon them with slow and deliberate relish. Then the feasting began.

When it was time to look away, when the horror approached its moment, she found that she could not, nor close her eyes, nor shut out the sound, for something suddenly had her in its fist, forcing her to look, forcing her to hear, forcing her to know, with horrific intimacy, the dark orgy of carnage as it unfolded below.

She wanted to cry, to scream her outrage, to fight the one that held her. But she could not. She was held where she was and the slow deliberate slaughter became a rape: a rape of sight, a rape of sound and, a rape of being.

Later, when it was over at last, when she eventually had strength enough to pull herself away from the horror, she stared back up at him for long moments, clutching at the only thing that she could to keep hold of her sanity – her hatred.

She reached out to claw at him, to strike him, to hurt him, but he knocked her aside with ease. He was far stronger than her.

"Why have you done this?" she sobbed. "Why have you betrayed everything?"

"This is not a betrayal!" he said, shaking her arm, shaking all of her. "You have failed to see. Still you hold on to the lie, the comforting lie that has been your existence. You do not look beneath its mask. I do now what I must. It is why I am here, to bring the truth and the way. Am I not the chosen of the Creator?"

"You are nothing of the Creator!" she said. "You are profane! You are a monster, a master of monsters. The Agdoain are yours!"

He smiled.

"The Agdoain? That is not what I call them."

"So they do have a name, then?"

"I see you," he said. "You are thinking that all names are a power, but you are wrong. Forget the little deceits you have learnt in your life, they will not help you here. My slaves are proof of that. Call them? They will not hear you! Summon them? They will not come! For a brief time they are born, but all too soon it is over again. They are so utterly empty."

He paused a moment, glancing back into the pit before turning to her once more.

"And that is their purpose," he told her. "That is why they are here. To clear it all away. But even they do not fully comprehend. Of all the creatures in all the heavens they come closest to the truth, but even they cannot attain it until the very end."

So that was it! She understood, and her comprehension burned her mind into another shape.

"So why not kill them all and gift them with your truth as well," she dared.

He laughed at that, a counterfeit of contempt.

"To fight a war you must understand the ground upon which you wage it," he answered. "In order to oppose, you must exist, but by existing you are corrupted. Learning this, knowing it, brings with it the wisdom to undo it. You must fight the strictures of the flesh and let the very purposes of life become your goad. You must live in the world in order to learn what it is you must destroy, and that is what they are here to do. They must destroy the world to which they have been born so that they may, at last, achieve salvation. That is the promise."

She hung her head, but her voice still rang clear.

"Salvation?" she said. "What salvation is there but the end? You are vile! You are diseased! You are a canker, a madness, a plague upon the bright heart of creation. All things are revealed by their opposites? You will end also. The light shall be turned upon you at last, and you will have no choice but to shrivel back to the nothingness from which you sprang."

She turned on him now, filled to the brim with her fury, and her eyes blazed.

"Hear me, you rotted thing! There will be an accounting for all that you have done. And though you hold my life in your hand, though you are able to slay me on a whim, I swear to you now that I will be there at the end, at the very end, when all hopes fail and all choices are done, to carve the name of justice into your foul and corrupted heart."

He laughed, and the sound echoed everywhere as though they had suddenly sunk through the world and down into the depths. Immensities reared about her, a vastness that lifted itself up to regard her through his eyes, older and deeper than time. She was a mote before it, crushed down to a dimensionless point, and it swallowed her whole.

"No," came the echo from the dark, "that will not happen. For all madness will end, as will loyalty, as will perfidy. There will be no darkness, nor light, nor an accounting either, for that also shall cease. And you will not carve your hatred for me into my heart, daring to call it justice in your petty arrogance, for that, too, shall be gone. For nothing will remain at all, and nothing shall come of nothing, ever again."

She sat upon the stone where he had placed her. He had carried her back inside the tower, or so he had said. She had fallen, he told her, her strength failing her at the last, an inevitable weakness of the flesh. So he had brought her here and bade her wait, telling her that many of her questions would be answered, that she would understand if she remained where she was. But then he had laughed quietly to himself and walked away, and his laughter had beaten the air about her head like two immense wings.

She was tempted to defy him, tempted to leave, but she knew that she dared not. Not now. He surpassed her for the moment. So she waited, and waited again, not daring to move lest she incur his wrath.

It was a long wait, and her thoughts circled in her head like wounded things. Images, words, a jumble of impressions. She tried to meditate, to calm her mind, but she could not, her mind would not obey. Finally it became too much. Though she dreaded the consequences, she stood up and turned to leave, only to discover that another was approaching. Was this why she had been told to wait?

She watched the shambling figure as it slowly made its way towards her. The head was bowed as though in pain, and it held out its hands before it as though to feel its way. With its deliberate steps and its ragged and tattered robes, she found herself thinking of aged seers broken by the power of their vision. Then she realised what it was that she was seeing. This one was blind.

She went to him, reaching out a hand to help, but he drew back from her and held up his hands as if to ward her off.

"I only wished to help," she said.

He lifted his head and with uncanny accuracy aimed the bloody holes where his eyes used to be straight at her. She stepped back. She could not help it.

"You are real?" he asked.

"Yes," she answered.

The figure lowered his hands.

"Then you are the one I was sent to meet. Who are you?"

"He did not tell you?"

"He tells me very little. I am here only for his amusement."

She reached out again.

"Let me help you."

The figure paused for a moment.

"Do I know your voice?" he said. "I have heard it before, I think, though I cannot place it. Please forgive my failing memory, but I have long been in darkness and it becomes harder to remember the light as time goes by. Who are you?"

She looked at him. He knew her voice? Did she know him? Long gone images of her past filled her, recollections of earlier, happier days. Then she had it, but the tormented figure before her hardly matched the one she remembered.

"Ponodol?" she asked. He flinched even as she spoke his name.

"Who is it that knows me?" he demanded. "Who is it that knows my name?"

"Oh, Ponodol! What has been done to you?" she cried. Tears came. She reached up to touch his face, but he knocked her hand aside.

"Please! Stop this! Tell me who you are."

His voice was desperate now.

"It is Obelison," she told him.

"No!" he hissed.

"But I am Obelison," she told him again. "Don't you remember me?"

He all but choked as she spoke her name. After long moments, he found his voice again.

"But Obelison is dead!" he growled. "What cruel phantom are you?"

"No, Ponodol," she answered, "it is me. In all truth it is."

She reached out and took one of his hands. He tried to snatch it away, but she held fast.

"Here," she offered, "here is my face, here is my mind."

Guided by her, he reached out – a single hand passing over her skin, a single thought piercing her mind. Then he sagged as he saw what he had already feared he would.

"Obelison!"

He breathed her name as though it both burned and soothed him.

"So you are here also!" he murmured. "I thought you dead. But then I thought I was dead also."

He paused, seeking hope.

"But perhaps I am wrong. Perhaps we are both dead, you and I. Has the madness I hear in this haunted tower cast me into the lingering place? But then how are you in here with me? You are flesh and blood. I know the touch. I know the feel. How is it that you are here also, beside me, living and breathing? Please tell me that you are some gentle spirit resurrected for my ease, that you are not really with me in this place of horror."

But she clung to him, holding him fast, crying quietly at his breast whilst he aimed his blindness at the unseen heavens and shook with rage and grief.

Obelison spoke at last, when she was finally able to.

"I am here, Ponodol," she said. "I am here with you. Both of us yet live, and maybe that is some cause for hope. Our tormentor may still be thwarted." The memory of a dreadful feasting filled her mind. "That is all I live for now," she whispered.

Ponodol bowed his head.

"Hope? I have precious little left of that." He aimed his sightless head at her and smiled. "But you are here, and you are alive."

"So why should I not be?" she asked.

"He told us you were dead, that Korfax had killed you in his mad rage," he answered. "Many believed him. But then Korfax came to me and told me another tale. That was when I first learned of his mad perfidy. But it all seems so long ago now, something that could only happen on the other side of the world."

Ponodol sighed.

"He did not show us your body. He would not let any other approach. But he wept over you and so we believed him. We convinced ourselves of his truth, but here you are now. How has this come to pass?"

"I do not know," she said. "I only know that I have slept for what seems an age. But now I am awake again, or so I believe." She looked down. "Then again, perhaps I dream also. The horror that dwells in this place can belong in no sane world."

"You do not dream," he answered at last. "I feel your warmth beside me, the flame of your life. I may have been blinded but I am not entirely bereft. This is no dream. No dream contains such terror. Only life can be so cruel."

She waited a moment before asking her next question.

"When I spoke to him, he kept talking about 'the other'. Do you know what he means?"

"I have felt that dreadful presence," he told her. "I do not know what it is. It is inside him. It blinded me."

"It blinded you?"

"Because I saw it. It talks to him. I heard it. Mother and child," he laughed grimly. "Mother and child."

"Mother and child?"

"That is how it speaks to him. I heard it. It punished me."

"Surely this is his madness? He believes he talks to his mother? But his mother died when he was born."

"No," said Ponodol. "Not that. It is something else. What it might be I cannot say, but it sits inside him like a grey hunger. It possesses him. It has driven him mad. It wants to eat the world. It wants to eat everything."

"Is it of the abyss?" she asked.

"No!" he said. "Remember what Korfax told you of his vision at Piamossin!"

She stared into the stone at her feet. She thought of the grey immensity, the void. Then words came back to her, words spoken far away to the north. An aged Arged stood in her mind and talked of dreadful things:

'You have seen them, I'm thinking. You know of what I speak. You have seen the grey void, just as I have. You have seen the infinite nothing, the well of dissolution. I saw it within you even as I healed you. Its servants have come amongst us at last: the foul, the vile, the upwelling spume. They are the unending hunger, the very heavings of Zonaa itself.'

"Zonaa," she said.

Ponodol stirred.

"Be careful what you reveal," he told her. "It does not enjoy the scrutiny of others."

"I cannot help what I know," she said. "It is what Mathulaa said to Korfax. He called the Agdoain the heavings of Zonaa. And Korfax saw the grey void, saw what was in it. I know. He showed it to me."

"Yes," he said. "He showed many that vision, but no one understood what it was that they saw. Whatever this 'other' is, it clearly sees Korfax as its enemy. It knows him. It reacts to him. He is our only hope. He is out there now, I am certain of it, gathering forces and building an army that he hopes will avenge us and cleanse the world."

Obelison looked up.

"You know something?" she asked.

"A little!" he said. "Enough to know that our enemy is not so mighty yet that he does not know fear, or doubt. They gnaw at him even as we speak. Will Korfax come, he wonders, and what will be the manner of his coming?"

Obelison started.

"He spoke to me of this. He told me things, terrible things. I did not believe them."

"What things?"

"How Korfax almost killed me. How Korfax has embraced the forbidden lore. How..."

She stopped. The words caught in her throat. She could not say it. Ponodol reached out a hand and gently touched her face, finding tears and brushing them away.

"Do not say it," he said.

"But I must," she insisted. "Nothing must be hidden."

She took a deep breath.

"He said to me that Korfax has taken the murderer of my father to his bed."

"He told you that?"

"Yes."

Ponodol grimaced.

"How can he know?" he said. "He is a thing of malice and spite."

He looked away.

"Korfax believed that you were dead and blamed himself for it," he told her. "There is pain in him now, the pain of loss. I saw it. It darkened his heart."

"But what of the rest?" she asked.

"There are many things you do not know," he said, "many things I have to tell you. None of it will be easy for you to hear, but believe it rather than the lies of our keeper. Not until Korfax can stand before you himself and tell you otherwise should you trust anything that you hear. There is more than one hatred at work in our world."

She waited in trepidation while Ponodol sighed and bowed his head again.

"Korfax has a heritage," he said. "He did not find out until after you were gone. But he told me what it was before the fall."

He smiled gently and squeezed her hand.

"Obelison, this will not be easy."

He looked up.

"But what is easy these days? All truths are hard now."

Ponodol turned to the window, unerringly catching the light with his sightless head. Suddenly he was a statue to her eyes, something carved from the finest stone.

"Before the fall of Emethgis Vaniad, Korfax came to the Umadya Semeiel and took the Kapimadar," he said. "He did this at the behest of Dialyas. It was a bargain between them. He would take the Kapimadar back to Dialyas and Dialyas would guide him to Doagnis. At that time we believed Doagnis was responsible for the Agdoain. Dialyas convinced Korfax that he could help, that he could use the Kapimadar against the Agdoain. Korfax believed him and came back here to take the stone. I only became aware of his presence when I felt the stone awaken at his touch. I rushed to the Hall of Memory to find out what was happening and confronted him. We had hard words together, but I was unprepared for what followed. He confessed himself to me. He told me the secret of his house. It was a brave thing to do, and dangerous, but I understand why he did it. I feel like Gemanim reborn. Trust such as that I can never repay, not even if I had a thousand lifetimes in which to achieve it."

"What secret?" she asked.

He turned back to her.

"The great secret of his house!" he said. "Where did the Farenith come from? From what great womb of power were they born? I would never have guessed such a truth, ever. He told me that he was descended, from father to son, in line unbroken, from Sondehna himself. Korfax is the last prince of the Mikaolazith."

Obelison felt the ground beneath her feet crumble away. An abyss suddenly yawned below her, not grey this time, but black, utterly black, all the way down.

"But his father, his mother..."

Ponodol smiled his sad smile.

"They knew," he said. "Sazaaim knew. Tazocho knew. It is all so clear to me now, all the things that were said, all the things that weren't. Even Gemanim knew, though he said nothing of it, not even when his death took him."

Ponodol bowed his head.

"Yet Tazocho wed with Sazaaim and bore Korfax in hope. If I had been told this tale, rather than witness it from afar, I would have dismissed it as fantasy. But strange as it may seem, there lies our hope now. Korfax knows."

Obelison continued to stare in horror at Ponodol.

"But... Sondehna?"

"Even so," he said. "Perhaps you do not know your beloved as well as you think. Korfax is not of such a temper. He is greater than that. Let him wield the lore that he has mastered and our enemy shall finally know the retribution of the Ell!"

There was a long silence.

"Does our keeper know?" she asked.

"No," he answered. "And here is something strange. He has looked into my mind many times but he has not seen it. Like the rest of us, I do not think he could imagine such a truth. It lies beyond his darkest imaginings."

Ponodol turned to her.

"You must not tell him, either. I believe there is advantage yet in keeping this secret."

He paused a moment.

"Let it run with the heavens," he quoted. She understood. It was for fate to speak.

They sat, side by side, hand in hand, and the long silence drifted on. She thought on all that she had been told. Finally, for want of something else to think on, she asked the inevitable.

"How long have I been gone?"

Ponodol sighed.

"Almost two years, I think," he said.

She clutched at him. That was far too long.

"What has happened?" she whispered. He sighed again.

"Many things, many terrible things! There are others here who tell me what passes in the world outside, whispering them to me in the quiet corners, here and there. He doesn't tell me anything, of course. Only riddles and spite pass his lips in my hearing. But I piece it all together eventually. He does not yet realise that, I think. He has not yet comprehended that others might think independently of him. In many ways, he is still a child."

"A child?"

"Yes. For all his power he remains a child yet. He has never truly grown up."

She held herself still. What a day of revelations this was becoming.

"But these others you speak of. Who are they?" she wondered.

"It is best that you do not know them," he told her. "All I will say is that a few, in their extremity, sold their souls to him at the very end. Only a few, a fragile few, but even that is enough. Such betrayals are bitter to take."

Ponodol passed a hand before her face like a warning.

"You should not seek them out!" he said. "You will not like what you find. They have paid dearly for their cowardice."

She watched the hand drop again.

"What do you mean?" she asked.

"They have betrayed themselves and they have paid for it," he told her. "Leave it at that."

"But you talk to them?"

A faint smile crossed his face. Obelison frowned. It suddenly seemed to her then that there was a hint of cruelty to it. Did Ponodol now relish the pain of others? Surely not! She silently berated herself for thinking such a thing. Ponodol could never be cruel. Or had he learnt such delights whilst incarcerated in this place?

"I am blind!" he finally said. "That is what I am here for – to listen."

He laughed quietly, but the sound was cold to her ears.

"Many of them have come to regret their decision," he continued. "Now they live in perpetual fear of what he might do to them, over and above what he has already done, and fear has ever fuelled rebellion, like envy before it. He thinks that their terror of him has silenced them entirely, so he feels free to mock them with tales from the world without. They keep their silence, of course, but then, later, much later, when I come upon them again, they tell me what he has told them. I have heard rumours, opinions, suppositions, half-truths and facts, all in equal measure. From them, and from his cruel riddles, I have gleaned much of what has passed in the land."

"And what has happened?"

"Enough grief and hope to fill the great ocean to overflowing."

Ponodol paused a moment, gathering himself.

"There was a battle, a great battle led by Noqmal, heir to the throne of Othil Ekrin."

He turned to her.

"Did you ever meet him?" he asked.

"No," she answered. "I never did."

Ponodol smiled.

"I met him once. He was tall and noble and courteous. And at the gates of Emethgis Vaniad he proved his valour. He fought the Agdoain right to the edges of the city itself. I would have given my soul to see it. Our captor must have raged that day to see so many of his slaves pass from the world. But, at the last, the long looked for victory was not to be. Noqmal was defeated, though his forces slew ten times their own number, and from that battle, from that defeat, dire consequences ensued. Othil Ekrin was the next to fall. The Agdoain, those that survived the battle, took many of the remaining sky ships and flew them back to Othil Ekrin. Othil Ekrin fell, but not by Agdoain hand. Someone destroyed the city by unseating its foundations rather than let the Agdoain take it."

Ponodol bowed his head.

"He lost a mighty army that day, almost all the forces he had in reserve, if what I have been told is true. That he has bred more I do not doubt, but the making of Agdoain seems to be a difficult art. They do not always wish to awaken. He, or the power he serves, has to coax them into existence. Their paltry spirits are ever reluctant to be caged in such unpleasant vessels. But, even better, he can only perform such makings at certain times. Our enemy follows some strange cycle I have not yet comprehended."

Ponodol offered her a grim smile.

"At the last the Agdoain are unwilling slaves, I think."

He dropped his head, peering into his sightless depths.

"When that army perished at Othil Ekrin I heard his rage from afar, and I relished it. But the Ell achieved a hollow victory that day, for who will be left to mourn the vanished beauty of the east? Who again will witness Rafarel rise over the Vasasan and so touch the Poamal Gevamah with the first light of morning? Who again will stand upon the seventh bridge and marvel at the great rift? Fifteen thousand years in the building! Fifteen thousand years!"

Ponodol bled empty tears. Then he turned back to her and she could see his rage. There was more to come, and she had already guessed that it would be bad.

"Othil Admaq has fallen also," he said, "but not by Agdoain hand. I do not know the whole truth of it, but another army was crushed that day, no less great than the one he lost in the fall of Othil Ekrin. Though I cannot find out how it was done, I do know that Othil Admaq was not destroyed by Agdoain hand, either. And, of all the things I have heard, that worries me the most. Was it sorcery? Korfax would not have done such a thing, but what of Doagnis? She would have no scruples in punishing those that would deny her will."

Obelison could barely believe what she was being told. Othil Ekrin and Othil Admaq? Both gone? Lon-Elah was being hurt in ways she had never dared imagine, not even in her darkest moments. And Korfax was with Doagnis? Obelison felt her heart sink.

"Is Korfax with her, then?" she asked.

"That much seems to be true," he answered, "but I imagine it would be an uneasy alliance. Remember who he is, and of what house he is born. But know also that Doagnis is born of the old north. Hers is a brutal heritage. I hope Korfax has tamed her, because if not, we may yet see one tyrant replaced by another."

Obelison tried not to think of it, but the words circled in her mind. 'He takes one of the Argedith to his bed.' She turned to Ponodol.

"You said that you hoped he has tamed her."

"It is not what you think, Obelison. Do not think that at all."

"But he is with her, the murderer of my father."

"I know, but how else will he achieve victory? The dark arts are the only weapon left to us, the only one that works."

"But he is with her," she insisted.

She could not get the thought out of her mind.

"Remember what I said," Ponodol reminded her. "Do not judge him until he stands before you. Do not count the cost of battle until you have fought it."

Ponodol did not let the silence lengthen.

"There is one last thing I should tell you," he said. "Lonsiatris is gone also."

"Gone?" she gasped.

"Vanished!"

"Vanished? Where?"

"Where?" he mused. "That is not apparent. But here is the thing. He fears its disappearance the most, though you will not hear him say so. He knows that he has been thwarted in some way, but he does not yet comprehend the magnitude of his loss. And he does not know that Korfax had a hand in it."

She looked up at him carefully.

"Korfax?"

"He took the Kapimadar to Dialyas. Dialyas must have used it."

"What is the Kapimadar?" she asked.

He smiled.

"The name speaks for itself," he said. "It is the fury of time caught within stone. With it, time can be subdued. With it, Zinznagah can be called down from on high and its waters navigated. It is the power of certainty."

"Certainty?" she asked.

"Complete and absolute," he answered. "The future revealed. All things known."

"Then why was it kept hidden?"

"Because it did not work. All thought it a failure, but little did they know."

"I don't understand."

"The stone silenced itself until the time was right. It locked itself down until the requisite moment arrived. It had already seen the future, and it would not move again until that future arrived. Looking back at it now, it is obvious, but then? Even Dialyas did not fully understand what he had wrought!"

"So how can Lonsiatris be gone?"

"Because the stone, in order to understand time, had to understand space as well. Being able to navigate time is not enough. You must also navigate space. So the stone had two purposes, one hidden beneath the other. That should not have been possible, according to the Namad Dar, but Dialyas was never one to accept a cage."

He leaned forward.

"Hear me well on this. With the Kapimadar, one could see the future. Vision, the art of the Exentaser, and purpose enough to use it. Even an Ell not gifted with the sight would be able to see with it. And not just see, it seems, for the stone had another power that was not so well known. Not only could it see the future, but it could take you there."

"But I thought you were one of those that made it?"

"Not always do we understand what is set before us. Four minds made the Kapimadar: Virqol, Ponodol, Sazaaim and Dialyas. It should not have worked at all, but Sazaaim was the key." Ponodol laughed bitterly. "And that did not please Dialyas! That did not please him at all."

"Korfax's father?" Obelison wondered. "What is this? What are you telling me?"

"Heresy! I am speaking to you of heresy. Sazaaim already had more than his share, though none of us knew it at the time. So once the deed was done he went his way and remained alone until his death. I do not know what he discovered in himself as he helped forge the Kapimadar, but it silenced his heart. And the rest of us? We did not understand. We carried on regardless."

Ponodol turned to her and his blind orbits pinned her where she sat.

"You are of the Exentaser. You are one of the inheritors of Nalvahgey, but even you have no idea of what is involved in the creation of such an artefact. We had to unlearn all that we had ever learned. We dared to go where even the greatest had feared to tread. There were four of us, four of us stirring a cauldron of power like a coven of Argedith. But when Sazaaim left us questions were asked, and we were all called to account. I, like the others, had to reveal what I knew to the council. But only Dialyas took the blame. In my darker dreams I sometimes think he actually enjoyed his martyrdom. He was ever perverse, was Dialyas."

"I still do not understand," she said. "What was your crime?"

Ponodol smiled his terrible smile back at her.

"The making of the Kapimadar relied upon one singular and unacceptable fact, namely that all the creations of the Namad Dar spoke with the very same abyss. The Kapimadar could shift its nature, you see, becoming a vehicle of both space and of time. According to accepted wisdom that should not have been possible. To do what the Kapimadar could do you should have needed two stones, one for space and one for time. But the Kapimadar was only one stone. The truth was inescapable. There was only one abyss, one nothingness, one void, and it must be that very same void from which the Creator divided creation. Do you see what I am saying?"

"You tried to touch the Creator!" she gasped.

"Blasphemy!" he answered. "But it was worse than that. By his own admission Dialyas was trying to explain Karmaraa, trying to explain how he could change the purpose of stone! Think of it! Who amongst the powers that ordered our world would accept such a thing? So I recanted, as did Virqol. Sazaaim had already confessed his part in all of this, so he was safe. But Dialyas did not recant, not entirely, and he was cast from our order for his honesty. I was a coward that day, and I have paid for my lack of judgement ever since."

He sighed again.

"Think what Korfax did in Othil Zilodar. He changed the purpose of stone. What if he discovered that power again? Is it any wonder that our enemy considers Korfax his foe? His entire strategy is based upon the Namad Dar. It is the only lore the Agdoain employ. But what if Korfax can subvert it?"

Ponodol paused for a moment.

"He comes!" he hissed.

She looked up and there he was, walking towards them both.

"Have you finished plotting?" he asked.

"No one plots!" Ponodol returned.

"Yes they do, but only in the darkest recesses of their hearts. You were ever faithless, all of you."

Obelison stood up, defiance written in her every line.

"We were not!" she said.

He looked at her for a moment.

"No, that is true. You were not. Once." He took a step forward. "Go, wander the tower. This blind fool and I will be having words that do not concern you. You can go where you will. It does not matter. But do not try to leave. That would be a mistake."

She reached out to touch Ponodol, but he intervened, slapping her hand away.

"Go, I said. Learn to do what you are told."

She backed away.

"Till we meet again," she said to Ponodol, but Ponodol did not answer. Instead he remained very still. No doubt there was some stricture on him. She turned about and walked away, not knowing whether she would ever see Ponodol again.

It seemed that what she had been told was so. She was allowed to wander as she would, so long as she did not attempt to leave. It was the first thing she tried, but the Agdoain outside snarled at her and attacked the door even as she pushed at it.

She did not try again.

She looked out from a higher window and saw how hopeless it was. The Agdoain surrounded the tower, restlessly orbiting it as if they could not keep still. She watched them for as long as she could bare it. There was something terrible in their relentless march, as though they were impelled to keep going but could not understand why.

She, too, felt restless, never wanting to stay too long in one place or another. Without realising it she found herself orbiting the tower also, just like the Agdoain.

The tower itself had darkened. Something was wrong with the piradar. They gave out a meagre light as though a veil had been drawn across their hearts. The only real light came from the windows. Corridors were now mottled with shadow, halls with pools of light. The tower lay in a dream of dust.

In her wanderings she noticed how all the great works of art had been defaced or defiled. Tapestries, paintings, even the statues, decayed. Most of the damage seemed random, but with some, particularly the finest and the greatest, there appeared to be some order to their defilement. Faces ran or blurred, expressions had been altered and even a few of the statues now looked as though they rotted, the stone of their eyes sunken, the stone of their flesh peeling back to reveal the bones beneath.

For a long while she met no other, and the tower itself seemed empty and bereft, but then she came upon two of them, all at once, and discovered what Ponodol had meant by his warning.

It was quite by chance. She had been looking for a weapon, any weapon, but there was nothing to be found. It seemed that everything had been removed – swords, lances and shields. There was not so much as a knife left, and it was in that search that she found them in one of the lesser halls, two of them, seemingly busy about some task or other.

They were dressed as servants but their clothing did not seem to fit them at all well. Their robes appeared too large for them, oddly gathered here and there as if the bodies underneath had been broken and bent. One was helping the other, letting her lean on him, though it seemed that he occasionally leaned upon her as well. They were silent, moving slowly, touching, feeling, deliberate and careful.

They turned, even as she saw them, and fled, scurrying away into the shadows. She tried to follow, but they were gone in moments. They knew the tower far better than she.

What had been done to them? She had caught strange glimpses. When they had first caught sight of her, she had seen their faces, and she was certain that there was something wrong with them. They moved strangely, too, bent over, crouching, their gait uneven.

She wanted to find them, to help them, but they would not be found. She listened, but there was no sound. They had hidden from her like wounded beasts, running off into the darkness in search of safety. She looked long and hard, but she did not find them again.

As she walked through the darkened halls and shadowed corridors, she listened as carefully as she could, listening for a sound, any sound that might lead her to the others, but the silence was complete. Or so it seemed, for after a little while she became aware of something else, something at the edge of hearing, faint and elusive. It would be like the smallest of echoes, as though something, somewhere, infinitely far away, beat at the air. At first she was uncertain that she had heard anything at all, dismissing it as a trick of the mind, but the impression came to her again, and again and again.

She began to look for it, but whatever it was, it also kept out of her way. She opened doors and turned corners, but she surprised no ghosts at play. Instead, each hall, each room she visited, was empty, as though whatever had occupied it had only just left.

Sometimes the feeling came to her that something waited for her just around the next corner, just beyond the next door. At such moments she kept herself as still and as quiet as possible, stealing up to the edge, before darting around to look, but she never caught it. It had already moved on, waiting around the next corner, perhaps, or through the next door. It became a most maddening play. But there was something there, she was certain of it, just beyond her limits, waiting beyond everything, waiting for her to hear it.

As night fell he found her again, walking easily towards her out of the shadows as though he had known where she was all along.

"Have you seen and heard enough?" he asked.

She did not answer him.

"Would you like refreshment?"

She still did not answer him.

"I see!" he said.

"Where is Ponodol?" she asked him.

"I have sent him away."

"I would like to speak to him again."

"That is a privilege you must earn."

"And how must I do that?"

"I would have thought it obvious. You must please me."

"I will do nothing for your comfort," she said.

"We shall see."

He looked at her then, almost as if he was peering through her.

"I have been watching you."

"Watching?"

"Yes! You have been listening."

"It is very quiet here."

"That is not what I meant. You can hear it."

"Hear it?"

"The other."

"I don't know what you mean."

"Yes you do!" he told her. "You stand and you listen, then you look. I have seen you." He smiled. "You are the only one. No one else can hear it, not even that blind fool whose company you would like to keep, and his hearing, since the loss of his eyes, has become most acute. It is a sign."

"A sign?" she asked nonchalantly.

"One of many that proves how right I was to preserve you. The other approves."

"You approve? I spit upon your approval."

"Not mine," he said. "The other. And you cannot spit upon the other. What nonsensical notions you entertain."

"Then I am becoming more like you, aren't I?"

"Are you?" He suddenly looked absurdly pleased. "Good!" he exclaimed. "For if you approach me, then you approach the truth."

"Such arrogance!" she said.

"Truth!" he returned.

"Madness!" she countered.

"Truth!" he repeated.

"Delusion!" she hissed.

"Truth!" he said again.

She gave him the most contemptuous look that she could.

"But surely even truth is no more," she said.

His smile became mocking.

"I would be careful, if I were you! You think this a silly game? It is not. You still dwell in the place where everything is judged against everything else. What is truth? What is falsehood? You think you know the answer. But in this place, in this time, such questions have meaning only because they are rooted in existence itself. Truth and falsehood are thus finite: they can be measured and they have substance, if only in our illusory minds. But remove existence and what do you have then? Such questions become meaningless. Such questions cease."

"So you espouse oblivion!" she said. "So why not kill yourself? That will end it."

Now he snarled, a scowl of lengthening teeth. Despite herself, she stepped back. When had his teeth become so long?

"Fool!" he snapped. "My soul would circle around and come back again. I would be born once more and the cycle would continue, for ever, and ever and ever. But destroy creation, destroy the vessels, destroy the traps of flesh, and everything ends. We return to the places we should never have left and gain once more eternal bliss – that place we knew before the womb. That is my desire."

He turned away and looked out of a window.

"If only you could understand!" he said. "This is why I am here! This is my purpose. It is why the other is here, for it is the voice of the one true god. We are here to end it all, all the pain, all the suffering, all the confusion. When we are done, the other and I, nothing will be left. You do not yet appreciate the beauty of it. You still cling to the illusion."

"What illusion?"

"The blind works of the blind artisan. Only that which does not move is eternal! Creation moves, changing, unfolding, finite and paltry. My purpose is a return to eternity. You still cling to mortality, the never-ending circle of pain. But even this I understand, and I forgive. How else can you be? It is all that you have ever known. You need to see with new eyes and learn again what you have forgotten."

For the first time since she had awoken, she found herself caught by his words. In his madness and delusion he had embraced the heresy of the fallen spirit! Him, the Velukor of all the Ell, had embraced heresy! If her predicament, and the predicament of all that she cared for, was not in such jeopardy, she would have laughed at the irony.

But it was also a lie, she was certain of it. His hatred, his malice, his contempt, these she could believe. But there was something else beneath his new-found creed, something deeper. There was a lie below it all, but she could not see what it was.

He gave her the very best apartments. When he had first taken her to the door, she had found herself wondering what decay and corruption lurked beyond, but instead she found them curiously unspoiled, as though the rot that held the rest of Emethgis Vaniad in its malicious fist had not come here at all.

There were many rooms, each fully lit by many piradar, each captive star held in great geometric arrangements that hung from the high ceilings. There were splendid wall hangings also, some depicting trees, others mountains, some the sea, a charge of ormn or a fair tower set amongst green hills. She looked at them all, but they seemed strangely innocent to her now. In this place, in these surroundings, they were alien.

The bed was set with the finest cloth, and the drapes that were gathered about the windows were finely embroidered. There was no hint of anything untoward here except, perhaps, the view from the window. Here she could see the desolation of the city, its grey streets and its sagging towers. No hint of the pulsing vines that strangled the Umadya Pir lay outside, but she knew they were there, withdrawn from her view by the command of their master, but not so far that she could not catch their stench when the wind blew from the north or the south.

The finest gowns were laid out for her or yet hung in the alcoves reserved for such things, but she ignored them – as she did the food. There were plates of delicacies, fruits, pastries and meats, all clearly fresh, set in abundance upon the table, but she would not touch them. Her hunger fled her as she thought again of those fleeing shadows, ruined things made to work his will and suffer his cruelties.

Her rooms were nothing more than a seduction. Here is comfort, said her captor, here are the things to which you once clung. But it was a lie. Beneath its surface lay horror, and she would not partake of it, nor know it. She went to the window and sat upon the sill. She gazed out at the far hills, the Leein Komsel, and let the tears fall as she wondered where Korfax was, and who he was with.

16

MESSENGER

Tham-honrax Avah-gie-in
Rabad-sob Nis-hon-akan
Fen-pl-velg Varmaq-garas
A-dar-nam Abai-zimji
Giz-traji Ana-od-vep
Zim-al-arp Daf-vimith-tha
Gem-dl-li Fen-brd-amap

They travelled the great highway that crossed the Piral Jiroks. The ruin of Othil Admaq lay behind them and the ruin of the north lay ahead.

Many marvelled at the great road, the great spans that leapt the desert, astonished that such a cool haven could exist above the burning sands. Only Korfax did not marvel. To him it was a sadness, another sign of the breaking of the world.

There were tokens of abandonment across the length and breadth of the highway: things dropped, broken pottery, a fall of rope, empty boxes. Though the way was easy enough, the wide road and the many way stations, Korfax found it harder with each step. Everywhere he looked he saw reminders of all that had been lost. The whip of guilt lay across his back.

It took many days to reach Fargur, the end of the great road. Though they moved with great speed, it was easily enough time for the Agdoain to grow again and forge another army.

Fargur, when they came to it, they found to be much like the great road, hurriedly deserted and emptied of life. No one remained within its walls.

They camped to the south and riders were sent out to scour the land all about for news. Almost within a day those sent to the north-west returned with grim tidings. Another army of the Agdoain was marching from Emethgis Vaniad, this time for the west. Though not as large as the one that had attacked Othil Admaq, it was still of a size that its numbers could not be counted.

They held a council. Some advised concentrating entirely upon Emethgis Vaniad, while others said attack the army because it was strategically unwise to have an enemy at your back. Korfax pondered the question. He also was tempted to attack the army. From what he had heard this was precisely what had happened to Noqmal's ill-fated attempt upon Emethgis Vaniad. Noqmal had forced himself almost to the gates of the city before another army had arrived at his back and defeated him in its turn.

Despite the ease of his victories against the Agdoain, Korfax remained wary. The power that ruled them knew something of what he could do. No doubt there would be a response to its losses at Othil Admaq, and he was certain that even now he had not yet seen all that the Agdoain were.

The choice was stark. Should they pursue this army or should they carry on north? He asked the others, but they remained divided, like him. Though the defeat of Noqmal's forces weighed heavily in their counsels, many also said that delay served only the enemy.

Afterwards he sat alone with Opakas.

"You are waiting for something!" she said.

"A sign," he told her.

"A sign?"

"One that tells me what I should do."

"Is this something you have read in the prophecies? I notice that you have kept those to yourself."

"And for good reason," he told her. "I am not playing that game again, nor shall anyone else. It never quite works the way that you think it will. Doagnis told me how it was when I was on her tail. She set traps for me according to how she interpreted the verses, and always she was thwarted. When she read the verses afterwards it was almost as if someone had changed the words when she was not looking. She enjoyed her games far too much, did Nalvahgey."

"Then what is this sign you speak of?" she asked.

He looked long at her.

"Another thing you do not know," he said. "And I have told no one of this."

"More revelations? You are full of them."

"I would rather not know this."

He took a deep breath, hardening himself for what he would say next.

"I have been visited by my dead," he said. "Each time they have told me things. Each time they have been correct, and each time it has proven dire."

Opakas drew back, frowning.

"By your dead?" she questioned. "The dead do not return."

"That is what I thought also. But still! Three times is the way of it. Doanazin, my old tutor who fell at Losq, Mathulaa, last Arged of the Korith Peis, and Adavor, Noqvoan of the Balt Kaalith. Adavor was the last. She warned me that I would have a choice to make and that I must make the right one, or I will fail. She told me that who wins loses, and who loses wins."

"You fear your death?"

"No, I fear failure. I fear loss."

"Loss is inevitable," said Opakas. "We all lose in the end."

She looked down.

"But to be visited by your dead?" she said quietly. "That is an omen of the end. Only at the end do the dead return, and then only to judge."

"This is not the end," he told her. "I refuse to believe it."

"I cannot advise you," she said, looking up again. "Like so much else to do with you it is too far outside my experience. All I can say is that a choice must be made – and soon. We have not far to go."

They went north from Fargur to the meeting of the southern ways, still without a decision as to which direction they should take. Korfax thought long and hard about the words of Adavor. He had a choice. One way lay victory, another lay failure.

They came to the southern crossroads. The road from the south went ahead to Emethgis Vaniad, the road east to the sunken ruins of Othil Ekrin, whilst the road west went to Othil Homtoh itself, where the new army of the Agdoain were going.

It was as they approached the crossroads that two outriders came back towards them. They stopped and bowed before Korfax and one of them pointed back the way they had come.

"My Haelok," he announced, "we have found a body at the crossroads. I am certain that it is one of the Balt Kaalith. I held my ralaxdo before him to see if there was any mischief present, but all I could think of was that I should bring you to see him. I do not know why."

Korfax looked ahead. He felt his heart quicken in his chest.

"I shall come and see," he said.

Aodagaa rode forward, his face resolute.

"Might I accompany you, my Haelok?"

Korfax smiled in return.

"Of course, and no doubt you would like to try to persuade me to ride west once more."

Aodagaa smiled in return, even as he bowed.

"We do not want the foe at our back, my Haelok."

"Agreed, but we might also lose precious time. I fear what we might find ahead of us if we delay too long."

He turned to Ambriol.

"Hold our people here for the moment. Let us remain wary. The Agdoain do not leave their prey behind, and the dead rarely linger. Maybe this one is here for a purpose. Maybe there is some intelligence to be gained."

"Perhaps, my Haelok, but perhaps not. I trust nothing where the Balt Kaalith are concerned."

Korfax looked ahead.

"Yes," he agreed. "You and I both have seen the truth of that."

Ambriol bowed and Korfax rode forward whilst Enastul lifted his head and neighed. He already knew what he wanted. He was tired of all this walking. Now he could gallop at last.

They came swiftly to the crossroads and halted in a cloud of dust. Before them reared the ancient pillar that marked the passing of the ways. The two outriders pointed at the dim, creased shape that sprawled unevenly against its base.

Korfax looked at the ruined bundle for a moment and then looked up at the pillar. That, at least, remained untouched. It still pointed, untroubled, at the sky, and its four sides still faced the four corners of the world.

Korfax rode forward and dismounted. Aodagaa joined him, along with the two outriders and three of Aodagaa's guard. Seven encircled the body, as was befitting.

Korfax lowered himself to one knee and looked carefully at the remains.

The corpse was only a few seasons old, perhaps, but its flesh had already shrunk upon its bones and its skin had dried to the thinnest of parchments. There was a tattered cloak about it, ragged from the incessant wind, but its armour still retained something of its polish under its coating of dust. The helm shadowed empty sockets, and each sunken pit stared at the left hand, where desiccated fingers tightly gripped two crystals of blue. Korfax leaned forward and gently prized the crystals free. They were kamliadar. He picked them up and looked at them. One was locked, its condition marked by the circling light within, a dim pulse of blue. The other could be used by anybody.

Whose voice was on here, he wondered? He touched the stone with his mind and awoke it. A voice rang out in the clear air, a voice in obvious pain.

"I, Noqvoandril Velgen Enay Tiarapax..."

Korfax staggered. He shut off the stone. Tiarapax? This was Tiarapax? But Tiarapax had travelled with the army of the east. What tale was this? After a moment he forced himself to listen again.

"I, Noqvoandril Velgen Enay Tiarapax, present my last confession under the Bright Heavens. The river awaits me, for I cannot travel any further. I have dragged myself to this place with my last strength and here I shall lie until the end. My time has come."

Korfax stopped the stone again and looked hard at the remains of Tiarapax. Then he bowed his head. Aodagaa leaned forward.

"My Haelok? You know this one?"

Korfax looked up and offered a sad smile in return.

"Yes, I knew him. He was honourable, right to the bitter end. Though he was of the Balt Kaalith, he knew the truth when he saw it, and he understood the deeper needs of his service. He stood beside me upon the wall and fought the Agdoain. He defended me in my trial with the Velukor. That he has died alone, wounded and without succour in this thirsty place..."

Korfax looked at the harsh land about him. He worked his jaw to fight back a sudden clench of grief.

"This is an unlooked for pain upon this journey," he muttered.

Aodagaa gestured at the body.

"Well!" he said. "If he honoured you, then I shall honour him. Shall we send him on his way with full ceremony?"

Korfax bowed his head a moment and then looked gratefully back at Aodagaa.

"Yes. That we can do at very least. And I thank you for your offer, Aodagaa. I shall take its mercy as a sign that all things can at last be forgiven. But there is time enough yet, I think, to understand this mystery. I think, perhaps, that Tiarapax has been brought to this place exactly for me to meet with him one last time."

Aodagaa withdrew with a bow and Korfax held up the stone again and let it continue.

"This Kamliadar contains the tale of my days, the tale of the great battle before the gates of Emethgis Vaniad. It also tells the tale of our defeat, and of the terrible revelation that I alone have had. I adjure that whosoever hears my voice to take these stones to Noqvoanel Soqial in Othil Homtoh and let him hear this tale in full. We, all of us, have been betrayed. The line of Karmaraa has betrayed us. Onehson is alive and is the master of the Agdoain. I, Tiarapax, swear this upon my immortal soul. As the Creator is my witness, this is the most solemn truth. I wish with all my heart that it were not."

Korfax fell forward and lowered his head to the dust. He wept openly as the darkness within swept out, sobbing his rage into the dried up earth.

"It was him?" he hissed.

Aodagaa knelt beside him.

"My Haelok?"

Korfax did not move for long moments. He was still grappling with the revelation. Onehson was master of the Agdoain? How? Why? He could not encompass it.

"My Haelok? What is it?"

Korfax pulled himself back up and looked at Aodagaa.

"I am sorry," he said. He looked back at the desiccated corpse.

"Though this meeting is a great pain to me, the words within this stone are an utter agony. That he should still live is bitter enough, but that he was the enemy we have sought from the very beginning is the hardest of all to take. It is almost as if we were doomed ere we were born."

He held out the stone and handed it to Aodagaa.

"Listen!" he said. "Listen for yourself. Then you will understand."

Korfax got up and walked away whilst Aodagaa set the stone in motion and heard what it had to say, and after he had finished listening, he looked back at his prince. He saw it all now, from the very first movement unto the very last, even as his prince had seen it. Another betrayal, and the greatest of all, as cruel as it was evil.

"Is this true, my Haelok? Is the last of the line of Karmaraa the master of the Agdoain? But how can such a thing have come to pass?"

Korfax took a deep breath but did not look back.

"I cannot answer you yet. I still do not understand it all. But it fits."

He turned about.

"I have been a fool! Such a fool!"

"My Haelok?"

"That all this, all of it, was foreseen and prepared against. The way was shown to me, long ago, but I did not see it. I could not see it. The time was not right."

"But is that not the way of all prophecy?"

"Know yourself! That is what they tell you. Do not be distracted. But I was. The Velukor was so obvious that I, that all of us, could not see him at all. His madness became our distraction, eating us from within and without."

He came forward, gesturing to the north.

"What I do not understand is why and how. How has he raised them up? And why? What is the grey void?"

Korfax stood now before Aodagaa and looked him full in the eye.

"And here we find a strange hope in all the madness. In all this time he has been curiously slow to act. Why did he not attempt to crush us all from the very beginning? Why has he allowed the rise of the Haelok Aldaria? We are armed with the one lore he has no mastery of. Why has it taken him so long to act? Either he has made a fatal mistake, or something else lies beneath it all."

Aodagaa looked at the kamliadar in Korfax's hand.

"What of the other stone? What does that say?"

Korfax lifted it up and smiled grimly at it.

"It seems you will have your way after all. We will go west. This is why Tiarapax is here. He has told me what I must do."

He gestured to the south.

"Come! Let us do the rites for Tiarapax. Then we must return."

Another council was held, but this time it was far more certain.

"Shall we do it?" Korfax asked. "Shall we save Othil Homtoh?"

"The west hates us!" warned Aodagaa.

"And we know the truth of it! Shall we follow in the footsteps of Doagnis?" Korfax answered.

"If we save them, they will hate it even more," Ambriol said. Many smiled darkly at that, even Korfax.

"Some of them," he said. "But there are many names in Othil Homtoh I would still honour. Valagar is one. He also fought beside me upon the wall."

He turned to Opakas.

"What say you now?"

"Go with your heart," she answered.

"Then I shall take a smaller force to Othil Homtoh. I shall honour the last words of Tiarapax and perhaps, perhaps, return with allies."

She held up a shew-stone. It gleamed with a pale light.

"Then I have a gift for you. I pulled this from the abyss. I have worked long at it. You will be needing it, I think."

He looked at it and then her.

"Why?" he asked.

"That way you can tell the rest of us what occurs, and we can tell you what the enemy does," she answered.

He took the shew-stone.

"Thank you," he said, "but I am no master of the art."

She smiled at that.

"I do not doubt that you will be soon."

With Aodagaa and Dosevax he took his vanguard, eight thousand mounted, and they rode for Othil Homtoh, following in the wake of the Agdoain.

They came upon the enemy just as they passed over the hills west of Bellor.

Looking down upon them, Korfax felt as if he beheld a crawling plague, with its swaying siege towers and milling hordes. He felt his anger rise once more, and turning to the others he felt their rage as well. Though the army below was vast, it suddenly seemed curiously insubstantial, as though a simple wind could pick it all up and blow it over the curve of the world.

He sent his thought to the others, telling them to prepare. This time, not only would they unleash their blades and their armour, but now they would summon as well, fires, corrosion and crushing forces. It would be swift, terrifying and unseen.

When all were ready he held up his hand in the gesture of attack and threw it forward. The Haelok Aldaria vanished from sight in a ripple of shadow and the Agdoain began to die. As it had been at Othil Admaq, so it was here. Through the grey ranks went the black fire, unseen, unsighted, invisible death that tore its way westward leaving nothing but ashes in its wake. Vast the army of the Agdoain might have been, but it took little more than a long hour to reduce it to shreds and tatters.

They pursued each fragment, scattering as the enemy scattered, for none was to be left alive. Korfax, with his honour guard, followed one of the larger groups up into the hills. They had streamed ahead, over a high pass. He followed quickly, expecting to overtake them upon the fields beyond, but instead he found himself staring down upon another battle.

Below him lay a long and wide meadow, a lush green valley still scattered with late flowers, yellow and white faces lifted up to face the sky. On each side of the valley the hills rose steeply, their sides set about with dark trees and crowned with airy seats of proud stone. But on the field before him a large force out of Othil Homtoh were fighting for their lives.

They must have met the fleeing Agdoain as they came over the pass. Now they were surrounded, the Agdoain attacking from every side at once, many times many, snapping at the flanks of the cavalry, or yet feasting upon the fallen.

Korfax saw it all in a single glance, positions, attacks and defences. He touched the others about him with his thought and then down into the meadow he galloped, unseen by any except his guard. They followed in his wake, a flicker of vague shadows that swept outwards in an ever-widening wave.

The Agdoain crumbled like statues of dust and the defenders looked on in astonishment as a wall of dim shadows thundered past them, a wall that undid their enemies like a storm of hidden fire. It seemed only moments but suddenly the Agdoain were ashes, and the Brandril that was in command found himself confronted by a rider in dark armour who appeared before him as if out of nowhere. Korfax let his helm roll back.

"May the light of the Creator shine upon you," he said.

The Brandril stared upwards for long moments, trying to collect himself. He looked at the face above him, searching it as if he could not quite believe what he was seeing. Fear filled his eyes, even as he tried to grasp what had just happened, and then he drew back, holding his sword before him.

"So it is you!" he said.

Korfax inclined his head somewhat.

"Do we know each other?"

The Brandril did not answer but looked to either side. His forces, what remained of them, were scattered here and there, many still clearly unable to accept their sudden deliverance. Some, though, cast worried glances back at the head of the pass as more riders in black appeared, and more after them, riding proudly down to the deep grasses of the meadow with banners unfurled.

The Brandril sighed and turned back to Korfax.

"It seems we have escaped the hammer and the anvil," he said, "only to be cast back into the furnace again."

Korfax smiled slightly.

"You have nothing to fear from me. I come to Othil Homtoh with messages, not to fight."

"So you say."

Korfax frowned.

"I do know you, don't I?" he said. "Your voice, I have heard it before."

He dismounted and stepped towards the Brandril. Two of the Branith leapt to his side to shield him, each drawing their blades and holding them aloft in the traditional attitude of threat.

Korfax looked at each in turn, marking how stern they were. But further in, in the depths of their eyes, he saw their fear. He withdrew a little, guessing what was in their minds. They now protected their master from the shade of Sondehna himself, expecting nothing but death in return. He turned to the Brandril.

"As I said, you have nothing to fear from me. Now, tell me your name."

"Nothing to fear?" said the Brandril. "That remains to be seen. But you already know my name, Korfax. It is Simoref."

He took off his helm and Korfax stared in astonishment.

"I would not have believed it!" he said. "It has been a long time since the seminary! You have changed!"

The other did not answer. Korfax looked him up and down.

"But you wear the habiliments of a Brandril," Korfax continued. "I thought they made you a Geyad, despite your dishonour."

"Nothing today is what it appears to be," Simoref answered. "I came out to spy upon the forces that were rumoured to be approaching, and I came as a Brandril because these Agdoain seem able to smell the very presence of anything that has been touched by the Dar Kaadarith. It was blind chance that such a large force came upon us here."

"Not by chance, I think," said Korfax. "They were fleeing us." He paused a moment. "So they can sense the touch of the Dar Kaadarith, can they?" he asked. "That is new. I have not heard of that before. How have you discovered this?"

Simoref regarded his hand for a moment as though the answer was written there. Then he looked at Korfax again, and his eyes were dark.

"Geyad Oanatom divined it," he said, "just after a messenger came to us, telling us the tale of Othil Admaq."

Now it was the turn of Korfax to suck in his breath. Here it came, just as he had feared it would, the trading of accusations. Now he would be called to account. He waited for approbation, and Simoref did not disappoint him.

"Yes," Simoref said, "we know all there is to know. That you destroy the Agdoain is one thing, but that you call up some foul nightmare from the abyss when Othil Admaq refuses your will is another matter entirely. Are you not satisfied with the crimes of your ancestor? Are the depredations of the old Haelok Aldaria not enough for you that you have to resurrect them again? Has Lon-Elah not suffered enough under the yoke of sorcery?"

With that, both Aodagaa and Dosevax rode forward, followed by many of the guard. Korfax raised his hand.

"Hold!" he said.

Aodagaa leaned forward.

"But, my Haelok! This one does not know of what he speaks!"

"Nonetheless," said Korfax, "let it pass for now. The truth shall be told, but only when I feel the time is right. Do you hear me?"

They bowed.

He turned back to Simoref.

"I did not do the deed," he said.

"Denials come easily to you as well, or so I have heard," Simoref answered.

"Then you have heard nothing," Korfax told him. "I have not forgotten you, do not think that I have. I have not forgotten what you did, nor the deeds of your father. I have no love for either of you, yet here I am, saving your necks from the Agdoain sword. I would think long and hard about that, if I were you."

"And I know who you are," Simoref returned. "That tale has already been told."

"Judge me by my actions, not by what you think you know."

"Then how did Othil Admaq fall if not by your hand?"

"It was Doagnis. She summoned Ash-Tel and bade it destroy the city. She desired to rule alone. She betrayed me."

There was dead silence.

"She summoned one of the Ashar?" Simoref looked horrified.

"Do you wish to hear the tale?" Korfax asked him. "The full tale?"

"Do I have a choice?"

"Yes."

Simoref looked about him.

"Just that? No threats? No demands?"

"Just come with me to Othil Homtoh," Korfax said. "I have a message for your father, for all of you. What you do after you hear it is your concern. You can come with me and hear my tale, or you can forbear. But do not think you can escape the consequences. We are come to the last play of all. On this everything that you know will stand or fall. But if we do not act, and act soon, the Agdoain will eat the world, and then it will be too late."

Simoref stared at the heavens. A clear day had turned into a brilliant night. He stood in the high meadow and looked up. The stars shone down in all their splendour and the night was glorious.

Around him the remains of his command went about their business. Food was eaten, wine was drunk, words were spoken and communion was had. But surrounding them, like an enclosing wall, the forces of the Haelok Aldaria shielded them from the outer world.

Simoref looked then from his own to the others that protected them and suddenly saw few differences at all. The same rituals were performed, the same practices were carried out and even the same songs were sung. He suddenly felt strange.

There were so many questions he wanted to ask. He wondered whether he should walk through the encampment and seek out Korfax so that he could ask them to his face, but when Korfax came towards him out of the night as if summoned by his thought, he found his desires other than he had believed them to be.

Korfax held up a dark bottle like a gift.

"A peace offering," he said. "I thought you might enjoy this."

"What is it?" Simoref asked.

"Girril," Korfax answered simply.

"I am not familiar with the name," Simoref said.

Korfax smiled.

"It comes from the south. It is very good, though not as good as Pelarr, if you have ever had it."

"I have not," Simoref said.

Korfax gestured at the seats set about the entrance to Simoref's tent.

"Shall we?"

Simoref bowed stiffly.

"Of course, my seat is yours, for the moment."

Korfax smiled drily at that.

"I have no intent other than to deliver a message. That is all. What you believe you know is not what you think it to be."

Korfax watched Simoref carefully as he went into his tent and came out again with two cups. Then Simoref and Korfax sat down and Korfax poured out liquid darkness for the both of them. Simoref tasted the wine and, once sipped, he stared at it in amazement.

"But this is magnificent," he said. "I have never tasted better. Wherever did you get it?"

"It comes from the fields of the Girrilith," Korfax told him, "far to the south. It was purchased there."

Simoref leaned back and looked hard at Korfax.

"So what do you intend to buy with it now?" he asked.

Korfax dropped his smile.

"I do not intend to buy anything with it," he answered quietly.

"Do you not? But I think that you do. If I am not very much mistaken I think you would like me to become your ally."

Korfax met the gaze of Simoref and held it.

"I am not sure that I would like it," he said, "given who you are, but yes, an alliance would be wise, given the situation."

He waited a moment. "So why haven't you accused me of heresy or told me to go back north and wallow in filth like my ancestors?" he asked.

Simoref looked away, a troubled expression upon his face.

"I am not the Simoref you remember," he said. "I have had to learn many a hard truth since that day."

"Many have!" Korfax told him.

Simoref took a long, hard breath, before looking back again.

"You are a mystery to me," he told Korfax. "The things you have done. The

creature that you are. You are the last person I would expect to see before me with
forgiveness in his heart."

"I am not sure I would call it forgiveness," said Korfax, "but I have made my
peace with it. Your father, though, is another matter."

"My father?"

"It was his hatred that set all this in motion. He has much to answer for."

Korfax watched as Simoref wrestled with his thoughts.

"My father is proud," Simoref said. "He has never accepted his lot in life. The
duel over your mother changed him, or so I was told. When he learned of your
father's death he was glad. I remember seeing his smile. It was as if I had never
seen him before."

Korfax did not move. His face was stone. Simoref found himself unable to look at
his guest with ease.

"Can you truly ally yourself with him?" he asked. "Can you reconcile such
hatred?"

"I can but try," Korfax answered.

"But you are a child of the line of Sondehna! No one in the west would ally
themselves to you, given what you are."

Korfax still did not move.

"The west does not know what I know. There are worse things in this world,
believe me."

He leaned back, eyes glinting.

"On my way here I found the body of Noqvoandril Tiarapax by the southern
crossroads."

Simoref started.

"I thought he fell in battle? I rode beside him for a while."

"You were there?"

"Yes!"

Korfax looked up with new respect.

"Then I honour your intent and your bravery. And also your good fortune. Few
walked away from that fight."

"I know nothing of bravery," said Simoref. "I did what had to be done. All
honour goes to Noqmal."

"But you were there, and that is enough," Korfax told him. "For even daring
such a thing you have all honour in my eyes. I would have been there also, but I
was hunting Doagnis at the time."

"Doagnis?"

"I believed she was the mistress of the Agdoain. But it was not so. The power
that controls them dwells in Emethgis Vaniad, as it ever has."

Simoref felt it in the air, like the presage of a storm.

"What do you mean?" he asked.

Korfax held up a kamliadar.

"Tiarapax recorded a message in this for Soqial. I do not know what it says, but I can guess."

Korfax put the kamliadar down and then held up another. "He spoke into this stone also, an explanation for all to hear."

He handed the stone over to Simoref. "You should hear it."

Simoref took the stone and listened to it. Then he listened to it again. Then he threw it away from him.

"If this is some play on your part..." he said.

Korfax went to retrieve the stone.

"This is no play of mine," he said. "This is his."

He pointed back east.

"He did this! Him!"

"I cannot believe it," said Simoref.

"Think about it," Korfax retorted. "I have. When the Agdoain first appeared they came from the west, from the direction of the Forujer Allar. If you remember I was sent on a mission to destroy their genesis, following the vision of Obelison. But who was it who went to the Forujer Allar before the appearance of the Agdoain? Was it not Onehson who performed the ritual of the cursing in his father's stead? Ermalei was too unwell to go."

Simoref still would not believe it.

"No!" he hissed.

Korfax smiled coldly.

"I am not done yet," he said. "So the war started in earnest, Othil Zilodar was besieged and I discovered a power I did not know that I possessed."

Korfax reached into his bag and drew out a piradar. He gave it to Simoref.

"What is that?" he asked.

Simoref frowned as if he could not quite believe the question.

"It is a piradar, of course!" he exclaimed.

Korfax took it back, held it up and it changed, its yellow light dimming to a faint green. Simoref nearly jumped out of his chair. Korfax handed the stone back to him.

"What is it now?"

Simoref stared at the stone as if it appalled him.

"It feels like a logadar," he said.

"It is," Korfax told him. "I can change the purpose of stone. Why do you think they made me Meganza?"

He took a deep breath.

"Othil Zilodar fell a year later. A womb grew up in the middle of the Piodo Mirul. We all thought that it was Doagnis that had done the deed, which was why I pursued her. But it turned out that she was actively engaged against the Agdoain, training her forces to kill them. An odd strategy that, if she was indeed the one that had called them up. I had to satisfy myself that she was not. Cruel and murderous she may be, but the Agdoain are not hers. She was not in Emethgis Vaniad when a womb appeared in the Umadya Pir itself. That was Onehson's doing, not hers."

Korfax leaned forward.

"Think about it Simoref, it answers so many questions. The Agdoain know the Namad Dar. They react to us as though they are our reflection. Every strategy we come up with, they counter, wearing us down, cancelling us out."

"Onehson broke your betrothal," Simoref said. "I have seen what such things can do. I have only to look at my father to see how the hatred eats him."

"You are right in what you say," Korfax answered. "I have no love for Onehson. But Onehson saw me as his enemy, and so did the Agdoain. They are an extension of his will."

Korfax leaned back.

"Did you ever hear tell how the Agdoain react to me?" he asked.

"I was told about that," Simoref said. "During the siege of Othil Zilodar they all advanced upon your position."

"It is true, but that is not the only thing. They attacked Losq, they assaulted Piamossin, they even conveniently turned up in the Pior Chanorus as Obelison and I fled from Emethgis Vaniad."

"But I heard that many slipped to the south, getting by the wall in small groups," Simoref countered.

"But to turn up in the Pior Chanorus?" Korfax asked. "In the right place and at the right time?"

"Chance, surely!"

"And who had now taken it upon himself to pursue me?"

"But why would Onehson do this?"

"That I cannot answer," Korfax said. "Onehson, when I knew him, was already strange. His mother died when he was born and his father went mad. As the war progressed he became increasingly unpredictable. At the end many said that he had already followed his father into madness. There is some sickness in the line of Karmaraa, some terrible sickness. I have seen something of the power that sits behind the Agdoain, a grey immensity dwelling in a void of absence. What it is, and what it has to do with Onehson, I do not know. But I intend to find out."

There was a long silence as Simoref thought of what Korfax had told him.

"It is hard to accept," he said eventually.

Korfax held up the kamliadar of Tiarapax.

"Do you doubt the word of Tiarapax?" he asked. "Once this other stone is unlocked, I imagine it will tell a tale few will want to hear." He leaned forward. "Now comes the bargain. I want you to do a thing for me."

Simoref looked wary.

"And what might that be?" he asked.

"Say nothing of this to your father," Korfax answered. "Merely tell him that he and I need to talk."

"I don't understand."

"I am uncertain he would not allow me into his presence if he already knew what I was going to say. I want them all there, all that are left. I want witnesses. No more hiding. No more plots behind closed doors. I want everything in the open. I want everything revealed."

"I am not sure that I can keep this secret," Simoref said.

"I am," Korfax told him. "You owe me this, Simoref. I saved your life today."

"And would you have saved it if you had known that it was me?" Simoref asked.

"Yes, I would," Korfax said. "We have both changed, you and I. I can see it, but what of you? What do you see?"

"I see you coming to Othil Homtoh. I see another Peis-homa."

"That will not happen. You have my word. Besides, the west has its own crimes to answer."

"What do you mean now?"

"Lontibir!"

Simoref frowned.

"Lontibir?" he asked.

"So they did not tell you?"

Korfax did not look surprised.

"I sent Odoiar to Othil Admaq with a message," he continued. "That message was the tale of Lontibir. When you get the chance, ask of the Balt Kaalith. Soqial, I am certain, knows it."

"More riddles?" Simoref questioned.

"Just ask!"

Korfax placed his cup upon the table and stared at it.

"Simoref, you have been fed lies all your life, just as I have. It seems we have become the same, but there yet remains one great difference between us. I was forced, by circumstance, by my blood, to confront the unpleasant truth. You were not. You think you know who I am? You think you know what I am? You do not. Your hatred of my ancestor has no place here. I am not Sondehna. I merely have his blood."

"But the blood is the life, or so they say."

"Do they, indeed?"

Korfax laughed and flicked his fingers in the air in dismissal.

"So much for what 'they' say," he said.

"Scorn?"

"A hard lesson learned from a harder task master."

"And what task master would that be?"

"Fate!"

Simoref looked away. He suddenly felt very unsure of himself. He took another draught of wine and stared up at the stars. Across the horizon was spread the Creator's gyre, the very fount of possibilities. Look at it one way and it was spiral, leading the eye ever onwards to its heart of fire. But look at it another way and it was a great cloud of scattered stars with no reason to it at all, no reason and no rhyme.

"It is difficult, isn't it?" Korfax said.

Simoref turned to look at him.

"What is?"

"To shed the lies of the past, to unlearn all that you have learned and to see beyond your boundaries."

Simoref drew back.

"So that much is true, it seems," he said. "Arrogance is your master. See my way and see no other?"

Korfax laughed gently and stood up.

"My old tutor once said that education was both the most unrewarding calling and conversely the most rewarding. So I will leave you now in reflection. Please, enjoy the rest of the wine. And while you are enjoying it consider all that has brought you to this place and to this time. What were the choices? What were the victories? What lessons were learned? But remember also that we are as much the sum of our failures as we are the sum of our successes."

Korfax turned about and left. Simoref watched him go. Then he lifted the bottle up in his right hand and stared at it for a long while. For a moment he was tempted to taste it again, but then he hardened his heart and carefully emptied its contents over the stones at his feet.

They followed the long road to the city, passing empty towers to the left and the right. As with the north and the south, the land had been emptied.

The small force under the command of Simoref was swallowed by a greater darkness. Those from Othil Homtoh would occasionally glance at their dark protectors, but little was said by either side.

After many days they came at last to the main pass to Othil Homtoh, and as the pass widened, so Othil Homtoh was gradually revealed. Korfax watched the revealing carefully. Here was another sight he had never seen. Othil Homtoh. The city was breathtaking, as dramatic as it was glorious.

The first of its walls, and the mightiest, seemed to fuse with the very stone at its base. It was as though some great jewel smith had polished a mighty mountain, cutting a vast ring of stone from the living rock. Beyond the first wall towers were reared as if to yearn for the heavens. And beyond them came the second wall, and more towers. And so it went on. Seven walls, each enclosing myriad towers, until one saw at last the pinnacle of the city, within the seventh circle, the Umadya Zadakal, the last unconquered bastion of the west.

Korfax looked up at it and smiled grimly. The city was a fortress, as he had heard, the mightiest ever made. The Agdoain, though, would not care. They would come, lay siege, climb its stone and break its power. Unless, of course, they were stopped.

He turned to Simoref.

"You will do as I ask?"

"I gave you my word, Korfax," Simoref answered. "I do not lie about such things, not even to my foes."

"That is all that I desire. I will await your word. We will camp upon the plain."

"You really are not what I expected at all," Simoref said. "The rumours I have heard paint you as a raging monster. In all our time together I have seen nothing of it, from you or your people."

Korfax smiled.

"Rumours should never be trusted."

Simoref fingered the hilt of his sword.

"If it was not for your armour and your followers, I could still believe that I shared this journey with one of the Farenith."

"One of the Farenith?" Korfax mused. "My mother might argue that point with you, I think."

Simoref looked away, his expression suddenly bleak.

"You really are not what I had expected at all," he murmured.

Korfax let his smile fade but did not answer.

Audroh Zafazaa sat upon the great stone throne of Othil Homtoh and stared down the seven steps and across the great hall to the great door beyond. At his side stood his son and heir, Noraud Simoref, a white stave in his left hand, a stone scroll in his right. About them both awaited the highest – Napeiel Valagar to one side on the step below, Geyadel Chirizar on the other. Beside Chirizar stood Noqvoanel Soqial, whilst beside Valagar stood Urenel Kukenur. And on the step below her waited Urendril Andispir. For some reason she had chosen to kneel. She was the only one that did so.

Branith lined the wide path to the throne, weapons held upwards, lances alternating with swords, and behind them waited the court, all the lords and the ladies, all the nobles and the courtiers, all eager to see the fabled Korfax, last scion of the Black Heart.

They had all heard the stories – how it was Doagnis, and not Korfax, that had destroyed Othil Admaq, and how it was Korfax and his forces that had saved Zafazaa's son and heir from the Agdoain. They had heard the tales, but few trusted them. Korfax was revealed, the last descendant of Sondehna, the last descendant of all that was said to be evil. So they waited in expectation and dread, all of them.

The great doors swung open and Korfax marched in. On his left was Dosevax and behind them both came five others of the vanguard, the shields of the Haelok. They approached the centre of the hall, where they stopped and bowed. No one responded, but all, whether they would admit it or not, were taken aback by this great black figure and his tall dark servants. There was an aura of power boiling in the air about them, unseen coils of force that filled the great hall with unease.

Korfax looked to Dosevax, who in turn bowed to his Haelok and looked back at Zafazaa. He stepped forward into the singular shaft of light that fell down from above and announced his embassy.

"Audroh Zafazaa, may I present Haelok Mikaolaz Audroh Korfax, hereditary ruler of the lands of Lukalah and Audroh of the Iabeiorith."

Dosevax bowed again with a great sweep of his hand and withdrew. No one moved. Korfax looked at all of the gathered faces in turn, seeing shock, anger, outrage and fear, all scattered in equal measure about the hall. He searched the faces for a moment, tasting the thoughts he felt around him, but he did not see her. His mother was not there. He did not know whether to feel relief or sadness.

Now it was his turn. He stepped into the light and looked up at Zafazaa. He thought back to the rites of death for Ermalei. An echo of the hatred swelled in him once more, but he put it back down. This was neither the time nor the place for such remembrances.

Korfax studied Zafazaa's face. With Simoref beside him, the similarity was obvious. They were father and son, undoubtedly, but their likeness was only skin-deep. Inside, within, they were not alike at all.

Korfax could see it now. Opposing spirits possessed them. Though he tried to be worthy of his title, Simoref was all doubt and regret, whilst his father had nothing in him but resentment and pride. Simoref held himself back, battling with uncertainties placed there by others, whilst his father caged everything except his certainty, utterly certain of his place in the world. They were so different within themselves that it was almost astonishing that they shared the same blood at all.

"Well?" asked Korfax at last. "Shall we speak together?"

Zafazaa leaned back and smiled as though the long wait had already given him every advantage that he desired.

"Yes!" he said. "We shall talk, you and I. We shall talk of many things together: of why you threatened the Velukor, of why you aided a known heretic, of why you destroyed Othil Admaq and yet saved my son's life. I am eager to hear it all – the accusations, the fantasies, the shams and the lies."

As if at a hidden signal the Branith around the hall raised their weapons, and a whisper of expectation filled the air. Dosevax glanced at Korfax before turning back to mark the forces that surrounded them. He and the honour guard assumed the posture of waiting, each facing outward, ready to receive their Qorihnas from their sheaths should the need arise.

"Is this treachery, my Haelok?" hissed Dosevax.

Korfax glanced back sharply and Dosevax turned away again. Then Korfax took another step forward and spread his arms wide.

"Would you attempt to kill me now, Zafazaa?" he asked. "I come here with messages, to treat, not to fight. Is this treachery?"

There was another ripple of expectation, but Zafazaa gestured nonchalantly.

"Karmaraa once sent three emissaries to the courts of your accursed ancestor, one leading, two following. Do remember what ensued? Would you like me to remind you?" Zafazaa did not wait for an answer. "The two followers were cut into pieces and placed in sacks. Then those sacks were placed about the neck of the third, who himself was bound about by many chains. They sent him back to us and by the time we gained him he was nearly dead, while the stench of rotting flesh that filled the air about him was all but intolerable."

Zafazaa leaned forward.

"Should I not visit that upon you?"

He glared.

"I do not desire your death here," he said at last, "and certainly not in this place. The last thing I want is for your accursed blood to stain these stones. But I do desire your death."

Korfax smiled darkly.

"That is not the reason," he said. "I know what lurks in your vengeful heart. My mother once rejected you. That is the real reason you hate me."

They looked at each other, measuring, searching and seeking. Then Zafazaa leaned back again.

"Say what it is you have come here to say," he said.

Korfax pointed back east.

"The future of our world is at stake. You can either aid me or you can thwart me, but know that I hold out the one last chance of victory. The Agdoain cross your lands now as they have crossed all others before. My forces have destroyed one such army that was on its way here. They will not be the last. Eventually the Agdoain will surround you in such numbers that you will not be able to deny them. Even the might of Othil Homtoh will succumb in the end."

Zafazaa pulled himself up again.

"So that is it, is it?" he asked. "An alliance? With you? I know your crimes!"

"The tale you have been told is not the truth," Korfax said, "and you are as wrong in this as you are wrong about so much more. I did not destroy Othil Admaq. That was no deed of mine."

Zafazaa all but sneered.

"So my son tells me. He seems somewhat inclined to trust you, I think."

Simoref stirred slightly at this, but no one else moved. Zafazaa smiled in response, a cold smile.

"But I," he added, "am not."

Korfax now turned to Kukenur.

"If it is trust that you want then let the Urenel look within me. Let her see the truth of me and so tell everyone else what it is that she sees."

The hall erupted in shock as Korfax stepped onto the first step and fell to his knees, his arms stretched wide. He stared straight at Kukenur.

"Look inside," he told her. "See the truth for yourself. I will not hinder you.

Open all the doors that you will. You shall see everything."

Kukenur looked thoroughly taken aback.

"You want me to see everything?" she asked.

"I trust you," he answered.

She looked at Zafazaa.

"Do as you will," he said. "The Exentaser have always been a law unto themselves. Wallow in him, if you can bear it!"

She almost said something back, but then turned away and looked at Korfax again.

"On your word?" she asked.

"My word!" he answered.

She came forward and sent a tentative probe into the mind of Korfax, locks and guards at the ready, but she met no resistance at all. She delved a little deeper, and then deeper again, increasing her power, burrowing further and further down into the depths, but still she was unopposed. So she committed herself to the task at last and went where she would, running through every room, thrusting wide each door she came to. But nothing was hidden from her and the house of his mind remained completely still, from its towering heights to its shuddering depths. She saw everything within it, all that Korfax was, and at the end she staggered away from him and sank down onto the steps before the throne.

All stared at her, awaiting her words. Andispir came forward and offered her support, but Kukenur waved her away. Kukenur stood up, slowly, shakily, as though her feet had suddenly forgotten their purpose. Then she stared back at Korfax and marked the look upon his face, the sad eyes, the sad smile. She closed her eyes for a moment as though to cage her own pain, but then she remembered herself again, who she was and where she was. The moment passed as quickly as it had come and she turned back to Zafazaa as though he was now the enemy. Her eyes darkened.

"Korfax speaks the truth," she said at last.

Many called out at that, some even raising their swords. She threw up her hands.

"ENOUGH!" she cried, her mind pushing out and touching them all. Some drew back in shock. Only Korfax smiled at it. It was masterfully done, a mental slap that shocked them all back to silence.

She stared at Korfax.

"What you have done!" she hissed. "What you have seen!"

Korfax did not answer. Instead he waited. Kukenur turned to the others.

"There are revelations here, revelations you would not believe."

She turned to Zafazaa and pointed at him.

"You have played your part in this!" she accused. "You should pay for your crimes also!"

She held up her hands in denial.

"But that is nothing now. What is done is done indeed."

She turned to the others.

"I will say only this. Korfax did not slay Obelison. Korfax did not destroy Othil Admaq. Korfax is the only hope that remains to us, the only hope we have against the Agdoain. Korfax knows who it is that we face, but I cannot, will not, speak of it. Let Korfax reveal this for himself. It is his to reveal."

She held up a finger like a warning.

"But once you have heard what he has to say, you will ally yourself to him or you will be damned for all eternity."

Zafazaa glowered like an old but obstinate stone, unmoved and incapable of moving. Eventually he gestured at Kukenur with his right hand.

"So that is it, is it?" he said. "You side with him? Are you so easily mastered, then?"

Kukenur drew herself up.

"Be careful what you say to me! I know what you are," she spat back.

"This is some trick," Zafazaa said. "He has fooled you in some way. Or perhaps it is possession! Doagnis once possessed Torzochil and fooled the entire high council. How do we know the same thing is not happening here?"

Kukenur almost ignited in shock and outrage.

"And I am Urenel, Zafazaa! No one possesses me. No one fools me. I am no one's puppet. I am the first of the Exentaser. Never, ever accuse me of such a thing again."

Zafazaa dismissed her with another wave of his hand.

"This proves nothing," he said. "I remember another tale. I remember how Korfax turned even Asvoan aside. And Asvoan was better than you."

Korfax clapped his hands together and stood back up. The sound was shockingly loud.

"Are you done, Zafazaa?" he asked. "The Urenel is telling you the truth. There are many others, were they here, that would tell you the same."

"No doubt, no doubt," Zafazaa said, "thralls and slaves and heretics all. I am unmoved by such fantasies. But I will hear what it is you have come here to say. So tell it to me, tell me this mighty revelation."

Korfax looked hard at him. He did not miss the contempt, or the scorn, so he said it as plainly as he could.

"It is simple. Onehson has betrayed us. He has betrayed us all."

Zafazaa closed his eyes as if weary.

"That tired tale again? Is that all you have to offer?"

Zafazaa opened his lips slightly and bared his teeth in a sneer, but Korfax let his own gaze strengthen in answer. Zafazaa tried to look away again, but then suddenly he found that he could not. Korfax held him now and taught him real contempt.

"This is nothing to do with my trial, Zafazaa. That piece of theatre is of less consequence now than it ever was before. My trial was a farce, a play, a comedy. We all watched the performance in fascination, but no one was any wiser afterwards."

He finally released Zafazaa.

"No!" he said. "That is not what I have come here to tell you. I came here to tell you that Onehson is not yet dead. Your precious Velukor is still alive."

The hall erupted. Many shouted in astonished disbelief, others in rapture, falling to their knees and praising the heavens. Korfax waited for the chaos to subside again. He suddenly found himself curious to see that Zafazaa had not moved. He understood Kukenur, of course, and Simoref. Both of them knew what was coming, but Zafazaa was fast becoming a revelation. What did he guess, and what was his true intent?

Zafazaa kept his face utterly still and not a flicker of emotion crossed it. The hall gradually became silent as the others realised that this was not the revelation they had been promised. The old stone of Zafazaa stared down at the rising storm of Korfax and awaited the worst.

"Say the rest of it!" he said.

"Onehson is the true master of the Agdoain," Korfax answered.

The hall erupted again, but now in outrage. Many of the Branith advanced with blazing eyes, their swords and shields ready. But Dosevax and the honour guard drew their blades and the lethal shadows of the Qorihna kept them back. The chaos subsided once more, but now all stared at Korfax as if he really was evil incarnate.

Soqial stepped forward, crossing the unseen barrier that marked his place beside the throne. That he could do so with impunity was also revealing, but Soqial did not care. He could contain himself no longer.

"I have lived to see many terrible things I thought I would never see. I have lived to hear many terrible things I thought I would never hear. But the blasphemy being uttered here, in these blessed halls, beggars all belief."

He stared down at Korfax.

"Are you insane at last?" he asked. "Does your hatred know no bounds after all? Would you profane even the memory of the holy dead?"

Korfax waited as Chirizar came to stand beside Soqial, his face twisted with fear and hatred, matching that of Soqial. Simoref, though, remained where he was, a look of resignation on his face. And Valagar also remained where he was, but then Valagar was stoicism itself. Korfax looked back at Kukenur and inclined his head.

"Well?" he asked.

She shrank from him as if suddenly plunged into the depths of torment.

"It is as Korfax said," she told them. "Onehson lives and is master of the Agdoain."

Soqial and Chirizar stared at her, twin expressions of disbelief and contempt. Korfax turned his gaze to Simoref.

"Simoref?"

Everyone stared. Simoref paused to gather himself up.

"Korfax has proof," he said simply.

Zafazaa glared at his son as though he had just been betrayed.

"You knew of this?" he said. "You knew of this and you kept it from me?"

"He asked me to keep silent until he could stand before you," Simoref answered, "and I said that I would. I owe him my life."

Zafazaa turned about and looked darkly at Korfax.

"Proof!" he hissed.

Korfax held up his hand. In it were two kamliadar.

"Do you remember Tiarapax?"

"What?" Zafazaa looked genuinely surprised for the first time.

"I thought it a simple enough question. Do you remember Tiarapax?"

"Of course I remember him," Zafazaa said. "He was one of the mightiest of the Balt Kaalith, but he died in the reckless attempt upon Emethgis Vaniad. Do not think to besmirch his name now."

Korfax smiled sadly.

"Besmirch? Never! One of the mightiest? Possibly! But I cannot judge that, as I am not of the Balt Kaalith. He was certainly one of the most honourable, though, and he did not die during the battle. He died afterwards."

Soqial narrowed his eyes.

"What new lie is this?" he said.

Korfax turned to him.

"No lie. But I have something for you, Soqial. Tiarapax died in the attempt to bring you his last words. His words we found and we have them still, but his flesh failed at the last and we buried his ashes with all due honour at the southern crossroads. However, his voice has not yet been laid to rest. He bade the finder of his body give you this."

Korfax held out one of the kamliadar. Soqial stared at it.

"This belonged to Tiarapax." Korfax told him.

He gave the stone to Soqial.

"You are the Noqvoanel. Only you can unlock it. Set it in motion, Soqial, and let the rest of us hear the last words of Tiarapax."

"Then you have not heard what it says?" Soqial asked.

"I have not," Korfax answered.

"But why?"

"Tiarapax did not give me the key. Besides, I am honouring the wishes of one of the dead. Tiarapax intended this stone to come to you."

Soqial drew himself up.

"Then I will listen to this later."

Korfax let his eyes flash.

"NO!" he roared, and his voice filled the hall.

"You will unlock that stone now, and you will let the dead words of Tiarapax speak to us all."

Soqial was daunted but not bowed.

"I will not," he said. "This concerns the Balt Kaalith, and no lesser order."

Some scowled at that, Valagar, Kukenur, those that did not wear the green. Korfax only smiled.

"So you are frightened of the truth, after all. I thought as much."

He held up the other stone.

"Then you will listen to this one, for it is unlocked. And after you have heard it, you will comply with my demand."

Korfax set the stone in motion and Tiarapax spoke once more. No one could mistake what they heard. Many eyes closed in grief, many cried out, or sank to their knees. When it was done, Korfax gestured to Soqial.

"Unlock the stone!"

Kukenur agreed.

"Unlock the stone!" she said.

Valagar stepped forward at last.

"I wish to hear also," he said.

There came a few muttered words from around the room. Korfax looked at Zafazaa.

"Well? Have you nothing to say?"

Zafazaa glared at Soqial.

"Unlock the stone!" he commanded.

Soqial sent his thought at the kamliadar and Korfax was suddenly caught by the actions of Andispir. She was listening to the thought of Soqial, carefully, subtly committing every single word to memory. Advantage for the future, no doubt.

The stone in Soqial's hand filled with a blue light, and a voice, unmistakably that of Tiarapax, filled the hall.

"I am dying," the stone said, "my wounds are too much for my body to heal. I send these words to Soqial, Noqvoanel of the Balt Kaalith, and to all that yet dwell in Othil Homtoh. May all your days be fruitful and all your nights be blessed. I, Tiarapax, send my greetings and my service to the faithful."

There was a pause. The great hall was utterly silent. The voice came again, and the pain and the effort in it were evident to all.

"I rode with the seventh parloh of Galath to the appointed place. There we met with Noraud Noqmal, and what a fair greeting that was. Never have I seen so many great captains all assembled together and set about with the panoply of war. I was proud to stand beside them all and be numbered amongst them. For our purpose was noble – we would take Emethgis Vaniad back from the grey demons and uncage its light once more. And what a mighty undertaking that was.

"How splendid were our banners, for the light of Rafarel caught each in turn, as it caught each polished helm, lighting the armies that stretched from horizon to horizon with the blessings of the Creator. My heart soared at the sight.

"We finally took ship at Belis. I have never seen so many sky ships gathered together and rising up as one. It seemed to me that a mighty flock of Vabazir, many sacred Vabazir, rose up to greet the dawn in praise of the very Creator that once gave them life. Though I live for ever and see all the glories of creation, I will never forget the sight.

"We came at last to Emethgis Vaniad and saw the evil. But I will not describe it, I cannot. Its horror is too great for the soul to encompass. Instead I will describe the valour of our forces, for we encircled the city in a ring of fire. Noqmal was a tower of strength that day, fighting ever to the fore, and all remained steadfast at his word. None would turn aside. And when the Agdoain fell from the opening gates at last, we slew them all, even to the very last. What a grim joy that was. Then we understood. We had done it. We had found our way back to the centre.

"The city was all but ours. We had opened the outer gates and would have passed within them, but then a force came at us from the north. Down they flowed, an army even greater than the one we had just slain. And they all but swallowed us whole.

"I saw Noqmal fall. I saw Orpahan stand over his stricken body, so that it could be carried from the field, holding back the foe as though he had lost all reason. He made a wall of bodies with his sword, but even he succumbed at last and they cut him into pieces.

"My wounds were great. Though I had been pierced by many blades, I still lived. I tumbled into a hole, some long forgotten passage under the earth, though it was by no design of mine. I lay there in the darkness, insensible, but for how long I cannot tell. After a time I was awoken by a voice, a voice I thought I knew, coaxing me back from oblivion. But the voice was not speaking to me, it was speaking to the grey demons. I had to climb up and look out of my hole. But what I saw then will remain with me for ever more. I doubt even the river itself could wash away such a stain."

There was a pause, a long one. The sound of faint breathing could just be heard. Then the voice started again, and it was cracked with pain.

"We are betrayed. The Ell are betrayed. Karmaraa, Zien Qadah, Audroh Eithar, is betrayed. For I saw an Ell walking amongst the Agdoain, taking his ease in their midst whilst laughing at their play. And as he came close to this one or that, they bowed to him in return, drooling at his feet in fear as though he owned them entirely. But when he had passed them by, they went back again to their dreadful feasting, consuming the flesh of the dead.

"But this was no mere turncoat, no mere traitor, for this was none other than Onehson himself, our Velukor, our holy Velukor, taking his leisure amongst the slain."

The voice cracked with tears of breaking rage and broken sorrow.

"His hands were slick with blood, and the great stave of Karmaraa that lay across his back was stained and sullied. But when he turned in my direction and held up a hand as though to display it, before licking the blood from his fingers, I found I could not endure it any more. I fell back again into my dark hole and let the shadow cover me.

"I have crawled as far as I can. These will be my last words, I fear. My wounds are too much. The grey poison is in me and I have lost more blood than my body can spare. The river approaches fast and I find that I desire its balm. I now wish to be washed of this life and to truly forget what I have seen. May the Creator look kindly upon this failed servant of truth."

The voice tailed off into a gasp and then finished. There was silence. Zafazaa looked up and met the eyes of Korfax. He drew back at last, and he felt the cold of the void clutch at him. For there were tears upon the cheeks of Korfax, glistening tears. Korfax wept for Tiarapax. Zafazaa looked away.

Soqial was appalled. He stared at the stone as if it were a nightmare. No one else moved. There was utter silence as they accepted the enormity of what they heard. Some cried in silent grief, some bowed their heads. All that was holy, all that they had believed in, was broken.

They stood together on a balcony, looking down over the city, just the two of them. The others waited on their word.

Korfax looked at the many spires, all white and blue, banners the colour of the sky, stone the colour of fresh snow. It was beautiful, a vision of air. Zafazaa looked also, but Korfax wondered what it was that he saw. Zafazaa had lived in this city all his life, Korfax had only just arrived.

Korfax was the first to break the silence.

"So there it is, Zafazaa, the dark truth at the heart of our world. We are the betrayed, both of us. Though you think of me now as Korfax of the Mikaolazith, you have forgotten that I was once of the Farenith, called the straight road by some, called the Salman Malah by others. Azmeloh began us and Anolei honoured us. Both our houses have served the throne faithfully for thousands of years. The weight of such service cannot be easily put aside, but put aside it must be if we are to preserve the world."

Zafazaa closed his eyes, a long, slow blink.

"I know your history. There is no need for you to repeat it."

"But I disagree," Korfax told him. "All you can see, even now, is the Black Heart. But I am not him."

He bowed his head for a moment.

"I was born in a high room in Umadya Losq, not in the Forujer Allar. I was given the name of Korfax, not Sondehna, and my naming seer was Ialpam of Tohus, not Umidar of Leemal."

He turned to Zafazaa.

"Shall I go on? Shall I name my father and mother? Shall I talk of the blood that runs in my veins? Shall I speak of the gift of Karmaraa, that I too can change the purpose of stone? How many of your walls do you wish me to batter down before you accept the truth of this and lift the shadows that surround you?"

Zafazaa closed his eyes again.

"Do not push me," he said. "I will go only so far before I break."

"One season, let it confound another," Korfax quoted. "It is the very nature of the world we live in. Every day, every hour, brings change. You either accept it or you fall."

"An alliance!" Zafazaa hissed.

"We fight together," Korfax said. "You and I may never have complete peace between us, but what of the north and the west? That might happen in the years to come, if we are successful."

"I need time," said Zafazaa.

"Very well," said Korfax. "But do not take too long."

He waited a moment before speaking again.

"I have one last question to ask," he said. "Where is my mother? Is she here? Or has she moved on?"

For the first time since Korfax had been with him Zafazaa looked truly unsettled.

"She is no longer here," he said quietly.

Korfax frowned. There was an odd tension in the air about him now, something newly arrived, something he felt he should know. But given what had been revealed in this place, was it any surprise that those about him were now strange and fragile themselves? The west had finally been defeated, and by the single brightest star in its firmament. Korfax put his feelings aside and looked back carefully at Zafazaa.

"Where did she go?" he asked.

"To the far west, I think," said Zafazaa. "She will not come here again."

"Then will you do something for me? Will you send her a message?"

Zafazaa shifted uneasily.

"I will see what I can do."

How humble he was now. Korfax suddenly felt a curious peace settle over him. He had come here full of vengeance and hope. But now, with the west's humbling, the longing for vengeance began to fall away at last.

Opakas felt the insistence of her shew-stone pushing at her, demanding her attention. It was time. She took it out and felt him there, within it. Oh, but he was strong.

They touched minds, and both knew everything the other had to say in moments. It is almost done, he told her, there is the promise of an alliance. The truth is known, and the evil of the past shall remain there. She allowed herself a smile.

She told him that all was quiet, that Emethgis Vaniad was silent and that no more Agdoain had ventured forth.

They parted, and she put away her shew-stone. She went to tell the others, Ambriol, Ralendu, Ortal, Vandalim and Dorlamu, all the chieftains that had remained behind.

As she walked through the camp, so she saw him, sitting alone outside a small tent. She paused. That was one of Teodunad's guards. She walked over.

"You are Tahlor!" she accused. "You served Teodunad. The others ran. What are you doing here?"

He glanced up. She marked the look in his eyes of fear and regret. His whole demeanour was wary.

"I serve the Haelok," he said.

"And that is what Teodunad said," she countered. "He even swore an oath before us all. What of you?"

"I am no oath-breaker."

She scowled.

"See that you remain so."

She walked off and he watched her go.

No one trusted him now, and it was rare for anyone to even acknowledge that he existed. But was that really so surprising? He had dwelt so long in the shadow of Teodunad that others now saw him as an extension of Teodunad's will. Until, that was, Korfax had slain his master.

He had become a ghost, a revenant, torn in half. He hated the place he found himself, but he feared the alternatives. A battle was coming, a great and terrible battle, and if the Iabeiorith emerged victorious from its jaws, none would look with any favour on those that chose not to fight.

"May the light of the Creator shine upon you," came a voice.

He looked up. A cloaked figure stood just beyond the light of his sorcerous fire. Another visitor? He was clearly in demand this night.

"And who are you?" he asked.

"A traveller," said the other.

"From where?"

The stranger paused.

"Many places. May I share your fire?"

"No, you may not."

The stranger folded his arms.

"You are not being very friendly. But I imagine you are like that with everyone. Why else would you be sitting alone?"

Tahlor stood up. He suddenly decided that he did not like this stranger. He was too still for one thing, and his voice had no life to it at all.

"If it is friendship you want," he said, "go find it elsewhere and leave me in peace."

"Very well!" answered the stranger. "But tell me this. What did you do that so angered the mighty Korfax?"

Tahlor started. There was venom in the lifeless voice now.

"Who are you?" he asked again.

"No one of consequence."

Tahlor made the gesture of dismissal.

"Then begone," he said. "I have nothing further to say to you."

The stranger held up his hands in the gesture of placation.

"I will leave, if you wish me to do so. But first tell me where I might find him."

Tahlor stood up, hand upon the hilt of his sword.

"Korfax has gone to Othil Homtoh," he said.

"Othil Homtoh?" asked the other. "Now why would he do that?"

Tahlor was beginning to lose his patience.

"Why do you want to know?"

"I have business with him."

"What business?"

"We have symmetry, you and I. You have angered him, and he has angered me."

Despite himself, Tahlor found himself wondering at what that might mean.

"You do not look very angry," he said.

"Sometimes one must look beneath another's mask, in order to truly see their nature."

"Very poetic," Tahlor sneered. "Well, let me offer you some advice in return. Whatever business you may have with the Haelok, I would think twice before you confront him. A more dangerous and powerful creature I have never seen."

"On that we are in complete agreement."

"Who are you?" Tahlor asked. "Who are you, really?"

The stranger came forward, drawing back his hood. Tahlor had never seen such a dark and unmoving face. If he had not known better he would have said that the stranger wore a mask. Then the light caught the stranger's eyes. There was a fire inside, a dead light that illuminated nothing. Tahlor felt his heart go still. What demon was this? But it had become too late to act, for the stranger was already inside his guard. Quicker than thought a knife pierced Tahlor's neck and he fell to the ground, unable to speak or even breath. He felt his limbs become flaccid, his jaw become slack. The blade must have been poisoned.

The stranger moved quickly now, removing the rest of Tahlor's clothing. Tahlor watched as the stranger dressed himself, before coming close and looking intently into Tahlor's eyes.

He felt the stranger in his mind, pulling at everything, especially everything to do with Korfax. It was like being raked by claws. The stranger was neither gentle nor considerate. He took everything.

Finally it was over. The stranger sat back and stared into the fire, no doubt reviewing all that had just been stolen. Tahlor had never met the like before. The stranger was demonic, ruthless and unfeeling.

Finally the stranger turned back to Tahlor and placed his hands on Tahlor's head, one on the jaw, the other at the back. Then, without a pause, he twisted Tahlor's head to the side and Tahlor felt his neck snap.

There was a dim rushing sound, a rising tide of cold, and the world began to fade. His last thought was that he still did not know who the stranger was. But it was far too late to ask now.

17

POSSESSED

Ag-oan-sa Ds-ip-ur-a
Gei-zidahz Tran-raf-gahdon
Homin-jon Loes-jo-othas
Tas-od-eil Hotch-son-diz-ji
Pim-najes Aran-groji
Krih-iambig Alk-fen-iul-je
Od-zaf-mia Farim-pirjon

Ponodol sat upon a bench of stone and Obelison sat beside him. Around them both stretched the hall of portraits, all defaced and decaying, leering down like a circle of demons. Obelison tried to ignore them, as she tried to ignore so much in this place, but it was hard.

Ponodol rested his hands upon his knees and sighed.

"So he has let you see me again. What did you have to do?"

"I had to please him," she said.

"I will not ask," said Ponodol.

"It is not what you think," she told him. "It was nothing grotesque. All I had to do was to spend time with him, to listen, to be present."

He sighed.

"Even that is not an easy thing, I imagine."

"He believes he is here to return us to eternity. He believes that we are fallen, that matter is base and corrupt, that the maker of the world is evil. He wishes to stop the cycle of pain."

"By creating even more?" Ponodol all but spat. "The creed of the fallen spirit? He has said that to me also! Lies! All of it! Not even a child would be fooled by it!"

"He believes it," she said.

"Part of him does."

There was silence for a moment.

"Did you know that he digs?" said Ponodol.

"Digs?"

"He has commanded his slaves to dig down into the world, down, ever downwards. They work unceasingly at the task. He seeks something."

"But what can he be looking for? There is nothing down there."

"I do not know, but the Umadya Pir is the centre. Perhaps there is some mighty periapt buried in the deeps, something that sleeps. Perhaps he seeks that which kept the Ell away from the Rolnir until the time of Karmaraa."

"I never believed that tale," she said.

Ponodol turned his empty sockets towards her.

"What? And you of the Exentaser? Nalvahgey herself wrote of it. Do you think that she lied?"

"It seems hard to believe."

"After all you have seen? I find it all too easy to believe now. Once upon a time the Rolnir was your altar, pristine and inviolable. Visions could be sought at its edges, but you dared not cross the boundary, not until the coming of Karmaraa."

"Legends?" she questioned. "Myths? Is that what we are reduced to, hunting around for scraps from our past? What hope is there in any of this? Perhaps the Rolnir was once an object of reverence and awe, but Emethgis Vaniad was built upon it and within it to mark the suzerainty of the Ell for all time. Before the coming of Karmaraa we were children, slaves to our ignorance and fear, but then we grew up and became slaves to dogma instead. And now that everything has fallen apart we haunt the ruin of our lives like ghosts, hanging on to elder memory as if it were the only thing left to us."

"Such bitterness," he said. "It does not become you. You have more cause to hope than I."

"I see little hope in this place."

"Then you have not looked deeply enough."

She let out a long breath.

"You think there is hope here, then?"

"Look beyond yourself," he said, "look outside. This is not all that there is. Retribution marches towards us even as we speak."

"But have you seen what he commands? Have you heard what he says? He wants to destroy everything, pull it all down. His betrayal has defeated us. We are lost."

"What he commands? What he says?" Ponodol laughed darkly. "Is that him? Or is it the other? Think! The other has him. Why? Why does the other not act on its own? It cannot. It needs him. It needs an agent in this world; otherwise, it cannot act at all. We are caught in the middle, caught between mother and child."

"Mother and child?" she asked. "You said that before."

"Because that is how he sees it. Because that is how he talks to it."

She looked down.

"But how does that help us?"

"Because he has a weakness."

She looked up again.

"A weakness?"

"Yes."

"You did not mention this before."

"Because I was not sure until now. I am not sure I should tell you either, given how little hope I hear in your voice."

"Then give me some."

"If I tell you this, it will force you to act."

"I do not fear action. I welcome it," she said.

"So be it. But be warned. You will not like it."

Ponodol held up a hand.

"It is you!" he said. "You are his weakness!"

She closed her eyes. He was right. She did not like it.

"Why did he bring you back?" Ponodol asked. "Why does he keep you and look after you? Why does he wish for your company? No other here earns such consideration."

She was silent for a moment.

"But you are here also," she said. "Why is that? Why has he preserved you?"

Ponodol kept his head down.

"I have thought about that, too."

"And?"

"I was once one of the teachers of Korfax."

"Just that?"

"In his mind he seeks to overthrow his enemy, so he would take everything that his enemy once possessed and despoil it. I am sure there are others he would like to keep also. Tazocho, perhaps? What better than the mother of his enemy to replace the one that he lost."

Obelison shuddered at the implications.

"But you said I was his weakness."

"You and he shared something once, and he remembers that."

"Friendship," she said. "I did have feelings for him. His loneliness touched me."

Ponodol spread his hands wide in the gesture of agreement.

"Exactly!" he said. "You were his friend, one of the very few he believed he ever had. I think he loved you for it. For a little while you became the only warmth in the coldness of his heart. You did not fawn upon him, nor compete with him, nor try to subvert his will. You were honest with him. You touched him as no other ever has."

"I have no such feelings now," she said. "His is the darkest betrayal of all. He has slaughtered mercilessly. Remember the arena? My hatred for him knows no bounds."

Ponodol dropped his hands. There was a look upon his face, sad and regretful.

"The arena?" he asked. "Yes, but was it him that slaughtered, or was it the other?"

"It was him!" she answered. "It was his choice. How can you even ask that?"

"Blind I might be, but not that blind. When he speaks to me I hear two voices, not one. How many choices do you think he actually makes for himself? Fewer than you might imagine."

"Then he willingly submits."

"Or has no say in the matter. The other has been with him since the beginning, or so he told me. Imagine his life, how it must have been."

"Why do you defend him?"

"I do not. But neither should I ignore cause and effect."

She did not miss the admonition. She was quiet for a moment.

"What is it you feel that I should do?" she asked.

"It is not for me to say," he told her, "it is up to you. But if I were in your place, I would play upon his feelings for you. Become his distraction. He has been lonely all his life. Play upon that. His power comes from the other. It needs him. But if you distract him from its whispers, who knows what might accrue."

She sat alone. How could she do this? How could she become his friend once more? His betrayal filled her. She thought again of the arena, the slaughter he had punished her with, so that she could punish Ponodol with it in turn. She could not do it.

Or could she? Perhaps it was this other that had done the deed after all, as Ponodol had said. How dark her life had become if such thoughts were her only comfort.

She closed her eyes and remembered back to the quiet soul she had once befriended. It was easier to think of him this way, before he had torn her world apart. Yes, he had been alone, but that was the world into which he had been born. No one could decide their fate before they were given it. You worked with the gifts you received. His had been the choice to bring it all crashing down.

Or had it? And that was the question. Ponodol's words sat on her like a great weight. She needed to know. Knowing, she could act. No doubt he would come for her soon, and then she would see.

He came as expected and suggested that they walk together. He led her down corridors, up stairs, until she realised where she was being taken. It was to the garden of Teluah, that high garden of astonishing beauty.

They came to the door and she began to hope that here, at least, would be a place where she could find some rest from the haunted world about her. But it was not to be. Through the door she went and found herself in a place of death. Nothing lived here, nothing at all. She closed her eyes against it and tried not to see.

Everything was almost as she remembered it – blossoms and leaves, stems and roots, trees and lawns – but all were frozen, all were grey, all were dead. Everything had been turned to stone. She stood at the edge of a burial ground where the tombs mocked the departed in exquisite detail.

He stood beside her and sighed as if utterly at ease.

"Did you know that I spent most of my youth alone?" he told her.

She turned to him and wondered what his purpose would be today.

"That was how it was supposed to be," he continued, "or so they told me."

He smiled.

"So I invented things, places to be, companions to fill them. And that is how I came to know of the other." He turned to her. "Imagine it," he said. "There she was, walking through my secret places and smiling back at me."

Obelison dared a question.

"She?"

"Yes! The very image of my mother, or so I thought."

He smiled again.

"It looked like her, I am sure of it, but I could not compare what I saw with any memory. I had none, nor even an image. That was not allowed. I asked once if there were any. My tutors looked shocked, perhaps even angry. Resurrect no true image, they said, the spirit will linger! I did not ask again."

He looked down.

"That was when I realised that I couldn't tell anyone else what it was that I saw. If a simple question could create such outrage, imagine what they would have thought if I told them that I spoke with her? So I kept quiet and let them tell me how things should be. They always told me how things should be, but they were never interested to see if I had anything to say in return. After all, I was only child, and who ever listens to children?"

Now there was an abstract look in his eyes, distant.

"I made a mistake once," he continued. "I did let another see. My father found me wandering through the tower, seemingly talking to someone. I should not have said anything, but instead I told him I was talking to my mother. He grew angry, really angry. He told me never to do it again, and he grabbed hold of me and shook me as his voice became louder and louder. I could do nothing, of course, until they came for him and took him away. He hurt me that day and I was glad that I did not see him again for a long, long while."

He turned back to the garden. Now his expression was regretful.

"That was the turning point," he said. "Nothing lasts for ever, and certainly not in this impatient place. With my father's admonition she vanished from my sight and I did not see her again. That was hard. Never having known a mother's love, having to imagine it, and then having it taken away again? You cannot conceive the pain. For a long while I was desolate. I had to imagine her all over again. But now I longed for more, a touch, a voice, movement, the scent of her. To hear with my own ears. To see with my own eyes. To feel with my own hands."

She watched the movements of his hands, small movements, reaching and grasping.

"I tried to imagine that she was close by," he went on, "just outside the door, or just in the next room, or just outside the window or in any such place that was just out of reach. But it did not work, for I would inevitably have to go and look. Such a disappointment. You cannot imagine the longing that I felt."

He reached out and touched a delicate leaf. It shivered, a brittle quivering.

"Then she came back to me, just as the longing became unbearable. But now she was the other and I could see it for what it was. I saw its true guise. I spoke to it. It answered me, and it answered me in all ways. I understood at last why things were the way that they were – the loss, the pain, the denials, the longing. I was answered completely. I have never felt so at peace as I felt then."

He turned to her and waited.

"Do you have nothing to say?" he asked eventually.

"What is there to say?" she answered. "You have said it all."

"I want more from you than that!"

"You care what I think?"

"Why else would I have you here?"

He looked at her fully.

"Listen to what I am saying!" he told her. "I spoke to the other and it answered me. It answered all my questions, each and every one of them. No one else had ever done that. The shallow creatures that flocked around me, ordering my life, telling me how things should be? They never told me such truths. They did not care. No one cared! They were too busy about their own wants and needs to care what I might think! I was denied! Is it any wonder that I went my own way?" He gestured back at the tower behind them. "Well, they have all now learnt the error of their ways."

She felt cold, as though the grey stone of the garden had seeped into her soul. What justifications were these? He had reinvented his past. He had been well-loved by those around him. Perhaps the mad grief of his father had made things a little difficult, but as for the rest? All had cared for him! Even her very own mother had been there, before her untimely death. Many of those that had been present at his birth had pledged themselves to his side, especially after witnessing the grief and the tragedy of his entrance into this world. Her father, Abrilon, had told her this, happy to tell such tales, especially if they involved her mother. No, this was a mad lie. But whose lie was it?

"Are you saying that nobody loved you?" she asked.

He looked at her, and his eyes glinted like hard stones.

"I was there," he said. "You were not. I remember what happened. The other showed me. And it did more. It protected me. There were so many threats it told me of, so many perils that had to be removed. I remember my dreams from that time, that sense of terrible danger surrounding me. But the other was with me, standing between me and the danger, helping me to be safe, showing me how. At first it was difficult to gain any influence at all. One had to punch a hole through the walls of the world, without fully understanding the whys and the wherefores.

That was hard. I am only thankful it is not like that now! You have no idea the suffering it caused me. I would feel ill for days afterwards."

She became very still inside. What was he telling her now? There were hints here, hints of something darker yet.

"I don't understand," she said.

He smiled at that.

"No one ever does," he said. "You tell them, but they never understand, because they do not see it as you do. We are islands of incomprehension, all of us, separated by a boundless sea."

He gestured to the far hills.

"Did you know that my path into this world was fraught with difficulty? It was not an easy birth. To lie so long in such blessed ignorance, in a warm place of comfort, only to suddenly find yourself thrust into a cold place of pain and death?"

That shocked her. Did he really think he was the only one ever to experience such a thing?

"We are all born," she said. "We all have to endure that transition. It is the price we pay for life."

His expression changed in an instant and he bared his long teeth at her in a snarl.

"Did you not hear what I just said?" he hissed. "Do you mock me?"

"And how would I mock you?" she returned. "There is no mock. It has ended."

"But you are mocking me," he told her. "I can hear it in your voice."

"How acute is your hearing?" she answered. "But hasn't hearing ceased as well?"

"Do not play such games with me, daughter of Zirad," he spat, "you have no idea how far they might go."

That caught her.

"Why do you call me that?" she asked carefully.

"Call you what?" he snapped.

"That!" she said. "Daughter of Zirad! She was my mother, but she died long ago, when I was very young. Why do you name her now?"

He looked at her for a moment with such appalling intimacy that she all but shrank from him. But then his expression lessened back to a hard smile and he looked away.

"I knew who she was," he said. "That was why I called you what I did. To remind you of your loss, so that you might appreciate mine."

She stared at him. What had she just awoken? Every time they played this game he revealed something else, something new, something never before imagined.

"What do you mean?" she asked.

"I meant nothing more than what I have already said," he answered quietly. "At least, nothing of consequence. It is old news now."

"Tell me."

"Why?"

"She died when I was very young," Obelison said. "I would know why you name her now."

"Died?" he asked. "Yes! In a storm, a great and monstrous storm out of the north, that took her ship and smashed it upon the unforgiving rocks under the tall cliffs of Lonzldor. She drowned. They all did."

"But why do you name her now?" she pressed, watching him, her mind alight for the slightest nuance.

"It is something we share," he told her, "the loss of our mothers. I was hoping to remind you of it. We share a pain, you and I, and I was trying to achieve common ground, but all you can think of is yourself. It was ever thus."

"But that was not what you meant," she said, her voice low.

"But it was," he replied. "It was one of the things that drew you to me."

His words flicked through her mind: 'the error of their ways', 'punching a hole through the world', 'so many perils that had to be removed'. What was he really telling her? Was it a warning? She sensed something, something at the edges of thought.

"You mentioned dangers," she said. "What could possibly threaten you?"

He looked into the distances.

"They could," he answered. "The other told me. If they had seen? They would not have understood. Even my father would not have understood. He went mad long ago, blind to everything but his own grief. No time to spend with a child whose only purpose was to remind him of what he had lost! Even he would have been a danger to me. I had to be safe."

There were lies and half-truths here. He told himself so many, how he had discovered the other, how it had always been there, how it had gone away and come back, how he had thought that it was his mother speaking to him, how he discovered that it was not, how he needed to be safe, how no one loved him. What was happening in his mind? She was tempted to look, but she knew that would be fatal. Better to use words. Words were her only option.

"What happened?" she asked. "What did you do?"

"Do?" he said. "I did nothing. I was just a child at the time, and what can a mere child achieve in this impatient place? One has to grow, become accepted, follow expectations, achieve what your fathers achieved before you. How paltry it all is! How repetitive!"

She watched him leave, slowly picking his way along the path. And as he turned this way and that, so she followed him with her eyes, watching and measuring. A suspicion grew inside her, then more than a suspicion. The storm that killed her mother, had he caused it? Was he responsible for her mother's death? Or was he saying that it was the other? She thought again of the tales her father had told her, happy tales of her mother's service to the throne. Bitterness filled her. Her father was dead also, one of the many victims of this evil war.

More words flicked through her mind: 'She drowned', 'They would not understand', 'I had to be safe'. Obelison went cold.

He gestured that she should join him. She looked down so that she could hide her feelings. He must not see, she told herself, not yet. Possibilities coursed through her mind. There were many ways to kill, quick ways, hidden ways, but he would see her, or the other would, and he would throw her down before she could act. Even with a blade in her hand it was not a certainty, and he had emptied the tower of everything and anything that could be used as a weapon. He wished to be safe! Better she do as he bid and bide her time, so she slowly mastered herself and came to stand beside him, but she did so in a cloud of hatred.

He leant against the carven wall and looked back at her with a pale smile resting on his lips. How mild he looked now, leaning on the stone as though he needed, or required, its support. He had become indulgent again, distracted and indulgent. He fluttered a hand at the frozen garden behind her, the one she had just walked through.

"So, now that you have wandered through my garden, how do you find it?"

She would have hurled herself at him there and then, striking with her hands at all the fatal places, but she knew how futile that would be; although he seemed vulnerable now, he still possessed that hideous strength. It was in there, inside him, ever waiting to assert itself when needed, like some unthinking reflex. She could not hurt him physically, not yet at least, so she let her hatred fall back down inside her and stared at the dead garden instead.

She shuddered. What could she say that she had not already said before? What had once been a place of astonishing beauty had fallen to desolation, its fragile mortality frozen for all eternity by a never-ending cold.

"I find your world vile and unspeakable," she said, involuntarily raising up a hand as if to strike him.

He regarded her lazily through lidded eyes for a moment as if she was of less consequence than a pebble. Then he glanced at her upraised hand and widened one eye slightly. She lowered her hand again and he watched it drop back down to her side, before looking back at her as if finally satisfied.

"Vile?" he mocked. "Unspeakable? You do not know what you are saying. Look around you."

He gestured with a flick of his fingers.

"I have preserved this place, preserved its imperfect beauty from the ravages of time. I have gifted this place with permanence, so that everyone who comes here can appreciate it, whenever they come. And all that you can say is that you find it vile? Has your reason been overthrown at last? You are base! You, like all the other fools here, do not know when you are in the presence of transcendent truth."

"Truth?" she questioned. "I thought your truth was the end of everything."

"You still do not understand, do you?" he said. "Shall I lead you like a child, again?" He looked at her with distaste. "Think, child!" he scolded. "The nothing from which creation has been pulled has the potential to be everything. The void holds everything within it. From nothing comes everything. Such a simple and obvious equation, I would have thought! You, of all of them, should have understood this by now. You have seen what dwells here. Is it not obvious to you now that all there ever needs to be is nothing? For nothing contains all truths within its single truth. The garden before you is merely a representation. Paltry, incomplete and imperfect as it is, it still aspires. Have you not yet appreciated the paradox of existence?"

She clenched her fists at her side. Child? No! He was the child here, not her, but she understood his meaning well enough. This was not a lesson in philosophy but a lesson in power. She gestured at the dead garden.

"But everything changes with time," she said. "And that is the point. I think it is you that have misunderstood."

He laughed at her. It was so affected and derisory that she had to bury her fingers in the palms of her hands to maintain her restraint. The pain did its work, calming her and clearing her mind. She could not afford anger or hatred at this time. She had to watch and listen, as she had once been taught.

Looking at him now was like looking at a mask. He had become the very thing he claimed to despise – a shell, hollow, hiding himself under layers of obfuscation. But it was his depths that she needed to see, something she could touch and affect.

She waited for him to stop laughing, which he eventually did. He glanced at her, clearly enjoying his own mirth.

"You have not listened at all, have you?" he said.

She looked pointedly at the garden.

"Then tell me again," she asked. "We have time, or has that ended as well?"

He continued to smile, but now there was a hint of a warning in his glance.

"You do not fool me," he told her, turning to the garden.

"Immortality," he continued. "Only that which does not move is truly eternal. Time is movement, the very agent of mortality."

He gestured at a frozen sapling, leaves as delicate as frost.

"Think of a tree," he said. "Before it grows there is an empty space awaiting its presence, but then comes the seed, followed by the sapling, then the tree itself, then its eventual death and decay, and then, finally, its absence, all in one. Now think again of the space before the tree grew to fill it. It is the void in miniature, a place of potential. But the void is mightier than this, because it, and it alone, contains the possibility to be everything. It is the all in one, and the one in all."

He stepped closer and his eyes were brighter.

"Even you are there," he said, "in the void. I see you now, child and crone, maiden and corpse. I see the space you currently occupy, the space before you existed and the space after you have long gone to dust. I see all of you."

She stepped back from him and clutched at the stone behind her. For a moment she had seen it, too, a brief flicker of images, one on top of the other, birth, life, death and decay. She closed her eyes. There was a great void around her, no up, no down, no left and no right. She was immense, she was tiny. She would have fallen if she had not been holding onto something. She gradually pulled herself back up from the depths.

It was almost as if she had been violated, as if the unwholesome spirit within him had traced its way down the path of her life so that it could bring back knowledge to her that she neither wanted nor desired. She shivered at the touch, insidious and pervasive, and it was a long time before she felt her heart beat again.

She looked at him, but he had already turned away from her to gesture at the garden around them both, hands sweeping to encompass it all.

"What you see about you here is a reflection," he told her, "the merest hint of what could be. Paltry and imperfect though it is, there is enough here to offer the perceptive mind a beginning glimpse of the underlying truth."

He looked back at her.

"All that changes and grows reaches a point where it cannot grow any further. It is the way of this world. Imperfection is inevitable, for nothing is ever finished in this place."

He pointed at the dead blooms.

"But here before you is an image of what could be, an image of a perfection yet to come, that yearning caught upon a single moment."

His smile deepened.

"So understanding moves on, seeing at last that there is only ever one true form, the paragon of its kind. How much that lives ever comes so close? What remains in the world all but falls away again, diminishing, ever departing from that perfect moment until it is gone at last."

He leaned over one of the flowers.

"But in the void there remains the shape and the form and the being to which it aspired, held in perpetuity, a single potential that is everything and nothing. There is no being, no doing, no actuality – only the possibility and the anticipation of all things."

He studied her for a moment.

"And you are not convinced!"

It was a statement, not a question.

"No," she said.

"Why?" he asked.

"You want a return to nothingness? You want the bliss of oblivion? I do not believe it," she said. "I do not believe that we are here merely to make an end of it."

"But that is the point," he said. "We should not have been here in the first place."

She was aghast.

"You think that creation should come to an end?"

"And what have I said?"

"But that is not what you want!"

He looked at her for a moment, eyes searching and seeking.

"Yes it is," he said.

"No. You would be alone, and that is not what you want at all."

He stood straighter.

"And if I say that it is?"

His voice had an edge to it.

"No," she told him. "I would not be here if that were true."

He subsided, but not for long.

"You were the only one that never made demands of me," he said, "not in the way that others did. All the others, they made demands. You never threatened me as they did. You allowed others to live, you did not order their coming and going. I found myself liking that."

"I did not threaten you?"

"No."

"And do I threaten you now?"

"That remains to be seen."

"And yet you have punished me," she accused. He looked surprised at that.

"I have been nothing but considerate," he said.

"But you showed me your arena. You made me watch. You punished me."

His eyes grew more intense by the moment.

"And you needed to understand," he told her. "Remember! You were the one left my side. You denied me."

"And you denied me!" she answered. "You took my beloved from me!"

He almost laughed at that.

"And how right I was to do so!" he countered. "Look at the creature he is! He left you for dead. He has forgotten you! You, though, are still infected by his desire. You are yet to be cured of him."

She held herself back. She could not continue on that road.

"But what of all those that have died?" she asked. "What did they ever do to you?"

The intensity increased.

"They never cared for me, so why should I care for them? Fickle creatures! As quick to give their loyalty as to deny it. But even in this I am merciful. I shall break the horrid cycle of life and death. It shall cease at my hand, and in the end they shall know who has done this, and they shall thank me for the mercy of eternal bliss, though they do not deserve it."

He turned and walked away from her, and she watched him go.

For a long time she stood, thinking on all that he had said, and then she looked around at the dead garden, before running all the way back to her rooms.

She sat alone in her apartments and pondered. He horrified her with his purpose, his belief. It was as if the world had been turned upon its head. Ugliness was beauty, pain and suffering were pleasure, beginnings were endings.

But he was also strangely vulnerable. The bliss of oblivion? That was not what he desired. It was as Ponodol had said: he was still a child in many ways. He wanted a world that would not interfere with him, but conversely he did not want to be alone. He wanted a kindred spirit, someone like him, someone who would approve. That was why she was here. But who had ordered her presence – him or the other?

Maybe that was her purpose, to keep him company in the darkness, to distract him from himself whilst the other went about its business. But that was also what Ponodol had said to her: 'Become his distraction.'

Her mind span. What was the truth? It was like sitting at the centre of a web of pathways that went off in every direction, the splitting of possibilities into ever smaller pieces until everything was nothing and nothing was everything.

The Exentaser had a word for it, Unchtonbanin, the confusion that lay in the contemplation of the unknown. Infinite choices. Nothing could ever be resolved in such a place. It was the antithesis of vision: undirected, shapeless and chaotic.

She had to find a way out, something onto which she could hold. The only lever she had, the only lever that she knew of, was his need for her. But how far could she rely upon it?

She went in search of Ponodol and found him in his usual place, upon his bench of stone, face turned to the light. As soon as she approached he turned to her.

"I feel your need," he said. "Do not speak of it to me. Whatever is in your heart, keep it there. I do not want to know."

She sat beside him.

"Why?" she asked.

"Whatever you have resolved to do," he said, "whatever you have discovered, keep it to yourself. If you tell me anything, he might see it."

"Why might he see it?"

"Because he goes looking. He looks inside me for perfidy, as he does with all the others here. He trusts no one."

"He does not do that with me," she said quietly.

Ponodol smiled.

"Exactly," he said

He leaned forward.

"I trust your insight, but it is yours alone. Whatever you choose to do, I will trust it. Have no other consideration. Be a sword, an arrow. Remember that your house is the bright firmament. Think only of that."

He turned away from her.

"Now go and do not come again. It is easier this way."

"But..."

"Go!"

His voice was hard, like the grinding of stone. She stood up. His command was utterly final; she could see it in him. She left his side and went back to her rooms. She stood at a window and stared out over the city, but she did not see it. Instead she saw a blind face and a snarl of teeth.

From that moment on her days became lonely duels. She kept away from Ponodol and remained either alone or in the company of her keeper. She debated with him when she could, probing, looking for understanding, a platform, a ledge, even a handhold with which to gain some purchase. She tried philosophies that would have been anathema to her, argued from positions that felt more like betrayals, trying to feel them and be passionate for them, but he remained essentially unchanged. No matter how she confronted him, he always found a way to twist her arguments back to the way he wanted things to be.

The only thing she achieved at all was his consideration. His manner with her clearly improved. He became more courteous, his smiles became less mocking and he showed more consideration for her feelings than he had before. But she knew it was only because she pleased him and did as he would have her do. The threat of his displeasure did not depart; it was always there in the background, like an uncurled whip.

She wondered how she could get closer, get inside and see what it was that she needed to see. But that needed trust, a shared covenant, and he was far too self-centred for that. She was his possession, his prize possession, and for all his enjoyment of their time together, she remained an indulgence, like the frozen garden.

Finally, when she could not think of anything else, she decided on a more dangerous strategy. She had spent her time attacking his position, his resolve and his belief, only to find that he had no position. He twisted and turned and shifted his ground with every thrust that she made. It was like grappling with fog. So why not pick another target, like the other, for instance.

It was not without risk. Ponodol's plight remained a hideous illustration of the other's displeasure. So what would the other do when she made her play against it? Would it even react? Could she draw it out? Or would that be the last thing that she ever did?

They were walking in the dead garden again, and he was talking of perfection as he liked to. She waited her moment, waited while he filled himself with his usual contemplations of the void, and then she struck.

"You speak of perfection," she said, "its glory, its possibility, but what of the Agdoain? What are they to you?"

He stopped and stared at her. In all their talks together she had never mentioned his slaves at all. They remained hidden, unspoken, like a dark and guilty secret, for ever there but out of sight.

"What do you mean," he said, "what are they to me?"

"Exactly that – what are they to you?"

Now he looked perplexed, as if such a question had never even occurred to him before.

"They are mere tools, of course," he answered, "an extension of my will. Nothing more, but nothing less either. I do not see why you even bother to mention them."

He gestured flippantly, dismissively. She watched him and smiled inside. An extension of his will? That was a lie. They were not his.

"Just that?" she probed. "Mere tools?"

She smiled slightly but did not continue. Less was more in this play. Let him follow her for a change.

"What game is this?" he asked. She wondered briefly if he had seen her thought, but she was sure he had not.

"No game," she continued.

She watched as her words penetrated the mask, sinking down through the layers. How his face changed as they fell, unravelling by degrees. Down here dwelt the child, the child that played in the courts of the mighty.

"What is it that you want from me?" he asked.

Was that petulance she heard? She had his interest at least.

"The truth," she told him.

He stopped where he was and gave her his full attention. Mockery waited at the edges, a child's inconsiderate spite projected upon his face.

"The truth?" he questioned. "You have had nothing but the truth from me ever since you rose from your sleep."

"Have I?" she countered. "I am not so sure." She allowed her smile to fade, but did not pause. Let him see the bait. "You talk of perfection," she continued, "keeping this garden as a reminder, but what about the Agdoain? They do not fit within your philosophy at all. They are too much, too corrupt, too distasteful, too debased."

His contempt dropped from him and he looked strangely at her now, as if he could not quite believe that she stood before him at all.

"Corrupt? Distasteful?" he mused at last. "No, they are not distasteful, except to those with narrow sensibilities."

He smiled indulgently, almost as if he had scored a point. "They merely have a shape and a substance that matches their purpose," he continued. "Does not all that live possess the same? You must remember that they inhabit the flesh and that the flesh has ideas all of its own. You must look beyond the flesh and see their purpose only, for that is all that really matters."

His smile deepened.

"And you should not forget that you are of the flesh also. Like them, you must learn to transcend the vessel and look beyond its selfish boundaries, if you are to see the inner truth."

"But look at them," she said. "They are hobbled things. They are deformed. Their flesh makes war upon itself. They are like a broken imitation. They confuse, they disgust for no reason and they pervert to no good effect. If you wish to convince others of your message, you must engender a purer breed. The Agdoain are too base, too vile, too grounded in the naked substance of the world. Your destroyers should be bright flames, not dark, corrupted flesh."

He stared at her now, almost with his entire being. Then she saw it.

Something behind his eyes swam sluggishly to and fro, from one eye to the other, before slowly swimming back again. It peered out at her from within his skull, vast and remote, and she could only watch it in horrified fascination. Was this the other come at last? She stilled an involuntary shudder. What was it? What was it really?

"I think I begin to understand you at last," he suddenly said.

His words brought her back and she focused on his face. He was looking back at her with sudden intelligence, and the thing behind his eyes was gone.

"You desire absolutes," he continued. "For you, the Agdoain do not suffice. Am I right?"

She took a long breath to calm herself. What had she seen? What did it mean? How could she use it?

"Yes," she answered, "I think that is it. No one questions the rain, the wind or the fire. But clothe such forces in flesh and they are deemed unnatural. They become abominations."

He stood straighter now and his eyes were brighter. He suddenly radiated force.

"Such insight!" he said.

He smiled at her and his expression was the most considerate she had ever seen on his face.

"Now am I repaid for the care I have lavished upon you," he said. "Good! Very good! I think I understand you all the better now. That was the attraction of Korfax, wasn't it? He also desired absolutes. I know. I saw it in him. Purity of service! Purity of rule! He worshipped at the altar of purity and you do the same."

He turned away from her and his eyes were grey flames in his head. She waited in stillness. Here, perhaps, was the turning point. Only the simplest answer would do.

"Yes," she said.

He smiled and looked back at her. The fire died within him and his face became a blank wall again.

"Then we are more alike than you had previously imagined. But do not concern yourself with that now, nor with the Agdoain. When the end comes they will be swept away and you will discover your heart's desire. In the great absence you will finally find the ultimate purity and the ultimate truth. The nothingness without will take you, and you will know nothing at all, and so know everything."

She remained silent. What else could she say? The debate had run its course.

What had she gained? His consideration? She spat upon it. His promises? She reviled them. His confessions, his lies, his spite, his masks? They were irrelevant, all of them. It was the thing behind his eyes that consumed her now.

POSSESSED

Back in her room she looked quietly out of the window, much as she ever did, but inside she was on fire with questions. Who had she debated with, him or the other? Who was the master and who the slave? Or was it as simple as that? Mother and child, Ponodol had said. Possessed, he had declared. But she could not agree. There was something else happening here.

She thought of how his moods changed. One minute he was indulgent, the next petulant, then angry, then cruel, then defensive. He debated the same way. And his desires? Part of him wanted to be with her. Part of him wanted to be alone. Part of him wanted to go back to the womb. It was as though he was no longer an individual, but a mob, a chaos of competing voices, each rising up into the light before falling back down again.

It was the influence of the other, it had to be. He had told her how it was, how the other was the voice of the void and that it had the possibility of all things within itself. She considered what that actually meant. All things, all at once. Chaos.

And that was why it needed him. It needed his voice, needed him to become its direction. It was the most fragile of relationships. It needed him to speak for it, but it needed him to give it direction. It had to submit and to rule, all at the same time.

So it walked the finest of lines. It had to hold all opposites in abeyance – there could be no reconciliation. If it actively sought for the thing that it wanted, the very act of seeking would deny it. It needed him to desire for it. But even its presence had divided him from himself.

Words came back to her, words once spoken with Ponodol.

"What he commands? What he says? Is that him? Or is it the other? Think! The other has him. Why? Why does the other not act on its own? It cannot. It needs him. It needs an agent in this world; otherwise, it cannot act at all. We are caught in the middle, caught between mother and child."

"Mother and child? You said that before."

"Because that is how he sees it. Because that is how he talks to it."

"But how does that help us?"

"Because he has a weakness."

"A weakness?"

"Yes."

"You did not mention this before."

"Because I was not sure until now. I am not sure I should tell you either, given how little hope I hear in your voice."

"Then give me some."

"If I tell you this, it will force you to act."

"I do not fear action. I welcome it."

"So be it. But be warned. You will not like it. It is you! You are his weakness!"

Now she understood. That was her purpose. She was here to help bring order to chaos. Without her, without others, his mind would collapse in upon itself and he would be useless.

Even as the answer dawned upon her she felt giddy, unbalanced and out of place. There was movement, but all was still. Out of the darkness it came and subsumed it.

Vision! Once before it had come to her and her world had changed because of it, but now it consumed her with breathtaking power and she fell from her body into a world outside time.

She could not move, she dared not. The vision took her with such rapidity that she dare not blink lest she miss it. It was on her and through her in moments. There was a knife in her hand, and the knife was in his throat. It was so clear, so vibrant, that it took all her powers to keep herself still at the shock. How, she asked herself, how?

The knife was outlined in light, and as it divided the flesh so it divided the spirit, dividing the one from the other. She saw what she had to do. She had to get between him and the other. Without the other, he was powerless. Without the other, the Agdoain could not be summoned. Without the Agdoain the war was over. And she was the knife.

The vision fled, leaving her breathless. So that was it! As the other had caught him in its snare, now she must catch him in hers. But she must be careful. She must hide her intent, make it her own whisperer in the darkness. As the other was to him, so her vision must be to her, unseen and unheard, but ever waiting to strike.

She must be subtle. Any sudden conversion to his side would be treated with utmost suspicion. She must be slow, gradual, a distant dance that comes ever closer. She must become his reflection, and in the light of his reflection he would lose her and see only himself.

No stratagem born of her order would work. No hiding pattern or hall of mirrors or illusion culled from the corner of the mind would do. He would see it, because the other would see it. She had to fool even herself in this. She had to send her desires deep down into the wells of her soul, down into the darkness and forget them, and then let them do their work in secret. Let her believe her distraction to be real and then her chance would finally come, and when Korfax arrived at last he would find his foe already defeated.

18

THE LAST ALLIANCE

Ors-gilren Alk-ar-uljo
Oach-zurji Od-muh-gruh-as
Krih-pla-st Ip-om-garzid
Koa-ridin Pim-do-teos-jes
Van-pir-hoa Mirk-mor-lai-in
Von-od-vep Chis-razax-jon
Ip-sorgie Od-lar-logix

Korfax waited in the ancient chamber. He was alone. He had been told to expect a visitor. When told the name, he had been surprised. It was to be Enay Osidess, wife to Zafazaa and the cousin of his mother. He found himself wondering if Simoref had had a hand in it.

The change in Simoref was profound now, and quite clear to see. Korfax saw it in the eyes of those around him: respect rather than subservience. How different to that of his father. Korfax found himself marvelling at it. Simoref was a very different creature to the one he had known in the seminary. It was almost as if he was trying to erase that part of himself, even the memory. Korfax chose to see hope in it.

Osidess entered through the western door, robed in dark samiss from head to foot. Veiled in the habiliments of grief ever since the death of Ermalei, she was hidden from view, even to her face. Until recently it had been a rare choice to make, but since arriving in Othil Homtoh Korfax had seen a great many similarly robed. The war continued to leave its mark upon the world.

He stood up and bowed to her.

"May the Creator's light shine upon you," he said.

"And upon you," she answered.

He looked at her. How like his mother she sounded. And she walked like her, too, with purposeful and graceful strides. Perhaps that was why Zafazaa had courted her, and why they were now estranged. Korfax suddenly felt a longing to look upon her face, to see if that was like his mother's also, but that was altogether forbidden. She would never show herself to any other this side of the river, not ever.

She came before him and waited for a moment. Then she spoke again.

"They tell me that you have the blood of Sondehna in your veins."

"It is true," he said.

"And how do you feel about that?"

Korfax frowned. No one had ever actually asked him that before.

"Blessed and cursed," he answered.

"I understand," she said. "Had I not heard the revelation of Tiarapax I might not have, but everything is changed now. What was once revered to the heights has now fallen into the darkest depths. Who here would dare to judge your heritage in the light of that?"

He could feel her eyes upon him, even though they were hidden by her veil. He could feel them searching his face, back and forth, this way and that. Korfax waited until he felt her gaze drop again.

"Yes," she said, "you are her son, I see her in you."

Korfax felt the threat of tears. He suddenly wanted to see his mother again with all of his heart, to see her one last time, to receive her final blessing. He dropped his head and squeezed his eyes shut.

"Have you seen her since she came west?" he asked.

Osidess came closer.

"No," she said. "I do not invite visitors. I have not invited any to see me since Ermalei passed into the river. I am estranged from Zafazaa. Simoref comes to me when he can, but that is all I will allow." She laid a gloved hand against him. "I do not know where she is. She has hidden herself away, I think, just as I have."

Korfax tried to hide his anguish, but Osidess clearly saw it, as she saw everything from behind her veil, watching it all burning within him, marking how it etched his face. She raised a gloved hand and touched him lightly upon his cheek, lifting his head again.

"I think she would be proud, if she could see you now. I see no evil in you, Korfax, only the rage of its temptation. Though you are dark with many sorrows, you have all but conquered the corruption that once tried to pull you from the path. You have won a victory not even Karmaraa could achieve. If ever you come into your own again, do this one thing for me. Make the north over in your own image. Strength, honour, fortitude and wisdom! Let those be the four pillars of your rule. They were your father's."

A single tear coursed down his cheek. She caught it carefully upon a fingertip.

"You are in such pain," she said. "I should not add to it."

Korfax did not know what to say, so he gestured to one of the two chairs that stood facing each other in the centre of the chamber.

"Please," he said, "sit with me. Let me take comfort in your presence."

He felt a dim smile warm him from within its shroud.

"Comfort?" she said. "I did not come here with comfort in mind, but now that I see you, I will do as you bid. You are in need, Korfax."

"And what do I need?"

"You need care."

"Am I so easily broken then?"

"You are already broken. Only love can mend such fractures as I see before me now."

"So tell me then, why you have come here."

And, as if satisfied, Osidess turned to the chair and sat down in it. Korfax sat in the other and awaited her words.

"I came here to tell you a single thing," she said, "the one thing you do not yet know. So here is my truth. Here is the thing that I saw in Ermalei. He gave it to me as he lay dying, the last gift of his soul."

She reached out with her mind and touched him. A vision came with the touch, and Korfax saw all.

The Umadya Pir. Above the city it reached, the very centre of the great seal that was Emethgis Vaniad, pointing at the heavens like an affirmation of rule.

Clustered about it were the seven, the towers of the great guilds, and around them the greater city, humble attendants bowing before their mighty lord. Beyond the walls reared greater heights, the Leein Komsel, the boundary of the Rolnir, bones strong enough to defy all the ages of the world. But in the heavens, above each tower's bitter tip, black clouds rolled like rebellion, spitting lightning back at the ground.

In a high room she lay, the fever of her travail nailing her to the bed. Fine linen covered her slender form, cruelly describing her famished limbs and wasted body. But in the midst of it all her pregnancy reared up in bloated contentment, happy to suck the very life from its host.

Above her the lights floated, a weave of flame and colour to gentle the unquiet air. About her figures knelt, robed suppliants watching and waiting, unable to intercede.

In a hall far below, empty of everything except a vast and ornate chair, lit only by the light of a single, flickering crystal, he awaited the outcome he could not face. He sat in the chair and stared at the crystal whilst his finely moulded features rippled with the light of its inner flames, even as his immense cloak enclosed the rest of him in its shadowy folds.

By the time it reached him, the scream had already traversed the entire tower, tumbling down from above in a cascade of echoes. He looked up at the ceiling in fear. Another scream followed the first. He stood up from the chair and ran to the door, discarding his cloak upon the floor like an old skin. From the door he took the stairs, the screams guiding him upwards as he made his way blindly through the darkness. Outside, beyond the walls, the storm had lessened and only the occasional tongue of lightning shattered the sky.

He reached her room and found the attendants weeping. He could hear them as he approached, quiet sobs falling through the cracks in the door, or through his mind. He thrust his way inside.

She lay upon the bed, a storm-tossed thing, a discarded rag. Her eyes were flung wide, dark pits empty of life. He went to her and stared down, before passing a hand across her face to close her eyes, hiding the oblivion he saw within.

He stayed by her for long moments, his head bowed. The attendants kept their distance and their heads down.

Finally he stood, crossing the room to the ornately carved crib. He looked inside. There was a shape in there, something small that moved. Vague motions beckoned and he leaned closer. An attendant came forward slowly, carrying a light, a small light that gleamed gently. He took it quietly and held it up. In the crib he saw a child shape, a pale roundness that the light could not resolve. He went closer.

The child turned to him and he fell back from it with a choking cry. By some trick of the light the child had seemed all but faceless, a blank sheet of skin unbroken except for a mouth, but even that was wrong, for the mouth grinned up at him as though amused by his horror, a glint of long, sharp teeth.

He dropped the crystal and it fell to the floor, bouncing upon the stone, tinkling quietly as it tumbled away. The attendants all rushed forward, helping hands and comforting words guiding him to a chair. He sat back in helpless shock whilst someone recovered the crystal. Another went to the crib, lifting out the child and bringing it to him. He looked again, he couldn't help himself, and when his eyes had focused on the tiny form held up before him, he almost laughed in relief. Here was his child, after all; eyes closed tight, a tiny nose, a mouth smiling in sleepy contentment. He reached forward and gently touched a cheek and the laughter turned to sobs in his throat. Then someone leaned over and spoke words to him, words that were meant to ease the ache in his heart.

"You have a son, my Velukor. The line of Karmaraa is assured."

Korfax did not know what to say. He looked at her.

"You saw this?" he asked.

"Some of it," she said.

He took a long breath.

"And you said nothing?" he asked.

"My grief was too great," she answered. "I discounted what I saw and considered it false, the imaginings of loss. We all look for culprits, after all, someone to blame. I dared to blame the child of Karmaraa. I thought myself cursed."

She looked up.

"But now I know that I saw truly."

She turned away.

"And I am still cursed."

"You also," he said.

"Yes," she answered.

They sat together in silence and thought of all the things that might have been.

Zafazaa sat upon his throne alone. The great hall was empty.

Some of Korfax's forces had entered the city and there was a calm of sorts. Few looked with favour on any of them, and some even muttered under their breath, but no one openly defied the truce. Besides, who would dare? Korfax was here, the last child of the line of Sondehna, wielder of unthinkable might.

Zafazaa stared up at the wall. Generations looked down upon him, portrait after portrait of his ancestors, all the way back to the founding fathers of the greatest dynasty the Bright Heavens had ever seen. What would they say now? Allow a scion of Sondehna to dwell within these walls? None of them would countenance it, were they here.

Yet what Korfax said was right. Why had there been a womb at the Forujer Allar? Why had there been a womb in the Piodo Mirul? How had the Agdoain invested the Umadya Pir so quickly? Though Kukenur had confirmed it, with all of the Exentaser in Othil Homtoh agreeing, only hard, cold facts would convince Zafazaa. That was why the testimony of Tiarapax was so damning.

Alliance! The word stuck in his throat. But all the others agreed, except for Soqial, and he only rejected it from fear. The Balt Kaalith were compromised in so many ways now, for not only had the perfidy of Vixipal stained them, but also he himself had misused them. If the truth ever came out, it would be ruinous.

He thought about Kukenur. The tales she told were astonishing. Korfax had slain one of the Ashar. Doagnis was banished. Korfax could change the purpose of stone.

He found himself wondering what else she knew. She had seen inside Korfax, seen his heart. Korfax had already mentioned Lontibir to Simoref. All the crimes, everything, would come out. He only hoped that his darkest secret would not, for that would be the end, if it did.

After Osidess had left, Korfax stared out over the city.

He marvelled at its might. No wonder the princes of the Iabeiorith had never set foot within its walls. All his life he had heard stories of Othil Homtoh, how it was the best fortified of any city of Lon-Elah, how strong it was, how tall. Now he could finally see it for himself.

Even from the inside it felt as if the whole had been carved from a single vast mountain, its many towers chiselled from the great ridges that might have once graced the long-vanished slopes. Othil Homtoh was everything rumour had made it to be, the very embodiment of might, the very spirit of fortitude. If the Agdoain ever tried to take it, they would pay a heavy price. But, at the end, he did not doubt that even Othil Homtoh would succumb to their hunger at last.

He walked to another window, a window that revealed the palace of Zafazaa in all its glory. How proud it was. He looked up at it. Seven tiers each set with seven spires, and the topmost spire, the Umadya Kansei, the tallest spire of them all.

He turned away and sat upon the stark stone-carved throne that dominated the centre of the room. It had an ancient look to it, coiled about as it was by many stylised Vovin. Someone in the past had attacked it with a sword. There were chips, dents and scratches on its surface. It was, no doubt, a spoil from the Wars of Unification, left here as a broken reminder of the north.

Korfax smiled grimly and caressed one of the arms. In all the time since then no one had ever seen fit to repair the damage. What a comment that was. Zafazaa was full of such plays. He had been the same in the great hall and when they were alone afterwards. He begrudged everything, not giving the least little thing that he did not have to. But Korfax found that he no longer cared. He was tempted to repair the chair, tempted to exert his power over the stone, but he did not. He was finally tired, tired of everything – tired of ritual, of tradition, of bloodlines and of meaning.

But this was not the void that called to him now. This was but the beginning of the end. He was tiring of the struggle, of the interminable fight with all those that he did not want to fight with. All he wanted now was to finish it. Onehson was his only care now, the only one that mattered.

He sipped at the wine they had brought with them, another cup of Girril, and waited. Time slowed around him and he gazed out of the window to the north once more. How clear the air was. He was high, as high as he had ever been. He thought back to another place on the other side of the world. Once, long ago, he had slept in the highest room of the Faor Raxamith and counted himself blessed.

Tears came to him then, and he suddenly found himself mourning for all that he had lost. How long these last few years had been and how far he was from that happy child who could see wonder in a single point of light. How beautiful the world had been in the days of his childhood. But now he felt old before his time, worn out and threadbare, his spirit spent. Where had it all gone?

He was nearly asleep, filled almost to the brim with dreams of regret, when the sound of many feet came to him, each stamping its singular authority upon the stone as they came closer to his door. He stood up and drew himself together. Curiously, his heart started beating faster, his body suddenly admitting what his mind would not, that the fate of the world now hung upon what happened next.

Korfax had made the gesture and offered up the proofs, but now it all lay in the hands of the lords of the west to save or damn the world. He looked at the closed door both in hope and fear. A hand rapped upon it, three strokes.

"Enter!" he commanded.

The door opened and in stepped Dosevax. Behind him came two of the honour guard. All looked grim, even Dosevax. Korfax frowned. This was not what he had expected.

"What is it?" he asked.

Dosevax bowed.

"My Haelok, you must come. There is something you must see. Aodagaa found it. He came upon it whilst searching the woodland near our camp."

"Why was he searching the woodland?" Korfax asked.

"He was practising theurgies," Dosevax answered.

"Theurgies?"

"Divinations, seekings, findings."

"And what did he find?"

"He says that he found a hidden place. It was heavily concealed, but he is certain someone was burned there. And they were burned alive."

Korfax felt the beginnings of trepidation.

"Someone was burned there? Is he absolutely certain?"

Dosevax bowed his head.

"Yes, my Haelok. There is something else, though, something troubling."

Korfax stared at him.

"What do you mean?"

"This was found buried in the ashes."

Dosevax held out his hand. In it lay a dull object. It was bent, metallic and looked as though it had been through a furnace. Part of it had been cleaned, though, and there it gleamed. Korfax could see a sigil, and when he recognised it the world went dead around him. The sigil was of a house, and that house was Faren.

Dosevax led his prince back out onto the street. They mounted up and rode out, a phalanx of black forms, a wedge of darkness.

The citizens that were still abroad at that late hour stopped and stared in curiosity as the darkness swept on by. Some looked fearful, some looked angry and some even cursed openly and turned their backs as the cavalcade approached, but none of the Haelok Aldaria looked either to the left or the right, and none in the city dared impede their progress. There was a shadow in the air about them now, a shadow that stank of the dark one. In their midst rode Korfax, the inheritance made flesh, preceded always by one of his dark heralds, and whatever they might think of his servants, Korfax inspired nothing but fear. All knew better than to get in his way. Let the lords of the city deal with it, this was not their concern.

Aodagaa met them at the edge of the camp. He had already prepared the way and took Korfax by the shortest route. They came to a darkened glade set amidst high rocks. There was a shallow pit in the middle, freshly dug. Under the soil lay grey ash, worried now by the swirling wind. Within the ash lay blackened chains. Once the glade might have been fair, but now it was a grim place. Death had happened here, and its stain would remain for ever. Korfax stared at the chains, the ash and the burnt earth.

Aodagaa stepped forward and pointed at the pit.

"Here is where I found it," he said. "My Haelok, forgive me."

Korfax looked up.

"Forgive you?"

"I used a revealing theurgy," he said. "I called up a vision. I saw what happened. If I had known what I was to see, I would not have looked. I do not want to cause you pain, or break your hopes, but this..."

He pointed at the ash once more.

Korfax looked down.

"There is nothing to forgive," he said. "You did what you should. You saw this and acted. We cannot hide from the truth, no matter what it might cost us."

He looked back at Aodagaa.

"Show me."

Aodagaa took out a small dark stone and gave it to Korfax, who in turn took it and held it tight. The vision rose up and entered his mind, an image of an image, summoned forms playing their parts once more. Time and space parted, and he saw the brutal past.

A march of shapeless robes and masked faces came, dragging others with them. Korfax recognised both of these. One was Baschim, the other was his mother. They were bound tightly about by chains. Baschim appeared to be wounded, there was blood on his face, but his mother seemed unhurt.

They were both dragged to the centre of the glade where a deep pit waited. They were thrown into it and then tightly bound to a stark wooden pillar which rose up from the centre. Wood was then piled up about them both, and then oil was thrown on the wood. Finally a fire was set.

The fire mounted, mounted high, heat upon heat upon heat, until all was burnt to ash and there was nothing left but glowing embers. As the embers died so soil was thrown back in and the pit was filled. A veil crossed the scene and Korfax saw no more.

He sank to his knees. His mother's face filled his mind, stretched in agony as the flames burned her up. How could he countenance this?

Before this moment he had dared to believe that perhaps all things could be forgiven, that all things might be reconciled at the end, but now he saw how shallow that was, how foolish and how arrogant. It was almost as if the world had turned upon him once more, to show him how much further he had to go. How could he forgive such a wrong? How could he contain it?

He felt himself shrink inside, his mind and soul compressing to some infinitesimal point. He became utterly still whilst the world about him flexed, fractures parting its substance, drawing back to reveal what lay beneath.

Like a parade through the courts of judgement, he saw his life as he had never seen it before.

His father had died because he had allowed himself to be distracted by the wrong things. He had been selfish and fearful of his own life, and that had made him too slow to save what should have been preserved.

His beloved had died because he had selfishly desired the destruction of his enemies above everything else, even her love.

Thilzin Jerris had died because he had trusted to the purposes of another.

Othil Admaq had died because he had not the strength to endure betrayal.

Now his mother had died because he had allowed Othil Admaq to fall.

He alone had dared the yoke of his heritage, he alone. His father had denied it and had everlasting honour. Korfax had embraced it, and now all about him suffered because of it.

Within him the seed grew, a dreadful flaming growth that boiled outwards, consuming him in its mad rush for damnation. Like a sudden furnace it coiled about the crucible of his mind, and there it cast its heat, a brilliant flame, ready and waiting to burn him alive.

He could see them all – his father, Obelison, the people of Othil Admaq, his mother – all in there with him, all staring back at him, imploring him to stop this terrible thing, to give it up, to forbid its continuance. But the fire within him burned them all to ash, erasing them from his sight. Then, with his mind consumed by its very own apocalypse, Korfax stood up. His eyes were fires now, fires that would never be eclipsed, ever again.

Great sorrow threatened him, a flood of tears awaiting their release, but they burned even as they approached, held in a swelling fist of fire. No deluge would quench this conflagration, for there was not enough water in the whole world to do so. Nor would any furnace contain it, for there was none mighty enough. Korfax felt as if he would burst. She had died. The one in all the world that had given him life had died here, here in this place, without help, beyond mercy, burnt alive by cruel, unthinking hands. And it had all happened because of him.

It was coming, it would not be denied. It was rising even now, making its irresistible way up from inside him, so he gave vent to it at last, opening up the doors of its confinement and immolating himself upon his very own pyre.

All of Othil Homtoh heard it, that terrible cry that shivered the air and shook the entire city to its very foundations. Those nearest to it saw dark lightnings claw their way up into the sky, even as they clasped their hands to their ears to shut out the terrible sound. Those with eyes still open saw dark flames writhe blindly up beyond the walls of the city, before climbing ever further. Up into the sky they went, above the trees, beyond the ridges of the neighbouring hills. Erect, impossibly dark, they flowed into the sky itself, impelled by the unleashing of loss and rage. For a brief moment they flickered over the whole city, reaching out like so many hands, clawed hands alive with the threat of endings. Then they tumbled back down again as though the very endings they had desired had taken them as well.

Silence came to Othil Homtoh, a silence more dreadful than the cry, and the city paused, subdued by the shadow that now covered it like a shroud.

But even that silence did not last, for out of it came gathering screams, screams that echoed across the city like an echo of that one terrible cry. The people ran this way and that with tales of black demons upon their lips. For none would dare withstand the darkness that now poured its way back into Othil Homtoh, tearing through the streets, a terrible darkness that aimed itself straight at the heart of the city like a bolt of night.

Zafazaa was with his councillors when he heard the cry. They all looked up and stared about in confusion until they saw the black lightning flickering upwards into the eastern sky.

Soqial looked out of the window.

"Sorcery?" he asked.

Others joined him.

"Is this treachery?" another wondered.

Zafazaa did not move. He, alone of them all, knew what that cry was. It was the cry of loss, and he was suddenly certain what had been uncovered. Ever since the coming of Korfax, ever since the truth had been revealed, his darker satisfactions had soured inside him. Now all he had were regrets.

Ever playing the part, he ordered his Branith to discover the truth of the matter, but he knew it to be pointless. He had sent his swords against a power greater by far than any under his command, so he waited at the centre, at the very heart, and wondered how he would weather the oncoming storm.

As the darkness grew, Zafazaa moved at last and went to one of the windows to look down for himself. The darkness was close now, and he could hear faint cries coming up from below. There was a sound like thunder, and then the darkness was within the walls of the inner city itself. It grew and it grew, a black storm that surged inwards, an absence of light that curled about this tower or that as it drew ever nearer.

Zafazaa stepped away from the window. Here it came, darker, blacker than he had ever imagined it could be, coming for him at last. Briefly, regretfully, he wondered why he had ever let it enter his city at all. But then he remembered that this was his doing at the last. He had done this, caused this. This was his failure and his alone. He had dared the monster. Now he would pay.

Faint cries of fear filtered up from below. The cries became louder and louder still until none in the chamber could mistake them.

Outside the great doors voices were raised in command, then in fear. Long screams shuddered the air and many around the table drew back as if to flee. The door to the council chamber trembled, shaking back and forth on its already breaking hinges, until it could take it no more. It finally crumbled to dust whilst brief fires flickered through its ruin. Darkness entered the room, a great darkness flanked by lesser satellites. In a mere moment every throat was marked by a black blade. No one moved.

"So it is treachery, then!" said Zafazaa.

Before him stood a black figure, pointing its long black sword at him. Zafazaa stared at the sword and the sword stared back. It writhed in the air, moaning and undulating, a vast black frond caught upon the swell of some invisible current of the deep. Zafazaa found himself wondering from what abyss it had originally been wrenched, from what dark womb, but the sword did not answer him. It did not care. It simply was.

Zafazaa could think of nothing further to say. This was his mistake, his alone. He should never have admitted the spawn of Sondehna into his city, never. Vile sorceries had entered a sacred place and the stones would for ever be defiled. He wondered vainly if he could still call upon the Dar Kaadarith to defend him, but no one else about him moved. They, like him, were held in thrall by the power that had so easily conquered their fortress.

The black figure relaxed its darkness and revealed its face. Here was Korfax once more, but oddly enough, his naked face was more terrifying yet, for some element had been added, or removed, from it, and it now hung mask-like, alone and naked in a cloak of night, a thing of dreadful stillness, as though its flesh had been transcended and transformed into something more absolute. Black eyes spat black fire.

"You lied to me, Zafazaa."

Zafazaa could hear finality in that voice. The very next words he uttered could well be his last, and he could do nothing to allay it. There was no time left in which to play games, for all games were void at last. He swallowed and licked his lips.

"And about what did I lie?" he said.

"My mother!"

Zafazaa closed his eyes. Here it came. He was doomed. There was no answer he could give, in this world or the next, that would satisfy the vengeful dark. Mother was the name of the Creator upon all the lips of all the children that had ever been or ever would be. Zafazaa might as well try to turn aside the wheeling heavens themselves.

Korfax held up his other hand and energies played within his grasp. All stared at the fires, wondering where they might be sent.

"You told me that my mother had left the city and had gone into the uttermost west," Korfax said. "But that was not the truth. She never left this city at all. She never went into the west. You lied to me, Zafazaa. When I asked you to send word to her, you already knew that she was beyond any border your messages could cross."

The room was silent. All dropped their gaze. Korfax took a step forward, letting the energies fall from his hand at last. Darkness covered him again, hiding even his face.

"Did you order it?" came his voice. "Was it you? Or was it Soqial? Which of you murdered her?"

"I do not know what you mean," hissed Zafazaa.

421

"I HAVE JUST COME FROM THE PIT WHERE SHE WAS BURNED ALIVE!"

The voice was terrible, rage that could not be contained, loss that could not be measured.

"I give you one last chance," said the voice. "Tell me the truth, or I will slay you where you stand."

There was utter silence.

"I did not order her death," said Zafazaa at last.

"Who did?" came the voice.

"No one ordered it," said Zafazaa again.

"But you knew about it."

"I heard tell of it."

"And did nothing?"

"Those who did the deed could not be found."

"And did you even look?"

Silence.

"I could enter your mind, Zafazaa," warned the voice, "and no power at your disposal could prevent it. I could enter your mind and turn it inside out. I could uproot everything, all your secrets, all your plans, all that you are. I could learn the truth of you, every single bit of it, but even I would rather not wallow in such filth!"

Zafazaa swallowed in a throat gone dry. His own cant, his own hatred, was being thrown back in his face. He felt the power about him, hovering just at his borders. The promise was clear.

"The truth, then!" he said.

The darkness receded. Korfax was standing there once more, dark armour and dark sword. Only his eyes betrayed him now, for they had become beacons in his head, blood-lit fires of judgement.

"I did not order her death," said Zafazaa, "nor did I seek out those that did the deed. At the time that it happened it was believed you had destroyed Othil Admaq. All we saw was another Peis-homa. Many were overborne by it. They saw your mother as the symbol of all that they hated. Some acted on that hate. I do not know who did the deed, truly I do not."

Korfax leaned in closer. He looked long and hard at Zafazaa. Then he drew back.

"I am done here," he said. "I want none of you. There shall be no alliance. I know who you are. I know what you are. I should wipe your foul city from the face of creation and let you watch as it burns, but I shall not. I am not Doagnis. I am Korfax, last prince of the Iabeiorith, and I know of what kind my people are. They are better than you."

He turned from Zafazaa and looked at Valagar.

"You at least I expected more of. We served together upon the line."

"I knew nothing of this," Valagar said.

"Yes," Korfax agreed. "Like so many others here there is much that you know nothing of. Othil Homtoh is a city built upon lies compounded in ignorance. So my last word to you is this. It is your turn now. Discover your heritage. Find out what kind of people your ancestors were. Ask the Balt Kaalith to open up their archives. Ask them what happened upon Lontibir."

There was a sharp intake of breath. It was Soqial. Korfax turned to him.

"Yes!" he said. "The truth! Kukenur has already seen this. She knows what really happened, so do not think you can hide behind your lies from this moment on. Your crimes are known. All the Iabeiorith know what it was that you did. The peace of unification was bought with bloody slaughter. You are no better than the creature that now squats upon the holy throne."

Korfax drew back.

"I want no more of you. Coming here was a mistake. Unification is done."

He turned to leave. His followers put up their swords and turned with him. Valagar called out.

"Korfax! What do you intend?" he asked.

"My intent?" Korfax replied. "You already know it! I will storm Emethgis Vaniad and unseat the demon that occupies its throne. Either that or I will perish in the deed. One way or another, we have come to the end of it all. This world will now live or die at my command."

He drew himself up and looked hard at Valagar.

"Of all here present, you know who and what I am. You have seen me in battle, you have seen how I once served. I can no longer forgive you, or any other here, your wilful blindness. Stay here and rot!"

Without waiting for an answer Korfax turned about and left the hall at last, the guards following in his wake. Only Dosevax lingered. He looked around the great hall for the last time, his eyes filled with the light of judgement. Then he left at last and the hall became silent.

By the time Korfax arrived back at the gates, all the Haelok Aldaria that had entered the city with him were assembled there. The fire within him had run its course and he was merely an Ell again, black armour, black sword, eyes weary with loss. He turned to Aodagaa.

"Do you understand the choice before us now?"

Aodagaa bowed.

"Yes, my Haelok. I understand. The west have brought themselves down by their own actions, as you once said that they would."

Korfax smiled sadly. He raised his left hand and gestured.

"Come, let us leave this hideous place behind us. The sight of Othil Homtoh sickens me and I am sorry that I ever came here at all."

Aodagaa bowed his head at that.

"But I am not, my Haelok. Our last uncertainties are gone. We know now who we are and what we must do. All our choices have brought us to this place so that we may see where we are to go from here. Our greatest hour is at hand. Alone, the Iabeiorith will conquer all. As it was before, so it will be again. We are the mightiest of Uriel's children."

They broke camp quickly. It was time for the long ride back to the others, and they would not tarry. Though unhappy at their prince's loss, most of the Haelok Aldaria looked thoroughly satisfied with what had occurred. The west had been humbled, and all knew it.

It was as they reached the head of the high pass that a lone rider raced to the front of the column. It was Simoref. All watched him carefully as he galloped by, but no one hindered him.

He came to Korfax, calling out.

"Korfax! Please! Do not leave in this evil mood."

Korfax turned about, his eyes alight with fires once more.

"Do not, you say?" he asked. "Then tell me what else I should do? Praise the murderers of my mother? Shower them with riches for slaying the one who gave me life? How perverted do you think I have become? What depravity do you believe is too much for the scion of Sondehna? Should I turn back now and embrace Zafazaa as a brother? After all, your father allowed that band of murderers to go unpunished! So should I not thank him for saving me the task of slaying her? All sons slay their mothers, after all, do they not?"

Simoref drew back. The fire was hard to endure, but the dark accusations were worse. He looked down. What could he do? What must he do to assuage such fire? So he dismounted and fell to his knees. He would beg.

"Then I implore you," he said, raising his hands in supplication. "We need you. And if you will wait but a little longer, you would find your numbers increasing."

Korfax leaned over the pommel of his saddle and stared downwards with burning eyes.

"And who would I wait for? The slayers of the innocent? Cowards with a thirst for fire still itching in their ready hands?"

He pointed back at Othil Homtoh and bared his teeth at Simoref. "Let them forget their names!" he hissed.

Simoref drew back. That was dark, one of the darkest curses of all, a call to the Creator for judgement and damnation. Simoref wondered what he could say to put aside such rage.

"You shared a bottle of Girril with me once," he offered.

"And you poured the rest of it upon the ground afterwards," Korfax returned.

Simoref blinked in surprise.

"You saw that?"

"I did."

"I doubted who and what you were," he explained.

"You doubted?" Korfax laughed. "And you doubt no longer? So what is it you desire from me now? Absolution? You'll get none here!"

Korfax gave him one last unanswerable look and then turned away. He rode off and the Haelok Aldaria rode with him, each passing by as Simoref knelt in the earth, and none gave him the slightest glance as they went, none at all. He had become the spurned and the scorned.

A feeling came over him as the Haelok Aldaria rode on by, a feeling he had known once before. He recognised its taste well enough, for it tasted of ashes.

Eventually Simoref returned to the city and sought out his father.

"This was ill done," he said. "We will rue this day. You should have saved her."

Zafazaa stared out of the window, and his voice seemed weary even as he answered the question.

"Save her? And how might I have done that?" he asked.

"I know you, Father," said Simoref. "I remember the look upon your face when the news came down from the north of Sazaaim's death. You were happy that day. I also remember the look upon your face when you heard that Tazocho had entered the city. You wanted vengeance. How happy were you when they told you she had been murdered?"

Zafazaa span about, his face bright with fury.

"Do not think to question me in such a manner!" he said. "You are the last person to talk to me of murder!"

But Simoref was not to be put off.

"You tried to make me over in your own image!" he answered. "Mother took the vows of grief as much to distance herself from you as she did for the death of Ermalei." Simoref now held up a finger, stabbing it at his father. "I remember what you said to me when you heard Korfax was to go to the seminary. I remember your hatred and how you infected me with it. It was my duty to make him pay, you said! It was my duty to do your will! The honour of our house, you said! I am only sorry that I did not see the truth sooner."

Zafazaa sneered.

"So now I am responsible for your actions as well, am I?" he asked. "It was your choice to call him out. You would have killed him. I did not tell you to do that."

"And would you have grieved?" asked Simoref. "You wanted the Farenith gone from the world! I was a foolish child."

"With a mind of his own!" Zafazaa replied. "Do not come here and lecture to me. You are no innocent."

"You lied to Korfax."

"Lied, did I? Lies given to the prince of lies are of no account to me."

"So you would rather see the world burn than admit you are wrong!"

"And so the taint spreads to my son!"

Zafazaa sighed.

"Were you there when the empire of the north was at its height? Were you there when Sondehna tore Peis-homa apart? Or took the Rolnir? Or butchered our people? Or threatened the entire world with his black hand?"

"No," said Simoref, "I was not. But neither were you. Only the victorious write the histories. So tell me, Father, what truly happened then?"

"Do you doubt what you have learnt?"

"I do now, having heard the words of Korfax, having seen him. He is not as I imagined him to be – him or his people."

"Never speak that name in my hearing again."

Zafazaa drew himself up, and the change in him was hideous. His face was filled with a sudden and terrible rage.

"Only the victorious write the histories?" he cried. "You arrogant and presumptuous youth! Do you think everything a lie now? The memories of those times have been preserved in imperishable crystal for all to see and all to know. The words, the deeds, the confessions, the horror! It is all there! We have them all! Do you dare to deny them? Do you dare deny your very own heritage? You shame your house and the memories of your ancestors!"

Once, long ago, such a display would have daunted Simoref, but not now. He had seen beneath the mask at last.

"Yes, I do doubt them," he said. "Such things can be staged. Memories can be edited by lore or they can be excised altogether. Entire chapters can be removed as if they never existed."

He leaned forward and matched his father's gaze.

"So tell me, Father, tell me of Lontibir!"

Zafazaa withdrew as if he had been struck. Simoref watched carefully and thought that he caught the briefest glimpse, the tiniest glimmer, of fear. But all too soon it vanished again as Zafazaa turned away from his son in apparent disgust.

"I will not!" he said to the window, glowering. "Nor will I allow you to talk to me in this manner ever again, even though you be my only son."

Zafazaa looked back over his shoulder with narrowed eyes.

"If you truly wish to honour your house and your heritage," he said, "you will leave me now and seek out a quiet place of meditation, where it would be wise for you to consider all the choices that are before you."

Simoref would have smiled, but all he felt was sadness. Even his father's rage was an act. Before this day his father had possessed the power to terrify him into submission and shame him with the sheer weight of his authority, but not any longer. Korfax had achieved one thing at least. He had exposed the great and terrible lie.

"So what do you believe my choices to be?" he asked his father.

"They are simple," said Zafazaa. "You can be my son again, to rule when I am gone, or you can become a traitor to your house and your heritage, for ever cursed and reviled by the Korith Zadakal."

"Is that it?" Simoref asked. "You think that is all? But there are other choices,

Father. I could also try to undo the mistakes of the past so that our people can be saved from the Agdoain!"

Zafazaa laughed quietly.

"And are you so certain, then, of our defeat? We will yet prevail. Othil Homtoh has never been taken by any foe, no matter how strong they were. And when you see how you have been gulled by the lies of the north, then you may return to my side – but only when your heart is filled with honest humility. Go now. Leave me."

Simoref did not move.

"And that is that, is it?" he said. "No answers to hard questions? No explanations? Deceit seems ever to be the way with you these days, and I find myself wondering how far back it goes. I offer you one last chance for redemption, Father. Tell me of Lontibir. Tell me what truly happened. Korfax has already whetted my appetite, but I would hear more. And I would have you tell me. I would hear it from your very own lips and from no other."

Zafazaa filled his face with anger again.

"I have warned you once already. Do not speak that name in my hearing."

"Or what?" Simoref scoffed. "Will the walls crumble? Will Othil Homtoh be swallowed by the outraged land? I think not. Korfax goes to save us from our own folly whilst you sit here like an old stone, nursing the lies of the past like a comfort, waiting for the blade of doom to fall upon your outstretched neck. Well, I am sorry, Father, but the doom you seek to avert has all but fallen. We await the final stroke even now. The line of Karmaraa has betrayed us all. Our holiest city, our mightiest jewel under the heavens, now crawls with demons whilst that which we once called Velukor crouches upon its throne and laughs alone."

Simoref took a step forward and brought his face to within a hand's breadth of his father's. His eyes never wavered, nor did Zafazaa's, and they held each other's gaze, and each other's mind, in seemingly unbreakable bonds.

"So, you will not tell me?" Simoref asked.

There was no answer.

"Then I will tell you what I already know!" he continued. "I went looking for answers before I came here. I demanded that Okodon throw open the archives of the Balt Kaalith to me. She was not happy to do so, but she acquiesced when I told her what I sought."

Zafazaa still did not move. But neither did Simoref.

"You know what I found, don't you? You know this story, as do a few others, I believe. Whatever the crimes Sondehna and his slaves committed, there was no excuse for that. The slaughter of an entire people? How many lives were taken in that one single act of horror? The Iabeiorith did not fight unto the very last, as the official histories state, most of them surrendered. Then, for their pains, they were burned alive, every last one of them! Is it any wonder that we are hated? Is it any wonder that Doagnis wrought in secret to overthrow the council and finally went mad with the destruction of Othil Admaq? She became the very monster of our own making. Hate begets hate, Father, as I know to my own cost. But this hatred has been festering for over seven thousand years, growing and feeding upon itself, passed down from generation to generation like a black plague. And now it is out and revealed at last, and the only thing stopping it from beating down our doors and murdering us all in our beds is the one Ell you would deny above all others. But your denial places you in the very same prison as that mad rage our ancestors once engendered. Korfax is trying, at the very last, to save our people and bring about an end to the cycle of hatred. But you cannot see that, Father, or can you?"

Simoref stood back and waited, but his father still did not speak.

"Well, there it is," he said. "I have my answer. My father is a coward. He sets others to do his will and refuses to acknowledge his choices when they fail. I no longer care whether you knew about Tazocho or not. What I care about is saving our people."

Zafazaa started, but Simoref was there before him, his hand held up in the gesture of denial.

"I am as ashamed of you now as I am of my heritage. If this is what it means to be a son of the Korith Zadakal, then I want none of it."

Simoref walked straight up to Valagar and placed himself directly in front of the Napeiel so that he could not be ignored.

"Well?" he asked.

Valagar folded his arms.

"I know what you are doing," he said, "but this will not work. Your father still speaks for the throne."

"Then disobey him! He is not worthy of such an estate."

Valagar frowned.

"Worthy or not, I must stand both by the law and our traditions. To do otherwise would be treasonous."

"And which would you prefer?" Simoref asked. "The extinction of our people or personal dishonour?"

"But that is not yet certain," Valagar countered. "There are still many chances in this world."

"And if it were any Ell other than Korfax I might have agreed with you. But this is Korfax we are talking about. He turned the battle for Othil Zilodar, he changed the colour of his father's stave, was sanctioned by Samor, by Asvoan, by every one of the Exentaser this side of Ovaras. He survived the fall of Othil Ekrin. He even defeated, in single combat, one of the Ashar."

Simoref held up his finger.

"Do you hear what I am saying, Valagar? Do you? Korfax slew one of the Ashar! There has never been an Ell so mighty, or so potent. If he says the storm is coming, then I, for one, believe him. If he says we should act, then I, for one, would act, even if he would deny me. The storm is coming, Valagar, whether we will it or no, and it would be folly to ignore it."

"So you say," said Valagar, "but my agreement with you has nothing to do with it. I serve, as do you! Besides, your own feelings in this matter are not without a certain prejudice. He also saved your life."

"And what has that to do with anything?" Simoref said. "I also denied him, until I came to my senses. But that means nothing now. In the great scheme of things my life is of small account. The issue here is of far greater import. We, the Ell, could live or die according to what you choose to do next."

"According to you," Valagar said.

"Not according to me, Valagar. According to Korfax! He came here with that exact intent in mind."

"I do not approve of many of the things that have been done," Valagar said, "either recently or in the distant past. But if I defy the one who now speaks for the throne, from whose authority do I then proceed? My oath was sworn to the throne."

"And what if the throne is itself corrupt?" Simoref asked.

Valagar did not answer.

Next he went to Okodon. She, at least, understood something of the matter in hand. Since escaping the fall of Othil Ekrin she had begun to look at everything she had taken for granted. The words of Tiarapax had become the tipping point.

"Would you ride with the Nazad Esiask?" he asked.

She looked back at him curiously.

"To what end?" she asked.

"To rid the world of the Agdoain and their master."

She looked momentarily dumbfounded.

"How?" she asked.

"Korfax will attack Emethgis Vaniad," he told her. "It is my intent that we should join with him."

"Even though he has rejected an alliance?"

"You know the truth of that as well as I."

"But you do not speak for the throne."

"I am second lord of this city and the first in line."

"You *were* second lord of this city," she said. "Your father has not long issued an edict removing you from that office."

Simoref laughed quietly.

"And so it begins!" he said.

Okodon smiled in return but then dropped her head.

"I also know that you have been talking to the Napeiel," she said. "I believe he has not yet joined your cause."

"His decision hangs in the balance, that is true enough."

Okodon paused for a moment and then looked back at Simoref.

"So why come to me? I am not a power. I am not the Noqvoanel."

"I knew my father would do this," said Simoref. "It is so like him. And I have even given him a good excuse, because I sided with Korfax instead of him. My intent was to be honourable. His never was." He waved a hand in the air. "So be it, then. So much for honour! My father has divined my plans and now desires to stop me. He is a coward, selfish with power and blind with hatred. He would rather the entire world be destroyed than lift a finger to aid the heir of Sondehna in battle."

Okodon sighed and looked away.

"It is not an easy thing to learn that your service has been built upon such rotten foundations. Since the fall of Othil Ekrin I have looked long and hard at all that I have had to do and the secrets I have had to keep. I have seen the results of misplaced pride and hatred for myself. I only have to consider my former master. Naaomir also mistook his hatred for duty."

Simoref stared at Okodon.

"And does that mean then that you will help me?"

Okodon pursed her lips for a moment.

"He saved my life also, even though I thought him both heretic and traitor. Perhaps, when it comes to the hardest choices of all, we are all heretics and traitors in the end."

"So you will help me?"

"I will try. Though what I can do for you, I do not know. Noqvoanel Soqial will always support Zafazaa. And without the sanction of my order..."

She let the words hang in the air. Simoref bowed as if that was all he required, and then he turned away.

"Oanatom," said Simoref. "I come to you in need. I intend to disobey my father."

Oanatom's habitual look of worry deepened.

"I know what it is that you wish to do," he said. "Even I, closeted away in the archives, have heard the rumours."

"You have always been a good friend and a worthy opponent."

Oanatom smiled slightly.

"Thank you, but do not think that our games of Avalkar together will sway my opinion. I believe you lost the last one against just such an occasion as this."

Simoref was in no mood for levity.

"I am not so politic," he told Oanatom. "But I do need your help. If the Dar Kaadarith rode with us..."

"Us? You have persuaded others to go with you?"

"I have spoken to Napeiel Valagar and to Noqvoan Okodon. I believe I can persuade them both."

"But you have not persuaded them yet?"

"I believe that I have! Okodon is certainly with me, whilst Valagar is still considering."

"And what of the hunter that promised the Vovin's hide?"

"I know, I know!" said Simoref. "But this is vital, Oanatom, vital. The future of our world is at stake. The more I think on it all, the darker become my nightmares."

"Ah, yes!"

Oanatom put his hands behind his back and looked out of the window.

"You have an ally in Thilnor at least," he said. "He has already spoken to me concerning this. He has the same nightmares that you do, I think."

"Thilnor?" Simoref looked up in hope. "His counsels weighed heavily in Othil Ekrin."

"But they carry little weight here. Chirizar is Geyadel, and Chirizar is a sayer, not a doer." Oanatom looked back. "My voice also carries little weight, so I will confer with Thilnor again. Maybe together we can come up with something. But, ultimately, whatever else happens, we will all end up disobeying the regent. And that is no small consideration."

"And what of saving our world? That, also, is no small consideration."

"Urenel!"

"Noraud!"

"Not for long, I feel," said Simoref.

"Has your father disinherited you, then?" she asked. "I think not. Nor do I think you will ever see it happen. He might incarcerate you in some far-off tower on some far-flung isle for the rest of your days, but deny your blood? Never! Not if I know Zafazaa."

"You understand why I am here, then?"

"Of course I do. I am the Urenel of the Exentaser. I am omniscient. Did you not know?"

Simoref stared hard at her.

"What?" he asked.

She glowered back at him.

"A jest, Simoref, a simple jest! You are far too serious. Didn't anyone explain humour to you at the seminary?"

He closed his eyes and smiled.

"No, Urenel. It was not one of the requisites."

"Pity!" she said. "But that at least explains Chirizar."

She settled herself in her chair and cast a bright glance at him.

"You require our support, I believe?" she said. "It is yours. We now see where we have erred and will act as we should have from the very beginning. But we are advisers; we do not make policy. Application is the calling of others; it is not ours." Her gaze sharpened. "Your father may not trust us, but our word has always been heard, so we have power enough yet. Nalvahgey made us, and the words of Nalvahgey still lie behind the workings of our world, whether the west likes it or not. She created us and then bound us all to her will with her words. So seeing the peril, and seeing you, I throw the entire weight of my order behind you. We will speak to the others."

Simoref looked at her in sudden shock.

"Then why didn't you say the same to Korfax?"

Kukenur gave Simoref a stabbing look as though he had intruded in places where he should not have. Simoref was not daunted, though. He had already gone further than he had ever imagined he could go, so he waited and watched. Kukenur bowed her head in approval.

"You have come a long way, son of Zafazaa, further than I would have expected in such a short time."

"And I will not be put off, either. Keep your fair words for those who are swayed by them."

Kukenur smiled grimly.

"You desire the truth? Good! Very good! The truth should be desired at all times!"

She looked away for a moment and then looked back. Her eyes were luminous now, luminous and dark.

"We did not act, because Korfax holds the prophecies of Nalvahgey within him!"

Simoref slammed his fist into the arm of his chair and stood up.

"What?"

Kukenur did not move.

"You heard me," she said. "He holds the prophecies of Nalvahgey. They are in him. They are his fate. I saw the cage, as did all the others. That is not something we could, or should, meddle with. But I have seen that which Korfax has not. The last vision has him now, as it has us all. That you come to me was also foreseen. We are caught within her vision, all of us. Her dead hand guides him and we cannot interfere. To step outside the light brings only chaos."

"I did not know," he said.

Kukenur raised an eyebrow.

"Of course you didn't," she said. "That is why I tell it to you now. Now is the time to act. But here is something you do know, Noraud of the Salman Zadakalith. We are the power behind the throne. On our word the throne is sanctified. Others forget this at their peril. So we join with you. Confront your father again and speak your heart. We will be there. And we will make sure that all the others are, too."

19

DEMON OF NOTHING

Ais-thar-jo Fen-on-sib-ji
Urqal-kleh Od-iol-saqihd
Krih-orpao Nimin-sizid
Porah-zod Qi-u-sonjo
Qis-linis Kah-tel-viufar
Krg-naral Tl-gah-tranaiz
Od-zien-a Torzu-nio-us

She was standing in her room, at the window, facing west, when he burst in behind her. The sound of wings came with him, a furious beating of the air. She turned to him, to ask what the matter was, but he did not wait. He came straight to her.

"What was that?" he demanded.

Obelison started.

"What are you talking about? she asked.

"You did not hear it?" he looked astounded. "Everyone must have heard it!"

She watched him carefully. What was happening now?

"I heard nothing," she told him.

He paused a moment, staring at her as if he could not quite believe what he was hearing, and then he seized her by her shoulders and shook her hard.

"You heard nothing?" he demanded.

"No!" she cried, trying to pull away from him, but she could not. Now she could hear the unseen wings beating the air about her head as well.

"THEN LEARN HOW TO LISTEN!" he shouted back, clamping his hands over her ears and lifting her off her feet. Though she struggled with all her might, he did not let go; instead, he held her fast and squeezed her head with his hands.

Now she could hear it, through his hands, through the pain, an echo of a voice the like of which she never wanted to hear again. So much loss! So much grief! It filled her up like a longing for death.

He released her and she fell to the floor. She clutched at her head, reeling with the pain of it. Her ears felt wet. She drew back her hands again and looked at them.

They were covered in blood.

"You know who that is!" he accused. "Do not deny it!"

Yes, she silently admitted, she knew that voice, but that was all that she would admit. So why cry out like that, she wondered, what new horror had assailed the world?

She looked up. He was standing over her, hatred and fear in his eyes, great hatred, but even greater fear. She found herself caught by it. How complete it was, how all-consuming.

"Have you nothing to say?" he spat.

There was only one thing she could think of, so she held up her hands and showed him the blood.

"You hurt me," she accused. "What did I do to merit such an assault?"

His face clenched. That was not what he had wanted to hear. She said nothing else, but kept her hands up before her like a bloody shield. After a moment he turned away and ran from the room, his hands over his head and his head bowed. The sound of wings vanished away into the distances. She remained where she was, staring after him.

What had just happened? All she could see was his face and his fear, circling in her mind like some stone-caught vision; and all she could hear was the frantic beating of wings, beating the air about them both like panic. Something important had just occurred, but she could not think what.

She thought of that voice, the power of it, the rage. No wonder he was scared. It was terrifying, a voice magnified a thousand-fold. But what did it mean? It was as though she had all the pieces in front of her but could not fit them together.

Then it dawned on her. The other had been with him, trying desperately to contain his fear, and his fear had consumed him to the exclusion of everything else. She grappled with the insight. How could she use it?

After she had collected herself, washing away the blood and cleaning her wounds, she went looking for him. She found him in the main hall, crouching upon the throne and staring at the floor as though it dismayed him. Dejection clouded the air. The child was here once more.

"Why did you hurt me?" she asked.

He did not answer.

"What has happened?" she asked. He glanced at her, sullen and suspicious.

"If I knew the answer to that," he hissed, "do you think I would have asked you?"

"You did not ask," she said, "you demanded."

Silence again.

"What has happened?" she repeated.

He glowered back at her.

"You are better suited to hazard that guess," he said.

She waited a moment.

434

"I cannot imagine," she told him.

"He is coming," he whispered.

Yes, she thought, he is coming. She heard again that cry. Such despair. But also, such strength. Who would not fear such a one? She remembered what Ponodol had said, that Korfax was born of the line of Sondehna. It answered so many questions. The beast lived on, its rage passing from generation to generation like a curse. Korfax had that curse. She had seen it, his rage, how all-consuming it could be. But she had also known how to calm him.

She went still inside, as though she had come upon a threshold. Was that the answer? Did the other want calm also? Was her keeper easier to influence when he was at rest? No doubt it was there now, crouching with him on the throne and trying to soothe him. What had Ponodol said? Mother and child?

Only when Onehson was perturbed did the other fully come, as when she had asked about the Agdoain. Disturb his equilibrium, ask questions that went to places he dared not go, and the other would rise up to ward him.

So what if she took the other's place? What if she was the one to offer solace? Where would that take her? But he would have to trust her first, as would the other. How then could she buy their trust?

There was a way, but it was a terrible risk. Fear burned inside even as she thought of it. If she awoke his anger, if he thought she mocked him or intended to betray him, he would fall upon her and his grey power would erase her from the world. But she had to take the chance. She had to.

She turned to face the throne.

"Do you know who he is?" she asked.

He looked at her, his face twisting slightly.

"Of course I know who he is!"

"But do you? Do you really know who he is?"

"What do you mean by that?"

"Why did he ally himself with Doagnis?"

"It was obvious that he would! He does not care what he does, just so long as he can oppose me!"

"But do you know why?"

"Power! He thinks he will gain power enough to defeat me. He thinks that the forbidden lore will serve him."

"So why did he destroy Othil Admaq?"

"They refused him, so he punished them."

"Doesn't that remind you of something?"

"What?"

"Such a thing has happened before."

"What do you mean?"

"Peis-homa!" she said.

He came closer.

"So he emulates the Black Heart? All that are slaves to their passion walk the same road. What of it?"

"But why do that? That is not who he is! Unless..."

"Unless what?"

"Have you never asked yourself where the Farenith come from?"

His intensity increased.

"What?" he asked.

"Why should the Farenith be so constant in their power, generation from generation? Where did they rise from?"

"What are you trying to tell me?"

"Ponodol gave me the answer, but I had difficulty believing it until now."

"That blind fool?" He did not hide his contempt. "And what could he possibly know? I have looked inside him. There is little of interest there."

"Then perhaps you did not look hard enough," she suggested.

He took another step towards her, but reluctant now, fearful.

"What did he tell you?" he asked.

"That the Farenith have kept a very great secret for a very long time," she answered. "You let me hear that cry. I know what it is. It is the beast. Ponodol told me, but I did not want to believe it. Now I have to. Korfax is the last in a line that stretches all the way back to Sondehna himself."

"THAT IS A LIE!" he screamed, coming at her, grabbing her and shaking her as he had before. This time, though, she managed to pull herself away from him.

"It is not!" she said. "The children of Sondehna did not die with their mother, as was thought. The line survived."

He seemed to stagger for a moment, fighting his disbelief. Then he moved away from her, as if to leave.

"He should have told me this," he hissed.

She swallowed. There was vengeance in him now, vengeance and spite. He meant to take it out on Ponodol, and that was not what she had intended at all. How could she turn him aside?

"No!" she said. "The fault is yours. If you do not look, you will not learn."

"He should have told me," he insisted.

"But in a way, he has told you. He told me and now I have told you. Doesn't that mean anything to you? This doesn't concern anyone else."

He went very still.

"Doesn't concern?"

"No, it only concerns us."

"Us?"

"Yes! Who else? Who are you? Who am I?" She took the plunge. "He abandoned me. You said it yourself."

He narrowed his eyes and looked at her. She could almost smell his suspicion.

"I do not believe any of this!" he cried, sweeping out an arm. "There is a lie here!"

He strode away.

"Wait!" she called out.

He stopped.

"I am telling you the truth."

"Are you?" he asked.

"When have you ever had cause to doubt me?"

"When you denied me and rescued your 'beloved'," he told her. "Now what are you doing? Denying him in turn? I do not believe any of it!"

"But I did not know then what I know now," she said.

"If you do not look, you will not learn," he mocked. Then he turned away.

"But you heard that cry," she called after him.

He stopped again. He looked back at her over his shoulder.

"It explains so much," she told him.

"We shall see," he said.

He left the hall and she sank to her knees. What had she done? She hoped Ponodol would forgive her for this, but she had to do it. She had to.

He found her again, as he always did, knowing exactly where she would be. He came to her and stood before her. She glanced up at him. He did not move, apart from his hands. They moved slowly, fingers curling and uncurling all the while. She wondered what that meant, but she did not wonder too hard. She could not afford regret, not now.

"What have you done?" she asked.

"Nothing!" he said. "I asked him for the truth, that was all."

"And he told you?"

"Not at first."

"Did you hurt him?"

"He was reluctant!"

"There was no need to hurt him," she said. "You could have simply believed what I told you."

"I had to know," he insisted.

"What did you do?"

"Nothing. Nothing much."

She could see that he would not tell her. There was a time when he would have revelled in his cruelty, but things had clearly changed between them. She sensed that this new state was fragile, though. She should not push. Now was not the time. She hoped she could find Ponodol again and that he would forgive her for what she had done.

"You have the truth, then?" she asked.

He looked down, almost as if he still could not believe it.

"Yes," he said.

"And?"

"It is as you said," he answered quietly. He looked at her, a sidelong glance.

"It seems my heart knew this all along. Though I denied it for a long while, something inside me knew that he was my mortal enemy. One cannot hide from one's own blood."

He bowed his head to her.

"I am sorry that I hurt you," he said. "I was wrong to do so."

She stared at him. He had never apologised for anything before.

"I have not been as good to you as I should have been," he continued. "I distrusted. I was wrong in that also."

There was a strange look on his face, almost regretful.

"It seems we are both the victims of our fears and desires," he said. "You loved him and now find that he is not what you thought him to be. Do you see what that tells you? Do you see what that means?"

"Betrayal," she answered.

He bowed his head slightly.

"He almost killed you. He takes another to his bed. You discover that he is born of the Black Heart."

He came forward, gently, slowly.

"Now do you see how I feel? Now do you see what I see?"

And she did. She understood exactly what he meant.

"Yes," she told him.

He almost smiled at that.

"Then let me make amends," he said to her. "I would grant you a boon. Name it."

She held her breath. He would grant her a boon? How far would he go?

"A boon?" she asked.

"Anything, just name it."

Anything?

"Then I want you to save me," she said.

His eyes widened, a look of amazement on his face. He had not expected that. She felt him look at her, look inside, so she let him see. She let him see what was in her, the memory of that voice, that terrible cry, how everything in her life had crumbled at its touch. Korfax was born of the line of Sondehna. He was the Black Heart come again. All her dreams were dust.

"I want you to save me," she repeated, even as he withdrew in confusion.

"But you are safe here," he said, "safe from everything."

"But you heard it?" she told him. "The beast? I want nothing of that. I would rather the world burn than submit to that."

"You want the world to burn?" he looked incredulous.

"Yes," she said. "It is too much. It is over. I want no more of it. I want what you want, a return to bliss. I want no more of this. No more pain. Let it end. Let it all end."

There were wings, distant wings, a heavy throb that circled far out, far away. There was a sense of satisfaction in the air. He smiled, really smiled, warm and generous, the kind of smile he had not bestowed upon her for a long, long while.

"So that is where you are now!" he said. "Then I must be content. It shall be so."

He took her arm in his and gestured to the door.

"Come, let us walk together as we did before."

She let him lead her and let herself be happy in his care.

They came to the long corridor between the third upper hall and the eastern balconies, and he stopped now and then to gaze in turn at each statue that they passed. Was he trying to remember what the statue had originally looked like, or was he remembering a similar walk they had once taken? Even then he had been fascinated by perfection. She looked at the statues. Like all the others in the tower, these had been defaced, and they slumped as though their stone was stricken by some creeping rot. She stopped and considered their decay. Something about it caught her attention.

"Why do you despoil the paintings and the statues?" she asked. "You have never told me. Why not keep them, like your garden?"

"The garden is special," he said. "It has meaning – permanence from impermanence. But as to the rest? I do not care, so I merely allow their decay. 'Their works and their pomp,'" he quoted, "'let them be defaced.'"

No, she thought to herself, that that was not the answer. The statues were an indulgence, an act of spite. But whose spite? His or the other's?

"A lesson?" she asked. "But why not make that lesson sharper and destroy them completely?"

He looked at her, searching her face for long moments. Then something clouded his eyes, something grey and potent. It swam back and forth, from one eye to the other, much as it had in the garden. She would have gagged at the sight had she not seen this before. The other had returned, and she had its complete attention.

"You have changed," he said. "Yes, you have changed. I find myself wondering how deep it goes."

Deeper than you know, she thought to herself. Yes, I have changed, just as you have, and the other sees it. She waited a moment, watching; not the one who stood before her, nor the child that had never grown up, but the one who stood behind the flesh, the one that held everything on its leash.

"You know how deep," she told him. "No more lies and self-delusion. No more betrayals. There is only one truth now."

The contempt, the cruelty, was utterly gone. Instead he looked bemused, as if he still could not quite believe what had happened. She had touched him, but had she touched him enough?

"Only one truth?" he asked.

The other was with him now, fuelling him, and she could feel its risen power about her, its fingers reaching out and enclosing her. It had never done that before. For a moment she clenched herself in readiness, instinctive, a reflex, but it did not enter. The power, though, was frightening. Even from within her thresholds she could feel it, the threat of it. If the other had really desired to know her it could have stormed her mind in an instant and she could not have stopped it, but she was ready even for that. I am honest, she told herself, honest in all that I say. See how honest I am.

"Yes," she answered. "Only one truth. I understand my choices better now. They are simple: absence or the beast. I have chosen absence."

He did not answer, and the other did not invade her mind. They both waited to see what she would say next.

"It is the only answer," she continued, "the only answer left to me." Then she gestured at the statues about them both. "Which is why I do not understand this. This is not who you are. Corruption is but another aspect of the imperfect world you so despise. Absence, surely, is preferable."

He became still, and she waited in fascination. There was a voice inside him, a voice she could all but hear, whispering to him, telling him things, prodding him. It was the other, the vast and distant swimmer in the flesh. She watched him. His face seemed to empty and then fill as though he breathed himself in and out of the world. Would he return with answers, and what would those answers be?

The dim beating of wings came to her ears. She looked behind her, back through the cavernous halls of the Umadya Pir, but there was nothing there. Nevertheless, it was back there now, the owner of the wings, lurking in the distant recesses, huge and monstrous. Having earned his trust, could she now earn the trust of his keeper? Would it then reveal itself to her, she wondered, and could she abide its coming?

She waited for it, almost eager for a glimpse. But then, as she waited, peering into the depths, a feeling grew upon her, a worrying feeling that she could not put aside. What would be the consequence? What if she truly saw it? What if she truly learnt its name? What would be the price?

She clutched at herself. Perhaps no one could see it. Perhaps no one was meant to see it. She shuddered and tried to put such doubts aside, but she could not dispel them entirely.

Her fears grew. Perhaps if she saw it she would die. But she must not die, not yet. She had to act. She was destined to act. She tried to tear her gaze from the empty halls behind her, but she found to her distress that she could not. Something had hold of her, holding her in place, daring her to see. The throb in the air about her was like that dim ecstasy of terror that waits on the edges of dreams. Great wings, immense wings, beat the phantom air, coming closer all the while, and she heard them, felt them shake her body. They were not there, they did not exist, but still they came.

She struggled against the compulsion, that terrible compulsion that bade her wait and bare witness. Her soul understood, but her flesh did not. She fought herself, battling, ever battling against the commandment to see. She told herself that she would not, but her body ever denied her.

It was only at the last, that last moment when thought gives way to sight, that she managed to turn away, only to find him before her, staring back at her with vacant eyes. He seemed to have been entirely unaware of her struggle.

"I think you have misunderstood," he said to her. "It is not I that does this."

He smiled, but only with his mouth. The other was telling him what to say, comforting him with well-chosen lies.

"No?" she asked.

"Creation resists," he replied.

"Creation resists?" she questioned, astonished.

"Yes," he answered. "The end is slow because creation resists. The war we fight is a war of attrition. If it were as simple as that, I would have done it long ago."

Obelison could not help it. She suddenly felt gloriously happy. Creation resists? A war of attrition? What a lie that was! Was it deliberate? Was the other testing her? If so, she knew exactly how to answer. Here was her way in, the act that would catch both him and the other. Here she would prove herself. She had no idea what would follow, not yet, but she knew, deep down inside, that something would. Here was where the world turned.

Letting nothing of her intent disturb her features, she walked over to the nearest statue, a delicate thing of crystal. It had not yet completely succumbed to the rot around it, a small island of resistance carved of brittle stone.

She stood before it, gazing up, and then she looked back at him. She saw the puzzlement on his face. He had not yet guessed what she was about to do.

"No!" she told him. "That is not the answer."

Then she reached up and toppled the statue.

It was not an easy thing to achieve, for the statue weighed much more than she did, but its pedestal had tilted slightly, slumping in the slow decay that had taken the rest of the tower in its fist. Unseated somewhat from its base, the statue was already leaning at an angle, almost as if it was waiting to fall. It was a gift of circumstance she dared claim as her own.

The statue fell. It tumbled from on high and shattered slowly. Thousands of pieces, large and small, danced across the floor before eventually coming to rest in many places, whilst the echoes of its shattering ran this way and that like frightened things. The tinkling of broken stone faded slowly away and silence fell once more. She drew herself up to her fullest height. She had done it. The statue had ceased to exist.

She had never felt so still, or so strong. There was a time when she would have been revolted by such an act, such callous vandalism, but not now. She had become another creature, made over by her plight within this place. In her mind she filled herself with joy, fierce joy at the destruction, joy that she had caused it. She let it flow outwards, downwards, subsuming everything. There were other joys inside her, deeper and more terrible yet, but she took them up before they could speak. She joined them, made them indivisible and indistinguishable, absorbing them in that one single, joyous act of destruction.

He stared at her in utter disbelief as though the possibility of what she had just done had not even occurred to him. She looked back and took her greatest chance yet. She bent down and picked up some of the pieces, small, long, sharp or shattered. She displayed them in her open hands like trophies.

"Do you see what just happened?" she asked him. "Creation did not resist me. I destroyed the statue. It is no more. And where it once stood? A glorious absence!"

He stared down at the pieces of the shattered statue for a moment and then back at her. He said nothing, but she could see the fear in his eyes.

"I understand," she told him gently. "I understand completely."

She took a step towards him.

"Creation does not resist. It is you that resists."

"No!" he said, the fear rising up.

"Yes," she answered, and she smiled gently back. "You fear the end, just as we all do, but you especially have never really faced that fear, because no one else has ever let you."

She felt it within her, the fearful child, and she held it to her, wrapping it in comfort.

"That first time that we met you told me that you were nothing more than a symbol. Others would act in your name, but your purpose was simply to be. You had no choice in the matter, or so you felt. All your life you have been a symbol for others to manipulate. They acted in your name, acted through you, but they would not allow you to act in return. They kept you caged so that you could serve their purposes, and they denied you the things that you wanted, because once you achieved them they would no longer have power over you."

She looked down.

"Even the other has done this, keeping you safe and preserving you so that you could fulfil your great purpose. But now another purpose must be served, and that is why I am here."

She looked up again and came a little closer.

"I am here to be with you. I am here to face the end with you. What did you say to me in your garden? Someone to be with, to share it all with, a voice to hear, someone to touch? Is that not what you have longed for all your life? For the brief time that we have left – would that not be a good thing?"

He stared at her, fear bleeding from every part of him, but he did not run. He stayed where he was and waited on her words with dread and with hope. She took another step towards him and reached out with her thought, opening her mind to him.

"See me!" she said. "Look inside. See for yourself. I have always been truthful to you. I have never lied to you."

She could see his doubts, he was full of doubts, but she did not care. This was not about power, this was not about what others wanted, this was about truth, her truth, and she wanted him to see it. She allowed only the deepest honesty within herself: no trick, no wile, just the memory of what had been. She reached out and touched his mind, taking him back to the very first time that she had met him alone, when he had stirred her heart with his loneliness and the quiet desperation of the life into which he had been born. That was the person she wanted to see before her now, the one that wanted escape, freedom, companionship and love. She let her feelings fill her up, and she let him see them.

"I know what it is that you want," she told him. "I know what it is that you desire, because I want it, too. You want a return to bliss, but you do not know how to achieve it. You think that you must be the master of all, that you must be the strongest, that your enemies should be thrown down. And once you have complete dominion, then, and only then, will your deepest desire come to pass. But that is the long road, and it is so uncertain. There is another way, a quicker way, and I can show it to you."

She filled herself up with all the compassion that she could. Like her joy she let it rise. Even her memory of kommah became a part of it, that flight of gentle arrows from her soul. But now she sent them to him. She let him see that love, its possibility. There was no guile, no lie. She honestly forgave him, forgiving the lonely child of madness, and, like a reflection of her thought, he saw her as the child would see. He saw his desire in her face, the light of a love he had never known but had always wanted. He reached out to touch it, daring to believe it was there, that what she said was true. The whispers and demands of the other could not compete, and they shattered upon the shores of his risen passion, his need for what was, not what could be.

"You see it, don't you?" she said. "Love! Love is the answer. Deny this place, this world. Throw it down, if you must, but in the end you know such acts are meaningless. There is only one thing that makes it bearable. Love. The joining of souls in bliss. This is what you really want. So let me show it to you. Together we can end our pain, you and I. Let us put an end to it. Like you, I want no more of this."

His barriers were down and his doubts were beginning to crumble. She could feel them, see them within. Is this really true, he was asking? Had he at last found in her the thing that he desired in his deepest self, a true companion, one who mirrored his thought? Like went with like, he reminded himself, and he suddenly saw her beside him, racing through the halls, the pair of them shattering the hateful past. Yes, he agreed, let it end, let it all be thrown down and let there be no fearful future either, just the two of them together in the unending moment, adrift upon the sea of potentiality, caught within the eternal now. The simple truth of it shook him. He had been blind. Here was a better answer. Let him accept it, let him admit that this was what he wanted with all his heart. He had been so alone. Even the other could not fill this need. Here was someone real, someone like him, someone he could touch, hold, caress and care for, someone like him.

He let the feeling grow within, shutting out everything else but her. The circling wings were gently thrown from his mind, and as his fear had consumed him, his desire did the same. It filled him from his depths to his heights, and the other could not compete. It fell away before the wish of his heart, here in this safest of places. Someone would come to him and comfort him as no other had. He was no longer alone.

He held up his hands to accept her, to embrace her, and she came into his arms. He stared into her eyes, into her thoughts, and found there not a mirror, not a reflection, but a spirit that moved as he did. It was all true. He reached up to touch her face, and she buried a long crystal shard in his throat.

She had forgotten she had picked it up, but her darkest shadow had not. Down, deep within, unseen and unfelt, it had waited for its chance, so that when the time came a weapon would be there when needed, long and sharp, in her hand, in his throat.

He gasped and staggered, falling back from her and thrashing his limbs, the shock silencing his mind. Having filled himself up with her he had denied the other, and by denying the other he had denied himself its power. Now it was too late. He fell to the floor, a hand clutching at the makeshift knife. He struggled and gasped and stared back up at her, seeing the love still there in her eyes, feeling it still in her mind. How can this be?

She watched his incomprehension as it became a rift between what had been and what was, watched as it grew into a chasm. As the blood flowed from his neck and pooled about his head, so he fell down into that chasm, down, down, all the way. Into the darkness he went, his last breath a long, drawn-out hiss. Then he lay still at last and did not move.

She stared down at him. She could not move, either. Hidden from herself, her sudden act seemed miraculous now. But it was a dark miracle, a bloody miracle. She had suborned everything to her purpose, even her love, profaning its sacrament. Love as deep as hatred, indivisible, rooted her to the spot.

The sound of great wings came from behind, and they beat at the air with rage. They were closer now than they had ever been before. The other was near, within sight, perhaps, leaning over the world and standing upon its borders. But she did not turn around, not this time; instead, she kept her attention wholly upon him. She willed herself not to look, neither to the left nor to the right. This was it, the last play. Would she survive it?

The wings beat louder and louder and she felt them behind her, along with something else, something that reared up, something huge, something monstrous.

She closed her eyes and bowed her head as vast wings beat above her. Surely the tower was too small to hold such immensity? Though her body was untouched, she fell to the floor and lay there, curled up into a ball and praying to the Creator that her end would be swift, that this terrible dream of life would cease and she would enter that far country beyond the river. But it was not to be. Her dream did not end and she lay still upon the cold stone floor whilst something moved across her and crushed her with its appalling weight.

For a moment she felt as if nothing of her was left, that she had been erased, removed, eradicated. But then it passed beyond, and the sound of great wings diminished until they were utterly gone. She remained where she was with her fists clenched and her eyes closed, and it was a very long time before she dared open them again.

She crouched upon the floor and glanced first to her left and then to her right, listening for a sound, any sound. There was nothing. The horror was gone and the tower felt utterly empty at last. Dare she move? She stood up slowly but kept her eyes downcast. She could no longer look at the body. She could not look at murder.

She went to the window and looked out over the city instead. It was silent. She beheld a forest of frozen stone. Nothing moved.

Had she done it? Was it really over? She could still scarcely believe it. And what of the Agdoain? She searched for them but could not see them. Where were they? Had they fallen into sleep, forgotten and bereft? Or had they decayed where they stood, leaving the world now that their purpose was overthrown? Would it be that simple? Defeat Onehson and so defeat the other? Defeat the other and so defeat the Agdoain?

A sound came from behind her, shockingly loud in the sudden silence. Something was moving, quietly and purposefully. She turned and found his body risen, standing there in a pool of its still-cooling blood. The knife of stone was gone from its neck and the ragged wound was closed and sealed. The body stood there as if nothing had happened, looking back at her with blank eyes.

She could not believe it. She refused to believe it. He was dead, and the dead do not return. She turned and ran.

How long she ran for she did not know, but eventually she stopped, lost in the emptiness of the tower, lost in her terror of what should not be. The dead do not return. The dead do not return.

She leant unsteadily against a window, breathing hard. For a moment she stayed there, looking down and hoping against hope that what she had seen was not so, but when she looked up again she saw what was outside. The Agdoain had reappeared. No longer restless, they stood now like statues, tall and straight as they waited for whatever commandment would fall from on high. She drew back from the window. She could not be certain, but it suddenly felt as if they were looking at her, all of them, every single one.

Something pulled at her. She turned and looked about, but there was nothing there. It pulled at her again. She bit back a scream and ran, but everywhere she went the sensation went, too.

Forces gathered about her. She was being watched, though the watcher was blind. She was being followed, though the follower did not move. She heard a voice, but the air was utterly still. She felt caresses, but nothing touched her flesh.

She was alone, but something stood where she did, not in the spaces she occupied, but in between them. It walked as she did, breathed as she did, but it was not there. She had never known such torment.

She sought surcease, somewhere, anywhere, but the sensation followed her wherever she went. The other had come to do battle with her itself. Her ploy had worked all too well and she had been noticed at last. Now she was paying the price. The other would not give her up. It had become a part of her.

Desire!

She stared wildly about. Behind her eyes, deep inside her was a feeling, but it was nothing that belonged to her.

Desire!

She could taste the sensation. She thought of all the meanings, all the feelings, but none sufficed. This was something greater.

Desire!

It was elemental, at a level below thought. It coiled inside her and gloated as it gazed outwards at the world, gazing through her.

Desire!

"LEAVE ME ALONE!" she screamed, holding her hands to her head. Her desperate rage threw it down, but it did not go away. It circled deep within and smiled. *You are mine*, it said, *I am yours*. She sank in upon herself and wept.

The corpse came to her then, walking slowly, quietly, and with a poise totally unlike the uncertain child she had come to know. She looked up at its face. It was calm and confident and powerful. All the fears, all the rages, all the smiles and the indulgences were gone.

How could he be here, she asked herself.

"You are dead!" she said. "I killed you."

She could not hold her terror in check. She clutched at herself and shook violently.

"And it was well played," came the answer. "You are almost as good a liar as I am."

It was not his voice. There was a strange quality to it, something almost feminine, and it echoed as though falling upwards from some deep abyss. It was not his voice.

"You cannot be here," she said.

"But I can," it answered. "One last gasp, before the end."

It leaned over her and she saw its eyes. She shrank from them, for they were truly blank now, grey pools empty of both iris and pupil.

"I see you," it said.

"What are you?" she whispered.

"You know the answer to that!"

"No!"

"But you do."

It looked at her with its hideous eyes and it smiled.

"You have seen," it repeated. "It was why you killed the child. Brave, daring, but utterly futile. The only thing you have achieved is to force my hand, and that is all that you have done. The house of Zilodar shall carry on."

"You are not of that house!" she insisted. "You are other!"

"But I am," it told her. "It is the body that is of the house, not the spirit. You thought to break the covenant, that the covenant was of the spirit, but you were wrong. The covenant was not of the spirit but of the flesh, and the flesh cannot be denied. What matter the will that drives it?"

"What covenant?" she asked.

"The one that was made long ago, the one that bound him and his line to me."

"Who?"

"Karmaraa," it said. "Karmaraa began this. He made this alliance. Without him, without his need, I would not be here at all. And neither would you."

She felt staggered by what she had just been told. What had she stumbled onto now? Karmaraa? Did the evil go back to him? Was everything a lie?

"You cannot grasp it, can you?" it smiled. "But it is true, nonetheless. To stop Sondehna, Karmaraa made a pact with me. And I have waited so long for this moment, when all the pieces were in their places once more. Vengeance is mine."

"What are you?" she dared.

"You have already asked that question. And you know the answer."

"Then who are you?"

Its smile deepened into something crueller.

"Now you shall see what your choices have wrought!" it told her, and it raised up its arms. Shadows, like wings, rose up with them. She felt a curious sensation then, as though wings rose up behind her also, but when she looked there was nothing there.

"I am that which has been born in this flesh," it announced. She looked back at it.

"I am that which fills this paltry shell," it told her. "I am Qorazon, the voice of the void."

It leaned over her and showed her its teeth. She felt a sudden urge to bare her own.

"Now I will take my due," it said. "Here, I shall create my desire."

"What desire?"

"You know what it is. You have spoken with the unsighted. He told you."

"But why?"

"You know that also. You have spoken with the child. He explained it."

She drew further away from it, but it was lightning fast. It stepped forward and its hand shot out, catching her in an unbreakable grip. She almost mirrored its action, her hand reaching out to grab in return, before she could stop it, but her hand was batted aside in utter contempt.

"No!" it said. "No more indulgences. You have summoned me, caught me in this failing flesh, so here I am. Take pleasure in it whilst you can, for from this moment on I shall be with you, as you shall be with me, until the end of everything."

It reached forward and embraced her, pulling her to it with a strength she could not resist. It leaned over her, kissing her upon her lips, and she felt the breath sucked from her body. She sank into darkness.

She awoke. She was alone in silence. She stood up and looked about. She was in her room. For a long moment she remained still, trying to understand what had happened, but she could not. She looked inside herself and it was as though she stared into a mirror, a twisted mirror where her own reflection stared back out at her, a reflection with blank eyes and long teeth.

There was only one hope in her now – that Korfax would come. Korfax would come and he would settle her scores. She closed her eyes and prayed that she was right. She had to believe in him. She had to. But if she was at all wrong in her hope, then all was damned.

As though in answer to her thought Qorazon came to her again, appearing at her side as if rising up through the floor.

"Your hope is no hope at all," it told her. "He is not what you think him to be."

She looked up and stifled a scream. Its eyes were no more. Its face was no more. Everything had been swallowed except for its mouth. A voice fell from it as if tumbling down from immeasurable heights.

"He will slay even you at the end."

Grey power passed over her and through her, and she tumbled to the floor. The world span about her and faded away.

She lay naked upon a bed and dreamt of a mask, a great blind mask that floated above her. About it lay a limitless heat that burned with an all but infinite cold, whilst its mouth opened up onto darkness, a gateway to unimagined deeps.

It decayed, that mask, but slowly, so slowly that the change was all but imperceptible, a decay that would never end but instead drift down into the void to lie there for ever.

It came close to her, a delirium of ecstasy and horror, the rift in her soul. It entered her and swelled inside like a poison. The stillness racked her, the rise and the fall, the collision of forces, the meeting of opposites.

She was enthralled, bound and gagged by her own flesh, felled by her divinity, exalted by her baseness. She straddled an abyss and was impaled by nothing.

On and on it went, never-ending yet ending at last. Something blossomed within, a fruit already rotted in the flower, a flower already rotted in the bud. Dead thorns uncoiled and pierced her with their need to drink.

She sighed in agony, she screamed in fulfilment. The end came, the moment that never moved, the gloating and the completion, all in one.

She had thought that she had known what the price would be, where her choices had brought her, the price she was willing to pay, but this was worse, far worse, and if she had known then what she knew now, she would have thrown herself from the tower. But it was too late for that, too late by far. The other had her in its clutches and would never let her go. Ever.

20

CRUCIBLE

Orm-aolaih Sor-ul-luh-jon
Ed-thilvar Vors-tra-odtran
Gie-tel-a No-ors-polmah
Fen-i-qas Lan-a-veldan
Krih-zona Ipvor-aspjo
Lan-torzu Korm-paloh-jir
Ged-vepmals Chis-dl-zah-us

They came to the end of the high passes of the Adroqin Ea whilst the world was still grey about them. Clouds hung over them, watery and vague, and a faint drizzle of rain erased the distances. It was cold.

Korfax stared out over the last foothills and shivered. There was little to see. Drifting mists shrouded the lush green valleys and made mere shadows of the hilltops. Nothing moved before him and little moved behind. The Haelok Aldaria awaited his purpose.

He turned back and looked at the long, thin, winding column that drifted back up into the hills. There were seven other such lines parallel with this one, three to his left and three to his right, each taking a separate route down to the wide plains of Ovaras and hidden by the mist from its neighbour.

Somewhere below they would meet again, a brief halt before the very last journey, a moment of peace and reflection before the assault upon Emethgis Vaniad.

Aodagaa leaned over and looked at Korfax.

"My Haelok? Something troubles you?"

Korfax gave Aodagaa a glance.

"No, no. Nothing troubles me," he said. "The world is become grey, like my mood. That is all. It is nothing more than that."

Aodagaa looked up into the clouds.

"The rain was never so persistent on Lonsiatris," he said.

Korfax smiled.

"The weather was more changeable there, or so I have been told. But this rain is not unseasonal. We are caught upon the edges of a storm that even now punishes the higher parts of the Adroqin Ea, far away to the west. The Adroqin Ea are almost the wettest of the great mountain ranges. Only the Adroqin Vohimar are wetter."

Korfax paused a moment.

"And higher!" he finished.

Aodagaa stared about at the hills around them for a moment, judging them in the light of his Haelok's pronouncement, perhaps.

"I have never seen the Adroqin Vohimar, my Haelok," he said. "I would like to see them before I die. I would like to gaze, just once, upon the mighty slopes of Adroq Vokaseas."

Korfax laughed gently.

"What a simple wish."

His eyes misted.

"I remember those."

He clenched his jaw.

"Once, long ago, I dreamed such dreams. Life seemed so simple then."

He turned to Aodagaa and placed a gentle hand on his shoulder.

"And may you be granted your wish, before the end," he said.

Korfax bowed his head briefly and then spurred Enastul on. Aodagaa waited a moment, watching his Haelok ride on with burning eyes. Then he rode on at last and the others, those waiting behind, followed in his wake, their steeds picking their way carefully down the steep path, and all that could be heard in all the grey stillness were the many faint footfalls and the occasional fall of stones.

Gradually, as they descended, the drizzle became a light rain. Soon they passed a few stunted trees that yet clung to the upper slopes, just above the line of the wider forests of Kannim and Bellor.

They came to Kannim and found the others waiting for them. Families were rejoined, tales were told, food taken and company kept. Korfax found a tent already waiting for him, with Opakas at the opening. Others were there also, heads bowed. The tale of the Haelok's grief had clearly been told.

Opakas bowed.

"Come, my Haelok, take refreshment and ease. All is prepared."

"You did not have to do this," he said.

"But I did. You are my Haelok."

She leaned closer.

"Remember, you are our prince, the lost that was found. You are our purpose. We do this gladly in your name. And as you serve us, so we serve you."

Inside he sat. Others had already set out food and wine and then withdrawn. Opakas sat opposite, watching him carefully.

"When do we attack?" she asked.

"When I account us ready," he said.

"Nothing has changed," she told him. "Emethgis Vaniad is quiet. No Agdoain have been seen."

He looked up at her, his face bleak.

"She is gone!"

"I know, my Haelok," Opakas said. "When Aodagaa told me I feared the worst. I feared what you would do, the madness, the burning. But my fears were groundless. You are a greater prince than your forefathers. Let it be as you once said. Let the west rot."

After he had eaten there was a brief council. Korfax looked at them all and answered the one question that concerned them most.

"This will be a different kind of battle," he told them. "We will storm a city. You have not done this before. No doubt you are thinking of the arts of siege. One attacks the weak points, wears down the defence and then invades. Other tactics there are: starvation, drought, fire, plague. All take time, time in which the master of the Agdoain can prepare a counter-attack or call up new forces, or react in some as yet unforeseen manner. We have defeated him easily enough in the past, and no doubt he expects us to be overconfident this time. I will not be. Nor will I wage this battle in any way he might expect."

"So what is your will, my Haelok?" asked Dosevax.

"We are creatures of power," Korfax said, "so I say let us use that power. One collective thrust of insuperable might. As Efaeis undid the stone of the Veludrax Mikaolazith, let us do the same here. If it stands in our way, we throw it down. If it rises up against us, we burn it to ash. One summoning, unending, a storm of fire. We will forge our own road to the tower of light and break it asunder."

They looked at him, all of them, their thoughts mingling as he showed them exactly what he intended.

"Is that possible?" asked Ambriol.

"Believe it!" said Korfax. "I have travelled this road before. A summoning to unknit the weave of the world. A new way to wage war, the lightning strike that cannot be countered."

Opakas held up her hand.

"I have a question. You know the Namad Dar. Will you use that power?"

"No," he said. "The Namad Dar will play no part in this – something I learnt from our journey to the west. The Agdoain are sensitive to it. Only those powers born of sorcery will suffice."

"But you can change the purpose of stone!"

"And our enemy knows it. I will do nothing our enemy might expect."

Opakas sighed.

"Then there is only one thing more. What if you are overborne? Will you then summon aid?"

Korfax looked down.

"I once swore not to do this," he said, "to summon another to a battle that was not theirs to fight."

"You may have to, if all goes ill," she answered. "As you have said many times before, we have not yet seen all that the Agdoain are. What if we are being deliberately misled? You have told us of all your encounters, how they can become a mirror."

"Then a summoning will be my last resort," he told her. He paused. "And I hope to the Creator that I will not have to use it."

"Why?"

"Because it will be dire."

There was a long silence. Korfax looked up again.

"So let us prepare. And before the last journey let there be a feast, a feast for all under the stars, one last feast before the battle. Let Kannim be filled with light, and let that light mirror the light of heaven. Let that which is below rise. Let that which is above descend. One last feast of joy."

Opakas smiled, her eyes glowing.

"Tomorrow is the last day of Ahaneh. What better time could there be than that?"

The feast was made. As twilight fell, so Kannim filled with light. Though not as ancient as Tatanah to the north, the forest of Kannim was far larger, vast enough to take all the peoples of the Iabeiorith under its eaves. The trees became pillars, their leaves the firmament, and under them were-fires were set, flames of every colour. Food was prepared, wine was poured and banners were raised.

In one of the many avenues of trees Korfax sat with his chieftains and their families. The Argedith under Opakas were there, as were many of the honour guard, and around them, in many a leafy hall, more gathered, and more besides them, all come to the feast, one last night of joy before the great battle.

Wine was drunk, there was laughter and song and around every fire the people of the Iabeiorith gathered and reclaimed the night.

There came a point when Aodagaa came to sit beside his prince.

"My Haelok, how is it that our power increases?" he asked. "How is it that I feel mightier now than I have ever felt before?"

Korfax looked back at Aodagaa and offered him a warm smile.

"I think that my good friend Aodagaa has suddenly discovered a delight in the asking of questions."

"If you would rather not answer, my Haelok..."

Korfax laughed quietly.

"It was merely a jest, my friend, merely a jest."

Korfax studied the cup in his hand.

"Why indeed do we feel mightier?" Korfax mused. "Perhaps it is because we have entered that special time, that time known only to those that know they approach death, that know they approach the time of endings. Perhaps your soul, like mine, knows that which your reason would yet deny."

"And what is that, my Haelok?"

"That you are closer now to the truth than you have ever been before."

"But why should that be? Why should the truth be closer now? Surely, any time, whether it be of endings or not, would be no different to any other in the great scheme of things."

Korfax let the smile drop from his face.

"In the great scheme of things?" he mused. "Ah! So why does the day seem brighter to the condemned? Why is the least thing of utmost consequence to those that are about to die? Why does the one that marches to his death see the world as never before?"

He turned to Aodagaa and held him with his eyes.

"I think it is because the mind hastens. I think the mind hastens because it desires life, any life, rather than death. The mind clings to any ledge for as long as it can. For the living desire life, Aodagaa, and it is as simple as that. The living cannot fully know what lies beyond the end of life. The living have only their faith."

As though moved by this answer, Korfax stood up and held his cup high. A hush spread everywhere as all felt the mind of the Haelok reach out to touch them. Far out into the forest went his thought, and all turned to listen.

"On this night," he said to them all, with voice and with mind, "in this place, there is joy. But let us not forget that we now stand upon the edge. Ahead of us the enemy waits, denying us our ancient home. Doom awaits us, but that doom is also the very thing that defines us."

He paused a moment, looking down, before meeting their eyes again, a sea of stars waiting upon his word.

"It seems to me, as it has seemed to many before me, I think, that the truth of everything becomes more certain the closer we come to our doom. He who knows the sword is about to fall knows the colour of his world with a certainty that is denied all others. He sees everything outlined in the light of ending, knowing that he will never see such sights again. We pass this way only once, in this flesh, in this form, and then, after a brief time, we are gone. So, if we have only one chance to make a difference, why should we not let the nearness of our end quicken our hearts, widen our eyes and fill us with power? Should we not have the full command of our being in that instant, that one last blinding instant, before the tide of death sweeps us away?"

He held out his cup.

"To those that are gone, and to those that are about to be."

He drank. All did the same.

That night he dreamt. He was back at Losq and both his mother and his father were there. He was kneeling before them.

"Was I wrong?" he asked.

His father smiled, that rare smile of care.

"You did what you thought best," he said.

His mother came forward and took his hand in hers. She was warm to the touch, alive.

"The dead do not blame," she said. "How can they? The same mistakes were theirs."

"But the world could end!" he told her.

"All things have their time," she answered him. "How else can we know what we have?"

Losq came apart around him, its stone flying away. His mother and father grew, and they filled with distance, cold and remote. Now the far reaches of the heavens lay within their eyes and they looked down upon him like gods.

"Do now what you know must be done!" said his mother, with a voice like all the winds of the world.

"Failure is its own reward," said his father, a roar great enough to hurl the stars from their courses.

Korfax awoke, breathing hard. His face felt damp. He had been crying. He lay a long time staring up. What had it meant?

It was dawn on the edges of Ovaras, and the growing light crept into the sky from the eastern distances. It was time.

Korfax rode out before the assembled masses of the Haelok Aldaria. To one side was Aodagaa, to the other side was Dosevax and behind them came Ambriol, Ralendu, Ortal, Vandalim and Dorlamu, all holding up the banners of their houses. Following the Haelok and the seven chieftains rode the honour guard, forty-nine of the best.

They all stopped in the midst of the great semi-circle and became still. Korfax extended his thought. All who waited before him felt his touch, sensing the waiting silence he invoked. Then Korfax sat up straighter and he spoke, and his thought carried his words to the furthest reaches of the great army of the Haelok Aldaria that now spread out around him.

"My companions, we come to it at last," he said. "Before us, to the east, is the grey heart of the foe, the rot and the canker that has eclipsed the brightness of our world these many years past. Before us it lies, forces unnumbered, a dark ocean filled to the brim with abomination. But we do not fear it. For we know what it is.

"It lies at the heart of our old defeat. The iniquities of the west are revealed at last for all to see, and we are become that which we should have been from the very beginning. For we are the Iabeiorith, and no shadow is so dark that we cannot pierce its heart.

"But hearts have been pierced, even now, for our sorrow is the fire that bleeds from us with every breath that we take. Great wrongs have been done to us, but now is the time to put those wrongs to right. We go to shake the foundations of the world and set the balance back.

"My father once told me that I was of the Farenith, and that the Farenith were quiet, followers all. We did the work of the day and asked for nothing more. We were satisfied simply to be!

"But I am satisfied no longer. I have been quiet long enough. Now I will shout, and my voice will rend the heavens asunder. For I am no longer of the Farenith and I am no longer a follower. I am of the Mikaolazith and I am born of the mighty. I am the mightiest son of the mightiest house, and all who follow me now will see their names carved upon the eternal stone that upholds the very foundations of creation itself."

Opakas came forward and raised her hands. In them were stones, winds, fires and waters, a great globe of elements held up in the air by nothing more than her will. She chanted the war blessing:

> Biaholuum beiith lujo
> Biaholuum beiith deral
> Torzuhol fasorith jo
> Oth holloes laajon igal
> Gol holim namad iada
> Gol holim faiin himeil
> Tevimith ommon vepein

Stand tall, lords of the north, Stand tall, lords of stone. Rise up from your shadows and face the four horizons. Lift up the Creator's sword, lift up your mighty voices and let the foe feel the fire in your heart!

She stepped back and Korfax held up his black sword, Matastos, the slayer of gods, and he pointed it at the heavens, and his sword cried out, howling its lust, singing its terrible song. The howl filled the air, and the world trembled at the sound.

Black lightning fell down around Korfax and his eyes became great lights in his head, their brilliance piercing the darkness of his helm like twin stars gazing out from beyond the flying rack of storm. Then his voice, mightier yet, rolled down across the darkened plain like thunder.

"Hear me!" he cried. "Hear me all! I shall not sheath my sword again, not until I have cleansed our world of the foe. Into the void I shall go, into that grey oblivion, but I shall not fear it. For the Creator is with me, and the Creator's sword is with me, as the Creator's sword is with us all. For we are become the Creator's sword, that blade, that vast and terrible blade that ever cleaves the void in two."

Korfax and his mount seemed to grow before them, a statue sheathed in shadow, enclosed by a gyre of ever darkening flame. On either side of him the seven chieftains drew their seven blades in turn, and each of them unleashed their seven dark fires. Then, at their master's behest, they all spoke their power and added it to the storm that swelled about him. And behind them the honour guard, seven times seven, did the same, summoning dark fires to add to those of their masters.

Now, on that low hill, in the midst of the Haelok Aldaria, there rose up a greater darkness, shapes written in silhouette against the eastern sky. And it seemed to the host assembled there that they stood upon a threshold, a threshold between the past and the present. And upon that threshold great shapes out of legend came to stand before them, an assembled might from ages past, towering forms that saluted them even whilst bidding them join in the last battle of all, where the light and the dark would descend upon the grey and formless void and defeat it utterly.

"Let the foe feel the fire in our hearts!" cried Korfax, and the host replied with but one voice, raising their blades into the heavens, swelling with the power that filled them.

Korfax wheeled about and Enastul reared beneath him, hooves challenging the heavens. Korfax raised his sword, and it sang of slaughter. He pointed to the east, spurring Enastul with his thought, before galloping away on the wings of night. And they followed him as one, the madness of their summoned power consuming them at last, even as it sent them on their way to battle and to death.

Across the plain they raced, a black storm of rage. Qorihnas were drawn and voices cried out. Here it came, the last battle of all. Here it came, the final act. On this, all would be won or lost. Their thoughts became a thunderhead above them, black and towering, as they called upon the powers, upon the fates, upon the Creator, calling up dark night from below and bright fire from above, setting each about them like blades and shields, and the black rage of their approach shook the world.

From the walls of the Leein Komsel it must have seemed as if the entire west had suddenly darkened, for over the wide plains of Ovaras a storm rolled in, a vast black storm that gathered itself up into mighty towers of shadow stretching from horizon to horizon, flickering with white and brilliant fires.

The storm roared in out of the west and over the plain, aiming its fury right at the very walls of the Komsel, black cloud, white lightning and the shuddering ground beneath.

The land and the sky were eclipsed as it boiled towards the walls of the high Komsel, the fury of its approach echoing from hill to wall and back again.

Out upon the field, at the storm's very tip, rode Korfax, his face white with fury, his eyes black with rage. He held Matastos aloft, the singing sword, the first and the only, its many blades writhing about him as it sang of death.

Below him, his steed, Enastul, echoed the mood of his master. Encased in armour of his own he swelled to a monstrous height. From each great eye red light fell whilst fires curled from each nostril. From his mouth streamed burning vapours, and from his single armoured horn energies flared.

Across the receding plain they went, eager for battle, eager for war, and in their wake came the very host of night.

All grew mighty, steed and rider, guard and guarded. A dance of shadows filled the air, and the black host rode up to the outer walls of the Komsel.

To the west gate came their fury, Qorihnas drawn, already pointing at the enemy above. On the walls the Agdoain hissed and snarled, uncertain as to their purpose. It must have seemed to them, then, that this sudden storm out of the west intended to rise up and over wall, picking everything up in its breath and blowing it away. But mere moments from the gate the Haelok Aldaria clenched their hands about their swords and uttered such a shout of power that even the giant at the end of the world should surely hear them.

They roared with one voice, one purpose, one desire, a summoning enough to unknit the very substance of creation, and against the great gate and its towers the power fell, one single and shadowy fist that passed into the stone and through it, before shaking it from the inside out. The gates rang, the towers trembled and shook, and the power undid them all, shaking wall from gate, door from lock, stone from stone.

The towers to either side fell back, walls tumbling and spires falling. Down they fell, walls and towers all, all crumbling in a shower of broken stone. Inwards they went, crashing down upon the inner slopes of the Leein Komsel, broken beyond redemption upon the heights of the encircling hills.

The Agdoain that had stood upon the battlements fell like rain, splashing onto the hard stone below, a rain of grey and broken flesh, whilst their siblings below were crushed where they stood. But it was not over yet, for even as Korfax approached the wreckage the fire about him blasted that wreckage aside as though it were chaff before a wind. Backwards and sideways flew the shattered stone, failed seeds from broken husks, taking with them the last few Agdoain that had dared to survive.

Onwards the Haelok Aldaria raced, charging through the gap in the outer walls like a flood, a deluge, a black tide greater than the grey, surging through the darkened breach, And out of the darkness pale faces stared, each eye blazing with the darkest of fires, each mouth roaring dark words of power. So, like Sondehna of old, Korfax stormed the Rolnir itself, racing headlong to meet his enemy with the power of the abyss at his beck and call.

To the city walls they came, once thought mighty enough to turn aside even the wrath of the Ashar. But no longer. Once more the Haelok Aldaria clenched their wills, raised their swords and called with wordless voices upon the abyss below, setting its naked power to their will.

The earth groaned and shook whilst waves of torment rippled outwards from their black assault. The gates and the towers, the walls and the battlements, all reared with ancient and cunning might, shuddered as they resisted. But the power mounted further, rage upon rage upon rage, until the stone could withstand it no longer and the gates and the towers shattered at last, riven asunder as though aeons of time had descended in a single moment, delivered by a single thrust of might. The walls were thrown down and a mountain was humbled. Great Emethgis Vaniad was pierced, and the rupture in its side opened like a mortal wound.

From within, from behind the failing wall, Agdoain swarmed across the breach like a sick fluid, pumped ever outwards by a mad and failing heart. They came in numbers uncounted, swarming over the wreckage with all the fecundity of a plague, but they perished even as they stepped up to the line, caught upon the edge by a withering heat of darkness, for the Haelok Aldaria pointed their Qorihnas at the foe, and from each blade flames shot forth and burned the enemy to ash.

Ever to the fore rode Korfax, stuttering now upon the borders of sight, a shadow of a shadow. His steed bore him on, vast and terrible, whilst about them both Matastos wove its darker snare, blades coiling like serpents, a flickering ring of nighted flame none could approach. Sondehna had come again to hold elemental night in the palm of his hand.

War beasts reared, claws flailing, mouths wide with teeth, but against Qorihna they were impotent; likewise their masters. Here came a force to which they had no answer, a power beyond their comprehension. All were swept aside and undone.

Into the city Korfax rode, and the Agdoain scattered before him, this way and that, trying desperately to regroup. He watched them run, cruel amusement in his eyes.

They were nothing to him now, mere tools, the wasted limbs of his foe. He only wanted one thing more, the mind that ordered them, the power that sat upon the holy throne. It had come to it at last. Now he would lay his long, grey nightmare low, for once and for all.

He reined in Enastul and looked about him. Emethgis Vaniad had changed. No longer was she the mighty jewel of Ovaras, for her beauty had fallen into vile decay. Leering skywards, the towers of crystal and stone were now shapes of delirium, fevered forms that twisted upwards like diseased roots, or broken limbs reaching for the heavens so that they could be dragged back down.

Great highways, once so straight and proud, now twisted thickly or lay coiled in confusion, sluggish rivers of stone dammed by heaped-up filth. Domes erupted like blisters, and squares lurked like quagmires or stretched like stagnant waters, and each glinted with a grey light, a rotted light that illuminated nothing but its own foul demise.

Korfax let his eyes wander across the city he had once considered the culmination of all his ambitions and desires, and let himself see fully at last the sickness and the blight that had taken the heart of Lon-Elah in its putrid fist. But when his eyes reached the Umadya Pir, even he blanched.

Like the deformed limb of some buried giant it pointed profanely at the heavens. Like failing flesh it decayed and perished even as he stared at it. Dark veins crossed its flayed surface, grey vines pulsing and heaving with slow fluids as they ate into the very stone up which they swarmed. The many windows gaped like sores, the many walls sagged and all the once proud spires curled like jagged claws.

Here it came. As the heirs of Karmaraa had swept aside the city of the Iabeiorith in their righteous fury, he would do the same here. Emethgis Vaniad had fallen beyond recall. It was utterly corrupted and only the fires of the abyss would cleanse it at last.

He sent his thought to the others about him.

"Burn it!" he told them. "Burn it all!"

From a high place they looked out across the city. They saw the storm of darkness take the walls of the Komsel and throw them down. They saw the darkness ride down from the heights and blast its way through the inner walls. Then they watched as the storm began to undo the city itself.

Stone crumbled and fell. Towers and walls, everything in its path was shattered. Night ate its way into the city and reduced it to rubble.

"So predictable," it said quietly. It turned to her.

"And you would love that, would you?" it asked.

She stared down at the darkness, watching as it slowly pulled the city apart. But she felt nothing except a dim satisfaction. What would have once horrified her, horrified her no more. Horror stood beside her. Horror dwelt within her. She welcomed the oncoming fire. It would burn away her pain.

"Vengeance comes," she said quietly.

It smiled, baring its long teeth at her. She looked back at it, back at the wasteland that had become its body. There was a faint odour rising from it now, the scent of decay. Its blank skin gleamed, like that of its slaves, and even its hair looked thin and wasted. Blank skin covered it, a sullen sea broken only by its lips.

"Is that all you can say?" it asked, lips parting, teeth glistening.

"You will end," she told it. "That will suffice for me."

"No!" it replied. "You have misunderstood. Your beloved is about to learn a harder truth than any he has yet endured. He thinks I have no answer to the lore of the abyss. But I do, and it is you that has brought this about. For you have unshackled me and I have no restraints upon me now."

It turned her so that she had no choice but to look.

"Witness!" it said. "See spirit fail, see hope die and see at what cost comes your hollow defiance. See my truth written in your flesh and your blood. See it written before your very eyes! For you behold the end of history itself."

It raised a grey hand, and she felt its commandments slither down to the city below.

Korfax felt it before he saw it. There was a change about him, a taste of something new. A wave crossed the city, unseen, unheard, the touch of the void. The Agdoain paused, turning to look back upon the Umadya Pir, and then they grew. Force swelled in them and they reared up, turning back, all as one, to face the night and welcome it with open jaws.

What had been easy became harder by the moment as the Agdoain began to fight back with ever mounting extravagance. Now they began to resist at last, both fire and blade, and the Haelok Aldaria began to die.

First came the Ageyad, rushing forwards in tangled groups, impaling themselves upon each black blade before erupting in grey force. For every Ageyad that died, one of the Haelok Aldaria would die as well. The mirror had returned.

Only by summoned power could the Ageyad be kept back, but now they blasted themselves apart where they stood, tearing holes in the ground and in the walls, destroying everything around them as they released the pent-up forces of their bastard limbs. At one point a ring of them, joined limb to limb, immolated themselves whilst huddled around an entire tower, bringing it all down in a slow avalanche of broken rock. Those that did not protect themselves, those that were caught unawares, were crushed and buried, Agdoain and Ell alike.

Warrior and war beast followed, growing and changing, their bodies warping, a burst of limbs and new mouths erupting. Some of them even merged, coalescing in strange union, their flesh and bone running like loose clay, before combining again to create new abominations, lurching horrors with all the ferocity of wounded beasts.

It felt now as though the Haelok Aldaria were caught at the edges of a sea of flesh, for ever burning back the twisted limbs thrown up by the bloody tide, limbs whose only aim was to drag them down and drown them. Though they could keep this assault at bay, their numbers continued to dwindle. They were finite. The Agdoain were not.

The further they went, the worse it became. A howl, dismal and deep, rolled across the embattled stone and even greater shapes reared up, greater by far. It was as though the towers themselves had awoken. Even the massed power of the Haelok Aldaria seemed inadequate for this onslaught. Things towered into the sky, horrible perversions gigantic in their new flesh, part siege tower, part war beast, part Ageyad. They lumbered up from pits or out of the very stone itself, wailing like an army of the damned, crushing friend and foe alike in their blind fury. Grey force fell from their knotted limbs like rain, undoing skin from bone and spirit from flesh, and they vomited up a liquid corrosion from their many gaping maws, a fuming slurry that ate its way through stone and armour alike.

Korfax was appalled. Never before had he imagined such perversions of mere flesh. Lunatic monsters suddenly walked, or stumbled, across his world. The very abyss of insanity had come to Lon-Elah.

Only by concentrated fire could the giants be felled, and even then, when they came apart, the acid that filled them flooded out and undid all those that were nearby. Hundreds died, and the warped streets sagged further, before crumbling at last as the stone of which they were made turned to vapour.

On and on it went, a delirium of mad shapes that had to be scoured from the world, a never-ending harvest of rotted things that howled their way into existence, only to be put back down again. The Haelok Aldaria were caught in the midst of a nightmare.

With his forces failing under the sheer weight of numbers, Korfax began to know the possibility of despair. The Agdoain resisted the massed power of the Haelok Aldaria at last, though how they did so he could not see. It was as though each had become a hole into which they poured their might, a great empty hole that swallowed their power and negated it.

The turning point arrived. Unsatisfied even with the groaning giants, the master of the Agdoain changed things yet again. Now the great womb at the base of the Umadya Pir vomited up an incessant stream of flesh and bone. No longer bothering with form, it spewed a living, liquid slurry out into the city, a howling, surging chaos that boiled across the streets, a grey and poisonous tide created for one purpose only, to swallow the invaders and eat everything that lay within its path.

Upon a shattered mountain of stone Opakas came to Korfax. Others joined them – Aodagaa, Dosevax and their guard. Around them the fight continued, scattered across the western side of the city, the black and the grey, the night and the void.

"We cannot win through," Opakas told Korfax. "We face the deluge itself. The Haelok Aldaria decrease, and as they decrease so their power diminishes. We of the Argedith can only help so much, but we remain shackled. Either you allow us to summon aid or we withdraw."

"No!" said Korfax. "I have not come this far only to be thrown back again. And only at the end of need will I summon."

Opakas made the gesture of appeal.

"But look around you," she said. "Is this not the end? Unable to match our power the foe will match our numbers instead. We will tire. We will end, and all will have been in vain. Will you lead your people needlessly to death?"

"But I said that I would not do this."

"No! You said not unless it was the end. So I ask again. Is this not the end? The world will fall if we cannot win through. This is our only chance. We must not fail."

"But to summon others to a battle that is not theirs?"

"And what is it to be? The fall of our world? The fall of creation itself? We stand upon the brink! Uncage the Argedith. Allow us to summon aid. It is well past time!"

Korfax looked back in obvious indecision, reluctance in his every line, but then

Dosevax stepped forward.

"Then if you will not summon," he said, "an attempt upon the womb itself must be made."

Korfax turned.

"And do you think me unaware of that?" he said. "But we are held at bay!"

Dosevax looked long and hard at his Haelok.

"Nevertheless," he said at last. "It must be done! It is the only alternative left to us!" And before Korfax could stop him he rode off and into the flood, followed by those of his command. They called up all the power that they could and rode into the grey sea.

With his sword raised and the name of his Haelok on his lips, Dosevax attacked the liquid chaos. With him went his guard and straight through it they went, burning their way towards the great womb, the dark fires of their summoning consuming the flood. It seemed impossible, even to Korfax, that this dark island of fire could surmount the infinite grey, but Dosevax and his followers did not stop. They rode on, through it all.

One by one they fell, but not Dosevax. Almost to the very wellhead itself he went, but there he was caught and could go no further.

He fought against the never-ending, the very fount of oblivion that lay at the end of everything, and though he held it back, it was clear he could not do so for ever.

With a great cry he erupted with force, burning against the very edges, a single black star surmounting the grey, but then his power failed him at last and the unending flesh reared up and over him and bore him down. Its acid touch undid him and he passed from the world.

Dosevax was gone. Korfax had to accept it. But he did not weep, he had no time. Opakas was right. It was come to it at last. He had no other choice. Now came the moment he had feared above all others. Here the game entered the last play, and all would be won or lost upon a single chance. Whether that had been his intent or not, Dosevax had bought him time, time enough for one last act.

He turned to Opakas.

"So be it!" he said. "But I will do the summoning! I will pay the price. I will allow no other to stand in my name!"

Korfax turned to the north. In his mind he saw again an aged Arged, burnt and torn but resolute. That was his final answer, the one that he dreaded. Maybe he would be spared in this, and maybe he would not, but here came the last chance. As Mathulaa had spent himself, as Dosevax had spent himself, so Korfax would spend himself as well.

He raised up his hands and uttered the call. The world about him fell silent and time itself seemed to stop where it was. Even the flood of chaos that surged over the city hung in the air, unmoving whilst the words were spoken. Creation paused, the river waited and everything bowed before the will of the Haelok.

Opakas looked up at Korfax in terror. She knew those words and what they portended. She would have cried out, tried to stop him, but she could not. This was the will of the Haelok.

The heat of the summoning burned the air and all fell back as Korfax became incandescent with summoned flame. Only Enastul remained to endure his master's immolation. Opakas glanced at Enastul and found herself marvelling at his fortitude. Rather than fearing the flame, Enastul dared even to revel in it, rising up and even assailing the sky with his hooves as though in utter defiance. Then Korfax and Enastul both erupted, and the flame flew outwards in a mighty ring of fire.

It passed over the Haelok Aldaria with a gentle heat, but the rising tide of shapeless Agdoain it burned and the formless sea fell back, mewling in pain.

Opakas watched the fading fire with sudden awe. How terrible it was, but also how wonderful. Was there to be an answer, though? She looked northwards.

A light was growing there now, an unexpected light, and Opakas thought she sensed another heat, something rushing towards her, towards the south, something more potent yet, something that beat against her with an ever greater fury.

She watched the clouds part, saw the sky break open, and then she all but cried out in wonder. She pointed. They had come.

Out of the fiery darkness they flew, and the sky to the north was suddenly filled, from horizon to horizon, with red avenging wings. A storm of fire hurled its tempest at the centre of the world, for Korfax, last prince of the broken north, had called upon the Vovin, and they had answered his summons – all of them.

Some of the Haelok Aldaria sank to their knees, whilst others wept with astonished wonder, but all eyes stared with awe at the greater storm now hurling itself towards them.

Korfax had not known how many he could call upon, and the memory of Mathulaa had sat in the back of his mind as he had issued the summons, a burnt corpse full of rage and failure. But then the summoning had taken him, and even he had gasped at its terrible power. He had hoped for a few, but his mind had touched all of them, all that yet dwelt amongst the peaks of the Adroqin Vohimar.

So they came to the call, letting it hurl them out of the world and then back again so that they could come with all due speed to the place of the summoning. Their minds joined with his – his rage, their rage, all one, red spirits of fire made to burn the world and to rejoice in that burning.

The thunder of their wings filled the air like the heralds of ending. They paused briefly to taste their summoner's desire, circling the sky above his head in a vast and towering gyre of wings. Then they descended as though already triumphant.

They turned upon the slurry of the Agdoain, upon the warriors and the Ageyad, upon the beasts and the towers, and with their flame and their fury the wreck of Emethgis Vaniad was lit from end to end with fire. Spirit was rent from flesh, even as flesh was rent from bone, and still the fires fell. Endless night hurled her winged avengers at the void, and the last child of Sondehna taught the grey slaves of dissolution the very meaning of destruction.

Fire filled Emethgis Vaniad. The Agdoain burned, the great womb burned, even the stone burned. Those that were left to witness the summoning named Korfax a god that day. They bowed before him, whether he willed it or no, even as he stood, etched into the firmament, a fleet of Vovin held in the palm of his hand, orchestrating their attack as though calling up the last judgement. Emethgis Vaniad was cleansed by purifying fire.

The Agdoain were gone, as was the great womb that had birthed them. All that was left of the city was burnt and broken stone. Only the Umadya Pir remained to stand tall, its strangling vines burnt from its worm-eaten stone. Everything else had been turned to ash.

But even now the master of the Agdoain had an answer, for from the tower of light grey fire spat. It arced across the heavens like a lethal finger, and every Vovin that it touched, it swept from the sky. They tumbled down, one after another, to crash upon the stone below, flesh burning and bones burning, great hearts undone.

Korfax understood. As he had once slaughtered the Agdoain upon the walls of Othil Zilodar, so the master of the Agdoain returned the favour here.

He screamed his denial at the tower even as the last of the Vovin turned to the attack.

Those that were left span through the sky, avoiding the grey power as best they could, though it picked them off, one by one, until there was but a single Vovin left.

With scalded eye, the last of the Vovin marked the spot from whence the grey fire came, and it hurled itself at the tower, heaving fire from its jaws. It did not stop, it could not. The summoning still held it. The enemy had to be destroyed.

It struck the tower and erupted. Fire blossomed where its body hit the stone, and the tower cracked from its sprawling roots to its broken crown.

Qorazon fell back from the window, turning away and dragging her with it, its mouth now turned downwards in grim rage, for a fire came after it, a fire it could not stop, a fire that licked, even now, at the very stone where it had only just stood. And the fire burned it, blackened it and broke it.

It ran from the flame, fled its ire, taking her with it, running deep into the tower, a grey shield of force ever at its back. But the flame pursued it still, daring even the deeps of the tower in its desire for vengeance.

She watched as Qorazon dragged her along, and she felt that she, like the stone around her, was being cleansed by the fire. She could feel the heat wash over her, could feel its delicious warmth as it scoured the cold grey from the city of her birth. It seemed to her then that she had been cold all her life, bound about by grey ice, caught in a frozen place. So she luxuriated in this sudden and miraculous warmth.

She caught Qorazon's displeasure and smiled back at it, relishing its sudden failure. This was a play it had never imagined, even in its darkest dreams. Though it might hurl its hatred at the Vovin's fire, Qorazon could do nothing about it. Here was a power that was utterly beyond it.

Qorazon reached the central hall and threw her inside. Then it slammed the doors and sealed them. Fire licked against them and even their stone began to burn. It drew back in shock, raising its stave and summoning a shield of nullity, but then the tower shuddered, the stone cracking and the floor heaving. With a great groan the tower split in half, cracking like the trunk of a burning tree. Stone fell from above and Qorazon stood over her, fending it off. Finally it was done, and only the dust dared move.

An ominous quiet fell about them all. No new shapes of horror erupted from the ruins about them, and the vines that had so recently strangled the Umadya Pir now lay in ashen heaps at its base, burned from the eaten stone by a greater fire. The tower itself was cracked from root to crown and the great womb that had lain against it was gone.

The drifting clouds of corruption fled before a fresh wind from the north, and the polluted skies drew ever further back until the cerulean vault of the heavens was revealed again. Around them all lay the rubble of war, still fuming from the fire of battle, and as the drifting ash settled back to the ground, a dim grey miasma rose slowly up into the sky on clotted wings. For a moment it bent over the ruin of Emethgis Vaniad, the ghost of an unsated hunger and unending lust, before consuming itself at last and vanishing utterly from the world.

Korfax stared up at the broken tower. He wanted to weep but could not. He had no tears left. The Vovin were gone. He sank to his knees. What had he done? Every Vovin he had called upon was gone. Victory was his, but at what cost?

He felt that terrible guilt again. Those wondrous shapes from his brightest dreams had been burnt upon the altar of his rage. He deserved to die. He deserved their wrath, but none remained to give it. He bowed his head and swore an oath before the Creator. He would never do that again. No matter the need, no matter the consequences, he would not do that again. Beauty and magnificence had passed from the world by his command, and he would never allow it again. The price was too much. Some things could not be borne.

After long moments Korfax bowed his head and closed his eyes, holding Matastos before him in an attitude of prayer. The others did the same, giving thanks to the Creator. Then the last of the Haelok Aldaria rose up as one and lifted their weapons to the heavens and sang their song of victory, their voices echoing throughout all the ruins of Emethgis Vaniad.

Of the tens of thousands that had charged into the city, barely a tenth of that number remained. Opakas, Aodagaa and Ambriol, along with the remnants of the vanguard, waited upon the shattered remnants of the Umadya Madimel and faced to the north so that they could honour all that had gone before them. Korfax stood with them, but he could only mourn for what had been spent.

She looked up. It was done. She could feel it. She looked at the faceless creature beside her and laughed.

"He has beaten you. Your slaves are no more. Now you will die at his hand."

Qorazon smiled its empty smile back at her, and its teeth lengthened even as it grinned.

"No," it told her quietly. "You have misconstrued what you have seen. Now begins the lesson in earnest, the bitterest of all. What matter that my slaves are gone? What matter that my womb is burnt from the world? I do not care what I spend, but he does. Already he grieves for his loss, but he does not yet understand how much more he has to lose."

It reared up and gestured behind her.

"Everything he has ever made, everything he has ever loved, I will have him destroy. He will lose it all, and the pain will grow and grow, until madness and death take him. But even then it will not stop, for I shall rend his spirit. I shall cast it into the lingering place and it will know eternal torment."

It laughed back at her, a hideous sound, shrill and deep and echoing.

"Now he must walk my domain. Now he must come to me and face me alone. Here is where the lesson becomes sharpest, more bitter than even the mightiest can endure. He must learn how much more he has to lose, discover all that has been wrought in his absence. Then he will learn my truth at last and finally know the wisdom of despair. The Agdoain are nothing. They can be made in uncounted numbers. They are mere tools, nothing more. It is not my enemy that has won, it is I."

It came closer, and its emptiness seemed almost to gloat.

"You are deluded!" she told it. "You are mad! He has defeated you!"

"Fool!" it spat back at her. "Do you truly believe that the forces that dwelt here were all that I had? Look to the north! Look with the eyes of power!"

It placed its hands to the sides of her head and squeezed. She almost screamed with the pain, but through her blood-drenched sight she saw what it saw, her sight piercing the stone about her and reducing it to translucence.

From the north they came, a grey flood of Agdoain in such numbers she could not see an end to them. They filled all her horizons, covering the north lands from the furthest east to the uttermost west. Not even all the Vovin ever spawned could burn such numbers. And they were, all of them, converging upon Emethgis Vaniad.

Opakas bowed before Korfax. All those behind her did the same.

"What is your will, my Haelok?" she asked.

"I shall seek out the dwelling place of him that is fallen," said Korfax.

"And we shall come with you," said Ambriol.

"No," Korfax smiled gently in return. "I confront him alone."

"But we would ward you."

"You cannot. This task is mine."

"Even so!"

"You defy me?"

"We do."

"Then you are thrice blessed, and an unlooked for benison in this desert."

"We merely do what we must."

"Then be warned. If you enter this place behind me, beware. There is great power here."

"That may be so. But if Onehson comes before me and mine, we will teach him fear."

Korfax turned to Opakas.

"Hold Enastul for me, will you?"

"But I would come with you also."

"No, my friend," he said, "you have done your duty seven times seven. I wish you to guard my back now, with all that remain. You are in command. Aodagaa and Ambriol will go with me."

Korfax looked at the others.

"When Opakas speaks, it is with my will."

All of them bowed.

Opakas fell to her knees.

"I do not wish to stay behind, my Haelok. I would ward you."

Korfax blinked back sudden tears.

"But you shall. You will be warding me. Here."

He touched Opakas on the brow with his left hand.

"Keep the Haelok Aldaria for me until I return. Be my voice in this place."

He walked off, Aodagaa and Ambriol following with the honour guard. All watched as they entered the tower, but none marked the dark shadow that slipped in behind them afterwards.

They approached the Rolnir and stared in fearful astonishment at the burnt sky above and the burnt stone below.

They all saw the breach in the great wall, the stone blackened, the ground strewn with grey ash. Simoref held up his hand, commanding a halt even as he reigned in his ormn. Valagar stopped beside him. Behind them both, the main forces waited whilst Kukenur rode her steed up to the edge of the scar.

"Noraud, you should see this for yourself," she called back. "I will not describe it."

Simoref rode forward, watching Kukenur all the while. Though she masked it well, he could tell that she was deeply shocked.

He came to the breach in the wall, others at his back. Some cursed under their breath, some averted their eyes, but none was unmoved by what they beheld.

It was as though a great ball of fire had rolled across the ground, leaving behind it a black swath of blasted earth as wide as the base of a tower. Where it had struck the wall the stone itself had been lifted up, shattered and then thrown back down again to either side. But the fire had not stopped there. It had continued on to the city itself and blasted a great hole in its side as well.

Emethgis Vaniad lay in ruins. The black fire had gone everywhere. Nothing remained standing, just so many islands of broken stone, the sad remnants of once mighty towers. Little was left of anything except ash and ruin. Only the Umadya Pir still reached for the sky, its stark silhouette a ragged claw. Of the Agdoain there was no sign at all.

Valagar was the first to speak.

"In the name of all that was holy, what has happened here?"

Kukenur clenched her jaws, fighting back the tears.

"You do not want to know."

All turned to her. Simoref reached for her, but he drew back his hand at the last.

"Tell me!" he ordered.

She looked at him.

"You do not know what you are asking," she spat back. There was a fragile look to her now and Simoref found himself wondering whether she had reached her limits at last. But then he looked back at the wreck of Emethgis Vaniad and found that he no longer cared. He no longer cared for the cost. He no longer cared for anything. All his dreams had failed, and all he wanted to know now was how it had come to this. He wanted to know the truth of it all before the end.

"Tell me!" he demanded.

Kukenur came to him and looked fully into his eyes. She showed him what she had seen and he shook with the force of it, all but falling from his mount. She finally released him and he tumbled to the ground at last, clutching at himself as if in utter agony.

"Now you know!" she said.

Simoref beat at the air with his hands. Valagar dismounted and took him by his shoulders, shaking him back to reality.

"I will know this truth as well. I must know what it is that we face. Tell me what you see. Tell us all what you see."

Simoref stared at Valagar for a long moment and then dropped his head. What horrors danced in his skull! Monsters lurched or staggered across his inner sight, things the size of mountains screaming as they were born and then felled by black fire. There was a battle in his mind, an assault of the darkness and the light upon the grey void, dark powers hurling bright flames, powers consuming the slaves of oblivion. He could not contain it.

"You cannot imagine," he gasped.

If this was what Korfax had contained within himself for all these long years, then Simoref was humbled to the point of insignificance. Only gods held such powers – powers enough to erase armies, powers enough to shatter cities raised for all eternity, powers enough to summon the very fires of retribution and have them bow down before him.

But Valagar did not know.

"Tell me what you see!" he demanded in his turn. Then he physically lifted Simoref up by his shoulders and shook him. "TELL ME!" he roared. Kukenur watched but did not intervene.

"Words are insufficient," Simoref replied as if already broken. Valagar lowered him gently back to the ground. Simoref looked back at him for a moment and then turned to the rest.

"Korfax took Emethgis Vaniad," he said.

They all waited, some with fear, others with expectation.

"He slew the Agdoain."

Many shook their fists in quiet celebration.

"He slew the monsters."

The fists shook again.

"He summoned Vovin."

The fists faltered.

"They burned Emethgis Vaniad."

No one moved.

"Nothing survived!"

There was utter silence.

They rode the black path to the Umadya Pir. Many looked ill at what they saw about them. The greatest city of the Ell had become a ruin. What had not been burnt to ash had been melted. What had not been melted had been warped. The malice of the foe and the fury of battle leered back at them from every broken stone.

At the west gate of the Umadya Pir a few thousand Ell, each clad in black armour, waited. Simoref turned to Valagar.

"Not all are dead, it seems," he said. Valagar did not reply, but looked grimly ahead.

They came to the west gate and dismounted. One stepped forward from the dark ranks to meet with them, clearly the leader. And though she was clad only in simple robes, there was a power about her and within her that burned the air. Simoref felt daunted.

"I am Simoref, son of Zafazaa, of the house of Zadakal," he announced. "I seek Korfax. I come to pledge my allegiance."

The leader spoke.

"I knew who you were when you declared yourself before the city walls. But you come too late! Emethgis Vaniad is already ours."

Simoref bowed his head.

"At least I have come," he said.

She inclined her head.

"Yes, that is true enough. But what else does it say?"

Simoref looked hard at her.

"Come now. I have given you my name. Tell me yours at least. Surely I deserve that, whatever else you may think of me."

"Deserve, is it? I know you. I know all of you. I know what you have allowed, and I know what has been bought with the blood of my people. What do I owe you?"

Valagar spurred his ormn forward.

"What bitterness is this? You are victorious. Can the rest of us not salute your valour in battle?"

"I will take salutation, but not from you. I am Arged Noje-eth Enay Opakas. We have not met before this moment, and you do not know me. But I know you. You are the sons and daughters of the slayers of my kin."

She looked at them all.

"I know you all. I have seen your likenesses in the mind of my Haelok. I have seen the grief that you caused him. No doubt he would be merciful and forgiving now that you are here, but I am not of such a temper."

There was dead silence now. All of the Haelok Aldaria that were gathered there arrayed themselves behind their leader, and their eyes were hard with the light of judgement. Every single sword was drawn, a crescent of darkness, two horns of shadow. Simoref swallowed hard.

"I know you cannot forgive any of us for what was done to you, but if you desire justice, then take it out on me."

"Justice is not mine to give," said Opakas. "Nor is forgiveness. Justice belongs to the Haelok alone. He is the only one that will decide whether your offer is mete."

"And where is Korfax?"

"Our Haelok is within. This battle is not quite over yet. Our Haelok still has your Velukor to subdue."

Valagar dismounted.

"The Velukor betrayed us also," he said. "He was our heart."

Opakas inclined her head.

"And that is why I allow you. But do not think to enter the tower. This task is for my Haelok alone. This is his desire. The Velukor is his especial foe."

"You do not tell me where I shall or shall not go," said Valagar.

Many of the Dar Kaadarith stepped forward, staves at the ready. Opakas laughed.

"You dare take offence? After the crimes you have committed? After the slaughter which brought you your peace?"

Simoref stepped into the breach, his hands held up in the gesture of supplication.

"I am Noraud!" he cried. "Hold, all of you. Remember why you are here. Raking up the enmities of the past will serve no purpose now."

A Geyadril, Balkoh by name, gestured at Opakas.

"But they are of the Argedith. We once swore oaths that they should not be."

"And in whose name did you swear those oaths?"

There was a long silence. Simoref now held up his hands in the gesture of warning.

"I have pledged my allegiance to Korfax. Do not forget who he is and what he can do. He can change stone. He has the gift of Karmaraa. Yet he is of the Mikaolazith. Be very certain of your ground. This is a new world we have come to."

It was as they stood there in uneasy silence, pondering their choices, that a rider approached, his demeanour wild.

"The Noraud!" he called. "I seek the Noraud."

Simoref held up his hand.

"I am here," he said.

"Noraud!" said the rider. "An army of Agdoain approach. They cover the horizon. I have never seen so many."

"Where do they come from?"

"The north!" came the reply.

"Which part?"

"All of it..." he answered.

Simoref stared at the messenger for a long moment, and then he turned to Valagar.

"As it was before, so it is again," he said.

Valagar agreed.

"Yes, but this time we are inside. We can defend from the walls of the Komsel."

Simoref turned back to Opakas.

"We need your aid," he said simply.

Opakas looked at her followers.

"It is as the Haelok said," offered one of them. "That we should guard his back."

Opakas bowed her head in agreement.

"So be it," she said.

She turned back to Simoref.

"It seems you will have your alliance after all," she told him.

They rode as quickly as they could back to the walls of the Komsel, but as they crossed the city boundaries they felt a tremor in the ground. Opakas reigned in her steed and looked back at the Umadya Pir in trepidation.

"It has begun," she said.

"What has begun?" asked Valagar.

She turned to him.

"My Haelok has found your Velukor," she told him.

The tremors increased, mounting by the moment. Stone began to fall from the Umadya Pir.

"The tower will fall," someone warned.

"Our Haelok will prevail," said another.

Then they heard it – a roar, a scream as if from a throat of metal. It tore the air and shook the stone. Such a sound. Many covered their ears. Then the Umadya Pir came apart. Light erupted where the tower had once stood and it hurled the broken stone of the Umadya Pir in every direction. Anyone standing was thrown from their feet. Anyone mounted was blown to the ground. The wreck of the city crumbled further, pounded into the dust by an immense hand of fire.

When they looked up again the Umadya Pir was gone.

With a scream of denial Opakas scrambled up onto her ormn and rode back to where the tower had been. Others followed as quickly as they could.

She came to the edge of the ruin and looked down into a vast crater of shattered stone. Kukenur was the first to her side.

"I should have been with him!" Opakas hissed. "I should have been with him!"

"And you would have been slain."

Opakas turned upon Kukenur in rage and grief.

"Then at least I would not have seen the purpose of my house brought to nothing! He was our prince! He was our dark centre, the night reclaimed. He was our Haelok!"

Kukenur shook her head.

"You believe him dead?"

Opakas gestured at the deep ruin.

"How could anything have survived that?"

"I saw what was in him. If anyone could have survived such fire, he could."

They looked at each other.

"Do you feel his death?" Kukenur asked.

Opakas took out her shew-stone. She touched it, concentrating, and the stone filled with darkness, night impenetrable.

"He lives," she sighed. She turned back to Kukenur.

"We should find him. We should seek him out."

Kukenur held up her hands in the gesture of denial.

"That is my task," she returned. "I will look. Your purpose is other."

"And what do you know of the matter?"

Kukenur smiled.

"More than you know," she answered. "I am a seer, and it is my business to know. So what was his last commandment to you?"

Opakas frowned.

"To ward him, to guard his back."

"Then go to it! The Agdoain come. Perhaps that is why he told you to remain. I will seek for him, as will others of my order. Let us do this thing. Let *me* do this thing. Too long have I pointed the way; now it is my turn to walk the path."

Opakas slowly filled herself with purpose again.

"So be it," she said. "Nalvahgey made you. He is born of her blood. I will allow it."

Opakas rode back to where the others waited for her. She rode up to Valagar.

"The Haelok lives!" she announced.

Those of the north raised their hands in salute. Many cheered. Those of the west remained silent.

"Kukenur will seek for the Haelok," she told her followers. "She is a seer. She walks the path of Nalvahgey. I have decided to honour this."

Many bowed in satisfaction. Then Valagar spurred his steed forward.

"So what will you do?" he asked.

"The Argedith and the Haelok Aldaria will guard the northern wall," she told him.

"But what will you do?" asked Valagar.

"We will summon," Opakas told him. She looked at his face, and then at those that waited behind him.

"Do you desire victory?" she asked.

"Not at any price!" said Valagar.

"Then leave the battle," she returned. "My Haelok told me to ward him. I, at least, will not betray him. He took this city with a flight of Vovin. He did it to save the world. If you cannot honour such choices, I do not want you beside me."

She looked to all the others of the west.

"We are come to it. Here we make our stand. Korfax, my prince, my Haelok, fights the demon that threatens us all. We are here to make sure that he succeeds. What are you here for?"

Simoref stepped forward, looking first at Opakas, then at Valagar.

"We have already lost so much. This battle needs to be won. None of us has seen beyond this day. All are tainted now, whether they know it or not. The Iabeiorith follow their lore, we follow ours. Do we wish to preserve the Ell or not? War is cost!"

"But to summon others to your will?" Valagar retorted. Opakas almost laughed at that.

"Do you eat of achir? Of gahbal? Do you blanch when you see them herded together for the cull? Do you take of tornrax and tornzl when they are given to you? Do you pull the cart yourself, or do you refuse to ride your steed to battle and war because it is bound to you in servitude?"

"But that is different!"

"How is it different?"

"It is not the same!"

"Is it not? Or do you only see the colours that please you? You are just as compromised in this as I. You use lesser creatures in the service of your will, just as I. But I do now what I need to do. Can you say the same?"

"But sorcery?"

"And is the Namad Dar any better?" returned Opakas. "Beyond the great wall to the north the land has been destroyed. My Haelok showed me. You shattered the land with qasadar. How are you any better than I?"

Valagar looked down.

"So be it, then. I may not like it, but that is how it is. We shall fight. That is what we came here for."

Up onto the walls of the Komsel they went. Those of the Argedith and the Haelok Aldaria spread themselves out and then called up their power. Along the northern walls of the Komsel green fires sprang into being, the circles of summoning. Out upon the plain the Agdoain came on, as heedless as ever.

The summoning began. Shapes rose up from the ground, or flew across the skies, or erupted from flames or coalesced from vapour. Those not of the Iabeiorith stared in horrified fascination as strange forms out of legend flew, shambled or rampaged northwards to meet the grey foe.

There were Pataba, the size of many Ell, giants with hides of stone; there were Barmor, great serpents of the sky, teeth, claws and tails like great scythes; there were Babemor, huge bags of flesh with a thousand mouths. There were freezing vapours, clouds of acid, swarms of crystal hooks that burrowed through the earth and crawling lakes of thorns that bestrode it. An ordered delirium crossed the grass of Ovaras and clashed with the Agdoain.

Demon horde after demon horde tore into the ranks of mad flesh, but it was not enough. The Agdoain stretched all the way to the horizon and beyond. The Argedith and the Haelok Aldaria could only hold the north. The Agdoain to the east and the west were free to close upon the Komsel at their leisure.

Seeing this, Valagar and Simoref took quick counsel.

"I have spread our forces to the east and the west," said Valagar.

"Then I will take the west," Simoref answered. "You take the east."

He turned to Valagar. Here it came. The time of parting. Simoref looked fully at Valagar and found himself wondering if, after this hour, he would ever see the first sword of the Nazad Esiask again.

"The light of the Creator be upon you," he said, holding himself as straight as he could.

Valagar bowed his head at that.

"I never believed that it would ever come to this," he said. "That all we ever held sacred would be thrown down, that all we ever held to be profane would save. I am not certain I would wish to live in such a world hereafter."

"Do not despair," Simoref told him. "We may yet prevail. And who knows what kind of world we shall build upon these ruins? I cannot, I will not, believe that this is all in vain."

"You have hope?" Valagar looked up.

"It is all that I have left," Simoref answered.

"Then I must honour that at least," said Valagar. "And I honour you, Zadakal Noraud Simoref, a better son of the line of the princes of the west than many that have preceded you. As you have risen from the ruins of your house, so I must believe that something will rise from the ruins of the world. A better peace and a better truth. May the light of the Creator be upon you."

And with that, Valagar turned about and spurred his steed into the east.

Simoref made his way into the west along the great wall of the Komsel, riding beyond the green fires of the Argedith. Occasionally he glanced to the north, shuddering at the screams and roars that echoed back south. As yet it was a distant battle, the forces of the Agdoain kept back, a wall of battling horrors far out upon the northern plains. But it would not remain so for long.

Eventually he came upon his own forces, all waiting for the enemy to arrive at the wall. Many of them glanced nervously to the north. Though the summoned forces of the Argedith held the line, there were so many Agdoain that it was all but a certainty that their turn would come very soon.

Simoref spoke to many as he went his way, words of encouragement and hope ever on his lips, but he saw the looks of desperation in each eye. There were so many of the foe.

Eventually he found the one that he sought. Oanatom.

"What news of the wall?" Simoref asked.

Oanatom gestured back to the south-west.

"The wall itself cannot be repaired, but we have raised a curtain of stone between the two sides."

Oanatom looked down for a moment.

"In order to make that place defensible we have reshaped part of the Komsel, splitting the stone, creating cliffs. None of the others was happy that we did such a thing."

Simoref gestured out to the horizon.

"Unhappy, were they? Ask them if they wish to survive what is coming! The Agdoain approach. There are so many of the foe that they will all but surround the Komsel."

"I am prepared, as are all the others. The Dar Kaadarith wait at each appointed place."

He gestured at the tall urn that stood beside him.

"Every Geyad, every Geyadril, has at least one of these at his disposal," he said. "Enough qasadar to shatter a host of armies."

They stood upon the outer wall and waited. There were thousands of them, each standing upon the battlements. Armour gleamed and swords flashed, reflecting the failing light of day in all its prismatic splendour.

But the oncoming Agdoain did not pause in their mad and headlong rush to the walls of the Komsel. Beauty was not their concern, nor the moment, nor truth. All they cared for was oblivion.

Behind the swarming ranks of warriors and Ageyad surged an insanity of forms. There were siege towers with mouths bellowing slime and bellies full of rot. There were war beasts, joined shoulder to shoulder, galloping waves of flesh washing in with the rising tide. And there was chaos itself, flesh unleashed, a flood of inconstant shapes that danced and leapt and reared, mouths open and limbs eager.

Simoref looked at it all and thought he beheld the parts and the pieces of a vast body, huge beyond imagining, rolling and writhing, unable ever to undo its dismemberment. He saw shapes like torsos, shapes like arms, hands and fingers, feet and entrails, all rolling in with the surge and screaming in agony from the rips in their broken flesh.

"So now we come to it at last," Oanatom looked at Simoref, who, still shaken by the sight, did not look back.

"Simoref?"

Simoref started. What could he say? He stared down at the enemy and wondered what it was that he saw. Finally he turned to Oanatom again.

"There are more Agdoain here than I have ever heard tell of before. This army dwarfs the one that lay siege to Othil Zilodar, and it is vaster by far than the one that defeated us when Noqmal dared knock upon the gates of Emethgis Vaniad."

"Do you have any hope in you, then?"

Simoref turned and smiled.

"I have hope." He laughed and raised his stave at the heavens. "Yes, I have hope. Though all seems fallen now, we can still have hope that better days will come from this – new days, new dawns and a world renewed."

Reckless abandon filled him. What did anything matter now? The world was undone and must be made anew. He saw the truth at last. Power came to those that had already abandoned themselves to their fate. Doubt was a shackle and despair was a jail. He even dared believe that he understood Korfax at last. Power depended only upon the will of those that wielded it, how infinite their desire, how boundless their hope. And Simoref suddenly discovered that he possessed a very great hope indeed.

The moment came. Qasadar were hurled, a great circlet of inconstant stars, glittering as they flew down from above. Over the foe they went, and then down upon them, a blossoming fire. White negation erupted and great holes were blasted in the enemy ranks, but the surging tide behind rolled in to fill them.

Those that escaped the fire came to the wall and all but surged up it, pushed on by the force of those that followed in their wake. Lightning fell, winds howled, ephemeral crystals tumbled down and the mad rush of the Agdoain was halted, but only for a moment. More came, and more came behind, and more behind them. Qasadar flew out, blasting the grey sea back again, but the grey was infinite and it returned again and again to lap at the walls of the Leein Komsel, howling with unending hunger.

Half-formed limbs clutched at the stone, only to be repelled by those behind the wall, Geyad whose mastery was that of earth, who fortified the stone itself with summoned energies. Fire of water rained down from above, torrent after torrent of golden heat, burning the slime of the foe back to the plain below.

And so it continued, order and chaos, the land and the sea, the acts of millennia compressed into moments. Stone crumbled, only to raise itself up again, and waves crashed and failed, only to return with re-doubled fury. The bones of the world resounded to the never-ending crash of flesh as the tide of the Agdoain washed ever up upon the shores of the Ell. The Ell remained where they were, withstanding the chaos below like cliffs of stone.

It was the eternal dance at last. But no gentle moon ordered this battle, for this dance was fiercer by far, and far more lethal.

21

GIANT

Zid-od-iam Sih-hul-monje
Lai-iran Nal-de-qahnjo
Ur-od-om Aod-jiz-uljon
Tolah-kaf Ahz-zia-bora
Mirk-basus Od-pan-aglas
Ring-torzu Dor-mirk-kaoji
Tol-telas M-korm-ged-chr

They entered the tower through what remained of the western gate. Korfax walked up the stairs to the entrance hall. Behind him followed the others, Aodagaa and Ambriol leading.

Inside, Korfax looked about him. All the stone of which the great tower had been made had been altered. Its substance had been changed somehow, losing its texture and its nature. It had become glassy, its matrix liquefying. Walls had fused with floors and statues had fused with their bases, sometimes seamlessly and sometimes not. In places the stone had flowed into whirling shapes, overlapping forms of fevered dream, each caught in the grip of its neighbour and inextricably linked together for all time.

Even the shape of the halls and the corridors had been transformed, for the ceilings sagged and the walls bulged. It made Korfax think of mouths, and worse than mouths. It made him think that he now threaded his uncertain way through the sagging innards of some vast and rotting beast.

This was it, he could feel it. The Agdoain had been but a prelude to this moment. Now he must traverse this ruined place and seek out its defiler. And the deeper he went, the worse it would become.

He came to a hall of portraits, each rendered in stone and crystal. He looked up at them and was horrified to see that each face, each body, had twisted like the stone about them. Features ran and blurred, their expressions suddenly impious; limbs were twisted out of true and hands curled as though irreparably deformed. All colour had faded down to a background of grey, illimitable grey, like a fog.

The tower was being erased and its contents were slowly being consumed by the power that now crouched at its heart. Given time, the whole mass would eventually slump into the ground, its substance leached away by the force that occupied it. Korfax shuddered. It was his dream from Piamossin all over again. This was the way the world would go – everything eaten alive by the void.

He looked at each of the portraits and heard their voices in his mind.

"Decay is the way of it!" they cried. "Let the world pass into nothing! Death may be empty, but life is emptier yet!"

As they went they heard occasional sounds, echoes of falling stone, the tower still settling after the assault. Many ways were impassable, blocked by rockfall or piled up debris, and they travelled a single path, winding and labyrinthine, that drew them ever downwards to its centre.

They were being led, Korfax was certain of it. They were being led along a road of ruin, and if the way had already been prepared then there would be traps and horrors lying in wait for them all. But that was the intent. Like its slaves, the architect of this destruction wished to show them the worst that it could do.

Korfax understood entirely. They were to be tormented, they were to be hurt. No doubt his enemy desired to weaken him to his utmost before he sprang whatever trap he had prepared at the heart of the tower. But if his enemy thought that this play would weaken him, he was sorely mistaken.

Sickly exhalations drifted by, fogs and mists that floated where they would, and there was even the scent of old rot in the air, or in his mind. But at least there was nothing left alive in this pile of corrupted stone. They walked through a tomb.

They came upon a body dressed in rags – all that remained of a Geyadril's robes. Broken and rotting, the body was set upon a pedestal, bound against the ruin of a statue by bits of torn fabric. There was a tight noose about its neck and the head was pulled up and sideways, lips drawn back in a grimace of pain. The eyes were gone, plucked from their orbits. At the base of the pedestal words had been rudely scrawled.

'Remember me!'

Korfax drew back. Did he know this one? He looked at the face again, looking beneath the scars and the pain. A name came to him, that of Ponodol. He hoped it was not so, but even as he thought it he knew that it was.

He said nothing to the others as he reached up and cut the body down. With their help he laid it out gently. Then he summoned fires and burnt it to ash. All of them said the prayer for the departed, albeit quietly, very quietly. No one wished to raise their voices in this terrible place.

They continued on their way, through the tower, blades at the ready. All their swords were silent, all except for Matastos. It still sang. Nothing could subdue it. Korfax took heart from that and reminded himself that Matastos had slain one of the Ashar.

A voice came, a distant voice, drifting through the corridors. A cry, a sob, a name. Korfax heard it and paused. It sounded familiar, that voice, especially when it called his name. He looked at the others.

"Wait for me here," he said.

"You will go to the voice? But what if it is a trap?" said Aodagaa. Korfax turned to him.

"And who am I?" he answered back.

He held up his blade as if that was all the answer he required.

"Wait for me here," he repeated.

"Let us come with you," Aodagaa insisted.

"No! I must confront this alone. I know that voice. Let the master of this place spring whatever traps he pleases. I am more than equal to anything he cares to try."

Korfax followed the voice. It echoed as if from far away, despair and regret in equal measure. He took a long corridor, then another that turned, until he came upon the cage. It blocked his way. Someone was inside.

They turned at his approach and came forward. He stared. He knew that face, though it was impossible. It was her, before him, within the cage. Obelison? But how could that be? He staggered back. She was dead! He had seen her death.

Her clothing hung from her in rags, and though her face looked haggard and old beyond its years, her eyes still blazed with well-remembered fire.

"You should not have come," she told him. "You should leave now. Deny it its vengeance."

Korfax staggered at her voice. It was hers. He would know that voice anywhere, anywhere. From the beginning to the end of time itself he would know it. Was this another of his dead? A memory? Some foul resurrection?

"You cannot be her!" he said.

"Yes!" she answered. "That is it. I am a phantom. It placed me here to torment you, but I shall not. That is its joy, not mine."

Her whisper barely reached him. He caught her scent. The illusion was damnable in its exactitude. Korfax took a step forward and clutched at the bars. If she was a phantom, she felt horribly real. He could almost taste her thoughts, but he was denied in some way. There were walls about her, both physical and spiritual, that he could not breach.

"How can you be here?" he asked.

She looked up.

"I thought you dead," he said.

"Dead?"

Her eyes lost their fire for a moment. She came forward and touched him briefly, a fleeting touch, before drawing back again. He shuddered. She was real! But she could not be! This was too much.

"NO!" he cried.

She sank against the bars of her cage and looked down.

"Would that I were!"

She stopped moving for a moment and then looked up again.

"What I have spent for you!" she told him.

He looked at her through the bars. His horror was all but complete. She was alive?

"I thought you dead!" he told her. "I THOUGHT YOU DEAD!" he cried.

She laughed, and her beautiful voice became a mad cackle.

"Did you? But that was its intent all along. Out of its chaos, out of its madness, comes the unguessed torment. I thought once that I had fathomed it, but then I discovered that I had not. Layers within layers within layers! It has planned even for this."

"It? What are you saying? Onehson did this!"

"Him? The mad child? The possessed? This was not his design. This is the work of the other, and I helped it."

"You helped?"

He stepped back.

"I killed him," she said to the floor. "I stabbed him and he died, just as I did. But then he came back again, just as I did, power and certainty and horror and cruelty. Except that it was not him, it was the other." She looked up. "You fight a corpse."

"What are you telling me?"

"It possessed him. Now it is him. Qorazon! The voice of the void!"

"Qorazon?"

"That is its name. It has been here since the beginning, possessing them all, all of them since the time of Karmaraa. He made the bargain, or so it told me. But it lies. Trust nothing that it says. Heart of chaos. All things and no thing. It uses others for its certainty. It has none itself."

She turned her back upon him.

"Did you lie with her?" she asked. "Did you lie with the murderer of my father?"

Korfax almost fled at that.

"I thought you dead," he whispered.

She became very still. He could not tell if she was even breathing any more.

"All true. Everything is true," came her voice. "You are cursed! I am cursed! You lay with her! He lay with me!"

She looked back at him.

"The seed grows within, even now. Did you know that? It commanded his body to take me. I am cursed. Like his mother before me, like Lavakon, I am cursed. The seed grows within."

The clash of events had him reeling.

"You have his child?"

She laughed.

"Not a child. A demon to suck the life from me. Of the house of Zilodar, but born of the heavings of Zonaa."

"NO!" came a shuddering cry of denial.

GIANT

"No good shouting," she answered quietly. "I am already deaf and dumb and blind. The nothingness has me, had me, will have me. Perhaps that is the answer, after all. Am I a child? Am I a crone? Do I still live? Or is my life yet to be? What empty space shall I fill, or shall I fill it at all?"

She looked up at him and her eyes were wet with grief.

"Which is it to be, my one and only love?"

Korfax screamed wordlessly as he wrestled with the cage. Energies erupted from his hands, burning fires of force that undid the cage's substance. But even as he tore the cage apart, a shadow appeared behind her and enfolded her with smoky limbs. She fought against the vagueness, beating her despair against it, but to no avail. Korfax shouted denial after denial, but his words had no effect. He entered the ruined cage at last and found no trace of Obelison.

He wept with rage and loss. He had not imagined this at all. It had to be an illusion, all of it. She could not be here. She could not! But tales came back to haunt him, how Onehson had brought back the body alone, how he had let no other see her, how he alone had interred her ashes in the vaults of the Sapaxith.

He was being played with. He must not submit. But how arrogant he had been, though. Equal to the task? He was not equal to this! The torment in this place had already cost him far more than he was prepared to pay, and that there was worse to come he did not doubt.

They waited, and as they waited quiet sounds came to their ears. For a while they wondered if they imagined it, but when they saw the shapes in the darkness, they understood, or thought that they did. The Agdoain were here, shuffling towards them out of the shadows.

But they were not Agdoain. Aodagaa stepped back and put up his blade, for the ragged shapes that came towards him were of another kind entirely.

What once must have been proud and beautiful were now defiled and ruined. Their limbs were twisted and uneven, their fingers and toes curled up as though broken. All of them were bent as though their spines had been deformed, and much of their flesh was crossed by open wounds. They wore simple robes, but these hung in tatters to reveal naked skin underneath. Aodagaa glimpsed more ruin beneath the torn garments, but he did not look too hard. Their heads, though, were the worst of it. Shaven and carved, they hung from their necks like rotten fruit. Their eyes had been plucked out, some still dangling from their roots, their noses and ears had been sliced off and their mouths crudely sewn up.

Aodagaa and the honour guard retreated from them. Here was a horror they had not expected. They had not thought to meet their own kind, and certainly not in such straits. The only mercy they could offer now would be death.

They all looked at each other, the same thought in every head. Some closed their eyes, others bowed their heads, but all extended their blades to do the deed. Aodagaa silently cursed the guilty as he gently ended the life before him. The body burned without a sound, all the bodies burned, and then they were gone, more ash to add to the ruin.

A distant laugh disturbed the air. All of them turned towards it. It came again, mocking and low.

Aodagaa looked at the others. He gestured at the ash at his feet.

"I want the one that did this!" he hissed.

Eyes burned in agreement.

They found the place from whence the laughter had come, the central hall, with its high balconies and many bridges.

Aodagaa walked into the hall. He held up his Qorihna and turned full circle. The others followed him, spreading out.

"It seems that we are alone. There is nothing here. Perhaps it was an illusion, after all."

He was about to turn away when a voice answered him, breaking the silence.

"But everything is an illusion! Did you not know?"

They all turned towards the voice and looked up. Above them, on a bridge of rotting crystal, something crouched. They could see a dull gleam of pale skin, but the rest remained in shadow.

The voice came again.

"You are surrounded by illusion. Your whole life is an illusion. Nothing is true, but everything is permissible!"

Aodagaa drew himself up.

"Who are you?"

"Who do you think?" came the reply, and they heard a quiet chuckling sound like the glut of a beast.

Aodagaa waited, as did Ambriol and the guard, uncertainty on all their faces. What had they discovered now? Then, as if in answer to their unspoken thought, the other leapt out into the air, somersaulting down to join them. The movement was so sudden that they all stepped back, swords at the ready.

The other landed lightly before them, grey cloak flapping, grey flesh glinting, before sinking to one knee, a mocking bow to the earth. Then it stood up and drew out a great white stave from some hidden place behind it. The stave was lofted high and held tightly about its centre. Dim energies rippled faintly along its length.

Aodagaa stared. This one had no face. There were no scars, no wounds, no subtractions. The only thing he could see was a mouth and the gleam of teeth. Blank skin covered everything else, rippling and flowing as though something squirmed beneath.

Aodagaa held out his Qorihna before him.

"You are a demon," he accused, but the other merely smiled. And the smile was so exquisitely empty that Aodagaa felt a shiver up his back.

"You are a demon!" he pressed.

The other bowed.

"How assertive you are! Far more so than many another that came to stand in my presence. Few have ever dared be so bold in this place, and certainly not with me. Demon, is it? Things are not always quite what they appear to be."

"Well, if you are no demon, then what are you?" Ambriol asked.

"Perhaps I am just an Ell, after all," and the other smiled again as though it had offered up the most exquisite of jests.

Ambriol raised his Qorihna.

"You are no Ell!" he said. "Look at you!"

"Appearances?" chided the other.

"And what does that mean?"

"Only that you clearly did not listen to what I said earlier. You are surrounded by illusion. Perhaps I can appear as I please. And if you truly believe what you see, then perhaps you should be concerned."

It hefted its stave, like a warning.

"You are no Ell," Ambriol repeated.

"This becomes tiresome," the other answered, drawing itself up. "If you no longer desire speech, then have at it. Let us see how you speak with that sorcerous blade of yours instead, though I am certain none has seen it do anything other than butcher children."

Ambriol roared and swept his Qorihna in an arc of flame. The other slammed its great stave into the floor and an earthquake shook the hall.

Ambriol was hurled backwards. He clattered against the wall with bone-breaking force, but his armour preserved him, absorbing the lightning that briefly flew up from the stone to undo him.

Then, in his place, Aodagaa and the others attacked, their blades weaving myriad dark patterns in the air. But each writhing tip was knocked aside by the whirling stave of their opponent. The grey Ell smiled with gentle mockery and span his stave about his head. He fired bolts of grey fire at them all, bolts hot enough to shatter stone, hot enough to undo matter itself, but the fire was caught and consumed by each of their Qorihna.

"Well now, you have mighty blades, it seems, and you know how to wield them. Perhaps this little diversion will be entertaining, after all."

Ambriol smiled mirthlessly as he got back to his feet.

"So it is entertainment you want? You will get more than you bargain for from us!"

He held up his sword again, but the other laughed.

"How kind you are. When I was a child, I was told that I should never expect to receive more than my due, as that way it would always be a delight and a surprise when more was given."

"You were never a child."

"But I was! And in this tower, no less. I was born here."

Aodagaa gestured.

"Beware Ambriol, I know who this is. This is the very one our Haelok seeks. This is the master of the Agdoain, none other than the Velukor himself. We have found Onehson, or what is left of him."

All of them hefted their weapons at that, raising their Qorihna over their heads, tips pointing forward in the attitude of preparation. The other drew itself up to its full height and smiled.

"Onehson, you say? But he is dead and already far beyond your reach."

"Then if you are not Onehson, what are you?"

"I am that which lives in his flesh."

"You are a corpse?"

"If such illusions please you."

"I know of theurgies that can raise up the dead and put them down again."

"Try them. I have always enjoyed the acts of futility."

"Enough of this!" said Ambriol. "It is as my companion said. You are Onehson, or what is left of him. We will take our vengeance upon you. Remember Lontibir!"

All the others advanced at last, each with their blades poised. There was no eye that was not now filled with hatred. Aodagaa spoke again, but his voice was for his followers alone.

"Hear me, all of you. Let us cut this thing into pieces and let its flesh be consigned to the dark places. It is time to end it. For the Haelok!"

"For the Haelok," they answered, and they concentrated their power upon the grey. But the grey gently raised its stave to bar their way, and energies flickered along its length.

"You speak of endings? So be it. For the Haelok, you say? No! You are witless fools, besotted with your sudden power. So your master has defeated my Agdoain? More are on their way to replace the many that have fallen! You have penetrated my demesne? You will be devoured! Though you call down all the forces of the Mahorelah upon my head, it will not avail you. I have more power in me than you can possibly imagine."

The great white stave spoke, a hiss like the touch of acid, and grey fire erupted, flooding the hall from end to end.

He came back to where the others had been and found them gone. He called out for Aodagaa, for Ambriol, but there was no answer except for a whisper drifting through the air.

"Come to me."

He followed the sound all the way to the centre, as he had known that he would. It was ordained. It had all been ordained. His fate had him by the throat and its claws were so deeply embedded that they would never come out.

There were others there before him, their bodies scattered upon the floor, many of them, thrown this way and that like so much bloody scrap. And, in the midst of it all, there was a mound, a single mound, a simple pile of heads.

He stepped forward slightly and his lips curled with nausea. He saw faces, faces that he knew. Aodagaa! Ambriol! His honour guard! Korfax went dead inside.

That damnable illusion had called him away too soon and he had paid again, a season of stillness and grief, leaves tumbling and sap retreating. He bowed his head and vowed no more, but then a voice broke the silence, a mocking voice from above.

"So here you are once more, mourning for your losses as you ever did, still not willing to admit that it was all your fault in the first place!"

Korfax looked up slowly. He saw a half-naked form looking back down at him from a high bridge. There was a cloak and a skirt, a dull ripple of grey fabric, but nothing else. He could not see a face, but that did not matter. He did not need to see one. He knew who this was.

Hatred blossomed, swelling inside, poisoning his thought as it filled his mind. There were no words to describe it, no words to encompass it. He moved without moving, his rage and his hatred shifting the substance of the world about him so that he could rise to the heights and stand upon the bridge. He stepped upon the stone, his sword before him, ready to confront the hatred of his heart, but then he paused, for the creature before him had no face.

Korfax remembered back to the vision of Osidess and the birth of Onehson. He remembered a child in a crib, a new-born child without a face, only a mouth, full of teeth. Though his fury boiled inside him, he suddenly could not move. He was caught by what had been and what now was.

So there they stood, upon the bridge, regarding each other – Korfax on one side, black armour rippling, sword coiling with flame, and the flesh of Onehson on the other, adorned in grey rags, the stave of Karmaraa in its hands, face blank except for a curling mouth full of teeth, smiling in cruel amusement.

"What are you?" Korfax finally said. "You are no Ell."

"But I am!" said the other. "This is the body of Onehson, and it is mine to do with as I please. And what I please is to horrify you. Your pain and your suffering are meat and drink to me."

Korfax listened to the voice. It echoed as though falling upwards from a great depth, and there was something else, some flavour, some texture he could not name. It was not the voice of Onehson.

"What are you?" he repeated.

"You know me," said the other. "We have met before."

"When?"

"Piamossin!"

"But what are you?"

"All in good time. Did you enjoy my messages?"

"I saw them. You will pay for that, as you will pay for a great many other things."

"I will pay? No! You will be the one to pay, for you are so deeply in my debt that even an eternity of suffering will barely suffice."

"I am in your debt? How can I be in your debt?" he hissed back.

"All in good time," said the other. "I believe I have something you want," it continued.

"Yes!" said Korfax. "Your life!"

"No!" retorted the other. "Obelison!"

"She died!"

"No!" it laughed. "She lives. You saw her. You spoke to her. She even told you who I am."

"Qorazon!"

"Yes!"

Qorazon waited a moment.

"So, Obelison – do you want her?" The words curled in the air. "I have so enjoyed her company," it continued. "I have so enjoyed her flesh. But all things must end."

Korfax held himself still. His world went dark. A tremor shook him and he could barely contain himself. This thing was baiting him. He must not rise, not yet. He had to hear what it would say. There were answers waiting for him here, answers he needed. But the fury was building and he would not be able to contain it for much longer.

"She is with child," Qorazon told him, licking its lips.

Korfax hissed. Obelison had said as much, but he had not believed it.

"Mine, of course," Qorazon continued.

"Another lie!" Korfax spat, but it hurt now, how it hurt. And as if conjured by his guilt he remembered Doagnis. He had got her with child. Symmetry. The mirror. Here it was again, that damnable mirror.

"You know it is the truth!" Qorazon answered. "I can see it in you. And do you know the best of it?"

It laughed again.

"When my child is born, Obelison will die and her spirit will come to me. Imagine it! She will be mine to torment for all eternity. How will you prevent it? Cut it out of her? Rip innocence from her womb? Every cut that you make, every exquisite cut, you would feel as if it were your very own flesh that you parted. How it would hurt you! What an agony that would be! Oh yes, I would like to see that! It is what I want with all my heart! I want to hurt you and hurt you and hurt you again. I never want to stop."

"Why?"

"No!" it laughed. "No answers for you. I want you to go to your doom in utter confusion, unable to comprehend anything that has happened. I want reasonless chaos to swallow you, an eternity of suffering, for you and for her, for her torment will increase yours a thousand-fold."

It smiled.

"Shall we duel now? Do you dare?"

It gestured with its stave.

"Know that if you die by my hand your soul will be mine, mine to torment for ever!" The smile widened. "Do you understand what that means?"

The smile became devouring as it pointed at itself.

"My servants are my hand. All that they slay become mine also. How many do you think I have in here? Every soul that died in the north? Every soul that died upon the wall? Orkanir? Ponodol?" Qorazon leaned a little closer. "Your father?"

It was too much. Korfax could hold it no longer. The taunts, the spite, the poison, he could no longer bear it. He flew at his enemy and they met at the very centre of the bridge, sword snarling, stave alight as they clashed. The air shuddered as the powers met. Matastos roared its passion like a furnace, whilst the stave of Karmaraa hissed back like a dousing flood.

Stray blasts of power smashed into the far walls of the tower, and with each clash of their weapons, the Umadya Pir shuddered and broke a little more. Walls crumbled and stone split, spitting dust, as Korfax hurled the many blades of his Qorihna at his foe. The other span the stave of Karmaraa about its featureless head, knocking the blades aside and consuming their fire, before hurling back fires of its own. Neither, though, could make any headway. They were too evenly matched.

Back and forth they went as the tower began to come apart around them. Walls cracked, stone fell and the ground heaved and shuddered.

Korfax thought of his power over stone. Perhaps Opakas had been right. Perhaps he could reach out and touch the stave of Karmaraa. But it was fraught with danger. Qorazon was already in the stave. It would stop him, or worse.

There was only one choice left to him, a gift gained from the death of a god. That which submits, rules. He must submit to his sword and let its power consume him. But this also was fraught with danger. He would lose himself, and he had no idea where the fury would take him.

He must take the chance, though, he had no choice. Victory must be his, so he threw everything he could at Qorazon and hurled his enemy back. Then he leapt back also and undid the power of his armour.

Qorazon paused, crouching where it had landed. For a moment it appeared puzzled, but then it smiled as it watched the armour unravel.

"What is this?" it taunted. "Have you had enough already? Do you retreat? Or do you surrender?"

Korfax smiled darkly at his enemy for a moment, and then he let the sense of his sword overwhelm him. The red mists came, the eternal moment that never moved, and he grew, and his sword grew, and together they towered over the grey.

Qorazon stared upwards at the dark shape in utter astonishment. A black giant with eyes of flame stared back down, a blade the size of a mountain in its hands, ready to strike and eager to fall. Qorazon held up the stave of Karmaraa in desperate defence, filling the air with the fires of nothing, all that it could summon, wave upon wave of grey fire, power enough perhaps to erase the entire city, but even that did not suffice.

Matastos fell, an arc of black flame like the ending of worlds. It divided the void and fell upon the stave of Karmaraa. With intolerable brilliance the stave shattered. Then the bridge shattered, the central hall shattered and the tower of light came apart.

Qorazon and Korfax fell, tumbling down with the broken stone, down onto the ruin below. Daylight erupted about them, daylight and dust. The tower of light was no more. All that remained were the foundations.

Qorazon stood up first, howling in rage as it fought its way back to its feet. Korfax followed, pulling himself out of the wreckage. He was back to his normal self. He turned to face his enemy and raised up his blade, and Qorazon stared back at him across the ruined stone with its blank skin, its mouth a snarl of dismay.

"You think you have won?" it cried. "I am not done yet; do not think for one moment that I am. This was but one play amongst many. We still have so far to go, you and I. Seek for me in the uttermost deeps."

Grey mists erupted about it like limbs and drew it away before the great blade of Matastos could touch it. Korfax watched as the grey mist sped off across the ruins, before vanishing down into a dark hole.

Korfax let out a long breath. He felt drained as though the previous confrontation had taken everything that he had. He paused a moment to consider what Qorazon had said. The uttermost deeps? He thought of the great caverns far below the city. Only one entrance had been discovered, and that had been under the Sal Kamalkar, but was there another entrance under the Tower of Light? They had searched long and hard and found nothing else. Who knew, though, what mischief had been perpetrated since that time.

He awoke his armour once more and walked across the ruin to the place where Qorazon had vanished. There was a hole that opened onto a set of broken stairs. They would take him to the lower levels. He readied himself and then dropped down, following the stairs to their end.

As he vanished into the hole a dark shadow disentangled itself from the ruin. It ran quickly across the rubble and then entered the hole itself, quiet, silent and all but invisible.

It took Korfax a while to reach the bottom, as the stairs were broken and half-choked all the way down, but eventually he arrived in the lowest hall and found his enemy waiting for him.

The hall itself was dark and wide, its many fat pillars bulging as though straining under the piled-up weight from above. At its centre a great pit had been dug and Qorazon crouched upon the opposite side, clutching Obelison in its arms. She was not moving.

"So you have come!" it said. "Good!"

"Is she dead?" he asked.

"Of course not!" it told him. "She but sleeps in the arms of her beloved."

"What have you done to her?" Korfax hissed.

"Nothing," came the answer. "Nothing much." The empty face leered at him from across the pit. "Do you want her?" it asked.

"You know the answer to that."

"Then follow!" it goaded, and it leapt into the pit, taking Obelison with it.

Korfax ran to the edge with a cry and looked down. The grey light of his foe fell slowly away from him and he heard an echoing laugh along with the beat of great wings.

Korfax stared down into the great pit before him. What game was this now? What was it Qorazon really wanted? To eat the world? To gnaw at it like a bone until everything worthwhile had been utterly consumed?

The pit went down as far as he could see, its sides gouged from the rock as if by many claws. Korfax could imagine its genesis. Qorazon had commanded the Agdoain to dig.

So, with terrible industry, they had delved deep into the earth, a pit leading into the depths, leading who knew where.

Once before he had leapt from the edge, two stones in his hand to guide his fall. Now he had his armour and his sword, and they would not let him come to harm, so over the edge he went.

He dropped into the nighted gulf, and as he fell his armour spread out around him, black wings to slow his descent. The sides of the pit fell away from him and the industry of the Agdoain came to an end. Their great hole, the work of uncounted thousands, became as nothing when set against the immeasurable cavern into which it opened, a cavern so mighty that Korfax could not discern its limits. How long it had lain here, brooding alone, brooding secret, he did not know. He felt as if he had entered the halls of eternity.

How paltry the works of the Ell were suddenly become; likewise the works of the Agdoain. Below him the grey light of Qorazon barely touched the sides at all. Korfax could just make out the shadows of great cliffs, great faces of twisting rock grinding against each other, four curving walls so immense they surely held the entire world in their mighty grasp.

Now it seemed to him that he fell through the navel of the world, down into the spiralling depths, for, like the coiled hills of the Leein Komsel, the rock here had been turned in upon itself. It was as though at Uriel's birthing some great hand had cut the cord of its life and cast it adrift in the heavens, letting it finally make its own way amongst the stars.

The descent seemed interminable: down, ever down into a night without end they went. Korfax wondered what his enemy's purpose might be. What secret lay down here? What advantage?

After what seemed an age, there came a light at last, a dim redness that grew out of the black depths, along with the beginnings of a great heat. They were coming to the end, the furnace at the heart of the world.

Then he saw it. There was a bright point of light below, a brilliant light like an earthbound star. Was that where they were going? What could it be? What fire, snatched from its place in the heavens, had been set down here in the red darkness?

The end arrived and Korfax found himself landing gently upon smooth stone, the floor of a wide shaft with many turning pillars of rock. Red fires shone upwards from below, shining dimly through the stone itself, but only a ghost of their insuperable heat shimmered the air. All was red and black but for the white light, that of a single white stone hammered deep into the heart of the world.

Here the world was impaled, locked in place by a single great crystal, vaster than any Korfax had ever yet seen, and its symmetry was the simplest: four corners, four edges, four sides. No legend, no myth, had ever spoken of it, but seeing it now, Korfax could guess of what kind it was.

The crystal had been forged of the Namad Dar, written in the very lore the Ell had dared to call their own, the very lore Qorazon had corrupted. For Korfax could feel the great crystal in his mind, and its slumbering might staggered his imagination.

On the other side of the crystal Qorazon crouched like a beast, its head thrust forward into the light. It held Obelison, her vacant eyes staring inwards as she lay under its clawed hand.

"Now we shall see what you are truly willing to spend," Qorazon said.

Korfax remained still. He did not know what the great crystal was, nor did he understand what possible advantage Qorazon saw in coming here. He looked at Obelison. She appeared utterly unaware, lost to the world in a deathly trance. But she was alive. He could see her breathing.

Qorazon could kill her easily, but obviously it had something else in mind. Obelison's life hung in the balance, so Korfax would take it slowly for now.

"What is this place?" he eventually asked.

Qorazon smiled.

"You do not remember? Of course you do not! Many before now have accounted the Dar Kaadarith the wisest of the great guilds, most knowing and most deep, but I always thought them arrogant in their presumption. So much has been forgotten, so much it was needful to know."

It gestured at the stone.

"Here lies the pinnacle of your lore. Here lies the beginning and the end, the first and the last, the ultimate expression of the Namad Dar. Here, at the bottom of the world, living stone has been set. It sees all. It knows all. It is both the receptacle and the received. It holds within it all of creation, and knows exactly what it is that it holds."

Korfax stared back at Qorazon.

"All of creation?" he questioned. "What nonsense is that?"

"Do not play simple with me," came the answer. "You once studied the lore of stone, or have you wilfully forgotten everything that you ever learnt in your willingness to embrace the abyss?"

"I remember well enough."

"Then you know full well what dwells at the heart of each stone. Infinity! And infinity contains all things."

Korfax let out his breath in a long hiss.

"How long do we go on playing this game of yours?"

Qorazon held up Obelison by her neck, its claws wrapped about her throat.

"As long as you are unwilling to hazard the soul of your beloved," it returned.

Korfax snarled and stepped to the side, circling the stone.

"You dare not hurt her," he said, holding up his blade. "You know what would follow."

"And you are in no position to threaten me," said Qorazon, dragging Obelison with it as it, too, moved around the stone, keeping the great white crystal between itself and Korfax.

"You dare not risk her," it hissed back at him, "not yet, not while hope still beats in your breast."

Korfax paused. Whatever Qorazon had in mind it involved this stone. Korfax could not imagine what that might be. He had tried to probe the stone with his mind, but he could feel nothing except a sense of great power. Beyond that, the stone seemed all but inert.

"Why are we here?" he asked.

"We are here because I want you to suffer as I have suffered!"

"You?"

"Yes, me!" it said, pointing at the stone. "Behold the instrument of my torment."

Korfax looked at the great white crystal and then back Qorazon.

"I do not understand," he said.

It leaned forward.

"Still?" it asked. "What is the Namad Dar? What does it do? It reaches into the void. What is in the void? I am! Every creation of the Namad Dar touches me. I know what I know because this knows."

It pointed at the great stone, a single claw stabbing in accusation.

"I am it and it is I. What I know, it knows. What it knows, I know."

Qorazon aimed its blank flesh upwards, its mouth twisting in remembered pain.

"Every time there was a forging I was torn by fires. Every time a stone was used I could feel it, sucking at me, pulling at me, bleeding me. The Ell are parasites crawling on my flesh!"

Now the claw was pointing at Korfax.

"And you were the worst. When you changed the purpose of stone I could not even scream to assuage the agony."

"No!" Korfax said.

"Yes!" said the other, and it wailed, a cry of such anguish that Korfax all but buried his ears with his hands.

"The pain!" the blank flesh cried. "The agony!"

Then Qorazon bared its long teeth again and aimed its blank flesh back at Korfax.

"And was that not your intent? An eternity of suffering?" It stared at him for a moment, a silent stare. Then it hissed. "But I forget. You do not remember." It drew back again. "Well, forgotten or not, you owe me. Now you shall reap the harvest that you have sown. Now you shall pay back all that you have taken, for I will make you do so. And you will pay it all back until time itself comes to an end."

"No!" Korfax said. "This is a lie!"

"A lie?" it sneered. "After all you have seen? Who is my enemy? Against whom have I set myself? Besides, what choice do you have?"

"Choice? I have you cornered."

It gestured at Obelison.

"You think? My child grows within. She dies as it grows. What will you pay to save her? You are two souls made one, sundered and joined again. The pain of that parting is beyond all understanding. Not the pain of the flesh, no. I speak of the soul. To save her soul, you must gain her. And to gain her, you must come to me." It leered at him from across the great crystal. "And time is running out, Korfax, for her and for you."

Korfax circled the great stone once more, but Qorazon kept pace with him.

"This body is failing," it said, pointing at itself. "Soon it will be beyond redemption, and when that happens she will be beyond you also. For I will take her with me and she will be lost to you for all time. She will never come back again from the void."

Qorazon leaned forward.

"But my child will," it warned.

Korfax felt his heart go still at the threat. He could not allow it. He could not.

They circled again. Korfax on one side, Qorazon on the other, clutching Obelison tight with long claws. There was a whiff of something in the air now, the stench of cold rot.

"So I must come to you?" he asked.

"Yes."

"Then stay where you are."

"No. The only way you can come to me is if you submit. Drop your weaponry."

"Release her."

"Come and get her."

Another circle of the stone. Korfax began to realise that the only way to get to Obelison would be to cross the stone itself, the great white stone that pinned the world. But every part of him seemed to cry out against it.

'You must not cross the stone,' came the warning. 'You must not cross the stone.'

But Obelison would die if he did not. And there was more. What of the child? What would happen if the child of Qorazon was allowed to live? How much more torment would be visited upon the world if that were to happen?

He had no choice, so he stepped up to the stone and tried to cross it, but found that he could go no further. His armour refused to move. It would not cross the stone. He drew back.

"What is this?"

"You must submit if you are to come to me."

Korfax stared across at the crouching form. It grew less like an Ell with every passing moment. In places its flesh had begun to crack, to warp out of shape, but its terrible facelessness still stared back at him, ghastly in the upwelling light.

Korfax let his armour unravel. Once it had reduced itself back to a collar he took it off and threw it aside. He took a step forward again and then paused. He felt a sense of anticipation in the air. This was what his enemy wanted. Would something worse happen if he touched the stone? He felt a rising panic. There was no way out.

"What happens if I touch the stone?"

"You gain Obelison."

Korfax circled again but the other kept pace with him.

"Do you want her? You have to come and get her," it teased.

"You want me to touch the stone. What happens if I do?"

"Obelison will be yours. There is still time to save her. But she is fading fast. Her time in this world grows short, as does mine. When I leave, so will she, and then she will be with me for ever. You will never see her again, though you span the heavens from beginning to end. So what is it to be? Her pain? Or yours?"

Korfax tried to leap across the stone without touching it, but something threw him back. His sword was moaning, pulling him away from the stone. It did not want to cross it, either. His panic mounted with every moment. There was some awful stricture here. What was the stone?

"What happens if I cross the stone?"

"Drop your sword!"

"WHAT HAPPENS?!"

"You must submit! Do you want her or not? Her soul is yours to save. Save it, or damn it. The choice is yours."

It began to laugh at him, a horrible sound, a hissing, gargling roar that echoed everywhere. His panic gave way to despair. He knew what Qorazon said was true. Obelison would enter the greyness and never return. Her soul would be racked by the forces of oblivion and she would know eternal torment. He could not let her suffer that, he could not. But what would happen if he crossed the stone? His armour would not touch it. His sword refused to go anywhere near it.

That was the worst of all – his sword would not touch the stone, nor allow him to touch it. That which had slain gods and demons would not countenance the great white stone. Korfax closed his eyes. He tried to drop his sword, but suddenly found that he could not. His hand was shaking. He stared at it for long moments, trying to open his fingers, but they would not budge. He fought with himself, and his enemy watched, gloating and smiling as war was waged. Then came the release as his hand finally relented. He dropped his sword and it fell down to the red stone and lay still.

"Now what?" he asked.

"Come and claim her," came the answer.

Clenching his hands he walked up to the stone. His enemy watched him with a terrible glee. Korfax paused at the edge. He knew that something awful would happen if he touched the stone, but what was he to do? He knew that this act, this single act, somehow ensured his enemy's victory. Too much, though, had been lost to allow such a thing. But if he did not submit then Obelison would be damned for all eternity and another child of Qorazon would be born. He briefly wondered if he could perform a summoning, call up a demon, or fires, or winds, but he knew, deep down inside, that it would be futile. If his sword would not countenance the great white stone, no other force from the Mahorelah would, either.

"Are you still considering your options?" came a mocking voice. "Have you not realised it yet? You have none. No summoning will work. The abyss is closed to you. The Namad Dar is closed to you. All other powers are subdued in this place. Even your sword knows when it has met its match."

Korfax looked down at his sword, lying at his feet. What should he do? He looked back up at Qorazon. There must be some way out of this, he thought, something he could do. But what?

He circled the stone once more and Qorazon kept pace with him, but its movements seemed ever more laboured and its sick flesh glistened. The stench of cold rot was now emphatic.

Korfax suddenly noticed that his sword now lay at the feet of Qorazon, still quiescent upon the floor of the cavern, its darkness impenetrable even to the light of the great white stone. Korfax paused.

"Perhaps I need do nothing," he suddenly said, looking up. "Perhaps this is all a lie."

"Then you will lose her," Qorazon hissed back. There was anger in it now, and a sense of thwarted desire.

"When my time finally comes," it continued, "I will know it. Do you honestly think that I will not take her with me? Do you honestly believe that I shall not torment her?"

Qorazon snarled its malice across the stone and then drew back again, holding Obelison up in its claws. It looked down at her, and then noticed the black sword itself. Qorazon let out a long hiss as though utterly satisfied, and then began to laugh. The laugh swelled until it echoed up into the blackness of the cavern that stretched above them all.

496

"And so you are utterly defeated!" it finally said. "Without a weapon you can no longer threaten me."

"Perhaps I do not need one," Korfax returned.

Qorazon clashed its teeth together.

"You think?" it spat back, "I am not so weak as you believe."

Then it reached down to claim Matastos. It dropped Obelison and stood tall, raising the sword up in a clawed hand.

"Now you are truly powerless to prevent whatever I desire," it said, just before the great black blade unravelled in its grasp and screamed with a thousand voices.

Qorazon stared in horror at the struggling darkness now rooted to its hand. It tried to drop the sword but it could not. It and the sword had become inextricably linked.

It became a struggle of powers. Matastos grew, its substance parting, a thousand blades and strangling roots, whilst Qorazon erupted, its flesh coming apart as the chaos within burst out.

Limbs sprouted like trees and wounds opened like mouths, claws and teeth and tongues, a whirlwind of forms that writhed up and into the air. Monstrous it grew, a great tower of howling flesh that leaned over Korfax and threatened to engulf him, but Matastos grew greater yet, an army of splintering blades to eat the grey. The blackness encircled Qorazon and slowly throttled it.

Down it fell, a long wailing scream from its many mouths. Stone cracked and the ground shook as a swarming mass of black blades undid the grey flesh of Qorazon. Back it went, down and down, until all that was left was a failing corpse, writhing in the black heat as it diminished, burned and turned to ash.

The sword fell out of the air and landed with a crash upon the rock below. Korfax gave it a quick glance and then ran to the side of Obelison. He knelt beside her and cradled her head in his arms. She was no longer unconscious. She stared up at him and their eyes met. He shook his head, tears falling from his eyes. He glanced at the cruel swelling of her pregnancy and looked back again. She reached out and touched his face.

"Welcome beloved," she said. "Welcome to the end of the world." And she reached out with her thought and pulled him into her mind.

They confronted each other upon a gleaming plain, he in black, she in grey. Above them burned a fiery sky, brilliant flames rippling, but the brightest light of all came from their eyes. In them lay their lives, reflections of reflections falling back into the far past.

"So that is how it was," she said at last.

"Yes," he answered.

He bowed his head and she stepped forward, cupping his cheek lightly with her hand.

"What's done is done," she told him. "We have both made poor choices in our time. But now we stand upon the other side of the divide and out of the darkness comes our last chance of salvation. You must grant me the river."

"But I cannot lose you again."

"I am already lost. It is the only way. The seed of Qorazon must fail."

"Is there no other choice?"

"No! If the child dies, so do I. If the child is born, then I will die also, and the sacrifices of this day, and all those that have gone before, will be made void. There is no other healing to be had."

"But you cannot know this!"

"But I can. Do you not yet understand the malice of the enemy? We have no choice in this. I know. Qorazon is still inside me, its child is with me. I see what it has seen. I know its intent. There is only one way to be free."

She stroked his cheek.

"Believe me in this. Know my truth as I now know yours. I see the grief in you. I know your regret. I know what is in your heart, but I cannot spare you. You must do this. You must help me to die. I cannot do this for myself. The child will not let me."

He stared at her in despair.

"But I cannot lose you again, I cannot. I have suffered the pain of parting once already. If I suffer it again, I will break."

Her face clenched as though she hardened herself against his words.

"But it is worse than you know," she said. "There is another army, another army of Agdoain, more than any have ever seen before. Qorazon showed me. Even now they surround the Komsel. The defenders fight bravely, but they are ultimately doomed. They fight against infinity. Even with you at their side there is no chance of victory."

She reached out and showed him her vision. He saw it, the Komsel surrounded, the desperate defence. He stared at the grey hordes. There were so many that he could see no end to them. Words came back to him, words from long ago: 'Enough to drown the north in blood.' He bowed his head.

"What do you think will happen after they have taken the centre?" she asked him. "The Agdoain will go where they will, and they will ravage Uriel from end to end until time itself ceases. Suffering without end. The malice of Qorazon. Having failed to slay you, it will burn all that you love instead."

More words came to him, words spoken in the heat of battle. 'I want to hurt you and hurt you and hurt you again. I never want to stop.'

"So that is it, then!" he said. "Qorazon has won after all!"

"No," she said. "Even in this, Qorazon has not won. There is still one more mercy left to us."

She pointed, and he saw again the great white stone, there in her mind, just as he had first seen it.

"That stone," she continued, "that crystal. Do you know what it is?"

She did not wait for his answer.

"It is the giant!" she told him.

Korfax felt staggered. The giant at the end of the world? The old fable came back to him, how the giant slept under the ground, how it heard all the tales and all the stories, and how one day it would awaken, throw off its slumber and gaze up at the heavens, just once, before dying at last. Korfax shuddered. The end of the world!

"Is everything true?" he asked.

"Perhaps," she answered. "I only know what must be done, though. Our time is almost upon us."

He looked darkly back.

"But I cannot do this, I will not," he told her. "Qorazon has taught you despair. I will leave this place. I will fight on. I will take up my sword and I will end the foe! I will not become like Usdurna. He destroyed Othil Ekrin rather than let the Agdoain take it."

"And you will fail," she answered. "You saw how many of the enemy there were. It will be war without end. Besides, you are down here. You have no food, no water. How long will it take you to climb back up? Can you, even? And what will you find when you get there? You must understand. This is a trap with no way out. If you truly wish to remove the taint of the void from all of creation, you must awaken the giant! Then all the Agdoain will be destroyed and nothing of Qorazon will be left. Out of damnation comes our only salvation!"

He turned away. He would not accept this. He could not.

"But Qorazon wanted me to touch the stone!" he said. "This is what Qorazon wanted."

The suspicion grew. He turned back again.

"You have his child," he said. "How can I know that this is not just another of its games?"

He saw only sadness in her eyes.

"Look at me," she said. "Look within. You know the touch of the grey void, better than any. Am I tainted? I may carry its child, but it does not own me."

Despite himself, he knew what she said was so.

"Yes," she continued. "Qorazon wanted you to touch the stone. But its intent was anything but merciful. If you had touched the stone and awoken the giant then Qorazon would have fled with me and kept the child. If you had not awoken the giant then Qorazon would still have fled with me, and the outcome would have been the same."

"But if the world is doomed, no matter what we do, then why keep the child? What purpose does it serve?"

"Because Qorazon intended to use the child for something else."

"And what was that?"

"Who fled this world?" she asked him. "Who lives even now? Qorazon's intent was to destroy the Ell, all of them. Now it knows that it cannot. You have defeated it. You have banished it. You have saved our people. Just not all of them."

He turned away. So that was it! He thought of Dialyas. He thought back to that bitter time, when he had discovered who he was, when he had brought the Kapimadar to Dialyas. What he had thought then was true. The exaltation had come and gone and only the cast out, the spurned, had been saved.

"So it has all been in vain," he said.

"No!" she answered. "Qorazon has been banished. You have won. But now the price must be paid."

"By your death," he whispered.

"Yes. And if you wish to destroy the Agdoain?"

"I must awaken the giant," he said.

"Yes."

He stared at the image of the stone that lay in his mind.

"So was it put here for just this purpose?" he wondered. "Was our doom written from the very beginning?"

"But that is how it is with everything," she told him. "All beginnings contain within them the seeds of their own ending. You know this. It is how the world is. I can only tell you that the stone has been here from the very first, hammered into the heart of the world, watching and waiting. Who made it and placed it there I cannot say. What their purpose was I do not know, but I do know this."

She looked at him, and her eyes flickered with many colours.

"Only you can awaken the giant," she told him.

"Only I?"

"Yes. Qorazon knew this. It is why it brought you here and bargained with you for my soul."

"But why me?"

"I cannot tell you. I only know what is."

Korfax looked down. A memory intruded, words rashly spoken in anger. 'One way or another, we have come to the end of it all. This world will now live or die at my command.' How little he had known when he spoke them.

"So everything must die?" he questioned. "I cannot do this. I will not."

"But the death of Uriel will not be the end," she answered. "Other worlds will grow from the ashes. The Bright Heavens will know life again, after we are gone. How I know this I cannot tell you, but I am as certain of it as I am of my own life. So do not weep, there is hope in death. Though this is an end, it is not the end. In some far off time we will meet again, washed clean and ready to begin anew."

"But Qorazon wanted the giant to awaken!"

Obelison took his face in her hands and held him with the lights in her eyes. Their brilliance washed away the words.

"Remember what I said," she answered. "It only wanted to cause you pain. Pay it no heed. Shun all its works. It is the liar, the corrupter, chaos unbounded. There will be no pain, not now. You have bought this one chance. So this is the choice before us: to be strong or to fall into darkness and cower in the pit."

Her face hardened again.

"Remember the first truth of all. Though the Creator's sword slices the void, making all things, light and dark, good and evil, what happens afterwards lies with us. To us is given the gift of choice. It is both blessing and curse, all things made known by their opposite. To live is to choose, and we have both lived. Now we must pay the price for our choices. Your final victory will be your death. My final victory will be my death. This is the only mercy left to us, the one grace given to us both. Do not deny it."

He felt the pain, the growing pain of loss. This was the least looked for end – and the most bitter. But in one thing he knew she was right. He had to end her life, otherwise the grey void would claim her. Here, before the giant at the end of the world, the tale of their joining would end.

"I love you," he said, as the pain mounted inside.

"And I have loved you," she answered, and she held him once more with her eyes, willing him to end her life.

So he reached out with his thought and cut the thread.

The grey was burnt from her in a blaze of white. Her eyes swelled with light, her gaze pierced him, a brief moment of sharing, and then she was gone. The gleaming plain and the fiery sky vanished and he was back in the red deeps, kneeling by her body. She was still.

He glanced at the swelling of her pregnancy and watched as it slowly diminished. Soon it would be gone entirely. With her death the birth could not continue. He had saved her and defeated the grey. But now she was gone beyond his reach, so he bowed his head and wept.

A hollow voice intruded out of the darkness.

"Is it done?"

Korfax looked up, startled.

"Who is that?" he called out.

They appeared, stepping out of the shadows of the cavern, a gleam of black armour. It was one of the Haelok Aldaria.

"Who are you?"

"I was sent to find you," came the reply.

"Sent?"

"By Opakas," the figure said as it stepped further forward.

"Is it done?" they asked.

"The master of the Agdoain is no more," he said, "but my beloved is dead."

The figure came to stand behind him.

"That is good," they said.

Korfax turned to answer, but then something hit him in the back. He stared down in disbelief as the tip of a long knife protruded from his breast. There was no pain, though, only shock and amazement. The voice came again.

"And so to the end," they continued. "When a tool has served all the purpose that it can, when it has been used up and can be used no more, then it should be cast aside at last."

Korfax staggered and fell away from the body of Obelison, the long knife still in him. He lay upon cold stone and there was light all about him.

"No," he said quietly. "No."

He turned to look at his assassin and felt a foot land upon his neck.

"Who?" he asked as his body began to weaken.

His assassin leaned forward, and Korfax could see he was armoured from head to foot in Qahmor. Then the armour rolled back to reveal a face, a mask from which all passion had been drained. Korfax stared up at a dark face and saw the glittering eyes and their pale, dead light.

"What demon are you?" he asked.

"No demon!" came the reply.

Korfax knew the face, he was certain of it, but he could not recall who it reminded him of. He closed his eyes.

"Who are you?" he hissed.

"Who am I? You do not recognise me? Look beyond the vessel, my love, look beyond the shell."

My love? Korfax felt it then, a sense of duality, not in the voice, but in the spirit. The suspicion grew. He had felt this once before. The realisation grew within, even as his life slipped away. It was true. Doagnis! He should not have spared her. Now she would take her vengeance.

"Betrayer!" he hissed.

"Thief!" she returned.

"Who did you suborn this time?" he asked. "Whose life have you stolen?"

"You do not recognise the face of your old friend? How slow you have become."

Friend? It was a long time coming but he finally saw it. Ralir – it was Ralir. He stared up at the dead face and its dead eyes. No wonder he had not recognised it.

"What have you done to him?" he gasped.

"Why should you care?" Doagnis returned. "He was a coward. I saw what was in him. He wanted to die but feared even to take that step. He was a coward, unworthy of you."

Yes, he thought to himself. Ralir had been a coward, but it had not been his fault. He had seen the abyss, the grey void. Who would not tremble before such horror? Who could endure in its shadow?

"I found him upon the wall of his city," Doagnis continued. "How he survived I do not know, but I am not one to dwell upon irrelevances, nor to waste a gift when it is given. So I took him. I emptied him and I filled him, and what a surprise he was. A fully trained sword? I have never lived in such a place before. All these skills!"

It was her voice that he heard now, forcing its way out of its stolen body as though in spite of it. Ralir was gone. Doagnis had all but slain him. It was hopeless. There was nothing he could do.

"And so I bid you farewell," she said, leaning in closer. "Your time is done, brother mine. Now it is my turn."

For a moment the memory of an older darkness filled him. It was as though he stood upon the walls of Othil Zilodar once more, a sea of foes below. But now the body of his beloved lay at his feet, not the body of his father, and before him was the face of Doagnis reflected across the world. Dark fire rose up inside, black fire, enough to burn all of creation. But it did not escape him. It was sucked away, downwards, down and down into infinite depths. No summoning could he call up, no fire was his. He was dying and there was nothing he could do to prevent it.

He looked back at her.

"Why?" he whispered. His strength was leaving him, drop by precious drop.

"I have already told you! No purpose outlives its completion, no tool its task."

Korfax could not think.

"What do you mean?" he asked.

"Your purpose was to win this war! This you have done. Now it is time for you to end."

"No," he answered, a hiss of breath. Then he began to laugh in bitterness and regret.

"The war is not over," he told her. "Even as we speak the fight goes on. You have slain me too soon. You have doomed the world to endless suffering. You have lost. Everyone has lost."

His sight blurred. Were there tears? He could no longer move at all. He was leaving, going away. He had both won and lost, in equal measure. Qorazon was defeated, but the world was doomed. He lay back and struggled no more; cold stone accepted his dying body like a comfort. He looked across and caught sight of the body of Obelison, lying a few paces from where he lay. He could only see her face. It was calm now, still and at rest. That was the sight he would take with him into the river, and he was glad of that at least. All this pain, all this suffering, let it end here, here at the bottom of the world.

The light swelled about him. Was this the river? Was it coming for him? Then he realised that he was moving. He was sinking down. He looked up. The foot was gone from his neck and Doagnis, in the guise of Ralir, was standing back, staring down with a look of utter shock on her stolen face. Korfax felt hardness about him and a light that took away the pain. What was happening? Then he realised where he was. When Doagnis had stabbed him he had fallen upon the great white stone. He had touched it and now it was pulling him down. He was being pulled into the stone, as was his blood. He could not stop it; he did not possess the strength. Soon he was within, sinking through veils of crystal. He was not going to the river at all; instead, the great white stone had claimed him. Healing energies filled him. Blood coursed through him once more. But he was enclosed and unmoving, wrapped about by translucent stone.

Below him there was fire, a molten boiling sea of flame. Above him there was darkness. Then the fire rose.

Fire encircled him, but did not touch him. Doagnis and her stolen body were gone. The body of Obelison was gone. Everything was erased as it rushed on by. What was happening? He tried to move, but he could not. He reached out with his thought, but it touched nothing. All he could see was a moiling inferno. Was he falling? Was he rising? He could not tell.

They stood upon the wall and around them surged the grey sea. Elements fell from on high – crystalline air, winds of fury, thunderous energies and rivers of fire. Sorceries blasted down, and demons and powers were pulled from the abyss. The limitless foe hurled its grey hunger into the chaos of destruction whilst above them the light of fury burned in uncounted eyes. The ground shook, the air roared and chaos stormed the walls of the world. But then a greater hand reached up from below, and Emethgis Vaniad began to shake.

Kukenur felt it first. She had been walking the ruin of the Umadya Pir, seeking a sign, any sign, of the whereabouts of Korfax, when the feeling came upon her. In her mind she felt it, a sense of completion she could not describe. It passed through her and for a moment she saw everything – all the stories, all the tales, everything that had ever happened, everything that had ever been, creation pulled to a point and held upon the eternal moment. She staggered, clutching at her head as a wordless cry filled her.

'The Giant awakes!'

The others around her felt it also, and all turned to stare at the centre, unable to move as the moment passed through them. The feeling grew, rising, swelling, and soon those that stood upon the wall, those that fought upon the Komsel, felt it.

Valagar turned from the battle to look back, as did Simoref. Oanatom and Thilnor lowered their staves and Opakas lowered her hands, releasing her power as she felt the moment strike. Wherever they were, whatever they were doing, they all turned to the centre as they heard that wordless cry.

'The Giant awakes!'

Great fissures opened, all across the Rolnir, vast mouths swallowing its stone. What remained of the city began to fall as the ground beneath it gave way. They all understood. This was it. The end of days had come.

'The Giant awakes!'

With one tumultuous surge, what was below flew upwards and outwards, and all saw, with their last sight, a fountain of fire, vaster than seemed possible, erupting from the very place that the Umadya Pir had once occupied. Up, up it went, its long-buried heat searing the heavens. The Rolnir heaved and crumbled as the world's heart pumped out its lifeblood. Emethgis Vaniad crumbled and broke, and all within or upon her died at the instant of her immolation.

Beyond her crumbling walls the Agdoain briefly howled before the fire took them as well. Their ending had come, feared and desired, all at once, and it erased them utterly.

He was high now, higher than any sky ship could reach, and he was still rising. The world unfolded before him, its marvellous symmetry spread out for him to see in all its glory.

There were the four great mountain ranges, radiating out from their fiery centre, four great curves of lofty stone, proud in the brilliant light. In between them stretched the many-coloured lands, all the hues one could imagine, beautiful beyond compare. He stared down at a sight he had never seen before – the immense and intricate jewel of his world set within its starlit darkness. He watched it recede, his hands set against his prison walls.

Below him the pillar of fire on which he had risen had long fallen back. Now he could see the Rolnir as a lake of incandescence, a furnace, a crucible into which the blood of the world flowed. Emethgis Vaniad was gone, consumed, and the hills of the Komsel were soon to follow.

He watched the land fall away beneath him, saw the four great mountain ranges – the Vohimar, the Ea, the Perisax and the Chiraxoh – all erupt as brilliant fire spread out from the Rolnir and along each of their crests. The land was coming apart, four equal segments ripping themselves away from their neighbours. The great ocean fell inwards, down upon the rising fires, and was consumed.

Korfax hammered upon the crystal wall of his cell as each great quarter broke away from its neighbour, but the unyielding crystal remained heedless. He bowed his head and wept. He could not watch as the broken parts of his world tumbled away into the void, fiery rock fleeing the last eruption of the world's heart, before its flame guttered and went out.

Korfax hugged himself and cried. It was over, he told himself, it was over. But it was not over yet.

Now great Rafarel itself began to change, its light stuttering as though the death of its brightest child could not be borne. Its light diminished as it shrank, faster and faster, crushing itself down as though to hide its grief from the heavens. Then it erupted and intolerable light erased everything from sight. Out from the light, out into the void, came a great wall of flame. Nothing survived its touch.

First to die was angry Qaomael, burnt to a red smear in moments. Then came Hanael, its mysteries unveiled and undone, all at once. Mikael quickly followed, the speed of its death mirroring the speed of its life, but still the fire did not stop. All the children were to die, all of them. Sweeping aside the remnants of Uriel and Gahburel, the fire surged on to Great Zadkarel, mightiest world of all, but its swirling wrath was powerless against the unstoppable grief of its maker. Last of all was Zafkarel, heavy Zafkarel and its rings of darkness, blown from the heavens as if its ponderous weight was meaningless.

The fire raced on, faded and went out, leaving behind it glowing filaments like shrouds, fiery cerements for the scattered ashes of the dead. Down into the night everything fell, and all was dark.

She awoke, staring up at a paleness she did not recognise. Where was the stone? Where was her crystal cage?

It slowly dawned upon her. She was here, back in her house, looking up at her ceiling. Something sat upon her brow, a cold dark stone. She cried out and flung it aside, but it was too late. Ages had descended. She had seen everything.

The final images still sat within her – death, destruction and the end of beauty. If she had known such sights awaited her, she would never have looked. Loss and horror filled her. She saw him briefly, looking back at her from the other side of the room. He was all that was left, and she could not bear the sight of him. She fled the house.

Korfax watched her leave and felt again that terrible grief. He mourned for his long-vanished world, for the ancient and beautiful places he would never see again, for the marvellous cities that reared their crystal towers at the sky, for mountains that were greater than imagination and for rivers that were mightier than dream. He mourned for the unstained places that had borne the mark of the Creator, for he knew, at the last, that they had all passed away under the torment of time.

The sullen world about him gave no comfort. A small distance away from where he stood lay the very image of a hill he had once known, a single image moulded again in all its intricacies by the caprice of time. But even that was not enough. Out there, beyond this low house, ran the soul, and perhaps even the substance, of his beloved. But that was not enough either. He clenched his fists at his side and cursed.

After a long moment he looked out of the window. She ran now, running far, to the edges, to the sea, grieving for what had been, knowing that it was gone and that she could never return.

He retrieved the mapadar from where she had thrown it and put it back in its keeping place. Then he frowned as he drew out its twin. Dare he tell her that there was so much more to this tale? Would she ever want to know the rest?

Here ends

LAND OF THE FIRST

The tale continues in

TO TOUCH THE CREATOR

Made in the USA
Charleston, SC
11 March 2016